Tessa Barclay is a former publishing editor and journalist who has written many successful novels, among them the four-part Craigallan Saga – *A Sower Went Forth*, *The Stony Places*, *The Good Ground* and *Harvest of Thorns*; the Wine Widow trilogy – *The Wine Widow*, *The Champagne Girls* and *The Last Heiress*; and the Corvill Weaving Saga – *A Web of Dreams*, *Broken Threads* and *The Final Pattern*. She lives in south-west London.

A Professional Woman

Tessa Barclay

HEADLINE

First published in 1991
by HEADLINE BOOK PUBLISHING PLC

First published in paperback in 1991
by HEADLINE BOOK PUBLISHING PLC

10 9 8 7 6 5 4 3 2

ISBN 0 7472 3552 X

Typeset in 10/10¾ pt Plantin
by Colset Private Limited, Singapore

Printed and bound by
HarperCollins Manufacturing, Glasgow

HEADLINE BOOK PUBLISHING PLC
Headline House
79 Great Titchfield Street
London W1P 7FN

A Professional
Woman

Chapter One

The door slammed shut. The key turned in the lock. Young Christina Holt, thrust into the room so that she almost lost her balance, whirled around. She threw herself against the thick mahogany panels.

'Let me out!' she cried. 'You can't treat me like a child! Unlock this door!'

'Not a child, eh? Then behave like a responsible adult!' Her father's voice was loud, angry, resentful.

'I've done nothing wrong – Dr Childers asked me to help—'

'And he ought to know better, by heaven! Just wait till I see him – I'll give him the rough side of my tongue.'

'Father, you've got to understand – it was an emergency—'

'No emergency is so great that a daughter of mine has to be dragged into a place like that! Childers should have more sense. And as for you – until I have your word you'll stop all this nonsense, you stay in that room.'

'Let me out!'

She stood back from the door, a disconsolate figure in a high-necked white blouse and a skirt of navy serge. The skirt rucked up to display slender ankles in black woollen stockings, long-boned feet in soft leather house shoes. She was rather thin, quite tall for her age and, in the opinion of almost everyone except her father, an exceptionally pretty girl. Very fair, pale-skinned, she had the look of someone gentle, almost ethereal.

In a way, this was one of the things Herbert Holt held against his daughter. She *looked* like an angel, but those dark

1

sea-blue eyes could flash with fire. She looked fragile, but she had a steely strength – stubbornness, her father called it. To him she seemed a trick that Nature had played on him, giving him the fairy-child every other father would envy but endowing her with a character he simply couldn't subdue.

She put out her hand to shake the doorknob. 'Father, please open this door.'

'Do I have your promise not to see Dr Childers again?'

'But you gave your *permission*—'

'That was before I knew what you and he were going to get up to. He's behaved abominably, letting you in for an experience like that. And as for you . . . !' She could hear her father gasping for breath in the midst of rage and shock. 'How any daughter of mine could be so unwomanly . . . !'

'How can it be unwomanly to help somebody in trouble?' cried Christina. 'Wasn't that the whole point of letting me go on his rounds with him?'

'Saints preserve us, haven't you any sense of propriety at all, girl? Visiting the sick is one thing. Going into a house of depravity is quite another.'

'But I don't understand what you mean!' wailed the girl. 'Why are you so angry? What have I done?'

'Never mind the ins and outs. I want your solemn promise to stop seeing Dr Childers.'

'No! We've been friends all my life! You can't ask me to do that.'

'He's not a suitable friend. I want you to tell me on your word of honour that you'll cease going on these jaunts with him.'

'No! Let me out!' She hammered on the door with her fists.

'Don't waste your efforts on the door. There you are and there you stay until I have your promise to treat your father with a proper respect for his authority. I want a promise to behave like a lady, to heed what you're told, and to give up this totally unsuitable friendship. Is that clear? When you're ready to confess your faults, just send Falmer down with the message.'

She heard his heavy footsteps on the carpeted landing, the thud of his slow descent to the hall. She beat upon the door. 'Come back! Come back! You can't lock me up like a naughty schoolgirl any more! I'm nearly seventeen years old!'

But she knew her words went unheeded, even if they were heard through the thick polished wood.

For a moment she stood there in the grey light of the late November day. She leaned her head against the panels. Very faintly came the sound of the drawing-room door being slammed shut. Her father had gone to vent the remains of his wrath upon her mother.

She pulled herself erect. The cinders of the morning fire still held some warmth in the bedroom grate. From frequent experience she knew she'd better add some small coals and revive it, for she might be locked up a long time in this cold room.

Kneeling on the plaited rug, she pushed some scraps of newspaper from the kindling box in among the clinker, blowing gently the while. It took a lot of effort, but by and by a tiny flame began to lick up. She added three or four little black slivers of coal. By careful tending she brought a little fire back into being.

Then she sat back on her heels, her breath faintly visible in the chill air as she sighed. She dusted thin hands together to get rid of the coal dust, then clasped them in her lap while she stared into the little flames with a sombre blue gaze.

What had she done? What was her crime? She was in an angry confusion. Her father had *given permission* for her to go out on rounds with old Dr Childers. He had, in fact, been quite pleased. 'Keep you out of mischief, maybe,' he had grunted when she had asked him. 'School holidays are always a time for you to get into some scrape or other. But I can't see you can do any harm by visiting the sick.'

So she had put on her thick coat and her muffler and her woollen gloves, and off she'd gone with the doctor in his dog-cart each afternoon since the middle of last week. Sometimes he had made her sit outside – that was if the patient awaiting him in the house was a man. This she quite understood.

It wouldn't be suitable for her to be present while Doctor was sounding the chest of bronchitic old Mr Bishop.

But on about half of the calls she'd gone inside with him. 'My little assistant,' he said with a teasing smile as she stood by, holding bandages for him to apply to Mrs Atchison's ulcerated leg, or lulling the baby while he examined some ailing mother.

The list of complaints was in itself interesting. Ears to be syringed, poultices to apply, a strange rash on the laundry-woman's arms after she tried a new brand of yellow soap, splints on Tom Graine's fingers after he got them caught in the springs of his butcher's cart, drops to put in the eyes of Mrs Lisson's five-year-old, a mysterious throat infection at the Simpsons' house. . . .

On Sunday, of course, there were no rounds. Christina had gone to church as usual with her parents. On Monday she went out after lunch expecting the usual list of family ailments, and so it had proved, until as dark was falling a woman had come scurrying out of Candle Alley.

'Doctor! Doctor! Thank God I've found you! Come quickly, come – it's poor Molly, she's dying – oh, quick, quick, she'll slip away if you don't hurry.'

The pony, startled, snorted and veered sideways on the cobbled street. Dr Childers reined up. 'Who's that? Oh, it's you, Beryl. What on earth's the matter?'

'Molly Tyler – she's been at it all day – God knows why it don't come – she's in agony. Please, doctor, I don't know what to do!'

Christina at once began to get down out of the dogcart. Dr Childers said, 'Heigh-o, where do you think you're going, miss?'

'Somebody's very ill—'

'Doctor, come *on*, she's dying while you sit there shilly-shallying!' And Beryl turned, lurching off into the alley.

Without waiting for more, Christina set off after her. She heard Dr Childers make a sound, half a grunt and half a laugh, then next moment his footsteps were coming after them.

The house in Candle Alley was a narrow one on a corner,

4

the door a bright though shabby red which gleamed under the light of a gas lamp on a bracket over it. The door stood ajar. On one side of the passage were curtains of heavy velvet, closed but with chinks of light showing at the sides. Through these chinks, glimpses of the room within could be seen – a strange rainbow mixture of ornaments, paper flowers, faded wallpaper, dusty mirrors.

Beryl led the way straight past this room to a narrow, steep flight of stairs. 'Up there, Doctor, the door on the right.'

But the direction was scarcely needed, for the moans of pain were guidance enough. Shoving Christina aside, Dr Childers ran up two at a time.

As he entered the little room, Christina was at his heels, unheeded. There was a narrow, untidy bed, and on it a girl was lying, writhing in agony, whimpering and crying out in an exhausted wail. Even in the flickering light of the gas jet her pallor was alarming.

'Good God, how long has she been in labour?'

'Dunno, doctor. Mebbe the middle o' the night. She took herself off early, saying she weren't feeling too good – and leaving me with my hands full, I can tell you.' Beryl's tone was aggrieved, anxious, yet her words were slurred. 'I got woke up fine and early, I can tell you – and I sleeps heavy, when I can get me rest – so she musta bin in a bad way already.'

'So she's been like this for about twelve hours?'

'Reckon.'

'Why the devil didn't you send for the midwife?' Childers said, stooping over the patient to catch a waving arm so as to take her pulse.

'Well, she's young and hearty – I thought she'd a done all right. But about dinner-time I got anxious and went for Lisbeth Munson, only to find she were out at Stentram wi' some other poor soul.' She began to sob. 'Oh, poor Molly, poor, poor Molly! She's going to die, ain't she, doctor?'

'Shut up, you fool,' said Childers. Christina had never seen him so angry. 'What have you been giving her?'

Beryl reached for a bottle on a cluttered side table. She held it up. It contained about an inch of some clear liquid which Christina in her innocence took to be a sedative.

'You've had a hair or two of that dog yourself,' grunted the doctor. He opened his bag, took out the stethoscope, leaned over the girl and, to Christina's astonishment, began to listen not to her chest but to some area around her middle.

The question, 'Is she going to be all right?' hovered on Christina's lips. But she knew the doctor hated to be spoken to when he was using the stethoscope. Thinking to help him as she often did, she took out the silver thermometer-case ready for his use. As she moved to offer it to him, she was able to see the girl's naked body.

It was swollen and rounded. She drew in a startled breath. The girl was expecting a baby! Of course, 'in labour', Dr Childers had said.

When Christina's body began to change in her twelfth year, her mother had said defensively, 'It comes to every woman, Christina, you must just put up with it.'

'But why must I? Is it a punishment for something?'

'Perhaps it is, child, perhaps it is,' sighed Mrs Holt, and would say no more.

That could never satisfy an inquisitive, intelligent child like Christina. She turned to Dr Childers for enlightenment.

Christina had been friends with the doctor as long as she could remember. He had brought her into the world, and her brother Elwin before her. When her mother had one of her bilious attacks, it was Dr Childers who prescribed the magnesia mixture. When her father was suddenly stabbed by pains in his back, it was Dr Childers who punched and pummelled him into fitness. Measles, chicken-pox, whooping-cough: Dr Childers had seen the Holt children through them all.

He in his wisdom told her enough to satisfy her at that point. In the following years, other knowledge had been added, seconded by what her alert mind noted from seeing the animals that abounded in and around Market Bresham:

sheep with lambs in the fields, horses with foals, domestic pets with their offspring.

The other girls at Bresham Ladies' College were shocked when she first told them what she knew. 'Nonsense, Christina, how can you!' So she never spoke of it to them again. They thought her odd, in any case – a swot, a teacher's pet, a mugger-up of French verbs and Latin declensions, actually keen to learn more botany and do such chemistry as Miss Greatrush thought fit, actually eager to paddle about in muddy ponds looking for newts, to watch butterflies emerge from the cocoon.

But all that Christina knew about having babies was theory only. Now, seeing this exhausted girl on the rumpled bed, she saw what the words meant. 'The child in the womb . . .' It was there, she could see it, and she understood with a sudden startling insight what she had walked into.

'Beryl, get a hold of yourself. You've got to help me save this baby.'

'Not me, doctor, not me,' sobbed Beryl. She bent double on her rickety chair, knocking her forehead on her fists. 'I don't want to be mixed up in a death! She's going to die, I see the sign on her!'

'Look, I can't do this by myself—'

'Naw!' roared Beryl, throwing her head back. She leapt up, overturned the chair, and fled.

The girl on the bed cried out in pain. Her body arched, she threw her arms above her head, seeking something to grasp and pull.

'Ye gods,' groaned Childers, 'it's hopeless . . .'

'I'll help you, doctor,' said Christina. 'Tell me what to do.'

The doctor grasped at his thinning hair with two hands. 'You'll have to do, there's no one else and we haven't much time. This is very serious, Christina.'

'I understand.'

'You know we've talked a little about this. You remember I explained that a baby's head comes first because it's the widest part of its body and once that has come through the rest is easier.'

'Yes.'

'This young woman's baby has got itself turned around.'

'But how can that be?'

'Never mind that for the moment. The poor creature is coming feet first and its little limbs have got tangled on the way.' To say nothing of the umbilical cord which must be wound round in knots. 'The mother's been struggling for hours to finish the birth and now she's pretty near exhausted. The baby too – you saw me listen for its heartbeat, it's very faint.'

'You mean it might be dying?'

'Right. So we must help the mother to bring it into the world, but first she must get a little respite so as to get enough strength to push when I free the limbs. You understand?'

'But how will you—?'

'I'll have to use instruments. One tries not to, but in this case . . . So you must help me. First you must go downstairs and try to find a clean apron or a towel to tie round yourself. Roll up your sleeves and wash your hands and arms thoroughly. Bring me up a bowl of water and some soap. Can you do that?'

'Of course, that's easy!'

'Yes, but there's more afterwards. Still, first things first. Go down and scrub up, nurse!'

Heartened by the little joke, she ran down to the kitchen. It was a grubby, untidy little place but there was an iron kettle singing on the rusty range. She took off her coat, rolled up her sleeves, and with an old scrubbing brush she found in the cupboard under the sink she scrubbed her hands and arms. She found a clean tablecloth in a drawer. This she tied about herself.

Carefully she went up with the bowl of water. In her absence Childers had done what he could to tidy and clear the room. All the rubbishy trinkets on the side table had been thrown out on the landing. On it now stood his open bag, and on a sheet of brown paper some instruments. The girl on the bed was lying peacefully, drugged with the only medicine known to women of her class, the one they call

Mother's Ruin, sixpence-a-pint gin. She was half covered by a single sheet, her nightdress of mercerised cotton and frayed ribbons tucked up about her waist.

There was nowhere to put the bowl. Christina set the chair upright, put the bowl on the seat and a clean rag over the back for the doctor to dry his hands on. He put disinfectant in the water, then as he washed he said over his shoulder, 'Do you see the gauze mask on the table?'

'Yes.'

'And the green bottle?'

'Yes.'

'I've given her a few drops of anaesthetic. She'll come to in a moment. I want you to stand by the head of the bed with the mask and the bottle. When I nod at you, you must put the mask over her nose and mouth, then drop two drops on the gauze. Do you understand?'

'Yes.'

'The time will come when Molly must push her baby into the world. She has to be conscious to do it, so when I say so, put down the anaesthetic. I'm going to give her this sheet to pull on. You can help by pulling against her. Is that clear?'

'Quite clear.' Christina heard herself say it with complete calmness, yet inside her spirit was trembling. This girl was very ill, close to death. They were trying to save her, save her and the baby, and it was almost too big a thing to contemplate. Yet there was no one else to help. It must be done. So she would do it.

Years afterwards she was able to reconstruct the scene from knowledge and experience gained later. But at the time it went by in a haze of anxiety. The smell of ether and lysol and, over them, the sickly smell of gin. The flickering gaslight, the shadows playing on the rumpled bedclothes, the gasps and screams of pain, Dr Childers's low-spoken commands.

And then the shriek of triumph, the soft rushing sound, the thin wail of the baby, and the doctor's grunt of satisfaction.

'Quick, wipe its nose and mouth – by heaven, I'm not letting it suffocate!'

9

There was nothing to use but her handkerchief. She tugged it from her skirt pocket, wiped mucus from the tiny features.

'Here, take it!'

Instinctively she pulled off the tablecloth-apron. Into this she accepted the crying baby. Its limbs jerked weakly, the little mouth was open in a cry of misery at being thrust into this cold, dark, dismal world.

Childers busied himself tying off the umbilical cord. In a moment the child was a self-contained unit, a new human being. Christina wrapped the cloth around it, held it close. 'Hush, hush,' she whispered, 'don't make such a noise.'

'Let her cry,' Childers said, snipping catgut. 'Gets the lungs going, you know – and tells us she's alive and well.'

'A girl?'

'A girl – about five and a half pounds, I'd say. We'll wash and weigh her later.'

And they did, with a spring-measure from which she was suspended in an underskirt Christina found in a cupboard. By that time the mother was quiet and half-watching, the baby was asleep with pink fists in the air, and the medical equipment was back in the Gladstone bag.

'Go out and see if you can find that half-witted woman. Tell her it's all over.'

'Shouldn't we send word to the father? I'll find out where he works.'

'I shouldn't bother,' the doctor said with a sardonic grin. She tried to catch his sleeve as he turned back to his patient. The words, 'What do you mean?' were on her lips. Not fetch the husband? Surely the man would want to hear the news, even though, as she knew it would be phrased, it was 'only a daughter'. She had learned in her own family that daughters were not nearly as important as sons.

But the new mother murmured to the doctor and the moment of inquiry was gone.

By now it was six o'clock. Christina was expected home so as to wash and change for dinner, which was served at seven in the Holt household. They hurried to the dogcart, left tied up to a lamppost at the corner of Candle Alley. She clambered in, strangely tired and yet in a glow of elation.

'Well,' said Childers as he shook up the reins, 'that was an unexpected event, eh?'

'Oh . . . it was wonderful!'

'Wonderful, was it? Well, I must say I agree with you. That must be the thousandth child I've helped to bring into the world, but it still thrills me.'

'It must be marvellous to be a doctor.'

'It has its moments, Christina, it has its moments.'

At home, she didn't mention the episode. In the first place she felt her mother wouldn't approve because she thought it indelicate to refer to anything concerning the functioning of the human body. The experience was too new, too precious for her to share just yet. She had been present at the birth of a new life; she had helped another creature into the world. In her arms she had held a tiny scrap of humanity whom no one else had held, except the mother, within the safe walls of the womb.

It was strange, mysterious, awe-inspiring . . . And not to be talked of for fear it should be spoiled by thoughtless comments.

But Christina's father heard of it through street gossip the next day. Someone had seen the doctor's trap hitched at the entrance to Candle Alley, had seen Christina and Childers come out and drive away. Neighbours in the alley fleshed out this titbit by explaining that Molly Pritchley in the corner house had dropped her kit but had had a bad time of it: the doctor had been called; a girl had helped him.

A girl? What girl? Who else but the strange, blue-stockinged daughter of the town's solicitor, Herbert Holt.

Herbert Holt came storming home from his office at mid-morning. His office-boy had sniggered the story out to the chief clerk, and the chief clerk had felt it his duty to tell the head of the firm.

'What is this disgusting story I hear? Answer, miss!'

'What disgusting story, Father?'

'You went into a house in Candle Alley yesterday? A house with a lamp over the entrance?'

'Yes, Dr Childers was called in.'

'It's true? You went into *that* house?'

'The one on the corner, where the footpath leads off across the smallholdings, yes. A woman called Beryl stopped the trap—'

'Don't mention that woman's name!' roared Mr Holt. It was the name of the only madam in the town of Market Bresham: Beryl Travers, who with the help of a single companion accommodated the male population when they needed a little comfort.

Of course Christina had never heard of her. She had no idea the house with the red door and the hanging lamp was a house of ill-repute – the only one in the district. She was at a loss to understand why her father was so angry.

She knew of course that she was a disappointment to him. From the age of four she'd been aware that he disapproved of her. On the first occasion she remembered, she'd been dressed up by the nursery maid in her best dress and white buttoned boots, to await a visit from Aunt Beatrice who was coming all the way from America. Instead of sitting like a good child in the nursery, as her brother Elwin did, Christina had set off to visit the hen run so as to see the chicks peck their way out of their shells.

She had been brought back in disgrace and a state of crumpled untidiness by the maid. 'Why can't you sit quiet and behave?' her father had scolded.

'But if I'd sat and waited, the chicks would have been hatched and I would have missed it.'

'But why on earth should you want to see the chicks being hatched?'

'But it's *interesting*, Father.'

He couldn't understand it. He felt utterly at odds with her. Why couldn't she be like her brother? Elwin, four years her senior, always did as he was bid. If there was any mischief in which he was involved, you could be sure it was Christina who had led him into it. Many a scolding Elwin endured rather than confess Christina was to blame, many a time he rescued her from trouble by a whispered warning.

She wished she had him here now to help assuage her father's wrath. What had she done? Why was he so angry? Surely he could *see* that to help bring an innocent baby into the world was a good thing? His harangue about wickedness baffled her. Because Herbert could see she was innocent, he was the more angry: he couldn't explain it to her, couldn't tell his already wayward young daughter that the girl she had helped was a prostitute and the child she'd nursed in her arms a bastard.

No, even in this day and age, six years into the twentieth century, one didn't speak to young ladies of such things.

'Well, that's the end of this jaunting around with Childers. You're not to see him again, Christina.'

'Why not? You were quite in favour—'

'That was before I knew the kind of places he was taking you to.'

'If only you'd explain what you mean by that. It was just a house.'

'That's enough! I want your word here and now that you'll give up this nonsense.'

'No, you can't say it's nonsense. It's *interesting*, Father. It's doing things for people.'

Interesting – that word again. The watchword of his clever, eager daughter, whose mind worked faster than his, who soaked up knowledge like a sponge, who made him feel dull and slow-witted.

'You'll promise me not to do it again or it's upstairs on bread and water for you, my lady!'

'You can't frighten me with threats like that. I'm too grown up now.'

'Oh, you think so, do you?' He seized her by the upper arm and thrust her upstairs ahead of him, uncaring of his wife's hand plucking at his sleeve as he passed and her voice pleading, 'Herbert, my love . . . It's hardly suitable now . . .' Herbert never by any chance listened to his wife. Particularly over the actions of his wayward daughter. Time and again Mildred tried to excuse her selfish, inconsiderate actions.

'Be so good as to keep quiet and stay out of the way, Mother,' he directed, pushing Christina ahead of him.

He felt her resistance, and the thought came to him, 'She's strong, she's not a little girl any more.' And to quell the thought he grunted out, 'In you go, my girl!'

'No!' At the room door she hampered his movements so that he couldn't get it open. 'I won't!' she gasped. 'I won't!'

'You'll do as I say. I *will* be master in my own house!'

'No one denies that – what do you mean?' she countered, totally bewildered.

'I mean that when I say you are not to see that buffoon of a doctor again, I am to be obeyed.'

'Buffoon? How dare you! Dr Childers is respected.'

'Not by me, by God, not after this disgusting episode.'

'But Father, I don't understand – what's wrong with helping in an emergency?'

'We won't discuss it! I have given you my orders, I expect them to be obeyed. And you'll stay here until—'

'You mean I've got to obey blindly!'

'And why not, I should like to know? Good heavens, child, who do you think you are, to question the right of your parents to choose your friends? Do I have your word that you'll stop seeing Childers?'

'No, I refuse!'

So here she was, locked up in her room to repent her sins. It hadn't happened for nearly a year, but before that it had been a regular punishment for disobedience, recklessness, lack of respect.

The clock on the mantelpiece showed it to be lunchtime. She went to look out of her window which gave on to the back garden. The scullery-maid was going down the garden with the scraps for the hen-run. Beyond, the spire of St Martin's reached up into the cloudy November sky. She could hear the bustle of the market.

If only Elwin were at home. He would steal bread and a cup of hot soup for her from the kitchen. But Elwin was staying with university friends until Christmas. He was at Cambridge these days, wrapped up in his own affairs.

She was hungry now, and would be hungrier before Falmer, the housemaid, brought her her supper: bread, as her father had decreed, although scraped with butter, and weak tea in lieu of water. Nursery fare at its plainest, and not much of it.

Generally she gave in after one such meagre meal. She made her apology, her father accepted it, her mother smiled tearfully and ordered an extra little snack for her at once.

But this time she would not give in. This time she was right. She had done nothing wrong. Besides, the conditions of being forgiven were too harsh. Never to be friendly with Dr Childers again? It was impossible. He was the only person in Market Bresham with whom she could talk on equal terms. He was intelligent and well-informed even though he was old – and none the worse for being what her father termed 'a bit of a Radical'.

Dr Childers hadn't thought it wrong to let her help with the birth of the baby. True, it was very unusual – Christina couldn't deny that it was so unusual as to make her unique among her schoolfellows: when she went back to Bresham Ladies' College after the Christmas break she had no doubt she'd be the subject of much giggling and pointing of fingers.

But nothing anyone did or said could reduce the wonder of it. A new life, a living, breathing human being. . . How could it *possibly* be a sin to have helped?

She took a book from her bookshelf. She was reading *Kipps* by H. G. Wells – another 'Radical' of whom her father couldn't quite approve. But she found it difficult to lose herself in the story. At the moment real life seemed more dramatic.

The hours went slowly by. Just before seven, the door was unlocked. On the threshold stood her father with, just behind him, Falmer holding a tray. From below came the enticing smell of roast lamb.

'Well? Are you prepared to mend your ways?'

'If you mean pretend I was wrong yesterday—'

'Pretend?' His square face went dark with angry blood. 'I should have known better than to expect remorse from you.

15

Very well. Here is your evening meal.' He stood aside to let the maid go in.

A white plate with two slices of bread thinly spread with butter. A mug of weak tea. Falmer kept her head turned away as she set this down on the dressing-table.

'I hope in the morning I shall hear some sense from you,' said Herbert Holt, backing out as the maid withdrew. The key turned in the lock.

On former occasions she had leapt on the food and eaten it eagerly, only to know the pangs of hunger again in an hour or two. Experience had taught her to eat the bread and butter half a slice at a time. The tea she drank at once. There was water in the bedside carafe if she needed more liquid.

Tired out by the arguments and emotions of the day, she was getting ready for bed at around nine when there came a tap on her door. 'Yes?' she called.

'Are you all right, dear?'

'Yes, thank you, Mother.'

'Christina . . .'

'Yes?'

'Do say you're sorry and be done with it.'

'No, I can't.'

'But . . . but . . . this is serious, dear. Your father is really angry.'

'I know that, Mother. But I can't give in.'

Even through the thick door she heard the deep sigh. 'Oh, Christina . . . Well, goodnight, dear.'

She slept well. At eight o'clock she was up and in her dressing-gown. Her father came to the door with Falmer. 'Have you come to your senses, Christina?'

'If you mean, do I agree with your view – no, I don't.'

'Come along now, child. Breakfast is waiting downstairs.'

She could smell the bacon. She hesitated.

'All you have to do is say you're sorry for behaving so badly.'

'But I *didn't* behave badly!'

'Christina,' her father said with great solemnity, 'I am

very sorry to have to mete out punishment to you. But I must do it, because if you aren't checked now, God knows what will become of you. So please, admit your guilt and promise not to see Dr Childers—'

'No!'

He sighed. 'Very well. Falmer will supervise. You may go to the bathroom while she tidies your room and makes up the fire. I shall come to the door at lunchtime to hear your submission. If you still haven't come to your senses, you'll receive nursery tea at seven o'clock. Is that clear?'

'You're talking like a gaoler!' Christina exclaimed. 'Don't you understand that this is 1906? You can't treat your children like this!'

'I'm the head of the family and I must do what I think best for it. I cannot have a daughter of mine running about the town making me into a laughing-stock and a subject of scandal. I act as you force me to act.' He paused. 'Do you apologise and admit you were in the wrong?'

'No, I don't, and I won't, ever! You'll have to keep me locked up for the rest of my life!'

'Very well.' He stood aside to let her pass him into the corridor. She went along to the bathroom, where she luxuriated in a long bath and a hair wash simply to infuriate him. When she came out half an hour later he was of course gone, and Falmer was standing outside looking distressed.

'I'm to lock you back in and take the key down to the master,' she said. 'I'm sorry, miss.'

'It's all right, Falmer, it's not your fault.' Almost jauntily she went back into her bedroom. It was a tussle of wills now – and she would outlast her father this time. She wasn't a child any more, in disgrace for some schoolgirl prank. She was grown-up, and she was defending her right to be regarded as an adult.

As she opened the room door for her Falmer whispered, 'Look in the coal scuttle.' Next moment the door had closed, the key had turned again in the lock.

Eagerly Christina went to the coal scuttle. All she saw was coals. The fire had been frugally made up, the room tidied, her bed made. She stood staring at the scuttle. Then, frowning, she picked up the top two or three lumps with tongs to set them in the hearth.

There was something among the coals wrapped in newspaper. She picked out the little parcel, unfolded it. Greaseproof paper inside the newspaper, and inside again, a thick bacon sandwich.

She ate it all in one go, too hungry to be careful with it. She drank water from the refilled carafe. Then she gave a little laugh and danced a little jig. She had allies among the servants. She wasn't going to subsist entirely on bread and water. And that being so, she knew she could win this fight.

Her father came to stand outside on the landing at lunchtime. 'Christina? Come along now. Let's have an end of this nonsense.'

'It isn't nonsense.'

'Look here, your mother is very upset. You've given her one of her sick headaches. Come now, child, say you're sorry and promise to be good.'

'Be good, what does that mean? Turn my back on my oldest friend?'

'Oh, you're incorrigible!' shouted Mr Holt, and stamped off.

Boredom was Christina's chief enemy. She finished *Kipps* and began on a life of Florence Nightingale. When her father came up at seven to supervise the awarding of the bread and weak tea, he saw what she was reading.

He snatched the book from her. 'It's this kind of reading that's given you these strange ideas!'

'Father! Please give it back! It was a school prize!'

'Yes, a school prize, and that's another thing – that school has given you ideas above yourself! Top of the class, first in French and chemistry – I won't have it!'

She stared at him. In his pin-stripe lawyer's suit and grey cravat, he looked so ordinary, so respectable. 'You surely can't grudge me my schooling?'

'My God I do, if it's turning you into a mad misfit! Let me tell you, young lady, once this is all over and behind us,

18

there's going to be some changes! No more going about with your nose in a book, no more carrying on as if you're cleverer than everybody else and don't care who knows it! You're going to know your place, my girl, and don't you think otherwise!'

He went out, taking her book with him. Then came the now familiar sound of the key turning in the lock.

Christina was shaken. This was something new. More than a battle of wills now, she sensed. Some old grudge, some long-felt need to put her in her place . . .

It was many minutes before she sat down to eat her supper. And then she discovered, under the tray-cloth, a layer of ginger snaps.

Tears came into her eyes. Her throat closed up. How kind of Falmer, how kind of Cook – and how typical to get more kindness from the servants than from her own father.

Next day the same routine was performed. Her father came to her at breakfast, lunchtime and dinner, to demand her submission. But now he was quite calm, very much in control. He entered into no argument, he simply asked the question: 'Do you admit your irresponsibility and promise to do as I tell you?'

'No.'

'Very well.'

Her mother came at eight o'clock, tapping on the door. 'Christina, please give in! It's making life so *unpleasant!*'

Well, thought her daughter with some grimness, it's more unpleasant for me than for you. 'I'm sorry, Mother, but I'm not giving in.'

'Why do you have to be so rebellious? Why can't you be more like Elwin?'

It was a question to which she had no answer.

'Unlock the door, Mother, and let me out.'

'I don't have the key, dear. Your father keeps it, and when he's out Falmer has it.'

That, of course, was typical. Her mother played almost no role in the household except as figurehead. Father controlled the household finances, Falmer controlled the household cleaning and the woman who came in to do the scrubwork, Cook ordered and cooked the food, the gardener ordered the shrubs and the bedding plants and decided which vegetables to grow. Mildred Holt drifted among them, a pale, somewhat invalidish figure, important only in that she was the mother of the children of Herbert Holt.

'Are you all right, Christina? I mean, you're not getting enough to eat – do you feel weak or unwell?'

'I feel quite well.'

'Well then . . . Goodnight, dear.'

'Goodnight, Mother.'

She slept badly that night and rose early. When her father came as usual at eight, she was up and dressed and, out of desperation, reading a school geography book.

'Have you changed your mind?'

'No.'

He studied her. 'The bathroom is free. Falmer will clean your room while you are gone.'

'Very well.'

When she came back under Falmer's convoy about fifteen minutes later she saw, to her dismay, that the row of books on her dressing-table had been taken away. Her father was determined not to let her have any escape from boredom.

'Oh, no!' cried Christina.

'I'm sorry, miss, he ordered me,' said Falmer.

Christina swallowed the sob that had welled up. 'It's all right, I know you had to.' She hesitated. 'Falmer, forget to lock my door when you go.'

'No, miss, I dessn't do that, I'd lose my place.'

'Well then . . . we can have a struggle and I'll take the key from you.'

'And do what?' said Falmer. 'I'd have to make an outcry and he'd stop you afore you stepped outdoors.'

'That's true.'

'Look among the coals. Extras today,' Falmer said with something like a wink, and went out.

The 'extra' was a note from Dr Childers.

This is a pretty kettle of fish! Your father has been to see me and read me the riot act. I've agreed not to take you on my rounds with me any more because, to tell the truth, some of my well-off patients have been very disapproving. I don't venture to advise you on what to do, my dear child, because I think you've more tenacity than I have, but I wish you well.

Yrs, George S. Childers, MD.

She read and re-read it. Should she give in? Dr Childers had given in. But for him it was to do with his livelihood. He couldn't afford to offend old Colonel Varney or Lady Pleshett. From her point of view there was nothing to gain by submitting except a more restricted life, a circumscribing of her activities and aims. She was sorely tempted. Without Dr Childers's support she felt alone and vulnerable.

Perhaps, she thought . . . perhaps when her father came up to stand outside her door at lunchtime she would say she was ready to yield.

But the decision was taken from her. Half-way through the morning, the key turned in the lock and her door was thrown open wide. In swept Aunt Beatrice in a flurry of outdoor furs and the scent of lavender.

'My poor little angel! What has that stubborn brother of mine been doing to you? Come out of that dreary room this minute!'

Chapter Two

Christina threw herself into the outstretched arms. Her cheek came to rest against artificial violets pinned on wolf's fur; she was pressed against a cape front trimmed with frogging and large metal buttons. A gloved hand stroked her hair.

'Oh, Aunt Bea! I'm so glad to see you!'

'I should think so – I've come to rescue you from durance vile. Come along at once! Falmer! Have coffee brought into the parlour immediately.'

So saying, Mrs Beatrice Kentley ushered her niece out of her impromptu prison and downstairs to the room where her sister-in-law was awaiting them in floods of nervous tears.

Aunt Beatrice came to spend Christmas in Lincolnshire every second year or so. She had been expected, but not for another two days. Having set off a day earlier than planned, though, and being a passenger on the *Kaiser Wilhelm der Grosse*, star liner of the Norddeutscher Lloyd line, she'd put in at Liverpool thirty hours ahead of schedule. Impatient to see her relations, Mrs Kentley had taken the night train south.

Beatrice Holt had married against the wishes of her family. Eighteen years ago, at a Cambridge boating party, she had met a handsome, earnest young Quaker student from Philadelphia, Pennsylvania. Her parents had been outraged at the idea that she should go so far from Lincolnshire, and marry a young teacher to boot. But Beatrice was of age and, being determined, had married and gone to settle in Philadelphia.

Walter Kentley and their young son had been killed in a fire at the Quaker college where he had the post of head of English Literature. Distraught, Beatrice had at first thought of coming home. But Philadelphia was 'home' now – Market Bresham seemed far away and not terribly inviting.

With the money she was given in compensation for the loss of her family, she set up as a hotel-keeper in a respectable suburb of Philadelphia. She had made a success of it after some difficult times. Now she was able to allow herself the luxury of a visit home at intervals, brought to the sleepy little market town not from any love of her brother but out of affection for her niece and nephew.

Although she knew it was wrong to have favourites, Beatrice particularly loved Christina. The child had always been so pretty, so full of life and light, a light that matched her fair skin and fair hair. Always interested in everything, inquisitive, active, affectionate, she had endeared herself to her widowed aunt.

As soon as Christina learned to write, she had begun sending letters to Philadelphia – letters which were eagerly awaited, but not so eagerly as the chance to see her again in person.

Beatrice's first question when she'd kissed her sister-in-law in greeting was, 'Where are the children?'

'Well . . . well, Elwin's with friends until next week. And . . . and Christina's locked in her room.'

'Locked in her room?' echoed Beatrice. 'Mildred, what on God's green earth do you mean?'

'She's been naughty . . . wicked . . . Herbert was forced to take strong measures.'

'Strong measures? I'd call it that, to lock up a girl who's pretty nearly seventeen years old. How long's she been locked up?'

'Three days.'

'*What?*'

'Three days. On bread and water. This morning is the fourth. It's . . . it's so upsetting, Bea. I don't know what to do.'

'By the lord, *I* know what to do. Give me the key.'

'I haven't got it.'

'You don't mean that fool of a brother of mine has taken it with him to the office?'

'No, no – Falmer has it.'

'Falmer? The housemaid?' Beatrice whirled about, pressed the button that rang the bell in the basement. She stuck her head out of the parlour door calling, 'Falmer! Falmer! Bring that key!'

Instantly, from behind the baize door where she'd been trying to eavesdrop, Falmer emerged with the key held out. Puffing a little with exertion, Aunt Beatrice marched upstairs to set the prisoner free.

Mrs Holt was divided between relief and alarm when Christina came in with her aunt. She could see the girl was pale from lack of fresh air and even perhaps a little thinner in the face from three days of short commons. She had wanted her daughter set free, but would never have dared take action herself. So her sister-in-law's initiative had taken away any blame from her yet had solved her problem – although what Herbert would say she dreaded to think.

Falmer came in with a loaded tray while Beatrice was still voicing her opinion of her brother's behaviour and demanding to know Christina's crime. Christina explained as far as she understood it what had happened, but broke off to accept a large piece of cake and a cup of milky coffee from her mother.

'Are you saying that simply because you helped in a case of childbirth you got locked up?'

'Now, Bea,' objected Mrs Holt, 'think what you're saying. She didn't just help by making tea and fetching clean towels, she was in at the actual *birth*. A really nice girl wouldn't get mixed up in a thing like that. Besides, it was in . . . a certain house.'

'I beg your pardon?'

'You know, Bea,' Mildred said, arching her eyebrows and shaking her head a little.

'You don't mean it was a b—'

'Have some cake,' Mildred said hastily, pushing a plate at her sister-in-law.

But she was laughing too heartily to take it.

Hotel-keeping, even in a Quaker city, broadens the mind. Beatrice wasn't nearly as shocked as her sister-in-law by the idea that Christina had helped bring a prostitute's baby into the world.

'Was it a boy or a girl?' she inquired.

'A little girl. Oh, she was so beautiful, Aunt Bea – small and perfect and trusting. I wish I knew how she was getting on.'

'We can easily find out.'

'Bea, please don't encourage the girl! We'll be in trouble enough when her father comes home for lunch.'

'Oh, I'll handle her father,' Beatrice said with a toss of her head.

She felt herself to be the equal of any small-town lawyer. Tall, upright, in her well-boned Enchantress corset, her still-fair hair piled up and frizzed in front in the French fashion, she had had to make the best of herself and hold her own in a man's world for some time now. She had always thought her brother rather dull and conventional, and her nephew Elwin promised to be just such another.

But Christina was different, had always been different. Inquisitive, enterprising, affectionate, the little girl's character had endeared her to Beatrice. She certainly wasn't going to let her brother clap Christina back into her bedroom when he got home.

When Herbert walked in at one o'clock, privately dreading the thought of having to go upstairs and hector his daughter through her bedroom door once again, he found Christina walking with her Aunt Beatrice among the shrubs of the front garden.

It put him in a dilemma. He couldn't berate Christina for escaping from her bedroom without casting blame on his own sister, and that was scarcely the way to welcome a woman who had just come across the Atlantic to see him.

He contented himself with kissing Beatrice and saying he

was glad to see her, and then muttering to his daughter, 'I'll deal with you later!'

But nevertheless, when Christina sat down to lunch with them, no remark was made about it. The only thing Herbert could think of was to ignore her pointedly. He felt somehow as if he'd been put in the wrong. It made him all the more determined to make Christina pay for her misdeeds at some point in the future.

When he returned to his office, Mrs Holt retired to her room for a rest as she usually did. Christina helped her aunt unpack.

'You seem to have spread oil on troubled waters,' she observed. 'I don't know how we could ever have come to terms with each other if you hadn't arrived.'

'But I was due to arrive eventually.'

'Yes, but by then Father thought he'd have starved me into submission.'

Beatrice shook out a creased jacket. 'I'll have to ask Falmer to press this for me. Do you like it? It's the latest New York fashion.'

'Falmer was wonderful. Don't tell Mother, but Falmer brought me goodies hidden in the coal scuttle.'

'My word, didn't they taste odd?'

'No, of course not, Aunt Bea, they were wrapped in greaseproof paper—' She broke off, laughing. 'Oh, it *is* so nice to have someone to joke with! The house has been awfully dull since Elwin went to university.'

'So you thought you'd enliven it by taking up midwifery.'

'Honestly, Aunt Bea, it was an emergency. The girl was in terrible straits. Dr Childers had to act at once and I was the only person available to help.'

'Do you like this hat? Ostrich plumes are so rich-looking, I always think.' Her aunt set it on the dressing-table. 'Listen, Christina, your father doesn't know what to do about you. I can tell he's what Westerners call "hornswoggled". You've got to make some sort of apology to him or goodness knows how it will end. He might send you to boarding school.'

'I shouldn't care!' flashed Christina. 'So long as it was a good school, I'd probably even enjoy it.'

'There speaks my little blue-stocking,' teased Beatrice. 'On the other hand he might marry you off to the first available young man.'

'To Rupert Boles, I suppose,' Christina said with scorn. 'Well, he needn't imagine I'm going to marry Rupert Boles – I'd rather be locked in my room for ever. Anyhow, I'm never going to get married. I'm going to be a doctor.'

Beatrice was so startled that she dropped the curling irons she'd just unpacked. 'What?'

'I'm going to be a doctor like Dr Childers. I made up my mind a few days ago.'

'Christina!'

Beatrice's voice rose on a note of shock. Christina's pale cheeks coloured up in a mixture of embarrassment and irritation with herself. She hadn't meant to blurt it out like that. She hadn't even been aware she'd made the decision.

But somehow the idea had found a niche, like a seed carried by the wind. It had taken root, sent out tendrils that were full of a rich vigour. The determination not to give her father the promise he demanded had been founded on this new understanding of what her life was meant to be. Fate had given her the friendship of Dr Childers; Fate had taken her to that bedside where the baby girl had drawn her first wailing breath. She was to be a doctor. She knew it, in some deep level of her being that had nothing to do with logic. A doctor . . . Dr Christina Holt.

Beatrice was staring at her in dismay.

'What's the matter? There *are* women doctors, you know.'

'Name six,' returned her aunt with cynicism. 'My dear girl, it's a totally unsuitable calling for a woman. Granted, a few formidable females have got their degree, but one never hears of them. I imagine they find it so desperately unpleasant that they soon give up.'

'That's not so! There's a woman doctor called Elizabeth

Garrett Anderson – you see her mentioned in the newspapers – she's just given up the post of director of New Hospital in London. And there's—'

'I see you've given it some thought.'

'Of course I have! Ever since Dr Childers began to talk to me about medicine.'

'Christina my *dear*! If I had had the least idea he was filling your head with—'

'Oh, he never suggested anything about becoming a doctor. That's my own idea entirely.'

'I advise you to forget it. Your father would never agree. It's just not the kind of thing you could ever say to him. I know my own brother, my dear, I can imagine how he would react to a thing like this.'

But her aunt's words fell on deaf ears. Christina's mind was taken up with the revelation that had come to her when she made her announcement.

All her girlish adoration of Florence Nightingale for her nursing in the Crimea, the eager interest with which she'd read in the newspapers about first this woman and then that achieving the victory of a degree in medicine, the ease with which she'd picked up snippets of medical knowledge from Dr Childers – she knew the reason now, she understood why she'd always wanted to be part of that world. It was because she was *intended* for that world.

'I'll make him agree,' said Christina, and in that moment her thin fair-skinned face took on a look very reminiscent of her father's stubborn expression.

It wasn't a hopeful outlook.

That evening, after Christina had diplomatically retired to bed at an early hour, Beatrice broached the subject of Christina's future.

'She told me categorically she'd never marry Rupert Boles, in case that's what you had in mind, Herbert.'

'Huh! Rupert Boles wouldn't have her after the things that have been said about her in the last few days. Do you understand, Bea, that she actually went into a . . . a house of ill-repute, and assisted in the bedside procedures of the birth?'

'Yes, she told me. And she told me something else, Herbert. She told me she's decided to be a doctor.'

Mildred Holt gave a little scream of horror. Her husband said, 'Don't be absurd.'

'I mean it,' Beatrice insisted. 'She says she's never going to get married because she's going to be a doctor.'

'Well, she isn't,' said Herbert. 'I'll put a stop to that.'

'How long do you think it will take you?'

'What?'

'You had her locked up for over three days and she still wouldn't promise not to see Dr Childers again. How long will she have to be locked up before she gives up the idea of a medical career?'

'Oh, Herbert,' wailed Mildred. 'Oh, it's going to be absolutely dreadful. And with Christmas only three weeks away!'

Herbert had jumped up and was stamping back and forth across the parlour. 'By the lord Harry, I'll have George Childers strung up from the nearest lamppost. What does he mean by putting such rubbish into the child's head?'

'It's awful,' wept his wife. 'What will people say when they hear? They'll think her so *strange*!'

'I don't think Dr Childers suggested it. It's her own idea. All nonsense, of course, but she's serious about it. At the moment, at any rate.'

'I don't know what to do!' exclaimed Herbert, throwing himself back into his armchair. 'She's the most peculiar girl in the whole of Market Bresham. Why didn't you bring her up to be interested in womanly pursuits, Mildred?'

Mildred wept into her handkerchief. Beatrice suggested that a glass of sherry all round would be a restorative. Herbert rang for it, and when it had been brought and poured, looked gloomily into his glass. 'Nobody's ever going to want to marry her,' he said.

'Oh, my dear,' protested his wife, 'she's very, very pretty.'

'No man in his senses would want her once he'd found out what strange notions she has in her head. Good lord, I'm going to have to make provision for her after I'm gone – she's going to live out her days as an old maid.'

'Not she,' said Beatrice. 'That girl's got a lot of—' She'd been going to say 'passion', but decided against it. 'She's got a lot of warmth and affection to give. She'll fall in love and get married. But I don't think it's going to happen immediately and certainly not in Market Bresham.'

'We might send her to stay with Cousin Amy,' suggested Mrs Holt. 'Buxton is very agreeable.'

'Cousin Amy wouldn't have her,' grunted Herbert. 'Not if she knew what had been going on here.'

'I was wondering,' murmured Beatrice.

'What?'

'If you'd like me to take her back to Philadelphia with me?'

'Philadelphia?' echoed her sister-in-law in a little scream of dismay.

'It might be just what she needs. A change, an interesting journey to get there, a totally new environment—'

'And a chance to get into more mischief,' said Herbert.

'In Philadelphia?' parried Beatrice, raising her eyebrows. 'It's a town full of Quakers. There *isn't* any mischief in Philadelphia.'

It wasn't strictly true, and she knew it. The Quaker influence in the city was waning fast. Yet it was a sedate town, quieter by far than New York, though not so restrictive as Boston.

'I'd love to have her,' she went on. 'You know how fond I am of Christina. And a long break away from Dr Childers would give her a chance to forget this foolish notion of taking up medicine.'

'But she's only sixteen,' objected her mother. 'It's too young to go away from home.'

'Nonsense, Milly, hundreds of girls go away to finishing school at that age. A year or two away from her family would make her appreciate it all the more when she came home.'

She didn't quite believe this herself, and had to add, to salve her conscience, 'It may well be that she'd meet a nice young man in Philadelphia. She might even meet a young lawyer. Philadelphia is full of lawyers.'

'But we couldn't let her marry an *American*,' said Mildred.

'The fact of the matter is, she's not likely to marry anybody if we don't knock these silly ideas out of her head.' Herbert rose, refilled sherry glasses, and stood pondering. 'Would you really take her, Bea?'

'Gladly.'

'You wouldn't be out of pocket. I'd arrange for an allowance to reach her.'

'Herbert, you're not really thinking of sending our little girl to the other side of the world?'

'Yes I am, Milly. I think it would be the best thing for her. She's always saying that she feels stifled in Market Bresham. Very well, let her try a big city like Philadelphia. She'll find she's a little frog in a big pond there – it'll make her see things in the right proportions.'

'Herbert, you always know best of course, but do you really think . . . ?' said his wife, greatly daring.

'I do. I do indeed. But I'll sleep on it, all the same. If I still think it's a good idea in the morning, we'll tell Christina. *That'll* stop all these nonsensical ideas about Florence Nightingale and so forth.'

The idea still appealed to him at breakfast time. He told his sister that when he had gone to his office she could issue her invitation to her niece. 'Don't let her get the idea this is some sort of treat. She's being punished – I want her to understand that. She's being sent away because she just won't behave like a civilised human being.'

'Very well, Herbert, I understand.'

But none of that appeared in her manner when she told Christina she was to come back with her to Philadelphia after Christmas.

'Philadelphia?' cried Christina, in much the same tone her mother had used.

'Yes, I thought it would get you out of an awkward situation here. You must see, dear, that you've put your father into a hopeless predicament. You won't apologise, he won't forgive you, your mother is at her wits' ends, and the atmosphere in the house is, to say the least of it, touchy. So I thought you'd be better off in Philadelphia.'

'But that's wonderful!' cried her niece. Philadelphia! The City of Brotherly Love. The New World, where old-fashioned attitudes didn't prevail, where women had been pioneers on a wild frontier. 'How long shall I be staying?'

'Well, at least a year, it's hardly worth going for less. It's not at its best in winter in the first place, and you want time to get to know it. I suggested a year or two, but no definite time limit has been given.'

The atmosphere in the house lightened immediately. Herbert knew he wouldn't have to deal with a rebellious child any more, Mildred looked forward to quiet times, Christina herself ceased to be on the look-out for slights and disapproval.

When her brother Elwin came home for Christmas, he wasn't even aware of any shadows. Christina was going to spend some time with Aunt Bea, it seemed to him a perfectly reasonable plan, although he was surprised that his father had agreed to the expense of the journey.

He wasn't a particularly perceptive young man. His head was naturally full of his own plans, which included taking a law degree and settling comfortably into the role of junior partner in his father's law office. In many ways he was like his father: not much taller than Christina, squarer and physically sturdier to look at, but with the family good looks.

Between Elwin and Christina there had been perfect companionship until he went to university. But now they had grown a little apart. He had his new friends, a different environment. His little sister, left behind in Market Bresham, seemed less important among his Cambridge set.

Yet when in the first week in January it came time to say goodbye, he found himself genuinely regretful.

'I'll miss you,' he said. 'Now I come to realise you're really going, I hate the idea.'

'But you left home, Elwin. Why is it so different for me?'

'I don't know. It is different, that's all. More permanent, somehow. At least I could always drop home and see you, but you're going an awfully long way away.'

'Well, we can write,' said his sister, trying not to let her voice tremble with tears at the thought of the ocean between them.

'It's not the same. Oh, Chrissie, everything's going to be awful now when I come home in the vac. You won't be here.'

'But it's not for ever, silly-billy.'

'I dunno,' Elwin said, taking her hand. 'Shall we ever really meet in the same old way?'

'Oh, cheer up. You make it sound as if you're never going to see me again.'

'Well, I don't expect to see you again as little Christina Holt. It's Aunt Bea's plan to find you a rich husband among her hotel guests: you'll be a married woman next time we meet.' It was half a joke but half in earnest. He'd heard his mother say Aunt Bea would try to settle Christina down.

Christina was shocked. 'Don't be silly, Elwin. I'm never going to fall in love and get married.'

'Dear little sister, you don't have to fall in love to get married. And I think Aunt Bea will prove too clever for you.'

Christina wanted to tell him that things were different for her now. She wasn't the kind of girl who could be married off. One day she was going to be a doctor. But she couldn't explain this to Elwin, because of her reason, the witnessing of the birth of the baby, something she could never bring herself to reveal to him. One didn't discuss 'intimate matters'.

This term encompassed anything to do with the physical side of life, 'women's troubles', the troubles that included the monthly curse and the conceiving and bearing of children. Taboos hedged women in among their woes. It was

34

indelicate, unseemly, unladylike even to imagine that a man knew about such things.

No doubt that was one of the reasons her father had been so angry. He'd had no objections to her going about playing Lady Bountiful among the citizens of Market Bresham. Delivering broth and bandaging fingers . . . yes, that was permissible. But it was the birth of the baby that had shocked him.

To speak of the birth to any man other than Dr Childers, even to her dearly loved brother, was impossible. Unthinkable to say to him, 'I saw a baby born!' Though it was the most miraculous thing in the world, it could never be spoken of between them.

So she couldn't tell him that despite all that Aunt Bea might do, she wouldn't be married off to a suitable young Philadelphian. She knew she had to wait, to let Fate show her the way, and one day she would be a physician.

How sad to part from Elwin without being able to explain it to him . . . Her dark eyes filled with tears. Elwin said, trying to be cheerful in face of her distress, 'Come on now, snippet, I didn't mean you'd change all that much. You'll always be my special chum, now won't you?'

'Oh, yes, Elwin, I promise. I promise, we'll always be the best friends in the world,' she said with earnestness.

He smiled at her. Father said she was wayward and stubborn and cold, but then Father probably never saw her as she was now – the inward fire of affection showing through her natural cool pallor, the determined character wavering in the face of parting.

He hugged her. As he saw it, she had a lot of growing up to do.

Saying goodbye to her mother was a simpler affair. Mildred wept, begged her to be good, reminded her to brush her hair a hundred strokes every night before she said her prayers.

'I promise,' Christina said. But whether she was promising to be good or to brush her hair, she wasn't sure.

She was truly sorry to be leaving her mother. Yet Mildred

might have a quieter life once she was gone. Christina was only too well aware that almost every family upset in the recent past had been due to something she herself had done.

She wanted to say, 'Don't let Father bully you too much.' But daughters didn't say such things to their mothers. Poor Mother . . . And yet Mrs Holt would have the quiet pleasures she enjoyed so much: church bazaars, afternoon-tea parties, shopping trips to Cambridge.

Christina was leaving all that. Already it seemed a distant view, something she was seeing through the wrong end of a telescope. Already her mother seemed to have receded from her.

Aghast at the thought, she took both her mother's hands in hers. 'I'll write, Mother.'

'Yes dear, and when you do, send me any interesting recipes . . .'

'Oh – yes.'

'I know Americans aren't good about cookery . . .'

'Aren't they?'

'No, it's all maple syrup and beans, I hear.' Mildred laboured to keep the conversation going. She felt as if she were suffocating. Herbert should be here, here at the station to say goodbye. But Herbert had gone to the office as usual after saying a formal farewell at the end of breakfast.

Don't go, don't go, Mildred was saying within herself, the rhythm of the words like the soft chugging of the locomotive as it got up steam to take her only daughter away from her. Yet she knew it was best for Christina to go.

Her strange, fairyland child . . . Too clever, too independent ever to be subservient to Herbert. Better to let her go where fairer prospects might open out for her.

The guard called out to 'Close all doors please.' Christina helped her aunt board the train. Beatrice leaned out to her sister-in-law. 'Don't worry, I'll look after her.'

'Goodbye, Chrissie!' called Elwin.

'Goodbye, dear,' faltered Mrs Holt.

Christina waved and called goodbyes until the platform had been left behind. Then she sat back to watch the advertisement hoardings slide past. 'Collis Browne's Chlorodyne'. 'A Fountain Pen of Quality by Swan'. 'Erasmus, the Dainty Soap for Dainty People'.

What kind of soap, she wondered, did they use in Philadelphia?

Chapter Three

If Herbert could have seen his daughter's arrival in Pennsylvania, he would have been pleased. Christina was considerably over-awed.

First of all there was ice in the Delaware River, and snow on the Philadelphia quays. Nothing unusual in that – Lincolnshire had its cold winters. But to see an ocean liner nosing its way up-stream between ice-floes was a new experience. And the quays stretching out interminably up-river, the sheds and gantries and offices, their roofs white with the new downfall, these were impressive.

Then there was the episode with the Immigration Officer. Christina had never thought of herself as an immigrant, and indeed she was passed as a visitor as soon as Aunt Beatrice produced the papers confided to her by her parents. Christina was a white Anglo-Saxon Protestant with a relative to support her – the interview was over in moments. But it shook her. She suddenly understood what it was to be a stranger in a strange land.

The porters who took their luggage out to the cab rank were odd. They wore thick short coats and spoke very poor English.

'Polish or Hungarian or something,' explained her aunt. 'The city's full of foreigners, of course – and you mustn't forget that a large number of the Founding Fathers were German.'

The cab that carried them from the docks was horse-drawn. But soon came an astonishment. Before they had gone a quarter of a mile, she'd seen at least twenty motor vehicles!

In Market Bresham, only Colonel Varney had a motor car, and even that seemed to spend more time in the garage being tinkered with than out on the streets of the town. In London, where Christina had been a visitor for shopping or theatre visits, one could see two, or even three, at the same time in Piccadilly.

But to see twenty! Christina gave up counting. Clearly the Philadelphians were keen on new inventions and had the money to indulge themselves.

Money, yes. The Philadelphians had money. As they were carried along Wood Street the hackney had to draw rein often to allow private carriages or great commercial wagons to pass. Public transport, which she would have called electric trams but which Aunt Bea said were known as trolleys, were plying busily up and down and across from side streets.

She soon saw the city was like a huge chessboard, laid out in rigid rectangles. The only exception seemed to be Ridge Avenue, which surprised her by taking them off to the right. Her aunt's address, which she had written often on envelopes, was The Wallace Hotel, Wallace and North Thirteenth Street, and proved to be on the corner of two pleasant residential roads.

The hotel advertised itself by a painted signboard in its front garden. It was a two-storey building on a long frontage, built about twenty years previously. There were mansard windows in the roof for the attic floor, and many gables in the Cottage-Gothic style. Clearly it had once been a family residence, but the family must have been large and well-off to have needed anything on this scale. Christina thought it at least twice the size of her father's house, perhaps even larger.

The door was flung open by an elderly maid in a brown wool dress, crackling white apron, and unbecoming cap. 'Welcome home, Mrs Kentley! You brought the blizzard with you. Brr, it's cold, come in, come in, I got the fire goin' in your parlour and hot punch just awaiting. My, who's this?'

'My niece, Miss Holt. This is Letty, dear – head house-maid and my strong right arm.'

'Your niece, eh? Seen your picture, dear, but you're prettier in the flesh. Joe! Joe! The missus is here, get yourself out there and see to the trunks.'

Joe appeared. Another shock for Christina – he was coal black. Except for his hair, that is, which was a little woolly cap of snowy white.

'Aft'noon, Miz Kentley, sure is cold after the snow. You have a good voyage?'

'A little stormy, thanks, Joe. You know which is my luggage. That grey and brown metal trunk is Miss Holt's. You'll take that up to the back attic room.'

'Yes'm,' said Joe, with a martyred expression, and when Christina herself ascended to the attic room she knew why, for it was sixty-four steep stairs from the hall.

'Take off your things and get tidy,' suggested Aunt Bea, when she had allowed her niece a moment to survey the neat little room with its sloped ceiling and white iron bedstead. 'There's a bathroom on the floor below, at the end of the landing. Leave your unpacking for the moment, we'll have a hot drink and I'll show you the house.'

The hot drink proved to be rum and lemon juice mixed with sugar and hot water. It was delicious. The parlour in which they drank it was her aunt's private sitting-room-cum-office, immediately inside the front door and just off the entrance hall. Behind it was a small bedroom and bath-room. Christina was amazed – two bathrooms, and she'd seen a cloakroom with wash-basin further up the hall.

The hotel's public rooms were on the ground floor. A large entrance hall with a sofa and a hat-stand opened out into the dining-room, which had tables laid for supper. Beyond that on the other side was the lounge, furnished with armchairs and little tables and a piano, where well-thumbed copies of popular music stood ready on the carrier.

There was a little room opening off: 'The card room,' explained Aunt Bea. 'Gentlemen are mad on cards, particularly Captain Dinsdorf.' Captain Dinsdorf was a retired sea captain, a permanent guest at reduced rates.

The kitchens were in a semi-basement at the back. Here Letty ruled a staff of three: Joe the porter and handyman, Helmina the cook, and an under housemaid. Joe stoked the boiler in the basement proper and had a little room to himself. Kitchen stores, trunk storage, a little area under a window where Captain Dinsdorf was allowed to use fretsaw and sticky glue in the construction of model ships – these completed the basement area.

'Two waitresses come in by the day to serve in the diningroom,' explained Aunt Bea. 'There's a scrub-woman to do the floor-waxing and the window-cleaning. For the yard – you'd call it the garden – a local handyman trims the shrubs and mows the lawn. You can't see it properly because of the snow, of course, but in the summer we can sit out in the backyard under the mulberry trees.'

On the first floor were the bedrooms. The original rooms had been adapted to accommodate twenty guests, of whom two were permanent residents, Captain Dinsdorf and Miss Melville.

'Miss Melville has a small income, helps in a charity organisation for the Episcopalian church. The clients who come and go are chiefly visiting engineers and supervisors connected with the railroad.' Aunt Bea paused and laughed. 'The railroad, one of the most important factors of Philadelphian life, the Pennsylvania Railroad. It stretches from Chicago in the west to Washington in the south and brings us beef and bankers, provisions and politicians. Though we don't need anything to bring us politicians, we have enough of our own – all bad.'

'Aunt Bea!' exclaimed Christina in protest. She was accustomed to think of Members of Parliament with respect.

'Oh, it's something you have to get used to if you're a resident of Philly. Not that it need concern you, my dear. But we get one rotten bunch after another. Bribery and corruption, contracts for the water system and the gas supply handed out to whoever will offer the biggest kickback

. . . Even the education system is a disgrace. This is one of the oldest cities in America, but it can't construct laws that make it compulsory for a ten-year-old to go to school . . .' She sighed and shrugged. 'Well, that doesn't interest you. The first thing is to take a good look at your room and see what we can do to make it prettier. It's intended for a resident maid, you see – a bit spartan. But I've got cushions and curtains in store that will brighten it up.'

A big walk-in closet on the landing was opened up. Christina was invited to commandeer anything she fancied while Aunt Bea went below to catch up on business. Letty had of course run the hotel for her as she always did in her absence, but there were bills to be paid, letters to be answered.

By the time the gong was struck at six o'clock for supper, Christina had made up the bed in her room with a pretty frilled valance and bedspread, found a drape for the dressing-table, a rag rug for the floor, and two crocheted cushions for the wooden armchair. She had even made a start on her unpacking.

She washed hastily before running downstairs. Mrs Kentley introduced her quite formally to the two permanent residents.

'So, you kom to liff in Philly,' commented Captain Dinsdorf. 'I kongratulate you, Mrs Kentley. It vill be very pleasant to have such a little beauty among us.'

Blushing, Christina turned to make a little curtsey to Miss Melville. 'Nicely brought up, I see,' she said. 'But then, the English always have such good manners.'

Miss Melville, it turned out, was an Anglophile, doting upon the British royal family and all things aristocratic. It was simply because Mrs Kentley was English by birth that Miss Melville patronised her hotel.

American food was a revelation to Christina. The meal began with corn soup, then went on to honey-baked chicken served with stuffed egg-plant, skillet cabbage and potatoes. Dessert, of which she ate not a nibble, was angel cake accompanied by ice-cream.

The male guests ate enormously. With no idea of hotel-keeping, Christina couldn't help thinking that Aunt Bea's profits vanished into those ever-opening mouths. But when she mentioned the idea to her aunt, she was told, 'The climate's very cold here in winter, dear. People have to stoke up.'

The evening was taken up with unpacking. 'My, your clothes are kind of schoolgirlish, aren't they?' commented Aunt Bea. 'Still, we'll let down these hems or maybe put in a false flounce. When I've sorted out a few problems in the office, dear, we'll go shopping. Let's say tomorrow afternoon.'

To Christina's surprise, she didn't fall asleep the moment her head touched the pillow, although she was so weary she almost fell into bed. Instead she found herself washed by a wave of home-sickness. What was she doing here, in this totally strange house in a totally strange city on the other side of the world from where she belonged? Why hadn't she been a good, sensible girl and fallen in with her father's demands?

Since now, after all, she *had* given up her friendship with Dr Childers. She *had* cut herself off from her books and her education. Here she was, a guest in Aunt Bea's home, and as far as she could tell the outlook was one of helping her aunt, being a sociable companion, shopping, walking about the town . . . She could have stayed at home and done all those things with her mother.

But in the morning, those thoughts had vanished. Outside, the world sparkled with snow. Aunt Bea busied herself with account books and papers. Christina went into the lounge to look at the bookcase, for she hadn't dared to ask her father to let her have her books to pack in her trunk.

Captain Dinsdorf was there, reading. He looked up to nod good morning.

'I'm sorry, I didn't mean to disturb you.'

'Not at all, it is no disturbance. How are you this morning, Miss Christina?'

'Very well, thank you. And you?'

'Oh, I amuse myself with this foolish book, but I am happier to speak to a pretty young lady.' He smiled at her through his wealth of grey beard and moustache. 'You know, you remind me of a character in one of our Cherman fairy tales. You have heard of the Snow Maiden?'

'Yes, I think I read it once – is it by Hans Andersen?'

'Ach, he may well have stolen it! Many old North Cherman tales he took and used for himself. The Snow Maiden, this is a very old legend. She is fair and pale-skinned, you know? And there is about her a sparkle.' He rose, favouring his rheumatic hip. 'Look, like on the window-pane. You see the frost patterns? They sparkle in the morning sun, ja?'

'Yes, they do – how beautiful.'

Dinsdorf smiled and nodded his head. 'You are like that. A cool sparkle from within, but the sparkle means fire – fire in frost, that is you.'

Christina was blushing and making sounds of denial. 'No, no . . .'

'You think not? You don't know yourself yet. Well, well, who does at sixteen or seventeen? When I was your age, I was a little midshipman who wouldn't say bo to a goose. Yet in time I was captain of a merchant ship, commanding men and fighting the storms, ja?'

To deflect him from any further discussion of her character, she murmured that he had had an interesting life. 'Oh, ja, very interesting, yet every seaman can tell you yarns. And what happens in the end? We are thrown up on the beach, and have to amuse ourselves making little models of the beloved ship and reading silly novels. Haf you read this book?'

He held it up so she could see the title on the spine. *Die Leiden des jungen Werthers*, she read. 'No, I'm afraid I don't know any German, captain.'

'Ach, only French, eh? French is the language of young ladies, but Cherman is the language of men and of science,' he said, throwing out his chest to show how manly he was.

She laughed. 'Now captain, you know that Latin is the language of science.'

'Not at all, not at all. Of ancient science, ja, I accept that.

But of modern science, of engineering and chemistry and medicine – where do all the great discoveries come from these days?'

'I don't know,' she confessed. She knew he was going to tell her it was his homeland.

Instead he said, 'It is a difficult language, difficult to learn, difficult to pronounce.' He read out the book title. 'Could you say that?'

She tried to repeat it. '*Dee Lyden des yoongen Verters . . .*'

'Very good, very good! You are an exception, Miss Christina. You do not mind trying strange sounds, you don't fear to make yourself sound foolish. You will find it useful to speak a few words, you know. Many people in Philly speak Cherman, from old tradition. Well, if you wish, I give you lessons! And you will speak good North Cherman, and like an old sea-dog!'

They laughed, and as she turned to the bookshelf, the matter was dropped. Yet three weeks later she was learning German, because learning was so much part of her nature she simply couldn't do without it.

The shopping expedition took place in the afternoon. The marvels of Market Street were made known to her, her aunt bought her a pair of galoshes and a ready-made skirt of a length more suitable for a young lady who had left school.

'May we buy some books, Aunt Bea? I didn't bring any with me.'

'There are some on the shelf in the lounge, dear.'

'They're mostly stories of the Wild West, or else instruction handbooks for accountants. I wondered if I could buy—'

'My dear girl, there's no need to *buy*! There's a big Free Library on Chestnut. I'll show you on the way home.'

They took the trolley and stopped off at the library. There was no time for more than a glimpse of the huge circulation room with its many-bracketed gasoliers, crowded shelves, and busy counters.

'Oh, lovely,' breathed Christina.

Beatrice gave Christina a sidelong glance. On the girl's

face there was the expression usually called forth by a scene of magic at the theatre. Well, well, to each his own enchantment.

A routine became established. In the mornings Aunt Bea attended to business, while Christina made expeditions to the Library or sat with Captain Dinsdorf, laughing over her attempts at 'Cherman'. In the afternoon they went out – at first to the town centre while the snow remained, but as the weather relented they went to Fairfield Park or the grounds of Girard College.

Spring came, the mulberries and hickories put out fresh green leaves, gardens in traditional Germantown were full of neat beds of daffodils, and Christina had written home two or three times to tell her mother she was happy in Philadelphia.

She also wrote to Dr Childers . 'I hope you and Father have made friends again. I am so sorry I caused so much trouble, but it's only recently that I've begun to understand the problem. Some hints from Aunt Bea have led me to think that it wasn't so much what I did, but where I did it, that annoyed Father.'

She was very pleased when Dr Childers took the trouble to reply in his scribbly doctor's handwriting. He assured her he and her father were back to being polite to each other, told her the baby girl had been called Christina in her honour, and ended with, 'It's odd that you should have been exiled to Philadelphia. I should think it very congenial, since it has a long tradition of medicine. The University, as I dare say you've learned, was founded by Benjamin Franklin and has produced some fine doctors. There's even a medical school for women, I believe. So you see you've reached an interesting harbour.'

She was at once intrigued. Aunt Bea knew nothing about either the University or any other medical school, but Miss Melville was better informed.

'The Women's Medical College, yes, of course. It's absolutely no good, you know.'

'No good?'

'No, at the Episcopalian Medical Mission we've had two

women doctors who qualified there and, really, the stories they tell! Only one of the teachers gave his whole time to the school, the rest were only part-time – and not very highly qualified, I may say. It hasn't any endowment worth speaking about, and I believe Dr Kleinshelm said the laboratories left a lot to be desired.'

'But that's unfair! Just because it's a women's college?'

'Well, that's usual, my dear. Women always have to take the leavings. "You're sure to get married", that's always the cry. I wanted to train as a teacher, but my parents wouldn't hear of it. So here I am, an old maid as they say, and a lot more useful I'd have been in the world if I'd had a proper training.'

'I do so agree with you!' Christina cried. 'My parents—'

'Parents try to do their best for their children, Christina. But it somehow always works out that the boys get all the attention and training, and the girls have to hang about at home until it's too late. Don't you make that mistake, my dear.'

'But what's the point of taking training – at a medical college, say – if the teaching and facilities are second-rate?'

'Oh, everything is first-rate at the University Medical School.'

'But women can't train there, I suppose?'

'What makes you say so? I believe they can. Of course it's much harder for them, and I should think very few actually go there – how distasteful to discuss intimate health matters in a roomful of men! But I believe I'm right in saying there's no law against admitting women.'

It was a surprise, yet why should it be? The ancient University of Edinburgh had opened the doors of its medical school to women only last year. If it could be done in Scotland, then why not in America, the land of freedom?

Out of curiosity she went next day to look at the University of Pennsylvania. She walked to Ridge Avenue, took the trolley to Market, changed to one signboarded for W. Chester Depot and from there, by asking passers-by, found her way to the fine expanse of collegiate Gothic in its carefully tended lawns.

It was a warm day in early May. Young men in short striped blazers and straw boaters sprawled on their stomachs with books propped against a tree; bearded gentlemen in dark cut-away coats walked together in earnest conversation; from one of the windows floated a voice in mid-lecture, 'But the purpose of Greek drama was not entertainment, gentlemen!'

And, yes . . . one or two young women were to be seen, hurrying to classrooms after lunch, document cases under their arms, or bicycling purposefully towards the further reaches of the lawns.

Christina longed to stop one and ask the way to the faculty of medicine. But her nerve failed her. What would they think of this queer creature with the English accent, detaining them with silly questions when they were expected in Room 16 by Professor Prink?

She walked all the way home, about four miles, thinking vaguely about the University. Off and on during the next few weeks she thought about it, and by paying attention to casual talk and reading the newspapers with attention, became aware that women medical students were by no means unheard of in the United States. Women doctors working in the female wards of hospitals were quite accepted. She even read an article by Louisa Knapp, the editor of the *Ladies' Home Journal*, giving details of the career of a certain Madame Montessori and speaking of her with obvious approval. Maria Montessori, it appeared, had received her medical degree in Rome thirteen years ago, in 1894.

Thirteen years ago. And here in the United States, the training was available. Some of the medical schools seemed to have very high entrance requirements, though. For Johns Hopkins in Baltimore, for instance, you had to possess an academic degree already.

But from what she heard about Pennsylvania University, the requirements were much less strict. As Aunt Beatrice had said when speaking of the political situation, the state seemed to be in something of a muddle about its educational system.

Summer brought with it enervating heat and clammy humidity. It was too much trouble to think deeply. Instead there was the pleasure of lying under the shade in the backyard, or strolling in the cool of the evening with new-found friends from nearby.

Because it was so hot, Christina put her hair up. It was cooler than having it hanging in two thick plaits down her back.

'My,' said Aunt Bea, 'don't we look grown-up!'

And Captain Dinsdorf said, 'My little Snow Maiden is turning into a Snow Princess.'

Miss Melville said, 'My dear, don't English girls generally wait until they come out to put their hair up?'

'I suppose you could say I *am* out. I was seventeen in May, you know.'

'Humph,' said Miss Melville.

Christina experimented with hairstyles, copying them from the portraits of the actresses outside the Arch Street Theatre. Plaits round her head made her look absurdly regal, rolled curls and a high topknot were too contrived. In the end the best solution was to twirl her long hair round her hand and pin it in a loose bun on the crown of her head. Unfashionable, perhaps, but cool and practical.

Autumn came – 'fall', as she must learn to call it. 'We'll have to get you some new clothes,' said Aunt Bea. 'Your old winter dresses were too short to begin with, and you've shot up at least another two inches.'

It was true. And she had filled out, no doubt due to the good food provided by her aunt.

Her quarter's allowance had come through from her father, an order to draw on the Bank of Commerce. She and Bea went out to spend a happy afternoon choosing velveteen and alpaca, serge and gaberdine, with taffeta as skirt lining for visiting costumes so as to rustle expensively. Accessories such as leather gloves, jabots, satin ties, and stockings both woollen and silk, were carried home. The clothes were made up by a German immigrant woman with whom Christina surprisingly found she could carry on quite a sensible conversation, thanks to Captain Dinsdorf.

As for hats, Christina would have to re-trim those she already owned. Hats were too expensive to buy often.

On a morning in September she gave up in exasperation on a wide-brimmed straw which refused to be re-shaped. She pulled on her jacket, caught up a tam-o'-shanter and gloves, and ran downstairs.

'Aunt Bea,' she said, putting her head round the door, 'I'm fed up with being a milliner. I'm going out for some fresh air and exercise.'

'Good for you. Shall you be back for lunch?'

'Perhaps not – I've been eating far too much recently.'

'Now, dear!'

'Oh, it's all right, I'll grab a sandwich in the drugstore at Lit Brothers.'

'If you're going into Lit's, see if you can find me a lace edging for that batiste blouse, Christina.'

She waved agreement and hurried out. It was a crisp, bright day. The trees were still green but there was a tinge of gold beginning in some of them, especially the ginkgos. Dahlias flaunted their opulence in the public gardens in Franklin Square. The city centre was busy, with its inhabitants, soberly but neatly dressed, moving about with purpose and obvious enjoyment of the fine weather.

How it came about that she found herself at the University, she never could explain afterwards. Later in life, when she had studied psychology, she knew what Dr Freud called 'the unconscious' had been at work through all the preceding months. Or 'Fate' – that 'fate' which had given her Dr Childers as a friend, which had taken her to a childbed in a slum quarter of Market Bresham.

She walked through the grounds, and by an arched doorway she found a wooden stand with a board and an arrow: 'Registration'. She went in. There was a long mahogany counter, and behind it several gentlemen making notes on forms as young people answered questions. She was interested to see that out of eleven young people, two were girls. There was a short queue. She joined it.

'Faculty?' said the clerk when it came to her turn to step to the counter.

'I beg your pardon?'

'For which faculty are you applying?'

'Oh – medicine.'

'Name?'

'Christina Holt.'

'Nationality?'

'English.'

'Age?'

'Eighteen,' she said, telling herself he meant her age on her next birthday.

'Regent's Certificate?'

'Pardon?'

'Have you got your Regent's Certificate? Or equivalent certificate of education?'

'Oh . . . er . . . well, I was educated in England. I don't have . . . er . . . any certificates with me.'

'What education did you receive?' asked the clerk, sighing and dragging at his moustache in impatience.

'I attended Market Bresham Ladies' College.'

'Ladies' College, eh? High School?'

'I should think . . . it would be the equivalent of High School.'

'Did you graduate?'

'We . . . er . . . we don't call it that. I passed the London School Board matriculation exam.'

'Did, huh?' He studied her with some glimmer of respect. 'Subjects?'

'English, French, mathematics, Latin, combined sciences with geography.'

'German?'

'I didn't take German.'

'Sorry.' The clerk's hand began the motion of crumpling the form. 'Can't take medicine without German.'

'Wait! I study German privately. With a native speaker.' Captain Dinsdorf, ex-captain of a merchant ship – but he was a native speaker of German.

'Ah. What level have you reached?'

'I'm afraid I don't know. I can hold a conversation.'

'Conversation,' wrote the clerk against the item on the form. 'No certificate?'

'I'm afraid not.'

'In that case you'd have to take the *vicario*.'

'What does that mean?'

'Short examination, instead of a certificate, to ensure your knowledge is sufficient for admission.'

'How do I take the examination?'

'It's held here at the Wharton Building. I put your name down for it. Do you want that?'

'Yes please. When is the examination?'

'Lemme see, German, German ... Daily, from two-thirty p.m. in Room 104. Which day would suit?'

'Er . . . today?'

'Just a moment, I'll look at Mr Lander's schedule.' He went into an inner office. When he returned he said, 'There's a space at three. Please be prompt, Mr Lander has other responsibilities and mustn't be kept waiting.'

'I'll be there.'

'The fee for the examination is five dollars.'

Christina fumbled in her bag and produced a five-dollar bill. The clerk gave her a receipt.

He was turning away.

'Excuse me.'

'Yes?'

'Isn't there anything else I have to know?'

'Not until you pass the *vicario*.'

'When will I know that?'

He smiled and made a little dismissive gesture. 'Why, about three forty-five this afternoon, I'd say.'

She went out. The sun was still shining, the lawns still gleamed, her feet crunched on the gravel path.

A clock chimed the time from a spire. Twelve-thirty.

Only twenty minutes had passed since she first went in under the arched doorway.

She ought to get some lunch but she knew she couldn't eat. She needed something to settle the fretful fluttering in the region of her stomach, though. She found a drugstore nearby, ordered a vanilla ice-cream soda, and sat sipping it slowly through a straw.

She wouldn't let herself examine what she was doing. She couldn't afford to unnerve herself by the enormity of it. Instead she made herself rehearse the difficult irregular verbs of the German language: *Ich bin, du bist, er ist* . . . She tried to hear Captain Dinsdorf speaking in her head, or the dressmaker asking if the waist of her new skirt fitted neatly.

At a quarter to three she went into the University grounds. Only then did it occur to her that she didn't know the whereabouts of the Wharton Building. She stopped a stolid-looking young man in a sports jacket and brown derby.

'Wharton – over there to the right. What is it, a *vicario*?'

'Yes.'

'Don't look so scared, the worst they can do is flunk you.'

She walked on in haste, not at all encouraged by his humour.

The room was on the first floor. She tapped timidly, to be greeted with an impatient, '*Herein, herein!*'

The room was small, more like an ante-room than an examination hall. The examiner was a small, burly man. He looked at a list on his desk. 'Miss Christina Holt?'

'Yes, sir.'

'Private lessons in conversational German?'

'Yes, sir.'

'Sit down.'

There was a chair on the opposite side of his desk. She sat down. He had two or three books in front of him, with slips of paper marking a place. He opened one, handed it to her.

'Kindly read the marked passage.'

The angular German-Gothic script leapt up at her. There were an awful lot of long words, none of them the kind Captain Dinsdorf ever used. She began to read, slowly, taking each syllable at a time so that the words came out without the rhythm of good speech.

'Hm,' said Mr Lander. 'Please translate.'

'Yes, sir.' She ran her eye along the first sentence, looking for the verb. In a faltering voice she began, 'Friedrich Nietzsche was concerned – preoccupied – with the loss of faith among the educated classes of Europe and the New World.' The subject matter was dry as dust and meant nothing to her but she ploughed on.

'Yes. You study any philosophy?'

'No, sir.'

'Never heard of Nietzsche, I suppose.'

'I've . . . I think I've heard of him.'

'Really. Please pick up that pen and be ready to take dictation.'

'Yes, sir.' She picked up the pen, dropped it, found it again before it rolled off the desk, and dipped it in the ink. A single sheet of paper lay before her, over which she poised her hand. Mr Lander opened another book. '"*Wie erhebt sich das Herz . . .*"'

She'd been expecting something as dry as Nietzsche, not a prayer to the Almighty. Catching at the words she'd let go by, she began to write.

'That will do. Please lay down your pen. I will give you two minutes to read through what you have written, then I want you to read me your translation.'

'Yes, sir.' She read it from end to end at great speed, couldn't make sense of it, couldn't even read her own writing.

'Time's up. What does it mean, Miss Holt?'

'Er . . . How the heart rises, leaps up, when it thinks of Thee, unending . . . no, permanent . . . no, I mean, everlasting one. How sinks it . . . no, I mean, how it sinks, when it upon itself looks under. No, I mean, when it looks down on itself. Wretched . . . it seems . . . it seems wretched . . . that's the heart, I mean; the heart seems wretched.'

And so on for six painful sentences. She sat red with shame. What a mess. She didn't know a word of German.

'That was a piece by Klopstock. You've never read it?'

'No, sir. I've only read a local newspaper published here in German.'

'That would contain very little about the soul and the poet's misery, I feel sure. How long have you been learning?'

It suddenly dawned on Christina that he was speaking German to her, that she understood him quite well, and that she had replied in the same language.

'I've been learning since the beginning of February. It's been quite informal.'

'Your teacher is a North German, I take it.'

'Yes, sir,' she said, smiling. In her own intonation she could hear Captain Dinsdorf's.

'You're applying for the Faculty of Medicine?'

'Yes, sir.'

'Then I'm afraid I have one more torment to inflict. Please read this aloud and tell me what it means.'

Once more it was full of words she'd never heard or seen before. It was a medical text. Once she'd stumbled through it she stared at it hopelessly. 'Children sometimes suffer from a something – burning, inflammation involving the whole of the . . . I think it's pharynx, especially the . . . oh yes, adenoids. This condition is due to a . . . a . . . some kind . . . acute? infection causing strong fever and head-ache. I don't understand the next phrase, something about the interior of the throat . . . I'm sorry, it's too technical. Later on it talks about difficulty in breathing and swallowing.'

'Hm,' said Mr Lander. He leaned back in his chair, stared at her, then began to laugh with great barks from his burly chest. 'Damned if I understand it myself, in German or English,' he said, 'but it's the medical text I have to use as a specimen. Well, Miss Holt, your German is fair, and if you work at it it will be good. I mark you as a pass in the *vicario* in German. That is all.'

'That's all?'

'Yes, please go, another poor idiot is due in five minutes.' He handed her a small slip of paper with her name, the time of her examination, and the word 'Pass' written in the space left for the verdict.

'What should I do now, sir?'

'You go back to the registration hall, give this slip to one of the registration clerks, who will call up your application form and enter the result. He'll take it from there.'

'Thank you, Mr Lander.'

'Goodbye, Miss Holt. Good luck.' He shook hands and showed her out.

Dazed, Christina went down the stairs and out. She almost began to run as she made her way back to the registration room. Once again there was a short queue. She waited, and at last stepped to the counter to be greeted by a middle-aged lady with her hair done in earphone coils and wearing wire-rimmed glasses.

'Yes?'

'Christina Holt. I registered this morning. This is the result of my *vicario*.'

'I see. One moment.' She disappeared into the inner office, and came back with the form to which Christina had supplied answers earlier. She looked at the slip, entered 'Pass in German' alongside the notation about Christina's education, wrote a few other words.

'Right, that's all the information we require. Your book list and information about fees, dates and classrooms will be sent to you in a day or two.' She tore off the back page of the double form. 'If you will just get your parents to sign this and send or bring it in . . .'

'My parents?'

'Yes, see there, it says: If under twenty-one the applicant must obtain the permission of parent or guardian who should sign below. The fee for the first semester must be sent with the form.'

'Oh.'

'Do you require a lodgings list? If so, please apply at the Bursar's Office.'

'Thank you.'

She went out, holding the form that needed her parents'

signature, and understood that the dream she'd been allowing herself for the last three hours was now at an end.

On the trolley car she got out the form and read it. Regulations about strict attendance at lectures, good behaviour, participation in the University's activities were set out. Prompt payment of fees was of prime importance, except in the case of a student who had a scholarship or bursary. Parents or guardians were to be held responsible if there was any failure to pay fees or any misconduct or laxity on the part of the student.

The language was stately, but how seriously it ought to be taken, she wasn't sure. When she thought of some of the pranks that her brother and his friends got up to at Cambridge, she couldn't quite believe so much solemn dependence on parental control was genuine. But there was the matter of fees. Someone had to guarantee her fees would be paid.

And her father certainly wouldn't do it.

She got off the trolley car, needing to walk and think things out. It was about half-past five when she reached home. Her aunt came out to greet her as she came into the hall. 'There you are, Christina. You've scarcely left time to wash up before supper. Did you get that lace?'

'I'm sorry, Aunt Bea, I forgot.'

'Oh, what a nuisance, I've got the blouse nearly finished.' She held it out to show her niece.

Christina ignored it. 'Aunt Bea,' she said, 'I have something very important to tell you.'

Chapter Four

Beatrice Kentley was so startled that she pricked her finger with the needle she was still holding.

'You did what?' And then, irritated, 'If this is a joke, I don't think it's very funny.'

'I'm perfectly serious,' said Christina. 'I've enrolled in the Faculty of Medicine at Pennsylvania University.'

'Now, see here, that's quite impossible . . .'

'It's possible. I just spent this afternoon doing it.'

'That's not what I mean. You know it's impossible. Your father would never allow it.'

'Oh, I know *that*.'

'Then you know very well that you've wasted your time. I hope you didn't pay any money or—'

'I paid a five-dollar fee for a German exam. It's the money side I want to talk to you about.'

'There's nothing to say. You can't study medicine. The minute your father heard about it, he'd have you sent home.'

'Why need he know?' Christina said.

'Christina!' Mrs Kentley sank down on a hall chair, staring.

'Well, why? You only write at Christmas and birthdays, and when I write I write to Mother. She only wants to hear about what clothes I've altered and how many bottles of pears we've put up. If we don't tell them, they needn't know.'

'But that would be deceitful!'

'Oh, I see,' her niece said, with unexpected anger. 'Helping me do the thing I was put on this earth to do is wrong, but trying to marry me off so as to get rid of me, that's all right. Where's the morality in that?'

'Christina! There was never any intention to "marry you off".'

'Oh no? So why do you keep leaving me alone with Paul van Schuys, and why do you keep on telling me how much money Amos Horder is going to come into?'

'But Paul van Schuys is a very nice young man . . .'

'Paul van Schuys has the mentality of a ten-year-old and the ambition of a bathmat. As for Amos, if he tells me once more that his property in New York is bringing in more every day, I'll—'

'You're very arrogant, Christina. Other girls would be happy to—'

'Very well, let other girls put up with those two. That suits me, I want to study medicine.'

'Now be sensible. Just because you were taken with this sudden notion—'

'It's not a sudden notion. I told you about it before ever we left Market Bresham.'

'Yes but, my darling girl—'

'Don't *patronise* me!' her niece cried. 'Just because it's something you don't understand, don't take refuge in a lofty tone!'

'Christina, go to your room!' Beatrice cried, springing up in indignation.

High colour crept in under the girl's clear, pale skin. 'Not you too.'

'What?'

'"Christina, go to your room and stay there until you come to your senses". I thought you didn't approve of my father's methods?'

They stood staring at each other. The outer door opened and one of the hotel guests came in, taking off his hat as he saw the women. 'Good evening, ladies. Cool tonight, definitely cool.'

'Yes, Mr Sands, definitely cool.'

He hung his hat on the hall stand, then went into the lounge to wait for Letty to sound the gong.

Beatrice Kentley knew that she and her niece were on the verge of a terrible quarrel. What was being asked of her was, of course, impossible. She had brought Christina to Philadelphia to rescue her from a miserable existence at home and, if possible, find her someone better than a Norfolk Dumpling to marry. In no way had it been her intention to help the girl with this mad idea of being a doctor.

Seldom ill, Beatrice always called a male doctor if she needed one. It would never have occurred to her to look for a woman doctor, nor would she have trusted one if she found her. Doctoring was a *male* profession.

True, there was a term used these days, 'a professional woman'. She herself was by way of being 'a professional woman' in that she ran a business, a hotel. Other women had learned office skills such as shorthand and bookkeeping. There was of course the nursing profession, which did have its gruesome side. But doctoring . . . ! For fragile, ethereal Christina? Out of the question. One look at a bad abscess or a surgical incision and that pale face would be even paler . . .

Of course there had been that great adventure into midwifery in the red light district of Market Bresham. Well, the child might say what she liked, but Aunt Bea was pretty sure Dr Childers had shielded her from the worst moments of that.

It was time to take a firm line.

'Christina,' said her aunt, 'in a minute we have to go into the dining-room and make polite conversation with the guests. If you begin to badger me—'

'I wouldn't dream of badgering you. I wouldn't dream of talking about my plans in front of strangers.'

'Very well. I have to tidy myself and I suggest you do the same. Supper will be in about ten minutes.'

Throughout the three courses and coffee no one, except perhaps Captain Dinsdorf, could have guessed that the two women were at odds with each other. To her own surprise Christina found she was ravenous, and made a good meal, with the result that afterwards she felt far less edgy, less aggressive. She began to feel she had handled the episode very badly.

'I apologise, Aunt Bea,' she said when they went back to the private sitting-room. 'Of course I realise you were taken by surprise and perhaps didn't understand that I'm in deadly earnest. Can we go back and start again?'

'My dear child,' said her aunt, 'you know I want what is best for you but I can't see how – even if I agreed to it – we could keep your studies from your father for ever.'

'We wouldn't have to!' rejoined Christina with eagerness. 'Just a year, that's all. Then if I do well – and I *will* do well, Aunt Bea, I know I will – I'll write to him with the results of the end of term exams and he'll see it's what I'm good at and he'll agree.'

'But why on earth do you want to be a doctor?' cried Beatrice. 'It's so unsuitable for a well-brought-up young lady! You'd hate it, I know you would!'

'Then the sooner I try it and find out, the better – isn't that true? If after one term I find I can't bear it, then the whole thing's dropped and that's an end of it.'

'Oh, well, if you think you'd drop it after one term, why start?'

'I don't think I'd drop it. I think I was meant to be a doctor. I've thought so ever since I helped bring that little baby into the world. That's why I can't bear to have you shrug it off, Aunt Bea, as if it was a fancy for an excursion trip to Cape May. It's the beginning of my life, the real beginning. I have to do it, Aunt Bea.'

Mrs Kentley walked about the room clasping and unclasping her hands. 'I think it's so unwomanly! All that close proximity to death and disease . . .'

'But I want to work with children: you surely don't think there's anything unwomanly about wanting to help children?'

'No-o . . . But . . . but there must be some very sordid things you have to learn . . .'

'I don't deny that. But other women have done it, Aunt Bea. It's not unheard-of.'

'It's unheard-of in our family,' said her aunt, with the first faint beginnings of a smile. 'Your father would have a fit.'

'That's why I think he shouldn't be told until I've proved myself. You do see that, Auntie?'

'I see that you think it should be so. But I still think it's deceitful.'

Christina hesitated. 'I don't deny that,' she said at length. 'I ought to have the courage to tell him, I suppose. But would *you* like to tell him a thing like that?'

Beatrice made a movement of rejection.

'And remember when you wanted to marry Uncle Walter? How you had to fight against your parents for what you thought right?'

'Yes, but that was different . . .'

'I don't see how. You wanted to choose how you would live your own life. I want the same.'

'But I was twenty-one years old, Christina. I knew my own mind.'

'What has twenty-one or not twenty-one got to do with it? I know my own mind too – and you could say it's not clouded by romantic notions or the mental upset of being in love. I'm sane and in my right mind, and I want to study medicine. I know I'll still want to when *I'm* twenty-one.'

There was a pause. Mrs Kentley folded her afternoon's sewing, put it in her workbox, closed the lid. 'How long is the course?'

'Four years.'

'There are fees, of course. How are they supposed to be paid?'

'Out of my allowance, Auntie,' Christina responded, having already worked it all out. 'I've got enough clothes to see me through for a long time, so we shan't spend any money on things like that. The fees aren't high.' She produced the form she had brought home. 'But there is a slight problem.'

She knew her aunt was pleased to hear it. 'Let me see. Oh . . . signature of parent or guardian . . . that's the end of that, then. Your father would never sign it.'

'But you can sign it, Aunt Bea.'

'Me? I'm not your guardian.'

'Yes you are.'

'Only in the social sense. I mean, you're living here with me and I of course look out for you, but *legally*—'

'Legally, you are my guardian.'

'I'm not, Christina.'

'Yes, you are. Remember when I arrived in Philadelphia, and we had to see the Immigration Officer? He gave you a form to sign guaranteeing that I wouldn't be a charge on the city.'

'Yes, but—'

'At the foot, where you signed, it said, Relative, Sponsor or Guardian. And you signed it.'

Beatrice stared at her niece, her momentary hope swept away. She said, 'I don't think I ought to sign this.'

'Please, Aunt Beatrice. Please.'

'Look here, child, I know you believe in all this with utter seriousness, but people make mistakes, change their minds, find they've bitten off more than they can chew.'

'I can do it, I know I can. I've always done well in my studies. I've always been interested in doctoring. Ask Dr Childers.'

Once again there was a pause. 'Dr Childers?' said Mrs Kentley slowly.

'He'd tell you, I'm sure he would! He approved of my taking an interest in medicine. I never actually told him I wanted to study to be a doctor but I think he guessed, and he encouraged me by taking me on his rounds.'

Mrs Kentley sat down. 'If Dr Childers approved . . .'

'Write to him, Auntie! Better still, send him a cable! Ask him what he thinks. Oh, please, please – I know he'll tell you I ought to do it.'

'I don't know. And yet, he's known you all your life.'

'Yes, all my life, and better than Father ever knew me. All I ever did was make Father angry and get locked up for being rebellious. But Dr Childers understood that I'm not really rebellious, I just want to *know* about things, I want to be finding out, not accepting and standing still.'

Her aunt opened her desk, took out a piece of paper and a

pen. 'I'll send him a cable,' she said. 'Let me think what to ask. We'll send it in the morning. And you must promise to abide by his verdict, Christina. If he says no, it's no.'

First thing next day Christina took the message to the cable office at the corner of Chestnut and Ninth Street. It read:

> Christina enrolled Medical School. Parents not to know. Shall I encourage or prevent? Please reply soonest.

The next four days were the longest Christina had ever lived through. She tried to work on altering her hats and re-trimming her winter coat; she tried to pay attention to her lesson with Captain Dinsdorf; she got the laundry ready for the Chinese 'boy', and when the book list came from the University she horrified herself by pricing the books in the shops.

At length the telegraph boy in his serge uniform bicycled up to the hotel. 'Cable for Mrs Kentley.'

'Yes!' cried Christina, grabbing it and leaving Letty to give the boy his five-cent tip.

'Aunt Bea! Aunt Bea!'

Her aunt came up from the basement where she'd been inspecting the new delivery of coal.

'It's come, Auntie. Open it – oh, please, open it!'

'In the office, my dear,' said Aunt Bea. She ushered her in, waited until the girl sat down like a polite Christian. Then she herself sat, slit open the orange envelope, and read the contents.

To Beatrice Kentley, the reply brought no satisfaction. Her face did not light up.

'Oh, he's said no!' faltered Christina.

Beatrice handed her the form. She read:

> Christina a born doctor. Go ahead with my blessing.
> Geo. Childers MD.

'Yippee!' shrieked Christina and, throwing the paper in the

air, she seized her aunt by the waist and began to polka round the office. Despite protests, she went on until she was giddy and began banging into the furniture. Then she sank down, her arms still around Beatrice, on her knees beside her while she guided her into a chair.

'Won't be a minute!' she cried. Next moment she'd darted from the room. Her aunt heard her footfall on the oaken stairs, running up to her attic bedroom.

She's gone to get her precious registration form, thought Beatrice. It's all wrong, all wrong! It'll sicken her, all the gruesome details; she'll give up and it'll break her heart to see she made a mistake.

Christina came in. She laid the form on the desk, set the chair, held out the pen. 'Sign, please!' She was laughing.

'No,' said her aunt, 'I'm not going to sign, Christina.'

'What?'

'I can't bring myself to do it. It's so . . . unsuitable for you.'

'But you *promised*!'

'No, I didn't. I said if Dr Childers said no, that must be an end of it. But I didn't say I'd sign if he said yes.'

There was a silence that grew so weighty it seemed likely to make Beatrice bow her head under it.

'I shall ask Captain Dinsdorf to sign it, then.'

'Christina! Don't you dare! He has no standing, no legal standing – he's not even a relation!'

'What does that matter? He lives at this address, pays his taxes, his name is on the electoral roll.' The tone became icy, the dark blue eyes shone with the cold glister of slates in the rain. 'I should have preferred to keep it in the family, but since you've lost your nerve I've no choice but to ask the captain. And he'll do it. He'd do anything for me.'

'Haven't you any scruples, Christina? You're planning to make that fond old man a cat's paw—'

'Who are you to talk?' flashed the girl. She was very angry, but the anger was as cold as the blade of a rapier. 'You promised to help me start my medical training if Dr Childers approved – yes you did, don't try to wriggle out of it.

66

Now when it comes to the point you're going to tell me it's a wicked idea, that I ought to marry some empty-headed young man and give him his children. If you—'

'But what would be wrong with that, Christina? You say you want to help children – what's wrong with having your own?'

'Nothing, nothing – that's not what we're talking about. We're talking about your ideas of suitability. You say I've got good looks, I ought to use them to get a husband. But I've got *brains*: am I not to use them? Am I to flutter about in a houseful of servants worrying over the flower arrangement for the dinner table? Because that's what you wanted for yourself, must it be "suitable" for me?'

Beatrice huddled into herself a little. 'You're very hard, child: hard, and rather ruthless. I didn't know you could be like this.'

'I don't want to be like this,' her niece said, her voice suddenly full of tears. 'It's only that it's so important. We're talking about my *life*, Aunt Bea! I thought you understood. I thought you, of all people, knew how important it is to me.'

'But you're so young. You don't know what's best for you – truly, dear, truly. The path between youth and maturity is hard enough without choosing a thorny one at the outset. Wait a while longer, perhaps you'll change your mind.'

'Perhaps I'll fall in love with one of your Philadelphian mashers, you mean. Oh, for heaven's sake, Auntie, can't you tell after a year of it that it's a waste of time? I'm going to go to medical school.'

She held out the pen.

She had put a harsh finality into her voice. She wanted her aunt to face the facts. Before her lay a shining path – but the path didn't lead to the altar, nor to a cosy home with a white picket fence and a rocker on the porch.

Instead it took her into the portals of the University of Pennsylvania. Her feet had been guided there so that she could make a beginning on her life's work. Classes and lectures, study and books – she could picture it all, could feel it casting a spell as potent as that of the Rhine Maiden. She wanted it, that life of dedication. It was hers, made for her, meant for her.

And if Aunt Bea thought it was a mere infatuation, something that would pass like a schoolgirl crush, she would soon learn how wrong she was. No argument her aunt mustered could ever be as potent as the cry of that girl-child she had helped to deliver. It echoed in her heart always, sometimes faint, as when first she made the journey of exile to Philadelphia, and sometimes stronger. It called to her now, telling her to help again, and again; to help mothers, to help children, to help the sick and the needy.

What did it matter if she must seem cold and hard at this moment to her aunt? Coldness, coolness, this was the armour that would see her through.

Beatrice Kentley met that steady gaze. Something she saw there over-awed her. She rose from her chair, sat at the desk, took the pen and wrote her name at the foot of the registration form.

Chapter Five

There proved to be six of them, 'the lady meds' – five other girls besides Christina. Four girls and a woman, in fact, for one of them was twenty-four, as she was quick to let them know, with a book of poetry already published. Her name was Daphne Towers, and she explained that she had a questing mind. She left at the end of the third week.

The others were Susanne Wellsley, Euphemia Grant, Mary Mennem and Josefin Belu. Josefin had a thick foreign accent. 'Are you German?' Susanne asked innocently.

'German? Never! I am Serbian!' She explained that she had exchanged the intolerable subjection of Serbia under the rule of the Austro-Hungarian Empire for the freedom of the New World. 'Some of us, we are not so easy to subject.'

'Subjugate?' suggested Christina.

'Is this the word? Well, we have put together our family fortunes, sent in advance people to America. Here in Pennsylvania is good farming land. They have buy good farms, soon are making profit, they send for me and I take doctor training, then others come, we head out to the West where is still land very cheap, make a good Serbian community, Free Serbian community with doctor, lawyer, even priest for those that want this religiousness.'

'My, it sounds a big undertaking.'

'Undertaking? Is nothing "under". We do it openly . . .'

'No, no, Josefin, Susanne only meant it sounded hard work.'

'Oh, yes, hard work, and we are not used to it, some are not. Aristos, you know, we do not wish to work with the hands. Many problems.' She went on talking nineteen-to-the-dozen about Serbians and their problems. She soon became known as Jo-Jo, and they all learned to sound sympathetic to the woes of her compatriots, though none of them knew with any certainty where Serbia was.

Jo-Jo was dark, rounded, quite muscular but with small hands and feet. Susanne was half again as tall, with her hair wound twice round her head so that she looked as if she were wearing a beehive. Euphemia – Youffie – was vague, soft-eyed, untidy. The hem of her skirt always needed tacking up. Mary Mennem was small and thin and very dark indeed, her skin a soft copper, her eyes like great black plums. She said she came from a family of Assyrians.

When the lady meds came into the lecture room at eight in the morning of the first day, some of the male students were already there, grouped around an anatomical map of the human body, sniggering. An uneasy silence fell at their entrance.

The first lecture began without preamble. Dr Liam O'Donnell walked in by a door at the back of the room, called order, and said, 'The anatomical map which has been an object of such interest to some of the freshers is not needed at present. This, as your timetable shows you, is a class on pharmacology. Please, gentlemen, turn your thoughts from any salacious hopes and look at this diagram which I now put up on the easel. It begins with the word "anaesthetic". Can anyone tell me the derivation of the word?'

Naturally no one was going to be such a show-off as to put up his hand.

'Excellent. From perfect ignorance there is only one path, into at least partial knowledge. Anaesthetic comes from the Greek "an" meaning "not" or "without", and "aesthetikos" meaning "perception". Therefore we find that "anaesthetic" means "without perception", "without the use of the senses". You all—' He broke off. 'I beg your pardon, I must make an exception of the ladies. You gentlemen know what it is like to be without the use of the senses: it is a quite common state, is it not, after the use of alcohol?'

There was a faint murmur of amusement from the men.

'However, alcohol is not an anaesthetic, except in very large quantities. Can anyone tell me how it is generally categorised?'

'A depressant,' Christina said before she could stop herself.

'Very *good*,' said Dr O'Donnell, with far too much approval. It was clear he wanted to show he had nothing against women students by being kind to them at every opportunity. 'How, young lady, could you have learned such a thing in your no doubt sheltered existence?'

'Dr Childers told me.'

'Dr Childers. A lecturer?'

'No, sir, he's a general practitioner. He let me go on his rounds with him and we . . . er . . . we saw farmers who were somewhat the worse for . . .'

'For some easily obtained depressant. Quite so. The next on the diagram is antipyretic. This, once more, comes from the Greek "anti" meaning "against" and "pyretos" meaning "fever" and therefore means, not fire-extinguisher as I'm sure some of you imagined, but "fever reducing".'

So the hour went by, with a little joke for each of the terms used in describing drugs. The students laughed politely, took notes, and were glad when nine o'clock struck.

The second lecture, a double lecture lasting two hours, was the introduction to zoology. Only three months were to be given to this subject, which was regarded as the introduction to biology. The first hour was devoted to a description of what they were about to do and the second, given in the basement, was the dissection of a crayfish.

At eleven there was a break. The girls crammed into the ladies' cloakroom to wash their hands and fold their smocks of rough blue linen.

'Ugh,' said the poetess, 'how disgusting.'

'And smelly,' said Mary Mennem. She sniffed at her fingers. The Fels-Naphtha soap had not done away with the smell.

Two senior women students elbowed them aside. 'Out

of the way, babies, we're due at the hospital for a demonstration.'

'Stop pushing,' Jo-Jo said, pushing back.

'A demonstration of what?' Christina asked with interest.

'Physical diagnosis – stomach pains by palpation.'

'That's second-year work?'

'Heavens, yes, you've got months of pottering about with earthworms and giggling at O'Donnell's jokes.'

With that the two girls left in a hurry. Slowly the fresher lady meds came out of the cloakroom, looking at their plan of the building to see where they were expected next.

At the foot of the staircase they found a gang of young men. 'Excuse us, please,' said Daphne, to whom the other girls were deferring out of respect for her seniority.

'Why, what have you done?' asked one of the men.

'I mean, please let us pass.'

'Pass, friend, and be recognised,' said the student, and let Daphne go forward. She was immediately hemmed in by the other men.

'Stop, let me through – oh!' cried Daphne.

Jo-Jo surged forward. 'You,' she said, digging her elbow fiercely into the ringleader, 'be so good as to move.'

'Oh, fisticuffs, is it? How unladylike,' said his nearest neighbour as the boy staggered sideways, hugging his ribs.

Trouble was in the air. Christina took a few steps back from the crowd, looked about for a diversion, and found it. A carafe had been left on a table outside the door of a nearby classroom. She picked it up, rested its base in the palm of her hand, and walked rapidly towards the group. As she reached it she stumbled.

'Oh, dear,' she said, as the water went in a wide arc over the men massed at the stairfoot.

There was only about a quart of water, and it was already tepid by having stood in the carafe for two hours. But water is wet and unexpected. With yelps of dismay, the ambush broke up.

They were late for their next lecture. The chemistry lecturer was not pleased. 'Punctuality is expected, even from young ladies,' he remarked, looking at the six girls over his glasses. 'No doubt you've been accustomed to spend hours prinking in front of the glass, but medical students must give up such pleasures.'

'It wasn't *our* fault,' said Mary. 'We were kept—'

Christina and Jo-Jo broke into a loud fit of coughing. Mary stopped.

'If you are subject to a cough, please supply yourselves with sufficient pastilles to keep you silent through the lecture. Now, students, chemistry is that branch of science that studies the changes which matter is capable of undergoing. Chemistry and physics are convergent sciences, but chemistry concerns itself with alterations in the composition of substances. How many here have studied chemistry?'

This was a question to which a response must be given. Christina, Jo-Jo and Susanne put up their hands, something like a dozen of the men did so too.

'Laboratory work?'

One hand went down, one of the men's.

'About a quarter of my class. Very well, it means back to basics for all of us, I'm afraid. This will be less interesting for those of you who have already taken these elementary stages, but we must all know what we are talking about. Very well. All matter, solid, liquid or gaseous, is composed of minute particles . . .'

Christina had thought she was going to be bored at having to go over a subject which had been well taught at Market Bresham Ladies' College. But Dr Biddle, though impatient and inclined to be sarcastic, was one of the greatest experts in America and was never uninteresting.

At the lunch break there was a choice of going to the University refectory or finding a café where they could eat quickly and cheaply.

'Let's go out,' said Daphne nervously. 'If we go to the refectory the men might try more of their jokes. And I believe there is one section for men only and one for ladies only: we might sit in the wrong place.'

'I think there is no need to be so nervous about it,' Jo-Jo

said in a pugnacious tone. 'In Serbia, we have brigands and bandits, so it is needed to know how to deal with young men who are giving a nuisance. If anyone tries more joke, I give him kick.'

'No,' Christina put in. 'That's just what we mustn't do. We mustn't descend to their level. Somehow we've got to avoid confrontations whenever we can.'

'I expected something of this kind,' Daphne said, 'men being as they are so rough and rude. But I thought it would be inside the classroom. I didn't expect them to assail us—'

'Oh, come on now, Daphne, they haven't "assailed" us—'

'What do you call what happened when we tried to come up from the basement? They completely surrounded me. I was very frightened.'

'But they didn't actually do anything. They didn't push you or hit you.'

'Good heavens, if they had, I'd have reported it at once, and no amount of diplomatic coughing would have stopped me.'

'Yes, why did you prevent me from telling Dr Biddle?' asked Mary, turning big reproachful eyes on Christina.

'Hunh, you want us to be like little child, running to Mummee when big brother pulls hair? What is this called in English?' said Jo-Jo.

'Telling tales,' said Christina.

'Weak and foolish thing. We are here only six women. We must not look weak and foolish to the men, and not to the teachers. If we are, they say to themselves, Look, we have been right, women are nuisance, we don't want them in medical school.'

'And more than that,' Christina added to Jo-Jo's remarks, 'we have to work and study alongside those boys for the next four years. We'll have to be partners with them when we do lab work. We'll need to borrow their notes if we miss a lecture. Do you imagine they'd lift one finger to help a bunch of sneaks?'

'You're reducing this to schoolyard ethics,' protested Youffie.

'Call it what you like. I believe—'

'Schoolyard, yes, it is,' Jo-Jo broke in. 'These men – these boys – how old are they? Most of them not twenty. They are *children*. To them girls are . . . now what is this word? Not silly, not missy—'

'Cissy,' Christina supplied. 'Girls are cissy. You don't play with girls. Girls have no right butting in where boys are getting a game set up. You've got it, Jo-Jo.'

Mary said, with a little shrug, 'I've never had any trouble with boys before. You only have to smile at them and look shy.'

'Oh, lor', don't start using women's wiles on them,' Susanne burst out. 'The last thing we need is to have trouble over flirting. That's always been one of the arguments for keeping women out. Women distract the men from serious study. Women entangle men in unsuitable relationships. Women are weak-willed and get pregnant.'

'Susanne!' cried Mary, shocked.

'You think it hasn't happened?' said Susanne. 'I was actually told that by the dean of my college – that one of the main arguments against allowing women into universities had always been because many of them didn't complete their courses but got married or pregnant, not necessarily in that order.'

'Listen, time's going on and we still haven't had lunch,' Christina pointed out. 'I vote we go in a body into the refectory. By now it ought to be clear which is the men's side and which the women's because people will be half-way through their meal. Let's all sit together, and look calm and inoffensive. And let's be quick, otherwise we'll be late for elementary physiology.'

The refectory was a high-ceilinged, echoing room. There were big tables and small tables. One corner seemed to be the domain of the women students; perhaps thirty girls were having lunch.

Christina and her companions chose one of the big tables, sat down, and were unremarked except by a waitress.

'Today's special is meat loaf and hash browns, fifteen cents.'

They ordered sandwiches and coffee, and that was that. Later they learnt that good manners always prevailed in the refectory: even student hazing among the men was forbidden, for trouble in the past had led to threats that the refectory and its cheap meals would be withdrawn if bread rolls were thrown about or crockery smashed.

Professor Wandel, who took physiology, was big and fat and kind-hearted. 'We don't pretend we're comfortable in this lecture room, ladies and gentlemen, but for this three-month crash course we'll work here. When you know what you're doing, then we will all remove to the new building and enter into the larger aspects of biology. Would anyone like a window open? You're sure you'll all stay awake without? OK, here we go.'

Christina went home with her head spinning. Today had been like no other day. Full, busy, alarming, entrancing . . . Hints of so much yet to come. Great subjects, of which she'd had the merest hints. Twenty-eight pages of her notebook already filled with words taken down in a hasty scribble. Would she be able to read her own writing?

'Well?' said Aunt Bea as she came in. 'How was it?'

'Oh, Auntie, it was *wonderful*!'

Supper had been kept for her. She ate it in the kitchen, trying to reply to Aunt Bea's question while protecting the real wonder of it for later consideration. Images flickered before her mental vision like the motion pictures at the Franklin Square Theatre. Dr O'Donnell's fine-boned hand holding up a phial of yellow liquid and his voice spelling out 'c-i-n-c-h-o-n-a, a bark with a considerable bite.' The ligatures of the crayfish and the dissecting knife-point. Jo-Jo's, 'I am not understanding how white potatoes can be hashed browns?' as she looked with horror at the food on a male student's plate. The blackboard and its physiology notes. Sunlight on the college lawns. Linen smocks. Up in her attic room, she spread out her text books, opened her notebook, and tried to recall all that she had learned in so few hours.

Shameful to relate, she fell asleep over her books. Aunt Bea had to wake her at bedtime. Yawning and in a muddled dream she washed and undressed and fell into bed.

Tomorrow . . . tomorrow . . . !

Christina found next day that she was luckier than the other girls in her year. She could go home to the peace and quiet of her room in the Wallace Hotel. They had to sleep in the women's dormitory.

Since there were so few women students, the University had taken over a house in one of the residential streets hard by. In many ways it was pleasant if spartan. Large rooms, but they had to be shared. A big sitting-room, but a dozen different recreations took place in it. A study hall, but without enough lamps to make reading easy. And a large garden, in which male students could lurk.

'It seems there's a sort of tradition,' Susanne reported. 'At the beginning of term, the men get up to all kinds of tricks at the women's dorm. About nine o'clock last night some genius threw Chinese crackers in through the study hall window and scared us half to death. Then shortly after midnight somebody was trying to climb up the wistaria vine. One of the senior girls pushed him off with a broomstick and he went down with an awful crash: I hope he broke his leg, the silly fool. But worst of all, just when we'd settled down about one o'clock, a gang of them began howling and meowing like cats on the prowl.'

'Did you get any sleep?' Christina asked, appalled.

'They are keeping it going for nearly one hour,' Jo-Jo said grimly. 'And as my bed is lumps and bumps anyhow, I sleep perhaps twenty minutes all night.'

'It's awful,' Youffie said tearfully. 'I hung my hat on the hallstand last night and this morning someone's smeared the inside with treacle or honey or something.'

'You mean somebody got in? Surely the door's locked!'

'Daisy Cameron – she's a senior – she says they often get one of the smaller guys to dress up as a girl and slip in to do tricks like that. She says there was an awful row two years ago when they actually caught a boy up on the bedroom floor.'

'If my father ever hears of that, he'll take me away at once,' Mary Mennem said in misery.

Susanne said, 'Let's keep it in perspective. They do it to all the freshers, men as well as women. We just have to live through it for a week or so, and then it'll be over.'

'You really think so?' Daphne wondered, shuddering.

Today was the first lecture in anatomy. All the girls were frightened and, if truth were told, so were the men.

'Good morning, ladies and gentlemen. I am Dr Verrill. You are about to enter into the study of the most important of all the medical sciences, anatomy.'

He was a small, spare figure in a neat old-fashioned suit that might have come straight out of the *Tailor & Cutter* of the Naughty Nineties: high slim lapels, waisted frockcoat, narrow pin-striped trousers above cream-coloured spats. Later they were to discover that he never took off the frockcoat, even when he demonstrated dissection. Thick grey hair fell over his forehead; he had a pointed grey beard.

'The human body is the temple of the spirit. We must always treat it with respect, even in the dissecting room. However, I do not expect you to face that room as yet. You will all come with me, please, and we will make a preliminary tour of the exhibits in the anatomical museum.'

He led the way, they trooped after.

At the first exhibits, no one blenched. There was a male skeleton, a female skeleton, and the skeleton of a child about six years old.

Next came a glass case full of skulls and facial bones. Dr Verrill unlocked it, took out three or four skulls and jawbones, and invited his students to try fitting them together.

On to the next exhibit. On a table were six glass jars. 'We continue our observation of the human head. This, ladies and gentlemen, is the tongue of a native of Venezuela who died from what is known as chubta, a cancerous condition caused by cigar burns in the mouth. Note the lump still visible and the scar tissue caused by prior excision. I beg your pardon, Mr Simmons?'

'Nothing, sir,' said Mr Simmons in a trembling voice, thinking of the cigars in the case in his breast pocket.

'In this small jar, we see the eye of an elderly—'

There was a startled sound, a rushing of feet, and a male student went pounding out of the door into the corridor.

'Dear me,' said Dr Verrill, 'do you think Mr Wickbridge is unwell?'

So it went on. Their tormentor led them through the museum, explaining the significance of each case or jar. One by one, students fell out. At the end, of the forty who had gone in with him, only twenty-nine remained. Of these, four were women: Daphne and Mary had retired.

'Well,' Dr Verrill said cheerfully, 'I see it is eleven o'clock, breaktime. Coffee can be obtained in the refectory. Please be back in the lecture room at eleven-thirty, when I will show you the musculature of the male arm. That will take us up to lunchtime.'

'The wicked man,' Jo-Jo said, fanning herself vigorously with her notebook as they got out into the fresh air. 'He did that on purpose.'

'Yes, he did.' Christina sat down on the steps. 'But we've got to start some time and I suppose he's learned by experience that taking us through the museum gives us a glimpse of the horrors to come!'

'The human arm,' said Youffie. 'Does that mean he's actually going to have an *arm* in the lecture room?'

'No, no. That will be later, in the dissecting room.'

'I don't know if I can *do* this,' said Susanne, who had remained stiff-lipped and silent up to now.

'What did you think, you can study medicine without looking at bodies?' Jo-Jo asked.

'No, of course not. I always knew. And I was ready. Or I thought I was ready . . .'

'Where did Mary and Daphne get to?'

'I bet Daphne's in the dorm with a pillow over her head,' said Susanne. 'Christina, don't you feel queasy?'

'Yes, rotten. But I'm taking deep breaths.'

'If you take deep breaths in the dissecting room you'll get a lungful of formaldehyde.'

Drooping and unhappy, they went to the refectory, where they found Mary and Daphne drinking strong sweet coffee. More of the same did something to restore those who'd taken the whole tour.

They lived through the study of the human arm. When the moment came to remove to the dissecting room, the girls were taken to a separate booth at the end of the corridor.

'It isn't suitable for women to be working on the human body in the company of men,' Dr Verrill explained. 'This is the lady meds' dissecting room. You have exactly the same specimens as the men and when each of you have completed your section, the specimens are exchanged.'

'Yes, sir,' said the girls, putting on their smocks and tightening their resolve.

It was the mouse that finished Daphne. They were three weeks into the term. Daphne had been having difficulty with dissection, both human and zoological. She was also very poor at managing situations in which the men made fun of her.

They came into the basement zoological lab. They were to dissect a dead frog. She lifted the enamelled dish that shielded her specimen but something moved in a springing rush. She jumped back, fell over her tall stool, went sprawling.

The mouse scampered over her. In a moment it had vanished. Daphne scrambled to her feet, drawing her smock close against her body with one hand, holding her skirts off her ankles with the other, screaming in real horror.

'A mouse! A mouse!'

'Where, where?'

Christina had run to Daphne's aid. Jo-Jo picked up a

cleaning rag from a bench and went whipping it about the room after the mouse. Susanne stood as if turned to marble. Youffie and Mary were clinging to each other in startlement.

Some of the men were standing in a group by the bench nearest the door. Their laughter rang out. 'Gee, I thought we were dissecting *dead* animals. Did you know we were going to work on *live* specimens, Dave?'

'It's favouritism. I didn't get a mouse. Why should the girls get a mouse?'

Jo-Jo turned on them. Before anyone could stop her she used her rag to whip at one of the speakers. The end of it caught him on the cheek. It couldn't possibly have hurt very much but it stung enough to make him yelp and throw up his hand.

Christina left Daphne to grab at the angry Serbian girl. 'No, no, Jo-Jo, it's just what they want – uproar and argument. Come on, come back to the bench.'

Jo-Jo let herself be led back to work, uttering terrible things in her own language. The technical assistant in charge of setting out the specimens looked in, a frown on his face. 'Anything wrong, gentlemen? And ladies?'

The joke couldn't possibly have been arranged without his connivance. The room was kept locked if not in use. Christina said in a cool voice, 'Everything is perfect, thank you, Hankins, but I think you should tell the housekeeper that the standard of cleaning is pretty low if mice can settle in.'

Hankins had the grace to look sheepish. Daphne came marching between them, out of the door and down the corridor. Christina ran after her. 'Daphne, where are you going?'

'Away.'

'But you'll miss the dissection . . .'

'I have no intention of staying in a room with those . . . those barbarians.'

'But Dr Silver—'

Daphne shook off her restraining hand. 'Leave me alone.'

Next moment she was walking towards the stairs out of

the basement, unfastening the buttons down the back of her smock.

Christina went back into the laboratory. Hankins was walking about behind the students, watching them make their first incisions. She went up to him. 'How much did they pay you?'

'I don't know what you mean, Miss Holt?'

'I just want you to know, if they make you an offer, come to us. We might be able to top it so you *won't* play rotten tricks on us.'

Hankins was a senior student helping out in paying his fees by working as one of the zoology lab technicians. He had let it be known that money was important to him, that for a half-dollar here and there he'd make sure you got a good clean specimen to work on, that your scalpel would be one of the new ones.

He coloured at Christina's words. 'How dare you talk to me like that!'

'Oh, aren't you interested in making money? Or will you only take it from the men?'

He turned away. Christina went to her work-place to begin work.

'We don't really pay him any money, Christina. Rather I hit him hard with my book-bag.'

'No, Jo-Jo, keep your temper. It's best.'

'So you say. I think you are wrong. We should kick and hit.'

Christina shook her head, giving her attention to her work.

Daphne didn't turn up for the pharmacology class. At breaktime all the girls hurried to the dormitory in search of her. They found her in the room she shared with three girls from other faculties. She was packing.

'Daphne!' Jo-Jo tried to take the suitcase away from her.

'Get out of my way. I'm leaving this ghastly place with its ghastly people.'

'Daphne, don't do anything rash!' pleaded Christina, her pallor accentuated by her anxiety. There were so few of them, they couldn't afford to lose one. 'You must have known it would be difficult.'

'But I didn't know it would be disgusting! I didn't know you had to handle pieces of dead human beings as if they were joints of pork! I didn't know you had to take sections out of slimy frogs and toads and fish! I didn't know the men would be so beastly!'

If she had burst into tears, they could have crowded round and comforted her. But her rage and repugnance were like a barrier that kept them off. She threw a few items into the case, banged the lid down, snapped the locks shut.

'I'm going,' she said. 'And if *you* stay, you're mad. My uncle was right – it's distasteful, it's unsuitable, it's horrifying for women to mix themselves up in things like this. The men are coarse and rude, and you'll end up like them if you stay.'

'Daphne, it's only because we're at the beginning . . .'

'We'll get hardened to it, is that it? I don't want to get hardened! I came here to study, thinking I would be doing something noble to help my fellow man. But if I stay I know I'll end up despising my fellow man. I'm going home.'

'Please don't, Daphne. Stay and think it over,' said Youffie.

'I've been thinking about it for three weeks. I knew almost at the outset that I'd made a mistake. You too, Mary. It's wrong for you.'

'That's not fair!' Christina flashed. 'Just because you've got cold feet, don't try to—'

'Mary's not made for this sort of thing. She hates it, I can tell.'

'Mary?' Susanne said, looking inquiringly at her.

'Yes,' Mary admitted, her head down. 'I hate it. I absolutely hate it. When Wandel was talking about the circulation of blood the other day, and I saw it in my mind's eye, pumping through the heart – I felt sick, really sick. I thought, There's this machine in all of us, you, me, my mother and father . . . We're just a walking collection of bits of muscle and gristle and bones and red liquid . . .'

'You see?' Daphne said. 'Come on, Mary, pack and come with me.'

'No,' said Christina. 'How can you, Daphne!'

'No,' said Mary. 'I hate it, I absolutely hate it. But I'm not leaving. I look soft and silly, don't I? I know I do. The boys look at me as if I were some sort of velvet cushion they'd like to sink into. But I'm not, I'm going to be a doctor.'

Daphne shook her head. 'You won't last another month. Well, goodbye everyone. I don't suppose we'll ever meet again, and I don't wish you well because I think you're doing the wrong thing.'

'Coward!' Jo-Jo almost snarled at her. 'Coward, traitor!'

'Jo-Jo!' Christina said. 'Oh, for heaven's sake, Jo-Jo, stop making a drama out of it. Daphne's quite entitled to change her mind.'

'You are so reasonable! You know the men will sneer and say, We told you you weren't cut out for this medicine. Don't you care?'

'All I care about is learning what I came here to learn. I can live with sneers from the men. And it occurs to me we're already fifteen minutes late for pharmacology.'

The girls hesitated, looked at Daphne with uncertainty, but seeing her determination shrugged and began farewells. Youffie hugged her, Mary kissed her on the cheek, the others shook hands.

'What are you going to do now, Daphne?'

'Go back to civilisation,' Daphne said as she closed the door on them.

When they walked into class, Dr O'Donnell stopped what he was saying. 'How kind of you to honour us with your presence, ladies. Am I to have the civility of an apology?'

'We're sorry to be late. We were saying goodbye to a colleague,' Christina said, since no one else seemed willing to speak.

'Really? Which colleague is that?'

'Miss Towers is leaving.'

'In what sense, leaving?'

'Going home. Giving up her studies.'

There was ironic applause among the male students. O'Donnell took off his glasses, turned to look at them with interest, then said, 'Is there some reason why you gentlemen should be pleased that Miss Towers is leaving?'

No answer.

'Gentlemen, a lecture room is a place where questions are asked and answered. Why did you cheer when you heard Miss Holt's announcement?'

Someone at the back of the room said, 'Women have no business here in the first place.'

'Indeed? Is that the view of you all?'

There was a shuffling and a muttering. Another voice said, 'It sure is my view!'

'However much or little I may share that view, gentlemen, the fact is that for the present the Senate has decided to allow women to study medicine. I prefer no audible cheering when one of them changes her mind. Is that understood?'

It was difficult to know whether O'Donnell was saying that he approved of women medical students or merely tolerated them because he must. But the men took it as a declaration of support. They let their sense of triumph be known.

It didn't last long, however, because at the beginning of the following week, John Wickbridge had had to run out of the anatomy lab to be sick. He had given up the study of medicine, packed and left within two days.

Jo-Jo couldn't disguise her glee. 'So, poor fellow, he wasn't strong enough for this work. Men too feel uncomfortable. Very strange. I thought men were superior?'

'Why don't you learn to talk English like a human being?' grunted Tom Spires, who was a ringleader of the opposition.

Christina heard the unreasoning dislike that tinged his words. It troubled her, as it always troubled her when the male students and their prejudices made working conditions uncomfortable.

But comfortable or not, they were working. At the same subjects, in the same room except for anatomy. The term was going by, the knowledge was being gained.

And nothing anyone could do would make her give up.

Chapter Six

Towards the end of the third semester, two major events loomed. The first was the first-year examinations, which would weed out those who weren't academically fitted to go on to the second year. The second, in June, was an initial visit to the University Hospital, a hospital of three hundred and fifty beds, to observe clinical work and diagnosis on patients.

'They dangle the hospital work in front of us so as to make us forget the exams,' grumbled Jo-Jo. 'And I shall do badly because of my poor English.'

'Your English has improved by leaps and bounds,' soothed Christina.

Jo-Jo laughed. 'It's a strange language. Why should I leap and bound?'

'Why shouldn't you?' Youffie countered. 'Everything's going well, the men have let up on hassling us, and here we sit, under a shady tree with endless supplies of lemonade, while we mug up our physiology.'

To make life easier for her friends, Christina had persuaded her Aunt Bea to let her invite them over on Sundays. They came after church, were given a light lunch out of doors if the weather was suitable, worked fairly hard all afternoon, ate a substantial supper in the kitchen with Helmina and Letty, then read and worked until the light failed. Sometimes Captain Dinsdorf came out to sit with them, quietly smoking his pipe, enjoying the company of pretty girls.

It was true, everything seemed serene. They ought to have known there was about to be an upset.

It came next day. As Dr Verrill concluded his lecture he remarked, 'Tomorrow we enter upon our study of the reproductive system. As this is an unsuitable subject for a mixed class, the young ladies are excused. Gentlemen, I shall see you here tomorrow at our usual hour.'

The five lady meds were taken aback. They were already filing out of the room. They looked at each other.

'Sir,' said Christina, 'if we are not to attend the lecture, how can we begin study of the subject?'

'I recommend you make a thorough read of your textbooks. You will find it well treated. Good morning, ladies.' He went out by the door at the back of the room. The lady meds were left speechless.

Some of the men laughed loudly and with ribaldry. 'That's put you in your place, eh, girls? Good old Verrill!'

The girls made their way to the refectory. Christina was so angry she couldn't eat. 'I'm simply not having it,' she said.

'What can you do? It's always the same, so I hear.' Mary had friends among the first-year men, and also among the male students of the second and third years. 'I'm told the women are always shut out of this lecture.'

'And haven't they protested?'

'What would be the use?'

'Well, *I'm* going to protest.'

'To whom, for heaven's sake?'

'To Verrill – who else?'

'Are you out of your mind? Exams are coming up – he'll fail you in anatomy if you annoy him.'

'I don't care! I won't be pushed out of a lecture I'm entitled to hear – *need* to hear! I'm going to write to Verrill. Is anybody with me?'

'Christina, it's not worth it!' faltered Mary.

'No, she is right,' Jo-Jo said, her dark eyes snapping with annoyance. 'All the time we've been good, we've played the part of the reasonable being, but see what it gets us. I am with Christina. I will sign the letter with her. Who else?'

There was a troubled silence. Then Youffie said, 'I'll sign.'

Susanne pulled anxiously at her piled-up hair. 'I don't

know . . . You're right, of course. I ought to stand with you . . .'

'Let's do it,' said Mary, surprising them. She was the softest, the most pliant of them all. But occasionally she showed signs of a steel core.

Christina stayed in college with her friends after the last lecture to concoct the letter.

'Dear Dr Verrill,' she wrote, 'We, the undersigned first-year medical students, wish to protest most strongly at being forbidden to attend tomorrow's anatomy lecture.

'When you began your first lesson with us, you referred to the human body as the "temple of the spirit". In this country a temple or church is open to both sexes. To prevent women from worshipping would be thought both unjust and un-Christian.'

She paused, looking at the others.

'Well, that's good,' said Susanne. 'It makes him sound un-Christian. He won't like that.'

'What next?'

'Tell him if we wanted to learn medicine from textbooks we would have enrolled for a correspondence course,' suggested Susanne.

'Right – not quite that but, after all, we are enrolled in a University.' She wrote:

'When we enrolled in the Faculty of Medicine we signed a promise to abide by the rules of the University. We imagined that we had made a bargain whereby the University for its part would give us a complete education. We cannot understand how this can be fulfilled if we are to have recourse to textbooks only. Books have their value, but they do not respond to questions.'

'Right! Now we want to tell him we know very well that he only wants us excluded so that he and the men can tell each other dirty jokes.'

'Jo-Jo!'

'That's the reason – we all know it.'

'Well, we can't say it. Calling him un-Christian and a welcher is bad enough.'

'No, Youffie, in a way Jo-Jo's right. That *is* the reason Verrill told us to stay away. So let's tell him we won't stand for it.' She turned the pen in her fingers, thought for a moment, then wrote:

'We are puzzled by the fact that the information in the textbooks is the same you must present in your lecture. We take it that it is the manner of presentation that causes some difficulty. If you fear that the question and answer session might allow indelicacies to emerge, let us assure you that we are quite accustomed to those. Since coming to the University we have been subjected to both ungentlemanly behaviour and indelicacies of speech, but we have learned to ignore the one and close our ears to the other. We give you our assurance to treat anything non-medical that is said at the lecture in the same way: we shall close our ears to it.'

'Oh gee,' breathed Youffie. 'Oh, gee whizz, I wish I could be there when he reads this!'

'We don't want to go over the page. We ought to sign off now. How're we going to do it?'

'Tell him we're coming to his stupid lecture,' growled Jo-Jo.

'You mean, not wait for him to reply giving his permission?' Mary gasped.

'That's right!' Christina wrote rapidly:

'We shall present ourselves in the lecture room at the usual hour tomorrow, Yours sincerely . . .'

She signed her name with a flourish. The other girls did the same without a moment's hesitation.

'This is like – what is your idiom? – a red rag to a bull. We must expect trouble.'

'All right, if there's trouble I'm going to give as good as I get,' exclaimed Christina. 'I'm going to give it to the newspapers if they try to stop us going in tomorrow. The Senate won't like that. And I'll take care to let them know it's Dr Verrill's fault.'

Christina slept very little that night. For all her bravado, she didn't enjoy the idea of a confrontation. She always felt she had no energy to waste on such things. She was at

University to *learn*, not to fight for women's rights. Though she admired Jo-Jo's courage in demanding emancipation, she disagreed with her outlook. The lecture rooms shouldn't be a battle ground, except for arguments about medical knowledge and practice. The rights of women were of little concern to Christina – except the right of a woman to *learn*.

She was now about to join battle with the men of the Faculty of Medicine. With all her heart she wished it could have been avoided. But if the lady meds didn't fight, they would be excluded from an important lecture. And this established precedent would then be even more difficult to oppose.

So Christina would fight. 'And,' she murmured to herself as she tossed restlessly in her rumpled bed, 'by heaven I'll win, *we'll* win, or die in the attempt.'

Next day the other four were waiting for her at the front steps of the anatomy building, by arrangement a little earlier than usual. They went up the steps and into the passage. A small crowd had already collected outside the door of the lecture room to see what would happen, for the college grapevine had let it be known that the lady meds were challenging Dr Verrill.

There were some friendly faces in the crowd. Three or four girls from other faculties had come to raise a cheer on their behalf, and some of the senior men. Strange to say, there were also some members of the teaching staff watching.

The first-year male students were of course inside the lecture room, forming a phalanx through which the girls would have to make their way. One glance through the door was enough to show them what they had to face.

The clock on the college spire struck eight o'clock. The door at the back of the room opened and they could glimpse Dr Verrill stepping on to the podium. The men barring the door didn't move.

'Gentlemen,' said a voice, 'I believe your lecturer is waiting for you.'

It was Dr O'Donnell. His plump figure moved forward. The men backed away a little.

'Sir,' said one, 'this is the anatomy lecture.'

'So I heard. I have a fancy to hear some anatomy today.'

Still he moved on, like a stately merchant ship among fussy tugs.

The girls exchanged glances. He was cleaving a path for them! They fell in behind him.

Almost at once the male students began a move to get behind the lady meds and drag them away. Another voice spoke from the corridor. 'Gentlemen, I wonder if I might trouble you to allow me to come in?'

Everyone stopped and looked back. It was Dr Fehr, the great Dr Fehr, senior lecturer in pathology. Next year they would attend his classes, but until now he had only been a shadowy figure seen about in the quadrangle or the path. building. He was famous throughout the United States, had original research to his credit.

The men fell back in awe. Dr Fehr walked in, thin, spare, upright, pince-nez glistening in the sunbeams that fell across the lecture hall.

He walked on towards the front seats. The girls, neatly sandwiched between him and Dr O'Donnell in front, were convoyed in. They took their accustomed places on the right of the room. As he passed, Dr Fehr paused. 'I shall probably meet you in my audience next year,' he murmured. 'I thought I would introduce myself a little earlier than usual. My name is Gilbert Fehr.'

'Yes sir, we know,' breathed the lady meds in unison.

He bowed, then went to join O'Donnell on the front bench. The sound of footsteps and the creaking of seats told the girls that the men had come in, but not only the freshers, many of the people out in the corridor had come too. The lecture, after all, was in theory open to any member of the University.

Dr Verrill looked patiently out at his audience until everyone had found seats and settled. He could see he had many unexpected guests. It was cause for inner amusement, considering what they were about to hear.

The letter of protest had shaken him. It challenged a male privilege he had taken for granted for years. Indignant, he took it along to a colleague to ask his advice. Should he send a message to these absurd girls, telling them to do as they were told?

'Well really, old fellow, I don't see how you can forbid them to come into the building and take their places in the lecture room, if they want to. They have a perfect right.'

'But it would be so improper!'

'Not if you left out the bawdy remarks, Joe.'

He had expected support. To be told more or less in so many words that he ought to re-form his lecture – a lecture he had given every year for eight years, and with great success – was a blow.

But with few exceptions, everyone he turned to said the same thing. So he'd spent last night cleaning up the talk, which was now perfectly proper but damned dull.

He threw back the cover of the illustration on his easel, shuffled his papers, cleared his throat and began: 'The human reproductive system. The male germ cell is known as a sperm, or spermatozoon. It is of microscopic size . . .'

The fame of this event rebounded through the University for a few days, but everyone was too busy swotting to discuss it for long. When Christina sat down to do the anatomy paper she regarded herself as a 'delta-minus' from the outset. Nevertheless she answered all the questions. When she laid down her pen she couldn't help feeling that, but for the 'Battle of the Lecture Hall', she might have earned good marks.

'How do you think you did?' Youffie asked as they came out of the examination room.

'Well, I failed, of course, but the questions didn't give me any trouble. How about you?'

'I thought it was ghastly. What was that about the likely results of the introduction of radiology?'

'That was about bronchography – don't you remember, Dr Verrill said that after Roentgen discovered X-rays, new methods were invented, so we could expect further developments in the exploration of the body.'

'That's *history*, not anatomy,' groaned Mary.

'Your trouble is you don't pay attention,' Christina said.

'You sit there taking notes but you don't always note down the interesting bits.'

'But how do you know which are the interesting bits? How do you know which bits you're going to be tested on?'

'Oh, Miss Marvellous here knows everything,' said Susanne, with only a faint grin to denote that it was a joke.

Later, when Jo-Jo and Christina were on the trolley going into town for ice-cream in Market Street, Jo-Jo said, 'Be a little less clever, Christina.'

Christina had been watching the pretty soft voile and muslin summer dresses of the Philadelphia girls. She turned her head to stare at her. 'What d'you mean by that?'

'When Youffie asked you how you'd done, she expected you to sympathise with her.'

'How could I know she needed sympathy, Jo-Jo? It was a perfectly straightforward paper.'

'Not so straightforward. That's what I mean. To you it's easy, and you let it show that you think it's easy. People who find it hard will end up disliking you.'

'Oh, that's very deep.'

'I mean it, Chrissie. It makes enemies to be too clever.'

It was too hot and sunny to worry about Jo-Jo's doom-laden Balkan view of life. Christina put it behind her.

When the exam results were posted, she was at the back of the crowd round the notice board. She was tall for a girl, but not tall enough to see over the heads of the men. People were reading out names, groaning or giving cries of delight.

'Holt? Does anyone see the results for Holt?' she begged.

The young man at the front turned to stare at her across the throng. 'Holt?' he said. 'Who doesn't see the results for Holt? It's the first name on every list but one.'

They made way, looking at her with a mixture of envy and curiosity. She moved to the notice board. It was true. Anatomy, C. Holt, Beta. Physiology, C. Holt, Beta plus. Pharmacology, C. Holt, Beta plus. Chemistry, C. Holt, Alpha. Zoology, C. Holt, Beta Minus. Embryology, C. Holt, Beta.

The highest marks in every division except zoology, in which Peter Semmring, one of the less noisy male freshers, had beaten her. He was just behind her or very near in most of the others.

She was so happy that faintness overcame her. She couldn't speak. She knew she ought to make some offhand joke, to ease matters for those who had done less well or even badly. But her head was swimming, she couldn't catch her breath.

First in her year. It was what she had aimed at but never dared hope for.

She hurried home to tell Aunt Bea.

Her aunt, though delighted, was troubled. 'So what happens now, dear?'

'I write and tell Father.'

'Yes.' She hesitated. 'You really think he'll be pleased?'

'Well, you're pleased, aren't you?'

'Of course, Christina. Yet . . .'

'You surely don't still think Father will disapprove? Now that I've *shown* I'm good enough to do it?'

'Well, I don't think your ability to do things was ever in doubt. It was more that he felt marriage was more suitable.'

'But now I'll be able to show him that I'm not meant to be a wife and mother. I mean, Aunt Bea, with a year's med school behind me, I can offer proof that I'm meant to be a doctor.'

Beatrice Kentley sighed and let it go. Her brother Herbert would have to be informed sooner or later. Now, it seemed, was the time. She could only hope he would be as pleased at his daughter's news as Christina seemed to expect.

The letter was written, Christina put it in the mailbox. She tried to imagine the surprise it would cause at home. Of course her father would be annoyed at first to think she'd done so much without his approval. But fatherly pride would overcome his objections. The youngest in the class, yet first in her year! He *must* be proud of her.

She expected a letter by return of post, which meant the

time it took for a mail steamer to make the double trip across the Atlantic. She counted off the days. Jo-Jo had wanted her to come to stay for a week or two at the Serbian farm in the Alleghanies, away from the heat and humidity of Philly in July. But she didn't want to go until her father's letter came.

She came in from the Public Library at mid-afternoon on a Thursday. A heavy suitcase stood in the hall. She stared at it, recognised it: it was her father's.

Not a letter! He had come himself, to take her in his arms and tell her how proud he was. At last he would say, 'You're a good girl, Christina.' All the years, while she'd fought him, defied him, it had been because she wanted him to see her for what she was: not a poor imitation of her good, obedient brother Elwin, but herself, his daughter, with her own talents, her own gifts to make him proud.

Then she heard his voice, speaking in a tone she knew well: loud, thick with anger.

Her dream-world dissolved. She'd been living in a fool's paradise this past twelve months. She'd always known her hopes were foolish, but she'd held off the realisation, telling herself always, He *will* understand, he *will* love me, I'm his daughter, he *must* care for me, accept me, perhaps even admire me.

She heard in her memory Aunt Bea's words: 'You really think he'll be pleased?' She'd made herself believe he would, because part of the striving of this past year at University was to convince him, convince him utterly and finally, that she really was an important person, important to *him*.

Tears welled in her eyes. What awaited her would be another recital of all her faults, another dismissal as wayward, wrong-headed, obstinate.

So be it. Years ago she might have gained his approval by submitting, but something within her had forbidden that. Now it was too late: she had done something he would never forgive. And to say to herself that she had done it for him, to make him admire her, was only part of the truth.

She had done it for herself. If her father couldn't accept that, if he couldn't see how right it was, then it was hopeless.

There was no communication, no link of instinctual love between them. It had to be faced.

Bracing herself, she went into her aunt's office. Aunt Beatrice was sitting in her favourite little armchair, her face pale above the pale summer dress, her mouth trembling, tears glistening.

Her father was standing, a posture she knew well, to dominate the room. His hands were clasped behind him under the tails of his frockcoat, his shoulders were thrown back. He had clearly dressed to impress: she could imagine him in his cabin that morning before he disembarked, tying his cravat, smoothing back his iron-grey hair. He was not going to appear at a disadvantage when he presented himself at his sister's home.

As she came in, he wheeled. He studied her. His gaze ran over her like a steel rod.

'Well, miss? What have you to say for yourself?'

'Good afternoon, Father.'

'Don't be saucy with me, girl! What do you imagine you've been up to?' He brandished her letter at her.

'I've been studying medicine.'

Her aunt half rose from her chair. 'I'll get—'

'Stay where you are!' her brother ordered. 'You've got a lot of explaining to do. Don't think you can slip out of it!'

'Aunt Bea has nothing to explain,' Christina said quickly. 'It was my idea and my decision. I—'

'Your aunt is as much to blame as you are, perhaps more. She at least is supposed to be an adult, with a proper sense of responsibility. She should have prevented—'

'She couldn't have prevented me. I registered without her knowledge and if she had tried to prevent me I should have moved out and lived in the women's quarters.'

'Christina, I'm afraid I haven't been able to say much to—'

'Will you be quiet?' shouted Herbert Holt. 'I'm speaking to my daughter. I want an explanation of this absolutely scandalous behaviour and then I want an apology and a promise of better conduct before I take her home.'

The room door opened. Letty the housemaid came half in. 'What's goin' on in here?' she demanded. 'You want me to call the cops, Mrs Kentley?'

'No, thank you, Letty. There's no problem; only a little family quarrel.'

'Family?' Letty said, astounded.

'This is my brother, Mr Holt.'

Letty gave him a glower. 'Pleased to meet you, Mr Holt.' She began to withdraw. 'I'll be just out in the hall,' she said. 'I got some polishin' to do.'

Herbert was utterly taken aback. In England, servants didn't speak to you in such a fashion. In the pause, Christina spoke.

'Father, I think you ought to remember that you're not in your own home where you can throw your weight about and terrify everybody. This is Aunt Bea's house, and you're a guest here.'

'A guest! I'm here to—'

'We know what you're here for, Herbert,' Mrs Kentley said, her courage a little restored by the support of her servant and the statement of the case by her niece. 'You're here in my home to make a fuss about Christina, and while I accept that you have reason—'

'Reason enough to bring me half across the world to save her from further madness! By God, Bea, what have you been thinking of? The arrangement was that you'd take her away and find her a decent husband.'

'Father, would you mind speaking to me? If you have grievances – and I admit you have – it's to me you should recite them.'

'You,' Herbert said in a groaning whisper. 'You, I'll tell you what you've done. You've reduced your mother to hysterics and made me drop an important property negotiation to come here and pick up the pieces.'

'Are you picking up pieces? Is this how it's done – scaring Aunt Bea half to death and shouting enough to frighten the servants?'

'Now that's enough,' Herbert said. He took a step

towards her, his hand coming up to strike her.

She flinched. It was only momentary, but it was enough to make him realise what he was doing. He dropped his hand.

And Christina, burning with shame at her moment of cowardice, lost her temper.

'I thought you might have come to tell me you were proud of me,' she said. 'I should have known better. You've never approved of a thing I've done in my life, and it's too late to hope you will now. I've studied medicine for a year, and I've done well. I'm going to go on for another three years, and do even better. And when that's over I shall be a doctor, a woman doctor, and you'll have to live with the fact. So you may as well accept it now.'

'You're not going on with it. Don't think it. You're coming home with me.'

'No I'm not.'

'You are, madam, if I have to drag you by the hair of your head.'

'That's how you'll have to do it!' she riposted. 'I will not come with you, unless you bind me hand and foot – and how are you going to manage that, Father?'

'You'll come,' he said grimly. 'You're still a minor. I'll get a court order.'

'No, Herbert . . .' It was Beatrice, jumping up from her chair, throwing out her hands in appeal.

'The law in America can't be so different from England. I can get control of my own daughter, for God's sake!'

'I'll fight it every inch of the way,' Christina said with fierceness. 'I'll find a lawyer – there are plenty of them at the University. I'll get one to fight my case for me. I'll make it take for ever, if I have to. What's going to happen to your precious office in Market Bresham while you're carrying on a long wrangle in Philadelphia?'

'In any case,' Beatrice put in, 'I'm Christina's legal guardian in this country. I signed a document when she was first admitted to this country—'

'That was without my consent . . .'

'Do you claim I took Chrissie away without your consent? Are you going to stand up in court and say that?'

It brought him up short. He shook his head like a bull baffled by the banderillas.

'Are you saying . . . are you saying you back this child up, against your *own brother*?'

Christina had regained control of herself. She stepped close to him for the first time since she had come into the room and seen him, newly arrived from the other side of the world.

'Father,' she said, putting a hand on his sleeve, 'please. Let's talk about this calmly. Sit down. Please sit down.'

He glared down at her. But a little of the heat went out of his gaze. He took the chair she offered.

'What we need is some English tea,' Aunt Bea said with too much brightness. She went out to the hall, where she could be heard murmuring to Letty.

Christina sat opposite her father. She said in a low voice, 'Please don't take it out on Aunt Bea. She was utterly against it at first. I blackmailed her into it.'

He shook his head. 'So you admit it. You aren't even ashamed of it.'

'I am. But I had to do it.'

'You've always been a headstrong child. You don't care what you do to get your own way.'

'I do care, Father. I would rather you accepted, approved . . .'

'Accept that you went behind my back? I suppose it was my money you used for your fees and expenses?'

'Yes. I'm afraid so.'

He gave a snort of angry laughter. 'You're incredible. If you ever turn to crime, the world had better beware.'

'Oh, please – Father, try to understand! I admit I had to use my wits, but if only you would believe that I really have to be a doctor. I have a . . . a . . .'

'Next you'll say you have a calling, like a nun!'

She felt the tears start into her eyes, but blinked them back. 'It really is like that. Don't sneer at it.'

'Nonsense! Utter nonsense! Dr Childers let you get too interested in all the jiggery-pokery of putting pills into patients and you felt you'd like to do that because it would make you feel superior if people said, "Oh, you've done wonders for me, doctor".'

'You don't understand—'

'I understand you, my girl, only too well. You always want to show off, to be different. You never would behave like any other little girl. Now you've gone too far. Look here, Chrissie,' he said, changing his tone and using the name that had sometimes cajoled her as a child, 'it's time to admit you've been playing silly games.'

'No!'

Her aunt came in. 'Tea won't be a moment. I've ordered sandwiches: I don't suppose you had any lunch, Herbert?'

'Thank you, I'm not hungry. Look here, Bea, help me talk some sense into this child.'

Bea fetched a deep sigh. 'I might have gone along with you a year ago, Herbert, but now I see things differently. To me Christina's proved herself and I'm very proud of her. I'm convinced she mustn't change course now.'

'But surely you can't want any niece of yours to be a doctor!'

'At first I thought like that. I thought she was too young and delicate. But I was wrong.'

'What do you imagine would become of her if she went through with this? She'd be coarsened, hardened—'

Christina got up from her chair in irritation. 'Why do people say things like that? Women are nurses, and nurses see as much of the seamy side of life as doctors, but do you claim that nurses are coarse and hard?'

'Oh,' groaned Herbert, 'it comes back to Miss Nightingale again, does it? Damn that woman! Why couldn't she have stayed at home and been content—'

'And let thousands of men die in the Crimea?' Despite herself, Christina laughed: there was scorn and anger in it but genuine amusement too. 'Father, this is 1908. You can't put the clock back to medieval times. Women get education,

101

they take their place in the world. And one of the places they belong is in the hospitals, in the surgeries.'

Letty came in with a big tray of tea and sandwiches. She gave the visitor a hard stare as she laid it on the little octagonal table. Herbert returned the stare with dislike. He hated this room, this house, he hated having his daughter talk to him with enthusiasm about a way of life that disgusted him. Women belonged in the home. That was how God had intended it, and that was how it should be.

When his sister handed him a cup of tea, he found he was very thirsty. He drank it off, accepted a second cup. The everyday social act seemed to bring some calm to the situation. That, in fact, had been Mrs Kentley's intention.

'Now,' she said, some ten minutes later, 'let's talk sensibly. Christina certainly isn't going to give up her studies and she isn't going back with you to Lincolnshire. I think you have to accept that.'

'Not by a long shot,' said Herbert. 'She's my daughter and she's going to do as I tell her.'

'Be sensible, Herbert. What could she possibly do in Market Bresham now?'

'She could—'

'It doesn't matter what I could or couldn't do, I'm not going to do it. I'm going to stay here in Philadelphia until I finish med school.'

'Christina, you are going to do no such thing. Even suppose you finished the course and got a degree, what on earth are you supposed to do after that?'

'I'll get a hospital post in a women's hospital.'

'Doing what – bringing an endless succession of other women's babies into the world? Surely you'd rather have a husband and children of your own!'

'No, I don't think I'll ever marry,' Christina said with the total conviction of an eighteen-and-a-half-year-old.

'So you're going to end up a sour old maid doling out pills and potions to a lot of hypochondriac women, is that it?'

She made no reply to that. It was so silly, so belittling. Why couldn't he face facts? She felt a twinge of impatience.

Her father really was not a very reasonable man.

'I'll tell you my assessment of the case,' he said. 'You're beglamoured by the idea of doing something difficult and different – I see that. You're a clever girl, Christina, nobody ever denied it. Up till now I've thought your intelligence was a bit of a nuisance, because on the whole men don't like clever women and any husband you got was likely to find you a problem. But let's say you've got brains and want to use them. Come back with me. I'll send you to finishing school, let you go on a tour of Europe the way they do: art galleries, museums, opera in Milan, that sort of thing. How's that?'

To him, it was a generous and appealing offer. To see Christina shaking her head even while he was making it put him in a rage.

'Goddamnit!' he said, springing up and sending his teacup flying. 'You simply won't see reason! I don't know why I'm even negotiating with you. You're my *daughter*, you have to do what I tell you!'

'No, I won't.'

'You'll go upstairs and pack your things, missie, and in half an hour you'll be ready to go back to the docks with me, and we'll go aboard the *Terentia* and you'll stay there under lock and key till she sails!'

Mrs Kentley looked at Christina, who sat white and still under the words. They both heard the echo: Go to your room and stay there until you've come to your senses.

'I am staying here, Father.'

'If you defy me on this, that's the last of it. You needn't think of yourself as my daughter any more.'

'If that's how you feel . . .'

'And let me tell you, Beatrice, if you give shelter to this bad and wicked girl, you're no sister of mine!'

'Very well, Herbert . . .'

'You mean you're going to let her? You're encouraging her?'

'Of course. Can't you see? It's meant to be. It's silly to try to prevent it. Dr Childers said it. Christina is a born doctor.'

Herbert strode to the door. 'Very well. I wash my hands of it. Please tell that impertinent maid to go out and hail a cab.'

'You don't have to go, Herbert! You can stay here.'

'What for? To be flouted, to be told I'm thwarting the wishes of the Almighty? I wouldn't stay in this house if you paid me a thousand pounds.'

He went out to the hall. Letty, who had heard him shouting his orders, already had the front door open and was out on the sidewalk calling to a cabbie at the corner.

'You can't go like this, Herbert!' Beatrice wept. 'It's all wrong . . .'

'And as for you, miss,' he said, ignoring his sister's tears and turning on his daughter, 'not one penny more do you get out of me. My money isn't going to finance this farcical idea. And don't waste your time writing to me when you get your precious degree and want to impress me with it. From now on, as far as I'm concerned, you don't exist.'

His daughter stood silent under the tidal wave of words. She made no move as he picked up the heavy suitcase and stalked out.

The cab drove up, the cabbie leaned back and opened the door. Herbert Holt gave directions, then got in without a backward glance. The cab rolled away.

'Goodbye and good riddance,' said Letty in relief.

Only then did Christina come to life. She ran out into the road to stand staring after the cab, listening to the clop of the hooves and the trundle of the wheels. Bearing her father away, out of her life.

Chapter Seven

Dr Fehr looked out over his audience. His audience of third and fourth year students looked back in bafflement.

'I know that what I am saying at this point leaves the field of pathology and enters into psychology. Nevertheless we have all seen – haven't we? – patients who truly exhibit symptoms for which there is no evidential basis.'

A hand was raised. 'What reason could there be for non-existent symptoms except pretence, sir?'

'Of course that happens. We've all had to deal with malingerers and hypochondriacs. What I'm discussing here is a man who truly believes he has tuberculosis, exhibits all the symptoms of tuberculosis, and yet microscopic examination of his sputum reveals no Kochian bacilli. Dr Sigmund Freud, whose work on dreams caused some scandal a few years ago, relates these cases of extremely convincing but non-existent disease to hysteria.'

The class moved and rustled. Some looked sceptical, some were uneasy. *Dr Freud! For heaven's sake, don't let's get into Dr Freud*, was the thought in many a mind. That idiot off in Vienna . . . Here in Philadelphia medicine was based on practical experience, not imaginative and unprovable theory.

All the same, Dr Fehr was apparently taking him seriously.

'There was a very interesting paper by Dr Freud in a German medical journal. All of you, I take it, know German?'

Laughter. They were all supposed to know German, according to the entrance requirements, but that was something of a fable.

'Hands up anybody who speaks fluent German?'

Christina nudged Jo-Jo. Jo-Jo had been educated in the

Austrian school system and, though her native tongue was Serbian, spoke perfect German. Jo-Jo put up her hand.

Among the men, a hand was raised. Peter Semmring came from a Pennsylvania-German family of some standing, who kept up the tradition of speaking the old language and sent their children to Europe every year to ensure they spoke it well.

'Anyone else? Miss Holt?'

Christina sat back and shook her head. She spoke adequate German but she sensed that some task was going to be imposed, and she had enough to do without taking on extra work – even from Dr Fehr.

'Right then, Miss Belu, Mr Semmring. I should like you to take these cyclostyled copies of the article and translate it for the benefit of your fellow-students.' A groan from the audience. 'Believe me, ladies and gentlemen, although I cannot accept all the man says, it's well worth reading.'

Peter and Jo-Jo went to the podium to accept the sheets of paper. Peter was secretly pleased, first to be doing something to attract Dr Fehr's particular attention, and second to be doing something that for once The Holt couldn't do.

The Holt was the bane of his life.

Peter had been put in the world to excel, yet somehow since starting med school, The Holt was always there, one rung above him on the ladder. She wasn't even as old as Peter, yet she seemed to be ahead of him wherever there was an open competition: for original study, for voluntary papers on pathology or physiology, for hospital systemics.

Peter was and always had been the alpha student of his year at high school. Yet somehow the pleasure of that memory was diminished by the fact that there was a girl some three years his junior who now held that honour in their group without apparent effort.

And she was a *girl*. That was what really rankled.

'How long d'you think this is going to take us?' he grumbled to Jo-Jo as they walked out of the lecture room.

'Who knows. It'll be full of funny words he's invented for himself, I bet.'

'Well, we'll confer, shall we?'

'But we're supposed to produce two separate versions so as to check one against the other for accuracy, Peter.'

'What the doctor doesn't know the doctor won't grieve over,' Peter said with a shrug.

'Is that entirely honest?'

'Is the world entirely flat? Come on, Jo-Jo, don't be naïve.'

They parted outside in the corridor. Jo-Jo was shaking her head to herself. Peter Semmring was in many ways a splendid type: quick-witted, clever, amusing. And good-looking – my word, yes, with his muscular torso which he didn't mind displaying while rowing for the Penn U. Rowing Club, and his flashing smile while pursuing the pretty girls on the dance floor. Yet sometimes he said things that brought a twinge of uneasiness. He liked short cuts, he liked to be first with a result. He liked to catch the eye of the important faculty members. She knew very well he was absolutely dying to be chosen as Dr Fehr's assistant.

Everyone expected him to get this honour. Each year at the beginning of the fall semester, Dr Fehr would choose a student to be a sort of personal assistant to him – someone who would supervise the technicians' slides, keep files on work progress in the path. lab., see that his notes were translated into readable English so that his secretary could type them up.

It was a position of great trust, great prestige. The man who got it became a confidant of one of the foremost doctors in the University. There was a small salary, which was quite unimportant to Peter: his family had money enough to cater for any of his needs or luxuries. What mattered was the high mark it put on your abilities. Any man who could go to a hospital and say, 'I was personal assistant to Dr Fehr,' was assured of a hearty welcome.

It was now the second week of term. Any moment now Dr Fehr should announce his choice. And Peter was pretty sure he would be the man. The fact that Fehr had just given him this translation to do was a signal – yet no, Jo-Jo Belu had been given the same task. But that was only because she spoke German.

Peter joined his friends, who were waiting to go for lunch. For some time now they'd been using a bar about ten minutes' walk from the medical faculty – but they didn't walk, they whizzed there in Peter's spanky new 9hp Oldsmobile.

'Who was a good little boy and put up his handie when Papa asked for a volunteer?' teased Virgil Jessup.

'Oh, we all know why,' Andy said. Andy White, big and plump, always liked to sound a wise old owl. But on this occasion the other two nodded agreement. They knew Peter had his tongue hanging out to get the post of assistant.

'What's wrong with that?' Peter was signalling to the bartender to bring their usual: four great mugs of beer and four thick sandwiches. 'See, the invitation's usually given by the end of this week. I want him to know I'm still as bright and eager as I was at the end of last year.'

'Your Mama would be shocked to the core if she knew you were translating something by that dreadful man Freud. I think I'll blackmail you a little,' said Stu Greysdell.

'Say, wasn't it funny The Holt didn't volunteer? I expected her to.'

'Oh, she nudged her chum into it. That's enough – one of that gang of little angels showed willing.'

'Jo-Jo's bright,' Stu said. 'Not as bright as The Holt, but a lot cleverer than Susanne or the Mennem girl, though I'm not knocking Mennem – she's a pleasure to the eye.'

'Well, so's The Holt. I mean, fellers, let's be honest, there's not one of us who hasn't tried to get his arms around The Holt and won't keep trying.'

'Waste of time,' said Peter, wiping beer froth from his upper lip. 'I spent almost two months last year laying siege to her. Not a hope.'

'What he means,' Virgil explained to his friends, 'is that if he can't do it, nobody can.'

Peter looked down with mock modesty. 'Can I help it if I'm irresistible?' he said. 'It's my manly beauty and my big brown eyes.'

'Hey, but seriously, all that time you wasted on her, you really didn't get *anywhere*?'

'She thought I was offering her platonic friendship—'

His companions hooted with laughter.

'You, platonic?' Stu said. 'By Canaan, she doesn't know you!'

'What's that thing in the poem?' suggested Andy. '"Something, something, chaste and fair." That's her.'

'Well, it doesn't signify, does it? There's plenty of others if she wants to waste time being chaste and fair.'

'And platonic.'

'And platonic. Down with Plato and all his notions.'

'Here's to that!'

They all raised their mugs and drank to it. Then it was time to wolf down their sandwiches – 'Chicken again,' groaned Andy – and be driven back to class by Peter.

While Peter and his friends of the fourth year were drinking confusion to Plato, Christina Holt was waiting in the ante-room of Dr Fehr's office. As she was about to leave the pathology building, a note had been brought to her by a college porter. Dr Fehr wished to see her before classes resumed, if that was convenient.

Of course it was convenient. Anything that Dr Fehr wished would be convenient. Only she hoped he wouldn't try to persuade her to take on the translation of the Freud paper. She didn't want to have to produce excuses. It would be embarrassing to have to say, 'I can't take on the translation, sir, I'll be too busy peeling potatoes.'

The withdrawal of her quite substantial allowance had made a big difference to her financial situation. Aunt Bea hadn't dreamed of charging her for her board and lodging, but times weren't quite so good for the Wallace Hotel as they had been. New, big, efficient hotels had been opened in the city centre, hotels that offered amenities such as telephones in every suite and room service at all hours of the day and night. Naturally businessmen preferred them.

Aunt Bea still had her two permanent boarders and a small but faithful clientele who had been using the Wallace

Hotel for years and didn't want to change. But in the nature of things, during the last year or two it had often happened that the Wallace Hotel was by no means full, even at the height of the busy seasons of spring and fall.

Some of the help had to be let go. It was Christina's idea that she should act as kitchen-maid and assistant chambermaid to Letty.

'But dear, your classes.'

'Well, if I do kitchen chores before I go in the morning and chambermaid chores when I get home, that should fit in nicely.'

'But what about your studying?'

'I'll fit it in. Don't worry about it, Auntie.'

When it came right down to it, there was no other way they could afford college fees and expenses: they had to economise, and use for Christina's books and fees the money that might have been paid to servants.

She tried not to let it show when she was tired or under stress. But there never seemed to be enough hours in the day except in vacation time. A couple of holidays at the Serbian settlement in its peaceful valley of the Alleghenies had helped give her back her energy, but even then she and Jo-Jo had read and studied in the evenings.

As her third year of medicine opened out to her, she found herself worried, over-stretched. She knew she had lost weight because her clothes, carefully valeted over the last twelve months, were loose upon her body. She couldn't take on anything else, not even an interesting translation, not even for Dr Fehr.

She looked about the small ante-room, seeing yet again the pencil sketches of Roman ruins, said to have been done by Dr Fehr himself in his youth. His secretary worked away at her big typing machine, filling the air with clatter. Christina stifled a sigh. It would soon be too late to get anything to eat before classes resumed.

The door of the inner office opened. A student came out. 'Dr Fehr said for you to go right in, Miss Holt,' he said.

'Thank you, Mr Shires.'

Dr Fehr was at his desk. He half rose to greet her. He was punctilious, always treating the lady meds with the respect he would have shown to women in his social circle.

'Thank you for dropping by, Miss Holt. How are you placed as regards voluntary tasks?'

Here it comes, she thought: Why don't I undertake the Freud? 'I'm helping to edit the Medical Students' Journal and I have a clinical study going on in collaboration with Bernard Yates.'

'Is that the one into infant recognition capability?'

'Yes, sir, but we haven't got very far as yet.'

'It should be interesting. I look forward to seeing the report. I wonder if you feel there's space among your activities to take on yet another?'

She began to shake her head. I'm going to have to tell him about the dusting and the bed-making, she thought.

'Please don't say no until you've heard me out. I was hoping you would take on the voluntary role of assistant to the Senior Lecturer in Pathology.'

There was a long pause during which she could hear the clock on his mantelpiece go tick-tick-tick.

'You don't like the idea, Miss Holt?'

'You can't mean it!'

He smiled. He was a tall thin man with pince-nez through which his eyes twinkled with a sharp, alert brightness. 'I won't take offence and tell you I do in fact know what I mean.'

'But sir!'

'Yes?'

'The post always goes to a fourth-year student.'

'How long have you been a student, Miss Holt?'

'This is my third year, sir.'

'Then you can't possibly know what "always" happens. The post has gone to a third-year student in the past. I had a third-year student in – let me see – 1903. And before that my predecessor had third-year students on two successive occasions.'

'But they were men.'

111

'Quite true. Are you saying that because you're a woman you can't do the work?'

'Oh, no, sir!'

'I thought not,' he said with quiet amusement. 'My impression of you, Miss Holt, is that you feel there's very little you can't do.'

She didn't know whether he was saying she was brave and determined or arrogant and stubborn. She sat looking at him out of her thin, fine-boned face, and he was struck with the notion that perhaps he ought not to ask her: she looked hard-pressed enough already.

But, damn it, she was the best choice. She was a brilliant diagnostician and her neatness and diligence in a pathological inquiry was remarkable. Moreover, she was dependable. The fourth-year students were dependable – but dull. He had decided to choose his assistant from the third-year class.

Semmring, who would have been his choice otherwise, had a certain frivolity about him – well, perhaps that was unfair: the boy just had money and spent it on frivolous things. He worked well, his marks were very high. And yet . . . and yet . . .

'Do you need time to think it over, Miss Holt?' he inquired. 'I generally have this matter settled by the end of the second week of the fall semester. If you'd like to think it over until Friday—'

'Oh, no, sir! No! I'd *love* to do it.' Her voice almost trembled on the words. Love to do it – what an understatement – she would give her right arm to do it.

'Good. That's settled. If you would like to report to this office after class this evening—'

'This evening?'

'Have you something arranged for this evening?'

'No, no, only my aunt. She'd be expecting me home, doctor, but I'll send a note . . .'

'We could begin tomorrow morning, if you'd prefer.'

'No, sir, if I'm to be your assistant I must be available when you need me. I can send a message home, Dr Fehr.'

'Excellent. I'll give you an outline then of the work at

present under way in the path. lab., although you're aware of most of it. And you have a good idea of what's involved because you saw McPherson doing it last year.'

'Yes sir.'

'I'd like to have you here on Sundays – I often catch up with things on the Sabbath and need someone to take note. Gifford will be here too – well, you know as well as I do, the path. lab. is seldom empty, so there's no need to worry about chaperoning.'

'I wasn't worrying about it, sir.'

He gave a little laugh. 'Good for you. As to the vac., I may need you to be here over Easter, because I'm going to start a series of cultures early next semester. But at Christmas I myself like to be with my family and friends, so you can safely make arrangements of your own.'

'Thank you, doctor.'

'The salary is very small, but you know that. You might find time to go to the cashier's office before classes – they'll give you a form to fill in and tell you the payment dates. The hours have to be fitted in around your lectures and mine, of course, but in general an assistant does about three hours a day on weekdays and perhaps four on Sundays. Is that agreeable?'

'Oh *yes* sir,' breathed Christina.

Anyone who saw her as she came out of Dr Fehr's office would have thought she came from an assignation with a lover. Starry-eyed, flushed, breathing lightly and quickly, she looked in a seventh heaven.

And that was how she felt. Dr Fehr had chosen her. The great, the influential Dr Fehr. She'd almost blurted out, 'Why me?' when he made the offer to her. Why? Why choose a third-year lady med over the fourth-year students, or over the third-year men?

He wouldn't have given her this chance if he didn't think her worthy of it. It must mean that he thought her better—

No. She stopped herself from entertaining that vainglorious thought. There was so much she didn't yet know, so much still to learn. Under Dr Fehr's aegis she would learn all the faster. She would be in his confidence, she would work closely under his direction, she would soak up knowledge. What did it matter if she had to work twenty hours a day, twenty-two, twenty-four, to fit it all in? She would do it, she would respond to the honour he'd done her, she would work harder for him than any man could ever do.

And so, when the question recurred to her, 'Why me?' she answered it with, 'Why *not* me? I'll work harder to deserve it than anyone else ever would.'

By the time the afternoon class began, she had seen the cashier and signed the form. She still hadn't had any lunch, but she was too excited to notice.

'What was it about?' asked Youffie. 'Are you going to do that German paper too?'

'No. It was something quite different.'

'Well, what? Have you goofed somehow?'

'No.'

She didn't know how to tell them. It was too strange, too unexpected, too grand and glorious to put into words. All the same, it had to be told, because she was to begin at once.

'No!' gasped Jo-Jo when she heard the stumbling explanation.

'He's asked *you*?'

'He's chosen a *girl*?'

She nodded, unable to say any more.

Her friends all gazed at her in awe.

'My Go-o-od,' said Jo-Jo, 'I want to be there when Semmring hears this.'

Peter was popular on the whole with his fellow-students but there were one or two, or perhaps even three or four, who were quite glad to see him take a knock, who were quite willing to tell him that Christina Holt's name had been posted on the students' notice board as the year's assistant to Dr Fehr.

Luckily for Peter, the news struck him dumb. It was his little group of friends who broke out in a protest in which most of the fourth-year men joined.

'He's given the job to a girl? Is he out of his mind?'

114

'Good God, she's just out of sophomore year!'

'Peter, you've got to go and protest about this!'

'The Holt? He's taken on The Holt! My God, she'll be even more uppish than ever!'

'Can he actually take on a third-year student as his assistant?'

'Can he actually take on a *girl* as his assistant?'

The outcry had given him time to recover. 'Do you want to go and argue it with him?' he inquired. 'I think we all agree Dr Fehr knows what he's doing.'

'But you can't just sit back and let—'

'Say, Pete, everybody thought you were going to get the job. Did you do anything to annoy the old man?'

'Everybody thought, did they? They were wrong, then.'

'But what are you going to do about it, Pete?'

'What do you suggest?'

'If I were you I'd go to Fehr and tell him . . .'

'Tell him what?'

'Well, tell him he can't *do* this.'

It was one of the hardest things Peter Semming had ever done when he produced an easy grin. 'Come on, fellers, it's no big deal.'

'What? No big deal? When you're cheated out of what everybody knows is yours by right?'

'Aw, come on, what is it, anyway? Two or three hours a day at the old guy's beck and call, and Sundays all messed up. I can do without it, if you want to know.'

'But I thought you were keen about it, Pete.'

'Well, I suppose I was . . . But see here, you can bet old Fehr only gave the job to The Holt to prove some point: that he's a good, tolerant guy, that he's got no bias against lady meds—'

'Well, why hasn't he? Any way you look at it, it's peculiar.' Stu wrinkled his brows. 'You don't think he's got a thing for The Holt? I mean, she's some eyeful.'

'Talk sense, Stu!' Virgil protested. 'He's an old man, got grandchildren . . .'

'You think that makes any difference? I've got an uncle,

he must be sixty if he's a day, and he still—'

'Never mind your uncle. I'm talking about Dr Fehr. He's not like that, and if he were, The Holt would freeze him with a glance. Naw, it's nothing like that. I think you must have offended him somehow, Pete, and The Holt was the next best candidate. Mebbe if you went to him and talked it over, he'd change his mind.'

'I'm not going to beg him for the job,' Peter said with a shrug. 'I tell you, it's not worth the bother.'

But it was. To have lost it had made him angry. He couldn't let anyone see how angry – he was afraid of letting go and making a fool of himself.

He'd told his parents he was sure to get the assistant's post. They were going to raise their eyebrows when they heard he'd missed out. And to a girl. To a *girl*.

He told his father the bad news after dinner that night, while they were having a cigar together in the den. The old man was furious. 'You must have done something, Peter! No professor in his right mind would take on a woman assistant in preference to you if there wasn't a reason. It's what I've always said, things have always come too easily to you, boy, you just don't take life seriously enough.' And so on, the old, old lecture about being responsible and remembering the family name and living within his allowance.

His mother wept when she heard. He patted her shoulder, assuring her that it wasn't really important. Over her head he saw their reflection in the pier glass, Mrs Semmring still fair-haired and stylish even though now a little plump. And for a moment he saw Christina Holt instead of his mother, leaning against him, her fair head against his shoulder.

He slept badly. He kept waking from dreams which were always about Christina Holt. She was ahead of him on a long, dusty road, or looking down at him from an ornate balcony, or she was in the path. lab. leaning over a microscope which he wasn't allowed to touch. Only when he saw her as he had for that moment in his mother's parlour – when he felt Christina was in his arms, leaning against him – could he feel that things were right, that he was her superior.

In the morning, without knowing how, he had made a resolution. Christina must be punished for taking the assistantship away from him, and the way to punish her was to melt that armour of ice.

Once he had decided to put his mind to it, he found it was surprisingly easy. Previously, he had gone after Christina as he would any other girl: flattery, little jokes that only the two of them could share, invitations to the theatre or concerts. Now he planned and carried out a different campaign. She was a serious girl. She could only be hooked through serious matters.

First of all, he could see that she was often close to physical exhaustion by the end of the day. It was easy to happen upon her, to offer to carry her briefcase or book bag, to put her on the trolley for her home. Then he had a book she needed: he lent her his copy. Then came the time when Dr Fehr was going to attend a conference in Chicago: the treatise he wanted to deliver was still in handwritten notes; it had to be typed up and the old man hadn't left sufficient time.

By now, Christina was confiding such problems to Peter as he walked her to the trolley stop.

'That's easy,' he said. 'You give half to me, and I'll get one of the stenographers in Dad's office to do it.'

'But it's needed by Friday, Peter!'

'Stop worrying. It'll be ready.'

'Oh, it's so good of you! Poor Miss Peverill was at her wits' end, and of course it's my responsibility to see his notes are ready for when he wants them.'

'I hope he isn't asking too much of you, Christina. It's a lot for a girl to manage.'

She looked up at him in the light of the lamp at the corner. 'You know, you've behaved quite differently from what I expected. I thought you'd be angry that you didn't get the post.'

'Me?' He took the chance, put his arm about her to give

her a hug. 'I expected to get it, sure, but you know I've always admired you, Christina. I couldn't ever be angry with you.'

'Why, I . . . I . . .' She was flustered. 'I never knew you felt like that.'

'But I tried to be friends with you ages ago . . .'

'Oh yes,' she said, leaning away from him with a smile in which there was some irony. 'I've seen you "making friends". You always drop the girl in a month or so.'

'Now is that fair? You and I have been friends now for more than six weeks. I know it, because I've been counting the days. In fact, I was going to ask you to have a little celebration for our six-week anniversary next Monday.'

'A celebration? If it's a party or a theatre, I can't, Peter, I really can't. I've too much to do.'

'Look, Fehr's going to be away, you won't be needed in lab. on Sunday – why don't we go out on the river? The trees are looking so good this fall, and we could take a picnic . . .'

'No, really, I ought to catch up on my textbooks.'

'Well, bring them with you. What are you studying?'

'It's a chapter about endocarditis.'

'Oh, that thing, I did that last month – we can go over it together, there are a few pointers I could give you.'

As he went home with the sheaf of Fehr's notes for the stenographer, he thought to himself, Good old Plato. He makes a good smokescreen. Platonic friendship . . . That's one way of getting where I want to be.

He rowed her up the Schuylkill above Fairmount dam. Maple and ginkgo, hickory and oak, flamed and glowed in the winter sun. He and his passenger had the river almost to themselves for it was really too cold for boating. Christina was delighted. She'd never seen the trees from this angle before.

There was a popular song about the Schuylkill that claimed there were plenty of 'Bosky nooks for Beauty's looks, And quiet bays for lazy days.' Peter chose a bosky nook for lunch. He tied up the boat, helped his passenger ashore, put the leather-covered boat cushions on the bank, and spread out the picnic the Semmring cook had prepared for them.

In this sheltered spot, the November sun was warm. There were even some insects humming in the reeds, and a bird twittering overhead.

'My, this is luxurious,' murmured Christina as she accepted wine in a collapsible silver cup. The food spread out on the cloth was of a much higher standard than she was used to: flimsy puffballs of pastry containing lobster pâté, little crisp rolls spread with mayonnaise and turkey, tartines of white fish in aspic.

He was amused by her naïvety. He took the picnic goodies for granted. He refilled her silver cup and pressed her to try something else.

The wine made her drowsy. He was surprised when nevertheless she produced the textbook from the satchel she'd been carrying.

'You see it says here, page 101, that in cases of rheumatic inflammation the valves become swollen and may suffer distortion. Then later, page 112, it says there may be wartlike excrescences. I want to know whether a distortion is a wartlike excrescence, or something else? The line-drawing . . .'

He leaned his head next to hers to read the pages. They went back and forth between the two line-drawings. He told her what he could remember of the notes he'd bought from a fourth-year man. She was yawning a little, fighting a languor brought on by the wine and the unexpected sunshine.

When they'd dealt with two or three points that had been troubling her, he quietly closed the book, turned her face towards him, and kissed her.

Her first response was surprise, but almost at once there was eagerness, a welcoming softness. He wrapped his arms about her, drawing her close. She let herself be held against him, then after a moment her arms went about his neck.

'Darling,' he murmured, 'I've wanted to do this for ages . . . Say you care for me a little, Christina.'

She shook her head, but clung to him. She seemed to need the comfort of his warmth, his strength. She leaned against him. Gently he slipped a hand into the opening of her unbuttoned jacket. He cupped her breast through the embroidered linen of her blouse.

'No,' she said in a muffled voice.

'Darling, it's all right. We need each other, we were meant for each other. You feel it too, don't you? Life's been empty until now.'

'Oh, yes, Peter . . . I don't know if . . . But it's so wonderful to find someone to *be* with . . .'

He didn't hurry. They were alone on a quiet river in a sunny bower. The girl was innocent, vulnerable, longing for something more than simple friendship, although she knew not what.

He had intended to make love to her, had come out this morning with that precise intention. She would be his, she would belong to him, no longer a superior being to taunt him in his dreams.

She gave way to him in the end, overwhelmed by his inexorable gentleness. And then to his surprise she seemed to soar in passion when he took her at last. The ice maiden had melted in a fire of autumn, fire compounded of loneliness and longing, physical need and human weakness.

She was his. Her body belonged to him. But even more than that, it astonished him to discover that he seemed to have won her heart.

Chapter Eight

The idea of going away for some part of the Christmas vacation seemed to arise naturally.

'After all, we have the right to be together,' Peter said. 'We belong to each other now.'

'Yes, like man and wife, really.'

'And it's so difficult here at college: I've got my work and you've got yours, and we sure don't want to arouse any gossip.'

He had explained that his family would be very difficult if they knew he was dating a girl at college. 'Since way back, my parents have been taking it for granted I'm going to marry Ardeth Loring, you know how parents are . . .'

'Do I not!' Christina had told him about her father and his views on suitable husbands.

In fact, she had told him all about herself. Like a dam bursting, all her confidences had poured out. She told him how she'd always been determined to be a doctor, how she'd been sent away as a bad and disobedient daughter to her Aunt Beatrice, how her father had said in so many words that he washed his hands of her.

In return she got half-truths. About things that were well known, he was honest: that it was a tradition in his family for a son to study medicine; how his grandfather had used his medical knowledge to found the firm of Semmring Remedies; how he himself expected to head up one of the departments after gaining his degree and some experience in practice.

But about his freedom to come and go as he pleased, about plans for the future, he used a little ambivalent diplomacy. It was true his family wanted him to marry the Loring girl, but he could always get his own way if he worked at it. However, it made a good reason for keeping their affair quiet.

Christina hadn't been too happy about that at first, but he produced good arguments. 'See, you want to finish your studies and get your degree, honey. My Dad would go berserk at the idea of me marrying a girl who wanted to practise as a doctor, even after she was married. You've got to give me time to work round to it.'

'Of course I understand,' she assured him. 'You feel you can make him see reason?'

'Sure,' Peter said, dropping a kiss on her nose, 'don't worry about a thing. All it takes is time.' Some hopes . . .

Thanksgiving had come upon them while they were still in the first stages of their affair. They couldn't spend it together because they were already involved in the usual family plans. Christmas Day, the same – but after Christmas there was free time.

'I generally spend some of the holiday with Jo-Jo at the farm up on the Juniata – we do a little skating and get snug in the farmhouse for a long spell of reading. But I could tell her I've got other plans this year, and my aunt wouldn't think to ask. She'd take it for granted I was going to Jo-Jo.'

'I could get away easy. Let's do it, Chrissie.'

'But where could we go? It would never do to go anywhere close by – someone might see us.' She coloured as she said it. The deceit troubled her. She was proud of being Peter Semmring's girl, wanted the world to know it; but Peter said no, and he had good reasons, which he had explained more than once.

There was his blue-blooded family, old German-American stock, well known in Philadelphia's social circles. There were their plans for his marriage to a girl of an equally influential family. It would only cause untold difficulties for Peter if he had to explain to his parents that he wanted to be released from the unofficial engagement to Ardeth Loring. And with exams looming in this final year of med school, the last thing she wanted for Peter was strain and upset at home. She herself knew how hard it was to cope even with the wonderful stress of being head over heels in love.

Love was a difficult emotion. She sometimes wondered if it wasn't a kind of madness. Everything looked different to her. She had the feeling she was no longer quite able to make judgements, understand problems. Everything that happened, everything she heard of seemed to relate to Peter. Peter had become the centre of her personal universe.

And so if Peter said it was best to keep things to themselves, she accepted it, though she would have gloried in telling the world.

'Ever been to New York?'

'Aunt Beatrice took me a couple of times for shopping.'

'Let's go there! It's a great place to lose yourself. And at New Year it's great: big shows in the theatres, everything decked out with bunting and tinsel – you'll love it.'

They had to go separately. So Peter would motor up in his Oldsmobile while Christina would go by the railroad. He met her off the train in the early evening, conducted her with panache to the snowy kerb where the car stood. He put her travel bag in the trunk, helped her aboard, and made a sweeping turn that spurted wet snow up under the wheels.

To her surprise they went bowling through the city, over the bridge to Brooklyn, and thence by Ocean Parkway to Coney Island. Coney Island had come out of its hibernation for Christmas and New Year but would go back to sleep again until spring. At the moment it looked joyous, celebratory, and Christina exclaimed in pleasure at all the lights in the winter night.

But the reason Peter had chosen it was that no one he knew would have been seen dead in Coney Island, at New Year or any other time.

The hotel made Christina laugh. It was called The Elephant, and was in fact built in the shape of one. It was so huge and vulgar, you could only embrace it with open-hearted enjoyment.

The bellboy hurried out to take their luggage. On the way, Peter had given Christina a ring for her left hand, stolen from his mother's trinket box. When Christina asked where he had got it, he told her it had belonged to his old nurse.

She slipped it on, blushing. She hardly dared look up at the reception clerk. But he, cynical and uninterested, merely turned the register for Peter's signature. Peter wrote, 'Mr and Mrs Peter J. Semmring.'

Their room was about three hundred feet up. Out in the winter night, lights from shipping twinkled off West Brighton. The bellboy switched on lamps, closed the drapes, stood waiting for his tip. 'Anything else, sir? Anything I can get you, Mrs Semmring?' The young lady didn't respond. 'Mrs Semmring?' he persisted.

'Oh, no . . . No, thank you.' The lady was taking off her hat, shaking out her beautiful blonde hair. Some lady – didn't know she was supposed to be Mrs Semmring.

Peter tipped the boy, who touched his cap, winked knowingly at him, and went out.

It was now seven o'clock. 'What shall we do, honey? Shall we change and go into New York and paint the town a little? Or shall we stay here, eat in the restaurant?'

Christina shivered. He helped her out of her coat, a coat of English woollen cloth that had once been trim and stylish but was now a little worn.

'Oh, Peter!' She clung to him, frightened at what she was doing.

'What's the matter? Scared? Don't be, Christina. So long as we have each other, we've nothing to be scared of.'

'I know, you're right. It's only I . . . I've never done anything like this before.'

'Do you think I have?'

'Oh, no! Of course not! I didn't mean that.' She had never intended to hurt his feelings. She reached up on tiptoe, kissed him on the lips. 'We'll do whatever you want to do, darling. You know New York, I don't, so I leave it up to you.'

'I'll tell you what I really want to do,' he whispered against her ear. And he told her, softly.

She lowered her head so that it was against his chest. 'I want that too, Peter.'

So they went to bed, and in his arms she lost any sense of awkwardness or timidity. Outside the winter wind blew snow against the window, cars and carriages rushed along the boulevard, down in the restaurant a band was playing ragtime, but to them there was only the touch of skin against skin, the perfume of each other's bodies, rising tension and then release.

About eleven they put on dressing-gowns and had food sent in. Peter made her sit on his lap while he put little titbits into her mouth, kissing her each time as a reward, savouring the food through the sweetness of her lips.

She was so lovely. She was such an astonishment. He'd imagined she would be cool and languid, but her physical needs seemed to match his own. He almost thought he could really fall in love with her, if he wasn't careful.

But that would be a big mistake, because his parents really wouldn't accept her. What, a girl who expected to practise medicine as Mrs Peter Semmring? The roof of the Semmring house would fall down at the mere thought. And he himself . . . He couldn't live with a wife who might have interests outside the marriage. She might even surpass him in her career. It was impossible.

At midnight they dressed for outdoors and went out to walk along the beach. It was icily cold, but they raced along the freezing sand laughing like wild things. The boulevard was still busy, vehicles hurrying by with their lamps wavering, pedestrians out making their unsteady way from café to restaurant, a little group of strolling players entertaining an audience by a snow-covered flowerbed.

'Oh, Peter, it's so wonderful!' Christina cried, throwing out her arms as if she could embrace the whole world. 'I never imagined a place like this. We're shut away at the University, we never raise our heads from our books . . .'

'Yeah, there's a whole big world out there,' he agreed, 'and I'm going to get myself a piece of it once I've finished school.'

When they were in their room again they undressed each other slowly. Their skins were cold from the ocean wind. With kisses they warmed each other, wound themselves together by their eager arms, and fell into bed to make love again.

They had three days: New Year's Eve, New Year's Day, and the day after. At midnight on the great day they were in the restaurant, sharing the loud celebrations of the hotel, laughing, a little drunk, embracing strangers. Christina had never been in such an uproar before. Back home in faraway Market Bresham, New Year had been a restrained affair: late-night sherry in the drawing-room, handshakes and yawns and the ringing of the parish church bells.

But at the the Elephant Hotel, there was noise and laughter and camaraderie. She noticed that money seemed to be no object: champagne was called for, men signed bills without even looking at them. Everyone was well-dressed, so much so that she felt a bit like a country mouse in her 'best' frock and shoes that didn't quite match it.

But Peter made up for any deficiencies. Elegant in his perfectly tailored suit, he outshone every other man in the room. His light brown hair gleamed under the ballroom lamps, he moved so well, held her with so much easy strength as they danced. She let herself relax in his embrace, let the music carry her away.

Life was so wonderful, so perfect. And love was even more wonderful. To be able to linger in each other's arms knowing no one would call them away, to lie curved against each other as sleep overtook them . . . How right Peter had been to contrive for them this little glimpse of paradise away from the hard, demanding life of the University.

She hardly knew how she had deserved to be so lucky. To fall in love with Peter Semmring had never been any part of her plan. She'd scarcely even been aware of his existence, except as someone the other girls glanced at with too much interest. It was Peter who had sought her friendship. And from that, love had grown – for him, too. To be loved by Peter Semmring seemed too much of a marvel for her mind to take in.

Yet here she was, in his arms in the noisy ballroom of this funny hotel, waiting for the band to strike up 'Auld Lang Syne', for the new year to come which would at last bring them their medical degrees and their marriage.

Married to Peter! Mrs Peter Semmring. Dr Christina Semmring.

They would work as a team. She would take as her patients the mothers and children, Peter would deal with the men. Although she seemed to recall he'd said something about doing research for his father's pharmaceutical company . . . Well, she would still be able to specialise in women's complaints, and anyway, this wasn't the time to plan it all out, it was nearly New Year and her head was spinning from too much champagne.

When the band-leader brought the dance music to a halt with a roll of drums, the crowd turned to watch him. His eyes were on the clock. His drummer beat out the seconds. At the stroke of midnight the musicians struck a noisy chord then launched into 'Auld Lang Syne'.

Everybody kissed everybody. Peter kissed Christina, and that was the only kiss that mattered. She clung to him in the throng, arms around him, body close against him, no thoughts in her head, only a whirl of love and happiness and optimism. The new year had begun, the year that was to be their special year.

The first day of January they spent in each other's arms. 'Start as you mean to go on,' Peter said, grinning, and she laughed her agreement.

Next day they were more solemn. It was their last; in the morning they must go their separate ways, she back to Philadelphia, he on to some relations in Vermont.

Now the tawdriness of the hotel no longer seemed amusing. He drove her into New York to spend some money in the shops, but her heart wasn't in it. She tended to cling to him: it was a little irritating. He said, 'Cheer up. We'll try to see each other often when we get back.'

'But it's always so hasty, so constrained. Here we were able to be free for a few hours.'

'I know what you mean, Christina, but we have to be sensible.'

'Couldn't we . . . Couldn't we get engaged? I mean, officially? Then we could be seen around together at the University.'

'But my folks, Chrissie . . .'

'Yes, of course.' She looked up at him, trying not to look as if she were pleading. 'When do you think of speaking to them about us?'

'Who knows? The timing's got to be right.'

'When we've got our degrees? That would be a good time.'

'We'll see, dear, we'll see.'

They were walking along Fifth Avenue. He was carrying one or two packages, things he'd bought for her against her protests. She stopped, searched in her handbag, got out a handkerchief.

'Aw, gee, Christina, you're not crying, are you?'

She shook her head, her face hidden in the handkerchief. 'No, it's just a little cold . . .'

That was all he needed, a weepy girl on his arm in the middle of Manhattan. 'Come on, let's go in here, it's time for lunch anyhow.' He ushered her into a restaurant, and then to his horror saw an old friend of his mother's handing in her wraps to a hat-check girl.

'No, on second thoughts, let's eat in the Italian quarter. I know a great place.' He urged Christina out, hailed a cab, and got them out of there fast.

But it had been a near thing. It shook his confidence. He was over-bright at lunch as a consequence. Christina was still too dazed with misery at the thought of parting to have taken much notice of the incident. She took his brightness as an attempt to cheer her up.

They ate, as he had suggested, in a good Italian restaurant: at least he ordered the food, but she actually ate very little. Then they went back to Grand Central Station where he had left the Oldsmobile. She was rather silent on the drive back to West Brighton. From time to time he stole a glance at that pale face, but she was staring ahead under the brim of her felt hat, her eyes looking into a future that troubled her.

Their lovemaking that night was different. It had in it a sense of farewell. He for his part was as eager as always, but Christina seemed to sense that this was the last of their careless, wayward love. She strained her body against his as if she would make herself part of him, mingle their flesh, make them inseparable. At last, when they lay exhausted side by side on the great double bed with its flashy silken spread, he felt her lay her palm on his chest.

'What are you doing?' he murmured, half asleep.

'I'm listening to your heartbeat, my love. I want to carry at least that steady, sturdy rhythm into the dismal days ahead.'

They packed quickly and hastily next day. Christina was a little distrait – she didn't know how to explain the presents he had given her when she got home, and one or two of her own belongings seemed to have gone astray.

'Never mind about it, dear,' he urged. 'Come on, you're going to miss your train.'

They kissed goodbye in the station entrance, like two ordinary people taking leave. He turned away as she walked firmly into the echoing hall towards the trains. As he drove north out of New York he was in a strange mood, half triumph, half regret.

He had done what he wanted. He had reduced her to what she essentially was: a woman who could be dragged into bed if you went at it the right way.

But damned if he didn't feel a little sad about it.

His mood had changed by the time the new semester opened. Friends in Vermont had treated him as he liked to be treated – made much of him, admired him, showed him he was right to expect first place in the world. Yet when he got back to University it was Christina people were talking about: Dr Fehr had gone on record publicly as saying that without her work he couldn't have got his recent treatise ready in time for the conference.

'She's some babe,' said Virgil. 'They say she's likely to get the Crompton Scholarship for her last year.'

'She's not so much,' Peter said with a shrug.

'Think not? You're in the minority, kid.'

'She's just like any other girl. Play it right, and you can get in there among her petticoats.'

'You wish.'

'No, I report.'

They were in a corner of the bar in the Schuylkill Barge and Athletics Club, Peter and Virgil and the usual gang. His words made all the other men stop what they were doing to stare at him.

'When you say "report", do you mean as of an event that has already occurred?'

'You bet.'

'You and The Holt? You're kidding.'

'Not a bit. Where do you think I spent New Year's, friends and fellow-womanisers? In West Brighton with the said Christina Holt.'

As he said it, he almost bit it back. But after all, what was the use of having laid her if no one knew? How could he diminish her in the eyes of others if he didn't tell?

'Aw, come on,' Stu muttered. 'I know you can't stand the kid, but don't say things like that.'

'It's true. If you doubt me, go to that temple of elegance, the Elephant Hotel at Coney Island, and look at the register. You'll see the names – Mr and Mrs Peter Semmring, from 30 December to 2 January.'

There was a stunned silence. Then Andy Lelliot said, 'Well, anybody could take a girl to the Elephant and then claim later it was Christina Holt.'

It was the moment he'd been waiting for. He took from his jacket pocket something soft and delicate, held out his hand, opened it, and let the fabric fall about his fingers.

It was a woman's camisole.

The men gaped at it.

'It's hers?' asked Virgil in a whisper.

'Check the laundry mark. I think you'll find it's the one

for the Wallace Hotel, sacred abode of the divine Christina. Besides, there are her initials in a little circle of forget-me-nots: C.H.'

Stu took the soft garment from Peter's hand. It was made of batiste, a very fine soft cotton almost like silk but much less expensive. All of them had in their time helped girls take off garments just like that. It was a pretty, feminine thing; and there seemed no doubt it belonged to Christina Holt.

'Well I'll be shot for a jack-rabbit,' Stu said. 'I believe it's true.'

'Bet your life it's true. Three hot and steamy days, boys. And she gave me this little pretty as a souvenir.'

They gave a shout of laughter. 'She did? She wanted you to remember?'

'It wasn't something you're likely to forget. Boy, was she great in bed! You know, fellers, there's something to be said for making it with a medical student – she sure knows where everything ought to go.'

'I'll drink to that!' cried Andy. They ordered more beer and toasted each other.

Yet as the gathering broke up, Virgil Jessup was rather quiet.

'Anything wrong, Virge?'

'No, it isn't anything.'

'Come on, don't you think it's funny?'

'Oh, sure, it's funny . . . All the same, I can't help being kind of disappointed.'

'Disappointed? What in God's name about?'

'Well, tell the truth . . . I never thought she was like that.'

Peter snorted with amusement. 'Sonny, they're all like that.'

The word spread, as he had known it would. Others in his year looked at him with raised eyebrows. Gossip would stop suddenly as he came into a locker-room or a study, then there would be hints, veiled questions. Of course he couldn't come right out and tell the story to any except his close friends, but everybody got the message.

At first Christina couldn't understand the change in

attitude that she felt around her. Men who used to treat her with distant politeness now grinned at her, but there seemed no friendship in the grin. Once three male students made a kissing sound at her as she went by.

A lady med in the fourth year approached her on a day in the middle of January. 'There's a lot of talk, Christina. Among the men. Is there anything in it?'

'What sort of talk?' she demanded, colouring up.

'Well, of course, they don't let me in on it. It's about you and some man.'

'I can't think why anyone would want to talk about me in that way.'

'You're saying it's just idle gossip?'

'I don't have to defend myself,' Christina said hotly.

'I agree, but you know how it us for us lady meds – we have to be like Caesar's wife, above suspicion. If you've been doing anything that gives any grounds for this kind of thing, just back off, will you?'

Christina made a little gesture of dismissal and hurried away. But she was dismayed. How could the gossip have got started? Peter would certainly never have said anything. Perhaps it had had something to do with that day in New York, when he had hurried her out of the restaurant. She was almost sure he'd seen someone there who knew him.

Well, it didn't matter. She wasn't ashamed. She had known what she was doing when she agreed to go away with him, and in her heart she regarded herself as his wife. Let the world think what it liked, they were two people who had given and taken vows of passion that bound them for ever.

So, head up, she met the smiles and the stares. She went about her daily round: classes, laboratory, hospital rounds, office work for Dr Fehr, reading room, voluntary sessions at the free clinic for mothers and babies.

In snatched moments with Peter, she confided the problem. He soothed her with a hand running softly over her hair. 'It's nonsense, honey, don't trouble your head about it.'

'Well, if it comes to that, I don't care what they say. We've done nothing wrong.'

'That's my brave girl.'

But it annoyed him. Why did she have to be so damned brave? Why couldn't it bother her a little, put her off her stride? Something about her seemed so inviolable.

Moreover, the gossip stayed among the students. He'd expected it to reach the professorial ranks by now, but Dr Fehr seemed unshaken in his regard for her, and the other lecturers still treated her with that mixture of tolerance and respect they reserved for the clever women students.

Perhaps he needed to take one more step.

'What I think I'll do, fellers,' he said to his gang of faithful supporters one evening in Hennesey's Bar, 'is send a little note to the Dean of Medicine, enclosing this pretty little item.' He shook the batiste camisole in the air. 'That would get her out of our hair for good and all.'

'But Pete—'

'What'sa matter?' he said. He was a little the worse for wear, having switched from beer to rye whiskey earlier in the evening.

'If you do that she'll be plucked!'

'Well, what would be so bad about that? The fewer female filebones, the better – isn't thasso?'

Andy said in a doubtful tone, 'You couldn't write to the Dean about taking The Holt to Coney Island – you'd only get yourself in trouble.'

'I don't have to sign the letter, rockhead! I just say Miss Holt has been off at the seashore, but not so as to listen to what the wild waves were saying . . .'

'No, see here, Peter—'

'And enclose the cammy, asking him to note the initials—'

'You can't do that, Pete.'

'Sure can. What's to stop me?'

'Why are you so down on her all of a sudden?' Stu asked. 'I mean, you owe her for three or so good nights in the sack.'

'I owe her! Yeah, that's it, I owe her! Who walks around with her nose in the air? Who acts like she's better and cleverer than everybody else? Who took my job with Dr Fehr from me? Who, come on, tell me, who?'

His friends wriggled and looked uncomfortable.

'If you were out to pay her back,' muttered Andy, 'you've done enough, huh?'

'No, it's not enough. She doesn't care if people snigger about her in corners. So the thing to do is *really* make it public. A little note to Professor Minchen, and she'll be cut right down to size at last.'

'It's kind of a rotten thing to do, Pete . . .'

'What, unmasking the deprativy – the depravity – of these seemingly pure little maidens?'

'Well, I agree she's no better than she should be,' said Stu, 'but all the same . . . I mean, chickens, we get up to some tricks ourselves—'

'But we don't set up to be pure and perfect. What was that deathless "pome" you quoted: "Something, something, chaste and fair." Well, chaste, yeah – I chased her and she let herself get caught.'

'That's right,' said Virgil Jessup with a sudden snap to his voice. 'You chased her and you caught her. It took you two attempts and you were pretty experienced with the bow and arrow, bucko, weren't you! Now you've had her and you can't forgive her for being silly enough to give in. Well, let me tell you this, Peter – if you go to the Dean over this, I'll lay you stiff, so help me.'

The other men in the group drew back from him a little. This wasn't like old Virge.

'What's eating you?' demanded Andy in surprise.

'You can't see it? This louse lays traps for the kid, she falls in, but that's not enough, she hasn't been made a public spectacle. So now he's going to snitch to the Dean. Christina will be run off campus, and our hero will fall into the job with Dr Fehr.'

Andy said: 'It's a bit devious, I agree. But you know, if it gets Pete the job . . .'

'The ends justify the means? Is that it?'

'Look here, you don't like having women students here

any more than the rest of us, Virge. What are you getting in a rage about?'

Virge looked about him. He saw the group of friends with whom he'd spent most of his days and many of his nights for three years. He saw the dingy bar they'd made their gathering place. He saw their owlish looks, their not-quite-sober expressions.

And he felt all at once that to be loyal to this bunch was no great honour.

'OK, since you can't see it, I'll lay it out for you. I'm not in favour of women studying medicine, I think it's unsuitable in every way. But to defeat them, do we have to turn them into whores and then tell tales to the Dean? That doesn't seem a damn dirty trick to you?'

'All's fair in love and war, though I'm not sure which this is,' Andy suggested.

'What do the rest of you say?'

They murmured in uneasy uncertainty.

'Well, I can't accept it. And I want this made clear. If you write that anonymous letter, Semmring, I'll go to the Dean myself and tell him you were the writer.'

'Virgil!'

'I mean it. I just can't go along with it. Goddamnit man, I always thought that though you were spoiled up to your eyebrows you were a decent type at heart. But if you do this, I'll not only knock your teeth in, I'll never speak to you again as long as I live.'

Stu said, 'I think the boy's in earnest, Father.'

'You bet I'm in earnest.'

Nobody spoke for a moment or two. Then Andy said, 'I do believe it would be better if you didn't make any more moves against The Holt, Pete. In fact, it would be a good idea to drop her, if you haven't already done it.'

'Drop her . . . ? But there's still fruit on the vine, lads.'

'You know, you're sick, Semmring, you're really sick! It's difficult to know how to deal with you. Have I your word you won't send any anonymous letters to Professor Minchen?'

Peter sighed in drunken defeat. 'It was a good idea, though.'

'I want your word.'

'OK, OK, I promise.'

'You're all witnesses,' Virgil said. 'He promises not to write any anonymous letters.'

'I expect he'll find something else to amuse him there,' muttered Stu, who hadn't been enjoying the evening as much as he usually did.

'That's what bothers me,' said Virgil and, getting up, he stalked out.

He was at heart a serious young man. He was part of Peter Semmring's set almost by accident and, though he admired Peter's brains, had a lower opinion of his character. After tonight, he doubted whether he would be spending much time in his company. And some of the echoes of their argument kept troubling him.

Next day he sought out Christina Holt in the dispensary of the mother-and-baby clinic where, in company with Susanne Wellsley, she was preparing cough cures and stomach mixtures ready for the morning session.

'Miss Holt,' he said in a very formal tone, 'there's something important I have to tell you. Can we go somewhere private?'

Chapter Nine

Christina's reaction wasn't what Virgil had nerved himself for. He'd expected an outcry or a burst of tears. But instead a tide of colour rose up under the clear, pale skin, and then more slowly ebbed away.

At length she said in a stifled voice, 'How can you tell such lies? I thought you were Peter's friend!'

'I thought so too. But I'm growing more particular in my old age.' He watched her, then added, 'I'm sorry, Christina, this is hard for you. I can see you love him.'

'Of course I love him!' The words broke from her, then she narrowed her eyes. 'Is that what this is all about? To trap that admission out of me?'

He shook his head. 'I'm not much of a one for traps or tricks, Christina. That's Peter's department.'

'How can you *say* that! What are you up to? Are you getting your own back on him, is that it? You've a grudge against him?'

'Christina . . .' Virgil moved uneasily. They were in an angle of the corridor, near the windows of the clinic. Back along the corridor were benches already full of mothers holding or trying to control their children, waiting for free advice about ailments, and for treatment if that was needed. The women were concerned with their own troubles, but all the same it wasn't the ideal place to be having this discussion.

Christina made as if to go back to her work. He caught at the sleeve of her rough linen smock. 'No, wait, you've got to believe me . . .'

'It's all a pack of lies.'

'Why on earth should I come here and tell you lies?' he

said with indignation. 'I'm trying to help you! Peter's been so weird these past couple of weeks, I don't know what he might have got up to if I hadn't . . . Listen, I made him swear he wouldn't go running to the Dean with his tale, and I think he'll stand by it. But I thought you ought to know how things are. He's not to be trusted, Christina.'

She shook her head violently. 'I can't believe it. I won't! No one would do such a thing. It's so *ugly*.'

'It sure isn't pretty. But you see you hit him where it hurts most – in his pride. He couldn't bear it when Fehr picked you instead of him. He had to pay you out somehow.'

'But he told me himself he didn't mind, that he admired me . . .'

Virgil's stolid features took on a look of acute embarrassment. 'Gosh, we all say things like that to girls, Christina. And Peter's better at it than most. See, it's the hunting instinct, you know? There's the target, and you sort of get close and find your range – I mean, you think out what will work with this particular quarry – and then bang! And all the more enjoyable if it's difficult: an easy kill's no fun.'

She shuddered away from him. 'That's horrible.'

'And there's trophies,' he ploughed on doggedly, determined to drag the scales from her eyes. 'Some guys are mad over girls' garters. Some like little bits of jewellery: an earring, or one of those glittery pins you do your hair with.'

'And you said Peter had a trophy?' she asked in a low voice.

'Yeah, a . . . an under-thing.' He couldn't bring himself to put a name to it, it was too indelicate. 'He produced it as evidence when we wouldn't believe him. Sort of soft stuff, with blue ribbon threaded through and your initials in a little circle of forget-me-nots.'

'Yes.' Her head drooped. She remembered only too well not being able to find the camisole when she packed to leave the Elephant Hotel.

'I didn't really want to get involved but I just thought you ought to know. I mean, you've been in the dark up to now.'

'If this is the light,' she murmured, 'it hurts the eyes.'

'I'm sorry, Christina, I'm real sorry.'

'Yes, I see you are. Thank you, Virgil.'

He took her hand, pressed it, and blundered out. He felt absolutely terrible. Such a straight, proud little kid – and he'd brought her life down about her ears.

Christina went back into the dispensary, where Susanne was rapidly writing labels for bottles of jalap.

'Susanne, I've got to go. Will you explain to Dr Aumant?'

'What d'you mean, go? What's the matter? You look as if you've seen a ghost.'

'I think I'm coming down with something. Tell Dr Aumant, will you?'

'Shall I call a nurse to go with you?'

'No, no, I'll be all right. It's just a chill.'

She was dragging off her smock as she spoke. She bundled it up, stuffed it in her bag, pushed herself into her outdoor coat and was gone while Susanne was still trying to suggest something helpful for a chill.

She had to see Peter. But they had had no engagement to meet today, since he was to be at the hospital assisting in surgery for the morning and then attending a lecture and demonstration in the afternoon.

In fact, now she came to think of it, she had seen Peter rarely since their return from Coney Island. It had seemed natural enough – beginning of term, each with extra courses to attend and work to do. Yet now she began to think about it she realised that he had not come to the trolley stop as he used to for just a moment's conversation before the day's end. He had not stopped to exchange a murmured word in the refectory. He had not chosen to walk through corridors of the University where they might run into each other accidentally, to exchange at least a secret smile.

She went to the University Hospital, hurrying past the janitor with only a nod. Peter was rostered to assist in Theatre A. There was an anaesthesia room and then an ante-room. No one stopped her as she went in until she got to the door of the theatre proper. There the nurse on duty to take messages barred her way.

'Operation in progress, please leave the ante-room.'

'I must speak to Peter Semmring.'

'Who's Peter Semmring when he's at home?'

'He's a third-year man, he's being allowed to assist.' She tried to get past the nurse so as to look through the glass panel and point him out.

'Please, miss, stand away. You know the doors of the operating theatre mustn't be obstructed during an op.'

'It's important. Please go in and tell Mr Semmring he's wanted.' She clutched at the nurse's blue-clad arm. 'It's vitally important.'

The nurse was perhaps twice Christina's age. She could sense near-hysteria in this girl's manner. The last thing they needed was a screaming fit at the doors of the operating theatre.

'Which is he?' she asked, allowing Christina to take a look at the white-jacketed and aproned figures round the operating table.

'The tall one with light brown hair, behind and to the left of the surgeon. Tell him it's Miss Holt.'

'All right. Stay here and not a peep out of you.' The nurse opened the swing doors a few inches, inserted herself through the gap, and went round the back of the room to Peter's side. She murmured in his ear.

To her dismay and disbelief she saw Peter shake his head with determination and move a pace closer to the surgeon. The nurse returned.

'Sorry, miss, he says he can't come out.'

'Please go back. Please say it's terribly important—'

'I told him that, dear, he doesn't want to leave. He's caught up in what's going on, I reckon. Not a good time to want him.'

Well, of course, that was true.

'I'll wait,' she said.

'Not here, you won't. This is surgical personnel only, and you ought to know that if you're a student.' Another student romance gone wrong, Nurse Fridolf was thinking. These kids, they thought they ruled the earth because they had the time and the money to go to college, but nobody was going to trespass on her domain.

Christina went out into the anaesthesia room, but the next patient had been brought in. The team preparing him for operation looked at her in annoyance. She muttered an apology, hurried out.

Above the operating theatre there was a gallery where students were watching the work in progress. If she sat there, she could see when the morning session ended and Peter left the room. She found herself a seat in the third row.

The operation would normally have been of intense interest to Christina. It was for the removal of an intestinal cyst, an intricate and difficult manoeuvre taking over two hours.

In the overhead mirror she saw the surgeon's hands moving, she saw the instruments slapped into the palm of his hands when he murmured orders. She heard his commentary as he worked. In front of her were the interns watching every move. Behind her were a few of the fourth year men taking note. She heard the scratch of their pencils on paper, heard their whispered comments.

Yet it meant nothing. All she could see was Virgil's face, all she could hear was Virgil's voice.

'There's trophies . . . garters . . . earrings . . . Your initials in a little blue circle . . . I'm really sorry, Christina.'

At eleven-thirty the surgeon signalled to his intern to sew up the wound of the last patient. The nurses were counting swabs and instruments, the men who had been operating or assisting moved together in two little groups to discuss techniques. Christina got up, went out of the gallery door, down the stairs, round to the corridor in front of the anaesthetic room of Theatre A.

The surgeons and assistant surgeons were slowly coming out, taking off bloodstained jackets, untying apron strings.

Peter wasn't there.

'Excuse me,' she said to a fourth-year man she recognised, Lars Jensen, 'I'm looking for Mr Semmring?'

'Ha, Semmring? He had to hurry avay.'

The corridor and the people in it swam before her eyes.

141

She went hot and cold. She felt a hand on her elbow. 'Something is wrong?'

'No . . . No, thank you, Mr Jensen.'

Peter had avoided her. There was no other explanation.

At that point she almost gave up. But he had to be back to attend the lecture and demonstration in the Agnew Clinic that afternoon. She simply waited, and when he came strolling up towards the lecture theatre with his group of friends about one in the afternoon, she walked up to him.

'I must speak to you, Peter.'

Her sudden appearance startled him out of his good-humoured conversation. 'Not now, Christina!' he muttered to her, turning half towards her.

'Yes, now. It's important.'

'But I've got to watch Dr Staves demonstrating an—'

'Peter, I must speak to you *now*.'

He might have argued, or shrugged her off, but Andy Lelliot and Stu were looking at them with curiosity.

'Oh, all right,' he said, and talking her elbow walked her quickly out of doors into the dark January day. There was an open-air courtyard behind the Clinic building, deserted in this weather. He paused once they were in its shelter.

'Now, honey, what's all this?'

'Peter, have you been telling other people about our trip to the Elephant Hotel?'

Perhaps he'd been expecting something of the sort. He put an arm about her and said gently, 'Now what put that silly idea into your head?'

'I was told you reported on it in detail to your friends.'

'Who said that?' He had coloured up, and the indignation was genuine, because he suspected at once that Virgil Jessup had been sticking his nose in again. He was annoyed, indignant at the betrayal – and perhaps a little apprehensive.

'Is it true, Peter?'

'Of course not!'

'You didn't tell anybody that we were there, or what we did there?'

'Would I talk about a thing like that?'

'Do you swear to me you haven't told anyone?'

'Swear to you? What is this? Do I have to put my hand on a Bible when I tell you something?'

'This person who told me about it . . . he said you had a trophy.'

'What?' That rat, Jessup. He'd *get* him for this.

'He said you had a camisole of mine.'

'A what?'

'A batiste camisole, embroidered with my initials and with blue ribbon round the neck.'

'Christina, I can't be held responsible for what some idiot—'

'The funny thing is, I can't find that camisole. It went missing on the day we left the Elephant Hotel.'

'Oh, honey, you just mislaid it.'

'No, it's gone. And how could this person describe it so accurately if he hadn't seen it?'

'Now look here, Christina, I don't know exactly what you're accusing me of—'

'I want to know whether you took that camisole and showed it to your friends when they wouldn't believe we'd been away together.'

'I didn't take it, for God's sake! What would I do a thing like that for?'

'Because . . . because it was all part of a campaign to cut me down to size?'

'Oh, if you're going to believe the kind of rubbish that Jessup talks, we might as well stop discussing it right now.'

'Peter.'

The flat coldness of her tone made him stop in his tirade of defence. He drew back a little, and his brown eyes held surprise at the way she was studying him.

'Peter,' she said, 'I never mentioned any names.'

'What?'

'You said I shouldn't believe what Jessup said. I never mentioned Virgil Jessup.'

Damn, he thought. Damn, walked right into that. 'Well,' he countered, 'Jessup's the kind of nosey-parker who—'

'What made you think he'd come to me with a story like that? Could it be because he's one of your cronies?'

'Not any more,' he burst out, furious. 'By God, if I get my hands on the stupe, I'll wring his—'

'Why?' she flashed. 'Because he told me a pack of lies, or because he told me the truth?'

Peter had had to deal with angry and reproachful girls before, when an affair was ending. He knew the best thing was to cut your losses and get out of it. He fell back on this hard-earned wisdom.

'I'm not going to discuss it,' he said, looking down at Christina with stern admonition. 'You're making absurd accusations and I just don't want to hear any of it. And I'm missing Staves's lecture.'

'Don't walk away from me, Peter. Have the decency to give me an answer. Did you tell your friends about New Year's at Coney Island?'

'You should have taken up law, not medicine, Christina. You'd make a great cross-examiner.'

'I see. So it was all a sort of joke, was it?'

'You're making all the judgements – go ahead and look at it any way you like.'

He gave her a little bow before walking off.

Some minutes later Christina became aware that a few flakes of snow were falling, that the courtyard's sky was full of soft downy drops gently filtering through the murk towards the ground. There were snowflakes on her sleeve, on her lashes.

Presumably that was why she felt so cold.

She'd missed the first lecture in the Department of Ophthalmology. If she didn't hurry, she'd miss the demonstration of the muscles of the eye.

Hugging her heavy bag of books and equipment to her, she walked as fast as she could to the University. It didn't bring any warmth into her body. She threw her coat on a peg in the lady meds' cloakroom, dashed hot water on her face to help her circulation, rubbed her cheeks vigorously with the towel.

Professor Juddson was just about to make the first incision as she came in. He said irritably, 'You're late, Miss Holt.'

'I'm sorry, sir.'

'Well, come in, close the door, get close enough to see. I hope the angle of the reflector suits you?'

The class went on. All the classes of the University had run their course while she had listened to two men: one had told her she had been a fool for the last three months and the other had confirmed the information.

'It doesn't matter,' she said to herself while the professor's voice rose and fell, the magnified reflection of his hands flickered in the big mirror, the instruments went snick-snick against the enamelled tray, the students rustled and drew in their breath at the fine network of muscles.

How could it possibly matter in the great scheme of things if one stupid girl lost her head and her virginity to a man who didn't care about her? The world would still turn on its axis, blood would course through human veins. Lectures would be given, papers would be written, fortunes would be piled up in the banks, trains would run, ships would sail to the far corners of the earth.

So why did her heart feel like a stone in her breast? Why was her face as pale as a winding-sheet? If it didn't matter, why were tears trickling down her cheeks so that she had to bend her head to hide them?

Ah, it was the sense of loss. Half her being seemed to have been cut away from her in some terrible surgical experiment. Yet that was silly. Yes, logically it was silly, because before she fell in love with Peter there had been nothing to lose, nothing to throb with pain and the shock of bereavement.

I'll go back to what I was before, she told herself. I can live by myself and for myself again. I don't need anyone else.

A mist of confusion clouded her brain. How could I have let him mean so much to me? And how could I have been so *wrong*?

Oh yes, it didn't pay to be too clever. Jo-Jo had said that to her a long time ago. Too clever to doubt her own judgement, too clever to need time to think what she was doing. Head over heels, like a clown, like a fool, straight into his arms.

Peter, Peter . . . You didn't really set traps for me? Not always? Those nights in that terrible, vulgar hotel . . . They weren't a trap? Some things in the world you needed to be sure about, otherwise you'd lose your mind. If she couldn't believe that Peter's body twined against hers had been proof of love and longing, she would die.

He loved me. He did. Even if he didn't want to, for those hours he loved me as I loved him. We gave and we took, and it was genuine, honest, single-hearted.

'Miss Holt? Miss Holt?'

She became aware she was being addressed, and not for the first time.

'I'm sorry, Professor, I didn't catch . . . ?'

'I was asking about the name of the paralytic ailment of the third, fourth and sixth nerves?'

'Ophthalmoplegia, sir.'

'Thank you. Now you see those nerves, exposed as one would never hope to see them by physical intervention on a living patient, at least in the present state of surgical technique. You will note—'

Christina looked at the reflection in the magnifying mirror. It had been specially made so that it reflected back with complete accuracy but in larger detail the work being done on the minute nerves. But as she looked, the reflection all ran together in a horrific distortion of colour and movement. She felt her gorge rise.

Hand to mouth, she ran out. Cloakrooms for the lady meds were few and far between. She scuttled into a cubbyhole meant for a lab. technician, and there she was sick into the cleaning sink.

She had recovered enough to rejoin class when it removed to the benches for microscopy.

'Fancy it catching you out like that,' muttered Jo-Jo with amusement. 'When old Dr Verrill did his act with the eye-in-a-bottle at the beginning of anatomy, you took it like a trooper.'

'She wasn't feeling good this morning either,' Susanne put in. 'Are you OK now, Christina?'

'Fine, fine.'

Classes dragged to a close. She had tasks to do for Dr Fehr. About eight o'clock she came to, discovering she had been sitting at the bench in the path. lab., lost to the world for nearly half an hour. Quickly she finished up, for once uncertain of the quality of her work.

'You're awfully late, dear,' Mrs Kentley said in reproof.

'I'm sorry, Aunt Bea, I lost track of time.'

She went upstairs to turn down beds, draw shades, ensure that the upstairs passage lights were all turned low. By ten she was in bed, but unable to sleep.

In the morning there were kitchen chores, sheets to get ready for the laundry boy, an urgent visit to the store for items that should have been delivered the previous day. No time to chat with Aunt Bea or Letty. For that she was thankful. She couldn't seem to make her voice sound normal: there was an edge of tears in everything she said, but she passed it off as the beginnings of a cold.

'I always do say you'll catch all kinds of things, peering down other people's throats,' Aunt Bea said fretfully, and made her wrap her scarf two or three times round her neck before she went out.

For the next week or so Christina lived her life on two different levels. The one which people saw was the one where she went to and fro, worked and studied, took part in class. The other was beneath the surface of her mind, an argument that went on all the time. How could I have been so stupid? How could I have been so easy to hoodwink? But then he set out on purpose to hoodwink me – me especially, not just any girl. It was a scheme carefully tailored to fit Christina Holt, the clever, self-confident Miss Christina Holt. But how could he know so much about me? How could he know what would work?

Because you were transparent, vulnerable, eager for someone to be especially understanding and loving. You laid yourself open to it. But surely everyone wants someone special? What's so wrong in that? And how could I know that Peter was a scalp-hunter? People speak so well of him: he's so admired, so well regarded . . .

She never saw him now, except at the far side of a lecture hall. Perhaps he took care to stay out of her way. But the expectation of happening upon him somewhere kept her in a state of nervous tension, so that she felt sick and edgy.

Having to work on Sundays for Dr Fehr had altered the get-togethers at the Wallace Hotel, but they still managed sometimes to come back with her from the University when she had finished her tasks. They would spend the afternoon either in some snug corner of the hotel lounge, or in her room on the attic floor.

They had been studying in preparation for a bacteriology test. Susanne, Mary and Youffie took their leave. To Jo-Jo's surprise, Christina detained her after the others left. Jo-Jo was the student to whom Christina was closest. Although they agreed to differ on the topic of women's rights and Serbian nationalism, other things they held in common. They were both hard-pressed for money. They were both determined to succeed as doctors. They were both hard-working, independent, open-minded.

Christina had spent several vacations at the Serbian community's farm in the Juniata Valley, working to pay for her keep in the daytime, working with Jo-Jo over their books in the lamplit evenings. It was an honour to be invited there: neither Mary nor Susanne had been asked, and even Youffie – to whom Jo-Jo extended a special kindly tolerance – had never been there. Christina had shared the sparse and badly cooked communal meals, making the others laugh with her efforts to speak Serbian. Somehow the fact that she had bothered to learn her language seemed to endear her all the more to Jo-Jo.

They had sat across a table from each other sharing their textbooks and notes. They had come to know each other very well. Yet they respected each other's privacy: Jo-Jo might give Christina orders about looking after her health,

Christina might caution her friend about preaching the Serbian cause too loudly, but they never intruded upon each other on more intimate matters.

On this special Sunday, Christina took Jo-Jo back upstairs again, made her sit in the one armchair, and looked at her with eyes strangely bright.

'Jo-Jo, I need your help.'

'*My* help? That makes a change, *mali doctoritza*,' Jo-Jo laughed. 'Usually I'm the one asking to borrow notes.'

'It's not about the work. It's about me.'

'What about you?'

'I'm pregnant, Jo-Jo.'

Jo-Jo gave an audible gasp. She felt as if she had been hit in the centre of the chest with a hammer. After a moment she said, 'Are you sure?'

'I'm a medical student. I've seen the signs often enough among women at the mother-and-baby clinic.'

Jo-Jo clasped and unclasped her muscular hands. 'And . . . and you know good reasons why those signs should be present?'

'Yes. And I've missed twice.'

'I can't . . . I can't believe it.'

'It's true.'

'But *when*? Who?'

'Over the Christmas vacation. As to who . . . I don't want to go into that.'

'Don't want to go into it? What on earth do you mean, Christina? The baby needs a father, you need a husband—'

'No. I'd rather die than tell him.'

Unable to sit quiet, Jo-Jo jumped up and moved restlessly about the room, squaring up the edges of books and papers. 'It's Peter Semmring, of course,' she said over her shoulder.

Christina threw up an arm in a defensive gesture. 'Does everybody know?' she groaned.

'No. No, there was some gossip about six weeks ago, but the rest of us lady meds just kept on saying it was all stupid talk and it died away. Peter Semmring, eh? God's gift to women.'

'Don't let's talk about him. I let him make a fool of me. I just didn't understand . . .' Christina broke off. Jo-Jo saw tears glinting in her eyes. She put an arm about her friend's shoulders.

'You fool!' she said, giving her something between a hug and a shake. 'You fool, Christina! Couldn't you see he was too good to be true?'

Christina said nothing. She was struggling not to burst into silly tears.

'You went away with him? Yes? So you're a medical student, why didn't you take precautions?'

'I did, at first, Jo-Jo. But then you see, it was New Year's Eve, and there was a big celebration in the hotel, and I had too much wine, and I didn't even remember. And then, we were going to say goodbye soon after that, and it just didn't seem . . . fitting . . .'

'Not fitting to prevent this selfish man from giving you a baby? Not fitting?' Jo-Jo's black eyes snapped with anger. 'You speak like an idiot child, like a simpering fool!'

'Call me any names you like, Jo-Jo. You can't say anything I haven't said to myself these last two or three days.'

'Oh yes I can. I can say very bad swearwords in Serbian. But that is little use, my dear. So what now? You want me to help with an abortion?'

'I couldn't ask that of you, Jo-Jo, it's too big a responsibility.'

'That is true, I should be very worried. Yet if we bring in someone else – a qualified doctor – that means one more person who knows about it. And the law might hear.'

'It seems the logical thing to do . . . Yet I can't bring myself to decide on it. You and I have seen things, Jo-Jo, women in the obstetrics department, ill and full of regrets.'

'Oh yes. It is a serious thing. There can be physical risks. And as you say, mental . . . spiritual damage.'

'But what else is there? I certainly can't tell Peter Semmring and expect anything from him; and anyhow I don't want him to know, I *don't*, it would be such a triumph for him . . . And there's the University. If I have the baby, I'll be expelled for "moral turpitude" like that girl in Modern Philosophy who only got herself in a compromising situation with a tutor. And I *can't* give up medicine, Jo-Jo. I can't!'

Jo-Jo let her thoughts go back over the past years. If ever a girl seemed intended by God to be a doctor, that girl was Christina Holt. To be prevented half-way through her training by such a cruel stroke was beyond endurance.

She made herself come back to practical points. 'Have you told your aunt?'

'No . . . Will you help me tell her?'

'Me? Oh, God, Christina, it will kill her!'

Christina began to cry. She covered her face with her hands and pressed her fingers against her eyelids, yet still the tears welled over. She said brokenly, 'I wish I was dead.'

'No. No, we don't say that!' commanded her friend. 'We say we are alive, and we are going to stay alive, and have the baby, and stay in medicine, and we shall do all this, and we don't give a damn how difficult it will be!'

By and by they went downstairs. It was a quiet time in the hotel, about five o'clock on a February Sunday afternoon, few guests about. Mrs Kentley was placidly embroidering under a lamp in her sitting-room.

'Aunt Bea, I have something very serious to tell you . . .' She paused, drew breath. Then, clinically, she said, 'I am two months' pregnant.'

The reaction was disbelief, tears, reproaches, desperation. 'What are we to do? I can't have a fatherless baby here in the hotel, Christina, this is a respectable establishment. Think what Miss Melville would say!'

Jo-Jo said, 'We have been discussing an abortion.'

'No!' wailed Aunt Bea. 'I forbid it! That's wicked, sinful!'

'Then what is the alternative?' Jo-Jo asked with asperity.

'Of course she must have the baby. Oh, you wicked, wicked girl! How could you? This means the end of everything. You'll have to be sent away . . . Oh, how shameful, how awful!' And Aunt Bea threw her sodden handkerchief over her face and wept in abandonment.

'Wait,' said Jo-Jo. 'Sent away, yes. Why can she not go

away and have the baby, and no one know?'

'Give up a year's tuition?' Christina sighed.

'No, wait, here we are in the beginning of February. The baby is due when?'

'I can give you almost an exact date,' Christina said with a wry grimness. 'It's due about the 22nd September.'

'Oh, Christina!' wept Mrs Kentley. 'How can you!'

'But it is, Aunt Bea.'

'Well, look, at the moment you are only just two months' pregnant. Nothing shows. We take our exams in June. You can leave as soon as those are over.'

'But by then the foetus—'

'Yes, yes, six months; but you are a small girl, and this is your first child. With luck and good dressing, it need not become obvious.'

'Good dressing?' faltered Aunt Bea.

'She wears a smock more than half the time, because of the laboratory work, you know. A loose smock, it covers everything, some of the girls even wear costume jackets under their smock on cold days. She must get into the habit of always wearing the smock—'

'Dr Herbert objects to lab. clothes in the lecture room, Jo-Jo.'

'Yes, that's a problem. Well, look again, have you seen these clothes Poiret is showing in Paris?'

'No—' said Christina.

'Yes—' said Mrs Kentley.

'The girls in the dorm were discussing them the other night. He says the weight of a dress should hang from the shoulders, the waist shouldn't be cinched in and corseted. Don't you see, Christina, if you wore clothes like that, the baby wouldn't show.'

'Jo-Jo, if I began dressing like a fashion plate all of a sudden, it would only attract attention—'

'But only for a week or two. And others among the lady meds are talking about wearing his styles because they feel they are more healthy, more in keeping with modern knowledge of the body. So it would soon be quite normal and no one would think anything of it.'

'But I can't afford a wardrobe of new clothes . . .'

'No, no, I'm not suggesting that. But one thing's certain, you can't go about in a skirt and a shirtwaist once the baby begins to make itself apparent. What you must do is to let out the waistbands of your skirts as much as is needed, and then you wear them with a loose jacket à la Poiret. One jacket, that shouldn't be too expensive. And perhaps *one* dress, for warm weather, falling from the shoulders in this vaguely Greek or Oriental style of his. And a good corset underneath holding the baby neatly.'

'To see her through until June,' mused Mrs Kentley. 'And then what?'

'Then she comes to our farm on the Juniata and wears big roomy gowns like a peasant and has the baby, and no one ever knows one word of it.'

'But after that?' insisted Christina's aunt. 'She can't bring a baby back to Philadelphia. I can't have it here. And if it became known she would be told to leave the University.'

'Yes. That is true,' said Jo-Jo with a sad shake of the head. 'And though we at Traskanya would have nothing against looking after the baby, we are busy enough, we couldn't take it on.'

They sat in silence.

Then Christina said in a low voice, 'There's only one answer, of course. I'll have to offer the baby for adoption.'

Chapter Ten

The baby's cry was lusty, strong.

'A boy!' cried Jo-Jo. 'A fine boy!'

'Let me see him, oh, let me see him,' whispered Christina from out of the haze of exhaustion.

'In a moment, little one, he needs a little attention—'

'Is there something wrong with him? Let me see!' She came up on her elbow, full of anxiety.

'Wrong with him? Not he, he's a perfect little thing.'

Christina sagged back. She closed her eyes. A boy . . .

She felt a blanket-wrapped bundle laid in the loose crook of her arm. She tightened her grip, raised her head, looked down at the baby.

Hair dark from the olive oil, but not dark hair. A round head, a snub nose, mouth open in the remains of a wail that had died as he felt the security of her arm. One small fist up close to his chin, folded, ready for a fight.

Yes, baby, she thought, be ready to fight. This world isn't easy even for a child who can stay with loving parents.

Jo-Jo was still at work. 'No stitches needed. You're a good patient, *mali doctoritza*. Soon we'll have everything tidied and perfect. He's a sweet baby, no?'

'He's lovely,' Christina said dreamily. 'But I knew he would be.'

In the three months during which she had stayed at Traskanya, she had come to know her baby well as he grew inside her. She had learned that he was strong, vigorous, eager for life. She had been sure almost from the first that it was a boy. Sometimes as she worked about the farm, she talked secretly to him. 'You'll have to do without me, baby, but you'll be all right because you're struggling already to make yourself known. That's right, push and kick – Jo-Jo always says you have to kick and hit if you're in a tight corner.'

At night when he woke her with his turnings and movings, she would smile to herself. An individualist . . . he didn't want to keep still and behave. But that was good, that was proof he was healthy.

She moved about the settlement, often alone, but never lonely. She had her baby.

She had always loved the Juniata Valley, with the Alleghenies sometimes visible in the clouds to the west. This was a world quite different from the one in which she was born: steep hillsides clothed with trees instead of the flat plains of Lincolnshire, swift running streams instead of the placid waters of the Witham, bright-feathered flickers instead of crows and starlings.

But this long stay at Traskanya had been more beautiful than any other, a dream time. The settlement had accepted her without question: Jo-Jo's friend, in great trouble, needing a refuge – of course they must take her in. And she for her part had taken her share of work for as long as she could. She had learned to herd cows, how to shepherd them into the milking-shed, how to milk in the old-fashioned way because the farm had no modern equipment. She was as good at it as Stefan, the settlement's leader – perhaps better, because Stefan still felt manual labour was beneath his dignity. He was a son of a noble Serbian house, exiled by the Austro-Hungarian rulers for his political views.

His wife, Martita, had been a lady of fashion. She did her best to be a farmer's wife, but her abilities were limited to looking after the poultry. Two of the men, Jovan and Peko, had taught themselves to plough and sow in order to raise winter feed for the milk-herd. There was another girl, Sofya, who tried to make cheese to suit the taste of the inhabitants of the nearest town, Duncannon.

They were all watched with ironic amusement by their neighbours in the next fold of the hills. Silly foreigners, who had bought a farm from an old German family who had given up because the youngsters were impatient with this limited, old-fashioned life. The farms in the Juniata Valley were small, because only by intensive and constant care of the livestock could a living be made. These foolish Serbians had taken on 500 acres on which they seemed to want to make every mistake in the book.

It was soon clear to Christina that what Jo-Jo had said was true: there was no way she could leave her baby here to be brought up. They scarcely made a living themselves, and none of them had any idea how to look after a child. Besides, by and by they planned to sell Traskanya and move out west. If she were to confide her child to them, they would take him with them to California, the other side of the continent.

So, early in her stay she had conceded that point. 'I'd been hoping I could make some arrangement to pay for his keep and come to see him often . . . But I don't think it's possible.'

'I'd be sorry for any child that had Martita for its foster-mother,' Jo-Jo said with a grin. Martita was apt to forget even to feed the chickens, and meals were never on time for the men. Sofya was too beset with the problems of the dairy house to be much help.

'It's not only that. When do they plan to move west?'

'It'll have to be soon. Even Stefan can see the farm's not paying its way well enough. Money's draining out. The best thing would be to sell up during the winter.'

'That puts a definite stop to any idea of leaving him here.'

'I'm glad you see that, Chrissie. It looks like adoption, then.'

'I don't want to, Jo-Jo. I hate the thought. But it's best.'

And Jo-Jo had said, 'Leave it to me.'

She went to the lawyer in Harrisburg through whom they had bought the farm. To him she had spun a yarn which was convincing enough to bring him into action.

'My little cousin, from the old country, a terrible thing, she found a job, straight off the boat, in a hotel – but one of the men, a hotel guest, you understand?'

'Dear me, dear me . . .' A common enough story, and

commercial men who used hotels . . . Yes, yes, only too common.

'She came to us at the farm. Naturally we take care of her. But she is shamed, you know? And who will marry her, Kristin Belu with a bastard baby? So we think it best to have the baby adopted when it comes. Can you tell me of a couple who are looking for a child to adopt?'

'Oh, surely. There are channels through which—'

'It must be a respectable pair,' Jo-Jo interrupted. Christina had been adamant on that point. 'They must be good people who will take good care of the child.'

'I'll see what I can do.'

A young couple was found, John and Estelle Charlford. 'Highly suitable,' the lawyer reported. 'A very fine Pittsburgh family, plenty of money. John is with the State Department, hoping to be sent abroad to an embassy. His wife, poor girl . . . Seems she can't have children. A great blow to them. So you see, they're ideal.'

Yes, ideal. A private adoption to a rich, well-connected couple. Every advantage for the baby: good schooling, horses and ponies, afterwards a career. No expense spared, love and care poured out.

'Very well,' Christina said.

That had been three months ago. But now, now that she held her son in her arms, it became impossible.

'I can't do it,' she sobbed to Jo-Jo the night before the Charlfords were due to come for him. 'I can't give him up.'

'My dear, my dear, hush . . . Don't cry . . .'

'He's mine! Why should someone else have him?'

'Because you can't look after him, Christina. Please, dear, be sensible. Your aunt can't have him at the hotel. If you were to move out and live somewhere else, how could you manage? You'd have to take a full-time job, and that would mean goodbye to your medical studies.'

'I don't care! I'll give it all up.'

'And hate him forever because of what you had to sacrifice?'

'No, I could never hate him. I love him, I love him.'

'Then give him up, Christina. You know in your heart of hearts that you *must* get your degree. You'd regret it for the rest of your life if you gave up now. And you can't look after Baby and attend University. And even if somehow you managed that, what about afterwards – who's going to hire an unmarried mother, even if she has a medical degree?'

'I don't care, I want him, I need him!'

Jo-Jo soothed and comforted, pleaded and argued. All through the night until the September sun was peeping over the rim of the hill, gilding the oaks and turning the larches to yellow fire.

Exhausted, Christina gave in. She knew Jo-Jo was right although her heart cried out against it. If she had had a family to turn to, if her own parents had been the kind to whom she could have gone for help . . . Ah, then, things might have been different. But they were far away across the Atlantic, and they were the last people in the world who would help an erring daughter. As for her aunt . . . She had asked too much already of Aunt Bea.

The early morning chores had to be done. The cows had gathered by the shed ready to be taken in for milking. Martita went out to throw corn to the poultry.

Later Christina went indoors, into the kitchen. There she took the kettle from the top of the kitchen range. She went up to the room where her baby was already howling for his morning feed. She undressed and bathed him, put him into a clean diaper and clean clothes, then unfastened the front of her peasant shirt and put him to her breast.

He suckled vigorously. She held him close, her throat clenched against the sobs that might rise and frighten him.

'My baby, my baby,' she said inside her head, again and again.

She knew it was the last time she would speak to him.

He went back into his Moses basket to sleep, face flushed, hunger appeased, fists curled. The light down on his head gleamed in the sunshine streaming into the room.

She leaned over him, swallowing her tears. Then, with an

effort that seemed to tear the heart out of her, she rose and left him.

She washed with water from the ewer, put on clean clothes, the clothes appropriate for the life she'd been leading these last three months: gathered cotton skirt, loose cotton blouse, a long bib apron with braid trimming. Her hair, as usual these days, was in two thick plaits down her back and kept out of her way with a piece of white tape that held them together at the nape of the neck.

She looked at herself in the old mirror that the farmer's wife had left behind. She saw a peasant – tall for a girl, slender again after the birth, rather drawn of feature but pleasing enough.

She heard the motor car labouring up the dirt road. By and by a brown sedan came into the open space in front of the farm stables. Jo-Jo was already there, awaiting the visitors. The other members of the Serbian community had tactfully gone to tasks elsewhere.

A murmur of voices as they were shown into the kitchen-cum-living-room, a substantial room but not well cared for these days. Christina sat upstairs by the side of her sleeping baby.

Jo-Jo's footsteps on the stairs. 'Christina? It's time.'

Unwillingly, limbs made of lead, Christina got up. She picked up the Moses basket. Jo-Jo laid a hand on her arm. 'Courage,' she whispered.

The Charlfords were standing together near the big kitchen table. He was a tallish, dark-haired man, well-dressed, well-barbered. His wife was rather thin, very fashionably clad in a loose coat of grey velvet and a matching toque.

Two men were sitting at the table. Their dark suits and sombre ties advertised the fact that they were professional men. One, Christina knew, was the lawyer, Wentway. The other was the family doctor of the Charlfords, come to check that the child was thriving, without blemish, suitable for his two young charges to adopt.

'Good morning,' Estelle Charlford said in an uncertain

voice. And then, to Jo-Jo, 'Does your cousin speak English?'

'Very little.' She turned to Christina to murmur in Serbian, 'Remember that. Say very little.'

'*Jeste, razumem,*' she said, in her halting Serbian, to let Jo-Jo know she understood.

'Ask her if I may examine the child,' the doctor said, getting to his feet and opening his bag.

'*Dobro?*' Jo-Jo said.

'*Dobro,*' said Christina.

She watched with an almost professional interest as the doctor undressed her son. The baby slept in uncaring bliss. His chest was examined, his skull was felt with probing fingers, his limbs were stretched and tested. Once he made a little protesting sound, but merely curled up into slumber again when he was let alone.

'A very fine child,' said Dr McGregor. 'I should say about seven pounds in weight.'

'Seven pounds four ounces,' Jo-Jo corrected.

'Oh, so you've weighed him accurately?'

'He has had good care, I assure you.'

'But no doctor at the birth.'

Jo-Jo hesitated. 'No,' she agreed.

'The birth has been registered?'

'Yes, we went into Duncannon on the day Judge Lemuel comes to town for such things.'

'What name did you give him?'

'We called him Stefan, in honour of the leader of our group here.'

'Stefan,' murmured Mrs Charlford. 'That would be Stephen in English.' She went to lean over the basket where the little boy slept. 'Stephen,' she said, 'Stephen, Mummy's here.' She put her hand down into the blanket, to touch his shoulder.

Christina made a move to prevent her. But then, recollecting herself, she sank back.

'Would you tell your cousin that we're very, very grateful,' John Charlford said to Jo-Jo but looking at Christina. 'We'll love her baby very much.'

Jo-Jo didn't translate but said instead in Serbian, 'Be brave. It will soon be over.'

'And tell her, I think she's very pretty,' said Mrs Charlford with a smile, 'and her baby is too.'

'Very fair for a Serbian, isn't she?' Dr McGregor said, as if Christina were some kind of animal they were discussing.

'Her mother was from an Austrian family: there are many blond Austrians,' explained Jo-Jo.

'Oh, of course, I see. Well, Wentway, everything's fine from the medical standpoint. You can complete the legal formalities. You've got papers there for the girl to sign?'

'Here they are.' Wentway produced them from his briefcase. 'Now, Miss Belu,' he said in an earnest manner to Christina, 'I want you to understand that this is irrevocable. Explain to her, will you, my dear?'

Jo-Jo translated word for word. Christina said, '*Razumem, da, razumem.*' She pressed Jo-Jo's hand and added under her breath, 'Get it over, Jo-Jo.'

'She understands perfectly, sir. She gives up the baby for ever.'

'She agrees to that?'

'She agrees.'

'Please ask her to sign here.'

The papers were spread out. There were two. One was an official form of adoption. The other was a formal letter as between Kristin Belu of Traskanya Farm on the one hand and John Charlford of 210 Sixth Avenue, Pittsburgh, agreeing that a boy child born to her on 21 September 1910 was given into the care of the said John Charlford and his wife Estelle with her entire and willing consent.

Christina could hardly see the space in which to sign for the tears that filled her eyes. Shakily, unwillingly, she wrote, 'Kristin Belu' in each of the two places left for her signature.

'Thank you,' said the lawyer. He turned to the doctor. 'Will you be a witness, Dr McGregor?'

'Of course.' McGregor signed.

'And now you?' He held out the pen to Jo-Jo.

As Jo-Jo took it, Christina made a sound of protest. Jo-Jo

turned to look at her. The black eyes burned into her: Be brave, it's almost finished, they said.

Christina met that burning gaze. Then she bowed her head in consent. Jo-Jo wrote with firm emphasis, 'Josafin Belu'.

It was done.

Mr Charlford picked up the Moses basket, his wife hanging on his arm in ecstatic encouragement. 'Careful, John, don't tilt it, you'll bump his head. Oh, look, he's waking up. Oh, how lovely, he's got beautiful blue eyes. Stephen, darling, you're going home now.'

Carrying the basket as if it were the Holy Grail, John Charlford went out to the car. He put the basket on the back seat. His wife got in beside it, stooping in adoration over the baby.

'Well ... thank you ...' He held out his hand to Christina, awkwardly, foolishly.

She took it, shook it once, then went to the car. She leaned in to Estelle Charlford. She wanted to say, 'Take good care of my baby.' But no words would come, only a mute sound of appeal.

She tried to read Estelle Charlford's character in her face. What was she like? An anxious, tense woman, perhaps, with an expression of something like awe as she gazed at the sleeping child.

I'm giving you the most important thing in my life, she wanted to cry to her. Make him the most important thing in *your* life. Love him, please love him ...

She felt Jo-Jo hovering anxiously just behind her. She understood: her friend was afraid that even at this late moment she would snatch her baby back. And she wanted to, oh, how she wanted to ...

Yet she knew it was best for Stephen to have both a father and a mother. What could she give him compared with this rich young couple? Nothing but hardship and need, a tainted name and burdens he would find hard to bear.

A memory flickered in her mind: the mother-and-baby clinic at the University Hospital, an unmarried mother taking refuge behind a pretended widowhood and saying,

'It's difficult on our own. I do my best but she keeps getting every infection that's going, and I sometimes wonder if it's more to do with us being alone and Kitty not having a father . . . A child needs a father . . .'

She wanted better things than that for her son.

Estelle Charlford already cared about him. You could read that in her wondering gaze as she looked at the child. Already she was thinking of him as belonging to her.

A cry of protest, of repudiation, almost burst from Christina's lips. But the silence imposed upon her by Jo-Jo seemed to have become a physical reality. No words would come.

All the love, all the caring, must go to other children she would tend in the future. God help me, she said inwardly, give me just enough strength for this last moment.

She touched Estelle Charlford's arm.

Estelle looked into the brimming, dark blue eyes. For the first time she looked into the depth of grief that this parting meant to the mother. She gasped, and then she took one of Christina's hands in hers.

'We'll love him dearly,' she said in a low voice, and kissed her on the cheek.

The men clambered in, arranging themselves with difficulty around the new mother with the baby in its basket.

In a moment they had gone. Christina stood looking down at the hard-baked soil underfoot, unable to move or think.

'They're a nice couple,' Jo-Jo said, trying to comfort. 'He'll be well cared for.'

Wordless, Christina nodded. Then she ran with all her strength out of the yard, up a path towards the hillside, to throw herself down on a carpet of fallen leaves in the shelter of the oaks. Her breasts, full of milk that would never now feed her baby, pained her. But she welcomed the pain. Anything to fill the emptiness that threatened to engulf her. Anything to make her forget her baby's little fist curled against the blanket.

Anything to make her believe she was still alive, when her very soul seemed dead.

Chapter Eleven

Fourth-year medical school was a time of challenge. Christina Holt went into it like a knight on a white charger, willing to take on anything that might enter the lists against her.

She had given up her baby so as to continue her studies. The only way she could justify it to herself was to do well, to achieve absolute excellence.

She'd nerved herself to see Peter Semmring again but he was gone from the university. After the end of third-year exams Peter had hosted a party at which he had physically assaulted a fellow-student, Virgil Jessup. His family had sent him to finish his studies elsewhere.

No one except Christina, Jo-Jo and Aunt Bea knew of Christina's pregnancy. If any of the other lady meds suspected something of the kind, they kept their thoughts to themselves. Life was difficult enough for women students, any hint of sexual laxity on the part of one could only make matters worse for all.

Sometimes Christina thought that Dr Fehr had had his suspicions. She had caught his eye upon her once or twice. But her year as his assistant had ended in June. Another happy student held the honour now, though Christina felt she still had Fehr's high regard.

This was proved to her after the fourth-year finals. He sought her out. 'I wonder if you have thought about your future, Dr Holt?'

'I haven't got the degree yet, sir,' she said with a faint smile. 'I don't deserve the title yet.'

'Oh, there's no doubt on that point. You haven't

165

answered my question. What are your plans?'

'I've applied for one or two internships.'

'Have you had replies?'

'Not yet, doctor. They'll be waiting till the results are out.'

'Of course. Well, perhaps I should have spoken sooner. I wondered if you'd care to stay on here?'

'Stay on?' she said, startled.

'As my assistant. You would be doing graduate studies and helping with classes – not a lecturer, a demonstrator.' He looked at her through his pince-nez, eyes bright and keen as a bird's.

His offer was so unexpected it took her breath away. She stood with parted lips, staring at him.

'I can see you are surprised, Dr Holt. I ought to give you time to think about it. But I had thought perhaps the idea would appeal to you. You have a great natural bent for pathology.'

'I . . . I just don't know what to say.'

'There is a graduate scholarship for which you can apply, if you have money worries.'

'I'm extremely honoured and flattered.'

'Does that mean yes?'

'I suppose . . . I ought to say yes . . . May I have a few days to consider?'

'Of course, of course.' He gave her his usual courtly bow before making his way off to his waiting class.

When Christina reported the conversation to her friends, the reaction was delight and envy.

'What an honour! My word, Christina, I believe you'll be the first woman graduate student doing research here in pathology.' That was Susanne, keener than the others on helping the cause of women's rights.

'Wait a moment. Have you accepted, Christina?' Jo-Jo asked.

'Of course she's accepted. She'd be out of her mind to refuse.'

'Have you, Christina?'

There was a pause while a waitress came and took away

their salad plates. They were having the fifty-cents special at their favourite restaurant, relaxing in the joyous thought of not having classes awaiting them now that exams were over.

'As a matter of fact,' Christina said, 'I asked for time to think it over.'

'What's there to think about?' cried Youffie. 'Take it, take it with both hands.'

'I felt like that when he first made the offer . . . But now . . .'

'Now, what? What? You aren't going to refuse?' Youffie was scandalised.

'Look here, Youffie,' Jo-Jo remonstrated, 'Christina isn't studying four years and getting a degree just to oblige Dr Fehr. I never in all that time heard her mention a preference for pathology. Did you?'

'No, but—'

'But nothing! Christina has the same right as the rest of us, to choose what she is doing and where she is going once she has her degree. Why should she suddenly have to change course just because Dr Fehr offers a job?'

'But it's a terrific honour,' Christina pointed out.

'What good are honours you don't want? If the King of Siam suddenly offers the Order of the Sacred White Elephant, you go rushing off there to get it?'

'Like a shot, if he was offering me a mother-and-baby clinic in his palace!'

'There you are. That's always what your aim has been – to take up obstetrics, to study and treat women's diseases.'

'But that was only because she never expected to get such a wonderful offer from Dr Fehr.'

'Is that so, Christina? Mother-and-baby work was always second choice?'

'You know better than that, Jo-Jo.'

'You're not seriously advising Christina to turn down this offer?' Mary Mennem said in amazement.

The broiled chicken was brought. They attacked it with relish. Years of rushed meals or studying with only a sandwich at hand made them enjoy opportunities to eat like ordinary people.

'I am not giving advices to Christina,' Jo-Jo said with her mouth full. 'All I am saying is that we shouldn't talk as if Fate is intending her to be a research pathologist. If she wants to do it, good and well—'

'That should be "well and good",' corrected Youffie.

'There is a difference? Well and good, good and well. Christina wants to do pathology, she takes the post, she works in a University lab, shut away from the world, she helps give demonstrations to first-year students . . . But me, I don't think Christina is an academic.'

'I don't think I am either,' agreed Christina.

'But Chrissie, if you say no, some *man* will get it!'

'Susanne, we've all paid our dues to women's rights by sticking it all the way through medical school. I don't think it's fair to press any particular course on Christina because it would look good on the suffragette front.'

'Look here, Mary, you slid through these last few years with very little trouble. And why? Because you flapped your eyelashes at the men and they all melted. That's just using your femininity . . .'

'Well, why on earth shouldn't we?' Youffie cried. 'The men use their masculinity.'

The conversation followed a familiar course: how the campaign for equal rights for women should be conducted. In the event, Christina's decision on the research job was left for her to make on her own.

She put on her good summer dress, her re-trimmed straw hat, her new gloves, and went to see Dr Fehr.

'Oh,' he said when she told him the news, 'I *am* sorry. I more or less took it for granted you would accept.'

'I'm sorry, doctor. I have always wanted to do mother-and-baby medicine and feel it would be wrong to take up pathology. You were kind enough to say I had a talent for it, but I don't feel it in myself.'

'It's one of the most important departments of medicine. Without it, doctors and surgeons would still be groping in the dark over hundreds of medical problems.'

'I quite agree, sir. It's not for lack of respect for the work, or lack of eagerness to see information brought to light about some of our more intractable diseases. I just don't feel I'm cut out for that kind of job.'

'I see.' He fell silent, rolling his pen back and forth across his blotter. 'Suppose you took more time to consider it?'

'I don't think so, doctor. I've thought about it hard and long.'

He rose. 'In that case, there's nothing more to be said. I can't deny I'm disappointed. Time will tell whether you have made the right decision, but whatever branch of medicine you take up, I wish you success in it, Dr Holt.'

'Thank you, Dr Fehr.'

He held out his hand. She took it. They shook across his desk. Then he came round to escort her personally to his door.

Posts in medicine weren't easy to come by for women. Most general practitioners seeking a junior partner wanted a man, therefore the hospitals were the best source of employment. But they too preferred male doctors and certainly male surgeons. Women had their place in a hospital so long as they wore nursing uniform, that was the view. Christina was still going for interviews when graduation came round. She went to the ceremony, received her degree and two prizes: a silver cup and a handsomely bound copy of *Diagnosis and Prescriptive Practice* by Elias M. Prendergast. Then she hurried home, put all these new possessions in a cupboard, and took the train to Chicago for an interview next day.

'You applied for the Maternity Department I see, Dr Holt?' remarked the hospital director, glancing at her application.

'Yes, doctor. I particularly want to work in that field.'

'Very commendable. You seem to have done more of your work in the mother-and-baby outpatient clinic, however: you only put in the requisite time prescribed on the syllabus in the maternity ward of Pennsylvania University Hospital.'

'That was because the schedules were arranged without consulting the students. I would have done more hours if I had had the opportunity.'

'Ah.' Dr Keesing didn't seem to warm to her. 'I heard that Dr Fehr, the Senior Lecturer in Pathology there, offered you a post and then changed his mind and withdrew it.'

'Not at all!' she said, startled. 'I was offered the post but refused it.'

'Indeed?' said Dr Keesing, in a tone that meant, I don't believe a word of *that*.

'I'm sure if you wrote to Dr Fehr—'

'My dear lady, I have quite enough applicants for posts at this hospital without having to put myself out to write to anyone. It seems—'

'I will write, then, and bring you the reply.'

'I think by that time our decisions will have been made, Dr Holt. Thank you, nevertheless, for coming to this interview.'

Christina went out aghast. She had lost a job she wanted because she had refused a job she didn't want. And the worst of it was, if that sort of rumour was going round, there was practically no way she could counteract it. If she wrote after jobs, she might well be refused even an interview on the grounds that Dr Fehr had discovered something unsatisfactory about her.

And the only way to deal with that would be to ask Dr Fehr for a letter saying she had in fact refused him. And that was something, on consideration, she simply couldn't do.

She had no one to confide in now. Jo-Jo had gone off with her Serbian colleagues to California. Stefan had sold the farm, though at a considerable loss. With the money they intended to make a new start, offering a home to any other exiles who had to leave Serbia because they talked too loudly about independence.

Aunt Bea still remained, of course. But she didn't understand medical politics.

'Perhaps if you go to the West Coast, like Jo-Jo?' she suggested.

'I don't want to go to California, Auntie. I've nothing

against California, but if I'm going so far off I might as well go home to England.'

'We-ell,' said her aunt.

'What?'

'I had a letter from England yesterday.'

'You mean Father actually wrote to you?' It was enough to put every other thought, even that unsatisfactory interview, out of her head.

Ever since Christina had refused to return to Market Bresham with him, any letters they sent to Herbert Holt or his family had been returned unopened. In the end Mrs Kentley and her niece had simply stopped writing.

'Elwin wrote. He's in London, at a firm in Lincoln's Inn for a year to get special experience, he says. Look, here it is.'

Christina took the letter. It was three years since she had seen her brother's writing but it was still the same: neat, schoolroom writing which had always pleased his teachers.

He assured his aunt that he'd always thought the quarrel in the family absurd, but that while still relying on his father for an allowance, he felt it his duty to abide by his wishes. Now, however, he was out on his own, before starting with his father's firm. He hoped all was well, sent his love and admiration to Christina for her staying power. 'I should have given in by now if it had been me, but Chrissie was always the stalwart one. Write and let me know how she's getting on.'

'Oh, we must write at once!' Christina cried. Dear Elwin! She had missed him, although she was always so busy that he had only been in some secondary part of her mind.

'What I was thinking,' said her aunt, 'was that Elwin might know of jobs going in London for doctors.'

'It's not likely. Law and medicine are two closed circles. Besides, I couldn't practise in London. An American degree doesn't permit me . . .'

'But you just said a moment ago that England was no further off than California.'

'So I did.'

'You mean you could never practise medicine in England?'

'Oh, of course. I only have to take the qualifying examination there and they'd give me a degree.'

'You mean, do another four years' study?' cried her aunt in horror.

'No, no, darling, I've done the study. The questions would be more or less the same as in the American degree exams. I think it could all be got through in a few weeks.' She paused, struck by a thought. 'Why all this interest in practising medicine in England, anyhow? Are you trying to send me home, Aunt Bea?'

'Well, dear.' Her aunt refolded Elwin's letter, tucked it in its envelope, and looked thoughtful. 'You know, I can't help feeling it's wrong for you to be cut off from your own flesh and blood like this. I think of your poor dear mother: she must often wonder how you're getting on, and long to see you. I do feel, Christina . . . I do really feel you should go home and try to make things right between you and your parents.'

'But . . .' She let the protest die. She'd been about to say, but wouldn't you miss me? Yet if she were to find a post in, say, Chicago or New York, she would have to leave the Wallace Hotel anyway. Her aunt would have to do without her company.

The chief thing was the money. It had always been Christina's intention to pay back what it had cost her aunt to keep her over these past three years; but that could only be done if she had a job. And jobs were apparently not easy for someone who had the reputation of displeasing the great Dr Fehr.

If you came to look at it logically, she might stand a better chance of employment in England. And it was just as easy to send money from England as from, say, Detroit.

Another thought occurred. Perhaps, using the hotel as a base and going on trips here and there for interview, she was costing her aunt a lot of money she couldn't afford. She wasn't always available to help the hotel staff as she'd done in the past, so Aunt Bea had had to get in a temporary girl, and pay wages.

Perhaps it was time to think less about her own prospects

and more about Aunt Bea's present difficulties.

'How long have you been thinking about this?'

'Since you took your finals. It made me remember how proud you'd been when you did well in the first-year exams and your father came rushing across the Atlantic for you. He was *so* angry.'

'Well, doesn't that seem—'

'But you know, we never once in that conversation mentioned your mother. It was as if she didn't count. But she does count, Christina. She's lost a child. Even though she probably doesn't dare say so, you know it must grieve her.'

Oh, yes. Christina knew that grief. She looked at her aunt with eyes dimmed by unexpected tears. 'Oh, Aunt Bea . . .'

'I'm sorry, dear. I didn't mean to remind you of that. But I lost my son too, years ago, and I know what it's like. I often think of your poor mother.' Mrs Kentley sighed. 'And then when Elwin's letter came . . . It seemed a sign. I felt I ought to put it to you. I hate the thought of your going, dear, but you're probably going anyhow, aren't you? It doesn't seem as if you'll get a medical post here in Philadelphia.'

'No.'

'And your mother's health has never been good, Chrissie.'

'Oh, mostly it's just nerves: she gets in a state . . .'

'You know better than I do, of course, but all the same, someone who's been ailing almost every time I've seen her . . . You couldn't forgive yourself if you left it too late to see her again.'

'Aunt Bea! That's really looking on the dark side.'

'Well, my love, we're none of us getting any younger. I often think I ought to sell up and live a nice quiet life on the proceeds.'

Christina jumped up to throw her arms round her aunt. 'Come on now, stop depressing yourself. You know you love this hotel! Where would Captain Dinsdorf and Miss Melville go if you sold up?'

Having nearly reduced herself to tears, Aunt Beatrice now gave a shaky laugh. She gave her niece a kiss on the cheek. 'You're a good girl, Chrissie. I'll miss you if you go.'

'But you think I should?'

'Yes, I do.'

The practical problems here in Philadelphia were almost enough to convince Christina her aunt was right. The undeserved reputation of having somehow offended Dr Fehr, and the mere fact that she was a woman, made chances of a decent career in or near Philadelphia very slim.

But, hearing Elwin's words read out to her, she experienced a surge of longing to see him again. She remembered telling him as they said their goodbyes that they would always be the best of friends. Yet she had let her father's anger part her from him totally. He, of course, had obeyed the command not to keep in touch with her: well, Elwin had always been the biddable one.

Her mother too . . . Poor Mother . . . Left alone at home to cope with her overbearing, self-important husband. How good it would be to see Mother again, to hear that soft, plaintive voice.

Aunt Bea was right. She ought to go home.

The problem was, how to find the money for the boat ticket. Christina had no savings, and she certainly wasn't going to take any more from her aunt. The first thing was to get paid employment. Miss Melville came to her aid. A stand-in medic was needed at the missionary clinic where she did voluntary office work. Christina could have the post of doctor-in-charge for six weeks while they found a more suitable – which in this case meant more church-minded – physician.

With this money, and having sold her silver cup and one or two other prizes that had come to her over the last four years, Christina amassed enough for a second-class berth on the *Mauretania*, which that year had gained the Blue Riband for the fastest crossing of the Atlantic, in four days, ten hours and forty-one minutes.

Parting from her Philadelphian friends was more difficult that she'd imagined. Aunt Bea was closer to her than anyone else in the world, closer even than the companion of her childhood, her brother Elwin; closer than the friend of her student years, Jo-Jo Belu. Even saying goodbye to Letty, to Captain Dinsdorf and Miss Melville, brought out emotions Christina found hard to handle.

There was a farewell party. Captain Dinsdorf and Miss Melville both gave her going-away presents. Miss Melville's was a beautifully embroidered collar to wear on dark dresses. 'I thought it suitable for a professional woman, my dear.'

Captain Dinsdorf produced a small old-fashioned box, long and narrow. 'I could not make anything delicate like Miss Melville's present,' he said, wrinkling his nose and tugging at his beard. 'But I hope you will wear this sometimes, little Snow Princess.'

She opened the box. Inside lay a gold chain, quite delicate but plain. 'But – this is beautiful, Captain Dinsdorf!'

'You like it?'

'I can't take this.'

'Please, please . . . It belonged to my mother. Who else should I give it to? No daughter, not even a distant great-niece. No, you must take it, my Snow Princess, and sometimes wear it if you go out somewhere pleasant, to a theatre or a party, and with a young man – yes, with a young man, for I am sure you will have many young men at your feet.'

Miss Melville shook her head a little, as if she feared a formidable woman doctor was unlikely to have success with young men.

'I will wear it, Captain, and I'll think of you each time I do.' Her throat closed up as she gave him a daughterly kiss on his bristly cheek.

'And write to me sometimes, eh? About your triumphs and adventures.'

Miss Melville sniffed. 'Adventures? Anyone would think she was going to the wilds of Borneo, not the capital of England.' She clasped her hands in gentle supplication. 'If you see the Queen, send me a line,' she begged.

'Of course.'

Letty held up well until they were about to board the New York train at Grand Depot. 'Now be careful,' she wept, 'and don't work too hard and get thin and peaked. An' remember to air that blue dress well before you wear it, otherwise it'll smell of mothballs in a warm room.'

'I will, Letty, I promise.'

'And be careful in New York. Rob you as soon as look at you, a New Yorker.'

'I'll look after her, Letty,' protested Mrs Kentley. 'Now stop sobbing over her, you're making her coat collar all wet.'

With a last hug, Letty let go.

There was an overnight stay in New York before the ship sailed. Aunt Bea took the opportunity to go window-shopping. 'Something wrong, dear?' she asked when Christina drew up as they strolled down Fifth Avenue.

'No, nothing, Auntie.' It was here, just here, that she had asked Peter Semmring when he was going to speak to his parents about their getting married.

What a fool she had been. And yet, it didn't hurt her now to think of it – at least, not much. It had all happened in another world, to a different Christina Holt.

That girl had been naïve, bedazzled. That girl had really expected Peter to marry her.

Now she knew different. If there had been any real love on Peter's side, it was short-lived, linked to physical conquest, nothing more. And, as for herself, she'd been in love with some young Norse god of her own invention.

Sometimes she hated herself for her own foolishness. But far more important was the loss Peter had inflicted on her. She had had to give up her baby. Beside that, everything else paled to a shadow. Her own stupidity, her gullibility, had led her into a trap from which she would bear the scars for ever. Not a day passed without a thought about Stephen – a hope that he was happy, a longing just to see him. He would be a secret grief all her life.

But as for Peter . . . She gave herself a little shake. She had outgrown him and all the naïvety that went with him. At least she had learned from the experience.

They were determinedly cheerful during their meal that evening. Aunt Bea talked about staying on another day in

New York, doing some shopping, visiting an exhibition of catering equipment. They went early to bed, had an early breakfast, and were taken in a motor taxi to the docks.

There Mrs Kentley's fortitude gave way. 'Oh, Chrissie, Chrissie, you're going so far away!

'It's not for ever, darling. I'll be back.'

'Yes, when you're a rich and fashionable Harley Street specialist,' her aunt replied with a quavering laugh.

'We won't wait for *that*,' said Christina. 'It's not in the least likely. But we'll see each other again soon, Aunt Bea.'

'If you can make it up with your father, I'll come for one of my visits,' said Aunt Bea. 'I sort of miss them, you know. Family *is* important. Blood is thicker than water.'

'But not half so easy to deal with!'

'You will be patient and tactful when you see your father?'

'It's more a question of "if". We still don't know whether Elwin was able to talk him into seeing me.'

'He will, dear. He must.'

Christina was by no means so sure. Nor, in fact, was that her only reason for returning to her homeland. She had decided that she did want to obtain an English degree: somehow it had become important to her, to prove to herself and anyone else who cared to know that she could practise medicine in her own country. With that degree, the possibility of gaining a suitable appointment at home opened up. No one in England was going to know she had refused a position with Dr Fehr, so it couldn't possibly affect her chances. Whether opportunities for lady meds were greater or less in England, she would soon find out.

At the same time she would try to gain her father's forgiveness and be allowed to see her mother. What Aunt Bea had said was true: she ought to make an attempt to repair that breach for her mother's sake at least.

When at last the great ship was under way, she sat in the cabin she was to share with three other women, and tried to take stock.

She was twenty-two years old. She held a degree in medicine from the University of Pennsylvania. She had made love with a man to whom she was not married and had borne and lost a child.

Christina Holt was no innocent, inexperienced waif. Yet there was probably no one on the ship who faced the future with as much uncertainty, as much trepidation, as she.

Chapter Twelve

Elwin met her off the boat at Southampton. She recognised him at once in the crowd, despite the five years' gap since she had seen him last. About the same height as herself, but much more sturdily built, he was bareheaded in the December drizzle. His neat brown hair shone under the lamps on the quay. He was carrying a sheaf of hothouse carnations.

She had to tap him on the arm before his gaze focused on her.

'Christina!' He was so startled he dropped the bouquet. They both stooped to rescue it. As they straightened, he was staring at her with disbelief. 'Christina, how you've changed!'

'Well, when I went away I was still more or less a schoolgirl. Now I'm not a schoolgirl any more.'

'My word you're not!' He pushed the carnations at her, threw his arms around her, and lifted her off her feet in a great hug. 'Oh, Chrissie, Chrissie! I've just realised how much I missed you!'

'I've missed you too, Elwin.' She felt awkward, at a loss, full of emotion that brought a great lump to her throat but uncertain how to express it.

The crowd had parted good-naturedly around them. Her trunk had come off the ship, and the porter waited in kindly patience for her to say what he was to do next.

'We're going to the train,' Elwin said.

'Yes, sir.'

He trundled off. They followed on behind.

'How are Mother and Father?' Christina asked, not knowing how else to begin catching up with the world she had left five years ago.

'Mother's fairly well. Dyspepsia, as always, and she had a

bad migraine a few days ago – my fault, I'm afraid.'

'How was that?'

'Well, I went to see Father to tell him you were coming home and I was meeting you at the docks. He raised the roof. Mother kept crying and begging him to be forgiving, and he kept roaring that he could never forgive . . .'

'I see. So there's no chance of going to the house even to see Mother?'

'No, but . . . Mother's coming to London to see you!'

'Father's allowing that?' She was astounded.

'He doesn't know. Mother caught me as I was leaving the house and cried into my shoulder and told me she absolutely must see you. She's coming to London when I let her know it's convenient, and you're being taken out to tea at the Ritz.'

It was perhaps the bravest thing Mildred Holt had ever done, this secret plan to meet her daughter. All her married life she had been a dutiful wife, but now for the first time she planned to defy her husband. Of course she would never let him know, but all the same, it was courageous, and Christina acknowledged it with a tightening of her hand on her brother's arm.

The train was fairly crowded but they had no difficulty finding a compartment. The journey to London would take something over two hours, so they would have tea on the train. Soon after it pulled out they made their way along to the restaurant car, where pink-shaded lamps on the tables and shining silverware made for an elegance that impressed Christina. She had lived such a Spartan life for the last five years that even the gentility of a Pullman car impressed her.

The dark landscape rushed by outside, dotted now and then with the gas-lamps of main roads or the windows of farmhouses. Stations appeared and disappeared. There was a feeling of safety and seclusion in the restaurant car. Christina leaned back and relaxed.

'You've turned out a bit of a beauty,' her brother remarked as he watched her pour their tea. 'But you haven't much flesh on your bones.'

'I never was very well covered.'

'You've been working too hard, I bet.'

'Well, medical school isn't a rest cure, Elwin.'

'Aunt Bea said in her letter that you'd done marvellously well.'

She offered him his tea-cup. 'Really? Then why can't I land a job?'

'I don't know. Why can't you?'

'Mainly it's because men get first pickings. But there were other reasons . . . Never mind, I'm hoping it will be different here. And now tell me about the law.'

'What, all of Blackstone over a cup of tea?'

'Not Blackstone, you. Do you like being a solicitor?'

'It's all right,' Elwin said, dropping sugar lumps from the tongs into his tea.

'Just all right? Is that all?' She was scandalised. 'Surely you don't want to devote your life to something that's just "all right"!'

'Well, what else is there?' he countered. He sipped his tea. 'I'm not like you, Christina. I don't have any windmills to tilt at. Father quite rightly said that the law had given him a more than adequate living all his life and he had confidence it would do the same for me. And as I couldn't think of anything I wanted to do more, I went along with it. And I'm happy enough.'

Happy enough. What a way for a young man of twenty-six to look at his life. 'Elwin, if you really don't like it, you must . . .'

'Must what?'

'Try something else.'

'What, for instance?'

'There must be something you feel a strong inclination for.'

'Nothing that would earn me a living,' he said with a shrug.

The waiter came to replace the pâté sandwiches with hot scones and jam. Elwin spread jam lavishly and popped a scone whole into his mouth. 'Are you going to start applying for medical posts?' he inquired.

'That's the idea. You take *The Times*, I imagine?' He nodded. 'I must go out tomorrow and buy some medical journals. It's a bit late for any jobs beginning with the New Year, but there might be some locums.'

'Inez says what you just said, that GPs won't take a woman as locum tenens.'

'Who's Inez?' she asked with sudden interest. The only girl she had ever thought of in connection with her brother was Dorothy Spinshill, daughter of a landed gentleman with an estate outside Market Bresham. From the time she and Dorothy went to school together aged twelve, it had been an understood thing in both families that one day Elwin was going to marry Dorothy.

But everything had to wait until Elwin was properly established in the law. And now here he was, talking about Inez.

'Inez is the sister of the fellow you'll be staying with,' he explained. 'I've got rooms with Matthew and Inez Clareton. She keeps house for him. A bit of a tyrant, I'm afraid, though a good soul at heart. She's interested in women's rights, so when I told her I had a sister who'd qualified as a doctor she was delighted.'

Well, that didn't sound like a romance.

'She's right about doctors preferring male colleagues,' Christina said. 'But if anyone was hard pushed – if the junior partner had flu or had broken a leg, for instance, he might take a woman.'

'Poor Chrissie,' he said, laughing. 'What an outlook: second best to a man with a broken leg.'

He spent the rest of the journey bringing her up to date on the news. On the other side of the Atlantic, matters of great weight to the British had received scant attention. All Christina had seen of any importance was the announcement of the death of Miss Nightingale.

He told her that in the previous year offices called Labour Exchanges had been opened, where men seeking a job might find employers on the look-out for them. An Act had been passed enforcing a half-day holiday for shop employees. Her favourite author, H. G. Wells, had brought out a new book called *The History of Mr Polly*, which Elwin said was 'peculiar'. A novel by Max Beerbohm called *Zuleika Dobson* was even more peculiar, he told her, but a lot funnier.

When the train steamed into Waterloo, it was eight o'clock. People thronged the forecourt. As they threaded their way through to the pavement, Christina eyed them with interest. They were for the most part dressed with more colour than the Philadelphians, whose Quaker past seemed still to cast a shadow over their choice of clothes. London ladies wore plum, maroon, violet. Even the men had less sombre suits: she saw many country tweeds, checked Ulsters, bright chestnut-brown boots and bowlers as well as City suits of black and pinstripe.

Elwin summoned a cab to transport them to Devonshire Street, where the Claretons had a flat in Brice Mansions. En route she tried to get some idea of the city. She had never known London well and now it seemed very strange indeed. Instead of the regimented right-angled streets of Philadelphia, there were curves and crescents, angles and alleys. There were electric street lights in the main roads and gas in the side streets. The number of motor vehicles had greatly increased since she had last been there: she saw motor omnibuses and many motor vans with the names of great stores on their sides.

'It's bigger than I remember, Elwin. Big and . . . impersonal.'

'Scares you, does it?'

'No,' she said with determination, but without sincerity.

Now that she saw the city, she understood how unimportant she and her affairs would be in it. Re-establishing contact with her family, finding a job – to her these were of paramount concern. But if she were to fall under the wheels of one of those busy delivery vans, London would go on uncaring.

She felt once again that shiver of apprehension that often came over her when she thought of the future. Her goal, her intensely desired wish, was to be a good doctor and thereby help humanity, particularly the neglected and suffering children. But who was Christina Holt to think she could make any difference?

She clutched her brother's arm for comfort. And Elwin, thinking she was simply nervous of the traffic, pressed her arm against his side. She glanced up at him. He seemed so confident in the midst of this maelstrom.

Perhaps he was able to fit better into the scheme of things. He accepted life as it came. But she wasn't like that, she wanted to change things. Only . . . it all seemed too big for any action of hers to make any difference.

The Claretons were both at the door when Elwin opened it with his key calling, 'We're here!' They were in evening clothes. Christina soon learned that their social standards were high, much higher than the casual regime at the Wallace Hotel.

The taxi-man brought up the trunk, the maid took the hand luggage, Inez Clareton fussed about giving directions.

'Dinner will be ready in an hour. I'm sure you're starved. Don't do much unpacking, my dear. Nancy will help you with that in the morning. Come along, this way.'

Christina was ushered along a passage papered in dark red silk and lit by a handsome ceiling light. As they went, Inez counted off rooms. 'My brother's room, my room, Elwin opposite, bathroom and so forth, box-room, and here's yours.' Inez opened a door at the far end.

'It's rather small, I'm afraid, but I hope you'll find space enough for your things. If you need a full-length mirror I'm afraid you'll have to come into my room. Wardrobe,' she opened a narrow walnut wardrobe, 'bureau,' she tapped it with her fingers, 'wash hand-basin behind the screen . . .'

'Really, Inez, Miss Holt can see for herself that she's got a wardrobe and a bureau,' teased her brother. He was a large man, a little older than Elwin and very much the master of the household. Christina soon learned that Inez knew her place, even though she dabbled in women's rights. She had been sent to London from Somerset by her parents, to keep house for her clever brother.

By and by they bowed themselves out to let her change for dinner. 'Back along the passage of course, we're in the drawing-room, straight across the hall – drinks when you're ready.'

'Thank you.'

As the door closed she sank down on the bed. The flat was much more opulent than she had expected. Her clothes were nothing like good enough for it.

She took out of her hand-luggage the evening dress she'd worn last night aboard ship. It was not much creased because it was crêpe. It was pale green and home-made after the style of M. Poiret, with a ribbon under the bosom. A green rose marked the waistline – or rather the beginning of the skirt – which flowed down in two curved panels, crossing at the front to reveal a glimpse of ankle.

With it went silk stockings of a pearly shade and black strapped shoes which also did duty for daytime. She had a black satin purse which Aunt Beatrice no longer had any use for. When she had arrayed herself she looked in the small cheval-glass on the bureau – by tilting it she could see herself almost full-length . . . Rather plain and provincial. As a fillip to her self-esteem, she took out the chain given her by Captain Dinsdorf and, with a momentary smile for his kindness, clasped it round her neck . . . Better. But still no match for the quite elaborate dinner gown of Inez Clareton, nor the splendour of pearl shirt-studs and black bow-tie of her brother Matthew.

With a little shrug, she went out to find the drawing-room. This, as promised, was straight across the hall. It was a fine room with tall windows masked by curtains of crimson brocade, sofas and armchairs upholstered in the same fabric, half a dozen lamps with oyster-coloured shades, and a Turkey carpet. A glowing fire took up the whole of the gleaming steel fire-basket under the mantel.

Elwin had changed and was lolling in a chair with a weak whisky in one hand. Matthew was at the drinks tray pouring sherry. Without asking what she would like, he handed the glass to Christina. Inez already had hers. It was clear that ladies drank sherry whereas men could have spirits – either whisky or gin.

'Well, now,' Matthew said encouragingly to Christina, 'settled in for the moment?'

'Yes, thank you.'

'Good, good. It isn't a big room, but Elwin tells me you'll be looking for a job with some hospital somewhere and then you'll be off, eh?'

'That's right. It's very good of you to put me up . . .'

'Nonsense, nonsense, fun for my sister, cooped up here with only two fellows to look after, no female company. And you're just the kind of company she yearns for, isn't she, Inez?'

Christina looked puzzled. Inez said, 'He's always teasing me about my views. When he heard you were a lady doctor he said to me, "You'll lap it up, having a professional woman to stay."'

'I wonder if Cook knows Miss Holt has dressed and we're waiting, Inez?' Matthew said, looking at his watch.

'Oh! Yes, I'll just ring.' She did so, the maid appeared, and was told to let Cook know that the visitor was now with them and they were ready to eat. In a moment she returned.

'Cook says dinner will be served in five minutes, ma'am.'

'Thank you, Nancy.'

'Drink up, my dear. Time for another before we go in, if you like.'

'No, thank you,' said Christina, preventing him with a little wave of her hand from taking up her almost untasted glass. 'I don't really care much for sherry.'

There was a tiny silence. Inez looked at Christina and then, with some perturbation, at her brother.

'Oh,' he said, recovering, 'why didn't you tell me? You could have had a whisky.'

'Thank you, I don't like whisky either. In fact, I seldom drink – but you're very kind to trouble about it.'

The moment had been smoothed over. But Christina had learned that in this household she was expected to conform to Matthew Clareton's view of what a lady required.

The meal consisted of six courses. It was much more elaborate that at the Wallace Hotel but not so well cooked. She saw Inez glance in anxiety at her brother when the cheese soufflé arrived looking rather collapsed. But he was in good humour. He had taken a liking to Christina firstly because she was exceptionally good-looking and secondly because he could treat her as a colonial cousin. Five years in America. Everybody knew that the Americans were unsophisticated and lacking in *savoir-faire*.

Next morning she had the unwonted luxury of breakfast in bed. Nancy drew back the curtains to let in winter sunshine. 'I brought you coffee, miss, but if you'd prefer tea . . .'

'This is lovely, thank you, Nancy. But usually I'm up and about by breakfast time.'

'Yes, miss, but Miss Clareton felt you'd need a good rest after being on a boat so long. Ordinarily it's breakfast at eight-thirty.'

Christina looked at the bedside clock. It was well after nine. She felt absolutely sinful, sitting up in bed drinking coffee and eating scrambled eggs at such a late hour.

'I suppose my brother's gone?'

'Yes, miss, both gentlemen went out about nine. Mr Holt left you this note.' She took it from behind the toast rack.

'Thank you, Nancy.'

'I'll come back later to unpack for you, Miss Holt.'

'Oh, that won't be necessary, thank you, I'll do it myself.'

Nancy looked surprised. 'You sure, miss?'

'Quite sure.'

Elwin wrote that he would like to offer her lunch at a restaurant close to the Law Courts in Fleet Street. He would book a table for one-fifteen. He had written to their mother to say Christina had safely arrived and suggesting Friday, three days later, for the meeting at the Ritz.

Inez was in the drawing-room working on that evening's menu when she got downstairs. 'How did you sleep? Is there anything you need?'

'I slept perfectly; I didn't hear anyone getting up or going out. There's nothing I need, thank you, except some magazines, which I'll go out to buy shortly . . .'

'Oh, don't bother. If you give the names to Nancy she can fetch them from the newsagent.'

'No, thank you, Inez, I should enjoy going out. I want to find my way around. And then, as I expect you know, I'm meeting Elwin for lunch.'

'Very well. Shall you be home for afternoon tea?'

'Probably not. I have the name of an agency which specialises in posts for medical practitioners. I'll drop in on them.'

'I see you're determined to get to work at once!' There was envy and admiration on Inez's plump face. 'Well then, till this evening, what? We've invited a few friends in to make a little welcome-home party for you.'

Christina would just as soon have had a quiet meal. But she must fall in with her hosts' wishes. She went upstairs, put on her winter coat and her felt hat, took up her handbag and gloves and went out.

Marylebone High Street was busy, for it was now nearly eleven in the morning. The shops were delightful to her: florists full of familiar flowers, milliners with the hat prices in pounds, shillings and pence, a tobacconist with brands of tobacco and cigars she hadn't heard mentioned in five years.

She bought her magazines, spent half an hour looking through them in a Lyons tea-shop, then went by bus to Fleet Street. The restaurant had an unprepossessing façade, but inside proved to be cosy and welcoming. A vast fire glowed in an equally vast fireplace, oaken booths kept guests free from draughts and also from eavesdroppers, and in one of them Elwin was already installed with a glass of red wine.

She was one of only three women in the room. She was certainly the youngest and the prettiest. Heads turned as she moved between the tables to join her brother.

'Good afternoon, Christina, you're looking fresh and fair.'

'I've had a good walk through Marylebone and Oxford Street. Is this a haunt of legal men?'

'Yes, indeed. And, as you see, very few ladies come here.

Those you see are probably clients whose cases are coming on this afternoon across the road. The food is good.' He handed her the menu. 'Do choose something substantial to put a few ounces on those slender bones of yours.'

When they had ordered they plunged once more into the catching-up process. 'How is Dr Childers?' she asked. 'I wrote to him fairly regularly but only got very sketchy replies.'

'He's getting very old, Chrissie. He's taken on a junior partner – very glossy and brisk, scares the old people with his efficiency. Mother won't have him at any price, even though Father would like her to because he took against Childers, as you can imagine. But Mother always insists she'll only have Childers.'

She made a sound that was half a laugh, half a sigh. 'It's very difficult being a doctor. When you start, people keep saying they can't trust you because you're young and inexperienced, and when you get old they say you're out of touch and doddery.'

'The thing is to be about half-way between those two,' her brother suggested. 'But that means a long wait for you, my dear, before you can be in the right age group.' He drank some soup then added, 'And even then you'll still have the handicap of being female.'

She dismissed it with a wave of her hand and asked after some of her schoolfriends. They were all, with only one exception, married. The exception was Dorothy Spinshall, who regarded herself as unofficially engaged to Elwin.

'Why is it unofficial?' Christina inquired.

'No reason, I suppose . . .' He looked at his steak and kidney pudding, picked up his knife and fork, then put them down again. 'I'm fond of Dot, you know.'

'Yes?'

'Known her all my life, practically.'

'But?'

'What d'you mean, "but"?'

'There is a but, isn't there?'

'No, of course not. No buts. It's just . . .'

'What, Elwin?'

'I've never had a chance to get to know any other girls, really. Cambridge was all-male, of course, and then the law . . . No women in the law . . . I just wonder sometimes . . .'

'Whether you might meet someone you like better than Dot?'

He went red. 'Of course not! Dot and I are an established thing. She'd be heartbroken if anything was altered now.'

'That doesn't seem a very good reason for getting married, Elwin.'

'What's wrong with it? We suit each other, neither of us is likely to have high-flown notions of romantic love or anything . . .'

Christina said nothing to that, and after a moment her brother began to eat his lunch.

The dinner party that evening was an ordeal. Matthew Clareton insisted on putting Christina on exhibition. The guests were two married couples, two women friends of Inez's to make table partners for her brother and Elwin, and a fellow lawyer to partner Christina.

The men followed the lead of their host and asked arch questions about medical matters and independence and romantic entanglement. The wives looked down their noses at her, Inez's friends tried to ask sensible questions, and Inez basked in her reflected glory.

Next morning after breakfast Christina caught Elwin before he went out to his office in Lincoln's Inn. 'Elwin, I think I'd better move out to a hotel.'

'Move out!' His bland features took on a look of astonishment. 'You can't do that!'

'I think I had better.'

'But why?'

'Because if your friend Matthew makes one more patronising remark about ambitious little lady doctors, I shall say something we'll both regret.'

'Christina! You mustn't be so touchy. Matthew is a very decent chap.'

'To other men, no doubt. But he dominates his sister and

he thinks I ought to perform to amuse his friends.'

'Oh, come on, that's very harsh,' he said, offended. 'Matthew's a friend of mine.'

'I know, and that's why I think I should move out. I don't want to cause any unpleasantness.'

'But why should you? Good heavens, can't you take a joke or two, Chrissie?'

'Why on earth should I?' she flared. 'No one makes jokes to your face about *your* profession – why should I have to put up with it?'

'But that's quite different.'

'Why is it different?'

'Well, you must admit a woman doctor is something worth commenting about—'

'Elwin, I don't want to argue with you on that score. I just feel I shall stifle if I have to spend another evening like last night. So I shall look for a hotel today.'

'No, no, don't do that – it would be most unsuitable.'

'Unsuitable? Why would it be unsuitable?'

'Well, a single woman on her own in a hotel . . .'

'I shall choose a respectable hotel, Elwin,' she said with some coldness.

But he was very upset at the idea. 'No, no, please don't. I haven't got time to stop and argue it out now. We'll talk about it this evening.

'But I—'

'Promise me, Christina! I promised Mother I'd look after you.'

'But I don't need looking after!'

At that moment they were joined in the hall by Matthew. Both men wished her farewell and set off together for the office. Fuming inwardly, Christina went to her room for her hat and coat. She had an appointment with the medical agency for that morning.

The gentleman in charge there told her almost at once that he had no posts on his register for a woman doctor. 'I could find you something in a shop?' he suggested. 'As a pharmacist?'

'No, thank you.'

'Well, we get no call for lady doctors, and if I were to contact any of our clients, I know they wouldn't even want to interview you.'

'I see. Thank you.'

He relented as she was turning to the door. 'Your best chance is a hospital or a clinic, miss. Some of the hospitals are employing lady doctors in maternity wards.'

'Yes, thank you, I have written after one or two.'

'Well, I wish you luck,' he said, in the tone of one who is merely being kind.

When she got home at mid-afternoon, Inez was in the drawing-room eating buttered crumpets by the fire. 'Oh, do come in, how nice, we can have a cosy tea together.' Her chin – incipiently double – was smeared with melted butter. 'Have you had a nice day?'

'Not very,' Christina confessed, throwing herself into a chair without much regard for elegance or good manners.

'Something wrong?'

'I went to an agency that specialises in finding locums for general practitioners. I was told it was out of the question to send me to any of their clients.'

'Oh dear.' Inez rang the bell for fresh tea, but Nancy had heard the house-guest come in and brought it when she came, together with fresh supplies of crumpets. Inez poured tea, then looked thoughtfully at the other girl. 'I wonder if you'd be interested in something Hebe said last night.'

'Hebe?'

'Miss Grant, you remember – the taller of the two friends who came last night. She and Ursula and I, you know . . . we're trying to do our bit for women's rights . . . Hebe was saying to me last night . . . But I don't know whether you'd consider it.'

'What, Inez?' Christina said in hidden exasperation.

'Well, Hebe is Scottish, you know . . . born in Edinburgh. And she was saying they're opening a mother-and-baby clinic in one of the poor parts of the city . . . Supported by

192

public subscription, so they're having trouble finding staff
. . . can't pay much, you see.'

'Inez,' Christina cried, 'are you saying they're looking for
doctors?'

Inez nodded over a mouthful of oozing crumpet. 'Specifically, women doctors. Hebe told me privately that these
poor souls in the slums are very shy about telling their
private affairs to anyone, let alone a strange man.' Inez tried
to say this in a casual manner but she herself was blushing.
'Can't bring themselves to mention their ailments. So the
management committee have decided to staff the clinic
entirely with women. But I don't know whether . . . ?'

'Could you speak to your friend about it?'

'Of course. In fact, she wondered last night whether you
would be interested but didn't like to—'

'Oh, please, put me in touch! It sounds ideal!'

'But the money, Christina? It will barely be enough to live
on.'

'That doesn't matter. What I want is to work. Oh, thank
you, Inez! You *are* good.'

Inez coloured and looked embarrassed. Then she said,
leaning forward and lowering her voice, 'To tell the truth,
dear, it would please me very much if you got this appointment, because Matthew was saying he was sure you'd have
to give up medicine. He said no one would ever take on a
young and pretty woman. And it is so annoying when he
turns out to be right all the time . . .'

Urged on by Christina, Inez went to the telephone to call
her friend. An engagement was made for that very evening.
Much cheered, Christina looked forward to dinner with less
dread than she had foreseen. And matters improved yet
further when the evening post brought a lettter to Elwin
from her mother. She asked him to tell Christina she would
be in the Palm Court of the Ritz at four o'clock on Friday.

Christina guessed that her mother had said she was going
to London for Christmas shopping. Whether her father
believed her it was difficult to know. He might very well
suspect that Mrs Holt was going to see her daughter. But at

any rate he had not forbidden the excursion, and so long as she didn't actually tell him she had disobeyed him, he would ignore the peccadillo.

After dinner Inez called a cab to take them to Hebe Grant's home. This was a lavish property in Belgravia. Once again, in her home-made Philadelphian gown, Christina felt out-classed. But the welcome from Miss Grant soon put her at her ease.

'I want to tell you, Miss Holt, how much I admired you last night. You kept your temper like an angel!'

'I kept my temper,' Christina laughed, 'but there was nothing angelic about it. If you want to know, I was seething like the Devil!'

'Christina!' cried Inez in horror.

'Well, you didn't show it. Men are *so* contemptuous of women attempting anything outside the domestic circle.' Hebe Grant, tall and gawky, clenched and unclenched her fingers as if she would like to get some male antagonist in her grasp. 'So, Inez tells me you're interested in our mother-and-baby clinic in Edinburgh?'

'It's just what I've always wanted to do. I refused a very important post in Philadelphia so as to try and find work with women and children.'

'Has Inez told you that we have practically no money?'

'I understand all that. I'm simply hoping you'll consider a newly qualified practitioner—'

'Consider you! We'll embrace you with open arms!'

'But don't forget, my Pennsylvania degree doesn't permit me to practise medicine in this country. I shall have to qualify by taking a British degree.'

'And in the meantime there would be some drawbacks. I understand. But you see, we're having such difficulty finding enough women doctors, and we're aiming at a team of four. Two in the clinic, each taking eight hour shifts so as to have it open from seven in the morning until nine at night, and two out on visits. These two teams would alternate: it would be one day in the clinic and one day out, six days a week.' She looked at Christina out of anxious eyes. 'It really will be very hard work . . .'

'I should love it! I'm used to hard work.' She hesitated. 'Might I ask you to write soon to your management committee . . . ?'

'Write? I'll do better. I'll ring Lady Laingley this very minute!'

'Ring her?'

'On the telephone,' said Hebe, miming putting a receiver to her ear and holding the speaker. 'Please give me a moment.' She pressed a bellpush and a butler came. 'Sanders, please bring these ladies any refreshments they require.'

She vanished. They could hear her going into a room further down the hall.

'Can I bring you anything, ladies?' Sanders asked.

'I think I'll have a gin and tonic,' Inez said with a hint of rebellion in her tone. 'How about you, Christina?'

She shook her head. She was too strung up to want anything. Presently Sanders returned with the required gin and tonic. Inez took it, looked at it uncertainly, then sipped it as if it would bite her.

'If you don't really like it, why are you drinking it?' Christina asked.

Inez giggled. 'Because I shouldn't dare to do it at home. Matthew disapproves of women who drink spirits.'

'Inez, what is the point of supporting women's rights if you give in all along the line at home?'

'Oh, you don't understand,' the other girl said in some bitterness. 'You're never had to put up with a disapproving male!'

'You think not?' Christina said, but didn't pursue it.

When Hebe Grant returned, a broad smile split her horsey face. 'Lady Laingley is absolutely delighted. We had quite a chat. She says it would probably be asking too much to drag you away from your friends and relatives before Christmas, but wonders if you would take up the post from 2 January?'

'You mean . . . she said yes without even seeing me?'

'Oh, I told her how suitable you were, and all about your

Pennsylvania degree and all that. She quite understands you'll have to act as assistant until you get your British qualification. But that can easily be arranged. Her Ladyship has friends among the faculty at Surgeons' Hall. What exactly won't you be able to do, until you take the Edinburgh University exams?'

'Well, no operations, not even minor ones, and I shan't be able to prescribe . . .'

'What we'll do is, we'll get one of the other women to sign three or four prescription forms each day and you can enter the medicines above—'

'I don't think that would be entirely legal,' Christina laughed, taken with the other woman's enthusiasm.

'Och, havers, when there's poor women needing help, who cares about technicalities like the law? So long as we have doctors who are genuinely interested in women's complaints and don't keep telling them either it's all female imagination or else it's the will of God . . .'

'I guarantee not to tell them it's the will of God,' Christina said. 'That is, if you really are giving me this opportunity . . .'

'Giving you! My dear girl, we're begging you! Right, is it settled?'

'Yes, it's settled.'

Hebe Grant put out a bony hand. 'Shake!'

They shook. Inez sat by, beaming plumply.

When they reached home, Matthew and Elwin were comfortably settled before a good fire, listening to a disc recording of Tetrazzini on a fine modern gramophone with a scientifically corrected horn. Matthew raised a finger to impose silence until the last silvery notes had died away, then asked with mild interest, 'Have a nice little hen party with Hebe?'

'More than a hen party, I think, Matthew. Hebe arranged for Christina to start work for the Edinburgh Women's Clinic in January.'

There was a stunned silence. Then Elwin sat up from his lolling position in his armchair. 'You've got a job, Christina?'

'Yes.'

'Well, bully for you!' He leapt up, embraced her, and lifted her off her feet in jubilation.

'But I say,' Matthew was protesting, 'I say! You can't take a post in this country! You're not qualified . . .'

'That's all taken care of, Matthew,' Inez said with obvious satisfaction.

'But what sort of job is it, exactly?'

'It's working in a slum clinic.'

'But, my dear Christina! That sounds most unsuitable! I say, Elwin old boy, don't you think you ought to put a stop to this?'

Elwin let go of his sister, studied his friend with eyes that seemed to see him in a new light. 'Don't be an ass, Matt,' he said. 'If my sister can go all the way to America and get herself a degree, she can jolly well go to Edinburgh and handle slum kids.'

Matthew subsided, still looking unconvinced. Christina congratulated herself that in a little more than two weeks she would have left this obtuse man's home and wouldn't need to be polite to him any more.

That night Christina wrote to Lady Laingley at the address Hebe had given, enclosing copies of her certificates. She also wrote to Aunt Bea, reporting her good luck, and to Susanne and Mary and Youffie and, lastly, to Jo-Jo in California. She had no idea if the letter would ever reach Jo-Jo: it had to go care of a post office in Marysville, wherever that might be.

Friday came, and with it the engagement to meet her mother for tea. She allowed herself a luxurious bath using a great deal of Grossmith's bath salts, and spent a long time dressing her fair hair in a more elaborate style than usual. She put on her best costume of gunmetal wool neatened with matching braid, black felt hat trimmed with grey and crimson feathers, and her strapped black shoes. She didn't feel her winter coat was good enough to go to a hotel that had been patronised by the late King, so Inez lent her a sable stole.

She arrived in Piccadilly too early. The December afternoon was already rather dark, but the lamps shone bravely and the shops were alight for Christmas shoppers. A

Salvation Army band was playing with gusto before the Piccadilly Arcade. Horsebuses and motorbuses went by, interspersed with Rolls Royce and Lanchester cars. Outside the Trocadero, a flower girl was crying her wares: 'Vi'lets from Parma, lidies, vi'lets from Parma!'

As four o'clock showed on the clock of St James's, Christina walked back and in at the doors of the Ritz. The afternoon tea tables of the Palm Court were mostly occupied, but she found one under a great gilt mirror where her mother couldn't fail to see her.

'Tea, miss?'

'No, not at present,' she told the waiter, 'I'm waiting for my mother.'

'Very good.'

She had brought with her a medical journal. She opened it and began to read: the hard times in Philadelphia had taught her never to waste a moment. Half-past four chimed on a gilt clock at the far end of the room. She looked up from her magazine, a little startled. Her mother was rather late. The waiter, hovering, saw her gaze about.

'Were you wishing to order, miss?'

'No, I was wondering whether my mother . . . ? A lady asking for Miss Holt?'

'No, miss, no elderly lady has come in alone.'

'Thank you.'

'Do you wish to order tea now?'

'No, I'll wait a little longer.'

Sighing, he went away.

Five o'clock came, half-past five. Her mother didn't come.

At ten minutes to six the waiter made his final offer. 'Excuse me, miss, but if you don't order now it'll be too late for afternoon tea. We stop serving at six.'

'No, I—'

She saw his disappointment. For two hours she'd been taking up a table which might have yielded him not one, but two sets of tips. 'Yes, please, I'll order now.'

Immediately he was back with tea in a silver service, tiny

sandwiches on a paper-lace mat. He was so keen to be of service that he poured the first cup of tea for her. She found she was very thirsty, and drank it so hot it scalded her mouth. But when she tried one of the tiny sandwiches she found she couldn't swallow it. Her throat seemed to close up.

A great sob of disappointment welled up inside her. She put the white napkin to her mouth to stifle it. The magazine slipped from her lap. The waiter leapt to retrieve it. 'Anything wrong, miss?'

'No, thank you, nothing.'

'Don't like the sandwiches? I'll fetch the cakes.' He ran off, to return in a moment with a tray of pretty small cakes in all kinds of shapes and decorative treatments. He showed them to her, tongs hovering to pick one up and place it on her plate.

'No, thank you,' she said, shaking her head at them. They seemed to swim in front of her eyes, myriad little winking colours and gleams of sugared cream.

'Oh, *miss*,' sighed the waiter, and withdrew.

For a long time Christina sat there. The Palm Court emptied of its tea-time clients. Waiters hurried about taking off tablecloths, carrying away crockery and silverware, preparing the room to receive its evening guests, those coming to await friends for dinner. Christina became aware she was holding them back.

She signalled for the bill, paid it and added a substantial tip. The waiter said, 'Thank you, miss!' Then, seeing something in her face, he added, 'Perhaps your mother went to the wrong hotel, miss?'

She shook her head and went out. 'Taxi?' asked the doorman.

'No, thank you.' She shouldn't throw money away on taxis. Her funds were limited. Indeed, afternoon tea at the Ritz had cost her more than she could afford.

She set out on foot through the bustling Christmas crowd. Everyone seemed to be in laughing groups, husbands and wives together, mothers with children, friends and relations heading for pre-Christmas entertainment.

Christina was conscious of an intense loneliness. Without ever acknowledging it to herself, she had been looking forward too much to this meeting with her mother. It had symbolised a reunion with her past, a return to the roots of her being. Her mother had always been a faint, ineffectual creature, but she was part of Christina's heartland, loved for her deficiencies as much as for her gifts.

But she had failed to come to their rendezvous. And Christina could easily guess why.

At the last moment Mrs Holt's courage had failed her. Somewhere between her home in Market Bresham and her arrival at Liverpool Street Station, probably. A too vivid imagination had shown her a picture of what was likely to happen that evening: her husband asking, 'Well, did you enjoy your Christmas shopping? What did you buy?' And she, unused to deceit, stammering and flushing and making a mess of it . . .

She might even have been here, in London. At Selfridge's Store in Oxford Street, perhaps, choosing a shawl for old Mrs Cates or chocolates for Dorothy Spinshall.

Ah, why couldn't she have come? Why couldn't she have summoned enough defiance to meet her own daughter?

With tears often blurring her vision, Christina Holt walked slowly through the streets of London back to her brother's lodgings.

Chapter Thirteen

The newspapers Christina bought for her train journey north were busy reviewing 1911 which had just ended. *The Times* worried a little about the problems with Turkey, then talked in a lordly way about the foolish antics of the suffragettes who had rioted in Whitehall, and with whole-heartedly approval about the State visit of King George and Queen Mary to India.

The *Scotsman* was more concerned with the downturn in trade and with the World Missionary Conference which had taken place in Edinburgh. She concluded that the Scots were concerned hardheadedly with finance, and warm-heartedly with doing good. In those respects, they reminded her of Philadelphians.

She was met at the station by Lady Laingley and her secretary. 'You will recognise us,' the secretary had written, 'by means of a bunch of white heather which I shall be carrying.' Sure enough, there she was, a small dark woman in navy, carrying a little bouquet tied with tartan ribbons. At her side and towering over her was a middle-aged lady in tweeds, furs and feathers.

'My dear lass!' cried Her Ladyship, forging ahead at her like a battleship under full steam. 'What a dreadful night to be seeing Edinburgh for the first time. This is what we call a *haar*.' She gestured at the mist that was slowly curveting around her, dimming the station lights. 'Didn't make your train very late, luckily. Come, child, I've engaged a room for you next to mine at the North British, just so that you can be comfortable for at least one night. Porter!'

At her gesture a porter came running. Miss McNeill, the

secretary, took charge of having the luggage brought up to the hotel. Lady Laingley led Christina up a steep slope into Princes Street, which was visible through the raw yet romantic mist.

'I ordered a meal.'

'Oh, thank you, I ate on the train . . .'

'But that was two hours ago, and by the time you've unpacked a little and tidied yourself, I daresay you'll feel peckish. Besides, I want the chance to talk to you before you embark on this work.'

Seeing that it would be useless to argue with this formidable lady, Christina gave in.

When she came downstairs to join the two women in the dining-room, she found them at a quiet table in a corner of a lofty room painted a darkish green but well lit with gasoliers. There were many diners, yet more than one of the waiters were hovering attentively about Lady Laingley.

'Very well, you can serve now,' she said, waving her hand. Christina sat down, to be served at once with a plate of very thick, hot soup. 'Eat up,' commanded Her Ladyship. 'You're nothing but skin and bone!'

Christina tried to obey. The soup was much too salty for her taste. She was to learn quite soon that the Scots liked their food with plenty of salt and plenty of sugar. When she later saw the bad teeth in the mouths of the patients at the clinic, they didn't surprise her at all. Bad teeth and too many cheap sweets . . .

'Perhaps the beginning of January wasn't the best time to bring you here,' Her Ladyship began after quaffing largely of a sweet German wine served with the fish. 'The day after New Year is not a good time for us Scots. We're all suffering from sore heads and short tempers after too much self-indulgence.'

'But on the other hand,' prompted the secretary.

'On the other hand, as you say, McNeill, you'll see some typical cases at the clinic tomorrow. Women who are suffering the after-effects.'

Christina was a little surprised. 'Are you saying the women here are heavy drinkers?'

'No, no, not at all. They take a dram at New Year, of course – who doesn't? No, what I meant was you'll see cuts and bruises. They get knocked about a bit by their men.'

'Lady Laingley!'

'I mean it, my dear. When the men who live in slum buildings get drunk they hit their womenfolk. Normally you'd see three or four cases on a Monday, after the weekend's brawls, but at this time of year you'll mebbe see ten or twelve. I just wanted you to be prepared for it.'

Christina nodded. 'I have seen women after domestic disputes,' she said. 'I did voluntary work at a clinic in Philadelphia where we had some Irish families—'

'Ah, the Celts,' sighed Lady Laingley. 'It's our cross – we discovered how to make whisky and then couldn't withstand the temptation to drink what we made. Well, well, on the whole your work will not be stitching up cut cheeks or putting arnica on black eyes. The main problems are—'

'Malnutrition, poor hygiene, and too many babies,' Christina suggested.

Her Ladyship raised bushy eyebrows. 'You're no fool, for all you look as if you had just stepped down out of a cloud. Finished your fish, dear? Waiter, waiter!'

It dawned on Christina that the food had been ordered to suit her hostess's tastes. A substantial roast was wheeled up, slices were cut off, vegetables appeared in silver tureens. Claret was poured into glasses.

'My dear child, take a little more – it's Scotch beef, you know, the best in the world. Waiter, where's the gravy? And don't forget the horseradish.' Lady Laingley attacked her food with unimpaired appetite. Chewing, she went on, 'My dear husband always used to say we could stamp out impetigo and ringworm if only we could install a bath in every house in Edinburgh. Dear man, he knew we should never accomplish that. But one of your tasks will be to help the women learn how to cope with headlice . . .'

'Your Ladyship,' interposed the secretary in a tone of long-suffering, 'may we discuss such points after we've finished eating?'

'What? Oh, there's for you, McNeill! You're right, of course. Nothing ever puts me off my oats but I daresay our new friend finds it a bit—'

'Not at all. It's all quite familiar to me, Your Ladyship. In Philadelphia there are slums, believe me, and the ailments and diseases – particularly among newly arrived immigrants – were of the same kind.'

Lady Laingley began to cross-question her about the nationalities she had treated, trying to find out for instance whether it was true that Russians and Poles were really predisposed to tuberculosis, and if Jewish women were better at breastfeeding than Gentiles. She had all sorts of extraordinary little bits of knowledge, betokening an inquiring mind which had never been properly disciplined.

At midnight she at last rose from the table. 'Well, Dr Holt, I expect you're ready for your bed. McNeill and I will see you at breakfast, after which we'll take you to the Canongate. Shall we say nine o'clock?'

They went up in the lift together. Almost unable to stifle her yawns, Christina went to her room. Full of heavy food and a little drunk from too much wine, she fell into bed.

Next morning at nine the *haar* still persisted. Lady Laingley nodded grimly at the view outside the dining-room window. 'McNeill and I are driving back to Bannsie later – that's where I live, it's on the south side of the Pentlands. Too far to come to Edinburgh every day, I fear, but I keep in touch by the telephone.'

'You don't mean the clinic has a telephone?'

'Dear Dr Holt, if you imagine we can afford such luxuries on charity donations, you are an idealist! No, no, I telephone Miss Gurnard and she reports on how things are going.' She broke off to say to the waiter, 'I'll have the kippers, please, and rolls with butter, and a pot of tea.' Then to Christina, 'You should have the same, doctor. You need a substantial meal for the kind of day you have ahead of you.'

Christina submitted to having her breakfast imposed on her, happy in the thought that this goodhearted but bossy lady would be unable to supervise any more of her meals.

She learned with surprise that when they drove home, Lady Laingley herself would be the driver. Miss McNeill looked less than happy at the thought.

'But first we'll deliver you and your belongings at the clinic. It was formerly a shop, you must know, and the living quarters are above it. That's so that if a doctor is needed as an emergency at night, there's always someone available.'

'I see.'

'Ach, don't sound so apprehensive. It's not a palace, but you'll have your own wee room and I've installed a bath and the other necessary plumbing. I can tell you, it caused a proper sensation in the Canongate when the bath was carted in!'

The kippers came. Christina found herself unable to eat more than a mouthful. She was too apprehensive, too eager to get started on the day.

At last they were in the car, a Lanchester. Christina's trunk was in the boot, Lady Laingley was at the wheel. They sailed off in an erratic curve, frightening a van horse trying to come round the corner from South Bridge which Lady Laingley was negotiating. Miss McNeill went pale but merely clenched her teeth a little harder.

The shop was on the corner of a building known as Shoemaker's Land. It had been painted a serviceable green, its window had been cleaned and then papered halfway up on the inside so as to make it opaque. The door, half glass, bore the legend 'Edinburgh Women's Clinic' in the same green paint.

The appearance of Lady Laingley's car caused a furore. Windows were thrown up on the upper floors of the adjacent buildings, women hung out of them to view the proceedings, and the door of the clinic flew open. Out hastened two girls in wrap-around white cotton coats.

'Your Ladyship! On time almost to the minute! How do you do? And you must be Dr Holt.'

Christina found herself being shaken enthusiastically by the hand and dragged indoors. The interior of the shop was like its exterior: serviceable, neat, cheaply refurbished.

There was new brown linoleum on the floor, walls painted dark green to shoulder-height and cream thereafter, a bench along each of two walls, and a desk and chair occupying most of the third. There were cupboards and an alcove with a sink and a gas ring.

Beyond that was a curtain, which allowed access to the back room, which had been curtained off into three cubicles. There was a tall steel cabinet for instruments, a glass cabinet for medicines, and one chair. There were three doors. One was half open to reveal a capacious store cupboard, another led out to a backyard over which a glass canopy had been arranged to shelter wooden boxes and two folded camp beds, the third showed a short passage and a stone staircase.

'This way with the trunk,' said the women, manhandling it towards the staircase.

'Wait, it's full of books, it's too heavy . . .'

'All right, then, two people each end.'

Christina and Miss McNeill took one end, the two others took the upper end, and thus the trunk was jolted upstairs.

Over the shop there were two more rooms, and above that yet two more. Christina's was on the upper floor. By the time they got there, everyone was ready to flop down on the floor to recover.

'I'm Agnes Kirkland,' said the taller of the girls, extending her hand. 'It was Jessie who dragged you indoors – Jessie Brunton.'

Gasping after the exertion, Christina nodded and shook hands. When she had recovered she said, 'Did I see four rooms?'

'Yes, we use one as a sitting-room – the one immediately below this.'

'That means three bedrooms for four doctors?'

'It's all right, no sharing. I don't sleep on the premises,' Agnes said. 'I'm an Edinburgh woman, I go home to my family each night.'

She was a handsome, brown-haired young woman of about twenty-eight or twenty-nine. Jessie was older, perhaps thirty-five, with an imposing bosom and ample hips kept under control by a stiffly starched blouse and heavy tailored skirt.

'Where's the fourth member of the team?' Christina inquired.

'Smollett – Florence Smollett. She's not on duty till this evening. She's gone out to do some shopping – bread and milk and so on. We're still in the process of moving in, you see.'

'Lady Laingley implied you'd have a queue of broken heads after the festivities.'

'No-o,' said Jessie with a sigh, ' so far all we've had is a few kindly calls of "Get away hame, ye daft besoms!"'

'My dears!' came ringing up the stairs from Lady Laingley, 'I've put the kettle on the gas ring for tea. Come along down so we can have a chat.'

Miss McNeill leapt to obey. Jessie and Agnes rose to their feet more slowly. 'She's a dear, really,' murmured Agnes. 'It's just she likes to give orders.'

Down they went. 'There's no milk yet—' Agnes was beginning.

'Oh yes there is, I brought some. And biscuits.' From her capacious handbag she produced a small tin of Edinburgh shortbread and a flask which she had clearly had filled in the hotel before leaving. 'Never move without provisions,' Lady Laingley advised. 'If you'd looked after the men on shoots as often as I have, you'd know that.'

The kettle on the gas ring began to sing. Agnes brought out a brown pottery teapot, a blue paper bag of sugar, and a silver-paper packet of tea. The milk was flavoured faintly with the whisky which had obviously been contained in the flask previously.

The secretary and the women doctors sat on the benches, allowing Her Ladyship the luxury of the chair at the desk. Despite the fact that she had eaten a substantial breakfast only an hour before, she made great inroads on the tin of shortbread. Between mouthfuls she reminded the medical staff that they must keep careful records both of patients and of medical supplies, that Miss Gurnard or some other member of the management committee would drop in from time to time, that in any emergency other than medical they could telephone herself or Miss Gurnard, and that their behaviour must be beyond reproach in every respect.

'The local police are not greatly in favour of this project,' she told them. 'The Superintendent remarked that while he had no objections to a special clinic for women's complaints, he had grave reservations about four unmarried women living and working in this area.'

'Ha!' snorted Jessie Brunton. 'I'd like to see any of the local lads making himself objectionable to *me*!' She shrugged her powerful shoulders, making her bosom bounce under its starch.

'While I sympathise with your reaction, it's not the best one in this neighbourhood,' Lady Laingley counselled. 'The men don't like anything that they can see as "interference". One of the main tasks will be to get them on our side.'

'Good God,' Christina exclaimed, 'surely no man could object if we helped improve the health of his wife and family?'

'Of course not. But . . . er . . . there are personal matters . . . as between husband and wife . . . you know what I mean. They don't like to think their wives are talking about them to some strange woman.'

'Their wives will be talking to *doctors* . . .'

'But they won't think of you as doctors, that's the point. To them you'll just be one more set of interfering women. So I warn you to be very, very careful.'

The door opened and the fourth of the clinic's doctors came in, laden with packages in a string bag and carrying a pint milk-can. 'Hello, having a housewarming party? You might have waited until I got back!'

Introductions were made, fresh tea was prepared, and Florence Smollett produced a batch of sticky buns. Good heavens, thought Christina, is that all they ever think of here – eating? But after consuming a bun and a fresh cup of tea, Lady Laingley announced her intention of driving home to Bannsie, beckoning Christina to accompany her out to the car.

'I meant to say to you, doctor – get off that bonnet, you rascal! —that I spoke to Sir Joseph Bainbridge-Clark about getting your Edinburgh degree. There's no problem. Perhaps you'll drop in at Surgeons' Hall when you have some time off? Ask for the Medical Registrar's secretary, Mr Paterson. There are some papers to sign and you'll have to produce copies of your certificates.'

'Yes, I have them.'

'Joe said that—'

'Joe?'

'Sir Joseph – oh, he and I have been friends since we were bairns! Plain Joe Bainbridge he used to be, but as he's gone up the ladder he's added titles and appendages.' She grinned. 'But he's the same good laddie at heart. He said if you'd like to retake finals in the summer along with the rest of the University, it would give you time to bone up a little. He mentioned that some of the classifications are different here – an old-fashioned school, Edinburgh. But Agnes Kirkland can give you tips on that.'

'Thank you very much, ma'am.'

'There! Now you do sound as if you come from Philadelphia! Well, goodbye and good luck.' She hit out with her handbag at the urchins who were clambering over the Lanchester. 'I wonder where all the patients are?' she said with a last glance about. 'Probably spying on you all from their windows, wondering if they should come down to have a boil lanced! Goodbye, goodbye!'

She drove off with a lurch, Miss McNeill holding on grimly to the window trim on the passenger side.

That was Wednesday, 3 January. There were no patients that day, nor the next, nor the next. The girls settled down into a routine, those on duty sitting patiently in surgery waiting for clients, those off duty housekeeping, shopping for food and cleaning materials and a pot-plant to brighten the place. Christina duly paid her visit to the offices of the University to register as a student in the Faculty of Medicine sitting finals.

She went about on foot, trying to learn the geography of

the district. Her main landmarks were the Castle, which told her she was near Princes Street, and the Palace of Holyrood House which, ironically enough, stood at the top of the street of slums known as the Canongate, the thoroughfare of the canons of an ancient Augustinian abbey.

On Saturday, the appearance of the Canongate changed a little. Women were to be seen going into a doorway up the hill, then coming out with brown paper parcels under their arms.

'What on earth is it?' Christina wondered aloud. 'What are they buying?'

'They're not buying. Today's pay day. They're getting their Sunday clothes out of pawn to wear tomorrow.'

'Agnes!'

'I mean it. About Wednesday the family runs out of money. Mammy takes the Sunday clothes to pop at Uncle's. They eke out until Saturday. Daddy comes home with his pay-packet at dinnertime, Mammy runs to Uncle's to get back the clothes. Tonight Daddy will drink up all his wages except the few shillings Mammy has managed to screw out of him for the rent and food, and by Wednesday it's back to the pawnshop.'

Christina was appalled. 'That's no kind of life!'

'Times are hard in Scotland, Christina, and hardest of all in the old tenements where the poor have to live. Few of the men here have steady jobs, I imagine: if they had, they'd move out to somewhere better than the Canongate. They're casual labourers, cadgers, millhands. And yet it's ironic. This used to be one of the upper-class parts of Edinburgh.'

Christina gazed out of the window at the buildings where lamplight was beginning to glow as the winter evening approached. 'Yes, you can see they're built of fine stone, with curlicues and such. I wonder who lived here?'

Agnes nodded at Florence, who was on her knees tending the sitting-room fire. 'Florence's namesake, Tobias Smollett the author, lived near here about a hundred and fifty years ago. Courtiers lived in houses as close to the Palace as they could. Huntly House up the road was a noble's residence, and so was Moray House. Strange to see how it's come down in the world.'

'It's always the same,' put in Florence. 'In Paris the grandees' houses are full of poor people. Streets in Rome where Papal courtiers lived are let off to women of ill-repute.'

Christina returned to her book. She was rereading her medical textbooks and wishing she could get some practical work to keep her hand in.

She got her wish. About ten that night there was a tremendous uproar in the street, shouting, smashing, the trundling of cartwheels, screams, oaths, the neighing of terrified horses.

Agnes Kirkland had gone home to her family. The three other women were in preparation for bed. Christina threw on her clothes again, ran downstairs in the dark, and unlocked the clinic door. She was just about to open it when a fist hammered on it from outside.

'Doctor, doctor! Come on oot! You're sair needed!'

She flung open the door. On the threshold a fat middle-aged woman leaned, panting. Beyond her, about a hundred yards down the Canongate, lights were swinging about, people were running to and fro, a vague square mass could be seen across the pavement.

'What on earth has happened?'

'A drunken carman juist drove his waggon through the window of McLowery's Bar! Come on, doctor, whit are ye staundin' there for?'

'Just let me get my bag!' She darted indoors, shouting up the staircase, 'Florence! Jessie! There's been an accident! Hurry up!'

The woman in the doorway was gone. Christina picked up her skirts from about her ankles and ran. Outside McLowery's Bar three or four men were helping a pair of horses to stand up. Smashed glass lay about everywhere. Two men lay unconscious on the pavement under the remains of the van, another was groaningly trying to get himself to his feet.

Christina helped him up. 'Are you all right?'

'Ma heid, ma heid!'

In the flickering light of lanterns she examined him. He was bleeding profusely from a scalp wound but not in immediate danger. Florence came rushing up and knelt by one of the prone figures. Jessie took over the examination of the other.

'Inside, missus, inside here,' called an urgent voice.

She picked her way over the glass and shattered joinery. A fire was springing up inside the bar, lit by capsized lamps. Men were beating at it with their jackets. Heavy marble tables had been overturned, their surfaces smashed. Under the debris lay three or four men, one moving feebly, trying to crawl free.

But worst hit of all were the two figures at the front of the bar. One had been impaled by a great shard of plate glass through the stomach. The other had two daggers of glass through his arm and sleeve, pinning him to the floor.

Christina put her head to the chest of the man with the stomach injury. His heart had ceased to beat. She turned to the other. He was cursing and swearing horribly, giving clear notice that he was alive, if kicking.

'Keep still!' she ordered. 'If you writhe about like that you're going to cut your arm off at the shoulder.'

'Ach, God, git me oot o' here! Ma airm, ma airm!'

'Keep still, you fool!' She captured his good arm, which was flailing in his efforts to wrest himself free. 'Here, somebody, hold him down.'

A helper appeared, threw himself down to use both hands in keeping the patient still.

A voice spoke from behind her. 'Now, now, this is no place for a lady . . .'

She jerked her head round. A uniformed police constable stood behind her.

'I'm a doctor,' she said sharply. 'Help get this glass out. He's got to be taken to hospital or he'll lose that arm.'

'But, look here, miss—'

'*Do as I tell you!*'

There was no arguing with that tone of voice.

Dumbfounded, the constable knelt at her side.

With infinite care she drew out the dagger of glass from the forearm. She wound a bandage quickly round the site of the injury. But it was the shoulder wound that mattered.

'Hold him,' she warned her helpers. Her patient shrieked in agony, and she wished – oh, how she wished – that she had some morphine in her bag to give him. But she had only a basic medical kit, and she must act quickly before in his pain he made the wound utterly irremediable.

She took hold of the upper end of the piece of glass with hands wrapped in bandages. She said to her helpers, 'On three, hold him.' Then, quickly, 'One, two, *three*!' and with a jerk the stalagmite of glass was uplifted and thrown aside.

There was the clanging of ambulance bells. Motor ambulances drew up in the causeway. Two attendants came running in.

'Quick, a stretcher – have you got morphine?'

'No, miss, but who—?'

'Never mind, a tourniquet; two men, one to apply, one to hold him down. You there, take hold of this stretcher . . .'

'I'll take it, miss.'

Another dark blue uniform appeared. 'May I ask what the de'il you ladies think you're doing?'

He had silver buttons on his shoulders – a superior officer, an inspector, perhaps. Jessie Brunton came up behind him, supporting a lad of about eighteen whose arm was in a sling.

'We're attending to patients, inspector. We're the doctors from the clinic down the road.'

'What, from Shoemaker's Land?'

And that was how the Edinburgh Women's Clinic in Canongate became known as the Shoemaker Doctors.

Chapter Fourteen

The doctors' popularity following the accident at McLowery's Bar, and the confidence in them that it engendered, brought a sudden flow of patients to the Clinic. Christina found to her amazement that she was incapable of helping them. For one reason: she could scarcely understand a word they said. And when she in her turn spoke, she was greeted with a flood of nervous giggles.

'It's because they're speaking broad Scots,' Agnes said, trying to comfort her. 'And more than that, it's a special dialect of broad Scots. They live in a kind of enclave here, especially the women. They only ever talk to each other, you might say. You'll just have to learn it, as if it were a foreign language.'

'But when *I* speak to them, they don't understand *me*.'

'Why should they? You're speaking English.'

'But surely, when they're at school, the teacher must speak English?'

'But not with your accent. You're speaking English English, or even English with an American tinge. And don't forget, when they had to listen to a teacher at school speaking good Scots-English, she never asked them personal questions about their intestines or their breasts!'

'Oh, Lord,' groaned Christina.

She never really learned Canongate-Scots. But she did learn to speak in a very straightforward fashion so that she could be understood. She thereby at last reached a day when she could be of some use in the Clinic.

Even so, she knew she sometimes shocked the patients. Mrs Nicolson, mother of ten, was aghast when Doctor told her she ought not have any more children. These were matters on which no one spoke: even medical students received no directions on how to deal with marital problems. Mrs Nicolson went red at Christina's advice.

'But it's the will of God, doctor!'

'Not exactly. You can take steps to prevent conception.'

'Whit's that ye're saying?'

'You can prevent your husband giving you a baby . . .'

'Och, get away wi' you! Prevent ma Jock? It wad tak the whole o' the Hundredth Hussars!'

'No, I mean that even though you and he make love, you needn't get pregnant. You can use something to prevent it from happening.'

'Whit-like a something? A perfoom that'll put him aff?'

'No. A small sponge soaked in olive oil.'

'Eh?' Mrs Nicolson shifted her one-year-old from one arm to the other. 'And whit do I do wi' that?'

'You put it where it'll do the most good.'

'But whaur's yon?'

A long pause.

Then Mrs Nicolson said, affronted, 'I couldna bring masel to do sich a thing! Whit an idea!'

Out she marched. All the same, Christina couldn't help thinking that the notion might stay with her. Particularly for those nights when Jock Nicolson came home a little the worse for the whisky, looking for the comforts of home.

The doctors soon noticed that some of the patients had their favourites: Mrs McDowell would only come into the surgery if Jessie Brunton was on duty, likewise Nancy Brown, the shy daughter of Mary Brown. Little old Miss Hewett would only tell her troubles to Agnes. Florence Smollett was the choice of those adolescent girls who were having trouble with the onset of maturity.

But all the children without exception loved Christina. She could make a fretful baby lie still while its wheezing chest was examined. She only had to be called, and young Jamie with the ear-ache would stand quiet while Florence looked into his ear. Almost any crying child would fall silent if she took it in her arms.

'How do you do it? Is it hypnotism?' demanded Florence. 'Or do you utter silent spells?'

'Neither of those. I don't know what causes it.'

'It's kind of uncanny,' Agnes said. 'I think you're in a pact with the devil.'

'Don't be silly – with the angels, more like,' Jessie objected. 'It's a power for good, however you come by it, Chrissie. Have you always had it?'

'No,' she replied, thinking back. It had come to her with the birth of her own baby. Perhaps its purpose was to remind her of her loss each time a hurt child took comfort from her – a kind of punishment, a gift for which she had to pay with hidden guilt and remorse. In every child she saw, she felt she could trace in those unformed baby features some likeness to Stephen. Any child with fair hair, with dark blue eyes . . . And yet in *every* child there was something of Stephen: vulnerability, need, a trust that grown-ups would be caring and helpful.

Soon after she sat her British medical exams, a letter at last reached her from Jo-Jo Belu. It began by congratulating her on finding a post in Edinburgh, but almost immediately went on in a tirade about the injustice being done to Serbia by Turkey. 'My friends and relations on the borders of Macedonia write to say that Turkish troops carry out massacres without hindrance in those territories along the border and sometimes, even, across into Montenegro. It is shameful that the European nations do nothing to help their fellow-Christians . . .'

Christina was surprised. Jo-Jo had never seemed particularly 'Christian' while she was in Philadelphia. She had seldom gone to church, although there was a Serbian Orthodox priest who took services regularly for a small congregation in the suburb of Reading.

The European political scene meant almost nothing to Christina. From looking at newspapers she knew vaguely that the Turkish Empire was apparently crumbling, and that in its death throes it was crushing and strangling small countries over which it had power – Albania, Macedonia, Thrace . . . These small states had begged the great powers for help. The result, she seemed to recall, had been some kind of treaty with Turkey called the 'Peace with Honour'.

Headlines announcing 'Trouble in the Balkans' or 'Balkan Students Riot' had become so commonplace that one scarcely heeded them. Like rain or the toothache, they were part of the less pleasant side of life.

Yet here was Jo-Jo pouring out page after page of complaint. Only near the end did her friend remember to give her any news of herself. 'Here in Marysville we are learning to grow fruit. Our community now numbers fifteen, and I have been able to help first of all with our own health problems and also in bringing in income by tending the other inhabitants of the town. We think of moving to the San Fernando Valley if we can increase our numbers to twenty. I wish you had come with me, dear Christina, you could have had a good life here – though it is hard work.'

She ended with love and good wishes, begging Christina to send news and also any medical journals for which she no longer had any use.

From that time on Christina paid more attention to Balkan affairs in the newspapers. In October, she read with astonishment that the tiny state of Montenegro had declared war on Turkey. A few days later Turkey retaliated by declaring war on Serbia and Bulgaria.

'Serbia! I have a friend who's a Serbian!' gasped Christina from behind her newspaper.

'Will he go for a soldier?' Florence inquired.

'It's a she. And no, she's actually in California. But I imagine she'll take this business very much to heart!'

'Much good that will do, if she's ten thousand miles away,' muttered Florence, refusing to take it seriously.

All the same, it was a serious war, a dreadful war. Correspondents sent back horrific accounts from the front lines. Casualties were very heavy on both sides and the state of the wounded was little better than at the time of the Crimean War. Yet it was the great Turkish Empire that was suffering most. The little kingdom of Montenegro captured a string of towns with extraordinary names: Detchitch, Skiptchank, Tuzi, Beranei, Tarabosh and then – ah, one that any admirer of Florence Nightingale had heard of – Scutari. The Serbian Prince Alexander won a great victory at Uskub. To the disbelief of most newspaper readers, reports came through that flying machines had been used to spy out enemy positions and give directions to gunners. It was a strange kind of war, a new kind of war.

Christina's second graduation day came. For this she needed a white dress to wear under a borrowed student's gown. She had no money to buy one, so Agnes suggested she should buy some cheap material in one of the shops in the Grassmarket. But how to get it made up?

The women patients, now much more friendly than when the Clinic had first opened, came to her aid. Little Miss Hewett had been a dressmaker before arthritis forced her retirement. Mrs Allerdyce had done plain sewing as a housemaid. Between them they cut out and made a simple gown, ankle-length of course, with a plain, slightly flared skirt, nipped-in waist, round neck, and bishop sleeves. The trimming, which fashion made absolutely obligatory, was devised from pieces of curtain net bought as remnants in the same shop. Worn with Captain Dinsdorf's gold chain, the dress looked surprisingly elegant.

Elwin came up to Edinburgh for the ceremony, which was held in the stately MacEwan Hall standing between the School of Medicine, which Christina had attended only for the written exams and the vivas, and the Students' Union, which she'd never visited at all. Christina sat in one of the front rows with the other students receiving their degrees: alphabetical order, men and women mixed as they seldom were otherwise.

Elwin thought they looked impressive, in their black academic robes and fur-edged, magenta hoods. He thought it less impressive when his sister almost tripped over her student's gown, which she had to hold up with both hands as she mounted the podium. Student gowns, he learned afterwards from a disgruntled Christina, were only made in men's sizes, and this gown, although it belonged to Agnes Kirkland, was too large for Agnes and twice too large for her.

There was a small celebration afterwards at the Clinic. 'Does Father know you're here?' Christina asked as he sipped the inevitable strong Scottish tea.

He shook his head. 'But Mother does. I told her I was going to attend your graduation and she gave me this for you.' He produced a little packet.

Unwrapped, it proved to be a tiny silver-framed photograph of her mother. A note was tucked in the back. 'Dear child, Forgive me for failing to keep our appointment at the Ritz. I bitterly regret it. I'm so proud of you and know your father will be too, one day. Your loving Mother.'

The other girls crowded round, admiring the gift. Christina tucked the note in the bosom of her dress. It was the only letter she'd had from her mother since she had left home six years ago.

Elwin's graduation present was a cheque. 'Seems to me you need cash more than kickshaws, Chrissie. I don't believe you're even eating properly.'

'Oh yes I am. I just burn it off, that's all.' She laid a thin hand on his sleeve. 'When shall I be sending you presents, Elwin? Wedding presents?'

He moved awkwardly in embarrassment. 'I don't know . . . Things have gone sort of cool between me and Dot . . .'

Privately Christina didn't wonder at it. Dorothy Spinshall was the same age as herself. At twenty-three most girls were married, or at least engaged. 'What happened? Did she find someone else?'

'Nothing like that. It's just that . . . I can't seem to see myself settled down and married. After all, what's the rush? There's plenty of time.'

For a man, perhaps. For a woman, no. She wondered how

to explain this to him without making him feel trapped into the marriage with Dorothy.

'You do want to get married? Eventually? I mean, you don't see yourself as a lifelong bachelor?'

'Maybe, Christina . . . Maybe that's what I am . . . And yet I like girls, you know. I . . . I'm quite *normal*.' He looked at her with an anxious sideways glance.

She didn't really understand what he meant. Of course he was 'normal'. It was only many years later she came to know what he was trying to tell her – that his sexual persuasions were not unusual.

The year rolled on. In the Canongate the policemen still patrolled in pairs, although the Shoemaker Doctors hurried to and fro unmolested. The infections of summer – chicken-pox, scarlet fever – gave way to the infections of winter: whooping cough, influenza, pneumonia.

A strange little epidemic began among the children. It was Christina who identified it as osteo-myelitis. She rushed the first case to the Royal Infirmary in a taxi, afraid to wait for an ambulance since the child was in such a desperate plight by the time she was brought to the Clinic.

Christina had seen it in the children's ward of the University Hospital in Philadelphia. The pale anguished look of the child, beset by pains in the joints for which there seemed no reason, the high temperature, the moans when the swellings were touched. She heard Dr Fehr's voice as they looked through a microscope in the path. lab. at the staphylococci: 'The symptoms are often mistaken for acute rheumatism, but the mischief is *not* in the joint and this child will develop blood-poisoning unless treated at once . . .'

Later the Casualty Officer sent her a note saying she had undoubtedly saved Betty Babson's life.

One evening soon after, she was in one of the tenement buildings attending a child in a very bad state from pneumonia. The parents, a rowdy pair normally, were weeping by the bed. They had not been to church since they were married, but now they felt the need of religious comfort. Someone had sent for a minister, but he hadn't come.

'Say us a wee bit prayer for the bairn, doctor,' begged Mrs Taylor.

'Me?' Christina was startled.

'Aye, a few words frae your lips, it wad be a comfort.'

She was at a complete loss. Although she'd gone to church regularly with her parents all through her childhood, in Philadelphia Sundays had become too precious to waste on hymn-singing while there was study to do.

But the parents, and the other children of the family, were gazing at her beseechingly. She searched in her mind, and at last words arose to help her.

'I will lift up mine eyes unto the hills, from whence cometh my help. My help cometh from the Lord, which made heaven and earth. He will not suffer thy foot to be moved; He that keepeth thee will not slumber . . .'

She looked at the family, hoping that would be enough. But they were standing about the bed, eyes closed, hands folded, expecting more.

What came next? She tried over some phrases but knew she had missed a verse when she began again. 'The Lord is thy keeper, the Lord is thy shade . . . thy shade . . .'

'Upon thy right hand,' took up a strong voice from the doorway.

They all turned. A young man in a dark suit and high starched collar was standing there, bareheaded. 'The sun shall not smite thee,' he recited, 'nor the moon by night.' He went on with perfect confidence to the end of the psalm.

'Thank you, minister. And thank *you*, doctor,' murmured Mr and Mrs Taylor.

'I'll take over now,' the newcomer said in a low voice to Christina as she made her way out. 'The child is dying?'

She nodded wordlessly.

'I'm very sorry. My name's Douglas Fairforth, by the way, and I'm not a minister, I'm a divinity student.'

'Christina Holt.' They shook hands.

'It's good to meet someone who takes religion into the sick-room,' he commented.

It wasn't the moment to correct him. And from that

misunderstanding arose a friendship that proved a great trial to Christina.

'But you *are* religious!' Douglas would insist whenever the incident was recalled. 'The fact that the right words came to your lips when you needed them – that proves it.'

'No, it doesn't, it only proves I've got a retentive memory.'

'You don't know your own nature.'

Douglas was always sure he knew best. He was older than Christina by some seven years, already a qualified doctor and now studying divinity so that he could go to the Congo as a missionary. His missionary work had already begun, at a centre run by the Church of Scotland in a disused warehouse. Here the drunks and derelicts of the Canongate could get a bowl of broth and a slice of bread at any time of the day or night, and here each evening Douglas or one of his colleagues held a service through which the drunks and derelicts snoozed in comfort.

Christina, on being invited to inspect it, couldn't help but smile to herself. She'd come to know the inhabitants of the district quite well. She guessed they thought Douglas a poor, misguided soul, wasting his time on men who didn't even want to be saved.

'I don't mind,' he told her when she murmured something of this to him. 'I've worked amongst them ever since I was a medical student, I know they're a bunch of hard cases. But you're here yourself on something of the same kind of lost cause. You're trying to persuade the women to stop giving their children "dummies" dipped in condensed milk. You're trying to change the men's attitudes to their wives. You must believe it's possible, surely?'

'*Touché,*' laughed Christina. Though over-earnest, he was no fool. You had to admire his perseverance.

The other women doctors quite liked him. They were more accustomed to being preached at than Christina. Besides, he was undeniably handsome with his tall spare figure and penetrating blue glance.

'He can save *my* soul any time,' muttered Florence Smollett. 'How can you be so argumentative with him, Christina?'

'What's the matter, I'm not allowed to argue with a divinity student?'

But she didn't enjoy the arguments. Douglas had got it into his head that Fate had sent him the ideal wife to accompany him to the Congo when he took holy orders.

'Don't you see, you could treat the women and children, I'd handle the men and get the church built—'

'Douglas, I don't want to go to the Congo.'

'But why not? There's work waiting to be done.'

'Good heavens, don't you think there's enough work here?'

'But there are people here to do the work, Christina,' he countered in a grave tone. 'There's no one to save the souls of those poor savages.'

'It seems to me they've got along quite well without having their souls saved until now. Really, I can't see that we have the *right*—'

'It's a God-given right.'

And so on. Douglas was totally convinced that he had a direct summons from the Almighty to convert the heathen. Christina was very dubious that the Almighty wanted everyone in the Congo to be a Scottish Presbyterian.

In her hours off duty, she liked to go to the theatre. It was possible to get into the gallery at the Lyceum Theatre for sixpence. When Douglas heard of it, he was shocked. 'The theatre is the abode of moral laxity,' he scolded.

'Where do you advise me to go on my time off, then?' she said in annoyance. 'A prayer meeting?'

'Why not?'

'I hate prayer meetings!'

'Have you ever been to one?'

'Well . . . no . . .'

Nothing would content him except that she must come to one he would be attending next Saturday night. That happened to be 5 July 1913, and on that Saturday the British newspapers came out with banner headlines: RENEWED FIGHTING – BALKAN WAR BREAKS OUT AGAIN.

Because it was now well known that Christina was interested in matters concerning the Balkans, Jessie Brunton brought in the evening paper on her way home from her rounds. The report stated that on 30 June, Bulgaria had attacked Serbia and Greece.

'Bulgaria? I thought Bulgaria and Serbia were *allies*,' said Agnes.

'Oh, it's impossible to say who's on whose side in the Balkans,' Christina sighed. 'Jo-Jo's letters are full of explanations but I never really get the hang of it. I think she said in her last letter that Bulgaria was being tempted into friendship with Austro-Hungary—'

'Austro-Hungary, that's the German lot?'

'Well, yes. Lots of money, a big trained army: you can see Bulgaria would want to be friendly with them.'

'But your chum Jo-Jo isn't, I think you said.'

'No, she hates the Austrian government because she always said it trampled on the rights of Serbia.'

'But Serbia is a kingdon in its own right, isn't it? With a king.'

'King Peter. But Jo-Jo doesn't like *him*. She wants a republic.'

'Great Scot, it's like knitting in a tangle.'

'Not to the people involved in it,' mourned Christina. 'Men and women and children are being killed out there.'

'It's not really our business,' Douglas Fairforth remarked, coming in at that moment.

'Oh?' Christina said dangerously.

'Well, after all, these Balkans are unbalanced and temperamental.'

'Oh, you know a lot of Balkan people, do you?'

'No, but it's well known—'

'To whom?'

'Well, to everybody.'

'Is it? Is it indeed? Just as it's well known that the Congolese natives want to become Presbyterians, I suppose.'

'There's no need to sneer. It's an injunction upon the Christian Church, to go forth and spread the Gospel.'

'But Christian charity doesn't extend to the people of the Balkans? They can be killed and maimed and forced out of their villages by bombardment, but it doesn't matter?'

'I didn't say that. I said it wasn't our business.'

'That's splitting hairs.'

'Really, Christina, we've only so much time and energy to use. It's pointless to waste it on the squabbles of a bunch of bandits.'

'I think you'd better go, Douglas. I shall say something very hurtful to you in a minute if you don't.'

'Now, Christina,' soothed Agnes, 'Douglas is right. If these people can't settle down and work out their problems in peace, they must just be left to fight it out alone.'

The argument was ended by a patient in need of attention. 'I'll wait outside,' Douglas said, putting on his hat.

'Don't bother,' said Christina over her shoulder as she led her patient to the cubicles in the back premises.

'But the meeting begins in ten minutes—'

'I'm not going.'

'But you promised.'

'I'm busy, Douglas.'

'But you're off duty!'

She came back out to the front shop. 'Douglas,' she said with a heavy sigh, 'can't you take a hint? I don't want to go to a prayer meeting, I don't want to go anywhere with you, I'm not interested in your missionary career and I'm not even sure it's justified.'

'Christina!'

'If you feel what I've said makes it unsuitable for us to be friends, I shall quite understand.'

He took one of her hands in his. 'I forgive you, Christina,' he said.

Douglas kept on forgiving her through the rest of that year and into the next. But in fact they didn't see each other so much, for Douglas's finals were looming and despite

Christina's view of the matter, divinity was a very wide-ranging and difficult subject requiring a knowledge of Greek, Latin and Hebrew.

When they did meet, they avoided discussing the unrest in the Balkans, even after an armistice was signed in Bucharest. Douglas nobly said nothing when Serbia, Christina's pet Balkan state, invaded Albania. Some time in the spring of 1914 there was a peace treaty between Serbia and Turkey. When the Archduke Ferdinand of Austria and his wife were shot to death at Sarajevo on 28 June, it seemed just one more brutal and absurd twist in the tangled story of the Balkans.

But from then on through July the great powers somehow became involved. The Austro-Hungarian government issued threats against Serbia. Serbia appealed to Russia. Austria mobilised troops along the Russian border, then two days later declared war on Serbia. The German government called on Russia to cease the mobilisation of its troops.

The British people, half-irritated by such goings-on and half-diverted, went on their merry way. It was a gorgeous summer. Children were taken to the seaside, ladies wore gauzy gowns and carried floral parasols, the consumption of the suddenly fashionable drink, iced lager, rose enormously.

In Edinburgh, the towers and pinnacles of Holyrood Palace gleamed in the sun. The steamer *William Muir* plied to and fro across the Forth with excursionists. In the Canongate, the Shoemaker Doctors took turn about to sit out in the backyard with lemonade to quench the thirst.

No one expected Britain to be involved in hostilities. When the newspaper boys ran through the streets on 4 August crying 'War Declared!' they were greeted with disbelief. And then, strange to say, with cheers. So, they were going to fight the Germans 'for little Belgium'. Quite right too. Time those bullying Prussians were taught a lesson.

To Christina's astonishment, men began to queue at the enlistment offices. 'But they can't *want* to go to war?' she cried.

'Of course they do. What else do you expect, Christina?'

'But haven't they read in the newspapers about the terrible things that happen in modern war? Didn't they read about the Balkans? The death, the destruction?'

'Oh, but this will be different,' Jessie assured her. 'You must realise that what was going on in the Balkans was a very uncivilised affair.'

Christina was dumbstruck. Could anyone believe in a 'civilised' war?

Before another month had passed, her views were justified. The newspapers were full of the casualty lists from the Battle of the Marne. It was clear to anyone with medical insight that the wounded were being brought to the base hospitals in almost overwhelming numbers. None of the armies was really prepared for the casualties: the onslaught had been too sudden and too powerful, medical teams had not had time to get into position and in any case were too few.

On 14 September, Christina got a letter from Elwin. He wrote that he had joined up with the Lincoln Fusiliers; that, thanks to Officer Training at university, he was being taken in with the rank of Lieutenant. 'I expect to be in France within ten days, though perhaps not in the front line as there may be some training to do. Mother is very upset but Father said it was just what he expected of me. Write to me, Christina, letters will be sent on through the Army Post Office.'

She rushed out to the General Post Office to ring him at the Claremonts' flat, but the difficulties of getting a trunk call put through proved too great. She wrote, but received no reply, but that was to be expected since he was on the move.

By and by she received a scribbled note from her mother:

Dearest, In case you haven't heard, Elwin has gone in the Army. He writes that he is quite comfortable in a hotel that has been taken over near Cambrai. Dorothy Spinshall has promised to wait for him which is a comfort to me because I really thought they had broken up. If you write to me, dear, write care of Mrs Giles, who has agreed to send on anything that comes for me.

When Christina told Douglas that her brother had joined up, it seemed to perturb him deeply. He felt it his duty to volunteer, yet his vocation as a missionary was still strong. 'What should I do, Christina?' he asked.

'You could enlist as a doctor,' she suggested. 'I think they're in desperate need.'

'No, I meant about my Christian calling. I could go into the Army as a padre – yet I know nothing about ministering to soldiers. All my training's been directed towards more simple souls.'

He was so distressed that she checked the remark she'd been about to make – that in her opinion no human being was simple, whether black or white. Instead she murmured, 'I thought you would have guidance? I mean . . . from above.'

'Oh, I have prayed for it! Yet I can't help wondering if it isn't cowardice to want to go to Africa, far away from the war.'

'You'd probably have trials there too, Douglas. Different from the front line of a war, but serious nevertheless.'

'Come with me, Christina.'

She shook her head.

'If you'd agree to come, then I'd know I was doing the right thing.'

'Don't be silly, Douglas! What has my coming to do with it?'

'I'd feel it was a sign.'

'Perhaps you're being tested?' she countered. 'A test of moral conviction? If you can make up your own mind, then it's what God intended.'

He gazed at her in wonder. 'How quickly you go straight to the heart of things, Christina.'

But next time she saw him he was in doubt again. He renewed his plea: marry him, go with him, he needed that to persuade him he was in the right.

She was almost impatient with him. 'I've told you, Douglas, I can't! I refuse to be used as a sign from Heaven. Either you know you're "called" or you don't – but please don't drag me into it.'

'Christina!' He was hurt. 'You know we're summoned to go forth and preach.'

'I'm not summoned to that. If I'm summoned anywhere, it's to help the men who are being maimed and damaged in the war.'

'There's no chance of that, Christina, they would never accept women doctors in military hospitals. Come with me to Africa.'

They parted in irritation. She went for a walk alone round Arthur's Seat to soothe herself and think things out.

The work she did in the Canongate was worthwhile and necessary. But there were other women who could do it. Men were dying in France, not only in the front line but in field hospitals and base hospitals, simply because there wasn't enough medical attention available. Shock and blood loss, gangrene, the ravages of extreme pain – all of these could be alleviated if only there were doctors there to administer treatment.

She had the training. She was a free agent. She felt what Douglas apparently lacked: a firm call to serve in the war zone.

And, contrary to what he said, there *was* a way for a woman to be accepted for a military hospital.

There was an organisation in Edinburgh recruiting for the Women's Service Hospital, medical units staffed entirely by women. She walked into their offices in St Andrew's Square, volunteered, and was immediately accepted.

Chapter Fifteen

The uniform was a sober blue, trimmed, in honour of the Service's Scottish founders, with tartan. There were many buttoned pockets on the jacket, the skirt was straight and ankle length. Under the jacket went a white shirt with a stiff collar which was held down by a tie-pin across a tie of the same tartan as the uniform trim. With it went a soft peaked cap in the same cloth.

Beneath the uniform, 'basic garments' were worn: a cotton chemise, short boned stays, navy lock-knit bloomers fastened at the waist by buttons to the stays, a camisole, black woollen stockings held up by garters and a cotton petticoat.

Gloves were to be worn or carried at all times. A canvas bag with a shoulder strap was supplied for the carrying of military passes, identification documents, smelling salts or other restorative, a handkerchief, and necessary currency. Feminine trivia was to be kept to a minimum, although a small mirror and a comb were not frowned upon.

The necessary currency turned out to be francs. Christina was posted to the medical centre for French casualties in the Champagne region. On the outskirts of the city of Troyes, a tented village had been set up, whose streets ran where the vine had flourished. Troyes itself wasn't a very picturesque city, Christina noted as she taxied through it from the station: though it was the capital of the Champagne region, it was noted for knitwear and machinery rather than wine. But the wine itself was plentiful enough, as Christina soon learned on seeing drunk *poilus* staggering around even in the hospital area.

The ward tents were not a uniform khaki. Some had come

from storage after the South African War, bleached by the scorching sun and tailored by former users for maximum ventilation. Others were brand new and much preferred by the French patients, who were obsessive about draughts.

The 'gatekeeper's lodge' was a little shack like a workman's hut, with a sloping roof of galvanised tin. Later Christina discovered that when you tried to speak to the gatekeeper on a rainy day, you could hardly make yourself heard above the din of the drops on the roof.

It was necessary to sign oneself in and out with the gatekeeper so that the whereabouts of both staff and patients were known at all times. Needless to say the audacious Frenchmen, as soon as they were ambulant, set out in search of wine, women and song, but took great care not to sign themselves out. Later Christina spent many an hour on hue and cry after some missing French patient.

She noticed a variety of uniforms: the blue of the French troops, the greyish-blue of the Women's Service Hospital staff, the khaki of the British and of the First Aid Nursing Yeomanry who drove the ambulances, the black of a visiting priest and even, sometimes, the scarlet of a cardinal from Troyes Cathedral.

Supplies were piled up inside the gate. This was France and the staff were catering for French patients, so the food in the heaped baskets shouldn't have surprised Christina. Bundles of tiny carrots, fresh river fish wrapped in moist cabbage leaves, bunches of fine grapes, truffles ... And, of course, cases of champagne. The place certainly didn't offer the scene of wounded and dying that she had expected and dreaded. These soldiers, it turned out, were mostly suffering from medical conditions that had made them unfit for service.

'I see in this c.v. that came with you, doctor,' the senior physician remarked, 'that you did extra path. work at the University of Pennsylvania?'

'Yes, ma'am.'

'Splendid.' Dr Bellhaven sat back with a grin of triumph. 'You're a gift from the gods. We've got these chaps coming in, offering all kinds of symptoms – some of them, I'm afraid, due to a misspent youth! We need someone to organise and run the path. lab. – are you on for that?'

Christina was surprised to have it offered as a choice. She'd taken it for granted that she was more or less in the Army, and that she would have to do what she was told or face the equivalent of a court martial. 'I'd be glad to take on the path. lab., ma'am.'

'Excellent, excellent, Morton will show you the way. Medical quarters are at the side of the camp nearest the town – that's for ease of registration when the transport brings in patients, not so that we can rush into the town if the Gerries come.' Dr Bellhaven got up, offered her hand, then shouted past Christina. 'Morton! Morton! Show Dr Holt to Section A. Don't put her in that tent with the leak, now!'

Morton appeared, a tall girl in the VAD version of the Women's Service Hospital uniform. She gave a sketchy salute to the senior physician. Christina soon found that military manners were not strictly observed in the WSH.

The tent had an occupant already. A head could be seen on a pillow on a camp bed. Morton said in a half-whisper, 'Dr Sibley, she's been on night duty. Just leave your things and I'll take you to the path. lab.' Christina was about to ask how Morton knew she was to go to the path. lab. when it dawned on her that anything said in the ringing tones of Dr Bellhaven could be heard through the walls of any tent. In fact, privacy would prove to be almost impossible in a tented city.

The path. lab. was another tent. Apart from wooden boxes and trestle tables, it was empty. 'It's waiting to be set up, ma'am. The equipment's in the boxes. If you'll tell me how many bods you need, I'll round 'em up. And there are some ambulant patients longing to be helpful.'

It was a warm October afternoon. Christina set down her shoulder-bag, took off her jacket, sat on one of the boxes, and surveyed her kingdom.

'If you could let me have two VADs,' she suggested, 'we'll

sort out what's what according to the labelling and get the boxes open. I should think it could be set up by morning. Is there any material awaiting analysis?'

Morton didn't know. 'I'll ask, shall I? It would be in Admissions, I think. But of course nobody's been taking specimens much, ma'am, because there's been nobody to handle 'em.'

Christina walked round the tent inspecting labels. 'Glass – With Extreme Care'. 'Medical Supplies – This Way Up'. 'Dangerous Chemicals'. A large packing case announced itself to be 'Cabinets'.

Well, there was no need for the 'Dangerous Chemicals' until they'd got the equipment out. First the cabinets to house the stores and, she hoped, a refrigerator. Then she needed to find the microscope and other metal tools. Then the glass.

When two girls arrived she set them to work at once with screwdrivers and levers borrowed from the Maintenance Department. Three French patients came in, anxious to be of use. Between them they set up the cabinets, unloaded the gear, laid out the benches, gingerly unpacked the glassware from its wood shavings.

'Tea up,' said a voice. Morton had reappeared with a tray of mugs. It was the usual strong Scottish tea. The Frenchmen tasted it with disbelief. '*On boît cela*?' asked one.

'Of course we drink it,' said Christina in her schoolgirl French.

'*Ah, les braves dames écossaises!*'

Not all the staff were *écossaises*, as Christina was to discover in the mess tent that evening. Several women from England and Ireland had joined the WSH so as to 'get into the war', as they expressed it. But for the most part the staff were Scottish, and because of this the hospital was generally known as the Scottish Hospital. The nurses had special little tartan bonnets with strings to tie under their chins, which earned them the nickname of the 'Scottish Widows'.

When Christina came into the mess a conversation was

already under way. She could hear indignation in the voices.

'. . . And told Dr Dyer that no British soldier would ever submit to being examined by a woman doctor.'

'He didn't!'

'His actual words, I believe, were "No British soldier would let a woman doctor touch him even if he were dying." Dr Dyer asked him how it was in that case that women nurses were able to save the lives of seriously wounded men. He said that was different, that a soldier didn't have to take orders from a nurse. So Dr Dyer said, "Do you really think that women doctors are going to waste their time ordering men about when there is work to do?" But she couldn't persuade him.'

'Who was that?' inquired Christina. She knew Dr Dyer was the intrepid Scotswoman who had set up the Women's Service Hospital, but wanted to know the identity of the wooden-headed male.

'Oh, some wallah in the War Office. So HM Government refused the services of the WSH and that's how we come to be here under French military jurisdiction.' The speaker paused to study Christina. 'I think you tiptoed into the tent while I was asleep this afternoon. I'm Jane Sibley.'

'Christina Holt.' Introductions were made. She met the administrator, Mrs Gibson, who was a non-medical member of staff, the radiologist Dr Maynes, the surgeon Edith Paterson. She was able to report that the path. lab. would probably be in action by noon of the following day.

Jane Sibley spoke across the table to Christina. 'You're the first American woman I've come across in the WSH.'

'I'm not American. I spent five years in Philadelphia, but I was born in Lincolnshire.'

'Lincolnshire? I have friends at Grimsby.' The usual exchange followed – possible acquaintances in common, what members of their families were 'in the war'. When Christina said that her brother was in the Lincoln Fusiliers, Dr Bellhaven said, 'I believe they're the first British regiment along the line – next to the French, I mean. Your brother's probably only about fifty or sixty miles north-east of here, on the Marne.'

Christina brightened at the idea. 'I'll drop him a line,' she said.

'Don't get optimistic. The letter'll probably take a month to reach him and anyway, you won't get time off to go hunting for him, my lass! Not for a bit. That pathological department has got plenty of work waiting for it.'

Of course. Ashamed of herself, Christina returned her attention to the steamed chicken and mashed potatoes.

Yet there was time off after a few days. She went to buy some soap and take a look at Troyes.

The town was full of refugees from the Marne villages. Men and women were sitting with their bundles of belongings in the cafés and in the one cinema. On the square before the Cathedral, some were offering goods for sale: small pieces of jewellery, a fox-fur stole, a pair of handsome hunting boots. These were offered in exchange for cash, perhaps to buy a train ticket to relatives in some safer area.

The ancient walls were mellow in the October sunshine. Even though the streets were over-full and the refugees gave them a sad look, nothing could detract from the beauty of the place. The stained glass with which every church seemed to be blessed glowed like clusters of gems.

But there was no soap. There was no toothpaste. Supplies of almost everything were scarce. Wine, yes, there was plenty of wine, for this region produced wine, the best in the world. Champagne was made from the grapes of the Marne region, and was still being made under the guns of the German artillery. And food was not scarce, for this was a country district with plenty of livestock. Manufactured goods, however – small luxuries such as nail scissors or a china cup – these were already vanishing from the shelves.

Not that there was much need to buy things in Troyes. The French government, who had accepted the services of this unit of the WHS, was their quartermaster. They received ample supplies of day-to-day requirements: disinfectants, laundry soap, flour, sugar, coffee. Tea wasn't supplied, but members of the team had alerted the home front to send that indispensable commodity.

By the end of the first week Christina had the path. lab. established. One of the nurses volunteered as a part-time assistant, and Christina was training up an exceptionally intelligent VAD in the art of preparing slides and cultures.

This being so, she was available for some work in the wards. Dr Bellhaven accepted her gratefully. The senior surgeon needed an assistant – would Christina take it on?

It was three years now since she'd done any surgery more serious than removing a cyst. But Dr Bellhaven waved that aside. 'You'll soon get it back. It's like swimming: once learned, never forgotten.'

So it proved. She assisted at an appendectomy, mended the jaw of a soldier who'd got in a fight in Troyes, and by the following day was wondering why she'd been nervous. But her nervousness returned when she was called as an emergency to a patient in the medical ward who, about to be discharged, was exhibiting symptoms of acute dilatation of the stomach, and writhing in pain.

Miss Paterson, the surgical chief, was off duty. Christina sent the man to be X-rayed. Dr Maynes brought the plate out to Christina, who held it up to the lamp with anxiety. She expected a perforated ulcer.

The two women stared at the shadow in the stomach. 'What on earth is it?'

'Well . . . It's an irregular rounded mass—'

'Apparently solid . . .'

'Certainly not as fluidly funnel-shaped or overhung as I'd have expected in that site.'

'And he's young to have an ulcer in any case.'

'Although that isn't a contra-indication . . .'

'Let's start from the other end. What could have caused it?'

'He's swallowed something.'

'But how could he swallow something that shape without knowing it and coughing it up? I mean, a chickenbone, yes, but a lump the size of a florin and with nobbly sides?'

'It's a bezoar,' said Christina all of a sudden.

'A what?'

'A bezoar. Something formed in the stomach or intestine from swallowing something else.'

'Sorry,' said Dr Maynes, frowning. 'I have either never heard of it or I don't recall it.'

'Well, I've never actually come across one but I was told the most common was caused by swallowing hair.'

'Swallowing hair? Did I get that right?'

'Yes, men with beards sometimes swallow hairs and then they get compounded with other substances, like vegetable fibres, and the activity of intrinsic stomach acids causes—'

'But your patient doesn't have a beard.'

'No. But I'll tell you this much for nothing. Whatever that lad has swallowed, it's done him no good at all. I think we'll have to operate.'

Miss Paterson arrived before he went into theatre. She listened to the story with interest, but declined to take over the operation. 'I'm very intrigued. Let's see what you bring out, Dr Holt.'

Two hours later the patient was in the recovery ward, and Christina was bending over a microscope, examining a section of the strange little mass she had removed.

At dinner in the mess tent everyone was agog to know the result of her tests. She looked at them with a hidden grin.

'I'll give you three guesses what it was.'

'Hair?'

'No.'

'Coagulated seed from fruit.'

'No.'

'Give up,' said the table as a whole.

'Resin.'

'Eh? What? What did she say?'

'Resin.'

'Are you telling us the man swallowed a lump of mastic?'

'Come on now, Dr Holt, you're pulling our legs.'

'I assure you,' said Christina, 'it's resin. Anyone who likes can go and have a look at it through the microscope.'

'Fat lot of use that would be,' said Dr Bellhaven. 'I've no idea what resin looks like through a microscope.'

'Well, it's almost the first time I've seen it myself, but I looked it up for comparison and there's no doubt that's what it is. I'll tell you this – that young *soldat* would have been a very sick man indeed if we hadn't done that op.'

The verification came when the patient was well enough to answer questions.

He had wanted to celebrate or drown his sorrows, whichever way you liked to look at it, upon hearing he was to be discharged as fit. He soon spent all his money in the bars of Troyes. Back at the hospital he had prowled around looking for something intoxicating to drink – surgical spirit, for instance. But everything was safely locked up.

In a cupboard he found some furniture polish. He was well acquainted with furniture polish, having drunk it before now for its alcoholic content when funds were low. He emptied the bottle and then, feeling very thirsty, drank two or three pints of water at intervals in the course of the night.

Result: next morning he had turned the suspended copal in the polish into resin in his stomach by precipitation.

Surgery began to play a larger part in the life of the hospital. With the coming of November, the rain began. The whole region became a sea of mud in which men and horses floundered. Motor vehicles were brought in, in the belief that they could do better in the poor terrain. Then the roads would be blocked when a *camion* got bogged down in a narrow village through-way. Patients were off-loaded to be sent by cart or wagon to whichever hospital could be reached. Troyes received a share of them.

The injuries were shocking. Christina had to take part in amputations that appalled her. Chest wounds meant desperately ill patients both before and after operations. Belly wounds were almost hopeless from the start.

Edith Paterson and her assistant laboured through each influx of casualties. Then there would be an interval of comparative peace if the blockage on the roads was cleared or if the surface dried out. They would supervise the nursing of the patients so as to get them well enough to be cleared to base hospital where there was a larger staff and better opportunity for follow-up work.

Then it would all begin again.

In December the patients well enough to sit up or walk about decided they would have Christmas celebrations. Bandages were secreted under pillows, to be tinted with green dye. Someone brought in a tin of silver paint from the town. Twigs and pine cones were dipped in this. Red flannel blankets were draped above doors and windows.

'It all looks very festive,' Christina wrote to her aunt in Philadelphia. 'The weather has turned intensely cold so we can hardly spare the blankets for decoration, but Mrs Gibson hasn't the heart to make the men take them down. There's a rumour that hostilities will cease for twenty-four hours on Christmas Eve but we don't know whether it's true – of course rumours fly like carrier pigeons all around the wards.

'This being a Scottish organisation, the really big celebration is being planned for New Year's Eve, or Hogmanay as I've learned to call it. Tell Captain Dinsdorf I shall wear his gold chain with my party dress, which is in fact the only dress I had room for and is of maroon crêpe with Miss Melville's embroidered collar stitched on.

'Have you had word from Elwin? He's a poor correspondent – or perhaps it's just that his letters take a long time to go round the long circle from his part of the line, back to the depot, from there to the Army Post Office, and thence to me only fifty miles away. I expected to go and see him before now, but the railway is being used by the army or else the train is needed for refugees, and the roads are in a mess . . .

'Because the roads are so bad, we've had some British wounded who should really have gone west to Chateau Thierry. It was strange to go into a ward and hear English being spoken after only French for so long. We're trying to get special supplies so as to give them a traditional British Christmas dinner, but the French don't eat the same things as we do at Christmas so it's a bit difficult.'

She ended by sending her love and begging for letters.

One of the hardest things to bear was not to have any news from home. Her mother had written once in answer to one of hers, but it was a short letter, as if the writer feared to be discovered. The other women had letters with every mail. She saw them look at her sometimes with veiled pity for her lack of correspondents.

Yet in a way Christina was happy. She felt she was stretching herself, testing her abilities. The work was varied and demanding, and though nothing could excuse the stupidities of war, she felt that she was doing something towards alleviating the suffering.

What was more, she'd been able to make friends with a little group of refugee children. Their ages ranged from two to eleven. They had been brought to her notice when one of them, a toddler, fell in the street, grazing her knee. Christina bound it up with her handkerchief, asked where Mama was and, in taking her to her 'home', found three or four women housed in a small barn, their children with them.

One child had a bad cough, one had a badly bandaged cut on the arm. All were suffering to some degree from lack of food and warmth. Christina came back next day with all the spare clothing she'd been able to beg from her colleagues, and with bread and a pitcher of soup from the hospital cook.

She spent what time she could with them. One evening, as she sat watching over a sleeping baby, one of the mothers said to her, 'You have children, madame?'

She shook her head.

The woman looked at her left hand, shrugged, and smiled in apology. 'Yet you have the look of a mother, it seems to me.'

'Thank you. That is a compliment.'

'Ah,' sighed the Frenchwoman, 'in this place and at this time, it is hard, being a mother.'

It was hard for everyone. And yet at Christmas there was a definite lull in the fighting, the home-made celebrations in the wards lifted the spirits, and there was still the New Year Party to look forward to.

On Hogmanay the patients tried to be very good. No one

was to demand extra attention, so that the staff could have a chance to go to their party.

Christina changed out of hospital garb into her party dress, shivering the while. 'Would it be all right to wear my sweater under my dress?' asked Jane Sibley, trying to view herself in the small mirror hung on the tent pole. They surveyed each other, put a dab of Jane's perfume behind each other's ears, and went as fast as they could over the frozen ground to the mess tent.

The dining table had been cleared to one side. Dr Bellhaven's wind-up gramophone was playing – not one of Dr Bellhaven's classical records, but the current hit in London, 'Hello Central, Give me No Man's Land.' There were some medical and artillery officers from local French regiments, a representative from the office of the mayor of Troyes. But the men were outnumbered more than two to one by the women.

Despite that fact, Christina danced almost every dance. At midnight the floor was cleared, a ring was formed in which the Frenchmen took their place with mystification. 'Auld Lang Syne' was sung, hands were linked at 'Then here's a hand', and the second verse was well under way when the telephone began shrilling in the Admissions Office.

The doctors, both French and British, looked at each other. They knew what it meant. A convoy of wounded was coming in.

The party broke up at once. Everyone rushed to change into work clothes. The Admissions clerk sat down at her desk, pen in hand. Stretcher bearers lined up, lights were turned on in Surgery and in the operating theatre, and the autoclave was started up.

The first man unloaded was in pain from a bad leg wound, but conscious. 'Cor!' he said. 'What a way to spend New Year!'

So they were to receive English troops. The nurses began moving among the stretchers, giving reassurance, lighting cigarettes. The doctors looked at the labels tied on each man to give some idea of the wound and when received.

Christina approached a silent figure under an Army blanket. A bloodied bandage round the head signalled at least a scalp wound, concussion, perhaps worse. She stooped over him.

It was Elwin.

Chapter Sixteen

Christina gave a startled cry. One of the nursing sisters whirled. 'What's wrong, doctor?' Sometimes, men were in such pain that in flailing about they hurt the helpers.

'He's my brother,' Christina said.

'Oh, dear God!' Sister McFarlane sprang to her side. She leaned over Elwin. Then she straightened, putting an arm around Christina in quick encouragement. 'Looks like a severe scalp wound – but I see no skull depression.'

'No.'

'Skull injuries always look bad, doctor, because they bleed so hard.'

'Yes.'

It was absurd, receiving the simple comfort she had so often given to relatives in the casualty ward at Pennsylvania University Hospital.

The very absurdity of the thought brought her to her senses. 'He must be moved aside,' she said.

'Yes, doctor.' McFarlane knew what the doctor meant: into the non-urgent line. There were men here much more seriously injured, whose very life depended on getting into the operating theatre within the next hour or two. Elwin Holt, though unconscious and haemorrhaging, was not in such danger that he needed immediate surgery.

'I'll see to him,' she said, to let poor Dr Holt know that while she was in the operating theatre with Miss Paterson, someone would take care of her brother.

It was a long night that went on into the dark dawn on the first day of 1915. When at last the two surgeons emerged to take off the last blood-soaked overall, the ambulances had gone, the wounded were dispersed between the wards according to urgency. Steps had been taken to clean them up, to relieve their pain, to lessen shock.

Christina went to the far end of the Admissions tent. There lay Elwin, still unconscious. Fresh bandaging had been applied, and very little blood-staining was now visible.

A ward nurse sat on a camp stool by his stretcher.

'How is he?' Christina asked.

'He doesn't rouse, doctor. He's been sick several times and slightly convulsive.'

That pointed to a severe concussion. It might mean irritation of the brain tissues.

'Has the wound been examined?'

'Yes, Dr Bellhaven examined him. She said it looks as if he was hit by a rifle butt swung by the barrel.'

'It's not a bullet graze?'

'No, ma'am, the other patients from his unit say the Germans attacked about ten o'clock, took some trenches a hundred yards away, and then tried to over-run the British trenches. Seems their ammunition was low at the end so there was a lot of hand-to-hand – your brother was tackling one man when another smashed him down with his rifle.'

'I see. Thank you.'

She would have given anything to stay by the bedside, but all her training cried out against it. Besides, the ward nurse was waiting for her to go. Medical etiquette demanded that Christina leave her brother's treatment in the hands of the doctor in charge of the ward. It was always considered wrong – downright dangerous even – for doctors or surgeons to treat members of their own family for fear emotion would interfere with judgement.

Christina had always agreed with this law, until now. Now, when she saw Elwin's still, lifeless features against the coarse white of the Army pillowcase.

She was brought to herself by the quiet voice of the nurse. 'I'll be with him, ma'am.'

They exchanged a silent glance of understanding.

Christina hurried out.

She must go and get some rest, and then resume work on the next group of casualties. There was less urgency now: the men were being cared for and 'improved' so as to stand the shock of surgical intervention. As their wounds were less severe, they could be left for a few hours before surgery was resumed. Miss Paterson was already sleeping: she would be wakened at noon and resume by herself. Christina would replace her at four o'clock or thereabouts.

She went to the mess tent, forced herself to eat something, and went to bed. She slept from sheer exhaustion. She had been on her feet since nine o'clock the previous morning.

When she woke, she showered in the ablutions tent. The water was barely warm. She dressed quickly. Breakfast, although it was two in the afternoon, was supplied on request. She went to the Admissions tent. Elwin had moved forward in the queue. No nurse was now keeping an especially watchful eye on him.

The ward sister came to greet her. 'Your brother is much the same. The vomiting has ceased, but he's still restless. However, his pulse is good, ma'am, and I think you need not worry too much.'

'Thank you, sister.' Christina sat down beside Elwin, took his wrist in her fingers. What Sister said was true. She sat looking down at her brother, willing him to wake up. The earlier he woke, the less the brain shock implicated.

It was a very cold day with occasional flurries of thin, dry snow. The sun seemed unable to pierce the clouds and soon it would be too late, darkness would have fallen. Christina felt a heavy depression settle on her. It was so cold here, so uncomfortable, the setting on this great plain so close to monotony, and the outlook for the new-opening year was so dreary.

More rumble of guns in the distance, more fighting, more bloodied and butchered men to patch up . . . And what was it for?

For 'little Belgium'. And before that, for the Serbians who were threatened by the Austro-Hungarian Empire.

But when you said that, what did it mean? Why was Elwin lying here, his head battered by a German who had never known him as a man? The statesmen said they were engaged in the 'war to end wars': if it were true, it was a great, a noble aim.

But was this how it was done? To send a quiet-mannered, conventional lawyer from Lincolnshire into a foreign land, there to kill or be killed? While at home mothers and wives and sweethearts waited, frightened at the coming of the postman or the telegram boy for fear it was the news they never wanted to hear . . .

Mothers and wives and sweethearts! She must write to her mother, to let her know Elwin was wounded but not in mortal danger. She ought to do that straight away, to get the letter into the mail pouch that went by motorcycle messenger at six.

But on her way to her tent to get notepaper and pen, she was waylaid by Dr Mayne asking for a conference over the leg X-rays of one of the men. Was that shrapnel in the acetabulum? Had they missed it when they set his fractured bones? Should the man be taken back into surgery?

And then the operating theatre was ready for the session in which she was on duty, and the letter-writing was put off. As she worked, it came back into her mind. She comforted herself with the thought, 'His commanding officer will have written by now.'

When she got back to the Admissions tent at the end of her shift, her brother was up at the front of the queue. He was sleeping – not unconscious, sleeping.

'He opened his eyes about an hour ago, ma'am, and mumbled a bit. I gave him sips of water and he swallowed.'

All cheering news.

She went to eat, safe in the knowledge that for Elwin the danger was past. Soup, meat stew with dumplings and cabbage, and strong tea was plain fare but sustaining. She lay down in her blouse and skirt to rest. She would be back on duty at midnight.

When, shivering and with eyes full of grit, she went to

check on Elwin before going to the operating theatre, he was gone.

'Ah, there you are, doctor!' cried Sister McFarlane, raising her hands and waving them in a triumphant gesture. 'Lieutenant Holt has had his wound stitched up and is in the Recovery Ward. Dr Bellhaven made a careful examination – no fracture.'

Impulsively Christina seized Sister's hands. 'Thank you,' she said. 'Yes, thank you.'

'Aye,' said McFarlane, then tugged at her cap ribbons. 'Sich a thing to happen – a very severe concussion, and your own kith and kin! Luckily he didn't lose too much blood and there was no wound infection, so all's well that ends well.'

Yes. If you could call it 'well' for a man to be knocked unconscious by a blow that could have fractured his skull, Christina thought.

Next morning, all the injured from the New Year intake had been treated and were into their recovery, although for some it would be a long and dolorous process. The emergency state was cancelled, the hospital settled down again to routine.

Christina went to visit her brother. He had been moved on to the post-Surgical Ward. He was lying on pillows, head neatly bandaged, eyes closed.

Christina found a chair and sat down at his bedside. It was about half-past nine, long past hospital breakfast time. Rounds would soon be taking place. Nurses were making everything shipshape for the visit of Dr Bellhaven and Miss Paterson.

By and by Elwin opened his eyes. He stared at the canvas wall across the aisle, then let his gaze wander to the bed on the other side and the man in it. The man had the rails overhead for traction to his leg. A puzzled frown creased Elwin's brow.

'What—?' he said.

'You're in the Surgical Ward, Elwin.'

He turned his head on his pillow, winced, closed his eyes, then gingerly re-opened them. 'I've got a fearful headache,' he complained.

'Yes, I know, but it will wear off.'

'Who's that?' He had to work a little on focusing his eyes upon her. 'Christina?'

'What do you mean by it, coming in here in an unconscious state?'

'I . . . I . . . what happened?'

'You got hit over the head.'

'But by who?'

'A German, by all accounts.'

The frown came back. 'I don't remember.'

'You will. You've had a concussion so you don't remember what happened, but it'll come back after a bit.'

There was a little silence then he said, 'Do I want it to?'

That was a good question. She had no answer for it. 'Just get some rest and let everything take its course, Elwin. Your headache will wear off, you'll feel better in a day or two.'

She knew this was true. Her brother was a fit man, physically well able to take the wound he had received and make a good recovery. Yet something was wrong.

'Your brother's rather sensitive, is he?' Dr Bellhaven inquired about a week later as she and Christina were taking advantage of the January sunshine to get some exercise.

Was he? Much though she loved him, Christina couldn't have said if Elwin was especially sensitive.

'He keeps his feelings quite well hidden, as a rule,' she ventured. 'But perhaps he does feel things deeply. Why do you ask?'

'Well, he's making a slow recovery from the head-wound. His temperature goes up and down in a very odd manner. The night sister says he has nightmares.'

'But then so do a lot of the men.'

'Yes, I'm not saying it's unusual. Has he mentioned Goodman to you?'

'Goodman?'

'I thought perhaps – in his letters home? Goodman was his captain.'

Christina shook her head. Impossible to explain to Dr Bellhaven the strange ramifications of her family, whereby news in letters home to her mother wasn't passed on to the daughter.

'I don't quite understand the significance of it, but Goodman seems to have been a particular friend.'

'You speak of him in the past tense?'

'As far as I can gather, he was blown to bits at your brother's side about ten days before that New Year attack. On the day before Christmas Eve, in fact.'

She drew in a quick breath.

'I'm no expert on this kind of thing,' Adeline Bellhaven said. 'But it's upset your brother very much indeed. And then that hand-to-hand attack so soon after, and being knocked on the head . . .'

'I see.'

'Could you talk to him about it?'

'Of course.'

But it wasn't so easy. When she sat down to share the ward tea with Elwin, she found it hard to bring the conversation round to Captain Goodman.

The man in the next bed said jokingly, 'You're all right, chum, got a doctor all to yourself! What did you do to deserve that?'

Elwin made no response. Christina turned to laugh with Lieutenant Noland. 'You should get your sister to train as a doctor,' she suggested.

'*My* sister? Wouldn't trust her to look after a sick kitten. But while I've got you here – when are you letting me out of this dump?'

'You mean you're not enjoying our hospitality?'

Elwin said suddenly, 'You can't really want to leave and go back to that?'

'Back to what, chum? Blighty leave first. Home sweet home. All the girls fussing over you, telling you what a hero you are.'

Elwin hunched his shoulders and let them fall. In his hospital pyjamas he looked strangely young and vulnerable.

'What on earth could you say to them?' he wondered in a wavering voice. 'What could you tell them?'

'About what?'

'About what it's like. What it's really like. For instance, there's nothing *heroic* about it.'

'Speak for yourself, chum,' said the irrepressible lieutenant next door. 'I'm going to crack myself up to be all kinds of a hero. I didn't get my arm cut to bits just so as to forget about it. It's going to bring me lots of admiration and kindly chat.'

Elwin shook his head. The nurses brought tea – sweet tea in mugs and two thick slices of English-style bread and butter. Lieutenant Noland took the opportunity to flirt a little. Elwin and Christina were left to their own conversation.

'You hate it so much?' she said quietly.

He stirred his tea. Then he said, 'I don't want to talk about it.'

'Not even about Captain Goodman?'

His hand shook convulsively. Tea went all over the bedspread. The nurse flirting with Noland exclaimed in horror, came running to remedy the damage. And afterwards the opportunity to speak about Captain Goodman was lost.

It never returned. Try as she might, Christina couldn't get her brother to touch on the subject of the death of his friend. She had a feeling it was important to get him to talk, but the justification for the belief was instinctive. Most people would have said it was better put behind him.

But not if it haunted him so.

At the end of three weeks Elwin was well enough to be discharged. He was to go with a party back to railhead, for transport to the coast and home. He would get two weeks' home leave.

Christina thought he would be pleased. But the news seemed to strike him with momentary terror.

'What's the matter, Elwin?' she said, seeing the shudder run through him as he sat across from her in the patients' Recreation Ward.

'What will I say to them?' he muttered. 'They'll ask me what it's like – and what can I say?'

'Tell them the truth.'

He hugged his arms about himself. 'They couldn't bear it,' he said.

Next day the transport vehicles arrived to collect the 'Blighty' men. The sergeant in charge of the convoy checked off the names of his passengers.

Elwin was not in the group waiting by the hospital entrance.

Christina was in the path. lab. trying to track down a strange streptococcus which had suddenly struck a French soldier in the Medical Ward. When Morton came to ask if she knew where her brother might be, she looked up from the microscope.

'He's with the others in the Recreation Ward, waiting to go home.'

'No, ma'am, he ain't. The men are boarded, the sergeant's waiting to drive off, and Lieutenant Holt isn't there.'

'Well, then, he's in the Ward – perhaps he left something in his locker . . .'

'We looked there, ma'am. We can't find him.'

Christina looked at the slide under her lens. She wavered. Then she said, 'Just a minute till I put all this away safely.'

Two minutes later she was outside the tent pulling on her jacket. She hurried to the Recreation Ward but Elwin wasn't there.

'Did you see Elwin this morning?' she asked two men who were playing checkers.

'Yes, early on, just after brekker. Haven't seen him since – have you, Tom?'

'Nope.'

Christina made a tour of the wards. By and by she had to go to the entrance. 'Not found him, doctor? I'm sorry, I'll have to go without him. I've a schedule, a train to meet.'

'I understand, sergeant. Carry on.'

'Very good, ma'am.' He saluted, swung aboard, nodded at the driver, and the ungainly lorry trundled off in the winter morning.

'Where can he be?' wondered Morton. 'He *knew* he was being posted home today. Why would he wander off?'

'He'll be back,' Christina said with a confidence she didn't feel.

By dusk he hadn't reappeared. Now she was really worried. He was not a hundred per cent fit. The last thing he needed was to be wandering about in the cold and dark of a January night.

She asked Dr Bellhaven's permission to go looking for him.

'Oh, my dear . . . Do you think you should?'

'He is still our responsibility, ma'am.'

'But he's probably just gone into Troyes to celebrate and had one too many.'

'But he knew very well the transport was coming at ten a.m.'

'Oh, well, perhaps he thought he had time for a quick one.'

'But my brother isn't all that keen on drink . . .'

'He's been through a big shock, doctor. Perhaps he's not quite the brother you used to know.'

'No,' agreed Christina, 'perhaps not. Perhaps I never really knew him.'

With reluctant permission, Christina went into Troyes. She looked first in all the cafés and bars, in the hotels, the railroad station waiting-rooms, the churches. No sign of her brother. She stopped to have something to eat after midday, then struck by a random thought went to the barracks of the French regiment. If Elwin had desperately wanted *not* to go home, perhaps he would have sought the company of other soldiers.

The guards on the gate looked at her in surprise.

'Excuse me,' she said, in her careful French, 'have you seen a British officer come in?'

'Here, mademoiselle? To our HQ?'

'Yes, a British lieutenant.'

They exchanged glances. Was the pretty lady deranged?

'He's ill,' she explained. 'Not quite himself.'

Ah, they thought, drunk. 'No, mademoiselle, no British officer has come in.'

'Are you sure? Have you been on duty all morning?'

'We-ell, no . . .'

'Perhaps he came in when someone else was on guard duty?'

'He would have had to present himself to the officer of the day.'

'Could you ask?'

'Eh? Ask?' They muttered to each other, then the older of the two went into the guardpost hut. He rang through on a field telephone. A conversation ensued in French, too quick for her to follow. She thought she heard herself described as 'an eccentric young lady'. After a moment the soldier came out.

'*Je regrette, mademoiselle . . .*'

She retraced her steps through Troyes. As she passed the little barn where the mothers and children were camping out one of them, a little boy called Roget, came running out.

'I saw you go by earlier,' he said, looking cross. 'I thought you were coming to see us.'

'No, Roget, I'm sorry, I'm busy.'

He took hold of the sleeve of her overcoat. 'Come and talk to us. Ermine has a new doll Maman made for her out of a flour-bag stuffed with hay.'

'I can't, Roget, truly, I've got something else to do.'

'What else?' he demanded, clearly thinking nothing could be as important as paying them a visit.

'I'm looking for someone.'

'Who?'

'A soldier.'

'Oh, goodness, there are plenty of soldiers,' he said with the easy logic of the ten-year-old.

'No, it's a special soldier – an Englishman.'

'I see, different from the French soldiers. What does he look like?'

'Well, he's medium height, has light brown hair, and he's wearing the uniform of a British officer with green flashes on the shoulder.'

'I'll help you find him.'

'No, Roget.' She'd been thinking that perhaps she ought now to try the less respectable hotels, to see if Elwin was there with a girl. Impossible to let a child go with her on that kind of errand.

'Well, then, come and talk to us.'

'Tomorrow, Roget. I can't just now.'

He gave her a sulky look. He was a determined boy, son of a shopkeeper who had gone missing in the scuttle to escape from the German bombardment. He was accustomed to getting his own way. But this time he had to accept a refusal.

'All right, then, tomorrow. You'll come tomorrow.'

Christina went on her way. The early nightfall was coming on, and with it a cold rain. She went to the back streets of the town, entered the vestibule of a dreary little hotel, and once again went through the inquiry that now came almost parrot-fashion from her lips.

'And if I had seen him, what then?' asked Madame, a thin and watchful woman.

'You mean he's here?' Christina said eagerly.

'Who are you? His wife?'

'No, I'm his sister – oh, please, take me to him!'

'Mademoiselle, I didn't say he was here,' the other woman said, softening a little. 'I merely wanted to find out what you were up to. You shouldn't be asking questions in places like this – it's not suitable.'

'But have you seen him? Lieutenant Holt? Is he registered here?'

'*Eh quoi!*' she snorted. 'No, I have not seen him. And it is the woman who "registers", not the client. Come, mademoiselle, you won't find him in this fashion. Go home, send a man to search for this missing lamb.'

'No, I—'

'Mademoiselle, things are difficult these days. People we don't know are streaming into our town. I don't know if you are safe, roaming our streets unescorted after dark. Inform the police and let them do the searching.'

Shaking her head, Christina went out into the wet night. True enough, she received some strange looks from passers-by. And got a great fright when a burly Frenchman tried to pick her up. As she wriggled away from his casual embrace she was lucky enough to see a taxi.

'The Women's Service Hospital,' she gasped, falling into it.

Once safely back inside the confines of the encampment she was ashamed of her panic. Her first action was to hurry to Admissions to ask if Lieutenant Holt had come back.

'No, ma'am. We've kept an eye out for him all day, but there's been no sign.'

A glance at her watch told her it was too late to do any more today. She must have a meal and get back to work. There were specimens waiting for her in the pathology lab.

Adeline Bellhaven came to confer with her there. 'What ought we to do, doctor? Should we report it?'

'To whom?'

'Well, that's a good question, as a matter of fact. I suppose to the Transport Officer at railhead. He ought to have gone there to pick up his travel pass and so forth.'

'But if he didn't, would the Transport Officer care?'

'Dunno,' said Adeline. 'I don't really know too much about military rules.'

Christina thrust her hands into the pockets of her white coat. 'In fact, my brother is on official sick leave. That's right, isn't it?'

'Yes, since ten a.m.'

'A beneficent government was supplying him with transport home.'

'Yes.'

'If he chose not to go, does it matter to anyone?'

The two women thought about it, looked at each other, and shook their heads helplessly.

'Well, I'm not going to report it to anybody. I can't see that it's necessary. The only thing that worries me is . . . well . . . it's the lieutenant himself. He did have a tremendous bang on the head, after all.'

'You're saying he's not in his right mind?' Christina said.

'Don't take it the wrong way, my dear. I'm not suggesting

he's violent or anything. But I hate to think of him wandering about . . .'

So do I, thought Christina. Oh, so do I.

In her spare time for the next two days she searched for Elwin, without success. Dr Bellhaven reluctantly informed the police, but even they seemed unable to find *ce pauvre malade*.

It was little Roget who found him. Or at least, it was a friend of a friend of Roget's.

'Mademoiselle, mademoiselle!' he exclaimed, leaping out at Christina as she arrived to visit the little community in the barn. 'I've found the British officer.'

She summoned a smile. 'I only wish you had, Roget.'

'But I have, I have! Haven't I, Maman?'

Mme Sucheler nodded. 'I think it may be true, mademoiselle. You know, my husband had the village store in Praie-le-Duc, and we knew many suppliers and drivers on the roads. My little boy – alas, I can't keep him under control – he has been going about asking the lorry drivers to keep an eye open for an English officer. I tried to stop him, I didn't know it was serious. But then yesterday Armand Vernay told Roget such a man had been seen.'

'Where? Where?' Christina cried, seizing the woman's hands.

'About twenty miles up the road, mademoiselle. There's a village called Jerache which was badly damaged by shellfire early on. The houses are in ruins and the people – well, some of them are here, in Troyes, and I don't know where the rest are . . .'

'And this English officer was seen there?'

'Let *me* tell, maman,' insisted Roget. 'I told Armand and the others to look for an English officer with green on his epaulettes – yes, that was what you said?' He nodded in satisfaction when mademoiselle agreed. 'Well then, Armand says such a one was in the garden of the big house outside Jerache.'

'Thank you,' Christina said. She hugged him. 'I must go at once. How do I get there?'

'Well, that isn't so easy, mademoiselle,' said Mme Sucheler. 'There used to be a bus service, but now of course . . .'

'I'll get one of my friends to take you,' said Roget.

'Roget!' his mother reproved. 'That isn't suitable for the young lady—'

'What does he mean, take me?'

'On a *camion*, of course,' said Roget. He took her by the hand and dragged her out.

He was proved right. A lorry-driver, hearing her plight, agreed to take her twenty miles up the road towards the front, although strictly speaking he wasn't allowed to take passengers and she should have had a permit.

She sat beside him in the jolting, swaying cab. He was a talkative man, anxious to let her know how difficult it was these days to keep transport going, what with the condition of the roads, the lack of petrol, the shelling as you got closer to the front, and so on and so on. She was grateful that he needed to talk. She herself was too anxious to say a word.

The landscape through which they were travelling was desolate, ravaged. Houses sagging into themselves; gaping empty windows; blighted rows of vines. What was Elwin *doing* in this empty terrain? Wandering like a ghost, as empty as the dwellings, as lost as the vanished population?

They passed two nearly empty villages before he slowed for Jerache. There were of course no signposts – those had been removed for fear of helping the enemy. But as they came within sight of a gaping roof the driver said. '*Nous voici*, this is all that is left of the house of the owner of the vineyard of Jerache. You are sure this is where you wanted to get to, mademoiselle?'

'Yes, thank you.'

'What happens now?'

'I'd like to get down.'

'And then what?'

'I don't know.'

'I would stay, mademoiselle, but I have food supplies for the Army on board.'

'I quite understand.'

She clambered down, he revved up his ancient motor, and with a wave he rolled on up the road towards the front line. She could hear the guns clearly now. All around the countryside was empty, with the village about a quarter of a mile away, a panorama of wrecked houses and broken spires.

The gateposts of the big house still stood, although the gates themselves lay on the ground. She walked into a driveway edged with rather sombre laurels and other dark evergreens.

The front door of the house was gone – taken, perhaps, for firewood by some foraging party. She went into the hall. The dim winter day shed very little light indoors. The house stood silent, melancholy. Only the angry gunfire from a few miles north broke the stillness.

'Elwin? Elwin? Are you there?'

No answer.

She went into the house. There was no one in any of the downstairs rooms. Very unwillingly she began to thread her way upstairs. Clothing was caught on the banister, as if someone had run hurriedly downstairs clutching an armful. The bedrooms were empty, drawers hanging open, wardrobes agape. Someone had packed in a hurry and gone, before the German gunners found the range and wrecked the house. She looked up. She could see the sky through the roof above the bedroom.

She went downstairs again. It was hopeless, there was no one here. But she would make one more foray through the downstairs rooms.

In the kitchen, something caught her attention. There was a sensation of warmth.

The rest of the house struck chill and damp, yet here in the kitchen there was a different sensation – not of the warmth of a cooking range in constant use, but a lessening of the chill. She held her hand out over the plates of the range. A definite feeling of heat. Slowly she put her hand down on the iron top. It wasn't so hot that it burned her, but it was hot enough to tell her that there had been a fire in the range this very morning.

'Elwin?' she cried, whirling about, expecting to see him behind her.

But the kitchen was empty.

She stood still a moment. Had he been here, and moved on?

But the fire had been alight this morning. And Roget's friend Armand reported having seen an English officer the day before yesterday.

Where had he seen him?

In the garden.

She went back through the house and into the garden at the front. The sombre evergreens looked back at her. She suddenly thought, If anyone wanted to stay out of sight, they need only hide among these laurels.

She threaded her way among them, but found no one. And yet, as she looked, she saw that someone had recently pruned sprays from a viburnum.

With a sudden leap of hope she went round the side of the house to the vegetable garden. It stretched down to a greenhouse against its further wall, and beyond that the vineyard stretched on to the west. She stood looking at the straight rows where frost-bitten greenery told of carrots left in the soil, cabbage unharvested, beets frozen where they grew.

There! Something was moving.

Someone was in the greenhouse.

She started forward then, checking herself, moved in a slow saunter towards it down the centre path. As she went, the figure became more clear. It was a man in a khaki shirt bending over a plant, doing something – spraying, it seemed, with a brass gardening syringe.

She opened the door of the greenhouse. He looked round.

'Hello, Elwin.'

'Christina? Close the door, we don't want the draught to harm the plants.'

He smiled at her, held up the pot he was about to put back on a shelf.

'*Abutilon insigne*, I think. Good, isn't it? Putting out these great big flowers when it's as cold as death outside.'

'Elwin, what are you doing here?'

He gave her a perplexed glance from frank grey eyes. 'Well, I should have thought that was obvious,' he said in the tone of one speaking to the not-so-bright. 'I'm looking after the plants.'

Chapter Seventeen

He looked perfectly normal standing there, with his hair carefully brushed so as to hide the shaved area round his scalp wound, with his crumpled but clean shirt, his patient expression and slight smile.

Perfectly normal – except that he was in the grounds of a wrecked house which belonged to strangers, in a strange land, whereas he should have been safely at home in Market Bresham.

Trying to keep her anxiety hidden, Christina said, 'How exactly did you get here?'

'I walked. It took me all day.'

'You mean you knew about this place?'

'Oh no. I just walked until it began to get dark, and then I saw the outline of the house against the sky, and I came in and nobody was here, so I dossed down in the hall in my greatcoat, and then in the morning, you see, I had a look around – and this glasshouse was standing here.' His smile was brilliant. 'It seemed such a miracle: the house all shattered, shell craters all around, and yet only a few panes gone in the glasshouse. I tacked cardboard over the gaps – it's not bad, is it?'

'Very neat,' she agreed.

'The paraffin heaters had burned dry, so I cleaned and refilled them. Too late for some of the plants, of course.' He gestured to a row of pots of withered, strap-like foliage. 'Those were orchids. I don't know much about orchids, but I think that one's a vanda. A few nights' frost has put paid to them, poor things.'

'Elwin,' Christina said in a careful voice, 'you've got to come back with me to the hospital.'

'Oh no. Why? There's nothing to do there. It's much more interesting here.'

'But you need proper food and rest.'

'But I've got proper food here. There's a store-room next to the kitchen with sacks of potatoes and strings of onions, and smoked fish hanging from a line, and though the hen-house has collapsed the hens are still about so I've had eggs almost every day. No bread or milk, though – that's a bit of a nuisance. But I manage.'

'But where are you sleeping? You can't keep on wrapping yourself in your greatcoat in the hall, and the beds upstairs must be wringing wet by now.'

'I sleep here,' he said. He took her by the elbow, guiding her round the central display table to show her a sack stuffed with straw on which his greatcoat and uniform jacket were neatly folded. 'It's warm in here and I've got the plants for company.'

'But . . . but, Elwin, you can't show a light in here at night and it gets dark so early—'

'Oh yes, that's true, but the kitchen is pretty well blacked-out so I cook up a big pot of stuff about five o'clock and while it's cooking I have a wash and a shave – got to keep up standards, haven't I? And then after supper I have a go at the French newspapers – there's a pile of old newspapers for kindling. That soon makes me sleepy, and besides, it's pretty hard work keeping this garden going – the water supply's gone, you see, so I have to get water from the well, and carting buckets back and forth . . . Anyhow, I've been sleeping very well.'

He paused, waiting for her reaction. He had said it all in a tone of complete reasonableness.

She felt a deep sympathy for him. He had made himself a beautiful little world of his own. Why should she disturb him?

'Yet you can't stay here for ever,' she ventured, reluctantly.

'Oh, of course, I know that. My leave's up in three days. By the by, when you get back to the hospital, ring them for me, will you? Tell them I'll need transport to get back.

Trucks and lorries go past on the road but there's no way of knowing which might be going west.'

'Hadn't you better come back and ring them yourself?'

'That's not necessary. Get put through to Company D, the Duty Office. Ask for the company clerk. It'll probably be Corporal Mimms – he's very efficient, he'll see to it.' Then he burst out, 'Where are my manners? I ought to offer you some refreshment! Would you like some coffee?'

'Coffee!'

He picked a big vacuum flask up from under a bench. 'I make a big batch at breakfast,' he explained. 'It sees me through until evening. Only black, I'm afraid.' He looked at her in apology.

'Black will be fine.'

On a little table there was a mug, down-turned, a little tin, and a spoon. He unscrewed the cap of the flask, poured coffee into it and into the mug, handed the mug to her, took the lid off the tin and offered it to her. 'Sugar?'

'No, thank you.'

The coffee was quite hot but rather weak. Elwin said, 'I have to grind the beans every morning and it's such a chore, turning the handle, I think I skimp a bit on it. Tastes better with sugar.' He offered the tin again, like an anxious host.

She took a little, stirred it in. 'Elwin,' she said, 'why didn't you go with the other men on the lorry?'

He strolled away from her to gaze through the glass at his domain.

'I couldn't, you know,' he replied. 'Mother would have wept all over me, and Father would have clapped me on the back and told me what a hero I was.'

'Well, that would only be—'

'There was nothing heroic about it. If that Gerry had had his bayonet fixed, he'd have run me through instead of just bashing me on the head. It's sheer luck I'm here to tell the tale.'

'Well, you could have told them that.'

He shook his head. 'They wouldn't want to hear the truth,' he said harshly. 'They don't have any idea what it's like. I didn't, myself, when I joined up.' Then, with a sudden change of manner, 'Shall I top you up?' as if he were host at a cocktail party.

'No, thanks, I must be going. And I want you to come with me, Elwin.'

'No, no.' He shook his head. 'What would be the point of that?'

'What's the point of staying here?' she exclaimed, unable to prevent herself. 'You'll have to go in three days – the plants are going to die then.'

He gave her a glance of reproach. 'Someone else might come along,' he said. 'I did, didn't I? And I saved some of them. Anyway, another three days means another three days towards spring. The weather might go into a mild spell; quite a lot of the plants might manage. Although of course the watering . . . I thought of arranging a sort of reservoir under them so they could soak up what they need. I wonder if that would work. What do you think?'

'Elwin, please come back with me!'

'Do you remember,' he said, 'that cottage we used to be taken to for summer holidays – in Devon? Do you remember we put some of the potted geraniums in the stream in the shallows, thinking it was a good way of doing the watering? What a mistake! Took three days to get them back to normal. What was that place called?'

'I don't remember, Elwin. Listen—'

'Prinkington, something like that. Do you remember how the valerian grew out of the garden walls? And I planted some sunflower seeds, expecting them to flower before it was time for us to go home.'

'Elwin—'

'This is what I really want to do,' he explained, with a sigh. 'I never wanted to be a lawyer, I wanted to be a gardener. But of course you couldn't *say* that. Father would have gone through the roof!'

She found herself unable to speak, choked by tears. There was so much sorrow in his voice, so much regret.

He came to her, took the mug of coffee from her, kissed

her on the cheek. 'You run along,' he said, sounding kindly and responsible. 'I expect you're due on duty or something. Just you run along, I'll be fine.'

'But Elwin—'

'How are you going to get back? We'd better go out and flag down a truck.' He ushered her round to the front of the house, up the drive, and out on to the road. As luck would have it, almost at once a small van came tearing along. The driver applied the brakes in a screech at Elwin's wave.

'Be so good as to take this young lady to Troyes,' he said in passable French.

'Huh!' said the driver, but opened the door for her.

'Don't forget to ring Corporal Mimms about transport – Monday the 8th, I'll look out for it.'

When she got back to the hospital, Christina checked in. Before going on duty she made the phone call to Elwin's company. It seemed to take for ever, but at last a voice said, 'D Company Office.'

'I want to report the whereabouts of Lieutenant Holt.'

'Beg pardon? Lieutenant Holt is on home leave, miss.'

'No, he didn't go on the transport. He's at a place called Jerache, on the road between Troyes and Vitry-le-François. It's a big house, I think it's called *La maison Jerache*.'

'Oh, decided to stay with friends, did he?'

'He asked me to let you know he'd need transport on the 8th.'

'Ho, did he! How am I supposed to get transport to pick somebody up outside our own sector?'

'Is that Corporal Mimms?'

'Well, yes,' said the bossy voice. 'This is Corporal Mimms.'

'Lieutenant Holt said you were very efficient and would manage it somehow.'

'Well, I suppose I could send a motorbike messenger. He could hop on the pillion . . .'

'That would be fine.'

'Righto then, miss, leave it with me.'

After dinner in the mess she sought a private word with Adeline Bellhaven. She had already reported that her brother was safe and well further up the line.

'Doctor, I wonder what we ought to do about him?'

'In what sense, my dear?'

'Well, his behaviour was quite out of the ordinary.'

'Passing up a home leave? I suppose it was. But he's old enough to make his own decisions, after all.'

'But it was all so odd, doctor. He . . . He was living in a kind of fantasy world.'

'Fantasy world?'

'Tending someone else's plants in a deserted garden. All alone, living like a gipsy.'

'Did he seem . . . peculiar? Not aware of his surroundings? Was he neglecting himself?'

'No, no, not at all. In fact, he was managing very well. But that's just it. He was like a little boy on a picnic.'

'Dr Holt, most men are just little boys at heart,' Addie Bellhaven said with tolerant good humour.

'But this was different. I can't explain. I just think I ought not to let it go by as if it meant nothing.'

'What do you suggest then, doctor?'

'I wondered if he could see a specialist?'

The older woman sagged back in her canvas armchair and stretched out her legs to the paraffin heater. 'What kind of a specialist?'

'I don't know . . .'

'You think the bang on the head has unhinged him?'

'No, I don't mean quite that. It's to do with his mind, of course – a psychological thing.'

'Humph,' said Dr Bellhaven, 'that Dr Freud and all his rubbish. I don't take much heed of that, myself.'

'I understand your feelings. But when I was at university, we read some work he'd done on hysteria—'

'Good God, you're not saying your brother is hysterical!'

'No. I suppose not. It's something else. I don't know what. I just feel – he's under some sort of strain . . .'

'Aren't we all?' sighed the senior physician.

'I wondered, since he was your patient, if you'd recommend him for a specialist . . .'

'A nervous disease – a neurologist, you mean?'

'Well, yes,' replied Christina, wondering to whom else he could be sent.

'There's no neurologist hereabouts, my dear girl. He'd have to be sent back to a base hospital.'

That would be a very good thing, thought Christina to herself. To get him out of the front line, that in itself would be helpful to him. A disease known as 'shell-shock' was beginning to be talked about and, although some doctors dismissed it as a form of malingering, Christina felt there was plenty of evidence to suggest that soldiers of the line suffered from the extreme stress of battle conditions.

After some discussion, Dr Bellhaven agreed rather reluctantly to refer Elwin for further examination. But the request was passed on and on, with occasional letters inquiring what exactly the patient seemed to be suffering from, so that it was summer when the subject was broached again.

'I had a telephone call from a Dr Redout,' said the senior physician, 'about your brother. We had a bit of a chat. He said he'd like to talk to you before going further with this case. I made an appointment for you to see him in Paris. Here's the address.'

Next day Christina presented herself at a French military hospital in the Tenth Arrondissement. She was shown up to a handsome office on the first floor, where an English secretary announced her arrival to the neurologist. Dr Redout proved to be an elderly man with a George V beard and moustache. He wore a well-tailored uniform of the Medical Corps.

'Sit down, Dr Holt. Can I offer you something? Tea? Coffee? Sherry? I generally have a cup of tea at about this hour of the afternoon.'

'Tea would be nice.'

They made small talk until the secretary brought the tea – a different brew from that produced by the Scottish staff at Troyes. There were even proper cups, not tin mugs.

'Now, about Lieutenant Holt,' said the major. 'I'm not quite sure what it is I'm supposed to look into.'

'I thought you talked to Dr Bellhaven about him?'

'Yes, and she only reinforces the reports I've had from his company commander. Lieutenant Holt is thought to be a good, steady, sensible young officer. What is it you say he suffers from?'

'I don't know what to call it, major.' She gave a brief sketch of the episode at Jerache. 'He seemed sort of detached from reality.'

'Is there anything unusual in that? We all go off into little day-dreams of our own from time to time.'

'But he seemed to think . . . I don't know how to convey it. He seemed to think it was more important to look after those plants than to see his own parents.'

'Did you question him about that?'

'I asked him why he didn't take his home leave.'

'And he said?'

'That . . . I can't remember exactly . . . that he didn't want to be wept over and treated like a hero.'

'Does he in general get on well with his parents?'

She hesitated. 'Well enough.'

Major Redout looked at her over the rim of his teacup. 'What does that mean? Family troubles?'

'Not precisely. But my father isn't the easiest of men.'

He shrugged. 'A lot of children have trouble with their parents. I can't see it's particularly significant that Lieutenant Holt should want to stay away from them.' He set down his cup to pat the folder on the desk before him. 'The lieutenant's medical records are here. I note that he had a severe laceration of the scalp but that the X-ray revealed no fracture, no splinters of bone into the dura mater, and although of course the brain tissue was bruised, he made a good recovery. No disability of movement, no dizziness.'

She nodded. 'That's the physical record.'

'Ah!' He brushed his beard forward and then back with his knuckles. 'You are saying this is a mental problem?'

She made no reply.

'Because if you are, Dr Holt, I must tell you that his fellow officers report nothing of that sort. Lieutenant Holt plays his part well under battle conditions. He led his platoon well during the offensive at the beginning of the month – so well, in fact, that his commander thinks of promoting him to captain to replace an officer who went down. Does that sound to you like a man who has mental problems?'

'No.'

'The reason I asked to see you was this. Your senior officer tells me you have very good qualifications. She speaks well of you. So I felt I owed you the professional courtesy of a face to face discussion. If you insist, I can have your brother brought to Paris for an examination. But do you really want him to suffer the stigma of being considered a mental case?'

Of course she did not. When Major Redout suggested that she was worrying too much, Christina couldn't find any arguments against it. Perhaps she'd been a fool. In the end she agreed that perhaps Lieutenant Holt should be allowed to carry out his duties as a soldier without any interference.

The following month saw a lull in the work at the WSH base at Troyes. At the moment the battle seemed to be less extreme on the Western Front, or else the casualties were going elsewhere.

The news from other theatres of war was very mixed, however. The submarine menace had begun at sea, but on the other hand Italy had declared war on the Austro-Hungarian government which automatically made her an ally of Britain and France. A German airship called the Zeppelin had, unbelievably, attacked London from the air. In July came news that far off in South West Africa General Botha had accepted the surrender of the German forces which, though cheering, seemed to Christina almost irrelevant.

In August a letter from Jo-Jo Belu got through. First of all it was full of anxious inquiries about her welfare and good wishes from friends in the Serbian community 'who still remember you with kindness'. Then it went on, inevitably, to breathe fire and brimstone against the enemies of Serbia. Bulgaria, announced Jo-Jo, wasn't to be trusted. 'Mark my words, they will seize their opportunity, those scoundrels, to cause hardship and take territory from my poor suffering country.' She ended by saying she was trying to find a substitute doctor so that she herself could come to Europe and enlist to help the Serbian army if they would take her as a doctor.

Events proved Jo-Jo right about Bulgaria. No one else in Troyes paid the slightest attention to the news when it came through, but Christina was forced to give a grim smile when she read in a French newspaper that Bulgaria had signed a military alliance with Germany and Turkey.

'Bulgaria!' said Miss Paterson when Christina mentioned it to her as they were stripping off soiled operating gowns. 'Who on earth cares about Bulgaria?'

To the surprise of the hospital staff, three days later they were all given seven days' embarkation leave.

'Where will we be embarking for?' everyone asked everyone else.

But it was a secret.

Christina spent her leave in Paris in the company of two other members of the hospital. There was still gaiety there, although the Germans had been so near at one time. They went to theatres, to the cinema, they ate rather better than they expected, they attracted a lot of attention in their grey-blue uniforms and were followed on two occasions by admiring Frenchmen.

When they returned to Troyes, they found the hospital electrical supply being disconnected and the tents dismantled by a unit from the French engineering corps. At once the staff set to work putting precious equipment into boxes, piling sheets and blankets into baskets, making beds of straw and woodshavings for glass bottles and glass dishes. By the last week in September 1915, the Women's Service Hospital was packed and ready to move from Troyes.

'Any news yet on where we're going?'

Nobody could say.

They all tramped along the dusty road to the station. There was a clear blue sky overhead, a thin crowd of citizens to cheer them as they went by, and at the *gare* a farewell speech by a French general.

The train took them off on a journey whose end they couldn't foresee. Two days went by during which they were shunted from one line to another and back again. But in the early hours of the third day they puffed slowly into Marseilles.

'Marseilles!' cried Jane Sibley in delight. 'We're in the South of France!'

'What's more important,' said the hospital administrator, Mrs Gibson, 'we're in a *seaport*.'

The women stared at each other. Overseas?

In the morning a rumour began; in the afternoon the rumour became a known fact.

They were about to embark for Salonika in Greece. And Salonika, as perhaps only Christina knew, was the chief staging post for the war in Serbia.

Chapter Eighteen

The ship, *L'Etoile de France*, was already stacked with the horizon blue of French uniformed troops by the time the Women's Service Hospital embarked.

'What have we here, *mon commandant*?' murmured one of the officers. 'Women . . . and some of them quite pretty, I'm happy to say.'

'What can the uniforms mean?' replied Major Henri Darblier, studying them from his vantage point by the rail as the doctors and nurses and VADs in their grey-blue jackets and skirts came up the gangplank.

'It means, I hope, that they are accompanying us to this confounded Salonika. Ah, the pleasures of feminine company!'

'The fair-haired one is mine, captain,' Darblier said with a grin. 'I stake my claim now.'

'You wouldn't pull rank on me, would you? She's sure to prefer me – I'm younger and better looking.'

'You're also fond of living dangerously, my young friend. I repeat, hands off the blonde. I shall look after her personally.'

Captain Lemur shrugged. After all, there were about thirty women, and though some were decidedly long in the tooth, the plump brunette wasn't bad.

Dr Sibley, who wouldn't have been pleased to be described as a plump brunette, turned on the gangway to appeal to Dr Holt. 'Shouldn't we be supervising the loading of the equipment, Chrissie?'

'Would you know whether it was being stowed properly? Mrs Gibson has talked with the purser, and she seems confident he knows it's important stuff. Do get on, Jane, it's hot and smelly here.'

The oily water of the harbour – smelly indeed – glugged beneath the gangplank. The sun shone down with unexpected ardour on this October day. It was a slow business, boarding a ship. Passes had to be shown as they stepped on deck so that each member of staff could be assigned her quarters.

The assembled members of the *Corps Expeditionnaire d'Orient* watched with eagerness. Men whistled their approval, called out compliments or, the more ardent of them, demands for kisses.

'*Bonjour, bonjour, mes braves,*' called Dr Bellhaven, toiling up the gangplank behind Sibley. And to her colleagues, in English, 'Bunch of rascals! I suppose they think we don't understand what they're calling out!'

They were four women to a cabin, in a quarter of the ship reserved for women only. The French troops signified their disappointment by lamentations and the wringing of their hands.

'Never mind,' Major Darblier said to his friends, 'the dividing line is only a rope hooked across a passage.'

He learned different on the first night, which was spent in harbour. There was a ship's officer on watch by the rope.

Well, never mind. There they all were, cooped up together on a ship of the *Messageries Maritimes*, about to head east through the Mediterranean. The days would be sunny, the nights moonlit, there would always be some private with a mouth organ willing to play romantic Parisian waltzes . . .

But when they set sail next morning, Henri Darblier's mood was altered by the grim sight of a French destroyer acting as escort. Worse still, the sunlit Mediterranean tossed up a storm that lasted three days. Major Darblier and all his friends were monstrously sick.

So, of course, were *les belles dames militaires*. 'I never thought,' wailed Dr Sibley, 'that I'd hate the Mediterranean the first time I got to it!'

It took five days to reach Malta. By that time sea-sickness

was over, the weather had calmed, but there was something else to quench any ideas of romance.

'Have any of you had a look at what's in the hold?' Mrs Gibson said nervously at dinner one evening.

Some of them had had conducted tours of the ship. The officers of the merchant marine were as keen as the military officers to get on friendly terms with this unexpected gift from heaven – thirty or so goodlooking and, on the whole, young women.

'I think the cargo is munitions,' Addie Bellhaven said, lowering her ringing voice for once.

'I think so too, doctor. And you realise that makes us a legitimate target of attack?'

'Nobody would attack a hospital ship . . .'

'But this isn't a hospital ship. It's a troop ship that happens to be carrying a hospital; but no German commander is ever going to know that, is he?'

This wasn't reassuring. Nor was a survey of the survival equipment. There were insufficient life-belts, nor could the boats have taken more than a quarter of the passengers. It was probably for this reason that there was never a life-boat drill.

Morton and two or three of the other VADs were confiding their fears to Christina as they took the air by the boat deck.

'I don't know about you, doctor, but I can't swim!'

'I'm going to carry my haversack with me, empty, until we get off this death trap of a ship! If we do get torpedoed, at least that'll be something to help keep me afloat.'

'Girls, girls,' Christina admonished, 'we're not going to be torpedoed. We're almost half-way to our destination already, so you must think like the famous Dr Coué: *Tous les jours, à tous points de vue, nous allons de mieux en mieux.*'

'And what might that mean, when it's at home?

'Every day, in every way, things are getting better and better.'

There was a little light applause from a section of deck above them. They all looked round.

'You speak French very well, mademoiselle,' Major

Darblier remarked to Christina in French.

'Oh, lor', it's Passionate Pierre, wouldn't you know it!' groaned Morton, and made her escape with her friends.

Christina wasn't so lucky. As she was about to follow, Darblier swung down through the rail above and landed lightly in front of her.

He gave her a little bow. 'Henri Darblier, at your service, mademoiselle! May I say how charming it is to have you aboard?'

She could tell he'd rehearsed this speech dozens of times in the six days since they left Marseilles. She said politely, 'Thank you, major. Now if you'll excuse me, I have tasks—'

'Ah, no, not on this beautiful morning! Surely you can allow yourself to enjoy the blue of the sea, the song of the breeze . . .'

'Major, I believe this part of the deck is reserved for the staff of the Women's Service Hospital.'

'Certainly, I know that, but you don't forbid me to present myself and say how much I admire you?'

He was smiling at her with practised cajolery. His blue uniform nicely set off his blue eyes. His hair was smoothed down with the last of his pomade. He'd had his batman make a special effort with his boots and leather leggings, which sparkled almost as brightly as his eyes.

He was so goodlooking and so well aware of it that Christina began to laugh. 'Monsieur,' she said, 'if you need something to cool you down, I can supply a prescription. Likewise, I can come to your aid if you break your leg. But compliments don't interest me. Excuse me.'

She made as if to pass him. Taken aback by her response, he let her go and then, suddenly coming to his senses, caught at her arm to pull her back.

'Mademoiselle, don't treat my admiration with contempt. It is entirely sincere, I assure you.'

Now Christina was annoyed. 'Take your hand off my arm, major,' she said.

'Ah, come, the touch of a man cannot be unwelcome—'

'You seem to be making assumptions, monsieur. You had

better understand at once that you're also making a mistake.'

'It is never a mistake to be in love.'

'Oh, stuff and nonsense!' Christina cried in English. She jerked her arm from his grasp and walked off.

The major hadn't understood the English words. But he'd understood the tone. He'd irritated her. Now that was strange. He'd never irritated a woman before. Angered, yes, intrigued, yes; but irritated?

They were strange, these English women. It was rumoured some of them were doctors. That hardly seemed likely – women doctors being sent into a theatre of war. They must be some superior brand of nursing staff. That was encouraging: everyone knew that nurses were tender-hearted and ready to be kind to soldiers.

Perhaps he ought to turn his attention to one of the others. There was one among those who wore the little bonnets with strings, a rosy little girl with springing curls. Perhaps he ought to pay his compliments to her.

But then . . . the slender blonde was so attractive. Such fine features, such unusually dark blue eyes. And her expression – thoughtful, sometimes almost dreaming . . .

No, he would pursue *la belle blonde anglaise*. All it needed was time. By and by she would surely melt into his arms.

His next attempt was rather neat. He'd noticed that the subject of his affections generally rose from the breakfast table in the dining-room before her colleagues. He managed things so that he went out just ahead of her then turned, so that as she came out through the swing door she almost walked straight into him.

'Mademoiselle!' he exclaimed, managing a realistic stagger so that they had to hug each other to stay on their feet.

'Oh! I'm sorry! I—' But then she realised it was a trick. The apology died away. 'Let go, major.'

'Not yet, ah, not yet!'

'Let me go! Others will come out in a moment.'

'Let them! How can it be wrong to embrace one so beautiful?'

She brought her arms up inside his, intending to hit him in the chest with her fists.

At that moment the alarm bells of the ship began to clang. The first mate could be heard shouting through a megaphone.

'What on earth—?'

'Submarine!' gasped Darblier. 'Have no fear, mademoiselle, I will protect you!'

He held her fast, thanking Fate for the intervention. No woman would run away from a safe embrace when danger threatened. To tell the truth, he didn't believe in the submarine. There had been one or two false alarms.

'Will you let me *go*!' cried Christina. 'I have girls under my care who can't swim . . .'

'Oh, as to that, there are plenty of French soldiers to save them.'

'Major, if you don't let me go this minute I shall report this assault to the captain.'

'Assault?' he said, laughing. 'The captain is a Frenchman too, mademoiselle. He will understand . . .'

The escorting destroyer had swerved away from its little convoy of merchant ships. It rushed along about a quarter of a mile off on the lee side, dropping depth charges. The merchant ships put on what steam they could, according to prior instructions, trying to separate and present a diffused target to the enemy.

Major Darblier was suddenly sobered. This wasn't a false alarm after all. Destroyers didn't waste depth charges on false alarms.

'Mademoiselle, forgive me, I think you would be safer—'

'Monsieur, there's nowhere on this ship where we'll be safe. And I have duties to perform.' She ducked out of his embrace and was gone, running towards the part of the ship where the hospital staff had their quarters.

Darblier stood hesitating. There would be a good chance to pursue her in the turmoil of the emergency; get into the women's quarters, learn his way about . . .

The depth charges were exploding among gouts of water

to the left. Then all at once there was a louder crash. A strange sound, of metal tearing, wood rending, water roaring.

Everyone on the *Etoile de France* rushed to the rails to look. Ahead of them the *Marquette* was sending up a shower of splinters and shards and steam. She had been holed in the engine room.

Horrified, they watched. The ship began to settle into the water. Boats were drunkenly lowered. Crewmen and officers clambered in. The *Marquette* tilted over upon them. They saw the men working furiously to get out from under the sinking vessel.

There was a whirlpool effect. The ship was heeling over. The stern went down. Now the passengers on the other ships could see men on the far side straining at oars to get away. Swimmers in the sea were making despairing efforts to clear the danger area.

The destroyer went surging by. Depth charges thumped as she tried to gauge where the submarine might be, following the torpedo run.

A sound went up from the *Etoile*, part shout, part wail. A torpedo was tracking straight towards them. In stricken horror they watched it as it came . . . It would hit them on the starboard side close to the bows.

But no. Slowly – or so it seemed – the *Etoile* was turning to starboard. The angle began to be just enough so that the track of the torpedo might, just might, go along and past the prow.

Everyone on the decks stood as if turned to stone. Hands gripped hard at the rail. No one breathed.

And then it was gone, streaking on until the momentum of its charge wore out in the waters of the Mediterranean and it fell in a slow angle down to the sea bed.

The destroyer carried on with its counter-attack for some time after the second torpedo. Meanwhile the remaining two merchantmen picked up survivors. The Women's Service Hospital were brought into action to deal with injuries: steam burns, fractures, splinters of metal and wood imbedded in fragile human flesh. The *Marquette* was to have left the convoy at Lemnos. Now they all headed there, to land survivors and allow the skipper of the destroyer to make a full report.

It was early November when the *Etoile de France* finally sailed into the Gulf of Salonika.

A Greek official in a tail coat and striped trousers came on board to make a short speech in strongly accented French.

'What's he saying?' groaned Mrs Gibson, who despite her great abilities as an organiser could never make much headway with foreign languages.

'It's a little lecture on the political situation and how to behave,' Christina translated. 'This is a Greek city. The Greeks aren't in the war. The Turks, who still run the place even though they're supposed to have handed over to the Greek authorities by the treaty of 1913, are in actual fact "the enemy" – Britain and France are at war with Turkey.'

'I say!' muttered Dr Bellhaven. 'I don't much care for *that*.'

'What you mean is, we're in a neutral country where the top officials are not neutral.'

'Shsh,' said Christina, trying to catch what else was being said. The colonel in charge of the contingent was making a ringing response, thanking the Greek government for its friendship to France, and for allowing them to land and pass through 'this classic home of freedom' to help their friends in Serbia.

Cheers were called for, the national anthems of Greece and France were played.

'Can we go ashore now?' demanded Dr Sibley, who after ten days at sea was aching to stretch her land legs.

No, they could not. In the first place, there were quarantine regulations to fulfil. Then there was some objection to the presence of women in this military unit. Who were they, what right had they to be here? A medical unit? Composed entirely of women? Who had ever heard of such a thing!

Forty-eight hours later, long after their equipment had been unloaded and left standing on the docks, the doctors and staff of the Women's Service Hospital Serbian Division landed in Salonika.

Christina's first impression was: This is a Turkish town. She saw slender white minarets rising above the roofs of little houses which climbed a steep slope. As slender but less tall were the dramatic dark cypress trees. The sun was peeping through a silvery mist. To her it was like something out of the Arabian Nights.

On closer acquaintance Christina lost any fairy-tale notions. She found herself rubbing shoulders in the main street, Venizelos Street, with a throng of Greek soldiers in newly issued uniforms – cotton drill trousers worn with green khaki puttees, a green khaki tunic, and a visored cap; summer kit, quite unsuited to this cold November weather.

'I thought we were told they weren't in the war?' Miss Paterson remarked as the WSH doctors tried to make their way among them to their shore quarters.

At the house where they were to camp for the night, they were told the Greek Army was in process of mobilisation. 'Today and tomorrow, perhaps another day also,' said the house janitor. 'Salonika is in an uproar.'

He was absolutely right. Next day when they tried to get their own equipment through the town to the rail station, the two small converted Austins had to move at a snail's pace. Donkeys, mules, and ponies laden with packs took up the whole thoroughfare.

Morton and another VAD, O'Donnell, were the drivers. They edged their way forward, with the other women in rough formation behind them, supervising porters who pushed handcarts with the more fragile effects.

Christina was just behind and to the right of the second Austin. She had her own luggage – a haversack and a soft leather valise – and under her observation she had a somewhat rascally looking Greek porter who pushed a cart carrying caseloads of small pieces of equipment for the pathology department. In one of the cases was the precious microscope. It must be preserved at all costs, for it would be impossible to replace out here.

They came to a crossroads. Christina watched the first Austin accelerate into a gap in the slow, four-footed traffic and speed across the intersection. The second had to halt with a screech of brakes almost on Christina's toes.

She and her porter and her handcart of equipment were now on the main road, in direct line with the side-street coming down from the right. Trundling down the side-street was a cart pulled by a team of bullocks. The two cars were the first the creatures had ever seen or heard. The sudden screech of brakes, the sound of the petrol engine throbbing, scared them beyond anything they had ever known.

They bucked and snorted. Behind them Christina could see their rickety wagonload of firewood swaying. In the hubbub of noise it made a high creaking sound. The bullocks swerved, knocked into each other, and set off towards the crossroads, dragging the firewood cart pell-mell towards her.

The porter abandoned the handcart, leaving Christina alone with the precious equipment. 'Wait!' shrieked Christina. Too late, he was gone. She threw down her luggage, seized the poles of the handcart, and tried to shove it out of the way of the thundering bullocks.

I'm going to be smashed along with my microscope, she thought as the rampaging animals approached. Then a figure in blue hit the little handbarrow Christina was trying to move. She felt herself and the handbarrow being turned at right angles to the stampeding bullocks. A moment later the firewood wagon went rocking past, pulled by the two snorting, trampling beasts. They thrust their way between the handcart and the hospital's Austin. The car rocked on its springs, O'Donnell screamed, voices shouted in response, a cloud of dust rose up, half obscuring the scene.

And then, when it cleared, the bullock cart was tilted up against the wall of the shop opposite, with firewood cascading in all directions; one of the oxen was on its knees while the other pulled and strained to be free; the driver was holding on to its horns speaking soothing words, and the

Austin was gingerly proceeding to the further part of Venizelos Street.

From under the handcart a French officer in blue uniform emerged, dusting himself off.

'*Eh bien, mademoiselle,*' remarked Major Darblier, 'we meet again.'

Christina subsided, shaking, on the edge of the barrow. 'Was th-that you?' she faltered. 'Who pushed me clear?'

'At your service, *ma belle*,' he said, picking up his cap from the ground. He had made what he felt was a very fine flying tackle, hitting the cart with his shoulder.

'Well . . . thank you! It would have been awful if the wagon had smashed up my equipment.'

'To say nothing of yourself, if I may mention it. You were nearly gored to death.'

'I . . . I was?'

'Come, you have had a great fright,' he said. 'Come and have a drink.'

'No . . . oh, no, thank you. I must keep up with my colleagues . . .'

'Ah, there is no difficulty there. Salonika is a small town, I can find them for you at any time—'

'No, you don't understand, we're headed for the railbase.'

'Greek trains never leave on time. Come,' he urged, 'a cognac will do you the world of good.'

He had salvaged her rucksack and her valise. She couldn't go until he handed them over. She took hold of the handle of the valise, but he resisted.

'Please let me have my luggage, major.'

'Not until you have done me the honour of taking a drink with me. Come, you owe me that.'

She had been shaken by the accident, but once again irritation at his manner came to her rescue.

'*Will* you give me my valise?' she cried. 'I can't stay here arguing.'

'Then let us not argue. Let us sit down at the café table and learn to know—'

A voice interposed from behind Christina. 'Can I be of

assistance, mademoiselle?' it inquired in good though accented French.

She looked over her shoulder. A tall dark man in a uniform she did not recognise was offering her her shoulder-bag, which she had lost in the mêlée.

'There is no need, sir,' said Darblier, giving the new-comer an angry stare. 'I am looking after mademoiselle.'

'It seems to me you are delaying mademoiselle rather than helping her.'

Christina didn't say, 'Oh yes you're right,' but something in the glance she gave him let the dark gentlemen know she needed him.

He saluted. 'You wish a porter to handle this little cart, mademoiselle?'

'Yes, please.'

He looked about in the crowd. He was tall enough to see over the heads of most of the people in the street. He beck-oned and called in Greek. A swarthy man came up.

'Wait one moment, captain,' Major Darblier said. He had taken a look at the pips on the shoulder of the newcomer: two six-pointed stars on a pale blue background. A captain in some fifty-centime army, Henri thought. 'If mademoiselle needs to have a porter summoned, I shall see to it.'

'Please,' Christina said to the captain, 'ask the man to push the cart very carefully to the railway station. It has fragile equipment on it.'

'A pleasure, mademoiselle.' He gave instructions to the porter. Henri Darblier, feeling he was losing control of the situation, tried to talk him down, but he could speak no Greek. The porter nodded and took hold of the cart handles.

'Wait!' protested Darblier. This was damnable. He had practically fractured his shoulderblade saving the pretty Englishwoman and her pile of boxes. He wasn't going to let her go to some other knight errant.

'The lady's belongings, if you please,' said the captain, and took them from him before he could think to resist.

Next moment they were piled with the boxes on the hand-cart. The porter looked at Christina for instructions. She nodded and gestured ahead in the direction taken by the Austin. He set off at a sturdy trot.

'Thank you, captain,' she called back as she hurried after him.

Darblier needed only the very slightest encouragement to throw a punch at the captain in the unknown uniform. He glared at him.

Christina turned to look back. A momentary parting in the crowd let her see the tall captain saluting politely and turning away from the angry Frenchman with supreme indifference.

'Now who was he, I wonder?' she said to herself.

Chapter Nineteen

Major Darblier was proved correct in one respect: Greek trains didn't leave on time. The train for which Christina had been heading with so much urgency and anxiety was standing at a platform – that's to say, the carriages and goods wagons were there. But no locomotive.

Christina paid off her porter then sat down on the hand-cart to recover from the fright and shock of the near-accident.

'What happened to you, doctor?' asked O'Donnell with some curiosity at her pale looks.

'Nothing, there was a bit of a fracas, that's all.'

'That awful little porter ditched you, did he? You can't trust these people: they just don't seem to like us.'

At noon, when they should have left Salonika, there was still no locomotive.

'When are we likely to go?' Dr Bellhaven inquired of the station-master.

'Who can say, Madame Médecin-Chef?' He shrugged. He clearly thought it improper for this female to be asking such pertinent questions.

'But we understood the train was to leave at noon.'

'That has been altered.'

'But why?'

He sighed. Everyone knew that women were incurably inquisitive. The only way to have peace was to give her some information. 'We await troops for transport north.'

'Troops?' The same contingent who had come out on the *Etoile*, perhaps, thought Dr Bellhaven. 'French troops?'

'No, madame, the French troops have already

gone – three divisions, to Krivolak and Strumnitza.'

'Then who are we waiting for?'

'That is confidential information.'

'Confidential to whom? Dash it all, man, we've a hospital in those crates and boxes. It should be up at the front line helping to save lives. Who are we waiting for?'

Despite himself, the station-master was intimidated by this tall, loud-voiced lady. 'We await the British Tenth Division, which will go to Lake Doiran. Without them, the train cannot leave.'

'And where is the Tenth Division?'

'On a ship somewhere, coming from the Dardanelles,' he told her with satisfaction. 'Or that is what I hear.'

There was nothing for it but to settle down where they were. They asked and received permission to pitch a tent in the goods yard. One half was for use as a mess hall, the other was sleeping quarters. Washing facilities were available in the station waiting rooms. No food, however. For food they would have to go back into Salonika – either to buy from the shops or to eat in the restaurants.

One day went by, another. The days were warm still, although it was November. The nights were surprisingly chilly. They occupied themselves by checking and rechecking their stores, so far as they could. Some of their equipment was stowed in a wagon at the rear of the train, covered by a tarpaulin which it seemed best not to disturb.

A mail delivery caught up with them. It was a great treat, something that broke the monotony of unrewarded expectation. For Christina there were two letters, one from Aunt Bea and one from her brother.

Aunt Bea wrote that life was much the same in Philadelphia, though the families of German extraction were under some disfavour because U-boats had sunk the US merchantman *Gulflight*. Miss Melville was working hard to raise money for British causes. She had heard that Mary Mennem had married. They all sent their love.

The letter from Elwin was quite different. It wasn't exactly incoherent, but it had a lack of order that troubled

Christina. First he told her he was well, that he had been posted Captain unofficially, that the weather was good, that he had actually seen General Joffre the other day. This last sentence had been censored but it was possible to read it under the black ink. The appearance of a French general must mean an offensive on that part of the front.

The next line had several words scratched out by Elwin himself, as if he found it difficult to express his meaning.

'The roses are dying now. Autumn always means that things die,' wrote her brother. 'And winter lies ahead. But if you have a greenhouse you can keep things alive. Do you remember the greenhouse, Christina? If I'd stayed there I could have helped things to live instead of to die.

'In her last letter Mother said she'd heard from you – through Mrs Giles, I gather. Mrs Giles probably thinks you're a secret lover.

'And speaking of lovers, Dorothy sent me her photograph. It was strange. I looked at it and I couldn't think who she was. I carry it, of course. Most men carry a picture. An amulet, to keep out the bullets.

'But there's no amulet to prevent the bullet being fired. I fire a lot of bullets. And other men receive them. Pictures don't help.'

Something's wrong, thought Christina. Even though the malady doesn't have a name, he's suffering. There are some wounds that don't bleed.

She looked up from her letter. She was sitting on a campstool outside the mess tent, enjoying the sunshine on her face and head. A group of men – Turkish, she thought, though it was hard to tell in this mish-mash of a town – were staring at her in disapproval mixed with admiration.

It wasn't a new experience to Christina, all the women were stared at. The men of Salonika thought them outrageous, walking about the town without a husband or a father to see that they were safe, no servant to carry their purchases if they bought food in the shops, walking into restaurants and sitting down – sitting down any-where – among the *men*, even.

Here they were, these outlandish women, living in a tent and some of the railway carriages at the station. Christina supposed that, in a way, that was seen as proper: women should be together in a restricted area if they had no male relatives to guard them. Yet they didn't stay there. They went into the town, they spoke to strangers, they gave orders, they didn't lower their eyes when a man addressed them.

The fair women would be the most interesting. Fair skins, fair hair, eyes blue or grey or green: quite unlike the women of this region. That one, reading the letter – yes, these Ferenghi women could read! – was amazing. Quite tall, rather thin, but with hair like the young maize in the early summer sun. A serious woman, it seemed. Yet she smiled when she spoke to children. She often stopped to speak to children on her walks into Salonika. And she would give sugar lumps to them, or sometimes tiny hard sweetmeats, tasting of honey. And she gave sugar lumps to Greek children as well as Turkish.

A strange woman. She looked back at them now, surprised but unafraid.

'*Kalimara!*' she said to them. And then, since they refused to respond to Greek, '*Merhaba!*'

Shameless! To speak to a man she didn't know, to speak without being spoken to. The men shook their heads at each other, one or two making the sign to avert the evil eye.

'Idiots,' said Christina under her breath, and took refuge in the mess tent.

That afternoon the British troops arrived, cheerful and talkative although still in the cotton shorts and shirts they'd been issued with in the Dardanelles. They gave a cheer when they found the hospital encampment and heard English being spoken.

'There's a sight for sore eyes! How long you bin here, sister?'

'Nearly a week, waiting for you slow-coaches!'

'If we'd a known you was here, we'd a moved a lot faster!'

At once they set about brewing tea. It was bliss to have it

again – the strong, thick, sweet tea of the British Army. And bully beef. The hospital staff had grown heartily tired of stringy mutton or what they suspected was elderly goat.

At nightfall, the troops were mustered. Extra carriages were shunted in. The men embarked. So did the staff of the Women's Service Hospital. The French troops, with the regiment of engineers to which Henri Darblier belonged, had gone on ahead, the troops to take up line positions, the engineers to help establish a field hospital for the Serbians.

The locomotive had puffed out of the station but came back to be coupled to the head of the train. The citizens of Salonika – Turkish and Greek, male and female – watched with interest while it pulled out.

'By-ee! By-ee!' cried the British Tommies. But no one waved a farewell to them. Only the British consul stood at salute as they left.

By dawn they were in a little town in the hills called Ghevgeli. The hospital staff uncurled themselves from their uncomfortable sleeping positions and crawled out on to the platform. The British Tenth Division tramped out into the empty area in front of the station to be formed into order of march. Once again it was 'By-ee! By-ee!' but this time they had friends to cheer them off. The doctors and nurses stood waving until the rearguard had gone round the bend of the hill-path. They wouldn't see another British soldier for over a year.

Ghevgeli proved to be full of Greek infantry in their newish uniforms and men in brown homespun suits braided in black and with sheepskin caps. 'Who are *they*?' the women asked each other.

They were the Serbians. Reservists called up because their Army had been decimated by previous battles, they had no uniforms as yet. They looked fierce; Christina found them infinitely touching, with their soft-soled loose sandals and their ornate stockings of coloured wool patterned in roses or trees or prancing horses.

'Well now, to work,' said Mrs Gibson. 'Today I'll get the

equipment unloaded and stacked at the station. Then I'll see about transport. Will you send a message to me, doctor, when you've inspected the hospital site?'

Dr Bellhaven nodded, blew a short blast on the whistle she used as a rallying call, and they went off to find the spot for what would become the Ghevgeli Women's Service Hospital.

Christina went through one of the most disheartening days any of them had ever spent. They were offered a piece of level ground outside a disused factory. Christina at once commandeered part of the building for the laboratory. The dispensary and X-ray unit were in screened-off corners.

Stores would have to be kept on the first floor, which was reached by a vertical wooden ladder. Above that was an attic, filthy dirty, but which when cleaned would be the staff sleeping quarters. It had no windows, only rectangular openings with shutters. When the shutters were closed, there was no daylight. When they were open, they let in the biting mountain wind.

'Where are we going to cook and eat?' wondered Christina.

'It'll have to be done out of doors,' Mrs Gibson said. 'And the wards? Will we have to use tents?'

'Well, I can't see us using any of the structures. They're insanitary beyond words.'

'I'll have to bring the tents up from the station, doctor.'

'That means they can't be set up today . . .'

And that was a terrible pity; the doctors had been to inspect the injured brought down from the front line. There was no provision at all for Serbian wounded: no casualty station, no dressing point and, even when they reached the comparative safety of Ghevgeli, no hospital. Such nursing as was attempted was done in the military barracks.

The doctors and the senior nursing sisters went there to see what they would be taking on. Both the wounded and the dysentery sufferers lay on straw, unwashed and in their uniforms. Their clothes were bloodsoaked . . . worse, they were soiled with their own excrement. A team of Serbian military surgeons was attempting to deal with the wounded, without anaesthetics and with almost no antisepsis.

And to add to all the other problems, there was typhus among the population of the town.

They went back to their own hospital site greatly shaken. 'Well, we came here to do a job,' said Addie Bellhaven, 'and by God it's a job and a half. So don't let's waste any time.'

She sent Morton off at the run with a message for Mrs Gibson. They needed the ward tents at once, to start erecting them now so that at first light next day they could get to work.

While they waited, Christina Holt came to a decision. Or rather, two decisions. She hurried down the road to the town where, on their way to and from the barracks, she'd seen a clothing shop.

'*Kalo ste, gospodjo,*' said the shopkeeper, coming forward. He was a tall, stooped old man with a great grey-and-white moustache.

'*Kalo ste,*' Christina replied politely, and summoned up the remnants of the Serbian she had learnt among Jo-Jo's friends at the farm in the Alleghenies. 'I should like to buy some trousers. Do you have any?'

'Of course, *gospodjo*. For a husband? A brother?'

'For myself, *gospodine.*'

'Of course.' He went into the back of the premises, returning in a moment with some very baggy trousers in soft dark red wool.

Christina gaped, then burst out laughing. 'No, no, uncle! I'm not a Moslem woman.'

He was offended. He drew back. 'Trousers, you said.'

'I'm sorry. Please forgive me for laughing. I couldn't possibly wear those with my uniform jacket.'

He studied her. His lips twitched and so did the giant moustache. 'I see your problem, young one. What kind of trousers, then?'

'Do you have any boys' trousers that would fit me?'

He hesitated. He couldn't offer brown homespun trousers to this lady. They would not be suitable. But it so happened he had some uniforms, acquired through rather devious means; the dress uniforms of Greek officers who had now gone into khaki as they prepared to enter the war in earnest. The trousers of these were of good fine black broadcloth.

'Wait, young one,' he said, and disappeared once more into his store-room.

He came back with three pairs of trousers over his arm. There was nowhere to try them on since the shop was little more than a shack built on to the front of his house, so she held them against herself one by one. He nodded when she tried the smallest pair.

'How much?'

'Three francs.'

'Francs?' she said in surprise.

'Yes, francs. Serbian money has no value now. Francs, please.'

This was, of course, a French theatre of war. The WSH was attached to a French Expeditionary Force. But she was surprised to find French currency in use in this small town. 'You have French troops billeted here?'

'From time to time. At the moment, there is only the small detachment which arrived about a week or ten days ago. The officers are in the *gospodar*'s house, the men are in tents in his orchard.'

The *gospodar*, she knew from her sojourn with Jo-Jo's friends, was the elder or leader of the community. Lucky French officers, she thought.

Back at the commandeered hospital building, she clambered up to the loft, holding her cumbersome skirt clear with one hand. She undressed, exchanging her skirt for the trousers. They were too loose around the waist, but she used a spare necktie to hold them up. She then propped her pocket mirror against the window frame and with a pair of old surgical scissors she began to cut off her waist-length hair. It took a surprisingly long time. When she had finished, her hair stood up in odd little tufts around her head.

It felt strange: cool, airy, light, empty somehow, as if some important part of her had been cut away. But her hair was clear of her shirt collar. And it would make it easier to keep clear of headlice, which were carriers of typhus.

When she went down the ladder to the ground, a shriek of horror greeted her.

'Dr Holt!'

'Chrissie!'

'What have you done to yourself?'

She faced her colleagues. 'Look here,' she said, 'skirts are a death trap going up and down that ladder. We don't want to have to put each other in leg splints, now do we? So I bought some trousers. If anybody's interested, the shop in the town's main street has at least two more pairs.'

'But your hair! Oh, Christina, your lovely long hair!'

She had to swallow a sob before she could answer that. 'I'd rather have clean short hair than long lousy hair,' she said starkly.

'Oh . . .'

One by one, they came to Christina to be shorn. And Morton, Dr Sibley and O'Donnell went to the town to see if they could find trousers to fit.

Mrs Gibson had commandeered assistants from among the Serbian reservists. Bewildered, but understanding that these foreign women had come to help, the soldiers hefted up bales and crates, then came trudging up the path to the factory.

Catastrophe. The tent poles were missing.

'Those thieving, conniving Greeks!' roared Dr Bellhaven. 'They came poking around among our stores at Salonika Station . . .'

'It might equally well have been the Turks, Addie.'

'Damn them whoever it was. We can't put up tents without tent poles.'

A small crowd of townspeople had clustered round to watch these strange women at work. What a weird gang they must look, their hair cropped short like boys' and some of them in trousers, though not of the conventional Turkish kind but narrow, close-fitting, quite unsuitable . . .

'We'll have to get something as a substitute.' Edith Paterson turned to the crowd and began to ask in French for their help. The townsfolk stared back at her, interested in the peculiar sounds but quite unable to understand a word.

'We need help,' the very fair-haired woman said.

At last one of them was making sense. She might not speak good Serbian, but at least one could tell she was actually uttering words.

Christina could speak quite a lot of Serbian on a conversational level. But she'd never had to ask for tent poles before. She tried 'long sticks' and 'holding up pieces' but all she got was perplexity and a kindly murmur of '*Ne mari nista, gospodjo.*'

One of the little boys ran off. A few moments later he came back up the slope with two men in blue uniforms.

'Thank God,' cried Addie, 'Frenchmen!'

'Good Lord,' cried Morton, 'and one of 'em's Passionate Pierre!'

Major Henri Darblier and his friend Captain Lemur of the Second Company French Engineers came neatly to attention and saluted in greeting.

'May we help you, mesdames?'

'*Mon commandant,*' began Miss Paterson in her dreadful French, '*nous n'avons pas des tentes poles.*'

'What does she say?' Captain Lemur said to his fellow-officer. 'They haven't got any aunts for their chickens?'

Major Darblier gave a guffaw, quickly smothered. 'These poor souls are in dire straits, my friend. They must be, to have got themselves rigged out in such bizarre outfits.'

And Dr Christina Holt suddenly lost her temper.

'You!' she said, pointing her finger at him like an accusing attorney. 'Who do you think you are? Some superior breed of human being? You weren't brought here to see whether we look like fashion plates. We need your help. Do you understand that? *Help.* There are about sixty Serbian wounded up in that pigsty of a barracks, dying because we can't get our tents up. We need tent poles. Do you know what those are? Poles to keep up tents. If we can get our tents up, we might save those wounded men. Now laugh, you imbecile, laugh at that!'

Major Darblier went red. His friend gaped in dismay.

'I . . . I don't understand . . .'

'No, you're too busy cracking jokes. Go and find us something to use as tent poles.'

'Are you a nursing sister, then?'

'I'm a doctor, for God's sake, and this is a field hospital – or at least it would be if you'd stop wasting time. What are *you*, if it comes to that?'

Greatly shaken, Darblier introduced himself and Lemur as officers of the detachment of engineers sent to help set up hospitals and improve roads for the French Expeditionary Force in Serbia.

'We can provide makeshift poles, *docteur*,' he said, trying to make hasty amends for the derision with which he'd greeted the scene. 'I suppose you have no idea of the measurements?'

'Good God, of course we know the measurements! We've put them up and taken them down often enough. Morton!'

Morton stepped forward and with glee wrote down the measurements in metres and centimetres. The officers went off at the trot. A few minutes later a unit of ten men arrived, verified the figures, and at once began to chop down birch trees further along the slope.

It took them two hours to fell and trim enough slender birches to make poles for the ward tents. In that time, three men died in the barracks at Ghevgeli.

Utterly subdued, Major Darblier came to report that the tent poles were ready.

'Thank you, major,' said Dr Bellhaven, then without another word went to direct the transfer of wounded to the beds that the VADs were getting ready.

'Mademoiselle,' Henri Darblier said to Christina, 'I must be allowed to—'

'Oh, get out of my way,' Christina said, sweeping past him with a boxful of theatre instruments.

'But I wish to apologise.'

'Oh, do you?' That gave her a moment's pause. The previous opening had made her think it was more of his 'I must be allowed to tell you how beautiful you are' or some other such nonsense. 'Very well, I accept your apology. Now get out of my way.'

'But can't we do anything else to help?'

'Can you operate on wounded men?'

'Well, of course not . . .'

'*Then get out of my way!*'

He took himself off. Captain Lemur was rounding up the privates who had felled the trees. 'Well, *mon ami*, we managed to retrieve our good name after a very bad beginning, eh?' he remarked.

Darblier shook his head. 'I don't think so. My beautiful blonde thinks I'm an idiot.'

'What a change in her, *mon Dieu*! The hair short like a boy, the legs in the trousers – *très gamine*! I hardly recognised her.'

'The beautiful hair cut short . . . A thousand pities, that.'

'Well, it's interesting, there's no doubt of that.'

Darblier gave a heartfelt sigh. 'I'll tell you something, Jules. When she is angry, she is the most exciting thing I ever saw in my life!'

Chapter Twenty

The rumours were alarming. Christina was continually being asked by the others to find out 'what people say'.

People said that the enemy – the so-called Central Powers, consisting of the Austro-Hungarian Army, the German Army, and Bulgaria – had now invaded Roumania. Their resources seemed unlimited. The Serbians were being forced south-west. Bulgarian troops were making a pincer movement to catch the Allied forces heading for Salonika.

'The news is not bad, not bad,' the townspeople would say hopefully when they talked to Christina. 'Our army has seen bad times before. Everything will change for the better, as it did last time.'

Last time – in 1912 – they had had only the Turks to beat, not all the Central Powers in alliance. And if they believed that, why were they leaving their homes?

Worse still, they not only left their houses, they left their possessions. They took only what they could carry or load on to a pack horse. They didn't even attempt to bring out their ox-wagons: they knew the road south was too bad to allow the passage of wheeled vehicles.

The two Austins brought by the hospital proved useless. They had been intended to bring the wounded down the line quickly and with as little jarring as possible. But they either got bogged down in the mud in the valleys, or failed on the slopes of the mountains. Casualties had to be brought in by hand-held stretcher or, sometimes, on the back of a comrade.

The wounded were mainly French troops. They were retreating doggedly from Demir Kapa and Strumnitza to the south. But there were even more casualties from frostbite.

The French Colonial troops – from Senegal, from the French Congo – suffered horribly in the freezing temperatures. The smaller operating theatre was in constant use as amputations were carried out on frostbitten fingers, toes, ears.

The Vardar was blowing, a wind dreaded by the mountain people. Its icy breath swept through the valley on the slopes of which the town of Ghevgeli was strewn. It clutched at the ward tents on their makeshift poles, it flapped the shutters of the sleeping quarters back and forth, it brought a coat of ice to the packs of tethered animals. The sound of the wind was frightening – a mournful wail that seemed to prophesy doom.

But to the women of the hospital, unused to these surroundings, worst of all was another sound: the howling of wolves.

Christina didn't believe it at first. She asked who owned the dogs that kept howling at night. 'Wolves,' said the townspeople. She didn't even recognise the word, had to have it explained: yes, a wild beast, like a dog but fiercer, that hunted in a pack with others. 'Oh yes,' she was told with a shrug, 'the Vardar always brings them down the mountains. Game is scarce, they hope to pick off sick animals in the valleys.' Then, with a laugh, 'And any humans, of course, who are silly enough to be out at night in this weather.'

Day after day, the weather got worse, the news got worse, the outlook got worse. Despite all the WSH doctors could do, the death toll mounted. In this weather, badly wounded men, evacuated down mountain tracks, could scarcely survive to the entry of the hospital compound.

The French engineering officers were called in to help keep the electricity generator going. Without it there would be no electric light in the operating theatre. More than once, when it broke down, Edith Paterson and Christina had to operate by the flickering light of tallow candles. X-ray pictures became unreliable because of variations in the power supply when they were taken.

'This is no place for women,' Major Darblier said as, in

his greatcoat and with a shawl wrapped round him, he checked along the cable to find the fault.

'Please, major, don't go back to that sort of talk.' Since her outburst at him over the tent poles, the major had dropped his exaggerated *galanterie* towards the women of the hospital, and had been treating them more or less as equal human beings.

'No, I mean it literally. It is not even worth while repairing this generator – you won't be using it much longer. You and your colleagues should be packing up to leave. The news is very bad. We have had orders to stand by for evacuation.'

'We can't leave. If we leave, who will look after the wounded from up there?' She nodded towards the peaks, from which could be heard a constant thunder, the thunder of the guns.

'The Serbs are finished, poor devils,' said Henri Darblier, shaking his head. 'Our men have had to give ground on their front and – forgive me – but I hear the British are falling back towards Albania.'

'Albania!'

'And soon there will be no more wounded from "up there". The Bulgarians will be there, and the wounded will either be taken care of by their doctors or . . .'

He didn't specify the alternative. Christina didn't need to have it spelt out. The war between the Serbs and the Bulgars was a very fierce struggle: little quarter was given on either side.

'You really ought to go,' he insisted, straightening stiffly from his task. 'A few days more and the Bulgarian gunners will have got within range of the railway line. After that, it would be a difficult retreat.'

Before he led his team of men away, he shook hands very formally. '*Au revoir, docteur.* I don't think we'll meet again in Ghevgeli. Our orders will probably come through by tomorrow and we shall be gone.'

Christina was busy next morning. But when at noon she went to thaw out her frozen fingers round a cup of hot soup, she was told the engineers had marched off to the railway station at ten. And of course, the generator went wrong almost at once.

Four days later orders came for the hospital to evacuate. Addie Bellhaven protested and raged at the French colonel of infantry who gave the order, all the hospital staff exclaimed against it, but the reply was the same. Stony-faced, the colonel said, 'You are part of the French Expeditionary Force and you will obey. It is no wish of the French military authorities to leave women doctors and nurses to the tender mercies of the enemy. Your patients must be ready to leave by noon tomorrow. Those of you who can travel by road, please make preparations to accompany the bullock carts.'

The patients were taken down to the station where they were put on the train for Salonika, a train crowded and unsanitary, totally unfit for the seriously wounded. The senior physician and four nursing sisters accompanied them, though what they could hope to do in that setting, no one knew.

With the rest of the staff, Christina set about packing up the stores and equipment. They were so distressed at having to go that they dared not say a word to each other for fear of weeping.

Everything was loaded on to bullock wagons. When it was done, they took a last walk through Ghevgeli to buy what they could for the journey.

An eerie quiet held the straggling town. The shop where they had bought their trousers was shut, nailed up against Bulgarian looters. A few old people could be seen, using a bedspread as a container for a few clothes, a round of *karmak*, the local cheese, and a bottle or two of *rakia*. In the sloping fields, cattle and goats found what greenery they could among the ice. They had been left to fend for themselves.

'Roast kid for the Bulgarians when they get here,' Morton said grimly. She sniffed. 'Someone's house is on fire.'

304

They went quickly on the track of the smoke. But all they found was a Macedonian leather-worker, sitting cross-legged inside his shack with the ever-burning charcoal brazier keeping his Turkish coffee hot.

'Tell him he ought to pack up and go, Christina.'

She relayed the advice. He looked at her with stoicism. 'I am a Macedonian Greek. Bulgaria isn't at war with the Greeks. I have nothing to fear.' And, with sly humour, 'And the Bulgarians need bootmakers too, after all.'

They bought a bottle of home-made spirits from a departing farmer, and some dried fruit – plums and raisins and halved pears. Then it was time to go, for it was past mid-morning.

The ground underfoot was frozen solid. The wagon wheels skidded on the icy rock, the hooves of the oxen slithered and slid. The two Austins were simply left. The chances of driving them down to Salonika were almost nil, even apart from the fact that petrol was now very scarce. The few remaining Serbians in Ghevgeli fell in behind them: very old men and women, some girls, a few boys. Every able-bodied male of military age had gone into the Serbian army.

As they made their ponderous way down from seven thousand feet to six, and from six to five thousand, the weather became less cold. Now their way was sometimes blocked by snow instead of ice. The drivers would get down and stolidly dig a way through. 'Lucky it's only December,' one of them said through his woollen muffler to Christina. 'In February the snow is too deep to dig.'

They camped at just below five thousand feet, in a bend of the road where there was a little extra room to draw the wagons up. Fires were got going, the inevitable thick Turkish coffee was made by the Serbians. For once Christina accepted it gladly. Hot and thick and sweet, it revived her enough to get her into motion to help cook an evening meal.

Food was shared out among the travellers. Everyone was welcome to everyone else's fire. But when it came time for sleep, the hospital staff bedded down in the wagons, among the bales and boxes, with a tarpaulin over them to keep out the wind. They were so tired they slept well. Only in the morning did they feel the result of a night curled round a bale of bandages and with a crate-corner digging into the back.

Breakfast was more Turkish coffee and Serbian bread, a poor, hard bread made from maize. With the sun bringing a magnificent halo over the rim of the mountains on their left, they set off down the road.

Now the mud began to be their enemy. At the fords, the oxen staggered and heaved, but the wagons remained immovable in the mud of the bank. Half the load on each of the three wagons had to be taken off. Boards and thorn bushes were put under the wheels. Everyone got at the back. '*Gurnitje-e!*' roared the driver. They all pushed.

And so, bit by bit, the carts were levered off the bank and into the stony riverbed. The oxen trudged on. The loads were carried over in relays, by the hospital women and the villagers of Ghevgeli. The stores and boxes were put back aboard. The caravan staggered on.

They stopped at a village called Pezne for their midday break, and also to dry out soaked boots and skirts and trouser legs. Luckily it wasn't nearly so cold now, but the river water had been icy. The bullocks were given a reviving nibble from the sacks on which the drivers sat and which Jane Sibley had nicknamed the tuck-bags: they had proved to be full of clover hay.

About five miles beyond Pezne, the road deteriorated yet more. The surface was mud strewn with boulders, or boulders in a sea of mud. The wheels went down into it no matter how they tried to carpet their path with such branches and twigs as they could find on the almost bare slopes.

'What are we to do?' Mrs Gibson said despairingly. 'Should we send someone back to that village to ask for men to drag us out?'

'Or send someone forward to see if there's a village up ahead?'

'Ask, Christina. Ask the drivers if there's a village nearer than Pezne.'

Christina approached the oldest of the three waggoners, the one who seemed best able to understand her Serbian. She was continually being told she ought to learn to speak properly and not use words that only a 'townie' would use.

'*Mozete, chicha,*' she ventured, '*gdeh u najbliz selo?*'

'*Blizu, blizu,*' he said, nodding towards the valley below.

But she'd had experience with what the Serbians thought of as 'near'. To them, it was 'near' if you could walk it in six hours.

She began on a discussion of how to get help to pull them out.

'It will take another team of oxen,' he told her with a shrug.

'Will they hire out a team to us in the next village?'

'Oh yes,' he said, but then he added with a grimace, 'Macedonians will hire out anything – for a price.'

Macedonians, that must mean that they were very near the Greek frontier, Christina thought. In a way, it meant safety. Even if the Bulgarians were in full pursuit, they wouldn't cross over into Greece.

A jingling of harness and the sound of horses' hooves in mud came faintly from among the fir trees further up the slope. Everyone stopped speaking. They didn't expect enemy troops, but they'd become so accustomed to danger that they all felt apprehensive at the slightest provocation.

From out of the shelter of the firs came a troop of six horsemen. There was a mass sigh of relief as the hospital company recognised the green-khaki tunics of Serbian soldiers. With delicate precision the horses picked their way down the stony slope.

'*Dobar dan!*'

'*Dobar dan, gospodar!*' The waggoners took off their sheepskin caps, gave little bows of greeting.

'Who is it?' whispered Christina to the old man.

'Captain Varikiav, of the King's personal staff. Good morning, sir, good morning. How did you leave His Majesty?'

'What's this about?' Mrs Gibson asked, nudging Christina.

'It's somebody from King Peter's staff.'

'Michty me! Is he a noble or something?'

No, in fact it seemed the king's man was the very captain who had come to Christina's aid when Major Darblier was trying to detain her in Salonika after the traffic accident.

He had got down off his horse, as had his fellows. There was another officer and four cavalrymen. They stood in a group, talking to the people from Ghevgeli.

There was something about him that spoke of a long ride over difficult terrain. His bony face was rather gaunt and looked as if it hadn't felt a razor for three or four days. His riding boots were caked with mud, which meant he must often have had to get down and lead his horse. Some of the buttons were missing from his tunic.

Something the waggoner said made him turn and look at the women from the WSH. His dark eyes ran over them.

'Chirovitch tells me one of you ladies can speak Serbian?'

Mrs Gibson nudged Christina. She stepped forward. 'I can speak a little, captain.'

She waited for him to recognise her, but all he said was, 'Excellent. But you are not the *directrice*?'

Christina introduced Mrs Gibson and Edith Paterson. He saluted each and shook hands. Mrs Gibson said, 'And Dr Holt is our junior surgeon and pathologist.'

'Dr Holt.' He saluted and shook hands.

He simply couldn't have recalled meeting her. And when she came to think of it, that was no wonder. Then she had been neat and trim in a little blue long-skirted uniform with her hair braided up around her ears. Now she must look like some young shepherd boy, with short-cropped fair hair under a round sheepskin cap, black trousers tucked into locally made handknit socks, and a peasant jacket of untrimmed kidskin.

'I understand you are bogged down here. I suggest that we let our horses rest a little and then we'll harness them up and haul you out. Then we can all travel on to Salonika together, if you will accept our escort.'

'Are you saying we are in danger, captain?'

'Not at all, Dr Holt. I believe in fact that Greece is about to join the war on our side. All the same, we are going in the same direction, so may we not travel together?'

She put his idea to the others. It was received with enthusiasm. A fire was made, and while the horses grazed and drank at a stream, the Serbian tea, *chaj*, was made. It was a weak amber brew that was despised by the Scottish members of the team but which Christina always found very refreshing.

'I regret I as yet speak no English. However, I can speak French or German if any of your friends do,' offered Captain Varikiav.

Dr Sibley could speak passable French, the chief surgeon could speak passable German. In a triangular conversation of French, German and Serbian the doctors learned that Captain Varikiav was indeed on King Peter's personal staff – 'but please don't imagine that makes me important. I run errands for him.'

'Where is the King at present, captain?' they asked with some interest. It was known that King Peter had been with the troops during the recent battle.

'He is taking part in the rearguard action to the south-west. I was sent on detachment to give a confidential report to his Salonika legation and also to gather information about the war on the frontier which you have just left.' He sighed and frowned into his glass of tea. 'We have done very badly, I gather.'

There was no use denying it. A silence fell.

'Well,' he said, rousing himself, 'your services will be needed in Salonika, ladies, of that I have no doubt. And your equipment must be sent down with you. Let's see what we can do.'

The cavalry horses were harnessed with long traces to the swingletrees of the wagons, and then led up ahead but on the solid rock at the side of the road. Another carpet of thorn bushes was laid under the hooves of the bullocks. Everyone got behind the wagons to push as the animals pulled.

An hour's work took all three carts past the great pool of mud. The cavalrymen gathered up their horses but didn't remount. Instead they walked alongside the caravan.

After about another hour, covering about three miles at the slow pace of the bullock carts, Captain Varikiav said, 'I believe we have now left Serbia.'

Somehow they all came to a stop. Slowly, like figures on a stage, they turned to look back.

The sun was going down behind Mt Bitolia. The snow glowed with a rosy light. From the peaks nearer to them, a great gliding form swept out, its wings tilting and shifting to the evening breeze.

A strange cry arose from the Serbians, a wail that yet had triumph in it.

'What is it?' gasped Dr Sibley.

'It's an eagle, Jane,' Christina replied.

Captain Varikiav took off his cap, almost as if he were in church. His men did the same. They stood staring up at the eagle as it soared around the mountain tops that separated Serbia from Macedonia.

'Do you know our national poet? "It is not in the plains that Freedom lies, But on mountain crags where the eagle flies."'

As the captain repeated the words, the other men nodded and joined in at the end. 'We feel it is an omen, doctor. The eagle is telling us that we shall come back.'

After a moment they turned to the road leading south to Salonika.

They were still descending towards the town when Dr Bellhaven came riding up to meet them on a sturdy mountain pony. 'I heard you were on your way. I've come to guide you to our new hospital site.'

'It's been allotted already?'

'Mrs Gibson, we're nursing men on the open ground! The town's full of soldiers – wounded, sick with fever or dysentery . . .'

A piece of waste land on the seaward side of the town, to the south, had been selected. Without a moment's delay the unpacking was begun. It was easier to halt the bullock carts outside the confines of the town and have the equipment carried in at the trot by porters pushing handcarts.

'*Bienvenue à Salonika, mademoiselle docteur!*' called a familiar voice, as they knelt among the bales and bundles. The French engineers had come to connect a water supply to the hospital.

By nightfall they had also connected the town's electricity supply. No more reliance upon a tetchy petrol generator. It seemed the height of luxury. Yet no one felt able to luxuriate. Christina knew that she and her colleagues were thinking the same bitter thought: even now, while they were in the comparative warmth and security of Salonika, men were dying up there among the mountains, men who might have been saved if they had still been in Ghevgeli.

Soon the hospital staff became aware that the safety of Salonika was comparative indeed. The rumour was that King Constantine of Greece favoured the Germans. His Queen was actually the sister of the German Kaiser. Far from joining the war on the side of the Allies, Greece might well come in on the German side. Which meant that the soldiers of Serbia, France and Britain who had fought their way out to Greek soil might still find themselves prisoners of war.

Captain Varikiav, appealed to anxiously on this point, could give no reassurance. 'It is a bad situation. You may not know, but there are consuls of Germany and Austro-Hungary here in Salonika. They send back news to their masters about the British and French forces, and their information is exact because they counted them off the ships when they first arrived.'

'You mean that if the Bulgarians or the Austrians broke through into this area, they'd know exactly what they were going to meet in the way of opposition . . .'

'Dr Holt, all we can do is prepare ourselves for attack. But if there is a chance to get away by sea, I advise you and your friends to take it.'

Christina's chin came up. 'We ran away from Ghevgeli.

311

We're not going to run away from Salonika.'

To her surprise, Captain Varikiav laughed in delight. 'Tell me, Dr Holt, do you have any Serbian blood?'

Christmas came. There was no possibility of a celebration in the wards, for they were full of men too ill to care. They were the pitiful remains of the Serbian force that had retreated south after the hospital was evacuated. Gaunt, desperate, their feet raw after marching through icy rock in their light *opanke* sandals, these men needed constant and expert nursing.

Major Darblier came across to the hospital on Christmas Eve, to wish them '*Joyeux Noel!*' He was taken aback to find the wards lit, as usual, with only the night lamps. 'No decorations, Christina? No candles?' he asked.

'It hardly seemed suitable, Henri.'

'But this is Christmas!'

She shook her head. It didn't feel like Christmas.

'Come, it is more congenial at the French hospital.'

'No, I can't—'

'Come, just for an hour or so. It is so dismal here.'

Against her will she let herself be persuaded. The midnight service was held in an Army hut in the French compound. The altar was an empty box, the priest's mudstained blue uniform showed beneath his surplice. The congregation was a motley collection of French wounded, medical personnel, a few French civilians from the business section. The mood was subdued, the voices faint and quavering in the dismal setting. As the last hymn died away and the clock on the Town Hall chimed the hour, Christina thought, 'This is Christmas Day.' She felt her eyes fill with tears. She hurried out.

Outside Henri caught up with her. 'I am sorry,' he said. 'Perhaps I was wrong to think any of us could be cheerful in this place at this time.'

'Never mind, Henri,' she said, and walked swiftly back to the anxious quiet of the hospital wards.

When New Year came, somehow things looked a little

better. The enemy had not, after all, pressed the attack into Macedonia, and most of the patients in the Women's Service Hospital were beginning to pick up.

Best of all – though why she felt it should be so, Christina couldn't quite say – Captain Varikiav came to visit them. He was shown round the wards, exchanged jokes and stories with the men who were well enough to respond, and ended by offering an invitation.

'Would you like to attend Christmas service?'

Dr Bellhaven stared. 'But Christmas is over.'

The Captain smiled. 'Not for us Serbians. Tomorrow is Christmas Day for the Eastern Orthodox Church.'

'Oh, of course it is! I never thought of that.'

'Would you like to come?'

'It'll all be in Greek, will it?'

'I'm afraid so.'

After some discussion it was decided some of the staff could well be spared. 'You go, Christina. The captain can explain to you what's going on and you can tell the others,' said Dr Bellhaven.

But going into the service they were separated by the press of people. The church, to Christina's surprise, was almost underground, and rather bare. Edith Paterson and the VADs sat at one side, Christina and Captain Varikiav at the other.

'You must understand that Salonika was ruled by the Turkish Empire for a long time. Christian churches were frowned upon,' the captain explained in a whisper. 'But in any case, the glory of the Orthodox Church is in its singing.'

Nothing could have been more true. Compared with the service in the French hospital, this was like a choir of angels brought down to earth. Passionate and poignant, voices rose in strange harmonies that echoed against the stone roof. The priest, tall and bearded, chanted phrases to which the choir sang responses repeated with fervour by the congregation.

Somehow the depression which had enwrapped Christina since Ghevgeli was lifted. When she came up the worn stone steps into the starlight, she had the feeling that she had received a blessing, an exquisite gift.

'Thank you,' she said in a low voice to Varikiav. 'Thank you for taking me to the service. I'll never forget it.'

He took her arm through his. 'Your name is Christina, yes? That is from this part of the world. We have it in Serbia too.'

'It's a common enough name in my part of the world,' she said, rather awkwardly.

'My name is Laurenz,' he said.

She felt a warmth, as of a little flame. He was offering her his friendship.

Chapter Twenty-one

In Salonika that spring nerves were jangled and tempers frayed. Too many different nationalities were cooped up in the enclave controlled – with or without the consent of the Greek government – by the Allies. In time this area came to be known by its inhabitants as 'the birdcage', and a cage it was; suspicion was everywhere, tensions grew unchecked.

Major Darblier, without pausing to wonder whether she would appreciate his advice or even needed it, took it upon himself to speak to Dr Holt.

'If I were you, I wouldn't be too friendly with those Serbians,' he remarked. They were sitting at a café table in the chief square of the town, watching the passers-by. Christina never tired of it: the variety of costume and uniform, the animation of the Greeks, the impassive features of the Turks, the Jewish merchants in their long coats of fur, the veiled women from the Moslem quarter, the sturdy fisherwomen from the shore settlements.

Despite the fact that she was often exhausted physically, Christina loved to revive her spirits by breathing in the beauty of the place. She would make the effort to walk into the town, perhaps to chaffer for something in the bazaars, or to drink a glass of the indifferent Greek wine, or simply to wander among the brightly painted houses.

Naturally the members of the Allied community often met. Henri Darblier did his best to be somewhere about if he thought his '*belle blonde anglaise*' would be in the town centre. Today, according to his calculation, she ought to have had time off during the morning. And so it proved.

He saw Christina look up sharply at his words about friendship with Serbians.

'That's a strange thing to say,' she replied with a frown on her thin features. 'We're here, after all, to fight for Serbia.'

He felt the irritation that often touched him when he thought about the Serbian campaign. 'Speaking for myself,' he said crossly, 'I'm here because the generals sent me. But it's not in this absurd campaign that the war will be won. It's the battles in France that are important.'

'I understand, Henri. Naturally you worry about your own country. But that's no reason to mistrust the Serbians. I can't imagine what you mean by that.'

'Well, they didn't put up a very good fight, did they?'

'Henri! You saw them yourself – they fought to the death, many of them!'

'Oh yes, the common soldiers. They were defending their own fields, poor devils. No, I meant these officer types who flit around here, and then all of a sudden disappear for days on end . . . Who knows what they're up to?' He studied his wine with distaste. This was a terrible country. They couldn't even make decent wine. 'You know this whole region is full of spies.'

To his annoyance, Christina laughed. 'Is this what it's about? You're trying to say the Serbian officers are spies?'

'Well, that friend of yours is fairly mysterious, isn't he?'

'Now, Henri, Laurenz is on the King's staff. Naturally he can't go around discussing information with casual acquaintances.'

'But where does he get to? He's been gone for over a week.'

'He didn't choose to tell me.'

Christina was fairly sure Laurenz had gone to Corfu, where the main Serbian army was trying to recover from the retreat through Albania and ready itself for a campaign to regain its homeland. But she certainly wasn't going to say so to Henri, who was often indiscreet.

Christina was quite fond of Henri by now, but his

tendency to lay down the law was sometimes tiresome. He was quite sure that he as a Frenchman knew more about warfare than any highland peasant from Serbia. Or any Greek, or any Bulgarian, or even, if it came to that, any Briton. He and his friends would get into terrible arguments about how the war should be won, made all the more futile by the fact that here in Salonika it was almost impossible to get any hard news.

One of Henri's chief annoyances was that Christina seemed too keen on the Serbians. She actually spoke the confounded language, which was one of the most impenetrable he had ever come across. Not, of course, that he had made much attempt to learn it: French was the language of diplomacy and of love – what more did a man need?

It wouldn't have been quite so bad if Christina had spoken her Serbian only with the patients in the hospital. But she seemed far too friendly with the little group of Serbian officers, and particularly with Captain Varikiav. It was an added irritation that Varikiav was a cavalry officer. Damn all cavalry officers, thought Henri Darblier: women always thought them so romantic.

Christina got up from her place. 'I have to get back soon, Henri. You stay and finish your wine.'

'No, no, where are you going? I'll come too.'

'I only want to collect a blouse I'm having made to replace—'

'Then of course I'll come with you. You know I don't approve of European women going unaccompanied into the bazaar.'

He heard her give a half-sigh. Really, she was very independent. At first he had found that startling. Now it was one of the things that most attracted him to her.

The tailor had the blouse ready – a fair imitation of the WSH uniform blouse, in white cotton. He pressed refreshments upon them while they waited to have the garment wrapped in blue tissue paper. Henri was uncomfortably warm in his uniform due to the close confines of the little wooden shop with its charcoal brazier glowing for the preparation of Turkish coffee.

'Do you think in summer they'll serve sherbet or

lemonade?' he muttered to Christina. 'It must be insufferably hot otherwise.'

The shopkeeper, who understood French quite well, gave the officer a glare. He was sick to death of these foreigners who had taken possession of his town and who didn't even spend money freely to make up for their trespass.

The warmth that March day was a presage of what was to come. Flies were a positive scourge by mid-April. Local hygiene was very poor so, spread by flies, dysentery began to appear. Another troublesome plague was ants. They carried no diseases but their bites raised large and irritating swellings which were difficult to keep clean if once they were scratched and broken.

But the greatest danger came with the onset of summer. Mosquitoes abounded. At first no one was greatly worried: the local mosquito was not the one that spread malaria. But there were anopheles in the marshy regions up country. Greek troops moved from one area to another, French troops were carried down from the front over badly made roads. Men were moved to Salonika, sometimes bringing anopheles in their clothing and before long the infection had taken hold.

The death rate rose. Those who survived recovered very slowly. Stomach ailments due to poor food and the chlorinated water were very common. Nursing became a constant struggle to keep men clean, to keep them from becoming reinfected. Christina spent hours in the laboratory staring at slides, alarmed at the number of cases of cerebral malaria that she saw. It was almost always fatal. She wasted precious time on sand-fly fever because the symptoms often mimicked more serious diseases.

In the autumn, infective hepatitis appeared. When she passed on the news to Addie Bellhaven, the senior physician groaned. 'That's all we need! It takes men long enough to recover as it is. If they get jaundice they'll be convalescent for weeks, and we don't have the proper food for the jaundice diet.'

Salonika filled with troops from the new Serbian army.

They had recovered in health and resolve. They looked quite different now: carrying French rifles, clad in British uniforms, American boots and puttees, but still wearing the unmistakeable Serbian cap.

'Now you see what Captain Varikiav was doing while he was missing from Salonika,' Christina said with a grin to Major Darblier.

'Oh, you mean he achieved all this by himself?'

'He certainly helped. Admit it, Henri, the Serbians have done well.'

'We'll see,' he grunted. 'They look all right but they've still got to go into the fight again.'

'That's what they're here for, surely?'

'Yes, and you can bet the Austrians and the Bulgarians know all about it.'

'Henri, why must you always look on the black side?'

But she understood very well. He wanted to be at the front himself, not cooped up in a multi-national 'birdcage'.

'I suppose your friend the captain will still be riding about on errands for King Peter,' he sneered, and could have kicked himself, for he knew she'd only defend the man.

Christina sighed. 'He's going up with Voyvoda Misitch when they move out.'

'You mean he's actually going to do some fighting?'

'Goodbye, Henri, there's no talking to you when you're in this mood.' She turned her back on him and walked off.

Well done, Darblier, he said to himself, that's just how to make a good impression on her.

As winter approached, Serbian wounded began to come into Salonika. Now Henri found it was a good thing that Christina could speak some Serbian, because from her patients she could glean news about how the campaign was going.

'They marched up the Cornicheva Pass,' she told him, 'and pushed the Bulgarians back, though with heavy casualties. Now they're at Mount Kaimakchalan and they've had to stop, because they can't get the artillery up over the snow.'

'Mount Kaimakchalan . . .' About 2,500 metres or, as the British would say in their absurd measurements, 8,000 feet. True enough, handling artillery over mountain passes in the snow, without proper roads, that would be hard. Even the Serbians could be forgiven for failing.

Why didn't they send up the engineers? What else were they for, except for making roads and building bridges? Instead here they were in Salonika, attempting to win goodwill by improving the town's water supply . . .

He longed for activity, any activity. And on 18 August, he got it.

The fire began about five o'clock in the afternoon. No one bothered when flames were seen in the bazaar. It was only a merchant's charcoal brazier, overturned by a frolicsome donkey. Neighbours came with pails of water to put it out. None of the Europeans even knew of it.

The welcome evening breeze of Salonika's summer came up. All at once there was a wall of flame. The wooden shops and houses were swallowed up. The breeze was fanned into a wind by the funnelling of the air currents along the narrow lanes.

At first everyone was concerned to save their belongings. Market porters were earning fortunes carrying heavy goods away. It was clear there was no hope of saving the houses: the water supply was insufficient, there was no proper fire-fighting service.

One of the VADs came hurrying into the mess tent. 'Ma'am, I don't want to seem silly about it, but that fire down in the bazaar is coming this way!'

Mrs Gibson, the hospital administrator, leapt to her feet. Alarm seized her. The smell of burning was strong in the hospital compound. Fool, she said to herself, of course if the smell is strong that must mean the wind is setting in this direction. In the evening the wind generally blew from the sea towards the land; she should have noticed that today it was different.

Outside, the prospect was alarming. Flames were creeping up the hill towards them, feeding on tinder-dry

Crown of Thorn and scrub juniper. As she watched, the flames changed from a low tide to a leaping wave as they reached a group of birch trees.

'Ladies!' she called, hurrying back into the mess tent. 'We're going to have to take action.'

'We can dig a ditch, ma'am,' suggested O'Donnell.

A ditch? All round the hospital? They didn't have time for that. And the flames had only got to reach one tent . . . And there were inflammable liquids such as alcohol in the wards, God only knew what in the store rooms.

Others had gone out to look, while Christina and Jane Sibley ran to warn those in the operating theatre.

'What?' cried Miss Paterson, pausing with her gloved hands over a chest wound. 'I can't stop now!'

'Edith, close up and get out of there!'

'Chrissie, I can't!'

The VADs and some of the ambulant patients were beating at the flames with brooms and blankets. The nursing sisters were preparing the bed patients to be taken out. Already the smoke was causing trouble to those with wounds to the chest and neck: they were coughing and choking.

'We're going to lose the hospital,' groaned Mrs Gibson.

'We're going to lose some of the patients,' warned Addie.

A procession of pyjama-clad figures was being led slowly away from the tents on the side furthest away from the flames. But where were they going to go? Night was coming on, and though it was warm enough to sleep in the open, that would lay the patients open to infection from malarial mosquitoes, from sand-fly bites.

Blue-clad figures were running about on the hillside. They made a flanking approach on the fire, coming round so that they were between it and the hospital tents. It was the unit of engineers. The commanding officer, Colonel Juverne, dashed up and gave a sketchy salute. 'Madame, is there anything in your tents that will be damaged by the blast of an explosion?'

'We-ell . . . glass utensils, sphygmomanometers—'

'My microscope,' Christina gasped.

'Damn your microscope! If you can save the tents, colonel, please do whatever is necessary,' shouted Addie Bellhaven.

The light was fading in the sky a little so that the glow from the fire seemed all the more fiercely red. The heat from it was intense. A few more yards, and the tent fabric might begin to burn.

'Please move all personnel and patients as far away as possible,' the colonel commanded. 'This is guesswork to some extent, so keep away.'

The hospital staff and their patients tramped up the slope to a distance of about a hundred yards beyond the last of the tents. Beyond that was a gully in which, in winter, a stream ran down to the sea. If worst came to worst, thought Christina, we could escape down to the beach: the fire couldn't travel over sand.

The short Mediterranean twilight had ended. Weird fireballs blew along in front of the wind. By their light Christina looked at her watch and saw that it was nine o'clock. The men of the engineering unit were working by electric torch. Commands and warnings in French were called across the burning hillside.

A series of three loud reports. Earth, stones and burning vegetation went up in three scarlet and black fountains. The ground trembled. The tent nearest the dynamite charges slowly tilted and fell over into itself, a huddled mass of canvas on top of the hidden beds.

A cheer went up nevertheless. The fire died back on itself. The ground below the hospital, burned and black, could be seen to smoke a little. But the ground nearer them, although covered in sandy soil from the explosion, was untouched by flames.

The engineers ran towards each other, throwing up their arms in triumph and laughing with glee. They clapped each other on the back. Mrs Gibson, as hospital director, went forward to offer thanks to the commanding officer. Christina and the rest turned back to the work of bringing patients back to their beds. The VADs began disentangling the fallen tent, repairing guy-ropes and pulling it erect. The electricity supply had somehow been cut off, so they worked by oil lamps.

Somewhere around midnight, the hospital was more or less restored to order. Hot drinks had been served to the convalescent patients, sedatives had been given where necessary. Christina, having examined one or two of her special charges and reassured herself they'd come through well enough, went to check if her microscope was safe. In the lantern light she found it sitting in its oilcloth hood undamaged, although the hood was covered in grit. A case of slides had fallen to the ground and been smashed, some of her tools had been scattered. But on the whole the laboratory had survived reasonably intact.

Jane Sibley appeared in the doorway of the tent. 'I say, Christina . . .'

'Yes? Am I needed?'

'No-o . . . Not exactly . . .'

'What's wrong?'

'You know that friend of yours?'

'Laurenz?' Christina said in surprise.

'No, that Frenchman – the major.'

'Henri? What about him?'

'He's . . . er . . . he's been hurt.'

Christina wheeled about so suddenly that the oil in the lantern flooded and the flame nearly went out. 'Henri?'

'In that charge they exploded. He got hurt.'

'Oh, no!'

'I'm sorry, Christina. He and another man. The colonel explained they didn't have time to calculate the charge properly.'

Christina came to the door. 'Is he badly hurt? Can I see him?'

Jane put a restraining arm around her. 'He's in theatre now. Edith's doing what she can but he's pretty badly burned and there's a lot of soil and stuff in the wounds.'

'Oh, Jane!'

When Henri came out of theatre she was allowed to see him, though he was still unconscious.

'What do you think?' she asked Edith Paterson in a scared tone, for his torso and arms were swathed in bandages.

'Hard to say, my dear. I cleaned him up as best I could but there was an awful lot of dirt and fragments of uniform in the wounds.'

It wasn't necessary to say any more: septicaemia was one of their greatest enemies.

'And the other man?' she asked.

'He's fair – burns to his back and neck, but not so bad as Darblier.'

There was nothing more to be done. The night staff took over for a shift that tonight would be quite short, while the rest of the hospital settled down to rest. Even Christina, despite her distress over Henri, slept after a while.

In the morning, before going to breakfast, she went to the post-op tent. The sister in charge nodded assent when she asked to see Major Darblier.

He was moving restlessly. A nurse was trying to hold him still, for every move would make the damage worse to his burned flesh.

'*Tirez!*' he was muttering. '*Tirez, la mèche est mise!*'

'Keep still, major, please lie still.' The nurse looked in appeal to Christina. 'How d'you say it in French, ma'am?'

Christina leaned over him. '*Doucement, doucement,* Henri,' she said in a quiet murmur.

He tried with his bandaged hand to take hold of hers. 'Christina, *c'est toi?* he asked, his eyelids flickering. 'Christina, *ne me quitte pas!*'

Then his hand fell away as the delirium left him.

'Poor soul,' muttered the nurse. 'He's not doing very well, ma'am.'

'No,' agreed Christina. 'How is the other man?'

'Tarrault? He's gone to the General Ward.'

'That's at least something to be thankful for,' sighed

Christina, and reluctantly left to carry on with the day's work.

And that work was hard. The ravages of the night's shock and anxiety had to be dealt with. Smoke inhalation had damaged the lungs of enfeebled men. Movement had harmed some who should have had complete immobility after surgery. Miss Paterson's theatre case of last night had now undergone his operation and was in great danger due to extended shock.

And there was the usual daily intake of Serbian casualties from the mountain campaign, brought down in the dust and heat along the terrible roads, exhausted, thirsty, in pain. Luckily there had been few civilian casualties in the Salonika fire, and those few were treated in a civilian hospital.

It was after eight when Christina got back at last to the tent where Henri was being nursed. The night staff had just come on. Sister Michaels came forward as she saw Dr Holt enter the ward.

'You've come to see Major Darblier?' she greeted Christina, and gave a sad smile. 'I'm sorry.'

Christina went cold inside. 'He's gone?'

'About six o'clock. Shock and blood poisoning. I know he was a friend of yours. I'm very sorry, doctor.'

'But . . . but . . .' Henri, dead? It was impossible. All that energy, all that self-confidence . . .

Sister led her to a chair. She sank on to it.

After a moment she said, 'How . . . Was he alone?'

'The French padre was with him. But he didn't know him, he was delirious most of the time.'

'May I see him?'

'They asked to have the body, ma'am, the engineers. The funeral is tomorrow. You know they never hang about in this climate.'

'Yes.'

'I'm sorry,' Sister Michaels said again, and left her.

By and by Christina went out. It was late, she ought to wash and change and get something to eat. She couldn't remember eating anything since breakfast at six that morning.

She went to the funeral the next day. It was a very short affair, after the military fashion, with a volley fired over the grave. Afterwards she spoke to Captain Lemur and Colonel Juverne. The latter thanked her for her condolences, then put his hand into his breast pocket.

'Major Darblier left a letter for you, mademoiselle.'

'Henri wrote to me?'

It was the custom for men to write letters which would be delivered in the event of their death. Usually they were for their parents or wives. Christina drew back in surprise as the colonel held out an envelope.

He turned the letter so that she could see the name. 'Mlle Christina Holt, MD' was written in a firm, broad hand. She took the envelope. It was strange to think that she had never seen Henri's writing before.

Somehow she felt she had to be alone when she read this letter. She took it to her tent, sat down on the truckle bed, and slit open the envelope.

My dearly loved Christina, if you read this it will be because I have reached the end of my road. I want you to know that as I write this I love you sincerely and more than I ever expected to love any woman. I know that I made a bad impression upon you when we first met, and after I learned to know you better I regretted this very much. Fool that I am, I can't bring myself to apologise to you for that behaviour. I can't bring myself to say openly that I was wrong, although I sense it is a barrier between us.

I want you to know that if I had survived I would have done myself the honour to ask for your hand in marriage. I would have done everything in life to make you happy. In death I can only wish you well and hope that you will sometimes think of me.

Your devoted Henri.

The words began to run together. Tears slid over the rims of her eyes to trickle down her cheeks.

Poor Henri. Poor, poor man. She had thought him shallow, but she'd been wrong. There was sensitivity and depth in his written words.

If only he were here now! She would tell him she'd long ago forgotten his foolish manner when they first met. It didn't matter now; what did anything matter in the face of the loss she felt?

She held the letter against her breast, rocking back and forth on her bed in grief. If only she had known! She could at least have told him she was fond of him, that she valued his friendship.

Too late now.

Was there some fate determined to wreck her friendships with men? On Peter Semmring she didn't care to dwell, but Douglas Fairforth had asked something of her she had been unable to give, and now again with Henri . . .

To Henri she would gladly have given an open, welcoming regard. But she knew it would never have been enough for him. He had been incapable of thinking of a woman as a friend – she must either be wife or mistress.

She could never have been either to him. Yet the thought that he was gone was unbearable. He had wanted her, had called for her by name, had begged her not to leave him. And she had had to go, because other men's lives were in danger.

Sometimes she wondered if she were really cut out to be a doctor, when her heart could break like this over a man who had in truth had little claim upon her.

She sat staring at, but not seeing the far wall of her little tent. 'I wish I could have stayed with you, Henri,' she whispered brokenly.

A voice spoke at the tent flap.

'Ka koksta vi, mali doctoritza?'

She knew that phrase! She jumped up. No one but Jo-Jo ever asked that question in that laughing tone of voice: How are you, little doctor?

But it couldn't be – Jo-Jo was in California.

Yet there she was, sturdy and vigorous and real. The dear friend of her student days, Jo-Jo Belu.

In floods of tears, Christina threw herself into the out-stretched arms.

Chapter Twenty-two

Jo-Jo let her friend have her cry out. Then she began the process of comfort by teasing her.

'So,' she remarked, 'you found the prejudice against women doctors was too great, so you decided to be a little man, eh?'

'What? Oh!' Christina grabbed a handful of her short fair hair. 'Most of us have short trims now, Jo-Jo. It's safer because of the typhus.'

'But the trousers? Explain please the trousers.'

'Never mind about that. How did you get here? The last letter – oh, ages ago, in the spring – you were still in California.'

'I left almost at once. I've been in Corfu all year.'

'Corfu?'

'Of course!' said Jo, her eyes flashing. 'The Army of my country was in Corfu, so I was there also. Where else? Much to be done, because besides the wounded there were men suffering from the after-effects of a previous epidemic. But now, they are well, and I am here because your unit is going back into Serbia.'

Christina stared at her. 'We are?'

'You didn't know? Ah well, then, I am the bringer of news. Good news?' she added with a tinge of doubt.

'Oh, Jo-Jo, you've no idea how good! We all hated it when they made us run away from Ghevgeli. Wait till the others hear!'

The news was received with cries of triumph. Jo-Jo soon made friends among the medical staff, and soon satisfied a curiosity of her own about Christina's tears. She'd seen the letter in her friend's hands. Now other members of the staff told her that a French major had just been buried. Jo-Jo put two and two together, and got a wrong answer.

She was accepted as a colleague with open arms by the WSH, although she had come entirely as a volunteer, under no one's orders. She understood she must obey Mrs Gibson as hospital director and Addie Bellhaven as chief physician. She earned their appreciation by pitching in just like everyone else.

As she'd predicted, in the summer of 1917, orders came for them to move up into Serbia. Their convoy was heading for Ostrovo on the Monastir road. The women laughed when they saw this 'road': it was the remains of the Via Egnatia, built by the Romans in AD 100 or thereabouts.

At Ostrovo, the unit was split up. Mrs Gibson with Jo-Jo and the surgical team pressed on northwards and eastwards to set up a tented surgical hospital, urgently needed before winter seized hold. Addie Bellhaven refused to take on the job. 'I'm burnt out, kiddies,' she said in a joking voice that belied the truth of the situation. She was a big, heavy woman, but service in the WSH had taken the flesh off her sturdy bones. 'Quite prepared to go on serving,' she added, 'but I've lost my nerve for big responsibilities.'

The administrator, Mrs Gibson, was prepared to take on the direction of the hospital so long as one of the others would be Head of Medical Staff. Christina found herself voted in despite her protests, and British HQ in Salonika were far too busy with military matters to care what the WSH did. So Christina was given the title of assistant director and the task of setting up in Ostrovo.

Ostrovo Hospital, badly damaged in the fighting, was on the northern shores of a lake. It was a breeding ground for malarial mosquitoes. Christina began a fight to have the WSH moved elsewhere, but the French military authorities had other priorities.

'But colonel,' she protested to the officer of the *Etat-Majeur*, 'wounded men brought in here will almost certainly get malaria – we haven't nearly enough mosquito netting.'

'Madame,' he said – a title in accordance with her rank, though not, he felt, with her age or marital situation – 'it will soon be too cold for mosquitoes.'

Easily said.

Within two weeks about half the patients went down with malaria. Worse still, most of the staff were bitten and infected. Life became a nightmare of semi-delirium and weakness, kept at bay by too much quinine: they had to be able to carry on their medical and nursing duties. Complaints from medical staff near to collapse from malarial infection all fell on deaf ears and nothing was done about the siting of the hospital.

Returning from a trip to the Area Commander's office Christina found the hospital in a state of jubilation. The news was good – perhaps of the very best. Serbia had driven back the Bulgarians. How Jo-Jo must be rejoicing, thought Christina. Her friend was some miles ahead of her into the mountains, with an advance surgical party under the leadership of Edith Paterson, heading for the Serbian troops at the Bulgarian border.

Whether it was the good news lifting their spirits, or the usual recovery that comes after malaria has run its course, everyone began to feel better. There was plenty of work still to do, although everyone said that the war couldn't go on much longer.

They entered into 1918. Hopefully they asked for news as lorries came in from Salonika. Peace, everyone longed for peace, but meanwhile battled on against the ravages of war.

Christina caught glimpses of Captain Varikiav now and again. 'There he is!' she would exclaim, shading her eyes to watch a staff car go by.

'How can you tell it's the captain?'

Christina looked at Morton in surprise. 'But he's so different from all the rest!'

'Is he now?' murmured Morton, smiling to herself.

But it was true that Captain Varikiav was different. The

Serbians said so. Round the paraffin heaters at ward-ends the convalescent patients would sit, swapping stories about the war.

'Our war, you know,' said old Sergeant Kashjo to Christina, 'it started long before yours. And Captain Varikiav was in the fight from the very beginning. He spent four months in the mountains with his father when he was a boy, fighting the Turks.'

'The Turks!'

'Ah, *mali doctoritza*, we have had many enemies, yes, yes,' the men said, nodding their heads and swaying their bodies in emphasis.

'And the captain, he saved the life of our King, you know,' Private Memna took it up, 'on the great retreat of the winter campaign – yes, when the snow in the high pass at Jelaj blocked our way and a group of Albanian bandits—'

'Ah-h, the Albanians,' groaned the men, nodding and swaying, 'who can trust the Albanians?'

'What did Captain Varikiav do?' Christina asked eagerly.

'Ah, you like our captain, eh?' said the sergeant, sipping his pale Serbian tea. 'Yes, yes, our captain, a good man, a good soldier, he put himself in front of the King when the Albanians leapt down from the rocks, and their horses went down on the icy road, and we were all in a scramble—'

'And you lost your rifle to a little bandit in a fox-fur hat, Kashjo, eh, eh?'

'Maybe so, maybe so, but I stayed by my King and so did the captain, and I got one of the horses up and the captain shot two of the little brigands and we put His Majesty on the horse, God bless him, and the captain, he hit the horse on its rump and set it at the boulders, and up it went, God bless the creature, up, away from the ambush, and surely I thought, they'll kill us all now, me with no rifle, and the captain levelled his revolver at another of the band—'

'And that was when I ran up,' put in Memna, 'and the rest of us, and though we were in a bad way, God knows, what with the cold and the starvation – for not a bite we'd had for two days, *doctoritza*, and very little even the day before that—'

'Yes, even though we were staggering about on our legs, we were too many for the Albanians and off they ran, and the captain, think of it, the captain ran after them shouting, "Let's get them, men!" And we ran, though I don't know how.'

'But we never caught them,' ended Kashjo, 'and God knows what we'd have done if we had, we were that weak, *doctoritza*!'

'And you know he's in the King's confidence,' another man put in, 'for he comes of a very good family—'

'Ach, family,' Memna said, shrugging and pouring more tea, 'which of us has a family these days, eh? Gone, killed by the Bulgarians or the Austrians and the same for the captain. It's not for his family that the King trusts him, no, it's for himself. Ach, ach,' sighed Memna, 'if peace comes – when peace comes – I hope Captain Varikiav will still be at the King's side, for a hard time it'll be, putting our country back together again.'

'But don't you worry about that, *mali doctoritza*,' the sergeant said with a smile. 'Even a man who has to work close to the King has time to fall in love.'

'Fall in love?' Christina said, blushing for some unknown reason. 'Who said anything about love?'

'Ach, ach, some things don't have to be said, *gospodjo*. Some things can be seen, when a man keeps having reasons to drive by way of Ostrovo to visit the general though he could far more easily ride horseback over the mountain tracks.'

And with this the kindly veterans put their heads together and began to sing in gentle harmony:

> 'When my true love passes by,
> From afar I hear her tread.
> Tell me, true love, tell me why
> We are not yet marr-i-ed?'

They burst out into laughter as they ended on a long-held note.

'You're a bunch of old gossips,' scolded Christina. 'And here comes nurse to shoo you off to bed!'

No matter what the men said about riding horseback over mountain tracks, dusty cars would rattle by with officers in the passenger seats. Clearly there was great activity on the general staff. 'Despatch cases,' Addie Bellhaven boomed, 'what's in those despatch cases they clutch so earnestly?'

'A peace treaty, perhaps?' Christina suggested.

In September Bulgaria suddenly capitulated, and the Serbian Army was forging ahead into former enemy territory. The Women's Service Hospital unit was to move on to a village called Vranja. Morale soared. Even the hazardous drive in ramshackle lorries up hair-raising tracks couldn't dampen their spirits.

All around the hospital convoy, Serbian troops were on the move northward towards their homeland. In the opposite direction, thousands of Bulgarian prisoners were trudging down to prison camp. Hour after hour, as the lorries swerved and swayed round the mountain bends, the scene around the women became more grim.

Every bridge had been destroyed, but the rivers were low at this late season of summer and the *camions* and wagons got across. On and on they went. Three hundred miles of terrible terrain, a journey of eight days. Their bodies ached from the continual shaking and jarring on the stony terrain. Some were still weak and ill with the lingering after-effects of malaria.

Food was scarce, their own supplies soon running out. What they could obtain locally was what the Serbian peasants could spare: very coarse black bread, with all kinds of impurities in it because the mills had been destroyed by the Bulgarians; a little cheese. Water had to be boiled, and sometimes it was difficult to get fuel for a fire on which to boil it, and the chlorine tablets were hidden deep in a packing case.

On the ninth day out, the unit arrived at Vranja. They scarcely had strength to get down from the lorries. Morton, who had been driving the lead lorry of their team, staggered about on woolly legs when she touched ground. A colleague held her up. They stood gazing about them.

It was a horrific scene. Almost every house in the village

had been burned down or wrecked. Some attempts had been made at patching up by taking pieces from wrecked buildings. The village street was a series of shell-holes.

Slowly, people emerged from the houses. Gaunt, wary, some armed with sticks or knives.

It took only a few minutes' explanation to put their fears at rest. Slow smiles dawned. 'We've won? We've beaten the Bulgarians?'

On the winding road, the Serbian Army still marched by, the men with their eyes on the mountains where their homes awaited. Perhaps, thought Christina, their home villages would be like Vranja – mere shells inhabited by skeletons.

They went through the familiar process of establishing their hospital. They had to bring water from a nearby stream in buckets, but they were used to such things. Within four days they had wards full of casualties, as well as a medical ward for the villagers. With the onset of cold weather, a lot of the village children, to Christina's concern, came down with acute bronchitis and chest complaints.

One afternoon Morton came running into the medical ward. 'Doctor! Doctor! One of the drivers—!'

'What? An accident?'

'No. Doctor, he says there's to be an armistice in France!'

Christina drew in her breath. Henri Darblier had always said that the important campaign was the one in France. And so it proved. The rumour was confirmed. The fighting had ceased on all fronts, the Great War was over . . .

But not for the women at the hospital in Vranja. For them there was still a war to wage – against sickness and disease.

It was essential to have a meeting to plan a campaign for hygiene. They had to get a clean water supply. The Bulgarian Army, before retreating, had callously poisoned the wells.

Mrs Gibson didn't come to the meeting. 'You take it, Christina. You're assistant director, after all.'

'You look bad, Anne,' Christina said. 'Get to bed. We'll manage.' They were all suffering from some degree of dysentery but Anne Gibson, though she tried to hide it, was in a worse state than any of them.

While they were making their plans, the wind came up. They could hear it on the hillside, keening among the ruined houses. 'You know what it sounds like?' Morton said with a shiver. 'Like that devilish wind at Ghevgeli, the one they called the Vardar . . .'

For a moment no one said anything. The Vardar had always been the bringer of bad times. Perhaps winter was about to come upon them as they settled in at Vranja.

During the night they were awakened by a convoy coming down the track and trundling into the village. It was their first intake of wounded from the advance into Serbia, where the Allies were now rounding up Austrians and Germans in retreat.

They rolled out of their blankets, eyes still glued with exhausted sleep, and went to work. The VADs got the ward tents up, the nursing staff hustled about putting up beds and unpacking blankets, the surgeons put the sterilisers to work.

It was only hours later that Christina realised she hadn't seen Mrs Gibson. Nor had anyone else, when she inquired.

With Jane Sibley at her heels, she ran to Mrs Gibson's ridge tent. They called as usual before going in, but got no response. In the cold mid-morning light, they lifted the flap and went in.

Anne Gibson lay dead on her camp bed.

Afterwards Christina found it hard to forgive herself. She had known the director was very ill, yet she had done nothing to help her. If she countered that accusation by saying to herself, What could I have done, the answer was, probably, nothing. But it haunted her, that Anne Gibson should have gone to her tent that night and died with not a friend at hand to comfort her.

The villagers of Vranja helped to bury Anne. They stood around the stony grave with their heads bent while Dr Bellhaven in her ringing voice repeated what she could remember of the Anglican burial service. Only Edith Paterson, Christina, and Dr Bellhaven attended. The rest of the unit was busy looking after the new patients.

'You're director of the hospital now, Christina,' Addie said as they turned away from the grave.

'Me? Don't be silly.'

'You were her assistant.'

'But that was only a formality—'

'There's nobody else.'

'But you must take it on, Addie. You're far senior to me.'

'I'd be no good at it. Oh, yes, I mean it,' she went on quickly as Christina was about to object. 'I know I'm big and impressive but I can't plan ahead. I'm great on day to day things, I can throw my weight about when it's necessary – but I'd get in a hideous muddle if I had to order supplies or plan a removal.'

'Then if you won't, we must ask Sibley.'

'Sibley! Don't be daft! Sibley's a nice lass, but she's afraid of men with braid on their shoulders. No, it's your pigeon: for one thing, you speak this confounded language, and it looks as if we're marooned among sick and helpless Serbians.'

There was no escaping the logic of it. After some further useless argument, Christina accepted the title of director, though she kept on insisting it was purely temporary – 'until someone senior gets here,' she said.

'Oh yes. In the sweet by and by,' muttered Addie in response.

By noon next day the nursing sisters had swept out the hospital compound with brooms made from twigs, to make ready for the expected convoys. The tattered villagers watched in amazement as they cleared up shards of wood and all kinds of rubbish left by the retreating Bulgarians, together with the torn clothing of the new patients. It was all burned in a great bonfire on the hillside.

Inside the tented wards, VADs scrubbed and washed the tent poles and bed legs with paraffin to prevent an onslaught of bedbugs. The men coming in were infested.

Morton took over as sanitary officer. She gathered together the more able-bodied villagers to help dig latrines. She purified the well and arranged for chlorinated barrels to be filled for use in the hospital.

As for supplies, certain things could be obtained, some could not. Paraffin was available, but not petrol for a generator. Blankets and sheets could be found, but not pyjamas for the patients, wood for the stoves, or spare parts for the unit's vans. These had to be kept functioning by cannibalising those that broke down irretrievably.

At Christmas, the staff barely had time to raise their heads and wish each other the season's greetings. At New Year, a more important celebration to the Scots in the unit, a break was made and a small gathering toasted each other in *rakia* at what they thought was midnight. No one attempted to join hands and sing 'Auld Lang Syne': they all had a horrible fear they might break down.

Several days into the year of 1919 the constant passing line of trudging infantry and labouring lorries was brought momentarily to a halt. Christina, in the middle of a conference about setting up a child welfare clinic, heard her name called.

'Dr Holt! Dr Holt!'

'Excuse me,' she said to the villagers in her office-tent, and went out.

A familiar figure was walking up the icy path to the office door.

'Captain Varikiav!'

'Christina! How are you?' He saluted, took her hand, then stooped to look in her face. 'Are you well? You look thin. What a terrible place!'

'What are you doing here, Laurenz?'

'I'm on my way to Prilep. They told me as we came round the last bend that the Women's Service Hospital was in action here. I wasn't sure if you were with this one . . .'

Although he hid it well, he was alarmed at what he saw. She seemed to him to be nothing but skin and bones. The short-cropped hair was hidden under a uniform cap. She had a woollen peasant coat wrapped round her upper body and belted close. Her legs were in worn black trousers tucked into boots which were padded to fit her small feet with two or three pairs of peasant socks.

'Come in,' she said. 'I can offer you some *chaje*.'

He followed her into her tent, which was in fact a half-tent. It was furnished with a trestle table to one side on which documents and ledgers were piled, a smaller table which served as a desk, a chair, a small paraffin stove, and a camp stool on which stood teapot, mugs, a packet of tea and a tin of sugar. Standing round the desk were four gaunt Serbians, one man and three women.

These greeted him with eager respect. 'Good morning, *gospodar*! What brings you here?'

'I'm on my way north to join Voyvoda Mishitch. How are you, my aunts, my uncle?'

'Well, nephew, God be thanked and thanks to these heaven-sent women.'

As Christina busied herself pouring the weak tea and adding sugar, she listened to the quiet voices. She loved the way younger people addressed elders as 'aunt' and 'uncle', and how the elders named the young people 'niece' and 'nephew'. She herself had become quite accustomed to being spoken to as 'niece' by villagers older than herself. It was as if they were all part of one vast family.

She explained to Laurenz that they were in course of planning a mother-and-baby clinic. 'There are some terrible problems due to malnutrition and to previous infections not properly treated. Did you say you were going up to General Mishitch?'

'Yes, I have despatches for him.'

'Please ask him to send food and fuel to Vranja. We're living hand to mouth here, Laurenz.'

'I see that. I'll do what I can.'

He clearly couldn't stay long. She had a feeling that he had stopped a staff car on the road in order to drop off and pay this visit. She went out to see him off.

'Oh, I nearly forgot! I bring you a message from Jo-Jo Belu.'

'Jo-Jo? You know Jo-Jo?' she cried, amazed.

'Our paths have crossed. Of course,' he said, laughing, 'you realise she and I can never be friends. She regards me as a Royalist lackey. But she promises not to cut off my head after the revolution, because I am a friend of Christina Holt.'

'That sounds like Jo-Jo,' she agreed, joining in his amusement. 'But I thought she'd put her republican ideas aside?'

'Only to help win the war. Now that it's over, it will soon be "Away with King Peter!" and "Away with Royalist supporters!" as in Russia.'

'Do you really think there could be a republic, Laurenz?'

'There's a strong movement to unite the Balkan people – or at least some of them – into a new country. Whether that country would have a king, I don't know.'

'A new country? What would its name be – still Serbia?'

He shook his head. 'All kinds of ideas are flying about. Some people are suggesting our country should be called Jugoslavia. But so long as it is free from the Austro-Hungarians, and free from the Bulgarians, and free from the Turks, I won't argue about its name.

'Well,' he went on in a sudden change of tone, 'I was ordered by Jo-Jo to say, if I saw you, that she is at Strumnitza and hopes to be able to come west to rejoin you before too long.'

'Thank you. I'd love to see her, to say nothing of needing every extra pair of hands we can get.'

'Try not to overdo things, Christina—'

She cut off the advice with an impatient wave of the hand. 'We do what we have to do, Laurenz. You know that.'

'Of course. Goodbye for the present, then.'

'For the present? Shall you be coming back this way?' she asked, with a surge of unexpected pleasure at the thought.

'I hope to.' He saluted and was gone.

The prospect of seeing him again buoyed Christina up during the next few hours. But he didn't come back that day, nor the next. The day after that was Christmas Eve acording to the Orthodox calendar, and as she rose that morning she knew, as if a messenger had come to tell her, that Laurenz would be at Vranja for the service.

This time the celebration was held in the wards. Most of the patients were Serbian soldiers. As midnight approached, tables were set at the end of each tent, empty.

Outside in the freezing night, the villagers and some of the walking wounded gathered. There was a leader, a man they called 'pope' in Serbian – it seemed to mean some kind of lay preacher rather than the Catholic primate. He wore a rough linen smock over his uniform, with black crosswork embroidery on it. Each person carried a candle or a small lamp.

At a signal from the 'pope' the congregation began to sing. The wind carried off their voices, but from within the tents the hymn was taken up.

They went from ward to ward, singing, carrying their candles and lamps. At each of the empty tables, a few of the lights were set down and left while the 'pope' recited a blessing. When they went out, they left a symbol of the 'Light of the World' behind them.

They had reached the Surgical post-op Ward when a new voice was added to the choir. Christina narrowed her eyes to see against the flickering glow of the candles.

But she knew, without being able to see, that the figure in the long double-breasted greatcoat was Laurenz.

When the service was over he sought her out. 'I spoke to Voyvoda Mishitch. He will do what he can to send supplies but they will have to come from Belgrade and the railway lines are wrecked. It may be some time before they arrive, Christina.'

She pulled her woollen coat closer about her. The temperature was well below zero, and because food was so short, energy levels were very low. She felt the cold more each day.

'I don't know if we can wait long, Laurenz. The flour supply is going to run out in two days.'

'No bread?' he said, shocked. Serbian peasants lived mostly on bread, eked out these days with a little lamb or mutton if they could find a stray sheep not carried off by the retreating Bulgarians.

'We hear talk of a *gospodar* in a valley the other side of the mountain who has a storehouse full of flour – sugar too, Laurenz. Could it be true?'

'A *bogat*? Oh yes, we have such men – a rich peasant who thinks it is his duty to protect his *zagruda* no matter who else is suffering. But if this man exists, how did he keep his goods from falling into Bulgarian hands?'

'They say he's very crafty, he hid everything. His name is Donutzi. I sent a man last Wednesday with all the money we could scrape together, asking to buy some sacks of flour, but he denied he had any stocks.'

'It may be true.'

'No, Maltan says the people of the *zagruda* looked well fed, and though they had hidden them he heard poultry clucking.'

Laurenz frowned. If a man could keep poultry it meant he had enough corn to feed them in this winter weather.

'I think perhaps I'll pay this *bogat* a visit tomorrow,' he said. 'It seems a suitable thing to do on Christmas Day, to appeal to a man's better nature.'

'I'll come with you,' Christina said. 'I've seen the children here crying for food. Perhaps if I tell him about it, it'll soften his heart.'

Next morning a spell of freezing fog delayed them, and then they felt it best to have a meal first. They ate in the mess tent: a stew of vegetables and bully beef, provided by some British lorry drivers from a Transport Division working with the French, accompanied by tea sweetened with Nestlé's condensed milk. It was about noon when they set off in one of the two hospital vans, driven by O'Donnell.

'You'll have to direct me,' O'Donnell said as she looked at the remains of the fog up ahead. 'I've no idea where this village is, doctor.'

'Can you direct us, Laurenz?' Christina asked. She herself had only heard the route described.

He produced an Army map. 'There it is, it's called Tezelk. We have to go over the shoulder of this mountain.'

'What's this mountain called?' asked Christina.

'It doesn't have a name,' he said with a grin. 'To the people who live here, it's just "the mountain". We have to go over this pass and keep east of the crag. Then there's a river, do you see?' His finger was tracing the route along the map.

It was the river that proved their undoing. As the light was fading they came to a ford across a stream, not very broad, but with a steep approach. As O'Donnell was gingerly driving down, the ground under the van's left front wheel went into an unseen trough. There was a cracking sound, the van swayed, and then slowly toppled over on to its left side.

Sitting on the left of the driver, Christina and Laurenz were in the greater danger. Christina was pushed against the door. She kicked it open then felt herself shoved out by Laurenz. He too came tumbling out among the boulders on the bank.

O'Donnell should have been the safest. She had only to open her door and throw herself out on to the expanse of the bank.

But her hand in reaching for the door handle missed its mark. The momentum of the overturn sent her slithering along the leather seat. She dropped out of the left-hand door just as the van completed its fall.

She went down among the stones. The van bounced on top of her once, twice, and then settled.

Christina, out first and momentarily stunned, staggered up just in time to see the van rock and sway on its side, then stay steady. Gasping, she moved to give a hand to Laurenz, who had landed on his side and was hampered by the skirts of his Serbian greatcoat tangling among the rocks. She took his hand, hauled on it, and he got to his feet.

'Are you all right?' he asked.

'Yes, hit my elbow, I think I've cut my head, but I'm all—' She broke off. 'Where's O'Donnell?'

Laurenz turned. They were alone on the bank of the stream. There was nothing else to be seen but the wrecked van among the boulders.

He stared at the van. Christina put a hand to her mouth. 'Oh no!'

'I think so, Christina.' He took off his overcoat. 'Wait there.'

She watched him pick his way and wade to the van. He bent to look down, then, after a moment's hesitation, knelt and tried to look under the vehicle.

After what seemed an eternity he clambered to his feet, leaned against the van's bonnet with his eyes closed.

'Laurenz?' Christina shouted.

He shook his head.

She jumped up and tried to run towards him. On the rocky terrain she lost her footing. He caught her in his arms as she approached. 'No, don't, it's useless. She's squashed between the rocks and the van.'

'We must—'

'What? We can't lift the van. It will need a team of oxen, if we can find a village that still has any.'

'Laurenz, we've got to get her out!'

'Not now,' he said. 'Not today. We have to make up our minds what to do. We're on foot now, and it's very cold and getting dark. We have to decide whether to go on or go back.'

She sagged down on a boulder. She wanted to weep for O'Donnell, but no tears would come.

'How far are we from Vranja?'

'About eleven miles.'

'And from Tezelk?'

'About eight.'

She drew a breath and squared her shoulders. 'We ought to head for Tezelk, then.'

'Very well.' He picked up his coat, searched for the map in its pockets, opened it, studied it and nodded. Then he opened the van door that was accessible, to feel under the dashboard for anything useful for their journey, which would have to be completed on foot.

But there was only an electric torch which had been broken in the smash, one pair of woollen gloves, and a copy of *Little Women*.

'We must be careful,' he told Christina. 'There are tracks that lead off the one we should follow. In daylight, or with the van's headlights, we should have been able to tell which was the main track. Now we must do the best we can.'

They crossed the stream by leaping from boulder to boulder across the ford. Once Christina slipped in so that one boot went under the shallow water, but only a little washed in over the top.

Now it was almost dark. Laurenz had a box of matches in his greatcoat. By the light of one, they re-examined the map. They must bear to the right.

The going was very rough. The rocks on either side seemed to loom larger and larger. By and by the evening star appeared, bluish-silver against blue-grey sky. Then the mist came over again. The star disappeared from view, but after a while the moon in its first quarter rose so as to give a diffused light.

They had been walking for about an hour and a half when Laurenz said, 'Can you hear a waterfall?'

She paused to listen. 'I can hear something.'

He swore under his breath. 'That's Machestna Voda. It's upstream from that ford. We've taken a path that's led us round to the river again!'

'The wrong path?'

'We're only about two miles away from where we started.'

'Laurenz . . . Do you think we should wait until daylight?'

The same thought had been in his mind. He said, 'If I remember the map correctly, there are some trees close to the waterfall. Let's walk towards it, and then we'll find wood for a fire.'

Though they could hear the falls, it took them a long time to reach them, for either they had lost the track entirely or the track itself was strewn with boulders. But by and by they came out on to the banks of a stream, and to their left they could see the sparkle of falling water in the moonlight.

There were a few birch trees, so they hunted about and found a few fallen twigs. Laurenz broke off some of the lower branches. With the field skills of an experienced campaigner, he made a little pyramid, poked a few small very dry twigs underneath, lit them with a match, and in a few minutes there was a fire.

Such a small fire. As she sat crosslegged by it, Christina was aware of the vastness of the mountain pressing against her back.

From somewhere up the slope, a wailing cry arose.

'Laurenz!'

'Shsh,' he said comfortingly, 'it's not a mountain spirit, it's only a wolf.'

'Only!'

'Tell me about Vranja. Tell me in English. I am learning to speak English. You were going to set up a baby clinic last time I came.'

'Oh yes – it's such uphill work. The women come from miles around but what we need is milk and there's none to be had except tinned condensed milk.' She explained why sweetened condensed milk wasn't really suitable for babies, then went on to describe the making of makeshift baby clothes from pieces of sheeting, the explanations to mothers about boiling the water, the rationing out of Army biscuit and tea.

He in his turn told her about the normal life of the peasants: the flocks of sheep and goats, the orchards with their superb plums and pears and apples, the colourful costumes of the women on feast days. 'You know our saints are not the same as in your church. The *slava* is the patron saint of the family or the *zagruda*. On that saint's day the whole family will take a holiday. The priest comes on a visit, splashes holy water in every room. There's a special cake, a *kolivo*, of which everyone gets a piece, and then there's dancing – you know the *kolo*?'

She'd seen the *kolo* being danced at a Serbian wedding in Salonika. But while she was recalling it, the cry of the wolf was repeated, and this time it was echoed from further along the mountainside.

'Does . . . does that mean there's a pack?'

'Don't worry about it,' he said. 'It is their song. They call to each other to keep in touch while hunting.'

'What are they hunting?'

'Not us,' he said in reassurance. 'Wolves seldom attack human beings.'

'But I was told . . . someone said that they attacked in cold weather, when game was scarce.'

'Not if we keep the fire going.'

She looked at the little pile of firewood which she could pick out by the light of the flickering flames. Would it be enough to keep the fire going until morning?

Yet by and by the song of the wolves seemed to be more distant, as if they were hunting on a slope much further to the east.

She began to feel drowsy. She had been up very late last night for the Midnight Service, and up early for the usual hospital rounds. Then there had been the shock of the accident, the grief of O'Donnell's death, and the exhausting walk on the bad terrain of the mountain. All of it had taken its toll.

She settled herself down in her thick woollen jacket as near the fire as possible. Despite its heat, she felt the cold at her back. She drifted into sleep and out again.

By and by she felt something being wrapped over her, and knew it must be Laurenz's greatcoat.

'No,' she said, coming half awake. 'You mustn't, you need it . . .'

'We will share it,' he said in her ear. She felt him fit himself against her at her back. His arms came round her, the coat was settled against her neck.

'You mustn't mind that I do this,' he murmured. 'It is to keep from the cold.'

Chapter Twenty-three

The walk to Tezelk took them until about midday next day. As they came down the icy track to the village the dogs came out to bark. That was a strange sound: at Vranja there were no dogs because there was nothing to feed them.

Gospodar Dinas greeted them at the head of a small group from his *zagruda*. He was a tall old man but rather stooped in his thick, kidskin coat. He had the usual luxuriant moustache of the Serbian mountaineer, grey and stained yellow from smoking Turkish tobacco. 'Please enter my home,' he said, but in a grudging tone that belied the usual welcome.

His house was large, with additions built in the past to house the families of sons and grandsons. The kitchen, the main room of the house, was very large but bare. There was a very small fire in the hearth.

Laurenz introduced himself and Christina. There was an awed murmur of '*doctoritza, doctoritza*' from the crowd when he gave her her title.

'We hear you have food stores.'

'Not true,' said Dinas. 'How could we have stores? The Bulgarians left us nothing.'

'All the same, you don't look as if you're starving.'

'If we have enough to keep body and soul together, what business is that of yours?'

'*Chicha*, why are you so angry? We only come to—'

'I know why you come! Like all those who wear a uniform you come to take, only to take! I have seen enough of uniforms! Please go!'

'But, *Gospodar* Dinas,' protested one of the villagers, 'they have come so far, and on foot . . .'

'Let them go on foot! In war we have to go on foot, and bow our heads, and eat little—'

'The war is over, *gospodar*,' Laurenz said. 'There's no need now—'

'So they say, so they say. But if it is true, why don't the rest of our men come back?' His anxious, flickering glance went from his visitors to the villagers. 'I have the responsibility of this *zagruda*. So far we have survived. But we have survived with nothing, we are poor, we are cold and hungry.'

Laurenz stepped past him to throw open a door at the far side of the kitchen. It opened into a smoke-room, where sides of bacon and legs of mutton hung from a beam. Covered baskets were ranged against the wall. He pulled up the lid of the nearest. It was full of dried corn.

'So, you are hungry,' he said with cold anger. 'Hungry, with full store-rooms?'

The old man dragged him back, standing in the way of his entry to the room. 'Those are to see us through until spring. They are nothing to do with you.'

'We have money, we will pay a fair price.'

'What money? Turkish money? Bulgarian money? Keep it!'

'*Chicha*, I tell you, the war is over. We use Serbian money now.'

'*Chicha*,' Christina put in, 'please sell us some of your food. In the village where I work, the children are crying with hunger. They need bread, the babies need milk.'

'Babies need only the milk of their mothers.'

'But if the mothers are so weak and ill that they have no milk to give? *Chicha*, help us to save the babies.'

'No one helped us to save our babies when the Bulgarians came,' *Gospodar* Dinas said. 'It was only because I hid them in caves outside the village. Yes, and food too, I hid that. What we have now, we deserve to keep.'

'I am an officer of the Serbian Army,' Laurenz said. 'I have the power to commandeer supplies.'

'Ah!' cried the *gospodar*. 'I thought it would come to that!'

Despite his age, he leapt with agility towards the wall, and seized an ancient dagger that hung there as ornament. He held it up in his fist. 'Well,' he said, 'come on, try to take my food! I will kill you first.'

The small group of villagers gave a gasp of horror, but stood as if frozen. Laurenz looked at them then, shrugging, took out his service revolver. He stood holding it down by his side.

'Very well,' he said, 'kill one or other of us. But you can't kill two with one blow, *chicha*. So first you will kill me, and then Dr Holt will pick up the revolver and shoot you. Is that what you want, to be shot by the friends of your country?'

The old man looked from one to the other, holding the dagger up in his fist.

Christina stepped forward, despite a movement by Laurenz to prevent her. '*Chicha*,' she said, 'would you really harm me? How many women have you killed, *chicha*?'

His glance fastened on her. A look of dismay came into his face. 'Women?' he echoed. 'I . . . I have never killed a woman. Men, I have killed men, when I was young and fought the Turks. But women, no . . . that is a wicked thing to ask.'

'Then, *chicha*, why do you hold a dagger up against me?'

He wavered. Her gentle repetition of the word *chicha*, uncle, with its connotation of relationship and respect, unnerved him. 'It's not against you,' he said. 'It's against him, *him*; he who comes to rob us of our food! You heard him! He said he would shoot me, or you would shoot me. So, if you must, then kill me; I will not give up our food-stores!'

'*Gospodar* Dinas,' said Laurenz, with a gesture towards Christina, 'you told the *doctoritza* that you had fought the Turks. I too. We have been comrades in arms, perhaps. And the *doctoritza* is our comrade too. She comes from far across the sea—'

'Too many people come!' cried Dinas, slashing at the air above his head with the dagger. 'Invaders, armies, strangers! Here in our mountains we only have enough to keep ourselves alive. Go, go! Before I set the dogs on you!'

Christina had watched the old man with great attention. He was angry, yes, and frightened; but there was something more. He reminded her of some of the men she'd seen who had recently left the battle line; too recently involved in crisis and horror to be able to unwind. Shell-shock . . . If there was a similar illness that could affect civilians, this man was surely suffering from it. Yet, because he was the *gospodar* and must be respected, no one had dared to take his authority away from him.

She turned to the others who had crowded in. 'Friends,' she said, 'you have dogs to set upon us? In Vranja, we have no dogs, because we have nothing to feed them.'

'Mountain dogs,' said the *gospodar*, 'strong, with sharp teeth. They would tear you to pieces.'

'Then set them on us,' suggested Laurenz, with a hint of amusement in his voice. 'For we intend to stay, until you promise to sell us some food.'

'Sell us some food, *chicha*,' urged Christina. She laid her hand on his upraised arm. 'And put down the knife. You know you would never use it.'

The old man lowered his hand. He faltered, 'But we have so little, so little. I have endured so much, only to hold on to these few things so that my nieces and nephews might not die of starvation.'

'Others are dying,' Laurenz said. 'Dr Holt's friend died on the road as she drove us here to beg for your help.'

'Ah,' said the onlookers in a sigh of regret. 'Ah, her friend gave her life.'

Christina reached out and took the great old dagger from the old man. 'Come,' she said, 'we are friends. There should not be weapons between us.'

As he let her take the knife, he gave her a wavering smile. 'Niece, you are right,' he said.

'Good, good,' murmured his villagers in assent.

The atmosphere relaxed, *chaje* was made, bread spread with jam was offered, and a general conference ensued. It was agreed that pack ponies should come next day to transport about half Tezelk's supply of food to Vranja, at a suitably handsome price. More, the *gospodar* would lend a horse for them to ride back.

Laurenz took the reins, Christina was helped up behind him. Although the ground was slippery with ice and patches of snow, the horse picked its way sure-footedly down the mountain track. The lights of Vranja were already in view as darkness began to fall. They ambled into the village, dismounted, stretched cold and aching limbs.

Christina staggered on unsteady legs. Laurenz caught her in his arms. He held her a moment longer than was necessary before letting her go. She tried hard to read his face in the darkness.

'Laurenz, why were you so tremendously respectful about holding me in your arms last night?'

He stiffened. 'It is only right to be respectful to a woman who is still mourning the man she loves.'

'Mourning?' she echoed in astonishment. 'For whom am I mourning?'

'For the French major.'

'Henri Darblier?' If possible she was even more astonished. 'Laurenz, I'm not in mourning for Henri!'

'But you loved him.'

'I loved him, yes, but as a friend. I grieved when he was killed. But I grieve just as much for Kate O'Donnell who died yesterday by the ford.'

'As a friend?' he said in a strange tone. 'But Jo-Jo told me—'

'Ah! Jo-Jo!' Now she understood. 'I remember – she saw me with his letter. Come, Laurenz, there's something I want to show you.'

She led him to her tent. It was in darkness and he had to light a match so that she could find the pressure lamp. By its light she found the letter in her writing case. She handed it to him.

'I am to read it?' he said with uncertainty.

'Please. Then you will understand.'

She stood watching him as he read it. When he looked up, there was a smile of wonder in his eyes. 'Christina,' he exclaimed, half laughing, half dismayed, 'I have wasted over a *year*!'

'Never mind,' she said and, putting her arms about him, offered her lips to be kissed.

Nothing more was needed. The touch of his mouth upon hers told her: This is my love.

She had waited so long for him. Not just the years of the war, glimpsing him as he went about his duties, coming closer as they shared their tasks, but all her life – yes, even when she'd imagined herself in love before.

At university, when she had given herself to Peter Semmring – when she had let him take her – she had been seeking what she now found in Laurenz's arms. This certainty of body against body, heart speaking to heart . . .

She was no longer that silly girl starved of love. Here in Vranja, love was all around her, from her comrades, from the patients and the villagers, love given and taken as they struggled with the harshness of their world.

Everything about Laurenz was *real*, not romantic illusion: his strong tall body toughened by years of hardship, his endurance, his courage, his patience. Yes, his patience, for he too had waited for her, imagining but accepting that she must wear out her time of mourning for Henri before he could approach her. But though she had indeed mourned Henri, the only man to whom she could ever have turned in full and joyous surrender was Laurenz.

Their embrace was short. They had no wish to make a show of themselves in front of the whole camp, and there was no time for fervent declarations. They loved each other. She had known it last night when she felt so safe and sheltered in his arms. For the moment they must be content with that memory, for the life of Vranja claimed them.

Back in Vranja, their first sad task was to report the death of Kate O'Donnell and arrange for her body to be retrieved from under the wrecked van. And more happily they explained to the medical staff and the *zagruda* of Vranja what they had achieved at Tezelk. Next day the pack ponies were sent off but came back with only half of what had been promised.

'That miserly old man!' snorted Laurenz. 'He makes me ashamed—'

'No, no, Laurenz, don't blame him. He's ill.'

'He looked well enough to me!'

'He's mentally sick. Anxiety has overwhelmed him.'

'We are all anxious, Christina. You mustn't be so softhearted with people like Dinas or you will make *me* anxious. I have to leave you now, I'm expected in Belgrade on Thursday. Promise me you'll look after yourself while I'm away.'

'I promise, my love, but come back soon.'

'As soon as I can.'

Christina couldn't keep the promise to look after herself for long. Two days later she was arrested by the village council on a charge of aiding the enemy. She had been treating Bulgarian prisoners-of-war in the medical ward, and as Director of the hospital she had refused to allow armed guards to stand at the entrance. Some of the Bulgarians had seized the opportunity to slip out under cover of darkness and make their way north to their homeland. The frontier was only a few miles off.

Jo-Jo Belu arrived as the rest of the medical staff were meeting to decide how to react to Christina's arrest. 'React?' she cried. 'I'll show you how to react!'

Like a whirlwind she rushed out of the mess tent, out of the hospital compound to the village, and there stormed into the *konak*, the village hall or council office.

'How dare you!' she shouted at the elderly ex-soldier acting as gaoler. 'How dare you arrest Dr Holt! Have you no gratitude? After all she's done for you and—'

'*Gospodjo, gospodjo!* Who are you?' the man said, starting to his feet.

'I'm Dr Josafin Belu, that's who I am, newly arrived from Strumnitza where I became a personal friend of General Grozowitch, and when I tell him how you behave to my friend—'

'*Doctoritza*, your friend is charged with aiding the enemy.'

'What enemy, you fool? The war is over!'

'That may be so, but we still hate the Bulgarians and we don't intend to allow anyone to befriend them in *our* village. It's bad enough that Dr Holt should take them in as patients and treat them as the equal of honest Serbians. But to plot with them to escape—!'

'Dr Holt didn't plot. Dr Holt is not a plotter. How dare you speak of her like that! I'll have you in gaol, my man, for daring to speak of her like that!'

But nothing she could say would make them release Christina. In fact, she made matters worse with her anger. She shouted at them that the Hippocratic oath binds a doctor to help anyone who needs help, but they had never heard of Hippocrates and imagined he was some fellow-plotter. Christina must be held, they said, until the military authorities could take her and put her on trial for her offence.

Meanwhile Christina was kept in a rather smelly hut on the outskirts of the village, in a room with no heating and only a candle for light in the evening.

Laurenz came with the village elder after she'd been under lock and key for a week. He was white with controlled rage. The door was opened, the gaoler bowed and said, 'Please feel free to come out, *doctoritza*.'

'Laurenz!'

She ran into his arms. He hugged her, then drew himself upright and said icily to the elder, 'You may go.'

'Yes, captain.' Looking shamefaced, the gaoler and the village headman walked away.

'How did you achieve that miracle?' Christina asked as, with his arm about her, she was taken to the mess tent for her first hot meal in a week.

'I told them that in the first place every prisoner who escaped to Bulgaria was one less mouth for Vranja to feed. I then pointed out that if this new influenza attack comes to Vranja, it made more sense to have the hospital director out helping to deal with it.'

'Besides,' Jo-Jo put in, 'what military authority were they

going to appeal to? Nobody much comes here except medical staff, and even *Army* medical staff would never have agreed to your arrest.'

'They got carried away,' Laurenz said, trying to laugh about it even though he was still angry. 'Now, of course, they're terribly ashamed. Christina, I think it would be a good idea if you took some leave so that they could forget this episode.'

'God knows she has enough due to her,' Addie Bellhaven cried. 'Go on, my dear, take some time off.'

She let herself be persuaded, the more so that Laurenz urged it. He suggested she should come to Belgrade. It could offer at least some of the attractions of city life that she had almost forgotten: theatres, cafés, electric light, bathrooms with hot water . . .

She made the journey on the railway line, now restored, although the carriages themselves were badly knocked about. Laurenz was waiting for her at the station. He gave an address to the taxi driver.

'What did you tell him? It didn't sound like a hotel.'

'We're going to a little place called Topchidarski Brdo, outside the city. The King has a house there, so I have to have quarters nearby. I live in a little house with a wistaria vine along the front. Will you share it with me, Christina?'

She leaned her head against his shoulder. There was no need to put her reply into words.

Of course the wistaria vine was not in bloom because it was still only March. But there were spring flowers growing semi-wild in the neglected garden: snowdrops, iris, narcissus, and winter jasmine shoots covered with starry yellow flowers just about to fade. Indoors, Laurenz had set a great vase of hothouse roses on a settle in the hall. Their scent filled the little house.

It had been built originally as a hunting lodge. There was a large room downstairs with a kitchen beyond, and upstairs a large bedroom, a bathroom, and a balcony from which one could look along the valley of the Sava River. A maid came in every day to look after them, which she did with a tolerant smile, as if to say, 'Ah, lovers, we all know how foolish they are.'

If it was foolish to give themselves up to their love, then Christina and Laurenz were the greatest fools in Christendom. Every hour that they could be together was spent in each other's arms.

Sometimes Laurenz would be called away on duty, and then Christina would take a noisy little tram into Belgrade, to walk around the city.

Belgrade had been treated very badly by its invaders: everything transportable had been carried off. What they couldn't take, they blighted. Many of the gardens had had their rose trees cut down and rare shrubs uprooted; statues had been overturned and smashed, buildings defaced.

When Christina mentioned it to Laurenz his glance darkened. 'The Bulgarians have much to answer for,' he muttered.

Although they were as open with each other as possible in their circumstances, she never dared ask him about the past. So many Serbs had deep tragedies hidden behind a calm, stoic façade. His country had been at war since 1912, with enemy forces surging back and forth across the land, wrecking and pillaging and killing. Families had been broken up and dispersed, many had simply disappeared. A French diplomat attached to the Peace Commission had described Serbia as 'the land of missing people'.

Who might be missing from Laurenz's life, she didn't know. He appeared to be entirely alone. He gave himself to her as completely as she to him. Although as yet they hadn't talked about the future – because the present was so sweet – she knew that they would be together somehow. His duties at present held him here in Serbia. She served his country too and was glad to do so, in whatever capacity fate might choose.

By and by the four weeks' leave was over. She went back to Vranja, but not so unwillingly as might have been thought; she knew Laurenz would come whenever he could.

* * *

As summer approached, instructions came through from the French medical HQ. The Women's Service Hospital at Vranja was to be replaced by a civilian unit of Serbians. The WSH was to proceed to Belgrade where it would be disbanded and its stores and equipment turned over to the Serbian authorities.

Nothing could have suited Christina better. In Belgrade she worked each day in an office made over to her, as hospital director, in the Belgrade *Konak*. Each evening she dined in the mess with her colleagues, thereafter they dispersed. Sleeping quarters had been assigned to them in a hotel, but no one ever had the bad taste to mention that Christina was never to be seen.

Laurenz's little house in Topchidarski was a nest to which she returned at the end of each day. She would pause outside to admire the wistaria, which had come into ethereal bloom, mauve and grey, like the echo of some sweet old song.

Sometimes Laurenz was already there, ready to pour out the wine they drank together as a welcome-home. Sometimes she would arrive first, and then she would go into the kitchen and try to make some improvement to the meal the housekeeper Moja had prepared. Moja's cuisine was limited and the ingredients were poor – but what did it matter? Better a dinner of herbs where love is . . .

One night when they were lying half asleep in each other's arms, a lovely liquid music arose in the woods alongside the garden.

Christina stirred. 'What's that, Laurenz?'

'It's a nightingale.'

'A nightingale!' She slipped out of bed, went to the open window, and stepped out on the balcony to listen. First one sang, and then another replied, and then there was a chorus of burbling, golden notes under the silver moon.

A moment later Laurenz put his arm about her. 'Have you ever heard the old Serbian saying? "A maiden without a sweetheart is as unhappy as a nightingale without a wood to sing in".'

She turned to lay her head on his chest. 'Ah, but I have a sweetheart.'

The scent of the many-petalled Balkan roses lay on the night air. She was drowsy with the scent, with the magic of the night. 'Laurenz,' she whispered, 'is there an old Serbian saying about being almost too happy?'

'Dear one . . .' She could tell that he was smiling.

The nightingales sang on, rapture upon rapture. I shall never forget this, never, Christina said to herself. If I live to be a hundred years old, I shall always remember the nightingales of Topchidarski.

By and by they went back into the bedroom, arms about each other. Through the open window the song still came, pure and sweet and full of longing. The lovers sank down on the bed, body against body, heart against heart. The magic of the music seemed to enter them, sweep them along to a passion deeper even than their first coming together.

Christina loved those long strong limbs, those enfolding arms; they had become part of her very life. On this perfect night they gathered her to Laurenz's body with a certainty that changed them both. They became one, in body and heart and spirit. Nothing could ever part them now.

Moja was right to smile tolerantly at the foolishness of lovers, for nothing is for ever.

Next evening Laurenz was waiting for Christina when she came in. She could tell at once that something serious was afoot.

'What is it, my love?'

'I have to go away. The King has asked me to undertake some work concerning the repatriation of Serbians taken prisoner and now held in Bulgaria.'

'Oh!' She put out a hand. 'When do you have to go, Laurenz?'

'Tonight.'

'Tonight!'

'There's a special train leaving Belgrade at ten and I have to be on it. I'm sorry, Christina.'

There was something strange and tense about him. His face was often sombre, but this evening there was a shadow over it that seemed to dim the usually piercing black eyes.

'Is this . . . Is this something bad, Laurenz?'

'It's something that has to be done. As you once said to me: we do what we have to do.'

She nodded. There was no arguing with that. 'We must eat, then, and pack—'

'I can't eat, don't ask me to.'

'Then we'll have the wine.' She poured it, rich and dark, tasting faintly of iron. She gave him his glass then raised her own. 'To success in your mission.'

'Success,' he repeated, holding up his glass momentarily.

They drank. Laurenz looked at her, his eyes travelling over the fair-skinned features, the short light hair, the cheekbones that led the gaze to the remarkable eyes – dark, like a mountain lake under a thunder sky. It was almost as if he were recording every detail so as to hold her in his memory.

She asked, almost afraid of the answer, 'How long will you be gone?'

'There is no way of knowing. Negotiations will be difficult. The Bulgarians are of course unwilling to admit they did anything wrong, but there are many missing persons, both military and civilian . . .'

'May I come to see you, if it's a long time?'

He stiffened. 'No, Christina.'

She knew better than to argue. He wasn't a difficult man in any respect, but there was a tone of voice she had grown to respect; a tone that meant the question was settled beyond doubt.

'Will you write and let me have your address?'

'If possible. But we'll be moving around. It would be better if you wrote to me care of the office of the Royal Equerry.'

'Very well.'

The shock of their imminent parting seemed to make them awkward. To relieve the tension she said she would see to his packing. Upstairs, she began to fold his belongings into the worn leather valise.

All at once he took her by the shoulders, turned her to face him, and held her hard against him. 'I love you, Christina. You are the most wonderful thing that ever happened to me. Say you believe me.'

She was startled by his fervour. It was almost as if they were saying goodbye for ever.

'Of course I believe you. I know you love me. And you know that I love you, Laurenz – now and for always.'

'Yes. Yes. Nothing can change it.'

'Nothing, my dear.' She kissed him, he returned the kiss. The taste of the wine was on their lips, rich, strong, bitter-sweet.

When she saw him board the train at Belgrade Station, Christina was glad they had said their goodbyes in the little house at Topchidarski Brdo. There were others at the station, other officers with important document cases, their wives and sweethearts saying goodbye. It was no place for the deep emotion of their reluctant leave-taking.

She stood in the soft night watching the train steam out. Laurenz leaned from a window, saluted with his characteristic little movement of hand against cap. Then a curve in the track took him slowly out of sight.

Chapter Twenty-four

The weeks passed; Christina wrote regularly. She received two letters from Laurenz, but they couldn't be said to be in reply to hers. It could be that her letters weren't reaching him, because when she inquired for news from his fellow-officers still in Belgrade, they said he was 'on the move'.

The work of winding up the Women's Service Hospital ended. About half of the team decided to go home. But where was 'home' to Christina? Market Bresham? She wanted very much to see her brother, from whom she received short, infrequent letters; but to go to Lincolnshire would put many countries and a sea-crossing between herself and Laurenz.

She was given the opportunity to take a post at a Belgrade hospital, but it was in orthopaedics, treating war veterans. She felt no urge to become involved in orthopaedics. What she really wanted to do, and the wish became stronger every day, was to work with children.

Her own lost baby was often in Christina's thoughts. He came into her mind as a complete picture: soft fair hair on the skull, little fist curled against rosy cheek, snub nose . . .

The minute Laurenz gets back, she told herself, we'll find a priest, get married, and start a family of our own. She realised with something of a shock that during the glorious days and nights at Topchidarski Brdo, her thirtieth birthday had come and gone. She mustn't leave it too late to have her babies.

Jo-Jo had elected to go back to Vranja with the civilian hospital. 'After all, I came back to help my country, and places like Vranja are where the help is needed. Come with me, Christina.'

But she felt a reluctance to go there. Something seemed to

say to her that there was work for her elsewhere.

And soon it came; doctors were urgently needed for the Crimean Children's Clinic. The minute she heard of it, Christina presented herself at the office in Belgrade. It seemed a sign: she wanted, she *needed* to work with children, and in the Crimea there were children who needed her. And although she would be a long way from Laurenz, at least she would still be in a Slav part of the world, not lost in the furrows of some flat agricultural county in England.

She wrote telling him her new address: The Crimean Children's Clinic, Sebastopol, Crimea, Russia. As she wrote, she wondered whether this letter would reach him, or follow him, as the others had done, on some long pilgrimage through Bulgaria. It didn't matter. They would meet at last, when they both came back to Belgrade. The war had taught her that much: separation was a part of life, to be endured because reunion was all the sweeter then.

The journey was overland to Constantinople and thence by steamer across the Bosphorus to Sebastopol where the administration of the CCC had its offices, under the approval of the Russian authorities. It wasn't really clear to Christina exactly what Russia was at the moment. Since the Revolution of 1917, the Bolsheviks claimed to be the government. The White Russians denied this and fought on to hold what territory they could.

Part of their territory was this peninsula called the Crimea, a name well known to every British nurse and doctor. It was here that Christina's heroine Florence Nightingale had revolutionised hospital organisation by bringing in educated women to care for the sick and wounded. The harrowing thought that the peninsula had also been a slaughterhouse for fighting men was never far from Christina's mind as she journeyed towards it.

The CCC were just setting themselves up in the Crimea, and had almost no resources. How Christina regretted the loss of the stores and supplies she had handed over in Belgrade! They would have made wonders possible here in Sebastopol, for there weren't even tents available. A school building was given to them as a hospital for sick children; a small beginning.

Autumn in Sebastopol was a pleasant, mild season. Despite overcrowding and the fact that Bolshevik troops were advancing towards the Crimea, the atmosphere was full of gaiety. Almost the entire company from the Imperial Opera was here, and the Marynsky Theatre Ballet.

They gave performances in the city's main theatre late at night by candlelight; strange, darkly beautiful evocations of the splendour they had left when they went into exile. Damask roses, late-growing, were gathered to hand to the artistes as they acknowledged applause. Always the performance ended with the singing of the Russian National Anthem.

At first life wasn't very hard for the medical staff. But as winter approached, the CCC administrator, Lady Downing, confessed her worries to Christina and her colleagues. 'I hear there is typhus already among the Russian troops. The overcrowding in the town makes it almost certain it will spread to the civilian population.'

'But surely, ma'am, if the army doctors take proper precautions . . .'

Lady Downing shook her grey head. 'There's no carbolisation available, and the men haven't a change of clothing, so you see . . . I have to tell you that the Divisional Medical Surgeon says he expects 300,000 cases . . .'

'*What?*' It was a united gasp of incredulity.

'I'm afraid so, ladies. We desperately need money to buy medicines and bedding, because we're going to need about 20,000 beds . . .'

'That's impossible!'

'Will the French government give us any supplies?' asked Dr Birkett, an ex-missionary doctor from Dakar.

'It seems not. They back the White Russians politically, but as to money . . .' Her voice died away. The others in the crowded room looked at one another.

'Perhaps the DMS was exaggerating so as to get your attention,' someone suggested.

'Let's hope so.'

Efforts to get supplies were largely unsuccessful. The British forces at Constantinople sent blankets and disinfectants but it was a purely charitable act. What they needed, if the DMS, Dr Ilyin, proved to be right, was massive political help.

In October a bitter wind blew every day, bringing hail and snow. News came that a big battle was going on at the front, north of Perekop, between the White and the Red forces. At the beginning of November it was acknowledged that the White Russians had retreated back into the Crimean Peninsula and that they would be in a state of siege all winter.

The commanding general made a speech to the population. 'There is no action we can take until spring. Since Royalist Russia has no navy, any Russian wishing to leave can only go to the Ukraine. This means going over to the Bolsheviks, and anyone wishing to do so had better do it now.'

No one would even entertain the idea of going over to the Bolsheviks.

'My God, I'd no idea I was letting myself in for a siege when I came here,' Marion Agnew said to Christina as they huddled for warmth over a small wood fire in the hospital kitchen.

'Nor had I. But then I know nothing about politics.'

'Fine thing,' said Dr Agnew with a grimace. 'I came here at the beginning of summer and thought I was in for a sort of Mediterranean holiday.'

There was nothing Mediterranean about the weather. It grew colder and colder. A British naval commander came to the CCC to say that matters looked very serious indeed. General Wrangel had four divisions of troops, but the Bolsheviks had twenty-four and, moreover, seemed ready to continue fighting even in the sub-zero temperatures and snow storms that would become the norm in the following months.

'You must take it that British nationals will be leaving soon by sea, ma'am,' he said to Lady Downing.

Her Ladyship was indignant. 'We can't go! We've got a hospital full of orphans who—'

'Ma'am, the orphans are Russian children who must find

homes with Russian families. Perhaps it will be with Red Russian families.'

'Commander, that's too pessimistic . . .'

He went away, shaking his head.

Two days later he was back. Because of his warning, the staff had been trying to find families who would take in the foundlings, but there were still twenty-one little boys and girls with nowhere to go.

Commander Ainsworth saw it all with weary concern. 'I'm sorry, ladies. You are the only British women in the Crimea. Admiral Hope has sent an order that if there is the slightest resistance to evacuation we are to bring you down to the docks in chains. So you see, it's unavoidable.'

A sense of hopelessness pervaded the hospital. The wards were half empty already. The intense cold penetrated inside, for they had had no coal to stoke the big basement furnace. All at once they knew the commander was right: they had to go, they could do almost nothing to help even if they stayed.

'But we won't give up the children,' Christina said, protectively picking up a little girl from her cot.

At nightfall they went down the steps of the docks with the unclaimed children in their arms, to board a British destroyer and be taken to Constantinople.

The adults sat in groups on the deck. As if to mock them, the bitter wind dropped, the sun came out, the sea was blue and calm. 'We should have stayed!' Christina cried within herself.

But it was too late; Lady Downing had bowed to political wisdom. Constantinople was to be the home of the Crimean Children's Clinic now. It was soon renamed the Russian Refugee Clinic, for other children came to them clinging to the skirts of their mothers. The White Russians had somehow managed to find transport – tramp steamers, sailing brigs, fishing boats, anything that would put to sea – and came thronging into Constantinople, men, women and children.

Christina and her colleagues worked unceasingly. All through the winter they toiled at the basic routine of preventing typhus: bathing women and children, disinfecting, fumigating. One hundred and forty thousand refugees reached Constantinople and, Christina felt, at least half of them seemed to pass through her own hands. Constantinople was of course a Turkish city, but the Turks had nothing to give except shelter – the Turkish treasury was empty.

When at last the first desperately needed precautions had been carried out, Christina found time to write to Laurenz. No letter from him had reached her, but that wasn't surprising because the Crimean address was now in the hands of the Bolsheviks.

She said very little of the exhaustion that seemed to weigh her down these days. Instead she wrote about the beauty of the dark-eyed children, the happiness of coaxing a smile from one. She ended by begging him to write to her, even if it was only a few lines.

But no reply came. She sought out some of the Serbs stationed with the diplomatic delegation in the city to sound them out: did they know if there was still a mission in Bulgaria dealing with Serbian prisoners-of-war? Had it returned to Serbia perhaps? They knew nothing about it, promised politely to make inquiries, and then promptly forgot.

She wrote to Jo-Jo. Could Jo-Jo find out where Laurenz had gone? If she got an address for him, would she forward the enclosed letter?

After a long delay, Jo-Jo wrote back.

I went to Belgrade, but Laurenz isn't there. You know how it is, I'm not popular with the Royalists, so nobody would talk to me. I went to Laurenz's home near Skoplje. It's in ruins because of the Bulgarian bombardment and the members of the *zagruda* didn't seem to know anything. I asked if they expected the *gospodar* to come back. They just swayed their heads in that gesture that means 'Maybe, maybe not.' I know how important it is to you, dear, but I haven't been able to learn anything at all. I return the letter you sent for him. I just couldn't find out where to send it.'

What was to be done? Perhaps by and by, when replacements came to take over at the Refugee Clinic, she herself would go to look for him. He must be somewhere in Bulgaria. He must be alive and well; if not, there would have been official notification to his fellow officers.

She must wait. She would receive a letter, his letters had gone astray, that was all. Who could wonder at it in the confusion and disorganisation that seemed to reign throughout this part of the world?

In the autumn of 1920 the White Russians persuaded the French government to take over the care of the refugees in Turkey and Greece. Teams of French doctors and nurses came out to take charge of the sick and the needy. The Russian Refugee Clinic handed over its charges to them. And on the anniversary of Armistice Day, after an absence of six years, Dr Christina Holt embarked on a British ship to be taken back to the United Kingdom. She didn't argue against being taken 'home'. She didn't know where else to go. Laurenz wasn't in Belgrade, he didn't seem to be anywhere in Serbia, and if he was in Bulgaria still, there was no way to get in touch.

In any case, she was too ill and exhausted to struggle against authority. They said it was time for her to go, so go she must.

When the ship docked at Southampton, Christina discovered to her consternation that she was a celebrity. Reporters crowded round her as she stood at the rail watching the city come into view.

'Dr Holt, is it right that you served in five different countries? How do you feel about the medals, doctor? What are your plans for the future?'

She was too stunned to make sensible replies. Even more dumbfounding was the moment when the group parted to let her parents come forward. She stood amazed.

Her father kissed her on the brow while flashpowder flared. Her mother embraced her in floods of tears.

'How does it feel to have a heroine for a daughter, Mrs

Holt? Will you go with her to receive the medal? Mr Holt, you're proud of her, I expect?'

'Very proud,' said Herbert, putting a proprietary hand under her elbow. 'But of course she was always exceptional, even as a child.'

'What happens now, sir? Are you taking her home to Lincolnshire?'

'Yes, yes, of course, I've a car laid on, we'll do the whole journey in comfort. After all these hard times, my daughter deserves a little luxury.'

Still Christina had said hardly a word. She couldn't take it in. A small girl appeared to present a bouquet with a large card that said: 'Welcome, from the Women's Guild of Southampton.'

'Just pose for one last photo, doctor – there, that's right, hold the bouquet up. Splendid, splendid. Best of luck, doctor.'

The formalities of arrival were soon over. As they went out to the roadway, Christina said quietly, 'Father, I'm not coming back to Market Bresham.'

'Of course you are, my dear, it's your home.'

'No, I have to go to London to see a doctor.'

'Good heavens, child, there are plenty of doctors in Lincolnshire—'

'I'd rather see Dr Bellhaven.'

'And who on earth is he?'

'It's a she. She was my senior at Ghevgeli and Vranja.'

Put out by all these foreign place-names, her father looked annoyed. 'But I've arranged for the car . . .'

'You can drop me off in London.'

'But good Lord, your first evening home.'

'I'd rather, thank you.'

Her mother said with diffidence, 'She doesn't look well, Herbert. Perhaps she ought to see—'

'Oh, very well, very well!'

They got into the chauffeur-driven car and were taken smoothly to London. The luxury of being able to summon up a car, to drive on good roads in well-padded seats . . . It was all so strange.

She asked to be put down at the Nelson Hotel in the Strand. Her father insisted on going in with her to see that it was a suitable place. Her mother kissed her goodbye, murmuring, 'Ring us up when you've had a good night's sleep, dear. We have a telephone now.'

In her room Christina unpacked her few belongings; she had a long, luxurious bath, washed her short hair, lay on the bed in her shabby dressing-gown and asked room service for an omelette and a glass of wine. While she was waiting for it she looked in the telephone book for Addie Bellhaven's number.

It was a little after seven. Her call was taken by a receptionist who at first baulked at disturbing Doctor who had a patient with her. Of course, Christina remembered, it was evening surgery.

'Would you tell her it's Christina Holt? She'll want to speak to me.'

'Oh, very well.' A pause, a click, then Addie's booming voice.

'Christina! Is that you? Where on earth are you speaking from?'

'The Nelson Hotel in the Strand. I got in about an hour ago.'

'Ha! Saw your picture in the evening paper. You looked like something the cat dragged in.'

'That's how I feel. Addie, can I see you?'

'Not half! Just let me get rid of this bunch of hypochondriacs, and I'll fetch you and buy you the best dinner in London.'

'No, Addie, I meant can I see you as a patient? I'm pretty much run down. Give me an appointment.'

'Appointment? Fiddlesticks! I'll be there about eight. The Nelson, you said?'

'Yes, but Addie—'

'See you later.'

The phone went dead.

Christina had finished her meal and was looking at a copy of the evening paper when Adeline Bellhaven was shown up. The older woman engulfed her in a bear hug, then stood back to study her.

'My God,' she said, 'the camera cannot lie. You *do* look like something the cat dragged in. You're nothing but skin and bone. What on earth's the matter with you?'

'That's what you're going to tell me. I think it's just a sort of general exhaustion but I'm a bit worried in case I've got some after-effect of malaria or something.'

'Right. Off with the dressing-gown.'

Addie put her through a thorough examination. When it was over she said in her gruff way, 'You're anaemic, your blood pressure's low, your nerves are as tight as a wound-up watch, your teeth are loose in your head, and if there's anything in this new stuff about vitamins, I should think you're deficient in every one of them. What have you been doing with yourself, for God's sake?'

'Never mind that. What's the prescription?'

'Well, I'm going to slow you down and build you up. And to make sure you do as you're told, I'm going to put you to bed.'

'Addie, I can't stay in bed in a hotel!'

'Nobody asked you, sir, she said. Half a mo.' She picked up the phone and dialled. Within the hour she had Christina installed in a private room in the Charing Cross Hospital.

In a way it was delicious to let her life be taken over. Christina lay in bed for a week, sedated and sleeping a lot. Then she was allowed up part of each day. Little tempting meals were brought at regular intervals. Smoked salmon – when was the last time she'd tasted smoked salmon? And strawberry mousse?

She read, fell asleep over her book, woke to read a little more, and then it was time for her iron pills or her nerve tonic.

After the second week she was allowed visitors. Elwin came. 'How're you feeling now, Chrissie?' he asked, kissing her on the cheek.

He looked much as he used to: well-dressed in a dark suit and regimental tie, brown hair well barbered. He had brought her a bunch of red roses.

'I'm all right really. I just feel a bit woozy from time to time.'

'No wonder, from what I hear.'

'What do you hear, Elwin? There's really nothing to tell.'

'Not according to Dr Bellhaven. She can't speak highly enough about you. Father was very impressed.'

'Oh, Father . . .' She lay back in her cushioned armchair. 'I nearly dropped through the ship's deck when he came aboard to welcome me home.'

'He's delighted with you these days. Someone he can be proud of, you know.'

Something in the way he said it let her know that her father was disappointed in Elwin – Elwin, who had always been his favourite.

'How is everything going, Elwin? How is Dorothy?'

'Blooming! Motherhood suits her.'

'And you're happy?'

'Happy?' he said in a much too hearty manner. 'I'm the happiest man in the land! Loving wife, pretty baby daughter, steady job – what more could a man ask?'

When she tried to find out more he turned the subject to her own health, her plans for the future. 'I don't know, Elwin,' she told him. 'I haven't made any plans. I don't know what I want to do.'

'Father wants you to set up practice near home, so he can bask in your reflected glory.'

'Elwin!'

'Sorry. Did that sound sarky? I didn't mean to. You really have done well, Chrissie, and I'm proud of you too.'

When he had gone she thought over what he had said. There was nothing in the actual words, she simply felt that he was terribly unhappy.

Christmas was nearly upon them. Herbert Holt wanted Dr Bellhaven to say his daughter could come home for the festive season. Addie could see that there was nothing Christina wanted less, and solved the problem by sending her to a convalescent home in Devon. There she was to stay, eating lots of Devon cream and breathing lots of healthy Devon air, until her weight had come up to something more near normal for her height and Addie was confident she could cope with everyday life without keeling over.

Mail was sent on to Christina in this quiet retreat. She went through it eagerly, but there was never a letter from Laurenz. One day she stood staring out towards the sparkle of the sea and admitted to herself that she might never see him again. He seemed to have vanished.

In the spring she at last got up enough courage to go home to Market Bresham. It was strange. It seemed to have shrunk. Dr Childers was dead and she was introduced to the new man, who treated her with exaggerated respect.

Her mother had arranged a dinner party for her first night home. 'Wear something pretty, dear,' she said anxiously. 'Your father wants you to make a good impression.'

Christina had bought a few clothes. All she'd brought back from abroad were the worn overcoat that went with her uniform, and the kid-skin jacket that had seen her through so many hard winters. Certainly not suitable for civilised society.

For the dinner party she chose a short dark blue dress with the belt worn around the hips. To Market Bresham, it would seem almost scandalously modern. Her hair, still very short, was in fact quite the vogue: if a hairdresser had cut it he would have charged two guineas and called it The Eton Crop.

All the local notables came. They asked embarrassing questions, such as, 'Weren't you terribly frightened among all those wild people?' and, 'I suppose they robbed you blind – foreigners always do.'

Her brother and his wife were there, of course. Dorothy was quite willing to be taken aside for a little private conversation when they left the men to their port. What Christina wanted to talk about was Elwin.

'He's quite different, Christina. He used to be so steady and dependable. Now he's moody, never the same from one day to the next.'

'He had some dreadful experiences in the war, Dorothy. It may take him a long time to settle down.'

'But other men went through the war and have settled down quite happily.'

'Do we know that for sure, dear? Someone – I think it was an American author – said that most men live lives of quiet desperation. Since the war, that's probably even more true.'

Dorothy cast up her china blue eyes in irritation. 'But what's he got to be desperate about? I could understand it if he'd come back to unemployment, like so many of the servicemen. But he's got a good career ahead of him.'

'Perhaps he's not so sure he wants to succeed Father as the leading solicitor of Market Bresham.'

'You're being absurd, Christina.' After she'd said it, Dorothy looked perturbed. Perhaps you couldn't say things like that to an acknowledged war heroine. But her sister-in-law didn't seem to have taken offence.

'I don't think it's absurd. Be patient with my big brother, Dot. Please be very, very patient.'

Mrs Holt called Dorothy to help hand round the coffee. The men joined them, conversation became general. People began to ask Christina what her plans were.

'I want her to settle here,' Herbert said.

'But there isn't a vacant practice in Market Bresham.'

'Oh, she's too big for Market Bresham, of course, but I thought perhaps Lincoln? How about Lincoln, Christina?'

It was strange. Now, when she didn't want or need his money, Herbert was eager to offer it so that she would set up nearby.

The truth was, the more she thought about the future, the more she was attracted to psychiatry. It was a new branch of medicine, one in which there was still much to discover. Although some thought it mere foolishness, Christina had seen things that convinced her that mental illness existed in far more forms than was readily acknowledged.

Her brother Elwin, for instance: he had been changed by his war experiences. Now he was home, and she could see he felt trapped somehow. Yet most people would say he was a lucky man. That was perhaps part of the illness, that no one appreciated what it was he suffered from.

That old man wielding the dagger at Tezelk. He had been behaving quite out of character: the villagers had been shamed and astonished by his actions. Something had changed him – the dreadful responsibility of keeping his village safe in wartime. And the many children she'd seen, suffering from nightmares, reverting to infantile bed-wetting. And women still afraid to go out of doors, even to buy food. For no reason, no reason that logic could offer.

She came to the conclusion over the first few weeks of April that she would take up psychiatry. She would need training. It might be a long business . . .

But before that she would give up six months to unfinished business, to a kind of pilgrimage. She would visit the people connected with her past, exorcising old ghosts so as to make a fresh start.

She wrote letters to prepare her way. First to Jo-Jo, who was now in Geneva working on the secretariat of the newly founded League of Nations. She asked her for names of Serbian officials she might contact in Belgrade in hopes of learning something about Laurenz. She wrote to Aunt Bea in Philadelphia. She wrote to the parents of Henri Darblier.

While she awaited replies, she made it her business to be introduced into diplomatic circles. It wasn't difficult, she was something of a celebrity: a medal had been sent to the Edinburgh HQ of the Women's Service Hospital, to be sent on to Doctoritza Holt in honour of her services to Serbia. There was also a little ceremony at the French Embassy at which she was invested with the Legion d'Honneur. From such contacts and with the help of the press she met officials of other Embassies, notably the American.

By the simple expedient of asking about them, she learnt what had happened to the Charlfords, the couple who had adopted her baby from the Serbian community in the Alleghenies. John Charlford, she was told, was a second secretary at the Paris Embassy – a plum posting, which meant he was well regarded in official circles.

By and by she received replies to her letters. Jo-Jo sent what help she could. The parents of Henri Darblier said they would be delighted to meet her. Aunt Bea urged her to come and spend a long spell with her.

All her preparations made, Christina took the ferry from Dover to Calais and from there went on to Paris to catch the train to Belgrade. She tried to keep her mind a blank, so that she might neither hope nor fear.

All she wanted was to *know*. Was Laurenz in Belgrade? Did he think of her? Because if not, she must put away all thought of him and give the rest of her life, without stint, to medicine.

Chapter Twenty-five

The office of the controller of the Land Registry was quite prestigious for post-war Belgrade. It had a well-polished floor, a walnut desk, an upholstered desk-chair, a telephone, and brown velvet curtains at the window. There was a plain wooden chair for visitors.

Jo-Jo had sent Christina a letter of introduction to Mr Bersak, showing a great deal of shrewdness in her choice: 'It's no good my giving you the name of any of the Army officials because they're Monarchist to a man and disapprove of me. Mishka was at school with me so he may be kindly disposed. Also, the officials at the Land Registry know everything these days: disputes over post-war land tenure have given them inside information about everybody.'

So when Christina shook hands with Mishka Bersak she was willing to overlook his grudging manner. She could tell he disapproved of her: her title of doctor, her short skirts, her short hair, her inescapable look of being a professional woman.

He nodded towards the letter of introduction, which she had sent in when she requested an interview. 'Jo-Jo and I go back a long way. But I can't allow myself to be involved in any madcap scheme of hers.'

'There's nothing madcap about Jo-Jo these days,' Christina said with a smile. 'She's a very responsible official of the League of Nations.'

'So that's the reason for the Geneva address . . . Well, so much the better for Serbia if Jo-Jo is in Switzerland. Republicanism! When we're still putting the pieces together after a terrible war . . .'

'I was in Serbia for most of the war, *gospodine*. That's the reason I'm here. I'm trying to get in touch with someone I—'

'If it's a claim on land, I'm afraid only Serbian nationals—'

'No, no, nothing like that. I've been writing letters to a Captain Laurenz Varikiav but there have been no replies.' To her dismay she heard her voice waver. She bit her lip and went on more firmly. 'I wonder if you could tell me whether Captain Varikiav's home address still exists? I understood he had property at Ikjstar, near Skoplje.'

'Varikiav, Varikiav . . . As far as I recall there have been no legal proceedings involving that name . . .' He picked his old-fashioned telephone from its rest. 'Ilsa, would you look in the files for anything on the Varikiav family? If there's a file, bring it in.'

A pause ensued. Mr Bersak filled it by asking her about her war work. He knew some of the places she recalled, had had to visit them to solve family disputes about land rights. 'So many women were widowed, you understand. Under our law, their rights are claimed by their son or, if the son is not of legal age—'

The secretary came in with a thin cardboard folder. 'The Varikiav file, sir.'

'Oh, so there is something. Well, well, let's see – thank you, Ilsa – oh, one moment. Would you like tea, doctor?'

'Thank you, that would be nice.'

Ilsa looked at Christina with interest, gave a little smile of admiration for the courageous woman who could come alone and speak face to face with her boss, and went out.

Christina's attention was on the file. She watched avidly as Bersak opened it. 'Varikiav . . . Varikiav . . .' He was pulling at his full moustache with two fingers. 'Ah, I see why your letters have received no reply, *gospodjo*. The leadership of the *zagruda* passed without dispute to a Mikhail Gedin, who is the neighbouring land-user. Laurenz Varikiav is unable to carry out his duties as *gospodar* because of absence.'

'But absence where?' cried Christina, sitting forward on her chair.

'In Bulgaria,' Bersak said, consulting the file.

'But he went to Bulgaria in 1919! He can't still be there!'

'Why not? He may be engaged in—' He broke off, having turned over the second sheet of paper that was the file's contents. 'Oh. No, I see. Oh.'

'What?' she insisted. 'What, *gospodine?*'

'Er, I think perhaps . . . It's quite understandable that your letters were not forwarded . . . Well, well . . . It's not really for publication.'

'Mr Bersak, I've come all the way from England to find out what has happened to Laurenz. Please tell me. Please, I beg you, tell me why Laurenz is still in Bulgaria. Is he ill? Has he been in an accident? What?'

The controller of the Land Registry got up from his seat, walked to the window with his hands behind his back, came back, and looked at Christina with something like compassion. He was a kindly man, and moreover this was a friend of the love of his schooldays. 'I see it is very important to you, doctor.'

'The most important thing in my life!'

'Very well.' He sat down in his place. Picking up the sheet of paper in the file he read:

'Laurenz Varikiav, Captain, Royal Cavalry Regiment, *gospodar* of Ikjstar, Skoplje. Management of land and undertakings of *zagruda* under temporary control of Mikhail Gedin, farmer and orchardist, due to absence of said Laurenz Varikiav. Absence allowed without charge of absenteeism due to special circumstances, as hereunder stated.

'Said Captain Laurenz Varikiav is serving a five-year prison sentence under the Bulgarian State Prison Service—'

The world whirled around Christina. Mr Bersak and his piece of paper, the square of light from the window and the velvet curtains, all melted into a kaleidoscope of white and black and brown.

At that moment the secretary came in with the tea. Mishka Bersak's attention was diverted to the matter of having the tray placed on his desk, checking that the correct accoutrements were present. He watched with satisfaction while Ilsa poured the steaming pale liquid, picked up the requisite two cubes of brown sugar with silver tongs and dropped them in.

'*Chaje, gospodjo?*'

The question brought Christina back to herself. She focused on the hand which was offering her the glass in its silver holder. 'Thank you,' she croaked, and took it.

She sipped down the scalding tea. She needed something to hurt her, to take away the pain of what she had just heard.

'A very sad business,' Bersak said in polite commiseration.

'What . . . what is Captain Varikiav in prison for?' she managed to ask.

'He killed a man.'

The hand holding the glass of tea shook so that the hot liquid spilled over her wrist. 'Killed?' she gasped. 'You mean . . . murdered?'

'Oh no,' Bersak replied, shocked. 'It must have been a fair fight, otherwise the charge would of course have been murder. But it states here, "accidental homicide with a weapon" and so the sentence was only five years.'

Christina rose to her feet. She set the tea-glass down on the tray on Bersak's desk. 'Where? Where is he? I must go to him at once!'

'I beg your pardon?'

'Tell me what prison he is in. I must see him.'

'But, *gospodjo*, I'm afraid that's impossible. Bulgarian regulations are very strict; only family are allowed to visit prisoners.' Of course, she was a foreigner. She had no idea of the complexity of the post-war situation between Serbia and Bulgaria.

She clasped and unclasped her hands. 'But . . . they must let me see him. I'm a friend, a very close friend . . . We were to be married . . .'

Bersak frowned. 'You are upset, doctor – but think what you are saying.'

'He would want me to visit him. Surely a fiancée is regarded as—'

'Doctor Holt, you cannot possibly be Captain Varikiav's fiancée.'

'But I am, I tell you.'

Bersak used his most official tone. 'You are under some misapprehension, madame. Captain Varikiav is already married, has a son and a daughter. He cannot possibly be engaged to you.'

Married.

It had never occurred to her to ask Laurenz if he was married.

When the blur of shock cleared enough for her to pay attention, she discovered that Controller Bersak was agreeing with his own suggestion that she was in error over the family name, that Serbian names were often difficult, that though she spoke quite good Serbian it was easy to make mistakes, that they must have been talking about the wrong man.

'Yes,' she said in a faint voice. 'Of course. I'm sorry to have taken up your time. Thank you, *gospodine*.'

She shook hands with politeness but with a blank look in her eyes that alarmed Mr Bersak. When she had gone he called in his secretary. 'Ilsa, you may as well have that glass of tea, the lady didn't want it. And Ilsa, if she calls again, I am not available, do you understand? I am in a conference or have gone home for the day if Dr Holt comes back.'

So much, he sighed to himself, for trying to do a favour for Jo-Jo Belu.

Back in her hotel, Christina sank down in an armchair in the entrance hall. Her legs refused to carry her any further. She laid her head back against the lace antimacassar, closed her eyes, and let the world go away. Perhaps in the aftermath of shock, she slept.

When she opened her eyes again everything still looked the same. The same worn bourgeois furniture in the lobby, the same May sunshine streaming in mercilessly to reveal its frayed upholstery, the same wealth of flowers in the ornate vases, the same murmur of Serbian conversation.

Married?

Laurenz had never talked of his private life, but there was nothing unusual in that. During that long and bitter struggle, most Serbians had family tragedies; homes wrecked and burned, children separated and lost, fathers killed, brothers taken prisoner, sisters taken hostage, heartache and loss buried deep, so that ordinary life could be allowed to go on.

Sometimes in Laurenz's manner there had been glimpses of darkness. But in the Slav temperament there was more contrast of light and shade than in the prosaic Anglo-Saxon. She had taken it for granted there were parts of his life she didn't as yet know.

But not this, not this.

She went up in the little gilt lift to her room, lay on the bed, and tried to come to terms with it. He was a husband and father. She had never had any claims on him except as a lover. All her fine plans to marry and bear his children had been dreamstuff, woven from the song of the nightingales and the scent of the roses.

Hours went by. The sun's rays changed, the shadows in her room lengthened. The May evening came, with its gentle coolness. Outside, the people of Belgrade made their way home from office and shop. She could hear laughter and music from the café along the street, the sound of feet moving in the *kolo*, that dance of linked arms and swaying bodies.

She turned over on the bed, hiding her face in her arms, putting her hands over her ears. She didn't want to hear it; she didn't want to think of those brief happy times when the music had lifted her feet, when Laurenz's arm had been about her waist.

By and by she pushed herself up. It was late. She must wash and go down to the dining-room, otherwise she would get nothing to eat and she knew, her good sense told her, that she was weak and in shock. She ran a brush through her hair, picked up a wrap to help warm her chilled body.

Good sense might prompt her to order a meal. But nothing could make her swallow any of it. Only the wine seemed to help.

She went to bed about midnight, dazed, sick with misery and bewilderment.

Next morning she woke early, knowing she'd been a fool. There was an explanation. Of course there was an explanation. Mishka Bersak had been telling her she'd made a mistake in the family name, but he was the one making the mistake. He'd given her wrong information.

She bathed and dressed and went down to breakfast. Then she went for a walk, to fill in time until the government offices opened. At nine o'clock she presented herself at the office of the Land Registry.

The commissionaire at the big double doors refused to admit her when she gave her name and asked to see Mr Bersak. 'I'm sorry, *gospodjo*, you are not permitted to enter.'

'But I was here yesterday!' she exclaimed in perplexity.

'I'm sorry, *gospodjo*, my orders are that you are not permitted to enter.'

'Whose orders?'

He had no intention of telling her that the orders came from Ilsa Mirioj, secretary to the controller. 'That is confidential information, *gospodjo*.'

And he refused to say more.

Anger fuelled determination; she would not allow herself to be frustrated, there were others she could approach.

In the telephone book she found the name of one of Laurenz's fellow-officers. She rang him. A woman replied, clearly his wife, but after a few moments' delay Peko Javich came on the line.

'Doctoritza Holt?' he said uncertainly.

'Yes, Lieutenant. Do you remember me?'

'Is that really you, Christina? How strange to hear from you! Where are you?'

'I'm here in Belgrade,' she took a breath and plunged on, 'looking for Laurenz. Peko, what is this strange mix-up about Laurenz being in prison?'

There was a crackling sound on the line.

'Hello? Hello? Peko, are you still there?'

'Yes, still here.'

'Tell me about Laurenz.'

She heard his sigh. 'You know about Laurenz.'

'But they say he killed a man!'

'Yes.'

'It can't be true!'

'Yes, it is.'

'But Peko, there's more to it than that! Tell me, tell me!'

After a long pause he said, 'If you know about the prison sentence and the reason, what more do you need?'

'I have a right to hear about his family, Peko! I have a *right*!' She heard the shrill note on which she ended, wished she could call back the words.

There was a fractional hesitation, and then the phone was put down at the other end.

Her first impulse was to jump into a taxi and rush to confront him. But she knew it would be useless. He lived in one of the blocks in a good area of Belgrade. There would be a hall porter who would refuse entrance, just like the man at the Land Registry.

She was filled with a sudden revulsion. What am I doing here? Making a fool of myself, shrieking at people like a fishwife . . .

And they would tell her nothing. She realised now that she would be told no more than she had already learned. Those who knew Laurenz Varikiav were not about to discuss his private affairs with his ex-mistress. And officials, if she could reach any of them, would regard her as a madwoman.

She packed, asked for her bill, and took the next train westwards. She needed to talk to a friend. She needed to talk to Jo-Jo.

Jo-Jo's address in Geneva proved to be a very handsome flat near the lakeshore. She welcomed Christina with open arms, though it was the middle of the night. She tut-tutted about her wan looks and her deep-sunken eyes. 'You look as if you've had no sleep for a week. Come on, straight to bed, and we can talk in the morning.'

'Jo-Jo, I can't possibly sleep until I've got some sort of idea of what it all means. Everyone in Belgrade was so matter-of-fact, but I find it . . . terrifying.'

Her story poured out. Jo-Jo, resplendent in a red satin pyjama suit, heard her out with a frown.

'We-ell,' she said at the end, 'I can't explain it entirely, but . . .'

'But what?'

'It sounds like he killed a man in an affair of honour.'

Christina stared. 'You mean . . . a duel?'

'Something like that. We Serbians don't dress it up with fancy names, but the men exact satisfaction one way or another. The villagers at Ikjstar must have known about this; I understand now why they wouldn't tell me anything when I came around making inquiries about Laurenz.'

'Oh, Jo-Jo,' cried Christina, burying her face in her hands, 'why did you let me fall in love with him? Why didn't you tell me he was married?'

Jo-Jo sat down and put her arms about her friend. 'Because, dear little nit-wit, when I brought the subject round to things like that, he said he was a widower. Naturally I believed him. Serbians lie like troopers when they have to, but about important things – I always used to believe they told the truth . . .'

'The truth, the truth! The truth is, I never really knew him at all!'

Jo-Jo could offer little comfort. She understood now that it was no use ordering Christina to bed as if this was the end of an ordinary day. She poured brandy, and they sat in the light of a single lamp sipping it, trying to make sense of what had happened, trying to come to terms with it.

'It comes to this, Christina. You have to put him out of your head and start again – a new life.'

Good advice.

First Christina had to complete her pilgrimage. She stayed a few days with Jo-Jo, then went to see the parents of Henri Darblier in Bordeaux. They were a quiet couple, living in a home that they had made a kind of living memorial to their son.

'Mademoiselle, Henri wrote to us about you! It is such a delight to meet the girl who might have been our daughter-in-law!'

It didn't even seem to occur to them that Christina might have refused him. They gave her a small photograph of Henri in a silver frame which they clearly expected her to keep by her bedside for the rest of her life.

'It's easy to see, mademoiselle, that you have a good career ahead of you. Henri told us what a clever doctor you were. We are so glad to know he chose well and that, although you have lost him, you still have a life to lead.'

When she left Bordeaux for Paris Christina put the photograph at the bottom of her trunk, knowing she would probably never look at it again. Yet she was glad to have visited M. and Mme Darblier. She felt it had given them pleasure to meet their lost son's love.

She booked into a little hotel in Paris called the Chavas. From there it was a short walk to the American Embassy, where she identified herself to the duty officer as a friend of a friend of John Charlford.

'I wonder if you could just give me his address? I've a message to pass on to him.' Without suspicion, he gave her the Paris address of the Charlfords.

Any time she had chatted at diplomatic parties with acquaintances of the Charlfords, she'd managed to bring up the subject of their family. 'Oh yes, just the one, I believe. A good-looking little chap,' people had said.

She was going to see him.

Not to cause any trouble, naturally. She would never in the world do anything to harm her son. All she wanted was to see him.

Christina had given him up to the Charlfords eleven years ago. She tried to imagine what he would look like now. Would he have a nurse, a governess? His parents would be occupied with the obligatory social round of the Embassy, so there would be a considerable household staff. Should she wait for a time when both parents would be out, and then introduce herself as an old friend of the family, just passing through? But then the servants would report it to the Charlfords, who would be puzzled and perhaps alarmed. Besides, Stephen might not even be at home.

She took a taxi to the address in the Fourteenth Arrondissement. It was a very fine apartment block, with a garden in front and a concierge in charge of the hall. No chance of simply walking in and ringing the bell.

Uncertain, she sat in the cab. 'Isn't this the address you wanted, mademoiselle?' asked the driver over his shoulder.

'Yes, it's the right place. Just let me sit here for a while.'

'The meter's going, mademoiselle.'

'I know, it's all right.'

With a shrug he took out a newspaper and began to read. These mad foreigners . . .

What should she do? It had seemed such a simple undertaking when she planned it, yet when it came to the point, how did you introduce yourself into a strange household?

She leaned her head against the dusty glass of the taxi window. Perhaps she should get him to drive her back to her hotel. Her courage wasn't equal to it after all, or perhaps the events in Belgrade had made her uncertain of herself.

Then, coming along the pavement, she saw a schoolboy. He was dressed in a loose blue and white striped shirt and tweed knickerbockers. A leather satchel hung by a strap from one shoulder. One hand was in his trouser pocket, the other was running a stick along the garden railing so that it made a satisfactory plick-plick-plick.

Tall for his age, well-built, taking after his father, Peter Semmring. But fair-haired and dark-eyed like his mother. Her son, Stephen.

Hurriedly she paid off the taxi. She turned to walk in the direction that would take her to meet him. The words, 'I'm your real mother,' surged to her lips.

Instead she said in French, 'Excuse me, can you tell me the way to Avenue des Suisses?'

He stopped. His head already came to the level of her chin. 'Certainly,' he said, and then with a smile, 'Madame is not French, I think?'

'Why no,' she said in English, 'how did you know?'

'Well, I'm not French either.' Now he was grinning.

'You're not? Are you English, then?'

'I'm American,' he said. 'Couldn't you tell?'

'No, your French is excellent.'

'I wish you'd tell that to the teachers at my school! They keep complaining I speak French like an American. Where was it again you wanted to get to, ma'am?'

'Avenue des Suisses.'

'Oh, sure, that's quite close by. It would be best if you walk on up to the Rue d'Alesia, then it's a left turn, and Avenue des Suisses goes off on the left just before Rue Raymond Losserand. You know Rue d'Alesia?'

'Well, no . . .'

'Maybe it'd be better if I walk you up to the corner. Would that be OK?'

Oh please, she said in her heart, please walk with me. Take my arm and walk through Paris with me.

'Thank you, you're very kind,' she said.

He darted round her so as to walk on the outside of the pavement. His manners were beautiful.

'You know your way around the district,' she complimented him.

'Oh, sure, I live in it. My folks are at the Embassy, you know. You're just visiting?'

'Yes, I'm only here for a few days. I envy you, it must be lovely to live in Paris.'

'Yeah, it's keen, except that I can't get any of the kids at school to take an interest in baseball.'

'Oh, that's too bad. You have to follow it in the American newspapers, I suppose?'

'And they're a week old by the time we get them. But my Dad pitches to me sometimes, in the park in the evening. Sure is funny to see the French kids watching us: they think we're crazy, I guess.'

She drank in every word. His voice was still unbroken but it was a boy's voice, firm and strong. He had a way of smiling a little as he pictured himself and his father playing family baseball in the Parc Montsouris. His stride was long, athletic. He must take after his natural father in his physical aptitudes.

'Well, here we are,' he remarked as they came to the junction of the Rue Didot with the Rue d'Alesia. 'It's this way' – pointing – 'and you stay on this sidewalk, you know, and there's just one turn before you come to Avenue des Suisses.'

'Thank you. That's quite clear. I'm very much obliged to you.'

'Oh, it was no trouble.' He hesitated. 'Say, I hope you don't think I'm trying to be funny, but there's something kind of familiar about you. Have I seen you before?'

When you look in the mirror, she wanted to say. When you look in the mirror, it's my eyes that look back at you.

'I don't think so. I was only ever in Paris once before – in the war.'

'Gee, were you here then? Mme Tremoux, that's our concierge, she's always telling about what it was like in the war. I guess it was exciting, wasn't it? She says you could hear the guns!'

'That's probably true, but I only came here once. I was serving on the Marne, with the French forces.'

'You were?' He gazed at her in awe. 'How come, I mean you being a lady and everything?'

'I was with a field hospital.'

'A nurse! That's real romantic. Did you ever nurse any Americans? My Dad was over here in the war, but I guess you wouldn't come into contact with him, he was in the Navy.'

'No, I never had any dealings with American forces. Your father was in the Navy? I expect he can tell you some exciting things.'

'Oh, sure, it's keen when I can get him to talk about it. But he says the war's over and we must think about the peace – which is true enough, I reckon, only it's not so exciting, is it?'

She laughed, 'I think you should find your excitement in baseball.'

'It would be exciting if I could find enough guys to make up even one team,' he said with mock mournfulness. 'Well, I mustn't keep you here talking. I expect you've got someone waiting for you in the Avenue des Suisses. Nice to have met you, ma'am.'

'And very nice to have met you. Thank you.'

They looked at each other. After a moment he put out his hand in the French fashion.

She took it. I am holding the hand of my son, she said to herself.

They shook hands, he gave a little bow and, wheeling round, marched off the way they had come. She stood on the corner watching him go. After a few paces he looked back over his shoulder. Seeing her still standing there, he took it that she was uncertain of her way. He paused, pantomimed, 'That way, along to your left.' She nodded, and took the direction he had shown her.

As she walked towards the Avenue des Suisses, tears poured down her cheeks.

Chapter Twenty-six

During the voyage to New York, Christina was obsessed by what had happened in Belgrade and in Paris. It haunted her thoughts by day, and her dreams by night. She went over and over it in her mind, in walks on deck while the Atlantic shimmered in the sunshine all around, in long hours under the summer stars when the shipboard life was quiet.

Two earth-shattering things had happened: she had learned that the man she loved was out of her reach for ever, and she had seen her lost son.

She had brought these two events about by her own will. She had sought them out. Each had meted out its own punishment. Surely, she said to herself, surely now you see that you must leave the past alone?

The past was gone by for ever. Laurenz was lost to her; Stephen was lost to her.

She had tried to tell herself she was tremendously important to both of them. She had gone to find them. And when she at last came face to face with one of them . . . Stephen had looked at her and had seen a mere stranger.

Perhaps to Laurenz too she was a stranger now. What claim had she on his thoughts? A woman whose body he had known – well, she had never fooled herself she was his first and only lover. Now she knew there was a prior claimant. A wife. Mother of his children. A son and a daughter, Bersak had said.

And he had killed a man. That was her worst nightmare. It formed itself out of the episode at Tezelk, when they had faced the old villager protecting his food supply. Laurenz with a service revolver held casually at his side, waiting for the moment when it might be necessary to kill . . .

His antagonist in the dreams was faceless, unknown. He had *killed* a man. 'It sounds like an affair of honour,' Jo-Jo had said.

Strange . . . Alien . . . A man she had never really known.

Jo-Jo's command, to put him out of her head and start again, began to seem good advice. If she could do it, if only she could do it. If she could banish him from her thoughts, her dreams.

One thing was certain. She had no claim of any kind upon him. She had loved him, but love can make no claim. She had no claim on her son Stephen either. Vague hopes that he would feel some bond as he looked at her had vanished that day in Paris.

So what was left for her?

The words of the Darbliers came back to her. Although she had lost the man she loved, she still had a life to lead.

Still a life to lead. Still work to be done, skills to be learned. The world was all around, still in need of help from those who had the will and the energy to offer it. Lives broken by the war and its aftermath, lost men like her brother Elwin who scarcely knew how to cope with memories of the awfulness.

And children. Children who suffered, not in the body – though God knew there were enough of those. But children who suffered in the mind, in the soul: not every ailment could be treated with a pill or a potion. She still held in her memory some of the children she had tried to treat in Serbia: trembling, white-faced, afraid to go to sleep because of the nightmares that would shock them back to wakefulness; nightmares of retreat under gunfire, of bayonet attacks among the village houses, of a mother hacked to pieces, of a father marched away to be shot.

Wakeful herself, she looked back at her life and forward to the future. She would find something to do. Now was the time to restore and repair, now that the guns had ceased firing. She would be one of those who helped rebuild society.

She would spend some time with her aunt in Philadelphia

and then she would go home. She would train, she would learn what she needed to know so that she could be useful again. That was what she needed – a sense of purpose.

In New York she bought a few more clothes. It would be very warm and sticky in Philadelphia, so she chose voiles and muslins and a new fabric called georgette. She made herself take an interest in the styles. It was important, if she was to have any usefulness, to be attractive to the beholder. The dresses were short and straight, skimming the figure. With them went fine straw hats that hugged the head, coming low on the ears but with the brim turned up to show off the brow. Pale silk stockings were all the rage – pale silk stockings and pale kid shoes.

When her Aunt Beatrice saw her, she threw up her hands in amazement. 'Christina Holt! What have you done to yourself?'

'Aunt Bea darling, don't you like me?' They hugged each other, then Christina said with anxiety, 'Auntie, you've gone awfully thin!'

'So much the better! I always was too curvaceous for my own good. Chrissie dear, how you've changed! Of course I was silly to expect you to be the little fair-haired girl who sailed away ten years ago.'

They sat down to catch up on the news. The Wallace Hotel was flourishing at the moment, contrary to all expectations. Men coming back from overseas were on the move looking for jobs, and many of them came to Philadelphia en route to mining and shipbuilding centres. Hotels in the city centre were a little too expensive. The prices at the Wallace were more within their range.

Her aunt had built on extra rooms at the back. Finding the work too much, she'd brought in a manageress. 'Christina, I wish you'd come and take over from me, dear. Velma is fine, of course, but it's not like having your own family in charge.'

Christina shook her head. 'I'm sorry, Aunt Bea, I'm just not cut out to be a hotelier.'

'No.' Mrs Kentley sighed. 'You always wanted to be a

doctor, and a doctor you will be until the end of your days.'

'How is Captain Dinsdorf?' Christina asked, to change the subject.

'I wrote you that he had to go into a residential seamen's home, didn't I? And Miss Melville went to a niece in Chicago. She hates it there – she rings me about once a month to say she's coming back to Philly, but she can't afford it any more, you know . . .'

Her aunt had news of one or two of the fellow-students of her year at the university, but couldn't remember which. She burrowed in an untidy bureau for letters. 'Dear me, I'll forget where I've put my own head next.'

As Christina said au revoir, she felt that her aunt was failing a little. The sensible businesswoman of ten years ago was gone, to be replaced by a kindly, slightly muddled-old lady.

Christina was putting up at the Bellevue-Stratford. In her student days the hotel had over-awed her with its marble stairs and gilt ceilings. But now her bank balance was fat with the unspent salary of six years of service. She could afford the solid comforts of the Bellevue.

On her second evening she came back to the hotel from a long visit with Captain Dinsdorf at the seamen's home. She was tired and a little sad, for the old man had held her fast when it was time to go. 'My Snow Princess, stay a while longer, please stay . . .' But the kindly nurse had led him off to his evening meal.

She showered then changed into an after-six gown of midnight blue voile. In honour of Captain Dinsdorf she fastened his gold chain round her neck. But before she went in to dinner she must buy a magazine to read while she ate. She hated to be unoccupied at a restaurant meal – men kept trying to catch her eye.

She paused on the marble staircase leading into the lobby to look for the magazine kiosk. Standing in the hall were a group of men in dinner jackets awaiting their womenfolk who were apparently fetching their wraps. These must have been early diners.

Her eye passed over them idly. Then, her attention caught, she looked again.

Impossible not to recognise that upright figure, that fresh tanned face.

At the same moment, his glance crossed hers. He looked, his expression showed admiration and then, as she clearly was studying him, interest. A frown developed between his brows.

One of his companions dug him in the ribs and muttered in his ear. She could imagine what he was saying: 'Who's the lady friend, old chap?'

The women for whom they'd been waiting joined them. One in particular, smart, dark and svelte, caught in a moment the link that joined these two – the girl on the marble stairs and the man watching her.

'Peter? Is something the matter?'

'Seen an old light o' love, Ardeth!' laughed one of the men, not unwilling to get in a jibe.

Light broke on Peter Semmring's face. He dashed across the lobby, came up the steps two at a time. 'Christina? Christina Holt?'

Fool, she said to herself. Why didn't you turn away the moment you saw him!

'Well, Peter,' she said.

Now it dawned on him that perhaps he wasn't particularly pleased to see her. At first she'd puzzled him, this stranger, so fair and so very smart in her slight dress of summery fabric, faint gleam of gold at the breast, hair cropped short in the dramatic new fashion.

Now memory rushed upon him. Christina Holt. He had no reason to want to see her again. He had tried to banish every memory of her from his mind.

But now he'd committed himself, and Ardeth would wonder what the hell he was up to if he just tried to drop the whole thing.

'You must come and be introduced to my wife . . .'

'No, no,' she said, trying to take her hand out of his. 'I was just going—'

'It won't take a moment.' He urged her across the lobby. The others awaited his arrival with interest.

'Ardeth, people, I want you to meet a fellow student from Penn.U. This is Dr Christina Holt – it is still Holt, is it, or have you married?'

'No, I'm not married. How do you do, Mrs Semmring?'

'How do you do, Dr Holt?' Ardeth Semmring said, her anxiety abating. Some fuddy-duddy doctor from his university days. Although, looked at dispassionately, Dr Holt didn't seem the least bit fuddy-duddy.

The men eagerly introduced themselves by name, their wives smiled and looked polite. 'We've just been having a working dinner,' Peter explained. 'Planning a charity ball for the autumn. If only I'd known you were in town, Christina!'

'Are you staying long, Dr Holt?'

'Not long, I'm going back to England in two weeks or so.'

'You're in practice there, doctor?'

She shook her head. 'Not as yet. I've just come back from . . . well, from service overseas. I mean to set up in practice quite soon, though.'

Ardeth Semmring said, 'Do you find people like to go to a lady doctor?'

'Where I've been, Mrs Semmring, they didn't stop to ask if you were a man or a woman, only if you knew medicine.' She said it with a smile.

'Oh, missionary work, how laudable. Come along, dear, we're expected at the Grovers' by ten. Goodnight, Dr Holt, so nice to have met you.'

'Yes, indeed,' the others echoed as they made their way out.

Christina went in to dinner. Well, Peter, she thought, you got the wife you deserved, I believe.

Next morning she was looking at timetables for Chicago, preparatory to going to see Miss Melville, when her room phone rang.

'Dr Holt? Say, Dr Holt, I was one of that gang you met with Peter Semmring last night. I know you didn't catch my name, it's Weiler, Dr Edmund Weiler. Listen, Dr Holt, it only dawned on me as I was going to bed – are you the *Serbian* Dr Holt?'

Taken aback, she hesitated.

'Doctor? Are you there?'

'Well, yes . . . I suppose I must be the Serbian Dr Holt.'

'Good God! Listen, doctor – I mean, if the faculty knew – why didn't you *tell* us you were coming?'

'But why should I?' she asked, astounded.

'But surely, doctor, you must know how much we'd all be delighted to meet you. I mean, you're one of our alumni . . .'

'I'm not quite sure I understand, Dr Weiler.'

'I'm sorry, I'm doing this badly. I'm doing chemical research at the university, some of it for Semmring's firm. I know the Faculty of Medicine would adore to give you a little dinner or a reception of some kind.'

'Oh, no, no!' Her horror at the thought came through even on the telephone.

'Please don't turn us down, doctor! I spoke to the Dean about it before breakfast and he said he'd love to meet you. It would be quite an informal affair. Any evening you choose.'

'But I don't at all want to—'

'We should feel it such an honour, doctor. You see, you served longer than any other member of faculty – six years, I think I read? Is that right? Six years in the forces?'

'Well, I wasn't exactly in the forces.'

'With the French Army, as I understood it?'

'Well, in a way . . .'

'So you see, we'd love to meet you and hear about it.'

'No, I really couldn't.'

But in the end she found she really could, because he wouldn't take no for an answer. She agreed to go to what he called a cocktail party at the Dean's house the following week.

Between the phone call and the event, flowers arrived, boxes of candies arrived, messages of greeting and congratulation arrived. The reporters from the University newspaper came to interview her, and from them the city newspaper took her up.

Peter Semmring made it his business to happen upon her in the hotel lobby one afternoon. 'Well, so it seems you're a celebrity, Christina. I'd no idea.'

'It's all in the past now, it's a pity your friend Weiler caught on.'

'Could we have a drink together? For old time's sake?'

'I'm sorry, Peter, I'm just on my way out.'

'Look, Christina, I've been hanging around for almost an hour, squeezed out of taking the kids to the beach so as to be here. Come on, let's go to a little speakeasy I know and raise a glass to all those good times we shared.'

She drew back from him a little. 'I don't recall that we shared much, Peter.'

He smiled. 'You've got a short memory, then. I remember it all very well. And now I've seen you again, seems to me we should do more than just raise a glass to the memory of it.' It was clear he had been piqued by all the attention she received. Christina Holt – The Holt – still one up on him. But after all, she was a woman, and it was easy to put a woman in her place. All you had to do was romance them a little.

She found she could read him like a book. I once loved him, she thought. I must have been out of my mind.

She leaned close up to him, smiled into his brown eyes. 'Peter,' she murmured.

'Yes?'

'Did you ever show your wife that camisole you stole from me?'

The conspiratorial grin died slowly from his tanned cheeks. 'What?' he said uncertainly.

'If you ever come near me again, I'll tell Ardeth you took me to bed in that awful hotel at Coney Island simply to steal a camisole so you could brag to your pals about it. Because that's what you did, isn't it, Peter darling?'

She walked on, drawing on her gloves. As she went through the revolving doors she glanced back. He was standing in the lobby looking as if someone had rocked him back on his heels with an uppercut.

He was at the cocktail party given by the medical faculty, but had the good sense to avoid her. It was less of an ordeal than she had feared, and for one thing she was grateful: she met Dr Lucius Messiter, the Professor of Psychology. To him, in a moment of private conversation, she confessed her ambition to learn how to deal with the psychological problems of children.

'But I don't feel I have the right,' she said.

He was a stooped, balding man of middle-age. He stood frowning down at her. 'What a strange thing to say!'

'You wouldn't think it strange if you knew the reason.'

'Come, tell me the reason.'

'Oh, no, I—'

'I mean it. Come and see me. I think you need to talk.'

'But I couldn't inflict my—'

'My dear young woman, everyone "inflicts" their troubles on a psychologist. If you take it up, you'll learn that for yourself. Come and see me. Tomorrow?'

'We-ell . . . if you mean it?'

'About six.' He gave her his card. 'I'll look out for you.'

She meant to ring and put him off. But he had been right, she did need to talk, to ask someone if she was making a right decision with her career. For one of the things that troubled her was the feeling that she often made the wrong decision.

So she went to his consulting rooms, as nervous as any new patient, and told him why it was she felt unworthy to take up the work of caring for children.

'I gave my baby away.'

He sighed softly. 'When was that?'

'Twelve years ago.'

He made mental calculations. 'When you were a student here?'

'Yes.'

'The baby was adopted?'

'Yes.'

'Because the father wouldn't or couldn't marry you.'

'I wouldn't have married him if he were the last man on earth!'

'I see.' He paused. 'So you hated the baby?'

'Oh no. Oh, how can you say such a thing? I loved him. I've never stopped loving him. In fact, I made a special journey . . .'

It all came spilling out, the journey to Paris, the trip in the taxi-cab, the encounter with Stephen in the street. 'He's so beautiful, and I gave him away . . .'

Dr Messiter was listening and nodding, nodding and listening. 'You feel guilty.'

'Of course! It was wrong, terribly wrong! I should have kept him.'

'But then you'd have had to give up your studies, care for him as an unmarried mother.'

'Yes, and I didn't have the courage. I was a coward.'

'And it's because of this you feel doubts about taking up child psychology?'

'I wonder if it perhaps means I lack something . . .'

'My dear young woman, one of the things you must have noticed, if you've done any reading about psychology, is the problem of guilt. The human race is absolutely determined to bear a load of guilt. It seems to be instinctive. If a child says in anger to its father, "I hate you, I wish you were dead!" and then the father dies – at once, that child may feel he has caused the death. We pick up guilt as black velvet picks up lint. It's one of life's great mysteries. So the fact that you feel you were wrong, cowardly, to give up your baby, only makes you a part of the human race. It's not a lack in you, it's a bonus – because only through knowing it yourself can you help it in others.'

'But I've made so many wrong decisions in my life! How can I have the arrogance to think I can help other people?'

'Insight,' he said in his heavy, sighing voice, 'insight is what helps you to help other people. Only if you have insight into your own mistakes can you help others. Every psychologist, every psychiatrist, has to use his own life as a practice terrain for what he can do for others. We recognise and analyse our own mistakes. And because we can do that, we can be of use to others.'

'But children? Children are so special.'

'Yes, and the most difficult to help, because their needs are so great. I think that someone who is still grieving for the baby she gave up more than ten years ago might well be a very good person to help a child in dire distress.'

'You think so? You don't think I'm just . . . projecting my need to use my maternal instincts . . . ?'

'Oh, that too. Why not? Instincts are given to us to use for the good, surely? And you won't be working alone, there will be colleagues, consultants. You'll have a lot of studying to do, you can work out your own problems as you learn. Because we all have problems, Dr Holt. No one comes into the field of psychology a perfect, whole man, because there is no such thing on the earth.'

They sat in Dr Messiter's quiet consulting-room. He let a silence develop. At length she found herself forced to say, 'I want to do this work. But there's so much to learn . . .'

'Yes, a new science. You know in Shakespeare, Macbeth asks the doctor, "Canst thou not minister to a mind diseased?", and the answer is, "Therein the patient must minister to himself." That's still true, because it seems the cure must always come from within. But for children, there has to be special help. And perhaps you're one of the people who can give it.'

'You really think so?'

He smiled his slow smile. 'It's not what I think that matters. What do *you* think?'

Certainty gathered in her. She nodded. 'Yes,' she said, 'I think I may be one of the people who can help children.'

When she got back to London three weeks later she went straight to a property agent and took a lease on a set of rooms in New Cavendish Street. After that she registered for a post-graduate course in psychiatry at the Maudsley Hospital.

She would study, and she would see patients as a consultant

in children's diseases. As she learned, she would apply what she learned to treating those diseases that seemed not purely physical.

She would be busy, too busy to think about the past – except as an object lesson in mistakes to be avoided.

Chapter Twenty-seven

Mrs Landon was crying quietly into her handkerchief. Her little boy, aged seven, sat beside her on the sofa gazing with blank eyes at the mural of Beatrix Potter animals.

The hour-long session was drawing to a close. Christina was tired but dared not show it. Mrs Landon needed someone to lean on, and this was the role Christina was supposed to play. What Mrs Landon couldn't yet understand was that Christina would be giving her attention to the child, not the mother.

'I've done everything,' wept Mrs Landon. 'I've tried bribery, and smacking, and explaining to him . . .'

'How do you explain to him?'

'Oh, I'm so careful! You can't speak to a child about things like that. Don't imagine I've made the mistake of being brutal.'

'Do you feel he has understood what you were saying?'

'He understands,' Mrs Landon murmured through her sodden handkerchief. 'He's just stubborn and wilful.'

'But why?' Christina wondered aloud, with a secret glance at her wrist watch. If, in the course of this introductory session, she could at least get across the idea that there was a reason for the child's aberrant behaviour, something at least would have been accomplished.

'Oh, there's no reason except jealousy!' cried Mrs Landon. 'You don't understand, doctor. You're not married, you've never had children!'

Christina made no reply. Instead she turned to the seven-year-old, who had been sitting throughout the entire hour without ever once touching his mother, even by leaning against her among the cushions of the couch.

'What do you think, Martin?' she inquired.

The blank eyes turned towards her. Otherwise there was no response.

'It's no use speaking to him!' his mother wailed. 'He *never* replies.'

'Is that right, Martin? You never reply?'

'Why do you ask him? Haven't you understood what I've been telling you? He won't speak!'

'But he can speak. Can't you, Martin?'

Martin tilted his head a little so that he could look at the picture of Felix the Cat above the door.

'Of course he *can* speak – he just won't!'

'Well, perhaps he'll speak to me next week.'

'You're wasting your time, doctor.'

'We'll see. Next week, when you bring him, I want you to leave him with Nurse in the reception office.'

'Leave him? Oh, I couldn't do that . . .'

'That would be best, Mrs Landon.'

'No, no, I couldn't! You don't know what he's like! He might do anything – break something, attack you . . .'

'Mrs Landon,' Christina said, 'is your little boy deaf?'

'Deaf? No, of course not.'

'Then why do you say things like that in front of him? I'm sure Martin never even thought of doing anything bad until you mentioned it. Isn't that right, Martin?'

The little boy swung his legs back and forth against the front of the couch. He said nothing.

'I assure you, doctor, I know my own son, and it just wouldn't be right to entrust him to anyone else.'

'You mean you are the only one who can handle him.'

'Of course, isn't that what I've been telling you?'

And that was just what Martin wanted to achieve – to be the sole object of his mother's interest. It was apparently for this reason that, about six months ago, he had attempted to kill his baby sister.

In the last year Christina had had several cases as serious as this brought to her. Cases of last resort, it appeared.

One of the most difficult problems was to wean the mother away from the child. She understood it only too well. If she had a child in desperate trouble, she too would want to hold him fast and protect him from all the world.

Gently she said to Mrs Landon, 'Bring Martin next week. See if you can leave him with Nurse. After all, there will only be a door between us: if you feel he needs you you can always walk in.'

'Oh.' The mother looked uncertain. 'Oh, I thought you meant I had to go away . . .'

'Not at all. Martin wouldn't like that, would you, Martin?'

Martin's empty eyes met hers for just a moment, then he returned his attention to Felix the Cat.

When the Landons had gone, Nurse Lowther came in with a much-needed tray of coffee. 'He's a difficult one,' she observed, pouring. 'One of those who don't show the slightest interest in the toys in the waiting-room . . .'

'They're all difficult, Alice,' Christina sighed.

'He's coming back?'

'Same time next week. Put it in the book, will you? But she may shirk it.'

'Not she,' Alice said, shaking her head. 'She's nearly at the end of her tether, poor soul.'

'The father wanted to pack the boy off to some sort of boarding school. So there's some strength there – she was able to prevent that, to make some effort at proper treatment. And of course,' Christina sighed, 'she can afford it. Do you ever wonder, Alice, how many children there are who need help but never get it because their parents can't afford it? Or else are afraid to ask for help from a "mad doctor"?'

Alice made tut-tutting sounds at the phrase. Mad doctor, loonie doctor . . . She had had her share of taunts from her family when she said she was going to work for a consultant in mental complaints. Dr Holt must have even more to contend with. Even other doctors were disbelieving or patronising about the relatively new field of child guidance.

A good spanking was the recommendation most offered to parents who had troublesome children.

She pointed out the afternoon post, which had just been delivered as she showed out the Landons. 'One from New York,' she urged.

Alice had guessed what the envelope contained. It would be an invitation to the International Symposium on Juvenile Disorders. She wanted Dr Holt to go. Three years they'd been hard at work here in New Cavendish Street, and in all that time Dr Holt had never taken more than a weekend break. She seemed to flourish on hard work but all the same . . .

Christina put the post aside for later. Now she had to face Elvira Dawson, a thirteen-year-old of great physical charm who had convinced herself she was intended to be a great ballerina, even though she had no dancing talent at all. Her delusion, as strong as steel, held the whole family in thrall.

Three mornings a week Christina worked at a recently opened outpatients department for nervous disorders at the Deptford Children's Hospital. There she treated children whose parents had little or no money. It was often more rewarding than the work she undertook privately, but very tiring because of the problems of explaining things to the parents. The language of psychiatry was so new, the concepts so untried . . .

She was due to go to Lincolnshire the following weekend, to visit Elwin and his family. All at once she decided against it. She was weary, too weary to take on yet again the burden of Elwin's troubles, Dorothy's dissatisfactions, her father's disappointment and disapproval.

Instead she spent Saturday shopping in the West End, simply for pleasure. In the evening she had dinner with Addie Bellhaven. Addie asked if she intended to go to the New York conference.

'Everybody keeps nudging at me to go,' Christina complained ruefully. 'You, Nurse Lowther . . .'

'Well, it would do you good. You need a break. Besides, it's right up your street. Little heart-to-heart chats with all the bigwigs of child psychiatry. And that new dress you described, the one you bought this afternoon, sounds just right for the captain's table on an ocean liner.'

'Are you saying that my unconscious prompted me to buy it?' she asked, laughing.

'No dear, that's the kind of thing *you* say. All the same, it seems to me your inclination is to take some time off – you ought to be in Market Bresham right now, but you aren't.'

'That's true.'

'And after all, Chrissie, you can't go on and on listening to other people's problems without a chance to recharge your batteries. I remember what you were like when you came back from Constantinople: all skin and bone and nerves. You don't seem to have any idea how to pace yourself; it's all flat-out until you fall down in a heap.'

Christina felt herself flush. She knew Addie was right. Although she had a good mind, she often failed to use it in judging her own efforts. She worked until she fell down, that was the truth of it.

By the time they parted Christina had promised Addie she would accept the invitation to New York. And having once done so, she found she was looking forward to it. She had liked New York City on the one short visit of three years ago: its drive and energy enthralled her.

The symposium was to be held in the fall, so that as part of the extra-curricular pleasures the visitors could see the spectacular colours of New England in early November.

The attendees gathered on the Friday evening, were greeted and encouraged to mingle a little. Saturday morning there was a lecture, then came an official lunch with speakers. Saturday afternoon was free for amusement, then in the evening a cocktail party was to be given by a well-respected firm of medical publishers, who intended to serve good liquor even though the United States was supposedly in the grip of Prohibition.

It didn't occur to Christina to study the party guest list. She knew some of the conference members either personally or by reputation, but those coming to the party were from a larger field, some from medical publishing, some from businesses connected with medicine, some from government departments.

It came as a complete surprise to hear the name John Charlford. It floated over to her from a group a few feet away in the Crystal Suite. She turned her head. 'No, no, of course the State Department has no axe to grind here,' a voice was saying. 'They simply send John to keep an eye on all these peculiar foreign bodies – am I right, John?'

'Now, Al, don't be a troublemaker. I'm here to show our high regard for the work of international childcare. Do you know my wife, Estelle?'

Slowly and casually, Christina turned. She sipped her drink, then put the empty glass on the tray of a passing waiter. The move allowed her to leave her group and join the next one without causing comment.

John Charlford, tall and rather distinguished, was in the obligatory black tie and evening jacket. His wife Estelle was in a dark red silk dress that showed off her milk-white shoulders. Rubies glistened in her ears; she was smoking a cigarette in a holder studded with little garnets.

Christina would have known them anywhere. John was greyer and more lined but still essentially the same man who had come to the Serbian community in the Alleghenies all those years ago to claim a boy child. Estelle had changed more: she was more brittle, wore a little too much make-up, but still had the good bones and fine features of long-lasting beauty.

Christina watched her, asking herself, How old is she now? Forty, perhaps? A little more? And unhappy . . . ? It was there in her eyes, a restless dissatifaction. They were avid for something they seemed unable to find.

'Have you met the Charlfords?' inquired Dr Van Rohn, taking her by the elbow unexpectedly.

'No, I—'

'Allow me to present . . .' The introductions were made. Christina waited in apprehension, wondering if any lingering recognition would surface. But then the one and only time they had seen Christina Holt, she had been an eighteen-year-old, pigtailed girl clad in a Serbian peasant skirt and blouse and living in a farming community in the Allegheny Mountains. There was no similarity to the slender, sophisticated doctor at this New York conference.

Christina hadn't intended to be introduced. All she'd wanted was to see again the couple to whom she had entrusted her baby. She would never have sought them out, but chance had put them in her way, so she wanted just to look at them, to see if she had chosen wisely.

To be introduced was dangerous. She mustn't ever come too close to Stephen. She had done it once – madly, foolishly – and it had cost her dear in emotional trauma. Now, working as she did with damaged children, she understood the perils of interfering, by even the slightest touch, in the ties of family love. Stephen was the son of Estelle and John Charlford. He had nothing to do with Christina Holt. And Christina Holt would show good sense if she stayed away from the Charlfords.

But it wasn't so easy. Men outnumbered women at the conference by ten to one. The few women psychiatrists were mostly American, so that any foreign women visitors were much in demand: hosts and the friends of hosts wanted to show their hospitality. Christina was continually being singled out for some particular kindness, and all the more so because she was an English-speaker: it was easier to show friendship and hospitality to an Englishwoman than to a Lithuanian.

Over the week of the conference she found herself in the same group as the Charlfords more than once. By simply listening she learned much that pleased her. Stephen was often mentioned in conversation. He was at school, doing well; was a junior tennis champion; had many friends; was saving to buy a jalopy as soon as he was old enough to hold a licence: a perfectly normal boy.

Perhaps the gratitude she felt towards the Charlfords somehow coloured her contacts with them. They took to her. 'Listen, doctor, when the conference ends Friday, what are your plans?' asked John Charlford.

'Plans? I have none. I might slip down to Philadelphia, I have an aunt there . . .'

'You do? Well, isn't that a coincidence: Estelle and I are Pennsylvanians, originally. We still have a place there, you know, on the Delaware, always kept it as sort of a home base during all our moving around. We were wondering if you'd like to come and spend the weekend?'

'I'm afraid I don't—'

'You could go right on to Philly from there, no problem. It's pretty there – not far from a little town called New Hope . . . trees just turning there, the frost line's a little further south.'

'Oh, but I couldn't intrude . . .'

'We've asked a few others, haven't we, dear?'

'Yes, it's a regular house party, we always do it at this time of year,' Estelle put in. 'For the country colour, you know. And listen, if you're sick of talking to medical people, don't worry, you're the only one we've asked from this bunch.' Her smile flickered, faintly malicious but attractive. 'And we promise not to ask your advice about our wayward son, don't we, John?'

'Not that he's wayward,' he protested, 'but he won't be there, he's at school.'

'Oh, that means boarding school?' Christina said, having not realised it.

'Sure, we couldn't have him at day school. In John's job we've never known when we're going to have to pick up and go somewhere abroad, so we like to have Stephen safely parked.'

'It's awfully kind of you to offer.' She was sorely tempted, wanting to see their home, wanting to imagine her son in that setting. And what harm could it do? He wouldn't be there.

It was arranged that after the banquet with which the conference was ending, John and Estelle would pick her up at the hotel and drive her out to Bixbee. They seemed to think nothing of setting out on a 200-mile drive across New Jersey at midnight.

John Charlford drove the big Packard with almost contemptuous ease. Great trucks thundered by on the turnpike, towns came and went in a flicker of electric advertising. At a little after three they were climbing mountain roads with the grey dawn coming up behind them. The trees were an uproar of claret and crimson, gold and amber. Little Quaker church-spires peered out now and again.

Christina had expected the house at Bixbee to be a country cottage. It was more on the scale of a rural manor, built in the mid-Victorian era by Pennsylvanian coal-owners. Servants came hurrying out, although the surrounding countryside still seemed to be asleep. 'Good morning, Mrs Charlford, Mr Charlford. Did you have a good drive? Weather seems like it would be nice.'

It appeared telephone arrangements had been made; Christina was expected. Her belongings were unloaded and taken upstairs almost before she had been shown indoors.

'You'll want to get to bed,' Estelle said, waving her hand towards a handsome stone staircase with an oak balustrade. 'People will begin to arrive during the morning, so there'll be a running brunch from about ten onwards. If you prefer breakfast in bed, just ring. Mrs Goode will show you your room.'

Mrs Goode was a thin little lady with the look of being part Red Indian. She led the way briskly upstairs and along a corridor. 'Here we are. You shouldn't be disturbed – the brunch will be served at the pool which is the other side of the house. Bath and shower here, closets . . .' She opened doors, made little welcoming gestures. 'You won't want to unpack now, huh? If you ring when you want it done, I'll send Rosie up. Now, what can I get you? Tea? Hot chocolate?'

'Nothing, thank you,' Christina said, overwhelmed in the face of this overpowering hospitality. All she wanted was to fall into bed.

She woke about six hours later. Autumn sunshine filled the room. Stretching, she lay for a time watching the shadows made by the trees moving in the breeze. By and by she rose to examine the weather. It looked set for a fine day with a sharp wind.

After her bath she put on a plain tweed skirt, a cream silk

blouse under a thick Arran sweater, and brogues. The rest of her unpacking she left for the moment. She was only staying until Monday; she would need very few items from the trunk which had been placed in one of the big walk-in closets.

A manservant was passing through the hall with a big silver tray of food. 'Good morning, ma'am,' he said. 'This way for breakfast.'

She followed him, curious to see where this enormous supply would end up.

A long table had been set up under an awning on a terrace which was sheltered from the wind by plants in tubs. At the foot of the terrace steps was the pool: a big rectangle of old stone faced inside with blue tile. No one was swimmimg, the breeze was a little too fresh. But about half a dozen people were lounging about around the pool, braving the slight chill, eating, drinking, laughing.

John Charlford waved to Christina. 'I see you made it,' he called. 'Come and join us!'

He explained that Estelle was still getting up. 'She doesn't have to be here supervising,' he said, 'she's got it pretty well taped by now, running a weekend party. How did you sleep?'

'Like a log!'

'Let me introduce a few people . . .' He nodded at companions, named names, and Christina received a few smiles and one or two languid waves. The manservant came up to ask what she would like to eat.

'Oh, I'll come and—'

'No need, Howie will fetch what you want.'

Nevertheless, she turned back to the long buffet table to inspect what was on offer. Chafing dishes with eggs in various guises, bacon, sausages of three or four kinds, an endless variety of breads and rolls, breakfast cereals, hot biscuits, honey, maple syrup, fruit, tea, coffee, orange juice, apple juice, milk and mineral water.

It was brought home to her with considerable force that the Charlfords were rich. This had never been of importance to her: all she'd wanted was to entrust her baby son to a stable, respectable couple who would give him the care she could not. But in choosing the Charlfords, Jo-Jo Belu had scored an extraordinary success: they clearly came from old money, and knew how to use it.

A little later Estelle joined them, looking very smart in riding clothes. Good God, thought Christina, don't say they have stables too? But no, horses could be hired in the village, whither Estelle now intended to drive. 'Anyone else want to come?'

The only other enthusiast was a tall, handsome young man also in riding breeches. He sprang up at Estelle's invitation.

Christina thought she glimpsed a knowing smile between one or two of her fellow guests. John Charlford took care not to notice.

The morning, leisurely and pleasant, flowed on. A walk to the village was suggested, simply for the exercise. Christina joined the group. She wanted to see the countryside in which Stephen had spent his childhood, the roads where he had walked, the streams where he had fished and swum.

'Did you see how Victor was at the ready when Estelle suggested riding?' said a plump lady a little ahead of Christina on the dirt road. 'It just so happened he was in riding gear.'

'Honestly, Millie, they hardly even bother to keep it a secret any more.'

'What's John going to do?'

'What can he do, the poor lamb? He's no match for a Broadway beau.'

Christina caught up with the speakers. They glanced at her but, assuming she knew as much of the Charlfords' private affairs as they did, made no attempt to change the subject.

'Did you see his show? He's not bad, you know, Amanda.'

Amanda was the younger and more fashionable of the two. She rolled her eyes upwards. 'If anyone had ever told me Estelle would fall for a tenor at least ten years her junior,

I'd have said they were out of their heads. Don't you think so?' she added to Christina.

'I'm afraid I don't know her very well.'

'Oh, a friend on John's side. Stay with it, dear, he's going to need all the friends he's got if this thing ever goes public.'

'You don't think she's going to do anything stupid?' Millie asked, her plump face going pink with vexation.

'Who knows? She's at a dangerous age, Millie. And the trouble with John is, no one could ever accuse him of being romantic.'

'You think *Victor Garrett* is romantic? I think he's just carried away by the idea of getting a Pennsylvanian Puritan to back his next show.'

Christina wanted to say, Listen, don't talk like this, these people have my son to look after. But she couldn't say anything like that. Instead, she walked along at their side on the steep, tree-bordered road, with a stream rushing down the hillside in a sparkle of brown water. Idyllic surroundings, but with a cloud threatening them.

It had never occurred to her that the marriage of the two people who had the care of her son would ever break up. Before the war, the idea of ending a marriage except by death seemed absurd. Nobody got a divorce, except the very wicked or the very unconventional.

Was that what these friends of the Charlfords were talking about? Divorce? But how could that be? Surely these were conservative people, from old families, who upheld traditions and lived respectable lives?

Besides, John Charlford's career would suffer if there was a divorce. Little though she knew about the diplomatic service, she had divined this much: that, like doctors and lawyers, diplomats were supposed to lead exemplary lives. No scandal, no wandering from the straight and narrow.

But then, it wasn't John who was doing the wandering, according to the gossips. It was Estelle.

Alerted now, Christina observed them throughout the rest of Saturday and part of Sunday. There was no doubt John disliked having Victor Garrett in his house. Garrett wasn't the type he wanted as his friend, he was only here because Estelle had invited him.

The other guests seemed well aware of the problem. Some wished they had never come, others were enjoying the show. 'God's sakes, why didn't they cancel the party?' Christina heard one man groan. 'If I'd known how bad things had gotten, I'd never have come.'

'Trouble is, I don't think John knows how bad things have gotten,' was the gloomy response.

After dinner on Sunday, bridge fours were formed. Christina had never learned the game, so was left free to please herself. She went out on the lawn, where a big hunter's moon was silvering the grass. Whispers and rustling from a gazebo alerted her to the fact that she was in danger of spoiling someone's love scene. She went indoors to the library, looking for a book to while away the hours till bedtime.

She was sitting under a library lamp beginning on *The Fall of the House of Usher* when the French windows opened in a flurry of autumn leaves and Estelle Charlford came in, face flushed, hair in disorder, eyes alight with the pleasures of love.

She stopped short at finding an occupant in the library. 'Oh!'

'Sorry,' Christina said, rising. 'Did I startle you?'

'It's only that generally . . . there's nobody in here.'

'I was just finding a book for—'

'Don't apologise, I'm the one who ought to be saying sorry.' She busied herself closing and latching the French windows. 'You must think I'm a terrible hostess, neglecting my guests all evening.'

'Not at all,' Christina said, edging towards the door.

'The fact is,' Estelle blurted out in a voice full of tears, 'I can't stand the way they all keep eyeing me, wondering what I'm going to do next.'

Christina felt there was nothing she could say to that. She had nearly reached the door.

'Do you think I'm wrong to want to live my own life?' Estelle insisted, more firmly and with a rising note of anger.

'I don't know that it's any of my—'

'*You* do what you want to? You have a career of your own?'

'Well yes, but—'

'But you're a single woman, is that it? You don't have a husband who has to come first all the time!'

'Estelle, I don't think I'm the one you should be—'

'Yes, you're the one! You're a dispassionate observer! My friends think I'm being a fool and *his* friends think I'm being a bitch; but it's not true, I can't help having fallen in love!'

She put her hands up to her eyes, like a child, and began to sob. Now it was impossible to leave her. Christina came up to her, put an arm about her shoulders and urged her to the Chesterfield. 'Come on, sit down, don't upset yourself.'

'I . . . I'm going to ask John for a divorce!'

'I see.' She didn't want to hear this. Yet she couldn't prevent herself from asking, 'Have you just decided?'

'Yes, just today. I suddenly realised I can't go on for the rest of my life giving parties like this for John, moving house to wherever he gets posted, being polite to stupid foreigners I'll never meet again . . . It's not even as if he's ever going to get an ambassadorship – or if he does it'll be to some rotten little South American republic with gunmen behind every palm tree.'

'Surely he's still young enough to—'

'It's not that. He's young enough and he's got the right money, but you don't get to be an ambassador without influence, and at the moment his family haven't got enough pull. I've wasted enough of my life waiting for him to be called His Excellency.'

She wiped tears from her cheeks with her fingers. Her make-up was smeared.

'What happens about your son?' asked Christina.

'Stephen? What a funny— Oh yes, you're a child specialist, I remember. Oh, Stephen will be all right. He's fourteen years old, for God's sake. It won't be any surprise to him, he's seen it coming for weeks.'

'And how does he feel about it?'

'Feel about it? Well, he knows what a divorce is all

418

about – quite a few of his friends have divorced parents. At the moment he's being very cold towards me, but that's just . . . well, you know, he can't bear to think of his mother with another man. But why should I live my life according to the rules of a fourteen-year-old kid? I'm still young, I still have a right to love and happiness, don't I?'

Christina found herself remembering the words of the American Constitution: The right to life, liberty and the pursuit of happiness. She wondered if it was the only set of governmental rules that promised citizens happiness. Mostly, in other countries, the talk was of duty, of moral obligation.

'Are you so very unhappy with John?' she asked gently.

'Unhappy? I don't know that I . . . It just seems so meaningless! It's not as if we were ever head over heels in love to begin with. I got married straight out of finishing school because that was what my family expected, and of course John was just the right type: same kind of background as myself, full of ambition . . . We were expected to settle down and raise a family and be a credit to them all.'

'And that's what you've done.'

'No it isn't; it all went sour from the start! I couldn't provide the big family everyone was expecting – that's why Stephen's an only child.'

'It will be hard for Stephen, if you and Victor marry. Stepfathers are difficult to live with,' Christina said, from years of experience listening to the problems of emotionally damaged children.

'Oh, he won't live with us!' Estelle said, astonished. 'That would be great, wouldn't it, trying to start a new life with an adolescent son glaring at us all the time! No, no, Stephen wants to stay with his father, and since he's old enough to make the choice the divorce judge will go along with it, or so my lawyer says. Besides, he's off at school, so it's only the holidays that matter. Even if John's posted abroad again, he can always have Stephen with him for those.'

'It sounds as if you've thought it out.'

'What else do you think I've been doing for the past

couple of months? All I needed was to pluck up the nerve to go ahead with it. I'm going to tell John when the weekend's over.' She shuddered at the thought. 'You won't mention this to him?'

'Of course not.'

Estelle went hurrying upstairs to repair her make-up. Christina was left to reflect on the frailty of modern marriage.

On Monday morning the guests began to take their leave. John was to drive Christina to a branch-line station where she should get the train for Philadelphia. The perfect host, he undertook the task without complaint, though his mind was clearly elsewhere.

As they joined the main road he gave up small-talk and said in a weary voice: 'You and Estelle had a long heart-to-heart last night.'

'Oh, yes . . . I happened to be in the library . . .'

'Damn funny thing, that she'd tell a mere acquaintance about it before she told me!'

Christina studied him. He looked worn, as if such sleep as he'd had was proving little use to him.

'That sometimes happens,' she apologised. 'You can say things to a stranger you couldn't say to someone close.'

'I was the bad guy in it all, is that right? Trying to shackle her to a marriage that's withered on the vine, failing in the brilliant career I was supposed to make . . .'

'She didn't say that.'

'Something very like it, I bet. Look, it's not as if there haven't been other men—'

'What?' Christina said, startled.

'Oh, sure, there was a handsome Frenchman in Paris . . . But she always had sense enough to break it off in the end. This time, it seems she can't. She seems hypnotised by this guy Garrett.'

'I'm sorry,' Christina said.

'I think he's just after the money. She's got a lot of her own, you know. But she won't hear a word against him. Even when Stephen tries to say . . .'

'Stephen doesn't like him?'

'Is it likely? A matinée idol for a stepfather, and at that Garrett's too young for the role. I mean, tops, he's about fifteen years older than Steve. You're an expert on this kind of thing, doctor. What's your opinion? Is it likely he'd ever accept a guy like that as a new father?'

'The relationship between step-parents and children is a minefield. In England we don't have many cases caused by divorce, but even in the simpler instances, when a widow or a widower remarries . . .' She was shaking her head in anxiety.

'Estelle's view is that if Stephen doesn't want to be friends with Garrett, she can do without him.'

'If Estelle allows herself to be cut off from Stephen she'll regret it.' Christina tried to put all the earnestness she could into her voice. She knew what she was talking about. It seemed incredible to her that Estelle Charlford would throw away her son's love and friendship so cavalierly.

'That's what I try to tell her. But if you want the truth, Stephen is going to be the one who cuts off the relationship.' John hesitated. 'He thinks she's wrong in what she's doing. I don't know how to tell him she's right, because I don't believe it myself.'

They drove for a time in silence. 'We're going to have trouble, aren't we?' he said at last with a sigh. 'She talks about "a civilised divorce", but I don't know . . .'

'Are there any teachers at your son's school in whom he has a special confidence? Do they have counsellors or advisers? Or how about your church?'

'We're not particularly religious. You're saying I ought to find some kind of help, but I don't know where, Christina, I sure don't.'

'I could recommend a psychiatrist in New York.'

'Oh, say, it's not going to be *that* bad! He's not going to go peculiar – he's a well-balanced kid.' He paused. 'Pity you never met him, Christina. Never mind, I shouldn't be bothering you with all this. I can't think why I've poured out my troubles to you . . .'

'It's because I'm a practised listener,' she said with something of a laugh.

'Yeah, right. But you only expect to have people bending your ear in your office, not when you're having a weekend in the country.'

'It's all right. I only wish I could be of more help.'

'You have helped, Christina, you really have.'

When they parted at the rail depot he shook hands cordially. 'Perhaps we'll see each other some time?' he said.

'It isn't likely. I don't expect to be this side of the Atlantic again for a long time.'

'Well, maybe I'll look you up in London some day.'

'I hope you will, if you ever come to England.'

It was the usual meaningless chatter at the end of a casual acquaintance. She never expected to see him again.

A year later he rang her from a London hotel.

Chapter Twenty-eight

Young Stephen Charlford showed a lot of enthusiasm for his father's travel plans. 'Gee, Dad, that'd be keen: there were a lot of places we didn't get a chance to see when you were on post. Could we take in Egypt? I'd kinda like to see the Pyramids and the Valley of the Kings.'

If the enthusiasm was partly pretence and the interest in Egyptian antiquities only recent, that wasn't important. The important thing was to help keep his father on an even keel. The other fellows at school had been really doomy about the aftermath of divorce.

'Your old man will probably take a vertical nose-dive into a whisky glass,' Willis Hite told him. 'Or he'll get into the clutches of a line of floozies who'll take him for every cent he owns.'

'Yeah,' agreed Sutcliffe, 'or maybe both. Wine, women, and sad songs. He'll be as gloomy as hell, and he'll keep telling you it wasn't his fault.'

'And if he doesn't go for the floozies, he'll probably get married again in ten minutes flat – to some dame as like your Mom as possible. It's called the triumph of optimism over experience.' Hite fancied himself as a cynic.

While Stephen recognised the half-intentional malice behind the words, he knew there was truth in them. His father's life had been inevitably broken up by the divorce. Not only was the marriage at an end, but his career too – the career to which he'd given almost twenty years. No divorced man would ever be given an ambassadorship by the US government. Ambassadors needed capable, supportive wives, to go among the womenfolk of the host country and kiss the babies, to smile at recalcitrant government officials, to ease the social strain and smooth the furrowed brow.

John Charlford might stay in the diplomatic corps, but if he did he would never rise much higher. In certain countries with strongly Catholic traditions, where divorce was frowned upon, he would not be able to serve at all.

John had decisions to make: whether to resign, or to make a sideways move to the Washington offices of the State Department. If he took a Washington job, it meant starting almost half-way back to the beginning again. His connections, his influential friends, were among the overseas diplomats.

What he decided in the end was to take a Sabbatical year, which he would devote to his son. If Stephen was worried about his father, his father was just as worried about Stephen.

John had a good idea of the kind of thoughts and feelings churning through his son. He remembered his own adolescence, his own disbelief and near-disgust when he learned that his mother and his father – his *mother* and *father* – had sexual needs even at their advanced age, which must have been all of forty.

He tried to talk to Stephen about such things, but he made a bad hand at it. He wasn't accustomed to talking about the physical side of marriage. He didn't even take part much in the smutty talk in golf-club changing-rooms.

As to discussing his career with the boy, that didn't even occur to him. He had no idea that Stephen mourned for him, hated his mother for the double hurt she had inflicted. The triple hurt . . . For besides cuckolding his father with a Broadway beau and wrecking his career, she'd turned her back on her son. He'd told her: 'If you go with that jerk I never want to see or hear from you again!' And she'd chosen the jerk.

Stephen knew it was his duty to be supportive to his father. But more than that, he *wanted* to help. His old man had always been good to him. He'd always managed to find time in the busy round of social obligation abroad to take him out and about. Thanks to his father, Stephen had seen old fishing villages on the Brittany coast, had climbed rocky slopes in Austria to watch the lammergeyer sail over the peaks, knew the heat of the sun over the Argentinian pampas.

Sure, if he wanted to spend a year bumming around the world, Stephen would go along. He joined in planning the trip, and as he did so the pretence of enthusiasm became real. He showed his father a couple of books he'd bought recently about the work of Howard Carter who, three years ago, had discovered the tomb of Tutankhamun in Thebes.

'Wouldn't it be great to go to Thebes, Dad? I mean, we might get to see the excavations. I think they've moved most of the work to Sakara recently, but I don't think visitors are allowed there.'

John was pleased. His main objective had been to get his boy away from familiar places where memories of his mother might rise up to wound him. The flat in New York, the house at Bixbee – those were too painful now. The great family mansion outside Pittsburgh had less of Estelle about it, but the grandparents lived there still. The grandparents, shaking their heads disapprovingly over the divorce, wondering how their clever son John could have gotten into such a situation, continually mulling it over, hinting that if he'd done this or not done that, Estelle would never have strayed.

Father and son planned the journey with maps and lists of hotels and liner timetables. They sailed as soon as the divorce decree became final and there were no more papers for John to sign. They went to Bremen, and from there to Alexandria. John had written ahead to friends stationed in Egypt. By their help, he and Stephen were able to visit the digs.

To his own surprise, Stephen was enthralled. They had just found the statues of Queen Hatshepsut at Deir el Bagara. Gazing at that serene face, that smooth brow with its arched eyebrows, the steady mouth, he felt a thrill at his heart. She had been a real woman. Long, long ago, she had ruled here. She had loved, she had lived and died. His own anger and resentment dwindled before that calm stare. What did it all matter? The present with its ache and its hunger – this was as nothing compared with the eternity of history. He knew what he was going to do when he finished school. He was going to be an archaeologist.

His father went along with his enthusiasm. After all, why not? He himself had nothing else to do with his life at the moment.

They spent some time visiting the sites, were allowed privileged access, were invited to see the work going on at the University of Cairo. Egypt became too hot, there were too many flies and mosquitoes, and besides professors kept saying, 'You should see the statue of Ptah in the British Museum', or 'The Louvre has a splendid ceremonial throne from about the Fourth Dynasty.'

Europe beckoned. They sailed to Marseilles, where it was nearly as hot as Cairo and almost as uncomfortable. But they didn't rush to Paris, there were beautiful things to see at Arles and Avignon – Roman antiquities, not on the same scale as Egypt but fascinating all the same.

In the end, there was Paris and the Louvre. And then there was Pigalle and the Moulin Rouge; Stephen feeling very wicked at seeing naked women with paint on their breasts and the French treating him, at almost seventeen, as if he were a grown man.

Compared with the political and financial tensions in France that August, London seemed almost lethargic. True, the art world was deeply divided over whether the scupltures of Jacob Epstein and Henry Moore were art or ugly hunks of stone, but at least the government wasn't always changing and the value of money seemed steady.

The Charlfords' diplomatic friends made father and son welcome. Little parties were offered, dinner parties and boating parties and tennis parties and Charleston parties. It was borne in upon Stephen that he was 'eligible': the son of a rich American, too young as yet to be considered as a match for any of the girls recently 'out', but certainly worth cultivating.

He gave them partial attention, these pretty girls in their short pale frocks and flesh-coloured stockings. His thoughts kept straying to the Egyptian Rooms at the British Museum. He was there almost every day, filling notebooks with sketches of the artefacts, making friends with curators, buying books in Great Russell Street. His father tagged along, but by and by it dawned on Stephen that it must be pretty boring for him.

'Look, Dad, there's no need for you to pretend you're interested in Egyptian mummies! Why don't you take up some of those invitations we found waiting for us at the hotel?'

John shrugged. 'You don't know English hostesses, son! I only got asked to make up numbers at a dinner table.'

'Sure, some of 'em, but some were from your old colleagues. You want to keep up with them, don't you?'

'I don't know, Stephen. They'd think I was buttering them up to help me get a good post at the State Department.'

'Now, that's not true. How many of them have any influence at the State Department?'

'One or two, one or two . . .'

'We-ell . . . Wouldn't it be a good idea to keep in touch more? You could do with a little help for when we get back.'

'Perhaps not,' John said with a frown. 'I've been thinking . . .'

'What?'

'I don't know if I want to go back six rungs down the ladder. I thought I might . . . go into politics.'

Stephen was so surprised he was speechless.

'I thought of standing for the Senate. See, travelling around like we have, it's dawned on me the world is a damned dangerous place these days. And most of America just doesn't know what's going on. I could help tell them, perhaps. What do you think?'

'Gee, that would be keen!' Senator John Charlford . . . ! It sounded impressive. But then he remembered remarks by Willis Hite, that cynical sixteen-year-old. Hite always maintained that two-thirds of politics was bribery and the remaining third was corruption. Hite's uncle was a big wheel in the Republican Party. Would his father be able to stand that kind of thing? He was kind of unsophisticated in some ways, despite nearly twenty years in international diplomacy.

But leaving that aside for the moment, it was great that the old man was making plans for his future. When they left New York six months ago, his only idea had been to get away from America and stay in motion, so as to avoid thinking.

They discussed the idea of going into politics. They agreed it might take some time before there would be an opening for John. Meanwhile he might play some part in local government in Pittsburgh or Philadelphia. The family had the right kind of 'pull' for that. Any coal family had 'pull' in Pennsylvania.

'Wasn't there a guy we knew in Argentina, the one who was adviser on trade, Ewart or Stewart or somebody? Didn't he have a relative in the Mayor's Office in Pittsburgh?'

'That was Ewart, Gerald Ewart. And funnily enough, that cousin of his is working in London – Ewart wrote to me, asked me to look him up. It's something to do with education; he's working with a man called Cyril Burt who's a specialist in child psychology with the London Education Council.' His father paused. 'Say, that reminds me. There was somebody I met at a conference last year . . . a nice lady doctor . . . I ought to give her a call.'

'Pretty?' Stephen asked teasingly. Lady doctor – surely not a floozie, so nothing to worry about.

His father put his bunched fingertips to his lips and mimed a kiss towards the heavens. '*Exquise*!' he said.

'OK, call her, take her out and have fun, why don't you? You don't want to mooch around museums with me all the time.'

The two men stared at each other. The words echoed in their minds. A grin began on John's thin face, was transferred to Stephen's. They burst out laughing.

'OK, Grandpa,' John said when he recovered. 'Thanks for the suggestion.'

He could tell Dr Holt was surprised to hear from him. However, it was rather flattering that she didn't need reminding who he was. 'John Charlford? Of course I remember you. Where are you speaking from?'

'We're at the Dorchester, Stephen and I . . .'

'Your son is with you?'

Strange, he thought there was a change in her voice just there. 'Yeah, I thought it would do him good, get away from the old home places. We went to Egypt, now he hangs around museums, says he wants to be an archaeologist.' He laughed, inviting her to share the joke if she thought it funny.

'That's an interesting choice,' she said. There was amusement in the words but no ridicule. 'And your wife . . . ?'

'We divorced.'

'I'm sorry.'

'But you knew it was coming.'

'I hoped perhaps you'd sort things out.'

'No . . . Well, I didn't call to cry on your shoulder, I called to invite you to lunch. Got a free hour or two?'

'Oh, I . . .' Unwillingness? Well, that was natural. He knew from experience that the British never cared to be looked up by acquaintances they'd made abroad. They'd say politely, 'We must get together if you're ever in London', but they didn't mean it. Perhaps he should turn it over to her: Give me a ring if you feel like it, I'm at the Dorchester.

But some instinctive need made him persist. 'I wouldn't want to take up a lot of your time. I know you're a busy lady. Just thought it would be nice to see you, have a chat.'

'What would you do with Stephen?'

'Huh? Oh, that's no problem, he grabs a sandwich in the restaurant at the museum. Or he goes into the park, chats to the pretty girls. Or he watches cricket: he's trying to figure out the rules. He's making out fine.'

'Well, I . . .'

'How about tomorrow?'

'No, I have a patient then—'

'At lunchtime, for God's sake?'

'It's a child with a working mother, she can't come any other time.'

'Oh, I'm sorry, I didn't meant to . . . Well, how about Thursday?'

'Not Thursday, I'm at an all-day seminar at the Home Office.'

'Friday, then?' If she said no to Friday, he'd have to give up. It would mean she didn't want to meet him again. And he wouldn't blame her, because she probably thought he wanted free advice about how to care for his son after the divorce. She probably got a lot of that in her work – people trying to get free advice.

Christina caught a hint of something in his voice. He was a sorely troubled man. Normally she would have tried to avoid involvement because she had enough problems. But this was the man who stood in the role of father to her son. If he was troubled, it might affect Stephen. And anything that concerned Stephen was important to her.

'All right then, Friday,' she said with a lightening of her manner, to let him know she wasn't simply giving in to pay off a social duty. 'Where and when?'

'Can I pick you up? Say one o'clock.'

'I ought to warn you, John, that London restaurants get very full around then.'

'I'll take care of it,' he promised.

John knew London quite well from previous visits but he didn't know which restaurants were the best these days. Somewhere elegant and quiet, with preferably French food and wine. He consulted a friend at the Embassy, was recommended to Chez Giselle in Jermyn Street, and made the booking next day. He told his son about it.

'That nice lady I told you about – Dr Holt – we're having lunch Friday.'

'Good for you, Dad. Any more old flames to look up?'

'Dr Holt isn't an old flame,' he said, rather hurt. 'We only met for a short time last year. I told you, she was at a conference in New York.'

'You mean this is a *new* flame?' Stephen teased.

John laughed and shrugged. He wasn't quite sure under which category to enter Dr Christina Holt. He wanted her for a friend, that was certain. How much more he wanted, he couldn't quite tell.

The nurse who took in his name looked him over with interest. Dr Holt had mentioned that an American acquaintance would be calling for her and all Dr Holt's acquaintances were of interest to Nurse Lowther.

She saw a tallish, well-built man with brown hair going attractively grey at the temples, well-dressed in the new-style suit with pointed lapels and turn-ups on the trousers. He had a pearl-grey trilby in his hands and a taxi waiting.

'Dr Holt is just coming,' she told him when she returned to the hall. 'She's finishing a phone call – would you like to sit down?'

Sit down, she urged mentally, I want to ask if you're here for romantic reasons, because God knows it's time the doctor got romantically involved with someone.

According to Alice Lowther's calculations, Dr Holt had passed her mid-thirties by now, so it was getting late if she were ever to start a family of her own. And if ever there was a woman intended by God to be the mother of a family, it had to be Dr Christina Holt.

But Mr Charlford said he'd wait in the taxi. The consulting rooms unnerved him a little. He had never before become friendly with a professional woman: most of his women friends were wives or sisters of others in the diplomatic corps. Few of them ever thought of taking up a career of any kind, let alone something as unusual as psychology. Perhaps this wasn't such a good idea after all.

But when Christina came out into the sunlight of the early September day, his fears evaporated. To his mind she was stunning: pale cropped hair under a little felt cloche hat the colour of hyacinths, short straight dress of blue crepe with a big soft collar of white, matching blue shoes with little heels. Her fair skin gleamed – no cosmetics, as far as he could tell. John was old-fashioned enough to disapprove of cosmetics: it was an issue over which he and Estelle had fallen out more than once.

He handed her into the taxi. They made small talk until Jermyn Street. She glanced about with approval as they went into the restaurant. 'I think this place is fairly new,' he remarked. 'Have you been here before?'

She shook her head. When they were settled at their table she chose cold consommé, sole à la meunière, but refused wine. 'I never drink at lunch-time, I can't afford to get sleepy in the afternoon. In my work, I have to listen very carefully to what people tell me, you see.'

'Nobody would think to look at you that you were a doctor,' John said, intending it as a compliment. 'I thought female doctors wore dark costumes with starched white blouses.'

She laughed. 'One of the first things I learned was that children are frightened by women in dark formal clothes. They talk far more easily to someone in light colours.'

'Really?'

'Oh yes. "Mothers" wear print dresses and aprons of blue or green or white. "Teachers" – of whom one should be afraid – wear dark dresses with white collars and cuffs to keep the chalk from showing up.'

'My God, I should have tried that while I was abroad for Uncle Sam! Maybe I would have gotten better results if I hadn't kept turning up in morning dress!'

'Ah no. Important business must be conducted in important clothes. Nobody would trust a businessman in a blazer and flannels.'

'Have you ever thought of writing that up and sending it to a business magazine?' He was only half joking. She impressed him more than he had expected. He remembered her as kind, and what he would have described as 'womanly', but there was a brain there, shrewd and analytical.

Afterwards he couldn't quite recall how they got on to the subject of his broken marriage and his son Stephen. He certainly hadn't intended to unload his anxieties upon her. But she seemed genuinely interested.

'See, Stephen's OK on the surface. I mean, he talks and laughs and seems to enjoy life. But I don't know what goes on inside his head. Sometimes he comes out with very hard things about his mother. Now, I don't want him to hate Estelle. I mean, she's the only Mom he's got, isn't she?'

'Yes,' Christina agreed in a quiet voice. 'Does your wife keep in touch with the boy?'

'We-ell . . . Yes and no. She remembered his birthday OK and last Christmas she sent him an expensive camera.' He hesitated. 'Stephen never used it. He left it behind somewhere in Egypt. I think he lost it on purpose.'

She nodded. 'That would be a likely reaction. He doesn't want to be reminded of someone who let him down so badly.'

'But after all, we packed up and left the US; he can't expect her to turn up at Christmas and sing carols with him.'

'That's part of growing up, John – recognising the fact that you can go on loving people after they let you down.'

'Ain't it the truth,' he said ruefully.

'You still love Estelle?'

'I wish I knew! Sometimes I forget all about her for days on end and other times I lie awake missing her. I think I miss taking care of her. She needed a lot of taking care of. She was always worried about getting freckles, or finding a grey hair, or whether playing tennis made her look rowdy. She never could take more than two drinks, either. She relied on me to check up on that at a party and see she only got mineral water.'

He knew she was listening intently, and he wondered why he was unburdening himself like this. But there had never been anyone else to whom he could tell these things.

'When we first had Stephen,' he said, with a sigh of regret, 'life was wonderful. You see, all our friends were sort of settling down, they had little babies and when we didn't have any, Estelle kind of felt left out. She loved being a young mother, fussing about at home, buying little fluffy toys for him. It's the Madonna thing, I think – there's a feeling that you look beautiful when you're smiling down at your baby.'

'Do you think so? Most women get bored and vexed with

nine months of being heavy and ungainly.'

He looked up, startled, then down at his wine glass. He shrugged. For a moment he was tempted to tell her that Estelle never went through all that, because they had had to adopt a baby. But that was something that he'd been advised to put to the very back of his mind. Bring up the child as if he were your very own – that was the advice the child specialist had given them. And they had obeyed it to the letter.

'When you go home . . . Stephen will see his mother then?'

'Who knows? Estelle is all wrapped up in Victor, and seeing Stephen reminds her that she's older than Victor by ten years or so. And whether Stephen would want to, I can't tell. He sure wouldn't want to see her if Victor was anywhere around. He hates that guy.'

'He wants to see his mother,' Christina said. 'No matter what he says, he should see her, needs to see her. In the end, the need will lessen because that's the way of life, children grow up and leave home. But Stephen has had to "leave home" too early.'

'You mean I shouldn't have taken him travelling?' John asked, stricken.

She gave his hand a sympathetic touch. 'Home isn't only to do with place – it's to do with people. You're "home" to Stephen for the moment, but by and by he'll want to see his mother again, because she's part of his home-life.'

He was comforted. Someone had taken the trouble to hear him out, to listen without being bored or embarrassed by his problems. He felt as if there were some bond that held them together at that moment, which was strange, because this was the first time he'd had a proper conversation with her.

A sense of guilt at imposing upon her made him change the subject. He chatted about the antiquities they'd seen in Egypt.

'England's full of archaeological digs,' she told him. 'We had the Romans here, remember?'

'Sure thing, Julius Caesar and the Trilobantes – I learnt it in school. Is there much to see?'

'There's a lot at St Albans. Do you know it?'

'St Albans . . .' He shook his head. 'I don't think I ever went there during my posting in London. Is it far?'

'No, a short drive north. It's really worth seeing. Stephen would be interested, I'm sure.'

'Say, why don't we go there together! You could show us the way. This fine weather, we could take a picnic. What d'you say ?'

'Oh, no, I . . .'

He drew back at once. 'Of course, you see enough kids with broken families in your work, why should you—?'

'No, no, it isn't that.'

'What, then? Can't spare the time? I'm not asking you to take a day off: we could do it at a weekend.'

For some reason she seemed to have a struggle with herself. He could see she wanted to come but thought she ought to refuse.

'Come on,' he urged, 'a day out in the country. St Albans is the country, I take it?'

'To some extent,' she said, half laughing. 'But I sometimes have patients on Saturdays . . . I explained . . . working mothers . . .'

'Sunday, then? Say yes you'll come, before this English climate changes its mind and we get rain and hail!'

'Well, all right.' How strange it was, that note of something like surrender. She added quickly, as if committing herself: 'I'll bring a picnic lunch.'

'Oh, I wouldn't want to put you to the trouble—'

'No, really, I don't know whether we'd find anywhere to eat – some old pub, I suppose, but English cooking . . .'

'Yeah,' he agreed. Serving abroad had given him experience of many cuisines, and the worst was certainly the English. 'Well, OK, you bring the grub and I'll bring the wheels.'

'We can use my car.'

'Not at all, not at all, would you let me drive your car? I bet you wouldn't! And I don't want you to have to do any work. It's going to be a day out for you.'

She gave in, smiling and shrugging. He had the feeling she was still uncertain about it, and all Saturday he expected a message to say she wouldn't be able to come due to pressure of work. Stephen couldn't see that it mattered too much whether she came or not.

'We can find the place for ourselves, Dad. I mean, Roman remains, it's bound to be signposted.'

'But I want her to come!'

Stephen sighed to himself. Was this the beginning of one of the ailments he'd been warned about by his schoolfellows? The 'rebound', the eagerness to find someone else . . . But this Dr Holt didn't sound much like a direct replacement for Mom. A career woman, a professional woman . . . Gee, she was probably as grim as hell even if, as Dad insisted, she was pretty. Though what a middle-aged man thought of as pretty might prove to be a disappointment.

When she opened the door to them on Sunday morning, Stephen was quite taken aback. She wasn't at all like Mom, even though the guys had said that Dad would look for someone as like Mom as possible.

No, Dr Holt was very fair-haired, and had cool grey eyes, and didn't seem to care too much about clothes. She was wearing a sweater and skirt and dark thick stockings and clumpy shoes. Stephen immediately felt that he and his father were over-dressed in their immaculate flannel trousers and checked tweed jackets and collars and ties.

Introductions were made, Dr Holt handed over the picnic basket. Stephen waited to see whether she would expect to sit in the front alongside Dad but no, she said she could give directions equally well from the back, and she wanted them to see the spire of the cathedral come up on the landscape.

It was only a short drive. The little town – city, the doctor corrected, it was a city because it had a cathedral – seemed asleep in the sunshine. 'Most of the population is indoors,' she explained, 'reading the Sunday papers. The Sunday papers are full of terrible scandals which the British adore but don't allow themselves except on Sundays.'

'Isn't that kind of illogical? Shouldn't they be reading

improving books?' Stephen countered, intrigued.

'Yes they should, but somehow that seems to have died out. Of course some of the population is in church. And some people are still in bed; they love a long lie-in on Sundays. Turn to the left here, John, the road to the archaeological site is down there.'

Stephen hadn't known what to expect, and at first after the splendours of Egypt the grassy expanse seemed nothing. But then it dawned on him that only a hundred yards or so away the town still existed. This place wasn't in the middle of an expanse of desert, there was still a living and breathing city more or less where the Romans had built it.

And then, the thrill of picking up pieces of ancient tile from the hypocaust; holding in his hand a bent and rusty nail, which must have been hammered home by a Roman mallet into a Roman housebeam . . .

The museum he thought kind of makeshift, but the guide explained they didn't have much funding and were only at the beginning of the work on the dig. 'Masses and masses of stuff out there,' he said with a wave of his hand at the windows.

Still to be unearthed! Stephen at that moment wanted above everything else to be allowed to take part in the dig. 'Gee, wouldn't it be keen,' he breathed. 'To be the first to come on, say, a tiled mosaic, or a statue . . .'

Dr Holt didn't say, as Mom might have done, that this was just another of his passing enthusiasms. She listened and nodded and, where she could, answered his questions. They walked back around the excavations, pausing to examine the little notices pegged in place: *atrium, coenatio*, he wished he'd paid more attention to the Latin course at school.

They ate lunch on the banks of the little River Ver, and he had to admit that the food was pretty good. Sandwiches with really thick slices of ham in the middle, and pastry envelopes filled with lamb and vegetables, and rich fruit cake. 'You must have spent a lot of time baking up this feast,' he said admiringly to Dr Holt.

'Oh, I bought it all. I'm no kind of a cook,' she said with a smile that seemed somehow to turn her coolness into a bright sparkle. 'I never had time to learn, I'm afraid, except for brewing up strong tea Army-style and roasting bits of lamb over an open fire Balkan-style.'

Army-style? Balkan-style? He was mystified. His father explained that Dr Holt had been involved in the military campaign in the Balkans during the war. Stephen stared. It couldn't be true. This little woman with the fair skin and fragile-looking bones? But yes, it was true, she was nodding and saying she'd never been a gourmet, she'd always eaten whatever the trucks delivered.

After lunch they went to look at the cathedral, which she told them had been dedicated in the early twelfth century, though there had been a church there earlier. You could see the Roman brick that had been used in building it. St Alban, it turned out, had been a Roman soldier serving in the garrison of the Roman town.

Something about it seemed to soak through Stephen's skin. It was so old, so enduring. And the little town – *city* – was full of old things. Overhanging upper rooms shaded the little alleys. From the top of the clock tower they viewed the rooftops glowing under the sun. The trees seemed to cushion the old buildings, the jackdaws seemed to call in pleasure as they flew in and out of spires and towers.

On the way home they stopped for tea in a little place called London Colney, on the banks of yet another little river. They sat in a cottage garden where bees hummed in and out of tall hollyhocks, and Dr Holt poured tea out of a thick brown tea-pot. Stephen found he was going on and on about what he'd seen in Egypt, and in the Louvre, and in the British Museum.

'You should go and look at the Roman Wall,' Dr Holt suggested.

'Yes, Stephen, how about that – up north a-ways, built by the Emperor Hadrian.'

Well, that would be keen. Could they go tomorrow? He was beginning to realise that Europe was full of ancient things and he was *here* and he ought to see them.

By the time they parted from Dr Holt at her place in New Cavendish Street, a plan had already been drawn up for a week's travelling to see the Roman sites in the north. He shook hands with Dr Holt and promised to report to her the following weekend. Somehow it was taken for granted they were all going to meet again next weekend.

'Made quite a hit with you, didn't she?' John Charlford said with hidden amusement as they drove towards the Dorchester.

'Dr Holt? Well . . . she's different from what I expected. Knows a lot about old things, doesn't she?'

'Well, the British soak it up through their pores, boy. It's all around them.'

'Yeah, I'd no idea! There's such a lot to see, Dad! Look, we don't need to rush off to Italy, do we? I mean, we could hang on here in London and see some more—'

'It gets cold and damp in London, Stephen. Italy has better weather.'

'Huh, weather! What are we, a pair of cissies? We can put up with a bit of damp and fog, can't we?'

So they stayed on, and they saw Dr Holt frequently, and when they were away on archaeological trips Stephen sent her postcards to show her what they were looking at, and Christmas came and they invited Dr Holt to Christmas dinner at the Dorchester but she had to spend Christmas Day with her folks in Lincolnshire. So instead they took her out on what the British call Boxing Day, and then went to the theatre to see a genuine British pantomime which was weird, really weird, though a lot of laughs.

It was decent of Dad not to want to pack up and leave for the warmth of the Mediterranean.

What Stephen didn't know was that his father had his own reasons for being pleased to stay. He had made up his mind to ask Christina Holt to marry him.

Chapter Twenty-nine

Christina had known she was playing with fire, but the temptation to get to know her son a little had just been too much for her. It was upon her son that all her attention had been centred. By not the slightest word, smile or touch must she let him know she had any special interest in him. And in this she felt she had succeeded.

She hadn't thought too much about John Charlford. She knew, of course, that he was in post-separation limbo. She knew he was looking for some way to get his life started again. She should have remembered that he was probably looking for someone to fill the gap left in that life.

She had failed to exercise enough caution. She hadn't even been aware of the attraction he felt towards her. To her he was the man who stood in the role of father to her son, a man glad to have help in keeping the boy on an even keel. She had forgotten that he was a man who was used to a woman in his life, and who was, probably unconsciously, looking for the one who would replace Estelle.

His proposal, when it came, took her by surprise. She could tell that he for his part was surprised at her reaction. 'Christina, surely you've realised I care for you?'

'I thought we were friends, John.'

'Friends can fall in love.'

'That's true. But we've only known each other a short time.'

'Not such a short time. We met a long time ago.'

'But that was—'

'And over the last three months, going on four, I've felt we were building an important relationship.'

She took a moment to think. 'What about Stephen?'

'What about him?' he countered, frowning a little.

'Have you told him you're thinking of remarrying?'

The frown disappeared. 'I'm only thinking of it if you say yes,' he said. 'But it will be OK. Stephen likes you.'

'As an acquaintance who can talk a little about archaeology. As a stepmother . . . ?'

'Oh, that word! You'd be a genius at it, Christina! You of all people would know how to handle the situation.' Then, realising that sounded as if he'd picked her because she could use her expertise on Stephen, he amended hastily, 'I mean, you really get on well with him. It's not as if you work at it, he just seems to like you.'

'He does? I'm glad.' A pause. 'John, a boy of seventeen can like a woman he meets round and about with his father. But accepting her as a surrogate mother is quite a different thing. I think it would change our relationship entirely, and probably not for the better.'

'Well, we needn't rush into it, dear. We could give him time to get used to it. And in any case he'll be going to university soon, it's not as if he would have to see you—'

'In the places where his mother used to reign? At Bixbee, for instance?'

'Oh, we can give up Bixbee if you think it would make things easier. Cousin Burford would take it off my hands in a minute. We could live in New York, or Philadelphia, if you prefer. That's where you qualified, isn't it? And there's another thing: you could practise in the States, no problem about your qualifications because you have an American degree. Of course I shouldn't object at all if you wanted to go on with your work, I want to make that clear—'

'John—'

'Or it might be a good idea to settle in London. If Stephen is really going to get serious about archaeology, he'll need to study, and it seems to me that all the experts are in Europe and Asia Minor.'

'John, I don't think—'

'Don't dismiss the idea, Christina,' he said over her

protests. 'I see I was wrong to think you'd seen it coming. Perhaps I should have been more romantic.'

They looked at each other ruefully. They had never even kissed except recently, at meeting and parting, and her kisses were for Stephen as well as for John.

She didn't say, we're too old to be romantic, she didn't feel that to be true. There had been times over the past two or three years when she'd longed for a man's arms around her, for roses to come unexpectedly and brighten up her day, for someone other than a respectful male colleague to squire her to formal dinners.

She had missed all that. In her girlhood she had been too concentrated on learning to be a doctor; in her womanhood she had been in the thick of the clash of arms. Only those few weeks with Laurenz in Topchidarski . . .

She felt his presence now, between herself and John Charlford. Laurenz Varikiav, in his worn uniform, the Balkan cap crushing down his wiry dark hair . . .

'What is it?' John said, startled. She had gone pale, her eyes had ceased to see him though she was looking straight at him.

'Nothing, nothing. I was thinking of the past . . .'

'We ought to think about the future, darling. I could give you a good life. I don't want to talk about money, but it would never be a problem. There's a possibility I might go into politics, but it all pretty much depends on whether the Republicans would want me. In any case, you wouldn't have to play any part if you didn't like to. I feel there could be good years ahead, Christina. Please say you'll share them with me.'

He understood that he had spoken too soon, hadn't prepared the ground properly. He wished now he could go back and start again.

'I can't help feeling there are things you haven't considered, John. Chiefly how Stephen would react.'

'Good lord, people with children remarry all the time, dear! Things always settle down.'

'But in this case . . .' In this case the boy would be getting

443

as a stepmother the woman who brought him into the world. A woman whose emotions were far too complicated to be able to handle the inevitable difficult situations well.

Impossible to confess all this to John, however.

'Think about it, Christina,' he urged. 'I see I've taken you by surprise. Think about it and we'll talk about it again. In the meantime we can go on being friends.'

Can we? she wondered when he had gone. Can we go back to the old relationship? Her work had taught her that it was almost impossible. Once emotions were voiced, made fact, they couldn't be retracted. John felt more than friendship for her: perhaps not quite love, but something that urged him to bind her to him with the marriage tie.

But she didn't feel anything like that.

When Jo-Jo Belu came breezing into London, on a business trip concerning the League of Nations, she stayed, as she always did, in Christina's flat above the consulting rooms in New Cavendish Street.

In no time at all she had winkled out of Christina the story of her friendship with John Charlford and Stephen, and John's marriage proposal.

'My God, what luck! Grab him with both hands, my dear,' she cried.

'But Jo-Jo—'

'Why are you hesitating? From all you say he's a nice man, and *rich*, and he hands you back the son that you've never stopped grieving over. So of course you say yes.'

'Jo-Jo, have some sense! It's not as easy as that.'

They sat over the remains of a meal which Jo-Jo had cooked – a rich stew with cream and dried apricots in it, a cake concocted with halva and chocolate. Jo-Jo wiped the crumbs from around her mouth, swallowed a large mouthful of red wine, and glared at Christina.

'My little Snow Princess, you are too timid! You have given away your young years to mending the broken bodies of men in war, and your days now are spent listening to the troubles of naughty children.'

'They're not naughty – how often must I tell you?'

'Ah, ah,' Jo-Jo said, swaying her head from side to side in a gesture of rebuke, 'you don't like to hear it said. You always were too soft about children, Chrissie, always, and that is why of course you have never been able to blot out the memory of your baby. Now you have your chance. He is there, motherless – rush to his side!'

'Jo-Jo, you speak as if once I married John there would be nothing to do except hold out my arms and Stephen would fall into them. But that's not so! He would very probably hate me.'

'But you just told me he likes you.'

'But that's as a nice lady who can tell him about the Romans in Britain and listens when he plans a visit to the Parthenon. It would be a different thing entirely if he found me in his father's bed.'

'Ach, you make a drama of it.'

'I don't have to make a drama of it, it would be one from its own momentum. And besides, you talk on and on about Stephen. What about John?'

'Well, what about John? You like him, don't you?'

'I don't love him.'

'Who expects you to?' Jo-Jo got up, went to the little kitchenette for the coffee. She had made it, Christina saw thankfully, Swiss-style, not Serbian-style. Seeing her relief, Jo-Jo smiled. 'Oh, living in Geneva has taught me a lot, my little one. It has taught me to appreciate the good things of life. And also to be practical. And you must be practical too. Listen, Christina, you're not getting any younger. If you want to have a family of your own you must begin soon. Here is this nice man, who wants to marry you and who would make an excellent husband. You still have time to bear him children – two or three, even. You should stop thinking about the bad side and think of the good side. Here is a man who could give you the children you've always longed for.'

Christina's eyes filled with tears. 'Oh, Jo-Jo. That's hitting below the belt!'

'Don't I speak the truth? You do still want children, don't you?'

'But not his,' she replied in a shaking voice. 'Not John Charlford's, Jo-Jo.'

Her friend glared at her. Then she said, 'Dry your eyes, blow your nose, and drink your coffee.'

Christina obeyed.

'So, we are still thinking about Laurenz Varikiav, is that it?'

'I've never stopped thinking about him.'

'What? You tell me this? After the way he deceived and betrayed you?'

'He didn't deceive me. I never thought to ask him if he was married.'

'But in my country decent married men don't start affairs with decent women without first making the situation clear.'

'Jo-Jo, there was a *war* on! How do we know what the "situation" was in his marriage? Besides, that's got nothing to do with it. I can't give up loving him just because he didn't tell me everything. He was honest when he said he loved me. I know he was. What we had was real. And I can't turn to some other man as if that would somehow compensate.'

Jo-Jo drank some coffee, thinking over what her friend had just said. 'I hope, Chrissie dear, you're not one of those *silly* women who ruin their lives over a dead love affair.'

'I'm not ruining my life. I have an interesting career, I'm doing some good in the world . . .'

'But you could have so much more! You could have your own son back in your arms, you could have a wealthy husband and time to raise his children, if you weren't still obsessed with Laurenz.'

'Now, Jo-Jo, don't try to use terms you don't understand. I'm not "obsessed" with Laurenz.'

'But you're prepared to throw away an excellent match just because John doesn't measure up to him.'

'An excellent match! What sort of talk is that?' Christina roused herself to counter Jo-Jo's view. 'I don't need "an excellent match". I need work that interests me and the freedom to do it. John is talking about going into politics. I can't see myself as a good wife for an American senator, and not to play my part would be unfair on John. And besides, if I had to go to America, what about the cases I'm working on here? I can't just leave them!'

'You could, and you would, if you loved John enough.'

'Exactly,' Christina agreed.

For a moment Jo-Jo felt she had hoist herself with her own petard. Then she rallied. 'But you don't have to think about love to that degree. You have to think about suitability, compatability, a place in society. And the chance to see your son Stephen every day.'

Christina was shaking her head. 'I'm not attracted by any of the former, and I'm *too* attracted by the idea of living in the same house with Stephen. No, Jo-Jo, it would be a recipe for disaster. I'm going to say no to him.'

Jo-Jo let it go. She was sure that when she returned to the topic – and she would, as often as she could, during her stay – she would make some inroads on her friend's convictions.

But she was wrong. Christina remained firm. John Charlford accepted her decision but asked if he could be allowed to go on hoping. He decided that to absent himself for a while might be a good idea. He and Stephen left a wintry London for more attractive regions where Stephen could spend days on end in the Coliseum, at Paestum, at Pompeii.

Christina missed them almost at once. And all the more when after about a week the post brought her a little leather purse with her initials worked on it in gold. It was from Stephen, with a note to say he'd bought it in Venice where they stopped overnight on the long train journey south. It was to say thank you for all the time she'd given up to them during their stay in London.

To her own dismay Christina wept over the gift. If he liked her enough to bother to buy it, perhaps . . . oh, perhaps he liked her enough to accept her as a stepmother . . .

Yet in the end she dried her tears and accepted her own

verdict. All that she had learned in her psychiatric studies told her that the relationship between step-parent and step-child was one of the most difficult in the world. She would not roughen the tranquil friendship between her son and herself with those violent emotions.

Besides, she was uncertain whether one day, in some passionate argument, she might not actually say the terrible words: 'How can you behave like this to me? I'm your real mother!' And that would be a disaster so great she dared not contemplate it.

Jo-Jo Belu went back to Geneva very discontented with her own efforts. She had been sure she could talk good sense into her dearly loved friend. It had come as a decided shock to her to hear Christina actually defending Laurenz.

Laurenz Varikiav! She would never forgive him for what he had done to Christina. Wherever he was, she hoped he was suffering.

Jo-Jo Belu would have been angry and disappointed with the events that were taking place on a grey day outside Plovdiv in Bulgaria, between the Balkan and the Rhodopes Mountains. The gates of Plovdiv Prison opened; Laurenz Varikiav stepped out to freedom.

The gatekeeper gave him the usual good wishes as between warder and released felon. 'God take you under his care and keep you from any act that might bring you back,' he said.

The released prisoner grunted, put his ageing trilby hat upon his dark head, and strode away.

An ancient limousine in the care of a uniformed chauffeur was standing on the muddy road not far away. Laurenz walked towards it. An elderly lady in the back seat leaned forward to watch him. The chauffeur leapt out to open the door for him.

'Welcome, *gospodar*,' he said, touching the peak of his cap.

'Thank you, Tesda.' He got in. 'Good morning, Cousin Vela.'

'God be thanked,' Cousin Vela said, leaning forward to kiss him first on one cheek then the other. 'Your release was delayed, I thought you were never coming.'

'The Bulgarian prison system is like the mills of God, cousin, which grind extremely slowly.'

'You're too thin! What did they feed you with, thistleheads and brackenberries? Didn't you get the food parcels I sent?'

'I got the parcels, cousin. But parcels had to be shared: one couldn't feast while others fasted.'

'Ah, high-minded nonsense! Well, I'm going to see that you get good food and plenty of it so that we put some flesh back on those bones. Tesda, drive on, what are you waiting for? Let's get away from this detestable place.'

The car lurched a little as it turned on the poor road surface. Rain had misted the windows. Laurenz gazed through the hazy panes until the grim prison buildings were hidden by a bend in the road.

'I hope you'll be satisfied with the way the *zagruda* has been run in your absence. The land is in good heart, we have had fair fruit crops the last two years and some timber we sold has fetched a good price. The spring wheat has been sown, shoots are poking up. There's still snow in Gelubku Valley but we let the sheep into Marep and Solda Valleys because there was a good early bite. The lambs have begun to arrive, the shepherd says the number is about the same as always.'

She paused. He was sitting with his hands loosely clasped in his lap, on the fine twill of a pair of trousers that had once belonged to a military uniform. She wasn't sure if he was listening or not, but she went on because she couldn't have borne silence.

'The town council are improving the roads with money they got for war reparations, so we'll be able to get the fruit to market much more quickly. The property in Skoplje is being repaired: we had to wait a long time for electricians to put in the power cables . . .'

Her voice creaked on, detailing for Laurenz all that had

been done by the *gospodar* who had taken over as head of his community while he was in prison. By and by, he would have to pay attention to it all, to hear the arguments for and against his resumption of the role. The man who had taken over was a good man, no reason to push him out unless the rest of the *zagruda* insisted.

He felt no urge to take command again. Life was different now. The war was over, had been over a long time, but he had never had the chance to learn to live in peace. Six years had been lost – a year awaiting trial and five in the cells. No remission for good behaviour in the Bulgarian system, and in any case his behaviour had not been very good, he had been sullen, grim, arrogant.

A Serb in a Bulgarian gaol, a conqueror in the power of the defeated . . . He had served what his fellow-prisoners called 'hard time': he'd got none of the easy jobs, had never been promoted to the rank of trusty, had been given only the regulation allowance of everything – food, fresh air, clothing, soap. One shower in cold water each week and one shave by the prison barber, a haircut and two books from the prison library each month. Mail from family or legal adviser once a week, heavily censored to prevent any escape plots. Visits infrequent because of the distance his family had to come and the obstacles placed in the way of obtaining permits.

But he didn't bear any ill-will. He had killed a man who deserved to be killed, and had paid for it.

'How are the children?' he asked, breaking in on Cousin Vela's monologue.

'Well, God be thanked. I didn't bring them with me, I felt it might be too upsetting.' Whether for them or for him she didn't specify.

He nodded. Two children bore his name: one was his, one not. As to his wife, there was no need to speak of her.

At the frontier, the Bulgarian guards examined their papers with care and sneered openly when they saw the release document from the prison and the travel permit that went with it. Cousin Vela coloured up at their attitude, but

Laurenz stared straight ahead, refusing to let them rile him. What did they matter? In a few hours he would be home again in Horamesc, in the valleys beyond Skoplje, beyond the tumbling waters of the Vardar.

Already he could smell the keen mountain air, the grass wet with mist, the pine trees. He could picture the thunder clouds roiling over the peaks, hear the croak of the ravens as they wheeled above the rocks. He could see the sheep running down the hillside, looking from the distance like a white river; the cottage doorways draped with golden tobacco leaf as autumn came on, the sharp scent of it as it dried in the slanting rays of the sun. Home, the village where he was born and where his family had held sway for generations. He hadn't seen it since the Bulgarians seized it during the advance in 1914.

They spent the night in an inn just over the border into Serbia. He couldn't sleep because the bed was too soft, had to take his overcoat as a blanket and sleep on the floor. But he slept well in the end, awoke refreshed. They were in Serbia now, the voices below his window were speaking his native tongue. For the last six years he had had to speak the language of his gaolers. In defiance, he had spent his time learning English, a language his captors frowned upon. The prison chaplain spoke good English and, despite official disapproval, had helped him.

The drive to Horamesc took several hours. The car, an old German limousine, wasn't equal to the steep inclines. He wasn't impatient. After five years in prison, one year under pre-trial arrest, why fret about a few hours more?

At last they passed Skoplje. The sun had come out, the town shone, the white minarets in the Turkish quarter soared up towards the blue of the sky, the ancient bridge over the Vardar glowed, green ferns in its cracks.

He sat forward, looking for the road to Horamesc. There it was, with an ancient cart drawn by two oxen taking up most of the space. The old car fell in behind, Tesda giving impatient little toots on the horn from time to time, the driver on the cart lifting his whip in acknowledgement but making no effort to pull aside.

'Let him be, Tesda, I'm in no hurry, I want to see the land . . .'

Orchards in bud, vines showing green growth, a little veil of green shoots over the cornfields. Birds flying to and fro with pieces of straw in their beaks, wisps of sheep's wool: nesting time.

At the fork for Grasne the cart turned off. Tesda put on some speed. The dogs came out to greet them as they drove into Horomesc. Poultry ran fluttering across in front of the car, in the barns the milk cows lowed.

But there were no people. Where was everybody?

Tesda drove into the courtyard of the Varikiav house. He braked, switched off the engine and came to the door to help Cousin Vela out. Vela stood by the car, smiling. Tesda opened the door for Laurenz. He got out.

And at once the bells in the village church began to peal, the door of the house was flung open, and a horde of people in their Sunday clothes came surging out.

'*Gospodar, gospodar*, welcome home! God's blessing on your homecoming! *Gospodar* Laurenz, be pleased to receive our offering!'

The village priest in a long black cassock, tall hat and beard was offering him a huge bunch of spring flowers, tears streaming down his face. Laurenz knew him well: this was the man who had married him to his wife.

He accepted the flowers, looked around in bewildered thanks. A little silence fell. Cousin Vela clapped her hands.

'Children!' she called.

From the dark beyond the open house door, two children stepped forth, a boy about thirteen years old in blue shirt and loose Balkan breeches, a girl about ten in the traditional white linen dress and embroidered bolero of the district. They came forward timidly, down the one step at the threshold, the boy with a protective arm around the girl's shoulders.

'Father,' he said, pausing and looking up. He bowed. 'Welcome home.'

The girl dropped a curtsey. 'Welcome home, Father.'

'Thank you, Milovan. Thank you, Suza.'

They were strangers to him. The last time he had seen them was on a visiting day a year ago and then only from a distance, since children weren't allowed inside the main prison building. And Suza had been frightened by the place, was in tears, her face turned away.

There was an awkward hesitation. Cousin Vela covered it up by crying gaily, 'Come and see what we've prepared for you.' She urged him into the house, where in the main room off the hall a meal had been laid out: the table, with its best napery, was groaning under cold lamb, cold pork, a whole carp with fennel in its mouth, pilau rice, savoury breads and biscuits, fruits, nuts, candies. Wine bottles stood waiting to be opened, glasses were lined up alongside.

'A toast!' called the priest. 'A toast to *Gospodar* Laurenz! Welcome home, many happy years of freedom to come!'

In a moment the entire village was inside, pouring wine and taking food. Laurenz stood in the midst, dazed, unreceptive. He wanted them all to go away. He wanted to be left alone, to go from room to room so as to convince himself he was home at last.

But that wasn't to be. He had to eat and drink, and since it was years since he had had a glass of wine he was soon quite drunk. The rest of the day passed in a dream.

He woke next morning in his old room, the master bedroom of the house, the room he had shared with his wife until the war took him to Belgrade at the King's command. He got up slowly, his head throbbing with every move.

It was still early. The dairy-maid was at work, and he could hear someone singing to himself in the stables.

He washed and shaved and dressed, pleased to find his old razors set out for him in the bathroom and newly pressed clothes in the wardrobe. In the kitchen the cook was kneading bread. 'Yah, *gospodar*, I thought you would sleep late and have breakfast in bed!'

'If you knew me from the old days, you'd know I never do that.' He cut a piece of bread from one of yesterday's loaves to serve as breakfast and went outdoors.

He hadn't reached the gate when running footsteps halted him. He looked back. Milovan and Suza were running to catch up with him.

'Shall we come with you, Father?'

'No.'

'But we want to show you—'

'No.'

Hurt, the boy drew back. Laurenz looked at him. What did you say to a thirteen-year-old boy when you didn't want his company? No, Daddy wants some time to himself. Or, Daddy needs a quiet walk to cure his headache and get rid of the wine fumes. Or, I don't know you, I've hardly ever exchanged a word with you, so why should I want your company?

As for the girl . . . What did it matter about the girl!

It was after midday when he came back from his solitary walk. He had been greeted by everyone he met, yet he knew only a few of them. His *zagruda* had been destroyed by the Bulgarians after he left for Belgrade. Most had been killed trying to defend the village, some had been taken prisoner into the service of the Bulgarians, a few had escaped to tell the tale. It was a common enough story during the war.

Now the village had come to life again, with newcomers arriving to help replace the lost population: cousins and nephews from other regions; friends willing to invest their future in the prospects of these fertile valleys.

During his absence the role of leader had been taken over by a distant cousin of the Varikiav family, a man he had never even met until yesterday. Javich had done well. In the next week or so the decision would have to be made: should he continue as a *gospodar* or should Laurenz be reinstated?

But the real question was, did he want to be reinstated, to be head of a group of people he hardly knew?

The same was true of his immediate family. The boy Milovan had been head of the house since the place was restored to the Varikiavs after the armistice. Too young for it, of course, but that was the tradition – the son took over if the father was absent. Here there was no question: Laurenz had to resume his place as head of the house; it would have been unseemly otherwise.

Yet in the days that followed it was clear Milovan resented it.

His elderly Cousin Vela remonstrated with him. 'Milo, you must show more respect to your father. Your manner to him is not seemly.'

'I am respectful. What have I said that is disrespectful?'

'It's not what you say, it's the way you look when he speaks to you. You must be attentive, obedient.'

'I'm not disobedient.'

Of course he was right. There was nothing you could pin down. Vela sighed. She longed to be allowed to go back to Novi Sad, where she had once had a neat little apartment overlooking the Danube and a circle of friends with whom she'd played piquet tournaments. But duty is duty, and Cousin Laurenz needed her.

'Milo, of course it's difficult for you trying to be affectionate to a father you've never known. But you must make bigger efforts.'

'What about *him*?' the boy burst out. 'Why doesn't *he* make some effort?'

'Milo, he has suffered—'

'Oh, I know all about that. I know I've got to look up to him because he's a big war hero who served with the King, and he killed a man in an affair of honour! I know all that, I accept all that; but he looks past me when he speaks to me, as if I don't matter. And he never speaks to Suza at all!'

There were reasons for that, good reasons, but Vela felt she couldn't discuss them with a thirteen-year-old.

'It's not your place to criticise your father, child,' she said with more severity than she felt. 'It's your duty to love and honour him.'

'I do honour him! I do!' Milovan threw up his clenched fists to emphasise his declaration. 'But I can't love him if he doesn't love me!'

So Cousin Vela tried to talk to his father. 'Laurenz, the

children need you. Can't you spend more time at home?'

He looked at her with a faint smile in his dark eyes. 'I spent years locked up indoors, cousin. You must forgive me if I like to be out in the mountains where the wind blows free.'

'Then can't you take the children with you? They would love to ride out—'

'What's behind this? Have they been asking to go with me?'

'Laurenz, they wouldn't dare!' she burst out, her wrinkled face crinkling up in bitter amusement. 'They're overawed by you.'

'What do you want me to do? Trot out with my son alongside on a pony and the girl sitting in front of my saddle? Can you imagine me in that sort of group?'

'The war is over, my dear, it's time to relax and take up pleasant pastimes. Why shouldn't you ride sedately out with the boy on a pony and the girl sharing your saddle?'

'No.'

'Laurenz, if you can't even make a pretence at being a father to them, the best thing would be to send them to boarding schools.'

'Would that be a good thing to do?' he asked, truly needing to be told.

'No it would not! They've lived through a terrible war and a long separation. The last thing they need is to be sent away from the only real home they've ever had.' She hesitated. 'Perhaps you should speak to Father Kiril about the way you feel.'

'Father Kiril! He's so old he's forgotten what it was like to be young and have problems. No, Vela, the priest wouldn't be any help. But I understand what you are saying. I'm failing to do my duty by the children. I'll try harder.'

The meeting of the *zagruda* was held, Laurenz declined the honour of taking the headship of the region, Cousin Javich was confirmed in his post, and Laurenz set himself to spend more time with the children. They did, in fact, go riding together. He sometimes sat in the schoolroom with them when they were doing lessons with Father Kiril. He took to looking in on them last thing at night before going to bed.

Slowly, a relationship began to build up. But for Laurenz it was hampered because every room of the house, every meadow and field outside, spoke to him of his wife.

The dilemma was ended for him by a summons from Belgrade. King Peter had died while Laurenz was in prison but now the son, King Alexander, had requested to see him.

Town clothes were taken out of the wardrobe and freshly pressed. A barber was sent for from Skoplje to cut his hair. He was more or less indifferent to his appearance; nevertheless, he didn't want to look a country bumpkin in front of his sovereign.

The first few minutes of the interview were painful. Both men had served in the war. Both had seen their hopes of a 'Greater Serbia' crumble in the wrangling of the post-armistice period. The other nationalities had been against it and in the end the King had had to accept a government of Radicals over a country awkwardly known as the Kingdom of the Serbs, Croats and Slovenes.

Now the League of Nations was debating national boundaries. King Alexander was anxious to have a man he could trust as his representative in Geneva.

'I tell you in confidence that I can't place any faith in my foreign minister,' he explained. 'Trumvich doesn't like me and I don't like him. He only stays in the post because he's able to handle the Slovene faction. So what I want, Varikiav, is that you should go to Geneva for me.'

Laurenz drew back in reflex withdrawal. 'Sir, I don't know anything about diplomacy.'

'Nedjozic is there dealing with the diplomatic aspect. What I want is to have someone at his side to stiffen him up. He's too apt to give in when the pressure's on.'

'I appreciate the honour, sir, but truly, I think I'm the wrong man.'

'Varikiav, how many men of ability do you think I have

who are pro-Monarchy? This country is full of clever brains, but unfortunately they seem to favour a republic. Now I happen to think that would be a great misfortune for us. If you look at the mess Germany has got into without its king, and France with its governments coming and going like swallows in migration, and as for Russia . . .'

'What you say is true—'

'Of course it's true! And I need a man in Geneva who remembers that when the negotiations get tough. I want to have my boundaries where they belong, not where some rapacious Austrian Republic thinks they should be!'

'But I have duties at home.'

The King held up his hand. 'Varikiav, how old are you?'

'Thirty-seven.'

'You and I are the same age, then. And we've both seen tragedy. Listen, Varikiav, refuse me if you must. But I think you'd be better off doing something for your country than moping at Horamesc. Think it over. I don't have to send anyone until the end of the month, but you ought to read the documentation before you go, if you take it on.'

As though by divination, Cousin Vela knew he'd been offered a post. 'What kind of job is it?'

'Assistant to the representative at the League of Nations.' He shrugged. 'Can you imagine me on a committee?'

'Why not? You used to handle the committee of the *zagruda* well enough, so I'm told.'

'Cousin, that was entirely different. That was a group of men who knew each other, settling difficulties about which they had expert knowledge. What do I know about diplomatic protocol, or boundary negotiation?'

'You could learn.'

'But I ought to stay at home and learn to know my children.'

'Do you think you're getting to know them by sitting in the schoolroom lost in thought, or taking them for long silent walks in the pinewoods?'

'You said I ought to share my time with them. I'm trying my utmost to do that.'

'But you can't shake off the memories. That's the trouble, isn't it?'

'Vela, that's my business.'

'It is my business too! I care about you,' she insisted in her creaky old voice. 'I think you should pack up, take the children with you, go to Geneva where at least there will be no memories to chill you when you look around.'

This was her opinion. If she was influenced by the idea that, once they had gone, she could return to Novi Sad and the healing waters of its spa, she tried not to let it outweigh her concern for the family.

After a little more argument he fell in with her wishes, chiefly because he really didn't care one way or the other. Obscure landowner in the mountains, busy negotiator in Geneva – what did it matter?

In Geneva he was second in command to Dr Nedjozic. The doctor was a doctor of philosophy, which had taught him to see two sides to every question, or even three, or four. He was the soul of reasonableness, with the result that the Kingdom of the Serbs, Croats and Slovenes (or the KSCS as it was known for brevity's sake) didn't come out well in the long arguments over territorial rights.

At first Laurenz was scornful. All this talk, all these sheets of paper with reasoned statements and sketch maps – for him the places were battlegrounds, remembered with sadness and anger.

But as the days went by, Laurenz began to be irritated by the way everyone else ran rings round the KSCS contingent. The junior assistants looked respectfully to Dr Nedjozic for a lead in debate, but Dr Nedjozic was busy seeing the debate from everyone else's point of view. Laurenz began to nudge his chief, whisper suggestions in his ear.

There were officials on the staff of the League of Nations itself whom he saw moving busily about the corridors in the first few days after he arrived. Once he thought he saw Jo-Jo Belu, but that must have been his imagination. His country would surely never have been so mad as to send Jo-Jo to

Geneva on its behalf: she was a red hot republican!

Nevertheless, he was shaken by the glimpse of that rounded vigorous body topped by glowing black hair. She brought back memories of the war, of the tented hospital among the frost-rimed rocks, of the field kitchen where broth simmered in great kettles, of women in uniform jackets and trousers moving purposefully about . . .

And more particularly, one woman, in a peasant sheepskin coat over coarse wool trousers, her short fair hair tucked under a woollen cap. And later, in the country lodge at Topchidarski, those slender limbs that gleamed in the lamplight, that ardent heart that had beat so strongly against his . . .

Long ago and far away; part of a life he had put behind him, because to think of it was too painful. All that might have been, all the hopes and plans he'd built around that one woman, had gone beyond recall when he went into Bulgaria to look for lost Serbian prisoners. What he had found in Bulgaria had called for an action that had cut him off from that rosy future for ever.

Well, as the old Serbian proverb warned, joy in the present is paid for by grief to come. He had paid with grief and anger and despair a hundredfold for that time in Topchidarski. His defence against them now was to put it all behind him, to try to build a new life in this shining city of Geneva.

All the same, if he had really seen Jo-Jo Belu, perhaps he could find her and have a word.

Not about politics. What he wanted to ask was – do you ever see Dr Christina Holt these days?

Chapter Thirty

Dr Holt came to Geneva in July.

She stayed in a hotel rather than with her friend Jo-Jo, so as to be with the other delegates. She was attending a symposium, arranged by the League of Nations, on the care of children orphaned by war.

Surprisingly enough, after four years that had cost them a generation of young men, the French were at war again, in North Africa. News reporters and the recently popular newsreel camera had brought before the public the misery and fear of children in a war zone. There had been calls for the League to 'do something'.

The result was a conference of experts on child care. How did you gather up children wandering lost in front of rifles and machine guns? What did you do to help them back to ordinary life? Who should deal with them – hospitals, special centres, orphanages, schools?

The invitation to attend had at first held no attraction for Christina. She had work enough in London to keep her busy. But then came the Coal Strike in May and, a few days after that, a General Strike.

Because of the resulting transport difficulties, her patients often didn't get to her consulting rooms. Alice Lowther failed to turn up on two successive days, and that went to prove how bad conditions were becoming: Alice would have turned up through hail, snow or earthquake if she could.

So, Christina decided to go to Geneva, since it was better to be doing something half-way useful than sitting in her surgery waiting for people who never arrived.

Jo-Jo had been quite relieved when Christina said she would prefer to stay at the Hotel du Chevron. 'I'm going to be away myself,' she explained. 'The office is sending me to Lugano where there's a mini-conference on trade regulations. Of course you could use my apartment . . .'

'No, no, Jo-Jo, it's better to be with my colleagues. Sometimes interesting conversations get going late in the evening, and it would be a pity to have to leave for the Old Town.'

'Interesting conversations? You mean flirtations? Assignations?'

'Jo-Jo, you're incorrigible!'

'And you are incomprehensible! To refuse that nice John Charlford!'

'How do you know he was nice? You only met him once, seventeen years ago.'

'Oh, I know about such things,' Jo-Jo said wisely. 'He was nice then and such men don't change. But you'll lose him if you don't make up your mind pretty soon.'

'I'm not going to change my mind.'

'But he still keeps in touch?'

Christina shrugged. 'He sends postcards. Sorrento, Palermo. I think they're in Greece now.'

'Postcards! He can't propose on a postcard!'

'Jo-Jo, for someone who's never married herself, you're awfully determined to push me into it!'

'It's different for me,' her friend said with a gesture of dismissal. 'I'm not interested in children, never have been. I like to have a man about, of course, and that's no problem, but as for settling down to raise a family . . . No, no, one day when I'm fifty and losing my charms, I shall marry a rich Swiss banker and spend the rest of my life in lazy luxury.'

'I thought your greatest ambition was to bring republicanism to Serbia?' Christina teased.

'Oh, that will come, my friend, that will come. They can make fun of the Kingdom of the Serbs, Croats and Slovenes at the League, but one day it will be Yugoslavia, a united democratic—'

'Don't orate at me, my pet,' said Christina, satisfied to

have got her off the uncomfortable subject of John Charlford.

The symposium was to last two weeks: one week in lectures and discussions, one in compiling a report on their findings. Outside the sun shone on the lake, the chestnut trees were in rich full leaf, the mountains gleamed in the background. Inside the conference room of the hotel, men in frock coats and striped trousers mounted the dais, adjusted their eye-glasses, and droned on for twenty minutes about the establishment of temporary shelters, the laying of drains, the recruiting of nurses.

There were only two other women, one a voluble French paediatrician who asked questions and argued at every session. The other, from Ohio, seemed to have no greater ambition than to persuade them to adopt the American breakfast – cornflakes – for children in care.

By Thursday Christina was convinced that she was wasting her time. She was the only one present who had seen children in war conditions. She knew if she rose to describe the orphans she had seen in Serbia and the Crimea, she would be regarded with horror. Emotion must not be allowed to enter into the discussion. They must be academic, systematic, dispassionate.

During lunch, a rowdy argument arose between two of the male delegates. The afternoon session was delayed while the organisers tried to calm them down. Christina realised she had a headache coming on. She got up from the table, nodded to acquaintances, walked out of the dining-room, and straight out into the fresh air.

The sun was hot, but there was a breeze off the lake. She was wearing a linen skirt, a cream silk blouse, and sandals with cuban heels. No hat, but it was excusable to be hatless on such a day. She set off at a brisk pace so as to work off her exasperation.

By and by she found herself in the Park of Ariadne, whose formal gardens offered comfort to the eye and tranquillity to the nerves. She sat for a time watching a family of ducks and ducklings on one of the ponds. They were so comical, so self-engrossed, that her good humour was restored. She strolled on much more slowly, out on to the walk bordering Lake Geneva, on under the sweet-chestnut trees, past the tubs of glowing geraniums and the lakeside cafés.

Others were out enjoying the day. This was the beginning of the Swiss school holidays, so families were sitting picnicking. Some were out on the smooth waters of the lake in rowboats and dinghies, a few were setting out in boots and knickerbockers for the bus up to the lower slopes of Mont Blanc.

Above the easy chatter of French conversation she heard children's voices raised in shrill argument. Surprised, she turned. A boy and a girl were attempting to launch a rowboat off the end of the wooden jetty. The children were arguing in Serbian!

In automatic response she moved towards them down the jetty. The boy was making the boat sway dangerously as he attempted to settle himself on the thwart and put the oars in the rowlocks. The girl was complaining that he didn't know how to do it and should give up.

'Do be quiet, Suza, it's quite simple, anybody could do it!'

'You've never been in a boat like this before.'

'What's that got to do with it?'

His left oar slipped past its ring. He almost lost it, lurched forward to grab it, sent the boat down so sharply that a wave of grey lake water came over the gunwale.

'They're going to drown themselves,' remarked a burly old man lounging against the low wall of the esplanade.

'You could be right,' Christina agreed.

He strolled down the jetty. 'Wait, now!' he called in French.

The boy paid no heed. He had his left oar now, was trying to draw it back to engage it with the rowlock, but didn't have sense enough to see it must be held perpendicular first. The flailing wood narrowly missed the girl's head.

'Milo!' she wailed, throwing herself back. 'You nearly hit me!'

More water slurped aboard.

'Stop that,' Christina said in Serbian. 'Sit still, you'll have the boat over.'

The boy glared at her. 'Mind your own business!'

'What's he saying?' asked the old Genevois. 'Squawks like a parrot!'

'It is my business if you're going to drown yourselves. Lay down that oar.'

'We're going for a row on the lake.'

'You're doing no such thing. You obviously have no idea how to handle a boat.'

'Let me tell you, I've handled dozens of boats . . .'

'Got a temper, hasn't he?' the old man remarked to Christina. 'Hi, you, do you understand French?'

The boy turned to him. In very poor French he said, 'I understand, yes.'

'Then sit down, ship your oars in, and get out of that boat.'

'What?' The advice had clearly been incomprehensible to him.

'He says you should bring in the oars and get out of the boat.'

'What's it got to do with him?'

'He probably doesn't want to see you sink. Neither do I. Come on now, do as you're told.'

'Suza and I are going for a row.'

The old man solved the problem by picking up a boathook, catching the row-boat's painter, and tying it firmly to a ring in the jetty. He then offered a hand to the girl, who stepped out with so much alacrity that it was clear she'd been quite frightened. The boy, after glaring a moment, dropped the oars and came ashore with an unnecessarily showy leap.

'We could have managed perfectly well,' he said with a frown to Christina.

'Do you think so? We thought you looked likely to drown yourselves.'

'What language *is* that?' asked the Genevois who, like most of the citizens, spoke French, German, Italian and English.

'Serbo-Croat.' Christina studied the boy. 'You are Serbian, aren't you?'

'Yes, why, is there anything wrong with that?'

'Goodness, don't fly into a rage over a simple question,' she said. 'It's one of those coincidences, isn't it, that you protested in a language that I happened to speak.'

The boy relented. Natural good manners took over. 'I'm sorry. It's just that I'm used to looking after Suza without any interference.'

The old man stroked his white moustache and smiled. 'Everything all right? He's decided not to drown himself today?'

'Yes, we're restored to sweet reasonableness.'

'*Génève, cité de la paix*,' he said with a humorous bow, moving away.

'Come and have an ice,' Christina said to the children.

The boy hesitated. 'Oh, do, Milo! cried the girl. 'It's so hot and an ice would be lovely.'

'But you know we're not supposed to accept anything from strangers, Suza.'

'But she's not a stranger. She speaks Serbian.'

Christina admired the good sense of the boy and, in normal circumstances, she wouldn't have tried to override his doubts. But these were not normal circumstances. Serbian children . . .

'If you'd rather, I'll just give you the money and you can buy your own ices.'

'We have money of our own,' he said stiffly, then, boyish, 'But I don't know how to ask for a double scoop of chocolate ice-cream.'

'Come on then.'

They went to the café that bordered the lake by the jetty, where they found a table under a tree. The order was given: a double chocolate ice, a double strawberry ice, and a *citron pressé*.

'I'd really rather sit and eat ice-cream,' the little girl said. She looked to be about ten years old, dark, shy, rather plain. The boy was equally dark but handsome, with bones to his face that already foreshadowed the man he would become.

'You said you wanted to be cool. It's always cooler on the

water and the boat was just sitting there . . .'

'You mean it wasn't even your boat?' Christina cried.

'What do you mean, our boat? It was just sitting there. In Serbia, anybody can use a boat if it's just sitting there.'

'But that's because the boat belongs to the *zagruda*,' Christina said. 'In Switzerland, they don't have the *zagruda*.'

'Don't they?' He scooped a great mouthful of ice-cream up, savoured it, and crunched his wafer. He looked at Christina. 'You speak jolly good Serbian. Not many people do.'

'Where did you learn?' Suza put in.

'In Serbia, during the war.'

'You've been to Serbia?'

'Yes, I spent five years there.'

'Do you know Horomesc? It's near Skoplje.'

She felt an icy stab at her heart. 'Horomesc?'

'That's our home. We're only in Geneva because Father has a job at the League of Nations.'

'I see.' She put her hands round the cold glass in front of her, as if to reassure herself of its reality. 'What's your name?'

'I'm Milovan Varikiav, this is my sister Suza.'

Suza was chasing the last of the strawberry ice round her dish, but paused to stare at their benefactor. 'What's the matter?' she said in alarm. 'You've gone awfully white.'

To Christina, the voice seemed to come from a hundred miles away. The bright sunlight had grown dim, the boughs of the tree ran together in a river of green.

'It's the iced lemon,' she heard Milovan say anxiously. 'Cousin Vela always said you shouldn't drink ice-cold drinks on a hot day. *Gospodjo! Gospodjo!*'

She felt his warm, rather hard hand on hers, rubbing her knuckles. She blinked and focused her glance on him. 'It's all right,' she said through lips that didn't seem to belong to her. 'It was just a passing dizziness.'

'Can I order something for you? Hot coffee? Brandy?'

'No thanks. No, I'm fine, thanks.'

'Did everything spin round in front of your eyes?' Suza inquired. 'I get that sometimes. I did, for a minute, when Milo was flailing about with that oar.'

'Oh, you, you're always getting giddy or bursting into tears or something. And I wasn't flailing. I was just getting things organised.'

'Well, I'm glad we didn't go out on the lake because I feel sure you'd have done something mad and we'd have got all wet, and then what would Madame have said?'

'I'm not scared of Madame. She's just a silly old French woman.'

'She's Swiss.'

'Well, Swiss, then. And I'll tell you something, Miss Scaredy-cat, if we don't make off home this very minute, we're going to be late and we'll find out what Madame would say!'

'Oh no, what's the time?'

'It's just chimed half-past four on that clock over the café.'

'And we promised we'd be home by five! Oh, dear!' Her little face pinched with anxiety, Suza began to get up from table.

'Suza, Suza, where's your manners?' her brother rebuked her. 'Madame, excuse us, we have to go. We were to be home by five o'clock.'

'No, wait a moment—'

'I'm afraid we can't. Father has to go out this evening and he likes to spend some time with us, so we must be going. Thank you for the ice.'

'Yes, *gospodjo*, thank you for the ice,' Suza echoed, with a little bob of her head.

'Tell me your address . . . !'

But the children were running off hand in hand. Still too shaken to get up and go after them, she watched them disappear along the lakeside promenade.

When the waitress came to clear the table, she paid and asked for a taxi to take her back to the hotel. Once there, she disregarded the afternoon session which was winding to a close in the conference hall, but instead took the lift up to her room. There she put a telephone call through to Jo-Jo's hotel in Lugano.

Jo-Jo seemed to be out. She left a message that Miss Belu was to ring her urgently, then ordered tea in her room. It steadied her, the little ritual of measuring and pouring and sipping.

The clock went round, six o'clock came, half-past six. It was time for her to bathe and change. There was a reception that evening given by the Education Department of Geneva for the visiting children's specialists. If she were to be ready to leave at seven, she ought to get dressed.

She was fastening her short black evening frock when the phone rang. Jo-Jo's voice was full of anxiety. 'What's wrong, has there been an accident, what?'

'Jo-Jo, Laurenz is in Geneva.'

'What? I didn't catch that. What did you say?'

'Laurenz. Laurenz Varikiav. He's here.'

'Here – where? In Geneva?'

'Yes.'

'You've seen him?'

'No, but I came across his children in the park.' She told the story of the boating incident. 'They said their father was here at the League of Nations.'

'He is not,' Jo-Jo said almost with indignation. 'The KSCS team at the League is Dr Nedjozic, an assistant called Harav, and various minions in the office.'

'But they said—'

'Though, now I come to think of it,' her friend amended, 'I did hear that poor Harav was being recalled.'

'Could Laurenz have been given his post? How could it be, Jo-Jo? He's got a prison record!'

'No one in my country thinks any the less of him for that,' said Jo-Jo with irritation. 'I told you at the time, it was probably a matter of honour. It will never be held against him.'

'Can you find out if he's really here, Jo-Jo?'

There was a murmur of perplexity. 'The chief of protocol

at the League has left for the day by now. I can try tomorrow, if you like.'

'Please, Jo-Jo, try him first thing. And ring me! Ring me as soon as you have anything.'

'Christina, you're not thinking of—'

'I must see him, Jo-Jo.'

'No! I forbid it!'

There was a tap on her door. She called, 'Who is it?' and voices from the corridor said, 'We're ready to go, Dr Holt. Are you coming?'

'I have to go, Jo-Jo, there's a party on tonight. Ring me tomorrow.'

She didn't wait for a yes or no but hung up the phone and hurried to the door. Taxis were waiting to take them to the Town Hall.

The summer evening lay like a golden net over the city. The taxis bore them swiftly past the pavement cafés where the Genevois were sipping an aperitif prior to the evening meal. At the Town Hall hats and wraps were taken by white-gloved footmen, and they were shown up a wide staircase to a fine room on the first floor.

The director of Education and his wife greeted their honoured guests. The room was already half full. A junior official, directed to offer introductions, led Christina to a group. A waiter brought white Swiss wine in crystal glasses.

There was the usual small talk: how do you like Geneva, isn't it a fine summer, I hear you have a strike in England, is your conference making progress . . . ?

The junior official reappeared. 'Dr Holt, may I present Dr Nedjozic of the delegation of the Kingdom of Serbs, Croats and Slovenes. He is very anxious to speak with you of children in post-war situations.'

She turned and held out her hand. It was taken by a small balding man with an anxious expression.

Standing next to him was Laurenz Varikiav.

Chapter Thirty-one

If she hadn't had a scant few hours' warning of his presence in Geneva, Dr Christina Holt might have disgraced herself in front of her colleagues by fainting dead away. As it was, she still felt all the breath go out of her body as her eyes met his.

She didn't give her hand in greeting. She knew she couldn't stay calm under his touch. They bowed to each other gravely.

Talk flowed on amongst the group. Dr Nedjozic wanted to put up the case for Serbian orphans of the Great War. 'We have many, my dear lady,' he told her, speaking in French, the language of their hosts. 'You may not be aware, our country was occupied by the enemy. Whole families were eliminated, but sometimes merely broken up. Then the children, you see . . .'

She nodded and agreed and made sensible sounds. She didn't volunteer the information that she had seen the plight of the children of Serbia under war conditions at first hand. By and by, Dr Nedjozic was given a little nudge by a watchful Swiss official, realised he had taken up enough of the lady doctor's time and, with a smile of thanks, turned away.

Laurenz lingered a moment. 'We must talk,' he murmured.

'But not here.'

'No, but it will end soon. Have you a dinner engagement?'

'Yes, but I can break it.'

'I'll wait for you outside.'

She nodded, and he followed his chief. A perplexed

Belgian took the place of Dr Nedjozic, wanting to know if psychology had as yet learned how to handle word-blindness in children. 'We have recently become aware of this problem. Is it a result of war shock, or has it always been there unnoticed?'

She listened, offered what she knew, and so the reception went on until its climax, a little speech of appreciation by the director of Education.

The doctors began to filter towards the staircase. Christina had promised to go with a group to dine at La Perle, but excused herself on the grounds that something important had come up. The others collected hats and wraps and went off in half a dozen taxis.

It was still bright outside, though the shadows were long as the sun waned towards the west. The streets were busy with traffic as the Genevois set off for the sedate pleasures of theatre and concert hall. Music spilled out from cafés, there were street musicians at the corners. The lake gleamed golden in the sunset.

Out on the pavement, Christina looked about. A tall figure emerged from the shadows of the maple trees.

'Here I am.'

She joined him. They stood looking at each other.

'Where shall we go?'

'I don't know. I don't know Geneva very well.'

'Nor I. I only took up the post about a month ago.'

'Somewhere quiet, Laurenz.'

'Very well.'

He hailed a taxi. The driver nodded in understanding – a quiet restaurant for two unhappy lovers; for he could see by their faces that they were not happy.

He took them to a café on the other side of the Rhône, in a side-street leading from the Rue du Temple. It was the kind of place used by the locals: known for its good Swiss wine, its generous portions of food, its respectability. Laurenz's request for a quiet corner was easily granted. They were given a table outdoors in the paved garden, with a trellis of roses for shelter.

'Are you hungry?' he asked her when the waiter presented the menu.

'Not at all.'

'A bottle of the house wine,' Laurenz said, waving the man away.

They made small talk until the wine had been brought and poured. Then, in the chequered twilight, they sat silent. There was so much to say. Neither knew how or where to begin.

'Why did you never tell me you were married?' Christina asked at last in a weary voice.

'Because I thought Franzisca was dead.'

'But she wasn't.'

'No.' He seemed to shrink from further explanation, then drew a deep breath. 'How did you find out?'

'I came looking for you, Laurenz. An official in Belgrade told me you were serving a prison sentence, but that I couldn't visit you because only family were allowed. He said you had a wife and two children. I met the children this afternoon.'

'Ah. That's why you didn't seem surprised when you saw me.'

'You weren't surprised either. You were expecting to see me.'

'I saw your name on the guest list this morning. I . . . I longed to see you again. I rang the hotel this afternoon, but they said you were out.'

'Tell me about your wife.'

He took a long time before he began. 'This isn't an easy thing to tell. First I must explain that I loved Franzisca. I'd known her since childhood. We were married in 1912, Milovan was born a year later. He was still a baby in arms when the Bulgars overran my home at the beginning of their offensive.'

'Go on.'

'I had been called to the service of King Peter as soon as war was declared. What I know of the events after I left, I only learned by hearsay. There were practically no men left in our village, they had all gone to the army. But the old men and the boys put up a defence that made the enemy colonel angry. So he decided to make an example of the survivors. All males were to be shot, all the women . . . Well . . . You understand . . .'

Christina reached out a hand to cover the clenched fist that lay on the table by his wine-glass. It was the first time they had touched. 'I'm sorry,' she said.

'A few of the *zagruda* managed to hide and so they got away. They told me that the last thing they saw was Franzisca throwing herself in the river with the baby in her arms.'

'Oh God, Laurenz.'

'They thought she was dead and so did I. She and Milovan.'

'But the official in Belgrade told me you had two children, Laurenz.'

His face was grim. 'When I left Horamesc I had one child, a son. The girl, Suza, isn't mine. She's the daughter of the Bulgarian colonel who kidnapped my wife and made her live with him as his mistress.'

'But you said . . . you said she drowned herself!'

'She tried to, to get out of the hands of the soldiers. I don't think I said . . . she was a very beautiful girl. Colonel Paspelevh had taken a fancy to her so he had her fished out, on a whim, she and the baby who was wrapped against her body in the way our women do . . . you know, with a shawl?'

She nodded in recollection.

'She tried to fight him off. He told her he liked a woman "with a bit of spirit" and offered her a bargain – he would spare the life of her little boy if she would agree to sleep with him.' Laurenz stopped, staring down at the table top. 'I don't know if you can understand this, Christina, but she accepted.'

'Of course.'

He looked up. 'You think she was right?'

'To save her son? Of course!'

He sat unspeaking for a long moment, then drank some

wine. His voice was low and harsh, as if it came from a parched throat.

'I learned this after I went to Bulgaria to look for our missing prisoners. I found some in a camp, and they told me they knew my wife was still alive. She had agreed to the colonel's terms, given the baby to another of the women prisoners, and gone to his room. Next morning she took poison.'

'Laurenz! Laurenz, don't tell me any more. I don't have the right to put you through this!'

'No, I want you to know. I need to share it with someone, and you're the only person in the world I could tell it to, my dear one.'

Her grip tightened on his hand. He turned his over to twine fingers with hers.

'Colonel Paspelevh called the regimental surgeon to save her life but Franzisca was always in poor health after that. She bore him a daughter and later, so I'm told, there was another child which died. By this time she was only half aware of her surroundings. You must understand she wasn't the only woman carried off: some of them told me what she went through.'

'And the children?' Christina asked.

'The children – yes. Milovan was three when Suza was born. He seems to have learned early how to look after himself and pretty soon he took over the care of Suza, because Franzisca couldn't do it. They were tolerated by the soldiers, who dragged them around with them all through the Serbian campaign and then back into Bulgaria as they retreated. I came on the scene when Milovan was six: I was a stranger who drove up to the estate where Paspelevh was hiding out with them, and took them all away to more strangers in Sofia.'

The waiter reappeared to ask if there was anything they required. Laurenz shrugged, but Christina ordered coffee. She felt the break in tension would help Laurenz. While they waited for it she said, 'I'm a specialist in children's mental disorders now. That's what I decided to do with my life after the war. What you've just been telling me explains something I didn't understand this afternoon – Milovan's aggressive attitude, his protectiveness towards his sister.'

'Milovan . . . I don't know what to do about him. He resents me – and why shouldn't he? I took him and his mother and little sister away from the environment that he knew how to deal with, and gave them to people he didn't know. I told him it was for his own good, that everything was going to be better now. But then *I* disappeared.'

'Into prison?'

The waiter brought the coffee, and at a sign from Christina cleared away the empty wine bottle and the glasses. Laurenz had appeared indifferent when she ordered the coffee, but he drank it thirstily. 'I have to admit,' he said with a tired grin, 'that Swiss coffee is better than Balkan coffee.'

'Anything would be better than Balkan coffee,' Christina agreed, returning his smile. 'Tell me about the trial.'

He shrugged. 'It was really an open and shut case. I killed Colonel Paspelevh – I had no choice but to kill him or be killed by him. Fate was on my side. I pleaded guilty and that ought to have been the end of it, but some idiot in the Serbian Foreign Office thought there ought to be diplomatic intervention and so it was nearly a year before I was brought to trial. There were "extenuating circumstances" so I got five years.'

'And Franzisca and the children?' she asked.

'Franzisca stayed in Sofia with the children so as to visit me. But her health was undermined. She died two years before my release. My cousin Vela Kargiash took over the care of the children. They weren't allowed to visit – only children over sixteen were allowed. I used to see them from a window from time to time. So Cousin Vela took them home to Horamesc and looked after them, since there was no one else to do it. My grandparents and my mother died in the initial attack on the village, my father was killed in the war we were fighting back in 1912.'

'Laurenz, I'm so sorry. So sorry.'

He accepted the genuine sense of grief behind the conventional words. They sat without speaking.

Staring fixedly at the shiny brown coffee pot, Laurenz began again. 'In prison I tried never to think of you, Christina. I knew that at the end of my sentence it would be my duty to try to make a life with Franzisca and my son and . . . and the little girl. But after she died, I sometimes thought . . . But I expected you to be married and settled down with some respectable Englishman.'

She held out her left hand for him to examine. 'No wedding ring, Laurenz.'

'I don't know what to say to you. I haven't put my life together as yet. King Alexander asked me to take this post in Geneva because he felt Nedjozic was too easily swayed. I don't know if I'm going to be any good at it. And then there are the children. Milo is a difficult boy . . .'

'And no wonder!'

'Yes, I see that, but I don't know how to . . .' He gave up trying to explain his feelings. 'He doesn't like me. He knows he must respect me but . . . I don't seem to . . . And as for the girl, she's afraid of me. I think the only person she really trusts is Milo.'

'That's understandable. He's been the only constant thing in a changing world.'

'My cousin told me it was my duty to bring them here and get to know them. That's what I'm trying to do. Perhaps you'll give me some advice on how to do it, Christina.' He studied her. Over her plain black dress she wore an evening jacket of black and gold Japanese brocade which glowed in the lamplight of the café. Her short pale hair had taken on a halo effect. 'You don't look like a doctor specialising in mental disorders,' he said with something like a sparkle of amusement in his dark eyes.

'What should a specialist in mental disorders look like?' she countered. 'I've found that if I adopt a severe style it frightens my patients, most of whom are under sixteen years old. The world's frightening enough for children these days. I feel it's my job to help them face it.'

'How long have you been doing it? Did you go straight home from Belgrade?'

'No, I went to the Crimea.' She told him about her appalling year among the stateless children and her efforts not to let them be abandoned. She glossed over her subsequent illness. She told him Jo-Jo was still her best friend, gave him news of other members of the hospital staff.

They spent a long time reminiscing. She drew him out, learned about his home, that he had given up leadership of the *zagruda*, and from there tried to get him to talk about prison life. He shied away from it. 'It's too ugly, my darling.'

She knew she must get him to talk about it, that otherwise it would fester and haunt him, but there was no hurry. Now that she had found him again, she knew they would have many evenings like this, evenings when they could sit and talk without restraint, without pressure.

A cooling breeze arose from the lake. She shivered. 'Shall we go inside? Shall we order something to eat?' Laurenz asked.

She rose from the table. 'Let's go home, Laurenz.'

'Home?'

'To my hotel.'

He left money on the table. They went out through the café and into the narrow street. At the top of the rise they found a taxi. 'Hotel du Chevron,' Christina said.

On the drive, they sat close together, heads touching, hands clasped. They went into the hotel, Christina retrieved her key, and they went up in the lift in silence.

It was about eleven o'clock. From the bar, the faint strains of a piano playing American popular songs drifted up, but this was a respectable Swiss hotel, most of its occupants in bed and asleep.

She unlocked her room door, took the 'Do not Disturb' sign and hung it on the outside door knob. She closed the door, locked it.

As she turned, Laurenz took her in his arms. They shared their first searing kiss of reunion. Fierce and yet tender, they clung together, murmuring endearments, moulding their bodies to each other, binding themselves to one another with arms made stronger than steel in their ardour. Their cheeks were wet with tears – most were Christina's perhaps, but not all.

After lost moments, they became aware of their surroundings. Christina went to the windows, opened them, pushed open the outer shutter to allow the sweet night air to enter. A pale light came in from the streetlamp a few yards down the avenue. In its light they undressed, clothes thrown haphazardly on chairs and side-tables.

They gave themselves up to their love like desert travellers who have found an oasis. Avid, eager, they drowned in its welcoming depths. Clocks in towers struck the hours, but they scarcely heard. They were lost in each other, needing neither time nor space except what their bodies could encompass.

The pearly dawn of summer found them entwined in each other's arms, murmuring in argument.

'But why should we delay, Christina? We've lost so many years already.'

'But we can't just get married, not without preparing the children for it. Think, darling! Milovan is full of aggression already, and from what you say Suza has problems coping with life. How can they possibly deal with a stranger like me?'

'All I know is that I can't live without you now I've got you back! Christina, can't we live for ourselves just this once? Do we have to consider others?'

'You know we do. Your children have had a terrible life. We don't want to make it worse. Be reasonable.'

'I don't want to be reasonable. I want to be married.'

'So do I, oh so do I! But that's only a formality, after all. You know I belong to you and I know you belong to me.'

'Yes,' he agreed, holding her closer, 'that's true.'

Unwillingly he rose. It was time for him to go: the hotel would soon be stirring into life and he ought to be at home in time to share breakfast with his children.

'When shall I see you? Can we have lunch together?'

'I'm supposed to eat lunch in the hotel with the other delegates . . .' She was pulling on a soft silk kimono as she spoke. 'I wonder if I shall be doing the least bit of good by attending any of the sessions? I'm sure I shan't hear a word that's said; I'll be thinking of *you*, Laurenz.'

'Think of me all the time, until we see each other again. At lunch?'

'Oh, yes! Where? When?'

'Come to the Palais de la Paix. The restaurant there is good. Twelve-thirty?'

'All right. And Laurenz, ask the children to lunch too.'

'No!'

'But darling—'

'No, not yet. Not yet, Christina. Let me have you all to myself for a little while longer.'

'Well . . . All right. But soon, Laurenz. You must start talking to them about me so that it isn't a shock when we meet.'

'Oh, God,' groaned Laurenz, pausing with his evening tie in his hand, 'why can't it all be easy? Why do we have to waste time and thought on what others are going to feel?'

She put her fingers on his lips to still his lament. She kissed him lightly. 'Time to go,' she said. 'See you in another six hours.'

'Six hours! Already I'm beginning to feel afraid that it will all turn out to be a dream.'

'It's no dream, my dear one. No dream.'

When he left she went to the window to watch for him. He looked up as he came out of the hotel entrance. She waved, he waved back. She watched him walk to the corner. He looked up at her as he turned it and paused for a moment. Then the tall angular figure was gone.

Unable to rest, she bathed, dressed, and went out. The café at the station was open – the Swiss were early risers. She found she was ravenously hungry and ordered a *café complêt*, to still the immediate hunger pangs, then sat watching the city come to life.

I am happy, she said to herself; at this moment I'm the

happiest woman in the world. No matter what problems may lie ahead, I'll remember this moment and it will give me courage.

She bought an English language newspaper to keep her amused until the first session of the conference. She went back to the hotel unwillingly, and certainly most of what was said went straight past her. About ten o'clock she was called out of the conference hall to take an urgent phone call.

It was Jo-Jo in Lugano. 'Christina? I got through to the Palais des Nations first thing. You're quite right, Laurenz is—'

'I know, Jo-Jo, I know – calm down. I met him last night.'

'Met him?' There was a crackling pause on the line. 'What does that mean?'

'Never mind. Thank you for making the inquiry for me, but everything is all right.'

'How do you mean, all right? What yarn has he been spinning?'

'Jo-Jo, please! Don't talk like that about him. I assure you, all the suspicions you've had of him are quite wrong. I can't stop now, I'm supposed to be taking part in a discussion on Muscular Distress in Malnourished Children—'

'Chrissie, *please* don't let him hoodwink you.'

'I'll tell you all about it when you get back. You'll be sorry you talked about him like that. Bye for now, Jo-Jo.'

The morning session seemed to last for ever. As soon as she could, Christina got away from the little groups that always formed to argue over each lecture. She rushed up to her room, brushed her hair, put on her hat and gloves, and took a taxi to the Palais de la Paix.

Laurenz was waiting to meet her in the vestibule and guide her through the formalities of entering the building. The restaurant was a pleasant venue, their meal was excellent. From time to time people coming or going would nod to Laurenz. 'I'm just beginning to be known by the other "residents",' he explained. 'It's a little world of its own. Milo hates it – he says he can't understand why I want to work here when I could be looking after the farms at Horamesc.'

'Of course, now I understand why I met them on the Quai Wilson. They'd been here to lunch with you?'

He nodded. 'It's part of the campaign to get to know them better, but so far it hasn't worked very well.'

'Laurenz, give yourself time! You've only been home, how long?'

'Two months or so.'

'You can't expect to build up a family life in two months.'

'You wanted to get to know them,' he said. 'Will you come to church on Sunday?'

'Church?'

'Of course, church. On Sundays don't you go to church?'

'Well . . . no, as a matter of fact. Not often.'

'Well, one of the things I've discovered about the children is that they were brought up by their mother to go to church every Sunday. I suppose it was some comfort to poor Franzisca . . . And when she got them back to Horamesc, Cousin Vela of course took them.'

'I see. But is there an Eastern Orthodox church here?'

'Of course! Switzerland is full of refugees: White Russians, Balkan radicals, Albanian nationalists . . . We share a church and alternate services are held on alternate weeks. The Eastern Orthodox one is next Sunday. Will you come?'

It was a good way to meet his children on more or less neutral ground. 'Very well,' she agreed.

'I thought we could meet as if by accident.'

'No, Laurenz! No tricks! Tell them I'll be there.'

'But—'

'Don't make a big event of it. Try to be casual. What I'd like,' she said with quiet earnestness, 'is to be their friend before ever I become their stepmother.'

'Whatever you say,' he replied.

He came to her late that night, and the next. Their lives felt so intertwined now that she could sense when he was near; she would be at her room door opening it for him as he raised his hand to knock. Their lovemaking still had an urgency something like desperation, as if they were afraid they would lose each other again.

'I still can't believe I've found you again,' he murmured as they sat up sipping chilled wine in the middle of a hot summer night. 'I get a feeling ten times a day that I ought to rush here, to make sure you haven't gone.'

'I shan't go, Laurenz.'

'When the conference ends?'

'No. I shall stay.'

'I felt sure you'd feel duty-bound to go back to London.'

She shook her head. 'The General Strike's still on, everything is difficult. I rang my receptionist this morning, she's cancelled all my appointments. There's really nothing to take me back. Thank heaven,' she added, leaning against his shoulder with a little laugh.

'Tomorrow you meet Milo and Suza.'

'What have they said about it?'

'They don't show the least interest.'

'Really? Or is Milo keeping his feelings back?'

'No, they really don't seem interested.'

'Good.'

'Good? But I *want* them to be interested! I want them to like you.'

'All in good time, my darling.'

He let his intuition guide him. It told him she knew more about children than he ever would.

Sunday was a 'rest day' for the delegates: there was a planned excursion by lake steamer. She excused herself from it. When someone asked why, she said, 'I have to go to church,' which led her questioner to think she had a guilty conscience and needed to go to confession. He had a feeling this might be so – he was certain he had glimpsed a man coming out of her room early that morning.

It was now August. The weather was hot. Christina had chosen a dress of dark blue cotton voile with a white collar, and with it she wore Captin Dinsdorf's gold chain – for luck, she told herself.

The church was in Cité Val d'Arve. The taxi-driver

looked at her with interest when she asked for it. 'You a Russkie? You don't look like it,' he remarked.

There was a little crowd around the stone church, chatting in the sunshine. She saw Laurenz at once, formal in his dark Sunday suit. The two children were standing beside him watching sail-boats on the river.

'Hello, Laurenz,' she said, taking the initiative as she saw how uncertain he was. 'I thought I'd find you here.'

'Good morning, Christina. I believe you've met my son and daughter.'

'Yes indeed – Thursday afternoon, wasn't it?'

Suza Varikiav gazed at her in alarm. Was this smartly dressed lady going to tell Father about their boating escapade? She was sure they had been doing wrong, and was the more sure of it because Milo hadn't mentioned it to Father and had told her she mustn't either.

'How do you do?' Milo said politely. 'How nice to see you again.' He was looking at her anxiously. He knew grown-ups. They were apt to make supposedly jokey remarks such as, 'Learned to handle a boat yet?' or, 'So you didn't drown yourself after all!' Which would then call for explanation, and rebukes from Father because Milo knew – had known all along – that he shouldn't have been tampering with that row-boat.

'Nice to see *you*,' said Christina. And, anticipating his fears, went on with a smile, 'I enjoyed our ice-cream together.' She turned to Laurenz. 'I explained to you,' she said, so that Milo would know, 'that they attracted my attention because they were speaking Serbian.'

Milo relaxed visibly. She wasn't so bad, this stranger. When Father said 'an old friend of his', he'd expected someone sombre and reserved, like Father himself, but no, here was this nice lady who'd bought them ice-cream and appeared quite willing to forget about the boat.

They went into the church. It struck Milo afterwards that she didn't seem very sure of the order of the service, and certainly she didn't cross herself in the devout way Mama used to, but then she was a foreigner, after all.

Christina was often at a loss during the service, but she couldn't fail to be touched by the fervour of the congregation and the angelic singing of the choir. Memories streamed back of the Christmas service at the hospital in the awful cold of the Serbian mountains: the Serbian army chaplain in his worn uniform; the wounded men in their beds with their brilliant eyes fixed on him; the strong male voices raised in the hymns, tunes that soared and swooped like the rivers and waterfalls of their homeland.

The service seemed to end abruptly. All at once the congregation, standing all the while, now turned to each other and began talking and embracing. Laurenz embraced Christina. 'Never miss an opportunity,' he whispered in her ear.

Afterwards they went for a walk by the River Arve. Laurenz had wanted them all to go out to lunch together, but Christina didn't want to press matters so hard. Meeting a stranger and feeling at least a tepid interest in her was enough for now. To have to sit through lunch with her might be a trial.

They sauntered along in the sunshine. They talked about the boats on the river, about the probability of there being fish in it and whether they would be worth eating. Laurenz asked Christina if she remembered how they had tried to catch fish at Vranja. She laughed. 'It was like the parable, wasn't it? Eighteen fish among a whole hospital of sick men.'

'Vranja?' Milovan interjected. Vranja was part of an heroic Serbian story. 'Not during the war?'

'Oh yes. Christina was attached to the medical staff of the Serbian Army.'

'A woman doctor?' the boy said, aghast. 'Impossible!'

His little sister caught at his shirt sleeve in alarm. Clearly it was the first time the boy had ever dared contradict his father.

As she explained that, yes, indeed, she and a team of women doctors had formed one of the main field hospitals for the Serbians, that this was where she and Laurenz had met, Christina watched the boy. He in his turn was watching his father. She saw he was trying to piece together the story of this man's life, a man almost totally unknown to him.

Her heart filled with pity for Milo. The strict Serbian sense of family, of family duty, laid it upon him as a law that he must respect and love his father. But how do you love a man you don't even know? No wonder he was full of confusion and anger.

She kept the conversation going about the war, about how Captain Varikiav would ride in from his forays among the mountains on behalf of the King, how together they had gone to beg supplies from the *bogan*, the hoarder, at Tezelk.

'That foolish old man—'

'Laurenz, he was ill – I told you at the time.'

'Ill? He was as fit as I was.'

'He was sick with worry for his people. Worry can make you ill,' she added, speaking more to the children than Laurenz. 'And not knowing what's going to happen – anxiety – a lot of people have things wrong with them because they feel lost and anxious.'

'What kind of things?' asked Milo. 'Suza gets pains in her stomach sometimes, and gets dizzy . . .'

'Yes, that kind of thing,' Christina agreed. 'And sometimes it makes people angry and aggressive. The poor old man at Tezelk, he threatened us with a knife.'

'You're too softhearted, Christina,' Laurenz said, half laughing and half annoyed. 'He could have stabbed us full of holes.'

'Oh yes. Frightened people do all kinds of silly things.' But enough had been said on the point. She turned the conversation.

On the whole, when they parted, she was pleased at how things had gone. Milovan, the leader of the two, had not reacted against her: on the contrary he seemed to have found her interesting because she could tell him things about the main problem in his life, his father. Suza tended to follow Milo's lead and was in any case a more affectionate child.

It was at least a beginning.

Although Laurenz wanted them to meet again next day,

she avoided that. 'Not too fast,' she warned him that evening. 'It went well today, but we don't want to rush it.'

'When, then?' he demanded. 'I want us to be married, Christina. The way we're going on now, it's as if we were conducting an affair and you have a jealous husband!'

'No, you have jealous children.'

'Jealous? They don't like me enough to be jealous.'

'You're all they've got,' she told him.

The conference toiled to its close. The other delegates wrote up the report with at least some help from Christina, although her thoughts were often elsewhere. The doctors and orphanage-managers packed up and went home. Christina stayed on at the Hotel du Chevron, where Jo-Jo came to find her on her return from Lugano.

'So!' she challenged. 'You've met our Monarchist friend Laurenz and he's convinced you he didn't deceive you.'

'Jo-Jo, sit down and listen.' She told her friend the story, and Jo-Jo, ever emotional and ready to identify with suffering, began to cry.

'Oh, Christina! Christina, how could I have been so unjust to him! What he has suffered!'

'Darling, don't get in a state about it. You couldn't possibly know.'

'But *you* knew! You never would think ill of him.'

'But I love him.'

'And he? Does he feel the same?'

Christina nodded. Jo-Jo threw her arms around her, hugging her and weeping into her short-cropped hair. 'Oh, darling Chrissie, I'm so happy for you! When's the wedding?'

'Not until I've won his children over.'

'What?' Jo-Jo sat back, glaring at her with tear-bright eyes. 'My God, you're not going to let the children stop you?'

Christina groaned inwardly. The hardest part of her work was persuading adults that you couldn't treat children like bales of cotton or packets of groceries, to be handed about without concern. So little was known about the working of the child's mind, so very little. Harm done in infancy, in childhood, could reverberate through adult life with crippling effect.

She tried to explain some of this to her friend, but Jo-Jo was of the school of doctors who believed that most things could be treated with a dose of tonic and the injunction to 'pull yourself together'.

'Well, I see you're determined to do it your way,' she sighed. 'How long do you think it's going to take?'

'There's no way of knowing. But I think they quite like me. We've seen each other three times now, and Milovan seems . . . well, he doesn't trust people easily but I think he's beginning to trust me.'

'Are you saying that you're letting a thirteen-year-old boy put a brake on your life?'

'Yes, but only on the marriage. In other respects . . .'

Jo-Jo laughed. 'I won't ask,' she said.

Late in August there was a civic festival in Geneva, a day of processions and public entertainment. Already bunting was flying over the streets, garlands decorated lampposts and flags – the Swiss love flags – flew everywhere. Milovan Varikiav asked Christina what it was all about. He'd already asked their housekeeper, Madame Pluchet, but his French was so poor that he didn't understand her replies.

'It's a big event, I gather,' Christina told him. 'There's a procession, with giants—'

'Giants?' he interrupted, disdain on his face. 'There are no such things.'

'*Grosses-têtes* – have you never seen them?' She thought a moment. 'Perhaps they don't have them in Serbia. I was never there in peacetime so I don't know. And in fact we don't have them in England either.' She explained about the figures, ten times the size of real life, who danced and cavorted through a continental carnival.

'Really?' said Suza, her eyes wide.

'I'd love to see that!' her brother cried. Putting a casual arm round his sister's shoulders he added, 'It's all right, Suza, I wouldn't let them hurt you.'

'They hurt no one,' Christina said. 'They're big kind fools. I'll tell you what – let's all go to watch them, and we can take a picnic, and—'

'Oh, that would be lovely.'

'And afterwards,' Laurenz put in, catching the spirit of the thing, 'we can go for a trip on a lake steamer. Would you like that? We could go to Montreux and back.'

'Oh, *Father*, that would be great!'

'You're keen to go on a steamer?' Laurenz said, surprised.

'Of course! I've been dying to ever since we got here.'

'Why didn't you say so, Milo?' his father said in surprise.

No one pursued that point. They all entered into plans for the great day.

Christina went back to the Hotel du Chevron full of optimism. There had been a feeling in that discussion, like a family looking forward to a day off.

The receptionist handed her her key but detained her. 'Mademoiselle, there is a telegram for you.'

A telegram. Telegrams always brought bad news. She tore it open.

COME AT ONCE. YOUR BROTHER HAS DISAPPEARED.

She stared at it, horrified. Not only for the news it contained, but because of the signature.

It was signed, 'Mother'. Something truly dreadful must be in train, if her mother had taken it upon herself to send a telegram.

Chapter Thirty-two

The receptionist was standing by, attentive and anxious to be helpful.

'Please get this long-distance number for me,' Christina said, scribbling the number of the family home in Lincolnshire. 'Put it through to my room.'

'As soon as possible, mademoiselle.'

She was already packing when the phone rang. 'You're thr-r-rough,' sang an English voice, and she heard the click and the ringing at the other end.

The maid picked up the receiver. 'Mr Holt's residence.'

'This is Dr Christina Holt here. Please let me speak to my mother.'

'Just a moment, please.'

Crackles and hissings on the line, the sound of distant angry voices. Then her father, almost shouting. 'Christina? I was absolutely furious when I discovered that your mother—'

'Father, what's the news on Elwin?'

'That fool of a boy! I don't know what's got into him since he came home from the war.'

'Father, is he home again?'

'No he isn't, and if he does come here I can tell you he's going to get a piece of my mind.'

'How long has he been gone?'

'Four days now, but—'

'And no news of him?'

'None at all, and it's very inconsiderate.'

'Have you informed the police?'

'The police? Just because Elwin decides to play the fool?'

491

'Father, he might be hurt, have had an accident.'

'Then we'd have heard: he has his notecase and wallet.'

'I'm coming home at once—'

'Don't be silly! Travelling is almost impossible with this stupid strike.'

'It's not difficult on the continent. I'll manage somehow once I get to England.'

'No, Christina, I forbid you to upset your own plans.'

'Let me speak to Mother.'

'Oh, she's in floods of tears, you'll get no sense out of her.'

'Father, please let me speak to my mother.'

She heard him give a little gasp, then there was a long pause.

True enough, Mrs Holt was crying so hard she could scarcely enunciate. 'Oh, Christina . . .'

'Did Elwin say anything to you, Mother?'

'Nothing. Nothing, but then you know . . . Christina . . . he never talked about his troubles . . . Oh, I feel I failed him . . . my own son.'

'Have you tried to find him? What have you done?'

'I telephoned everybody . . . I tried to think . . . Dorothy is so shocked and angry . . . She says it's another woman but you know . . . Christina, Elwin isn't . . . Oh . . .'

'Try not to cry, Mother. Did Elwin take any clothes with him?'

'Dorothy says not.'

'You must inform the police.'

'The police?' cried Mrs Holt.

There was a muffled sound, then an annoying interlude which ended when her father spoke again. 'We certainly are *not* informing the police,' he cried. 'What, a respectable family like mine . . .'

She put the phone down as he was still expostulating.

Christina rang the hotel desk and asked them to prepare her bill and reserve a sleeper on the next train to Paris. When she got downstairs the receptionist had carried out her instructions. He looked at her single valise.

'Mademoiselle is not leaving for good, I take it?'

'No, please keep my room. I'll telephone you in a day or two to let you know my plans.'

'Very well, mademoiselle. Anything else?'

'A taxi, please.'

'It's too early to go to Cornavin for the train—'

'I have something else to do first.'

She gave the taxi-driver the address of Laurenz's apartment. She had never yet been there and, in a way, it was a necessary step she was now taking – the time would come when she would have to visit the family in their home. But not for such a reason . . .

It was about eight o'clock when she reached the apartment block off the Boulevard Carl Voge. She asked the man to wait, leaving her overnight case in the car. The door was opened by a buxom Swiss woman in a dark dress – Madame Pluchet.

'Would you tell M. Varikiav that Dr Holt is here?'

'Dr Holt, of course! Please come in.' She was shown into the vestibule but shook her head at Madame's offer to take her hat and coat.

Laurenz came hurrying out of the dining-room, napkin still in his hand. 'Christina! Come in, come in, we're just finishing supper.'

The two children were still at the table. Suza had a large glass of milk in her hand, Milo was eating a piece of cherry tart. They gaped at the sight of Christina.

'I've come to say I have to go home to England,' she plunged in.

'Go home?'

'It's an emergency.'

'How long will you be gone?' Suza demanded, putting down her glass with such suddenness that the contents slurped over on to the cloth.

'I don't know – a week, perhaps two . . .'

'But the festival! You promised to take us to the festival next Saturday.'

'I'm sorry, I can't. Something very important has come up.'

Milo threw himself back in the dining-chair with a gesture of disgust. 'It's always the same with grown-ups,' he grunted. 'Other things are always more important.'

Suza had got up from her chair. She came to take Christina's hand. 'I *want* you to take us,' she urged, staring up at her with dark eyes in which tears were beginning to sparkle.

Christina knelt so as to be on the same level as her. 'Darling, I want to take you. But something bad has happened at home.'

'Where you come from in England?'

'Yes, it's a place in the country. My parents live there, and my brother.'

'You've got a brother?' Suza said. She glanced at Milo. 'Older or younger than you?'

'Older. He's a grown man, his name is Elwin.' She looked up at Laurenz, who was standing watching the scene in bewilderment. 'Elwin has disappeared, Laurenz,' she said.

'What?'

'I got this telegram.' She held it out, creased from being thrust in her coat pocket.

It was Milo who took it. He tried to decipher it, but handed it on to his father. 'It's in English,' he said.

Laurenz read it. 'Perhaps it's not so bad . . .'

'You don't understand. My mother sent that telegram. She's never done such a thing in her life. She must be very frightened.'

Suza leaned closer to Christina. 'What's she frightened of?' she asked in a low voice. 'Is somebody shouting at her and saying bad things?'

Christina put an arm about her in response to the tremor in the child's body. 'No, dear, but she's afraid something bad may have happened to Elwin. I have to go so I can help.'

Milo approached, put a hand on Suza's shoulder to ease her away from Christina. 'It's all right, Suza, don't be afraid,' he said. 'I'll look after you.'

Christina let the little girl go to him. She spoke directly to Milo. 'You understand that I have to go. I'm sorry about the festival, but your father will take you.'

'Father?' he said in surprise, looking towards Laurenz as if the idea of being taken out by his father on a pleasure trip was unthinkable.

'Of course, yes, he'll take you to see the processions and then on the steamer.'

'Will you, Father?' asked Milo with a frowning glance at him.

'Certainly. We'll have the whole day together, doing whatever you want to do.'

'I want Christina to come,' Suza insisted, tears beginning to trickle down her cheeks.

'I wish I could, Suza, but I must go. You see that, don't you? It's my brother. Think if something had happened to Milo.'

'Oh no!' Suza clutched her brother's arm. 'Don't say things like that.'

Milo gave her a hug. 'I'm all right, I'm here, don't be silly, Suza.' To Christina he said somewhat grudgingly, 'I understand that you must go to England. It's a long way, isn't it?'

'Yes, at least a day's journey.'

'So even if you sorted things out quickly you couldn't get back for Saturday.'

'No, I'm afraid not, ' she said, trying with a tremendous effort to keep her own anxiety out of her voice.

'All right, I suppose we have to put up with it,' the boy said.

'Milo, that's hardly polite—'

Christina stopped Laurenz's reproof with a quick glance. 'Thank you, Milo,' she said, 'I'm glad you understand. Now if you don't mind I'd like to have a word with your father.'

'Well, we haven't finished supper anyway. Come on, Suza.'

'I'm not hungry any more,' his sister said in a voice that just failed to be a sob.

'Oh, come on, have a piece of cherry tart, it's awfully good.'

Laurenz took Christina into the drawing-room. 'What's it

all about, darling? It says "disappeared" – what does it mean?'

Quickly she explained her anxieties about her brother: the episode in France when he'd gone absent without leave rather than return to the front; his difficulties in settling down since returning from the war; his depression. She had no need to labour the point with him. He knew what war could do to a man.

'I don't think his wife understands his problems,' she ended, 'and as for my father . . . Well, I must go home, Laurenz, I must.'

He took her in his arms. 'You told me you would never leave,' he reminded her, but without reproach.

'I meant it. But I didn't foresee this.'

'Come back soon, my darling.'

'I will. As soon as ever I can.'

'There's a strike of some kind in your country, isn't there?'

'A General Strike.' Strange how something that loomed so large for the British meant absolutely nothing here in Geneva. 'But never mind, I'll manage.'

'Ring me as soon as you get there. And take care.'

'Yes, Laurenz, I promise.'

He went down with her to the taxi. They kissed, he handed her into the car and was about to close the door when she stayed his hand.

'Laurenz, will you tell Jo-Jo what's happened? I haven't had a chance to ring her.'

'Of course. Is there anything else I can do?'

'See that the children have a good time on Saturday.'

He gave a rueful smile. 'I don't think I know how to do that,' he confessed.

'Buy them ice-cream.'

Her travel problems didn't begin until Calais. Because of difficulties in docking and handling the ferries at Dover, long delays had built up on the French side. From a bistro Christina tried to put through a call to Geneva but the cranky French telephone system let her down.

To comfort herself she sent postcards to the children. For Suza she chose a picture of kittens with a message in Serbian on the back, 'By the time you get this you'll have had your lovely day's fun. I hope you enjoyed it.'

For Milovan there had to be a more business-like approach. She sent him a picture of the ferryboat with the message, 'Long delays here but when I get to the front of the queue I shall board a ship like this to cross the Channel. Affectionate greetings, Christina.'

She didn't send a card to Laurenz. She guessed the children would flourish theirs at him. She felt sure they would never have received a picture postcard from anyone in their life before.

The ship on which she eventually crossed docked at Folkestone instead of Dover. There was no help with the luggage and the Customs examination was brief. She was told there was no rail service. The queue for taxis was so long she didn't even join it but instead walked into the town, glad she only had her overnight bag. Once there she found a garage that was just about to close for the night and, at great expense, hired a car.

About fifty miles up the road towards London it dawned upon her that finding overnight accommodation might be difficult. She pulled in at the first respectable-looking country inn, was lucky enough to get a room, and fell into bed exhausted at ten.

She reached Market Bresham soon after lunchtime on the following day. Her journey home had taken about three times as long as normal. The door was opened to her by the maid but her mother came swooping around her to fall upon her daughter's neck.

'Oh, Christina, I'm so glad to see you! Things are so absolutely awful!'

The maid managed to take Christina's lightweight travel coat and her bag from her while her mother clung about her, weeping.

'Please, Mother, calm down . . . Now, now, it's all right . . .'

They went into the drawing-room. As she closed the door on them the maid said, 'Shall I bring some tea, ma'am?'

'Oh yes, please, Gracie.'

'And a sandwich, please,' Christina added.

'Haven't you had lunch? Oh, then of course, sandwiches—'

'Cook could probably make you an omelette, miss, if you'd rather?'

'Oh, thank you, yes. And coffee in preference to tea.'

When she had gone, Mildred Holt gave herself up to her tears. She lay back in her favourite chair with her handkerchief to her eyes, sobbing helplessly. The room was dim, the August light kept at bay by the half-closed curtains.

Irritated, Christina threw them open.

'Oh, don't, Christina.'

'We're not having the curtains closed unless you've got one of your migraines. It's as if we're in mourning! Now, now, Mother, stop crying . . .'

She could hear the practised ease of her mother's sobs. Mildred Holt was apt to take refuge in sobbing when things got difficult.

'Have you heard from Elwin?'

'Not a word!'

'What's being done?'

'Done? I don't understand—'

'Where's Father?'

'At the office, of course. And he's so *angry* with your brother! You can't imagine how awful it's been.'

'What do the police say?'

'The police? We haven't told the police!' cried Mrs Holt, shocked into sitting upright.

'But in heaven's name, why not? Elwin's been missing for over a week and you—'

'But Christina, suppose they found him and he was with another woman? It would be so *awful* and there would have to be a divorce – a *divorce*, in our family!'

'But is there any reason to think he's with another woman?' Christina asked, taken aback at this suggestion.

'We-ell . . . Dottie says . . . she feels sure . . . I mean, she and Elwin haven't . . . they don't . . . I can hardly go into it but . . .'

'You mean, she and Elwin haven't been sleeping together?'

'Christina!'

At this moment the maid Gracie came in to say that the coffee was in the dining-room and she was just about to bring the omelette.

In the dining-room Christina found the curtains half-closed. She opened them, saw to her pleasure that Gracie had had the sense to bring two cups, and poured coffee for herself and her mother.

'And you say there's been no word from Elwin. He hasn't written or telephoned?'

'No, dear.'

'Did he leave a note for Dorothy?'

'No, nothing.'

'What happened, exactly?'

'Christina dear, it was so *awful*! It was the day after their wedding anniversary. Can you imagine? Dottie says he left the house as usual, drove to Market Bresham, parked where he usually parks: the car was found there next day, but there was no sign of Elwin.'

The omelette was brought. As she ate Christina tried to coax information out of her mother, but it seemed that Mildred was more or less in the dark.

After the meal Christina announced she was going into town. 'I'll drop a prescription for a sedative in with the chemist and have it sent up. You must take a dose the minute it arrives, Mother.'

'But I don't need a sedative.'

'I think you do. And it's only mild. You must try to calm down, Mother, and stop working yourself up into a state.'

She walked into the town, glad of the chance to stretch her legs after spending so long in train compartments and ship's cabins and cars. The chemist promised the sedative should go at once with the boy on his bicycle.

The inns which the farmers and traders patronised were closed, because the market's activities ended by mid-morning. But the cafés and tea-houses were catering to the afternoon trade.

Christina went into the one that occupied the corner near where Elwin had parked his car. She ordered tea, which she didn't want, but when the waitress came back to tidy the table she started a conversation.

'Of course I know young Mr Holt,' the girl said, surprised at being asked such a question. Everyone in Market Bresham knew everyone else. 'Know his wife too – she sometimes comes in here.'

'Did you see him park his car outside one day, about a week ago? A week ago yesterday?'

'We always see him. Regular as clockwork. Hasn't been there for the past week, though. He ill or something?'

'Yes, he's ill. Did he do anything that last time you saw him – anything unusual?'

'Funny you should ask! First of all, instead of turning along the pavement here, towards his office, he turned the other way.'

'Towards the Market Square?'

'That's right. And then, funnier still, that evening he never came at five o'clock to drive off. In fact, the car was still there next morning. Young Mrs Holt came about eleven and it was her that drove it off.'

Christina drank half a cup of tea, then left, leaving a substantial tip. She walked towards the Market Square, in the direction of the railway station. Because of the strike, there was no rail service.

A market always has its odd-jobbers hanging about, wait-ing to earn an honest shilling by loading and unloading, pushing trolleys, running errands. Christina was pleased to see that some she recalled from her girlhood were still lounging on the steps of the market cross, older now but still puffing their pipes and enjoying the sun.

'Course I saw young Mr Holt,' said one worthy. 'Cadged a lift off Bailton's lorry, didn't he?' He puffed and spat. 'No train service, o'course. I s'pose his own car had packed up.'

'Which direction did he go?'

'To'rds Cambridge, o'course. That's where Bailton's depot is, outside o' Cambridge.'

And from Cambridge Elwin might have gone on in any direction.

She went back to her father's office. The receptionist, a new girl, didn't know Christina but hurried into the main inner sanctum to announce her. Her father rose to greet her.

'Humph. I expected you before now, since you seemed so set on coming!'

'There were travel difficulties, Father. Have you had any word from Elwin?'

'None at all. I don't know what he thinks he's playing at! But he's never taken himself or his work seriously since he came back from the war!'

He waved her to a chair. 'What good do you suppose you're doing, rushing home like this?'

'At least I can try to keep Mother from getting hysterics. She seems to have no idea what steps you're taking.'

'Steps? What steps should I take? If he wants to run off with some woman—'

'What's this about a woman!' Christina said sharply. 'Mother brought that up too.'

'Well, Dottie says things have been – how shall I say? – not quite right . . .'

'Oh, for goodness sake, just because Elwin didn't come up to expectation as a husband and they took to separate rooms, it doesn't mean he had another woman somewhere. It might equally have been some physical or emotional difficulty if he lost interest in sex.'

'Christina! I forbid you to talk like that!'

She shrugged. 'I'm a qualified doctor and a fully-trained psychiatrist. Sexual problems are quite familiar in my work.'

'It's disgusting! I won't have you talking like that!'

'Father, please stop barking and blustering at me and tell me what you've done to find Elwin,' she said in a flat tone.

501

'If he wants to be in touch, he's the one who—'

'Do you mean to sit there and tell me that my brother's been missing for over a week and you've done nothing?'

'Don't take that tone with me, young lady.'

'You haven't been to the police?'

'No.'

'But why not? Anything might have happened to him. He may be wandering around suffering from loss of memory, or be sick in a hospital.'

'He was perfectly fit. And let me tell you, if he stays away I shall be all the better pleased, because he had been doing some very odd things with his clients' money.'

'Father! Are you saying – something criminal?'

'Cooking the books, it's called. Now you know why I haven't involved the police.'

All at once Christina Holt lost her temper. She sprang up, took a step forward, thumped the desk with her fist. 'I don't believe a word of it!' she flared. 'My brother's not a thief!'

Her father almost shrank back, and looked grateful he had a desk between him and his angry daughter.

'How do you account for the missing dividends, then? I wouldn't have known about it except that he had an appointment with Mrs Dettram and of course didn't keep it because he was gone, and I looked over her papers, and her spring dividends are unaccounted for. So I looked at a couple of others, and there's the same thing. If the accountants were to see it . . .'

'So now he's not a philanderer, he's an embezzler! And this is your own son you're talking about! The one you thought the world of, who was going to be such a credit to you, take your place here when you retired. The war hero who came back to banners across the street – remember? But now he's run off with – how much? A fortune?'

'Well, no . . . A couple of hundred. I can make it up out of my own pocket and no one the wiser. Thank God there isn't an audit due until January.'

'There you are!' Christina cried, pouncing. 'You didn't suspect and he wasn't going to be discovered until January.

And it's not exactly the Crown Jewels, is it? Why in heaven's name should he disappear in the middle of August with a couple of hundred pounds?'

Her father could offer no explanation. Either it was a woman, or it was the money. What else could it possibly be?

Since she now understood his unwillingness to call in the police, she insisted a private detective must be employed. Mr Crouch spent a week of hard work on the case. He ascertained that Elwin had indeed gone to the outskirts of Cambridge with Bailton's lorry, and from there had taken one of the private buses heading south. But at what point he had got off and what he had done then, he couldn't discover. A man in a black jacket and pinstripes in a van or a lorry was nothing to wonder at in these days of the General Strike.

But where was he heading? Was he heading anywhere in particular?

Christina put that point to Laurenz when she rang him to let him know how things were going. As a disinterested observer, she thought he might notice something she was unable to see.

'My poor Christina, it sounds a miserable business. You told me your brother suffered from shell-shock during the war? I have seen men in that condition. Sometimes the world becomes too much for them to cope with.'

'Laurenz! You're not suggesting he . . . he . . .'

'No, no,' he said quickly. 'I'm not suggesting suicide. I don't know the man, it would be too much to think that. But we've all felt the urge to turn our back on our ordinary lives sometimes, just as you say he did. One morning he drives to town as usual but instead of going to his office, he walks the other way.'

'That's what I've been told.'

'I've felt the same impulse, my dear. When I have to go into the Palais des Nations, and know I shall hear the same old wrangling . . . You know that my country has just signed a Treaty of Friendship with Greece? Now all the negotiations over boundaries have to be looked at again, and it all seems so pointless . . .'

He broke off again, and she could almost hear him remonstrating with himself for bothering her with his frustrations. 'But if I were to turn my back on my life in Geneva, I would come straight to you, my love.'

That thought stayed with her long after the telephone call ended. If Laurenz were to turn his back on his ordinary life in Geneva, he would come to her. If Elwin had turned his back on his ordinary life in Lincolnshire, where would he go?

If it were true that there was another woman, he would go to her. But the only evidence for that – if it could be called evidence – came from his wife.

Dorothy was, understandably, very bitter. 'I don't complain about the way our marriage turned out because I never cared very much for that side of it, although of course I would never have been the one to *refuse* and of course it's always the man who makes the demands, isn't it? So I was really quite content when he stopped wanting to, you know, and since it was his idea I took it for granted he was quite happy.'

She wiped away a tear. 'But now of course I see he got tired of me because there was someone else. And what I'm going to tell his darling little girl, I don't know!'

There was nothing to support the myth of 'another woman'. No unexplained outings or nights spent away from home, no 'staying late at the office', no lipstick on collars, nothing.

So he had no fond mistress to turn to. So where would he go if he were in trouble – emotional, spiritual, mental?

All through the night she kept thinking about it, dozing off, and waking to think again: where would Elwin go for sanctuary?

About four o'clock she woke completely. The answer was bright in her mind. To a garden!

When he slipped away from the field hospital in France, he had found himself a garden. At a ruined house in a village called . . . what? . . . Jerache. And there he had talked nostalgically of the times they had played at gardening in their holiday cottage. A cottage in Devon. What was the name of the village?

She sat up, racking her brains. But the name wouldn't come to her. In north Devon, by a stream, with the rocky coast about five miles away.

She slipped out of bed, went downstairs to look for the family album in the bureau of the drawing-room. She turned back its pages to the photographs of their childhood, passing on the way photographs of Elwin and Dorothy at the church, Elwin in uniform, Elwin in cap and gown, Elwin in school clothes . . .

There! The cottage in the background, Mother holding the boy Elwin by the hand and grimacing into the sun. Under the photograph was written, in her mother's careful hand: 'Summer 1897, Hayhoe Cottage, Brinkington.'

Brinkington. She found a road atlas of the UK. South of Bideford, north-west of Torrington – there it was.

She decided to go at once. To wait and try to explain to her parents would only start an argument: What a ridiculous idea, why should he be there, I forbid you to go, if you go I'm coming with you . . .

In her nightgown and bare feet Christina went into the kitchen, made herself some tea, cut some bread and butter. She ate and drank hastily, hating to spare the time but knowing it would be hours before she found a roadside café to eat breakfast.

Upstairs she dressed in haste, packed her valise. She tip-toed downstairs to write a note, which she set prominently on the drawing-room mantelpiece. She went out to the hired car which was parked on the gravel.

There was a slight incline from the house to the gates. She took off the brake and let the car roll down. She braked, got out and opened the gates, tensing in alarm at the hideous shriek they made. But no one stirred indoors, no one opened curtains to look out at her.

She started the car. It sounded very loud in the summer dawn. But she was off down the road without having been delayed by a long family argument.

It was a cross-country journey of about three hundred miles, complicated by the fact that, since there were no trains running, everybody in Great Britain was trying to get about on the roads. But because she'd made such an early start she was well on the way by the time traffic got really heavy around eight o'clock. She stopped for breakfast south of Birmingham. After that it was a slow crawl to Bristol, with extra police and special constables directing traffic in an effort to sort out the jams.

She decided to stay in Bristol overnight although it was still early evening. It had been an exhausting day. She allowed herself a good meal and a good night's sleep.

Next morning the fine August weather had broken. Low cloud hung over the town, and a fine drizzle was drifting in from the sea when her early morning tea arrived, as she had requested, at six. She was on the road by six-thirty, but there was traffic to deal with already in this busy port.

By lunchtime she was in Bideford. Ravenously hungry, she had a meal surrounded by large Devon farmers and their wives. Before she left she asked for directions to Brinkington, and was given contradictory advice. All the same, she got there only half an hour later.

The village seemed almost exactly the same as she remembered it. A sloping main street with a shop, two pubs, several cottages – some thatched, some with more modern roofing. A row of little Georgian houses facing the green. On the green there was now a memorial to the men of Brinkington who had died in the Great War.

She drove on, trying to remember how to find the cottage – Hayhoe Cottage. Her childish feet had taken the route from the village shop to the house many times, but in a car everything was different, the scale was different, the speed of movement much greater.

But there it was, with the name newly painted on the gate. She parked, opened the gate, went in. A woman came from the cottage, a sturdy woman in a yellow print frock and bare legs. The famous 'other woman'? For a moment Christina felt a shiver of apprehension.

'Yes?'

'Is Elwin here?'

'Who?'

'Elwin. Elwin Holt?'

'Sorry, luv.' There was the unmistakable touch of Yorkshire in her speech. 'Bertie! Bertie!'

'What?' The response was an irritated bellow from upstairs.

'There's a young woman asking for sombody.'

Bertie appeared – a young man of about the same age as the woman. He was in flannel trousers and a short-sleeved shirt, pink with sunburn.

'Who were you asking for again?' prompted the woman.

'Elwin Holt.'

'Holt? Nobody of that name here, luv. Sorry.'

'You're here on holiday?'

'S'right.'

'Been here long?'

'Second week. Looks like it's broken up,' he said glumly, looking at the grey sky.

'Have you heard of a Mr Holt in the village?'

'No, not that I recall. Do you, Eileen?'

'What's he like?' Eileen asked.

'Tallish, brown hair, a round face, rather shy . . .'

They shook their heads. 'Try at the village shop. They know everything,' Eileen recommended.

'Thank you,' Christina said, turning to leave.

'Hey,' said Bertie. 'Does he talk like you – I mean, he isn't Devon or owt like that?'

'I suppose he does talk like me,' she said.

'Is he the chap does the jobbing gardening, is that it – you want to hire him?'

'Jobbing gardening!' She caught her breath. 'Yes, that's the man.'

'He's putting up at Mrs Poulter's – back into the village, go down the lane opposite the memorial, it's the cottage with the sweet peas all over the place.'

'Thank you. Thank you very much.'

'Only,' Bertie said, 'his name isn't Holt, it's Smith.'

'Smith. Yes, of course. How silly of me.'

She almost ran to the car. She had to drive on to a bend in the road before she could turn and drive back. She reached Mrs Poulter's cottage about ten minutes later.

The cottage had a riotous garden with flowers, soft fruit and a peach tree competing for attention. There was an overgrown path leading to the door and on the door a well-polished knocker in the shape of a galleon. She raised and let it fall.

After delay a plump elderly woman came to the door with flour up to her elbows. 'Yes, m'dear?' she said. 'Make it quick, I'm baking.'

'Is the gardener in?'

'You want Johnny? Round the back.' She waved at the narrow path going round the house, withdrew, and closed the door hastily.

Christina went round the house. The back garden was given up to neat rows of vegetables. Kneeling among the cabbages was a man in his shirt sleeves, with a flour sack tied over his head to keep off the drizzle.

She trod carefully between the rows of plants to reach him. He looked up.

'Hello, Elwin,' she said.

Chapter Thirty-three

Elwin rose slowly from his kneeling pad. He dusted off his knees, took the makeshift hat off his head.

'What are you doing here, Chrissie?'

'Looking for you.'

'I thought you were in Geneva.'

'I was, but Mother was in a state so I came home to look for you.'

'All the way from Geneva?'

'Yes.'

'How did you know I was here?'

'I worked it out.'

'Does everybody know?' he said, and for the first time instead of mild interest there was alarm in his manner.

'No, only me. But of course they're very anxious.'

'What about?'

'About you and what might have happened to you.'

'Well, I'm quite all right. You can tell them that when you get back.'

'I will, Elwin,' she said.

The drizzle was becoming heavier, more persistent. 'Could we go indoors?' she suggested.

He looked at his watch. 'Might as well. Mrs Poulter generally lays on a cup of tea about now.'

He led her to the back door. He wiped his feet very carefully on the scraper and she did likewise. They went into a kitchen scented with the smell of baking bread. Mrs Poulter looked up from a mixing bowl.

'Oh, dear souls, there you are. I've just put the kettle on.'

'Thank you, Mrs Poulter. This is my sister.'

'Glad to meet you, Miss Smith.'

'How do you do,' said Christina.

'Now, Johnny, fetch out the milk and sugar, you know where they be. How about a hot scone and cream?'

'Lovely.'

'You too, Miss Smith?'

'I'd love one.'

Elwin got out milk and sugar, cups and saucers. Mrs Poulter made tea, put newly baked scones on a plate, brought clotted cream from a pottery cooler. They all sat down at the end of the kitchen table not taken up by the mixing bowl and pastry-board.

'Now, Johnny, be you wash you hands before sitting down?'

'Oh, of course,' he said, and obediently went to the steep staircase that led to the bedrooms above.

As soon as he had gone Mrs Poulter said, 'Now, soul, what's his real name?'

'Holt, Elwin Holt. You knew he wasn't John Smith?'

'M'dear, I've been letting out rooms to gentlemen this many a long day, and when he came here saying he was a gardener called Smith and needed a place to put up, I had no quiver about taking him in. Paid two weeks in advance, and 'as paid this week too. But you know, soul, he could never make a living at odd jobs in the gardens hereabouts, and from the way he spoke and all, I knew full well he were no workman.'

'Weren't you afraid to take him in?'

'He'm as harmless as a butterfly,' Mrs Poulter said roundly. 'But where do he belong, in truth?'

'Market Bresham in Lincolnshire. He just walked out on his home and his job.'

'Poor lad. There's another like him, Jessie Duckton's son: he can't settle to nothing and has the lost look on him. What shall you do, then, Miss Holt?'

'He has to go home. He's ill, you know.'

'Reckon so. What happens when he's gone home?'

'I think he ought to go into hospital, though I doubt if

he'll want to. But the first thing is to get him home.'

'If he wor so eager to get away from't, mebbe he won't be so eager to go back.'

'Oh, I know that. I couldn't force him. He must go back of his own free will.'

'Well, m'dear, I wish you joy of the task. If I can do aught to help, just tip me the wink.'

When Elwin came down again, washed and tidied, they were spreading cream on scones. He ate three, drank two cups of tea, chatting all the while about the vegetables in Mrs Poulter's garden. At a certain point their hostess decided the tea break was over. 'Now, I must finish the baking. It's not fitten to go out and work in that misky, so why don't you take your sister into the parlour and have a chat?'

Elwin rose like an obedient child. The parlour was furnished with straight-backed mahogany chairs and a great number of pot plants on a walnut table. They sat down on the two least uncomfortable chairs.

'What do you plan to do at the end of the summer, Elwin?' she inquired.

'Do?'

'Well, there won't be any work here in the winter. No gardening.'

He looked down. 'There'll be some. The estate agent who handles the holiday cottages needs someone to keep the gardens tidied up.'

'You think of staying on here, then?'

'Of course.'

'Don't you think you ought to tidy up your affairs in Market Bresham first?'

He didn't reply.

'You ought to have let them know where you were, Elwin.'

'No! And don't you tell, either!'

'You mean, you don't want Dorothy to know? She thinks you ran off with some woman.'

He gave a tremulous laugh. 'That shows how little she knows.'

'Don't you care about Mother? She's terribly upset, and Father suspects you of fiddling about two hundred pounds of your clients' money.'

For the first time he showed a spark of resentment. 'That's not true!'

'He does suspect you, Elwin—'

'I mean it's not true about doing anything with the money! I never took a penny!'

'I know that, dear. I never for a moment thought you did.'

'But . . . Father thinks so?'

'Well, there's something wrong with the accounts and he seems to think you took some dividends or something.'

He looked at her, blinked, and looked away. 'I don't think I did.'

'You ought to come back and clear it up.'

'I want to stay here.'

'But if you can't afford the rent?'

'I'll manage somehow.'

'Mrs Poulter may only take summer boarders. She may not want you here in the winter.'

'Of course she will!' He leapt up and crossed the narrow vestibule to the kitchen. 'Mrs Poulter, my sister is saying you wouldn't want me here in the winter!'

The landlady turned from taking a golden loaf out of the oven. She straightened, her face pink, but whether with the heat from the kitchen range or from having to tell a lie, Christina couldn't say.

'Dear soul,' Mrs Poulter said, 'I never yet had a boarder here in winter and I don't know as I'd care to have one. In winter I like to be snug and sheltered, and if snow comes I move in with my cousin Menlison. Was you thinking of staying on past summer?'

'Well, I . . .'

'If you were thinking of going on with the odd jobs, I have to tell 'ee that there's a many a man in the village wants to have the chance of 'em while farming slows down. I don't know as you'd be popular taking their livelihood from 'em.'

'Oh-h.' It was a long, despondent sigh.

'I thought,' Christina said to Mrs Poulter, 'that it would be best if he came home with me.'

'There's a job and so forth there for him?'

'He needn't go back to the office if he didn't want to,' Christina said.

'Needn't I, Christina?' There was a little flicker of relief, which quickly died. 'But I'd have to face Dorothy.'

'Who's Dorothy?' Mrs Poulter asked.

'My wife.'

'You're a married man?' she cried, astounded.

'I've got a wife and daughter. Helen's five.'

'But, m'dear, you wouldn't want to be away for weeks and weeks from your own little girl?'

'I suppose not.'

'She'll be missing you.'

'Yes, perhaps.'

'At least there ought to be a chance for everybody to know what you want,' Christina said carefully. 'You could explain what it is that troubles you.'

'I tried explaining. Dottie wouldn't listen.'

'Ah, but,' Mrs Poulter said, laying a hand on his sleeve, 'it would be different now. They'll listen for sure.'

'Do you think so?'

'Yes, m'dear, I do truly.'

Elwin glanced at Christina. 'We could go tomorrow, I suppose,' he murmured.

'Nay, if you're going, pack up and go. The little girl is perhaps crying now for her Daddy!' protested Mrs Poulter. 'I'll get your shirt that I was going to iron.'

Thus bustled by his kindly landlady, Elwin packed his few belongings. He had bought a couple of pairs of trousers and some shirts in a secondhand store in Bristol, together with an ex-Army knapsack in which to carry them. It was soon placed in the back seat of Christina's car.

Mrs Poulter gave them both a hug. In Christina's ear she whispered, 'Do 'ee write to me and tell me how he fares, poor dear soul.'

'I will, and thank you.'

* * *

They stayed overnight at an inn. What the landlord thought of this ill-assorted pair he didn't say. Late next night they drove into Market Bresham. Glancing at her brother, Christina saw he was pale with fear.

'Let me do the talking, Elwin,' she said.

He nodded wordlessly.

She had telephoned from Birmingham to say they were on their way, warning that he wasn't well enough to undergo an inquisition. She drove him to his own home a few miles the other side of the town. Her parents were with Dorothy, sitting tensely in waiting.

'Well!' Herbert Holt cried as his son came in. 'A fine business, I must say! And you look a sight! What did you do with your proper clothes?'

'Father!' Christina intervened. 'I thought we agreed—'

'Oh, Elwin, how could you do this to me?' wept Dorothy, throwing herself on her husband.

Mildred Holt sat sobbing quietly into her handkerchief – real sobs, not the theatrics she used when she wanted to avoid trouble.

Christina insisted that everyone must be calm. She undertook to explain anything that needed explaining, but most of what was said consisted of exclamations of wonder. Devon! How strange to go to Devon! And alone – this was from Elwin's wife, who still half expected to hear of a secret love nest. How absurd to want to cut himself off from his family!

'Where's Helen?' Elwin asked suddenly at this point.

'Upstairs in bed, of course,' Dorothy said. 'It's almost eleven o'clock.'

'Couldn't you have let her stay up to meet me?'

Dorothy went pink with anger. 'She wouldn't have had to "meet" you if you hadn't run off!'

'Dorothy!' warned her sister-in-law.

'Oh, don't "Dorothy" me as if it were my fault! You know he behaved totally irresponsibly! And now he comes back and we've all got to pretend it was perfectly all right.'

'I want to see Helen,' Elwin said and, getting up, walked out of his drawing-room and upstairs.

'Don't you dare wake her!' cried Dorothy, running after him.

Christina caught her as she was rushing through the door. 'Dorothy, for God's sake, let him look at his own daughter!'

'How do I know what he's going to do? He's just so odd!'

'Mother,' Christina said, 'go up and just be there with him.'

Her mother obeyed. Herbert said to his daughter-in-law, 'I understand you're upset, Dottie, but please try to—'

'It's all right for you! You're not going to have to share the same roof with him! I tell you, he isn't responsible for his actions!'

She was working herself up into hysterics. Christina looked in appeal to her father. 'It might be better if he went home with us, Father.'

'But good God, Christina, this is his home! I thought he'd need to be here—'

'Perhaps not.' She turned to Dorothy. 'Would you rather he went with us?'

Dorothy couldn't bring herself to say the words outright. But she nodded vigorously then took refuge in an outburst of tears.

They took Elwin to his boyhood home. The family doctor came next day, diagnosed nervous debility, prescribed rest and good food, and prepared to leave.

'Dr Mayles, don't you think he ought to have treatment?' Christina suggested.

'For what?'

'For depression.'

'Of course he's depressed. His marriage is breaking up, I gather.'

'I mean clinical depression – a functional disorder brought on by a situation he finds hopeless and impossible to deal with.'

Dr Mayles smiled. 'I'm just a simple country doctor,' he said. 'Of course I know of your reputation, Dr Holt, but your speciality is childhood disorders, isn't it? I hardly think a grown man needs more than a rest and a few good meals, to get the better of any depression.'

She knew she ought not to interfere too strongly, that it would be best if Elwin himself asked for help. But this he couldn't do. Nor could his parents quite see that he had an ailment that needed treatment. His father, in fact, after a day or two, decided his son was well enough to face the music.

'Now then, what about this missing money?' he demanded.

'Christina mentioned that. I don't know what you mean.'

'Three hundred and ten pounds, that's what I mean.'

'I thought she said about two hundred.'

'I took the trouble to do a thorough check and there are three hundred and ten pounds' worth of dividends that ought to have been reinvested for our clients. And let me tell you, that means they've also lost the interest on that money, and Mrs Wilkins has already mentioned she wants to withdraw the interest to pay for some roof repairs . . . So we shall have to make that good also, but first tell me what you did with the money.'

'I didn't do anything with it.'

'Look here, I haven't any idea why you wanted it, but if you were stuck for a few pounds, why didn't you ask me?'

'I didn't take any money, Father. I already said that.'

'Don't try to brazen it out, boy. Those dividend coupons have vanished and you've initialled the papers as having received them. If you banked them in your own name, tell me the number of the account and we can get it transferred.'

'I didn't take the dividends. Why don't you believe me?'

'Look here, my lad, you're going to come down to the office and see for yourself that you've initialled for the receipt of those coupons.'

'I suppose I did initial for them.'

'And then you took them?'

'No, I didn't.'

'But they're gone, boy! Gone! Three hundred and ten pounds' worth.'

Without telling Christina, Herbert Holt hauled his son into the office and confronted him with the evidence.

'Yes, I see.'

'So what did you do with the dividends?'

'I don't remember.'

'Oh, come on, Elwin! What did you do with them? You have power of attorney from the clients so you could bank them.'

'I didn't do that.'

'Then you invested them in your own name somewhere—'

'I didn't.'

'Understand me, son, we'll stay here until Doomsday, but I'm going to find out what you did with that money which didn't belong to you!'

Herbert's voice had risen to a roar. Pale and stricken, Elwin was standing like a prisoner in the dock. There was a tap at the door. Jervis, the firm's chief clerk, came in.

'Excuse me, Mr Holt—'

'Not now, Jervis—'

'But, sir, I couldn't help hearing what you were saying.'

'This is a confidential conversation!'

Mr Jervis forbore to say that Mr Holt was shouting so loudly he could be heard all over the office. He persisted, with considerable courage. 'I know it's confidential, but if it's about the dividend coupons for Mrs Wilkins, Miss Dagott, Captain Pryce and—'

'Jervis, I warn you—'

'I know where they are, sir!'

There was an awe-struck pause.

'*You* know?'

'Yes, sir.'

'How do you know?'

'Mr Elwin gave them to me, sir.'

Herbert stared at him. After a moment of struggling with himself, he turned his angry eyes on his son. 'Why did you give them to Jervis?'

'I don't remember.'

'Jervis, why did Mr Elwin give them to you?'

'I don't know, sir. He told me to keep them safe.'

'Why didn't you ask him his reasons?'

'It wasn't my place, Mr Holt.'

'And why the devil didn't you tell me this weeks ago?'

Jervis looked offended. 'I had no idea there was any problem, sir. You didn't mention it.'

'My God,' roared Herbert, 'for weeks I've been under the mistaken impression that my son stole those dividends—'

'I'm sorry, Mr Holt. I'll fetch them now if you wish.'

'For heaven's sake, bring them here and let's get them reinvested.'

When the clerk had gone, Herbert turned to Elwin. 'Well, I owe you an apology, it seems, but you must admit you brought it on yourself. Why didn't you tell me you'd given them to Jervis?'

'I didn't remember.'

'Didn't remember! And what were you going to tell Jervis to do with them?'

'Nothing.'

'What?'

'I . . . just gave them to Jervis to keep.'

'But you were instructed to reinvest.'

'I suppose I was.'

'But you decided not to?'

'I . . . didn't decide. I just . . . didn't know what to do.'

'What?'

'Can I go now?'

Herbert made a big effort to control his temper. 'We've got to sort this out, Elwin. Are you saying you just didn't *bother* to look after your clients' money?'

To his utter consternation, his son began to cry.

By that evening, Elwin Holt had been admitted as a patient to the Psychiatric Ward of the Anglian Hospital in Lincoln.

Christina had felt all along that it was inevitable. To Herbert and Mildred it was a blow from which they scarcely knew how to recover.

'He broke down!' Herbert cried. 'Right there in the

office, in front of Jervis! Cried like a baby!'

'My poor boy, shut up in a mental ward,' moaned Mildred.

'It's just an illness, like any other,' Christina tried to tell them. 'You can be sick in the mind just as you can be sick in the body.'

They couldn't accept it.

Dorothy took it even harder. She was bitterly ashamed of being married to 'a mental case'. 'I should never feel safe in the same house with him ever again,' she muttered.

'You can't imagine that Elwin would ever do anything violent?'

'Christina, it's all very well for you, you're used to these kind of people, and if you ask me it's a very strange sort of life for a woman, dealing with people who are out of their mind, but *I* never imagined myself involved with anyone like that, and I can tell you I'm not going to put up with it.'

The news inevitably got out. Some of Elwin's clients asked to be transferred back into the care of the senior partner; some simply went elsewhere. Mrs Wilkins, finding she had lost the interest on one hundred and twenty pounds, was talking about bringing a charge before the Law Society of negligence and incompetence against Elwin.

Herbert was so angry he wouldn't even go to visit his son in hospital. Nor would Dorothy. Only his mother, after a shaky start, was able to shoulder the responsibility.

Christina drove back to London to begin the business of winding up her practice. This was easier than it might have been because the General Strike had cause a big break. Patients had to be referred to other consultants nearer their homes. Some had simply stopped coming.

She rang Laurenz regularly to report on progress. 'I hope to be in Geneva for good by Christmas,' she told him.

'Your Christmas or my Christmas?' he teased.

'*Our* Christmas. If I'm going to be married to a Serbian I shall have to accept the Eastern Orthodox calendar.'

'It's nearly three months to Christmas. Shall I come on a

flying visit? I've some leave due, I could come for a long weekend.'

'Darling, there's nothing I'd like more, but the strike's still on: by the time you got here you would just have to turn around and go back.'

'It doesn't matter. I must see you or I'll die.'

He arrived the following Monday, half wild with irritation at his journey and half delirious at seeing her again.

'I should have been here thirty-six hours ago but everything was incompetent and wrong and so here I am – what is your English saying? – better late than never.'

She threw her arms around him. 'Laurenz! Darling! How well you look!'

'Well? I am haggard from lack of sleep and sea-sickness! But no, I am well, very well, for I am with you again. Christina, because the journey was so long I have to go back to Geneva tomorrow. Come back with me!'

'I can't, darling. I really can't. My brother's wife is talking about divorcing him. I can't leave poor Elwin until he's back on his feet again and able to cope with that.'

'In Serbia we would say that such a wife is no bargain even with a dowry of oak forests.'

'She's not to blame. She never expected things to work out the way they did.'

He shook his head and gave a sigh. 'This is how it is for all of us. How could I foresee what would happen to my poor Franzisca? Well, don't be sad, Christina. See, I've brought a bottle of good Swiss wine, and we shall go to bed and drink it and forget the world!'

When Alice Lowther let herself in next morning to continue with the discarding of patients' records, she was surprised to hear the sound of a man singing to himself in the upstairs flat.

Dr Holt came downstairs presently, blushing. 'Mr Varikiav has been staying with me,' she explained.

'Staying long, doctor?'

'No, he's leaving for Geneva later today.'

Alice smiled. At last she would have the chance to meet

Mr Varikiav, so often mentioned in Dr Holt's conversation.

The doctor had gone back upstairs and Alice was surrounded with piles of file cards when the doorbell rang. Puzzled, for almost no patients were coming these days and certainly none was scheduled for Tuesday at eleven o'clock, she went to the door.

The man on the threshold was somehow familiar. He had no child with him so he couldn't be one of Dr Holt's cases.

'Is Dr Holt at home?'

'She is, but her practice is suspended—'

'This is a personal visit. It's very important that I see her. Would you please let her know?'

Alice went into the office to put the call through on the internal phone. 'Dr Holt, a gentleman has come to see you.'

'A gentleman? Tell him to make an appointment.'

'Doctor, it's that American gentleman.'

'What American gentleman?'

'Mr Charlford.'

Chapter Thirty-four

Christina's first reaction had been mere surprise that Alice would bother her at a time like this. She must surely have guessed she didn't want to see anyone while Laurenz was here.

'Would you tell him I'm otherwise engaged this morning?'

'I wouldn't have rung, doctor, only he seems terribly upset,' the receptionist intervened.

'Upset?'

'Yes, not his usual self at all.'

Upset? Christina's thoughts flew immediately to Stephen. Something had happened to Stephen – an accident; or he'd got mixed up with a girl; or his mother was making trouble . . .

'Is his son with him?' she asked quickly.

'No, doctor.'

Laurenz, across the room, was watching her while she had this conversation. 'A patient?' he asked.

'It's someone whose son I'm interested in . . .'

'Please, see him,' Laurenz said. 'I'm just about to leave in any case.'

'No, no, Laurenz—'

'Yes, I have to buy presents to take home to Suza and Milo. Tell me which place to go to for that, and I'll be on my way.'

'Oh, please, Laurenz—'

'Doctor?' Alice was saying in her ear. 'Mr Charlford says—'

'Christina, I need your help!' John Charlford intervened, speaking over Alice's voice. 'I need to talk to you!'

Laurenz could tell that something dramatic was going on down in the consulting rooms. 'You see? You are needed. I ought to go, my dearest.'

'One moment,' Christina said into the phone, then set down the earpiece. 'Laurenz, I'm going with you to the train.'

'No, no, you are needed here. Which shop am I to go to for the presents?'

'Well . . . The Army and Navy Store is on your way.'

'And what should I buy? This is the first time I ever brought home a present to my children.'

'Well, for Suza that's easy: something pretty – a little sun parasol, or a silk scarf with flowers on it. Milo is more difficult – what are his interests?'

'Damned if I know.'

'Stamps? Fishing?'

'Riding, but that's not very convenient in Geneva . . .'

'Buy him one of those little box cameras,' she suggested. 'Even if he's not interested in photography, he won't be able to resist taking snaps at least until the film runs out!'

'Perfect!' He hugged her, then went to collect his overnight case from the bedroom.

Meanwhile Christina said into the phone, 'I'll be down in a moment, Alice. Ask Mr Charlford to take a seat.'

When she went down to the door with Laurenz, John Charlford was pacing about in the narrow hall. He was about to speak, but drew back when he saw she had someone with her.

They went out on the steps, pulling the door almost closed behind them.

'Ring me when you get back.'

'Of course, darling. Come back to Geneva soon.'

'As soon as I can.'

They kissed, he put on his hat, swung his overnight case, and walked away.

John almost seized her arm as she came in. 'I can see I'm a nuisance, Christina, but this is terribly important.'

'Let's go in and sit down. Would you like a cup of coffee?'

'What? Coffee? Well, I guess . . .'

Christina nodded at Alice as they went past her into the inner office. They sat down, John on the sofa, Christina on a cushioned chair across the low table. She had always found this casual setting helpful with patients.

'Now, what is this all about?'

'It's about Stephen! I don't know what to do with him! He seems to have gone out of his head!'

'Stephen?' Christina said, astounded. The boy was one of the most level-headed she'd ever known considering his situation.

'He's been drinking like a fish, I had to bail him out for smashing a café window in Athens, he won't get up in the morning, he goes out at night and I don't know where he is, and when I told him we were coming back to London if I had to put him in a strait-jacket, he punched me on the mouth!'

She listened to this with growing alarm. These were symptoms she had heard described before, only too often. She'd never expected to hear them of her well-brought-up son.

'I know kids are supposed to go through a kind of crisis when they get to . . . well, you know . . .'

'Puberty – yes. But Stephen seemed to have got past that stage.'

'That's what *I* thought. And as for, you know, girls . . . there was a girl in Paris, I think it all went well, he seemed OK, no bones broken if you see what I mean.'

'You say this began in Athens? Was there a girl there? I know the Greeks are very strict about their young girls.'

'No, nothing out of the way: he went around with girls from the Embassy families mostly. And in any case we were spending all our time driving around looking at the antiquities, he didn't spend much time looking for . . . well, anyhow, it's not about a girl, I'm pretty sure of that.'

Alice came in with the coffee. She looked at Christina for further orders. Christina shook her head and, when her nurse had gone, said, 'Did he have some sort of shock? Something about his mother?'

'Estelle doesn't make much contact. She sent him a

present for his birthday – that's September, you know.'

'Yes,' she said, nodding, and then recalled that she wasn't supposed to know Stephen's birthday.

John, however, was too taken up with his own problems to notice. 'The trouble all began the day after his birthday.'

'Yes?' She was pouring the coffee, not watching him, letting him come to it in his own way and his own time. She had understood almost from the first that John knew the root of the trouble but couldn't bring himself to say it without getting his anxiety established first.

'See, Stephen's decided he wants to take up archaeology. He wants to study it at university. But it's kind of early for him to go to Yale, so he asked if he could spend a year helping at one of the digs in Egypt.'

'It sounds like a good idea.' She handed him his cup, offered sugar and cream.

'Well,' he said, after an eager gulp that seemed to refresh him, 'I said OK to that. Professor Symes had said he would put him on one of the teams in the Valley of the Kings, just as a general dogsbody. But, see, Cairo University won't let just anybody on the digs. There's been a lot of pilferage – scarabs and little things like that: that go to collectors who don't mind if they're stolen. So the Department of Antiquities checks up pretty thoroughly.'

'Go on.' Christina began to have an idea of what might have happened. But she had to wait for John to lay it out for her.

'Well, we were in Athens, we'd had this good meal to celebrate his birthday, and he'd asked if it was OK to apply to the Department of Antiquities and I said sure, great, we'd write in the morning.'

He paused, colouring up. 'I guess I drank too much Greek wine. Anyhow, I surfaced kind of late the next morning. Stephen was up already, drafting a letter to send to Cairo. He said he needed his birth certificate and I was feeling so dopey I said, sure, in my document case.'

'He went to get it himself?'

'Sure, he saw no reason why not. When we left the States

for this long trip, I picked up this leather case from my private safe, just in case it was needed. It holds insurance papers, my passport – Stephen is travelling on my passport. I had my own birth certificate and Stephen's. It never occurred to me that they would really be needed but, being in the diplomatic corps, I've been in the habit of carrying stuff like that in this old leather document case.' He took a deep breath. 'And so Stephen opened the case and rummaged about and found his birth certificate and discovered he's adopted.'

He sat looking at Christina. She met his gaze.

'I see,' she said.

'He went to pieces. I never saw anything like it, I thought he was going to pass out. He held out his birth certificate as if it was dirty somehow and said . . . He said, "Is this true?" and I said, "Well, yes, but we didn't mean you to find out", and he turned around and walked right out.'

She felt a tremendous surge of pity – pity for this good, bewildered man, and for the boy who had seen his whole life suddenly warped as if in a distorting mirror.

'You never told him?'

'Of *course* not!' John was shocked. 'We were told to bring him up exactly as if he were our own son, and that's what we did. We almost forgot we adopted him in the first place. He was only two weeks old when we got him – I mean, he *is* ours, we always loved him, we always put him first.'

Not always, thought Christina. Estelle had not put him first when she fell in love with a Broadway actor. Coming on top of that hurt, this new wound was too hard for Stephen to bear.

'What happened then?' she prompted.

'He was out all day and most of the next night. When he eventually came home he was stinking drunk. I never saw him like that before.' John's blue eyes filled with tears. 'Honest to God, Christina, I was never so shocked in my life. Well, I got him to bed and helped him through the hangover next day, and then he started on me. How could I do a thing like this to him, lie to him all his life? Who were his real parents; he wanted to find them and ask them why they didn't like him enough to keep him, and so on – God, it was awful.' He stopped. 'I didn't handle it well,' he confessed. 'I told him to stop acting like a baby and accept the facts. So he walked out again. That was the night he got arrested for wrecking the café.'

'He was trying to punish the world around him for lying to him,' she said. 'It's not a criminal thing, don't imagine that.'

'Sure, I see that – he's just getting back at everybody. But I don't see why he took it so badly. After all, Christina, we've loved him and taken care of him for seventeen years. What's so bad about that?'

'The foundations of his life have been shaken. That's what's bad about it. He thought you were his father, but you aren't.'

'Of course I'm his father!' John cried. 'Who else has loved him as a father should? But now he hates me. I don't understand it.'

'And his mother? Does he hate her too?'

'Oh, God, you should hear him talk about Estelle. You know she sent him a silk shirt for his birthday. He tore it up and threw it in the trashcan. He says he'll never forgive her for as long as he lives.'

'Don't be so upset about it, John. His reaction is extreme, but it will grow less bitter in time.'

'Yeah, I hope so, but in the meantime, what am I going to do about him? I couldn't let him go on the way he was in Athens – the Embassy gave me a hint he was making a spectacle of himself, and the Greek police were getting kind of sick of him. So I said we'd better go back to London, because I thought I could ask for your advice, and he said he didn't want to go to London, and I told him not to sass me, and he punched me in the face . . . Oh, dear God, he was the sweetest kid! How could he change so much?'

She didn't reply to that. People change all the time, that was the answer. Warmed by love and encouragement, chilled by neglect and sarcasm, shaped by what they met with in life according to their innate abilities . . .

Stephen was one of the lucky ones. He had been given love in abundance all through his childhood and the years of his young manhood. Now it was as if he had crashed over a cliff on to sharp jagged rocks below. Yet the background of care and affection still remained. Fundamentally he was well-balanced and strong. He would recover.

But he would need help.

'I can give you the name of a colleague,' she said, going to her desk and opening a drawer for her address book. 'With good counselling from him, Stephen should—'

'But I want *you* to help him!' John cried, springing up. 'I came to London specifically to ask *you* for help.'

'It wouldn't be a good idea,' she began. 'Doctors shouldn't treat friends or relatives, and that's particularly true of psychiatrists—'

'Don't give me that! That's just damn-fool medical etiquette.'

'No, John, it's a safeguard against making wrong judgements.'

'How can it be wrong to help a friend? Good God, Christina, I know you didn't feel enough for me to want to get married, but I thought you *liked* us, Stephen and me!'

'I do, of course I do!' She went to him, took his hands. 'John, believe me, I want to do what's best for Stephen. And I *know* it wouldn't be best for me to undertake his treatment.'

'Who's talking about treatment, for God's sake? I'm just asking you to see the kid, as a friend – talk to him, see if you can get through to him. For I know for sure that I can't.'

'No, no.' She shook her head, pressing his hands to let him know she felt strongly about it, that it was a decision of concern and good judgement. 'He needs proper attention. And I know I'm the wrong person.'

He jerked away from her in anger. 'Well, this much is for sure. If you're the wrong person, nobody else is right. For I can give you 100 per cent assurance that he won't go to anybody else.'

'But you must persuade him—'

'Me? Persuade him? He treats me as if I'm his worst enemy!'

'But there must be moments when he lets his aggressive guard down?'

'If there are, I'm not good at spotting them. I tell you, I practically have to hold him at gun point to make him do anything, even when it's obviously for his own good. I mean, he won't eat – I try to get him to sit down to a meal but if he does, he just pushes his plate away. He won't look after himself – he looks like a slob—'

'Lowered self-esteem,' Christina murmured.

'You see? You understand what's making him act this way. I'm damned if I do! And I know I couldn't make him go see a stranger about this business. He would just walk out on me, maybe for good. Christina,' he said in agonised appeal, 'I'm losing my son! Help me!'

She knew he had no idea what he was asking . . . But she could see that this was a crisis, that the boy needed help *now*, before he did something irreversible in his sudden hate and resentment. It was true that it might take days, even weeks, to persuade him to see a psychiatrist, even if his father knew how to set about persuading him.

She knew it was wrong. But it seemed the only thing to do. 'Very well,' she said with great unwillingness. 'I'll see him.'

'When? Today? I'll try to find him and get him here this afternoon—'

'Not this afternoon,' she said. She needed time to prepare herself for the task that had suddenly been thrust before her. She saw his disappointment and went on at once, 'I've things to do. But meanwhile I need to know more about what he's been saying to you. First of all, Stephen never had any hint that he was adopted?'

'None, of course not. We asked a child specialist about it and he said we must bring Stephen up exactly as if he were our own flesh and blood and never think about the adoption, until he was old enough to be told.'

'Which in the specialist's opinion was when?'

'Well, I don't know that it was ever actually specified. When he was all grown up. I suppose we thought of telling him after his twenty-first birthday.' He frowned at her. 'Why? Was there something wrong with that?'

'I don't know,' she confessed. 'It's what's always been said – that to let a child know he's adopted would wreck his security. Yet recently there have been some studies . . . they seem to suggest it's better if a child grows up with the knowledge that he's adopted.'

John was appalled. 'How could you do that?' he demanded. 'Tell a little toddler he wasn't really your baby? You couldn't do a thing like that!'

She made a little gesture of perplexity. 'I don't know, John. There might be some way to tell the child . . . The studies seem to show that young people who suddenly learn, by whatever means, that they are adopted, in general have a bad reaction to it. And in Stephen's case . . .'

'Yes, what about Stephen's case?' he challenged. 'Why should the kid go to pieces like this? See, he's always been a good-natured kid, quite self-controlled and able to take his bumps like the best of them. I know this was a big surprise—'

'It was more than that. Think of it, John. It's the ultimate rejection.'

'Huh?'

'Well, from his childhood Stephen was always being uprooted from his home and friends and school, to travel with you in your job.'

'OK, yes, that's true. But it's true of all "diplomatic" kids.'

'Yes, of course. But then you sent him to boarding school—'

'Sure! I went to the same school myself—'

'But it was away from home. And then Estelle falls in love with a man only about ten years older then Stephen.'

'That was rotten, of course . . .'

'And breaks up the family. She shows she doesn't want Stephen by giving up custody to you.'

'Well, she wanted to be able to build up this thing with Victor.'

'And Stephen knew it, you can be sure. So from his point

of view, his mother rejected him for this other man.'

'Oh, you can't put it like that . . .'

'How would you put it? She turned her back on you and Stephen—'

'But it's not her fault, Christina. I mean, she loves this guy.'

'I'm not saying it's her fault. I'm just showing you – to Stephen it was a terrible rejection. And now, eighteen months later, he finds out his real mother rejected him from the very outset.'

'But it wasn't like that!' John tried to summon up that long-ago scene. 'She was a nice kid – a Balkan girl recently arrived in the States. I know she was cut up about handing the baby over to us, but it was the best thing for him—'

'No,' Christina said with a bitterness she couldn't prevent, 'as it turns out, it was not.'

John Charlford was silent. Then he said heavily, 'No, it wasn't. And in a way Estelle and I were kidding ourselves even then. We kept saying to each other that we would take some poor unwanted child and give it the best of everything and what a big, high-minded thing it was to do; but if we'd really wanted to do the kid a big favour, we'd have handed his mother a couple of thousand dollars and told her to bring the kid up herself.'

Christina's mind went back to those desperate days. If only someone had said to her then, 'Here's the money, hire a children's nurse to look after your baby while you keep on with your studies . . .'

And yet . . . There was the shame of having a bastard baby, the almost certain antagonism of everyone in the chaste, respectable circles of Philadelphia, the extreme likelihood of being dismissed from the University for 'moral turpitude'.

'Well,' John said, 'maybe Estelle's ideas about adoption were kind of phoney. The truth probably was that because everybody else about our age was starting their family, she felt sort of . . . deprived. And sure, I wanted a son. I really wanted to do right by him and, to the best of my ability, I

have. Estelle changed. But Estelle's always been . . . well
. . .' He sighed.

'What does Stephen have to say about her?'

'Oh gee! He says she never really loved him, she was
always off at a party or a weekend trip or at the opera. He
told me about once, in Paris, when she said she'd meet him
from school and they'd go see a new Chaplin film that had
come into the cinema, and he says he waited an hour and a
half at the school gate . . .'

'It still stays in his mind? It was two or three years ago that
you were in Paris.'

'How did you know that?' he said in surprise. 'Have we
talked about our Paris posting?'

Careful, she said to herself, drawing in a sharp breath.
Careful, you fool. 'Oh, I think it came up in conversation.'

'Yeah, sure, when we were talking about this recent trip,
to see the stuff in the Louvre – yeah, that must be it.'

'Do you remember that occasion?' she said. 'Was Stephen
very disappointed at missing the film?'

'He didn't miss it, I took him myself. It turned out Estelle
just forgot: she was at a dress show and stayed to buy a dress.
I don't recall it as anything special – see, he didn't make a
fuss that stays in my mind, but then, he was never one for
making a fuss. He was like most of the "diplomatic"
kids – he grew up fast, learned how to live with the ups and
downs of that sort of life.'

'But it seems he always sensed that his mother had other
interests . . .'

'Well, sure! A diplomatic wife has to play her part.' John
was always quick to defend Estelle. Christina knew he
couldn't get out of the habit of loving her even though they
were divorced. If there had been mistakes in the upbringing
of their adopted child, he was ready to take a large part of the
blame.

But that was one of the things she had to reassure him
about. No one was to blame. He and Estelle had done their
best. Events had so fallen out that Stephen had suffered a
double wound they had never intended.

And now Christina must try to heal that wound, or at least help the scar tissue to grow over it.

'Where is Stephen now?'

'Who knows? He was still in bed when I left this morning, sleeping it off. I guess he'll have a kingsize hangover when he wakes up.'

'This has happened before, you say. What's the usual routine?'

'Well, he surfaces around noon, he's usually as sick as a dog. I dose him with Seidlitz powders and pour black coffee into him. Takes him a couple of hours to get normal again.'

'Leave him to recover on his own today.'

'What?' John was shocked. 'He's only a kid, Christina!'

'He's getting drunk like a man, let him recover like a man, on his own. It ought to take a good deal longer – alcoholic poisoning is no joke. Let's say it takes him until late afternoon to get the better of his sickness and headache. You walk in, say he looks bad – which will be quite true – and ring me, as a doctor. I'll come at once.'

It needed a certain hardening of the heart, but John Charlford agreed. He left looking a little more cheerful.

Christina spent the rest of the day thinking about what she'd been told and looking up one or two cases in textbooks. The more her mind went over it, the more she knew she'd been a fool to let John persuade her into it. It was utterly wrong to be trying to treat her own son's mental disturbance over the trauma of his adoption. She must get out of it as soon as she could.

John Chalford telephoned. 'How is he?' she asked him.

'Looks like a ghost and says he feels lousy.'

This was a true assessment. Stephen, still in dressing-gown and pyjamas, was poorly indeed. Christina briskly took his pulse and his temperature, briskly administered spirits of ammonia in a wine-glass of water, and as briskly shepherded him into the bathroom to make him take a shower.

About half an hour later a shaken but recovering Stephen Charlford, dressed in shirt and trousers, sat down to a pot of black coffee.

534

'I feel rotten,' he said.

'No doubt.'

'There was no need to call you. I can look after myself.'

'Well, you can get yourself home from a bar – what do you do, call a taxi and tell him to unload you at your hotel?'

He drank his coffee, letting the question go past.

'Then of course you rely on your father to get you to bed, and to see you through the after-effects next morning.'

'He wasn't even *here* today!' It was a flash of childish resentment, somehow at variance with his tall, well-grown frame.

'Got fed up with it, I suppose,' Christina said with a glance at John.

John, taking the cue, said, 'It sure is no pleasure acting nursemaid to you.'

'Nursemaid? Look, if it bores you, don't bother.'

'So what will you do then, Stephen?' Christina asked.

'I'll manage, don't you worry.'

'But we do worry. And that's what you want, isn't it?'

'What?' The boy choked on his coffee.

Christina waited for him to recover. 'Who are you punishing, Stephen? Yourself or your father?'

'I don't know what you mean!'

'Things have gone wrong, so *someone* has to suffer.'

'It's none of your business what's gone wrong.'

'Your father has asked me to help. He feels things can't go on like—'

'He hasn't *told* you!' He was horrified. Red colour came up in his sickly cheeks. 'He had no right!'

'Why do you take it like that, Stephen? Being adopted is nothing to be ashamed of.'

He sat mute, the coffee cup clutched in his hand, coffee stains from his spluttering on the clean white shirt-front. Tears glinted in his grey eyes.

'You see, it means your parents chose you. Other children are born and their parents want them and love them, but you were wanted and loved and *chosen*.'

She waited.

After a long pause he said, 'It doesn't feel like that.'

She nodded. 'I understand.'

'You do?'

'Well, I think I do.' She managed a smile. 'That's one of the things that's wrong with people in my profession – we think we understand. But we can only *really* understand if the other person helps us.'

'Helps how?'

'By talking it over. Would you talk it over with me, Stephen?'

For a moment an eagerness flared in his gaze. Then he looked about at the hotel room – comfortable and efficient but not friendly. 'Not here,' he said.

'All right. Will you come to me?'

He hesitated.

'When?'

'Tomorrow.'

Another hesitation. 'All right.'

She stood up. 'There's one condition.'

She saw him stiffen. She could almost hear the thought that formed: Just like a grown-up, always making rules.

'Yeah,' he said, 'what?'

'Don't drink between now and then.'

He was unwilling to concede. He had realised quite early that his drinking gave him power over his father.

But then something in him seemed to relent a little. She stood there, watching him, and he saw that she somehow understood something of what he'd been going through.

'OK,' he said, 'it only makes me feel rotten next day anyhow.'

'Good. Eleven o'clock tomorrow morning then?'

'OK,' he said.

She went out with only a nod of goodbye to his father. She made her way to the lift walking briskly. But once inside it she almost sagged against its walls.

Tomorrow was going to be a hideous ordeal. And it was quite wrong to think she could help anyone, feeling that way about it.

Chapter Thirty-five

Stephen was early next morning. But he walked up and down on the pavement outside. He could hear the chiming clock in the hall giving out its eleventh stroke when he rang the bell. Alice showed him into the consulting room.

'This isn't going to do me any good,' he said to Dr Holt, with a full aggressive forward push of the head.

'Then why did you come?'

He shrugged. 'Why not?'

'You could have found some other way to spend the morning.'

'In a bar, you mean.'

'Would you have gone to a bar?'

'I promised I wouldn't,' he said angrily.

'You saw it as a promise?'

'Well, it was, wasn't it?'

'I'm glad you kept it. Can I ask you a few things?'

'That's why I'm here, isn't it? So you can put the hex on me.'

'What does that mean, "hex"?'

'Oh, cast a spell.'

'You mean you see me as a witch,' she said, laughing.

He knew he looked sheepish. 'Well, I suppose not. What did you want to ask?'

'I take it you've given up the idea of doing archaeology?'

Whatever it was he'd expected, it wasn't this. He was startled. 'No, course not! What a stupid question!'

'You still want to do it?'

'I sure do!'

'Then I think you ought to realise you're spoiling your

chances of being taken on any important dig. They want reliable people, and if you get a reputation for going on a blinder each evening and sleeping it off till noon next day, you aren't going to seem very reliable, are you?'

He glowered, then moved uncomfortably on the cushioned sofa. 'I'm not going to make a career out of being a drunk,' he said.

'When do you think you'll stop?'

'Don't be a smartass!'

'I'm only trying to get information. How long are you going to keep up the alcoholic haze?'

'Mind your own damned business!'

She nodded, and wrote a note on the clipboard on her lap. He watched, and said in great annoyance, 'What did you just write down?'

'Want to see?'

Taken aback, he stammered, 'Well . . . yeah.'

She held it out so that he could read the note. *'Takes refuge in aggression.'*

He was relieved. He had expected some very critical remark. Why he should value her good opinion, he couldn't have explained – but he didn't want her to make critical remarks.

'What am I taking refuge from?' he challenged.

'Pain?'

He felt some sort of struggle within him. 'I'm in no pain. Why should I be in pain?'

'Because you saw your birth certificate when you wanted to apply to the Department of Antiquities in Cairo.'

He closed his eyes for a moment. Then he said, 'OK, so you know what was on it.'

'You don't want people to know?'

'It isn't anybody else's business! It isn't yours! I don't know why the hell I'm here, letting you ask puerile questions!'

'You're here because I said I would try to understand.'

'And you're so clever, you think you do!'

'At least I'm trying to. Don't you want to try?'

'Try to do what?'

'To understand why you feel so much pain.'

He got up. 'Lady, you're talking horse-feathers. I'm going.'

She too rose but made no attempt to detain him, which took him by surprise. He looked at her. She smiled.

'Will you come back tomorrow?'

'Why the hell should I?'

'Beats getting yourself a reputation for being unreliable, don't you think?'

'You're making fun of me!'

She laid a hand on his arm. 'No,' she said, 'believe me, I would *never* do that.'

They went to the front door together, more like hostess and guest than doctor and patient.

He went out on the front steps, then hesitated. 'So long,' he said.

'Tomorrow?'

'No.'

'The next day?'

He tried not to smile. He was determined not to smile. 'You don't give up easy,' he grunted.

'Tomorrow,' she said. 'Seems silly to waste a day.'

He walked down the steps then looked back. 'OK,' he said.

Next day was a repetition of the sparring match. He had a lot of anger to work off, and now he had a target at whom to discharge it. Trouble was, she sat there and took whatever he threw at her. She let him tell her she was a fool, a busybody, and an old maid. His father, too, was a fool, a busybody, and an old maid.

'Left on the shelf!' he sneered. 'Replaced by a younger model!'

These oblique references to his mother and the divorce were all he could allow himself to say about Estelle. So it remained for the first week. Then, all at once, the breakthrough came.

They had paused because the consulting-room fire needed replenishing. He asked to be allowed to use the tongs, which he'd never done in America because all the various Charlford homes were centrally heated. He dropped a knob of coal into the embers and then heard himself say: 'What I can't bear is the thought that my mother – my real mother – just gave me away to a pair of strangers!'

'You think she just did it casually?'

'She couldn't have given it much thought! I saw from the papers in Dad's document case – I was only two weeks old when I was adopted.'

'How long does it take for a baby to grow in a woman's body, Stephen?'

'Nine months, of course.'

'You believe she didn't think about it during those nine months?'

He finished putting the coal on the fire, dropped the tongs with a clatter into the coal-bucket.

'You don't understand. I saw in the birth certificate, her name was Kristin Belu, Serbian nationality, father unknown. I lived all my life up till then thinking I was an American, but now I find out I'm not. I'm not my father's son, I'm a nobody. *She* did that to me!'

He was hurt, confused, sure that someone must be to blame for what was done, how he felt.

Dr Holt said carefully, 'You're a nobody, but your name is Stephen Charlford – that's right, isn't it? Those legal documents you saw prove that. You're Stephen Charlford, legal son of John and Estelle Charlford.'

'Well . . . yes.'

'If your mother hadn't given you for adoption, who would you have been?'

'Who? I don't understand.'

'What would your name have been on any legal papers?'

'Stephen Belu.'

'Stephen Belu, illegitimate son of Kristin Belu. "Father unknown".' She paused. 'Don't you think perhaps your mother was trying to save you from that?'

He said angrily, 'Don't give me that! She must have known who the father was! As far as I can make out, she was living on this farm run by Serbian immigrants – how many men could there have been who were to blame?'

'What are you saying? That she should have married the man?'

'Sure she should have married him!'

'No matter what kind of man he was?'

'Yeah, yeah, if he was good enough to go to bed with he was good enough to marry, for God's sake! I mean, it isn't as if she was a rape victim. Dad told me that – he had the lawyer look into it. She went to bed with some guy in a hotel or something.'

He had bludgeoned some information out of his adopted father but the details were a little hazy. It had hurt him to realise that by this time John Charlford didn't remember too well, even about something so momentous as the adoption of his son.

He knew Dr Holt was trying to form some kind of argument. He didn't want to hear it, and yet he did; because if she could persuade him his real mother had cared about him just a little maybe, it wouldn't seem so bad.

'Stephen,' she said, 'try to imagine what it's like to be an eighteen-year-old girl who's been starved of affection. Perhaps she's offered what she thinks is love, promises are made – or at least she thinks she hears promises of marriage. But it turns out all wrong, it turns out she was tricked. What if that was what happened?'

'Well, if he had said he would marry her, she should have made him keep to it . . .'

'But suppose she found out that he didn't care for her at all, so she felt she couldn't even tell him about the baby?'

He set his mouth in a grim line. 'That would make him pretty much of a rat to have as a father.'

'Are you going to set out to hate him too?'

'I reckon I've got good reason to hate him.'

'Yet she doesn't hate him. She's forgiven him a long time ago.'

'How can you possibly know that?'

The doctor seemed startled by his question. She sat back

on her chair, perturbed, and he watched in perplexity. Then she said, 'I'm trying to put what I think is a reasonable case to you. Bad things happen, but people get over them.'

'Not always! If people get hurt, they want to get back at the people who hurt them.'

'Do you think that's a useful attitude? We only have so much energy, so much time, in this world. Wouldn't you want to use your time and energy on something better than revenge?'

'Well, yeah, I'm not thinking so much of revenge. But people wouldn't forgive somebody who did a bad thing to them.'

'If they have enough strength they forgive whoever hurt them, and go on with their own lives. Don't you think your mother was perhaps a nice girl, a decent girl? Couldn't you think – perhaps I should say hope – that she's forgiven the man who was responsible for your birth?'

'For all you know she may still hate him to this day!'

'I hope not. Hate is a very wasteful emotion. I wouldn't like to think she wasted any of her life on hating anybody.'

Well, that was the psychiatrist talking, Stephen told himself as he walked back to the hotel. Of course she would say it was wrong to hate, just like a parson would say it was wrong. Her reasons were different. She was trying to put over a case that it was wrong to waste energy on unproductive things . . .

Funny, though. It somehow almost seemed she might be right. When he looked back on the two months that had gone by since he saw that birth certificate and was suddenly seized by anger and resentment, it sure did seem as if he'd wasted those scores of days.

He didn't see Dr Holt for two days after that. The strange thing was, he began to be anxious to see her. He wanted to get on with it, whatever it was that they were doing. He felt as if she had taken him by the hand in some dark maze, and was leading him towards the light.

He began to accept that his unknown mother might have had good reason not to want to marry his unknown father but instead give her baby up for adoption.

'You must remember she found John and Estelle

Charlford. If you looked for parents, would you say they were a good choice?'

'Well, sure,' he agreed. '*Then*, they must have seemed pretty ideal. But look at them now.'

He watched a smile turn the corners of Dr Holt's lips. 'You want your mother to have been a clairvoyant too?'

Almost against his will, he chuckled. 'I guess that's a lot to ask.'

'Of course things changed in that marriage. But things change all the time, Stephen. You yourself – you've changed. You couldn't have stayed a little boy living with two loving parents for the rest of your life. You grew up, and even if Estelle and John had stayed together, wouldn't you have left home?'

'I suppose so. To go to Egypt to study archaeology.'

'The trouble is, you were the one who should have changed. Instead it was Estelle.'

'You don't understand how awful it was. She just walked away from us. I thought she loved me.'

'She did, and she does still. Give her *time*, son. She loves you, and so does the girl who gave you up seventeen years ago. So much love has been poured out on you, don't you think it's a shame to push it away and say it's worthless?'

After that session he felt as if something had stirred inside him. Something in the way she talked to him seemed very special, very cogent. He said to his father, 'Dr Holt is a nice lady. It's a pity she didn't marry and have kids of her own.'

'It may have something to do with the war, Stephen. A lot of women lost their men in the war.'

When he next saw Dr Holt, she had bad news for him. 'I have to leave London for a few days. I'm needed at my home in Lincolnshire.'

'No!'

'I'm sorry. There's a problem there.'

'Don't go, doctor! I need to talk to you.'

'I wanted to suggest something to you. Since I have to go anyhow, wouldn't it be a good idea if I handed you on to a colleague of mine?'

The idea of talking to anyone else as he talked to Christina Holt was abhorrent to him. He shook his head.

'I think it would be a good move, son. Your case is so nearly – '

'I'm not a case,' he said in a sudden return of the old anger. 'I'm just a fellow who found out he had the wrong idea about his parents.'

'It was more than that, or why did you take it so badly?'

'It's not the kind of thing you can take well.'

'I quite understand that—'

The doctor's receptionist put her head in the door. 'Mr Varikiav is on the line. Shall I put him through?'

'Oh!' Her face lit up, then she looked at Stephen in apology. 'Would you mind if I took the call? It's long distance from Geneva.'

'Sure, go ahead.'

She picked up the receiver on her desk and spoke in a language he didn't know. That was kind of a surprise to him, because in the course of being dragged around the world as part of a diplomatic family he'd learned French, German and Spanish. This was something totally strange to him.

He rose and wandered to the window. It was growing dark outside, the streetlamps were coming on. Dad was probably thinking about going down to the hotel lobby for an evening paper. It must be pretty dull for Dad, hanging around from day to day while he came here to talk his head off to Dr Holt.

He heard her say something like *'Sbogom, voletjen'* then the earpiece was hung up on the speaker.

'I'm sorry about the interruption,' she said. It was clear she was happy. Her face glowed.

'I've been thinking,' Stephen said. 'You have to go to the country. Maybe I ought to sort myself out and go on my travels too.'

'Really?' She looked pleased and surprised. He realised it was the first time he'd said anything about making any positive decisions since first he began to come here.

'I thought I'd go back to the States and get Dad to take me to this place where my mother was living.'

'Oh, Stephen!' The pleasure suddenly vanished.

'What's the matter?'

'That was seventeen years ago. She probably isn't there now.'

'Sure, I know that, but just to see the place and maybe ask people round about if they knew her . . .'

'It's not very likely—'

'I want to go. I want to get nearer to her.'

'Is that a good idea?'

He had noticed that part of her technique was to ask questions, to make him query his own opinions and actions. He counter-attacked with, 'Got anything against it?'

'Only that it might be a disappointment.'

'Gee, I've had a few of those recently, I guess I can stand another.'

She sighed and accepted the decision. 'When shall you go?'

'I'll ask Dad. It'd probably be while you're off in wherever-it-is.'

'I see.'

'Can I write to you, tell you how I get on?'

'I'm planning to move to Geneva as soon as I can . . .'

'Wouldn't there be someone here who will forward letters?'

'Well, yes, my receptionist, Alice.'

Since it seemed as if it was going to be their last session, they shook hands when they parted. He thought she looked at him with a special sort of look – you might almost have called it affection.

She sure was a nice lady, even if she was a psychiatrist.

Out in the hall he met Alice picking the evening post out of the letter cage.

'Won't be seeing you again,' he said. 'Bye now.'

'Oh, goodbye, Mr Charlford.'

He paused. 'Say, that language that Dr Holt was speaking on the phone, what was that?'

'Serbian, probably. Dr Holt has a lot of Serbian friends.'

'Serbian? That's unusual, isn't it?'

'I suppose it is. Goes a long way back – her best friend, one she was at university with in Philadelphia, she's a Serbian.'

He nodded and went out. Alice closed the door. When he'd taken a step or two, his mind was suddenly crowded with questions.

But that would mean ringing the doorbell, and what would the nurse think of him?

Still, it was funny. It gave him a strange kind of little thrill to think that Dr Holt could actually speak the language of his unknown mother.

Chapter Thirty-six

The cry for help this time had come from Elwin's wife Dorothy. She had rung Christina that same morning.

'He was released from hospital yesterday, Christina.'

'Yes, I know that—'

'But what you don't know is what nonsense he's talking! As for his behaviour . . .'

'What about his behaviour?'

'He's so *odd*! I just don't know what he might do.'

'I told you before, Dot, Elwin would never harm you.'

'Do you think he hasn't harmed me already by his weird carry-on? The whole neighbourhood is talking! And little Helen . . . thank goodness she isn't old enough to know what it means to have a father in a mental clinic.'

'But you'd explain it to her if she was worried—'

'Explain? How can I explain what I don't understand to a seven-year-old? And don't start telling me it's only an illness like any other because it isn't. I never bargained for this when I married him and I don't think I can put up with it.'

Christina guessed that it was to say this that Dorothy had rung.

'What exactly do you mean, Dot?'

'I want a separation.' Having blurted it out, Dorothy waited for Christina's retort and, when it didn't come, said, 'Are you there?'

'Yes, I'm here.'

'Well, what do you think? Father-in-law says that when I tell Elwin, he's going to go straight off his head again.' Another silence. 'Hello? Hello?'

'Father may be right,' Christina said with a sigh. 'On the other hand . . .'

'Look here, Christina, will you come home and tell him my decision?'

'Good God no! You must tell him yourself.'

There was the sound of a sniffle. 'I can't. I'm afraid of him.'

'Oh, Dot . . .'

'Please, Christina. If he's going to go berserk you're the only one who can handle him.'

'He *isn't* going to go berserk!' Christina cried, angered by the word. 'You're so full of prejudice, Dorothy! Elwin has never raised his hand against anyone except in the war – and then he hated it so much it put him into a neurosis.'

'Neurosis! That's just a fancy word for being mental! And I'm not trained to handle mental cases, so if you want to see Elwin through this, you'd better come home.'

There was nothing to do but give in to this blackmail. Having seen Stephen for his last session and said goodbye to him – for the last time, she thought, as they shook hands – she put a few clothes in a suitcase and went by train to Market Bresham.

Her father was there with the car to meet her. He was in a state of suppressed rage. 'You can't blame Dot. She's right to want to live a life without continual apprehension about her husband's mental state. After all, she has a child to think of.'

'Father, for the last time, will you stop talking about Elwin as if he ought to spend the rest of his life in a strait-jacket? He's suffering from a well-known ailment: he's clinically depressed. He can be cured. And while he's getting better, the last thing he needs is anxious glances and shudders of apprehension.'

Herbert folded his lips together. He still couldn't get used to being spoken to in this fashion by a woman. And what made it worse was that she knew more about it than he did. He couldn't flatten her with the phrase, 'You don't know what you're talking about,' which had always silenced his wife Mildred.

Elwin was staying with his parents since Dorothy was unwilling to let him come home. He was in the hall to greet his sister. In her eyes, he seemed much better: still pale, and somewhat thinner, but calm and in control of himself. The improvement in his mental state was shown by the fact that he was taking care of his physical appearance – a recent haircut, a good shave, his clothes tidy though casual.

Their mother was hovering in the background. She hugged her daughter with fervour. 'It's so lovely to see you, Chrissie,' she sighed. 'Everything here is so *awful*!'

At this favourite lament, Christina couldn't help smiling. She hugged her in return, then went up to unpack the case which the maid had taken to her room. Her mother followed.

'Dottie said she rang you.'

'Yes.'

'You know what she wants?'

'Yes.'

'It's so *awful*, Chrissie.'

'Yes.' Christina busied herself shaking out her nightdress and dressing-gown.

'I'm disappointed in Dottie,' said Mrs Holt, hanging the dressing-gown on the hook on the door. 'After all, dear, marriage is "for better, for worse".'

'Yes.'

'Christina, do say something besides "yes"!'

Christina straightened for her task, faced her mother. 'What do you want me to say? The truth is, Elwin would be well rid of her! She's no help, she keeps telling herself he's going to attack her with a meat-axe.'

'Well, of course, that's nonsense . . .'

'You know that and I know that, but Dorothy doesn't seem to know it. It's not her fault, she's just subject to the general misapprehension about mental illness. Yet you know, love ought to drive out fear . . .' She shook her head in sadness. 'If you want my assessment, I think she won't face life with Elwin unless he's a successful provincial lawyer, and as he obviously doesn't seem likely to be popular with Father's clients, he's not going to be very successful, is he?'

'Your father says he can find a use for him in the firm . . . Clerical work . . . No responsibility . . .'

'Oh, I see! So that's what brought Dorothy to her decision,' Christina said in some cynicism. 'All right. She wants to live apart from Elwin but she doesn't want to tell him. So I'm elected to do it.'

'Oh dear.'

'And I'll do it. The sooner the better.'

'Wait till after dinner, dear. Cook's done a ragoût, and it would be such a shame if our appetites were spoiled.'

Divided between tears and laughter, Christina threw her arms round Mildred. 'Oh, Mother, you're such a gem!'

The meal was in fact good, and Christina was interested to see that her brother ate quite well. That was another improvement. When she first brought him back from Devon he wasn't eating enough to keep life in a linnet.

'Can we have a word in private, Elwin?' she suggested as they left the dining-room. 'We could have our coffee brought up to your room.'

'I'd like that,' he said.

He ushered her into the room he'd always occupied. It still held trophies from his Varsity days: photographs, a college scarf pinned above the looking-glass. He offered his sister the armchair. He himself sat on the hard chair by the writing desk.

'Well?' he said.

'Well what?'

'You came home on purpose to say this – whatever it is – to me. What is it? Have you conferred with your colleagues and decided I need the services of Sigmund Freud?'

'No, it's something about your private life. I have a message from Dorothy.'

'Dorothy, my loving wife.'

'She doesn't want to live with you in the future. In fact, she wants a legal separation.'

She watched him anxiously as she said the cruel words. She was looking for facial tremors, beads of sweat on his forehead, a glazed look.

He leaned back in his chair then took a deep breath, his reaction strangely subdued.

'Well, that solves one problem,' he remarked.

'I beg your pardon?'

'I was wondering how she'd take it but she's solved that for me.'

'Solved what? Elwin dear, what are you talking about?'

Something that might even have been a smile touched his pale features.

'Don't be so worried, little sister. I'm not devastated by what you just told me. If anything, I'm relieved.'

It was said in such a reasonable tone that she could scarcely believe it.

'Aren't you upset?' she burst out.

'Well, I'm not exactly bounding with joy. But I think I have to admit that if there ever was anything between Dorothy and me, it died of its own accord a couple of years ago.'

'Elwin!'

He nodded. 'Oh yes, I was a great disappointment to her. After waiting so long for me, she expected me to keep her in the state she was accustomed to, and bring credit on her and her children by my work as a lawyer – ending, she hoped, by my becoming Mayor of Market Bresham. I fell far short of all that.'

'Don't reproach yourself—'

'But I do. We should never have got married. When I look back, I see I never loved Dorothy. If I had, I'd have married her as soon as I came down from Cambridge. But I kept finding reasons why we couldn't name the day, and then came the war and off I went, almost glad to get away from her. And damn it, she "waited for me"!'

'Oh, Elwin—'

'When you're ill in hospital, Chrissie, you have plenty of time to think about things. I thought about my life with Dorothy. And I realised I did her a great injustice by marrying her.'

The maid came in with the tray of coffee. They waited in silence until she had gone.

'Elwin—'

'Pour the coffee, my dear. I've said all I want to say about my marriage, which can be summed up in one sentence – except for having produced a pretty little daughter, it's a flop.'

They sipped their coffee. Using the techniques of her craft, she said: 'How do you see the future, then, Elwin?'

He nodded his head at her. 'A good question. You'll be surprised to hear I have a good picture of it. The background of this picture is a country place, but far away from here. There are flowers and trees and a big lawn – and I'm there, working away with a lawnmower.'

'Elwin!' For a moment she thought he was babbling. Then, studying him, she could see he was amused.

'I mean it. I can tell you the name of the place. It's called Craikdown Hall, and it's in Cumberland. And I'm mowing the lawn there because I'm the gardener.'

'What? Gardener? What are you talking about, Elwin?'

'Look, Chrissie, if I don't have to stay in Market Bresham and be a good husband to Dorothy, I can go away and be a gardener. Right?'

'But – but—'

'I applied for the job while I was still in hospital. When I got home I found the letter waiting for me. I've been accepted as gardener.'

'Elwin!'

'I get fifty pounds a year, unlimited fruit and vegetables, meals at any time in the kitchen of the main house, and a cottage on the estate.'

'But *Elwin*! You can't go away and be a *gardener*!'

'Why not? It's what I've always wanted to be.'

'But you can't! In the first place, it's . . . it's . . .'

'Beneath my dignity?' He shrugged. 'A mental patient doesn't have much dignity, Chrissie.'

'Oh, but I meant – you were educated for the law . . .'

'And a fine mess I made of that. Well, I've educated myself to be a gardener. Any time I couldn't stand things, I used to retreat to the garden shed at our house and read books about the soil and cultivation and so on. I told our daily gardener not to come any more – I've been doing it all myself for ages.'

'But are those enough qualifications for . . . what's it called . . . Craikdown Hall?'

'Oh, they know I've never held a gardening post before. I was quite honest with them – war veteran a bit cracked in the head, can't settle down to the law, would like to try his hand as a gardener. And Lord Stoddesden replied that as an old soldier himself he understood perfectly and was willing to take me on. All I had to do was summon up the nerve to tell Dorothy that she was going to live in a gardener's cottage in Cumberland. And now I don't need to.'

He spoke perfectly coherently. She could hear no overtones of hysteria or panic. He had thought it all through.

A gardener? He could be right. When he had looked for refuge, it was always to gardens that he had gone. And the slow, inevitable procession of the seasons, the round of the gardening year with its set tasks and its renewed hopes each spring – that might be just what he needed.

Certainly almost anything was better than staying on in Market Bresham with a broken marriage and an inferior job in his father's office. Nothing was more likely to bring back his depression than daily reminders that he was a failure, daily urgings to 'pull himself together' and do better.

Besides, this was a choice he was making for himself. That in itself was important. All his life he had done what he was told, been a model son. Now he was at last speaking with his own voice.

'What about Helen?' she asked. To her, this was almost the most important point – the future of the little girl.

At the question the appearance of self-assurance wavered, the confident posture wilted. 'She's always been more Dorothy's daughter than mine.'

'Don't give her up, Elwin. She'll never forgive you later, if you just walk out of her life.'

He made a little defensive gesture. 'Dorothy would never let her come to stay on holiday. She's so sure I'm bats, she wouldn't trust me with Helen.'

'Then you must come home as often as you can to see her.'

'I'll try,' he said.

There was a pause.

'Do Mother and Father know your intentions?' she inquired, fiddling with the silverware on the tray.

'Don't be silly! Would Father be as quiet as he is if he knew what I mean to do? But I have to tell them soon. I'm leaving for Cumberland at the end of the week.'

'Have another cup of coffee,' his sister said with a wry smile, 'you're going to need it.'

When they went downstairs both parents were on the *qui-vive*. Mildred looked at Christina with an anxiety that was almost palpable.

'Yes,' Elwin said, surveying them, 'she broke the news you'd clearly had from Dorothy. And in return I'll give you some of my own. I'm going north to take up a job on Saturday.'

'What?'

'What kind of job?' Herbert demanded. 'Why wasn't I told about this?'

'I'm telling you now.'

'But before now, why didn't you say anything before now?'

'For the same reason that you didn't pass on Dorothy's decision – I didn't want an upset.'

'Elwin dear—' his mother began.

'Just a moment, Mildred. Now see here, Elwin, I don't know if I want you to go to some other law firm.'

'I'm not going to be a solicitor. I'm going to be a gardener.'

'Oh,' Mildred said faintly, flopping into an armchair.

'A *what*?' roared her husband.

'A gardener. A tiller of the soil.'

'What damn-fool nonsense is this?'

'It isn't nonsense. I've decided to be a gardener.'

'You can't be a gardener, dear, what would people think?'

'I don't care what people think, Mother. I've spent almost forty years of my life bothering about what other people think, and now I'm going to do what I really want to do.'

'You'll do no such thing!'

'Elwin, dear, a gardener—'

'It's all delirium! Something to do with the drugs he's been given in hospital—'

'I'm not under the influence of a drug. Am I, Dr Holt?'

'Not so far as I can see,' Christina said.

'Did you know about this?' her father thundered at her.

'He just told me.'

'Well, I forbid it! I—'

'How are you going to stop him?'

'I'll stop him! I won't have this sort of childishness! After all the money I spent on educating him!'

'If you had told me,' Elwin put in in a quivering voice, 'that I was going to have to pay for my education with total obedience for the rest of my life, I would have refused to go to Cambridge.'

'Don't you take that tone to me, boy.'

'And don't you take that tone to me!' Sudden temper flared. It was so unusual in the normally agreeable Elwin that Herbert actually drew back a step.

'Elwin,' murmured his mother, 'Elwin . . . !'

'Don't sound so tragic about it! I'm just going to try something different from the law.'

'But a gardener! A common labourer!'

Elwin made a helpless little gesture of the hands. Christina came to his aid. 'He's always been interested in gardens, Mother. He knows a lot about them.'

'Humph,' snorted her father. 'What good's that going to do him? A pound a week, twenty-two shillings if he's lucky: what good is that to a married man?'

'If you recall, sir, my wife has decided she doesn't want to live under the same roof with me. I don't have to support her.'

'What? What?' Herbert stuttered and seemed at a loss.

'She can have my savings. She can have the house. She can even have our daughter, because I don't suppose a cottage on an estate in Cumberland would provide the kind of background Dorothy would want for Helen—'

'A cottage?' Mildred broke in. 'On an estate? Elwin, how are you going to get on? Who's going to do the cooking and cleaning?'

'I'll manage.'

'Don't encourage him by asking questions as if he was really going to do it,' Herbert told her. 'It's not going to happen.'

'Yes it is. I got the letter offering me the job yesterday and I sent a reply by return of post to say I'd be there on Sunday ready to start on the Monday.'

'Who on earth would take you on as a gardener?'

'Lord Stoddesden of Craikdown Hall, in Cumberland.'

'What? Who?'

'Who'll do your mending?' Mildred persisted. 'And your laundry – you'll need dozens of clean shirts in a job like that—'

'Mildred, I forbid you to talk about it as if it were really going to happen!'

'Father,' Christina said in a cool tone, 'I think Mother is showing more sense than you in this case. Elwin is really going to Cumberland on Sunday.'

'No he is *not*. I won't have any son of mine working as a paid servant.'

'How big is the cottage?' Mildred demanded. 'Has it got running water? A bath?'

'It's been modernised, so it said in the advertisement I answered. All amenities, it said, and unlimited vegetables and fruit.'

'I think I'd better go with you, dear, to keep house.'

There was an amazed, an astounded silence.

'You'll do no such thing!' her husband roared.

'But I've made up my mind, Herbert.'

'Then unmake it! I never heard such nonsense. Whatever has got into you, Mildred?'

'I don't know, dear. It just suddenly seems . . . if my poor crazy son can do it, then I can.'

'Elwin isn't crazy, Mother,' Christina protested.

'Oh, I know that. In fact, I think he's saner than most of us at this moment. That's why I'm going with him.'

'I've told you, you're not!'

'What are you going to do, lock me up on bread and water as you used to do with Christina? I think you'll just have to stop raising your voice about it, dear. Elwin needs someone to keep his house and darn his socks, and as his mother I'm the best person to do it. Unless he finds some nice young woman who feels like taking him on, in which case I'll come home again.'

Her husband was gaping at her with his mouth open. 'Mildred! Are you saying you'd move out and let Elwin live in sin with some woman?'

'We'll just have to see, dear,' Mildred sighed.

Elwin suddenly awoke from the stupefaction her remarks had brought on. 'I can't ask you to do this, Mother—'

'You haven't asked me, I've volunteered.'

'Damn it, Mildred, stop talking like that! Elwin can't go to Cumberland and pig about in a cottage! He's a married man with a wife and daughter!'

'They're perfectly welcome to come and live in the cottage,' Elwin said. 'But it's quite clear that Dorothy won't even let me share our house on the other side of town. So I don't think it's likely she'll want to share a cottage in Cumberland.'

'Have you told her?' Mildred inquired, frowning a little.

'I didn't see the necessity. Just as she didn't tell me she was applying for a separation, I didn't tell her I was starting a new career.'

'I give it six months,' Herbert said in contempt. 'You won't stick it beyond June.'

'Herbert, I'd better write out a list of the people you ought to send Christmas cards to . . .'

'What?'

'I think you can give money presents to the servants: they

wouldn't expect you to go shopping for them—'

'What?'

'Don't worry about old Mrs Durman. I'll send her something from Cumberland.'

'Look here,' Herbert said, in a quite different voice, 'you're not really going?'

'Of course I am.'

'But . . . but . . . you can't!'

'Why not, dear? I know I suffer from migraine headaches and stomach upsets, but perhaps a quiet life in the country is just what I need.'

'You can't go, Mildred. What about me?'

'What about you?'

'Who's going to look after me?'

'You've got a houseful of servants, Herbert dear,' she said in the patient tone of one pointing out the obvious.

'But that's not the same at all! I don't want to be looked after by servants!'

'I know, dear, it will seem strange at first. But you'll get used to it.'

'But you can't leave me! I'm your husband!'

'And Elwin's my son. And as he won't have any servants, it seems to me quite clear that I have to go with him.'

'Mother, I wouldn't want you to do something you might regret . . .'

'I shan't regret it, Elwin. In fact, I'm quite looking forward to it.'

Christina had witnessed the exchange in astonishment. Not only had Elwin found his voice; at last her downtrodden mother had spoken out as well.

'You . . . you can't go,' her father said to her mother. 'I . . . I forbid it!'

'Let her try it for a few weeks, Father,' she suggested. 'If she finds it's too much for her, she can come home.'

'Oh, I don't think I shall want to come home,' Mildred said in a strangely certain tone of voice. 'But if you want to come and visit, Herbert, of course you'd always be welcome.'

The three-sided conversation went on until long beyond

bedtime. Herbert insisted that his son couldn't go to Cumberland to be a gardener, nor could his wife go to be his housekeeper. Mildred gave him instructions on how to manage once she was gone. Elwin talked calmly of the legal steps Dorothy would have to take to obtain a legal separation.

When at last the fire had died to ashes and they were almost dead with weariness, it had become an established fact: Elwin and his mother would both be taking the train on Sunday. Nothing the hitherto all-powerful Herbert Holt could do would prevent it.

Next morning before she left for the early train to London, her father got Christina to one side. 'Talk sense into them,' he said. 'They can't *do* this.'

'I haven't the slightest wish to interfere, Father.'

'But you can't think it's right? For your mother to disrupt the household . . . disregard my comfort . . . make me look absurd . . .'

Christina was suddenly sorry for him. Past middle-age, accustomed to his own way all his life, Mildred's rebellion would leave him stranded like a beached whale.

'It won't be so bad,' she urged. 'You can tell people it's only temporary, while Elwin settles in. By and by they'll get used to the idea.'

'But *I* shan't, Christina.'

'No. Well, it's not a perfect arrangement. I suppose nothing ever is. The thing is to appreciate good things while we have them, Father, not leave it too late and then have to regret them.'

'What do you mean by that?' he challenged, baffled.

Useless to try to explain that he had more or less brought it all upon himself. She patted him on the shoulder and hurried off to the station.

On the journey home her own words echoed in her mind. 'Appreciate good things while we have them, not leave it too late and then regret them.' What she and Laurenz Varikiav shared was one of the good things, one of the rare things in life. They had a strong, lasting love. It was wrong to put off their marriage for first one reason and then another.

When she got back to London she would hurry on with the winding-up of her practice and the selling of her lease. As soon as she could arrange it she would join Laurenz in Geneva and break the news about the marriage to the children. They might not like it, but somehow they must be brought to tolerate it. Thereafter she would devote all her energy to winning their affection.

But one thing she had learned for certain in the last twenty-four hours. Love was too precious to relegate to some hazy future. She would grasp it while she could, for fear she too might leave it too late and then regret it.

Chapter Thirty-seven

There was a fat envelope postmarked Geneva awaiting her. It contained a short note from Laurenz to say he was missing her, an even shorter note from Suza to say she loved the little Japanese parasol that Father had brought her, and a collection of snapshots. A page of writing was wrapped round the snaps, from Milovan.

There was nothing particularly friendly about his communication. It consisted of instructions about what she was to notice in his pictures. The snaps had a number on the back and she was to refer to the number. The pictures were mostly of Lake Geneva steamers – tying up, casting off, turning away from the pier, and sometimes so far out on the waters that only a little dab of white was visible.

But despite the stiffness of the language, she heard Milovan's message: I want to say a sort of thank-you for getting Father to buy me the camera; I want you to be interested in what I've photographed; don't laugh at the results, they're pictures of things that I admire.

She sat down at once to reply. To Laurenz she gave a brief description of the upheaval in her father's household. 'It means I shall have to spend Christmas with him, otherwise for the first time in his life he'd spend it alone. Soon after that I hope to have disposed of the lease of this house. With luck I should be with you for "our" Christmas in January.' She wrote two short notes to the children: the one to Suza was really a pretty card with room to write a few words, but the one to Milo asked questions about the timetable of the steamers now that winter had come. 'I'll bring your photos with me when I return,' she ended, 'unless you want them back urgently – perhaps you'll write to let me know.'

He might write, he might not. But at least they were in contact.

There were various official matters to settle. One was, could she practise medicine in Switzerland with a degree obtained in Philadelphia? The answer was no. Did this apply to psychiatry? No, it did not. She was free to practise psychiatry under Swiss law, but if it involved the prescription of drugs she must have a qualified doctor in consultation. However, she could enter for the degree examinations in Geneva for the following year, but must understand that the papers and the viva voce would be in French.

It was a challenge. At thirty-seven she was being asked once more to prove herself. All right, she would do so. But friends in London wrote letters of commendation to back up her application, with the result that she was offered a post in a private clinic at Chene-Bourg, a few miles east of the city.

At the beginning of December she got a letter from Pittsburgh. Stephen wrote to say that he had been to the farm in the Juniata Valley at which, according to his birth certificate, he was born. 'Almost nobody here remembers the people who used to own the place when it was called Traskanya. It seems it wasn't one family but a lot of different people. I met an old lady who seemed to recall the name Belu, but she says she was a plump little brunette and Dad is certain my mother was very fair. You were right, Dr Christina, it's been a disappointment.'

He came vividly into her thoughts as she read. She recalled his distress, his anger. Yet this letter was quite calm. Even when he went on to say that he'd been to visit his mother and Victor, the words were steady and without resentment. 'I can't say *he* improves on acquaintance, but Mom seems happy and I guess that's good enough. I've been thinking over what you said about giving her time to want me back in her life and I can't see it happening any time soon. But what the heck! I've got stuff to do, I don't have to hang around waiting on Mom's change of heart. Have a nice Christmas. Yours, Stephen.'

It was as well she wouldn't be seeing him again. She had made some bad mistakes during his treatment. She'd let herself show too much personal involvement in their conversations. She could hear the echo of her own voice saying 'son' as a term of affection. Well, that could be brushed off as the kind of thing an older person might say to a boy. Yet had she said it in that casual way? Hadn't there been too much tenderness?

And then that terrible gaffe when she'd said his mother had long forgiven the man who seduced her. He had said, 'How could you possibly know that?' How indeed! She couldn't recall how she had dealt with the question. Adequately, it seemed, because he hadn't pursued it.

If he had queried it further, he might have got some hint. He was a very normal boy, not particularly sensitive, but on a subject such as this he seemed to have developed special antennae. And if he had cross-questioned her, would she have blurted out the truth? And if she had, what would have followed?

Psychologists were divided on the subject of adoption. Was it good for the child to learn he had been adopted? If he learned that fact, should he be allowed to look for his natural parents? If he found them, would it be good or bad for him? And what would the relationship be after that?

It was like a minefield. The wrong move, the wrong touch, and a life – perhaps several lives – could be blown sky-high. Received wisdom was still that, if possible, the child should grow up without ever knowing he was adopted. Yet recent studies contradicted this belief. Christina had had to deal with a girl whose adopted parents unconsciously resented her failure to be the ideal fairytale child they'd expected – and the girl had no way of knowing how she was falling short.

December trudged on, dark and grey and chilly. Elwin wrote from his cottage in Cumberland to say that they were comfortable and that the work would be interesting and not too tremendously arduous because there were plenty of local boys to be hired for the hard jobs.

It appeared that the enthusiastic gardener in the

Stoddesden household was his lordship's sister, Lady Violet. Elwin described her as 'sixtyish, skinny, and spritely'. A friendship seemed to be springing up between her ladyship and Mrs Holt.

The cottage was described as two up and two down with modern additions. Mrs Holt had one or two ideas for improvement, mostly to do with the colour of the paintwork and some new curtains. For himself, Elwin was busy in the greenhouse since there wasn't too much to do outdoors at present. He sent his love and, in a carefully thought-out phrase, sent warmest Christmas greetings to all in Market Bresham. A present for Helen was in the post.

At the end of the letter her mother had added a few lines: 'Really a pleasant little house though draughty at the moment. Lady Violet wears very sensible shoes, she's given me the name of the firm so I can get some too. Your father says you're spending Christmas with him: very good of you, dear. Please try not to let him eat the dark meat, it always disagrees with him.'

Christmas at the old house in Market Bresham was more than just seeing that her father didn't eat the wrong food and chats about Lady Violet's shoes. Many subjects had to be avoided.

Dorothy came on Boxing Day with Helen. 'I feel it's my duty,' she explained to Christina as they watched the little girl play with the new doll Elwin had sent. 'No matter how badly Elwin's behaved, Mr Holt is still Helen's grandfather and it's my duty to bring her to visit.'

'It's always good for children to see as many of their relatives as possible, as often as possible.' Christina hesitated. 'I hope you're going to extend this goodwill to letting Elwin and Helen see each other.'

'Of course,' Dorothy said. 'Strictly supervised, however. I could never be easy in my mind if I wasn't there to see no harm came to her.'

'Dorothy, I hope you're not passing on this view of her father to Helen . . .'

'What view do you expect me to have?' Dorothy snapped.

'He's gone, isn't he? Without discussing it with me first.'

'But you had already said you didn't want to live with him.'

'That doesn't mean I want him going off and making a fool of himself! A gardener – I'd have to say I was married to a *gardener* if anyone asked me what my husband does.'

Christina was on the verge of saying she could substitute 'horticulturist' for 'gardener' but had a feeling it would be thought frivolous. 'I can see it's caused a difference to your standing—'

'Not just to my standing!' her sister-in-law interrupted with indignation. 'Have you any idea how expensive it is to run that house of ours? Of course when we bought it we thought we were going to have a large family and do a lot of entertaining but now . . . It simply eats money, and if you imagine that what Elwin made over to me from his bank account will keep it going, you're sadly mistaken!'

There was no doubt a problem existed. Herbert, when he got wind of it, would find yet another cause to be angry with his errant son. But an idea began to emerge from the back of Christina's mind.

There was her father, alone in a large family house and with plenty of money to run it. And there was his daughter-in-law, left without an income in a house she couldn't afford.

What could be better than that Dorothy and Helen should move in with Herbert?

Both of them could see great obstacles to the notion when Christina suggested it. She didn't press it. Either it would come about, or it wouldn't. She was fairly confident that two things would work in its favour. In the first place, Herbert was lonely and enjoyed the company of his little granddaughter. In the second, it was much more prestigious for Dorothy to be in charge of Herbert Holt's household than to be thought of as 'that poor Mrs Holt whose husband ran off and left her'.

Christina had very little left to do in London. Her belongings were packed up ready to be collected by the 'continental remover'. Case records had been transferred to the consultants taking over her patients; those referring to patients who had simply ceased to come were put in safekeeping with Alice Lowther, who promised to burn them if they weren't needed again within the year. The premises were to be turned over to a trichologist, who would move in during January.

She made a farewell visit to Market Bresham and then travelled on to Cumberland to say goodbye to her mother and Elwin. 'You're really going to settle in Geneva?' her mother mourned. 'It's such a long way away!'

Christina didn't say that she might eventually settle in Skoplje, which was even further away. For the present she simply made soothing noises about the ease of modern travel. 'Who knows, Mother? You might feel like coming to see me.'

'I don't think so, dear. We're living on what Elwin earns. I don't think I could afford trips to—'

'Oh, darling, I'd pay your fare, of course!'

'That hardly seems right . . .'

'Surely you'd want to come to my wedding?'

'Christina! You're getting married?' Mildred was over-whelmed. 'When? Who to?'

'Soon, I hope. His name is Laurenz Varikiav.'

'A foreigner?' Her mother sounded dubious. 'Chrissie, I hope you haven't fallen for some glamorous foreigner you met a few months ago in Geneva!'

'I've known Laurenz for years. I met him during the war in Serbia.'

'Don't say he's a Serbian!'

'Yes, he is.'

'Oh goodness! But I don't know a word of Serbian!'

'Never mind, Mother. He can speak quite good English. He works at the League of Nations.'

'A foreign diplomat?' said Mildred, greatly impressed.

'I suppose so.' Christina always thought of Laurenz as a soldier and a land-owner. It was true he was a diplomat too, but that wasn't his own choice of career.

She told her mother about Laurenz, leaving out the aspects that would upset her: no mention that he had served a prison sentence; that he had killed a man over an affair of honour; no mention of his wife and the fate that she had met. She explained about Suza and Milovan – 'handsome children, the little girl seems to be getting fond of me already, the boy is more difficult.'

'Oh, Christina . . . Why couldn't you choose someone more straightforward,' sighed her mother.

'I don't know. It just happened.'

'You love him. I can see you do.'

'Yes, darling. Very much.'

'Then it'll be all right.'

Elwin came in from an afternoon's work lopping dead branches from trees. She was delighted to see that he looked fuller in the face, with colour in his cheeks and an air of being at ease with himself.

'What do you think, dear?' Mildred cried, busying herself to provide fresh tea and hot scones. 'Christina's getting married!'

'Really? Congratulations!' He listened to a somewhat muddled version of the news from his mother. The evening turned into a little celebration.

Only as she was leaving next morning did he ask after his little girl.

'She's well, Elwin. You've heard that Dorothy is thinking of moving in to keep house for Father?'

'Mother had a note from him about it, didn't you, Mother?'

Mildred looked vexed. 'Really a very silly note! More or less telling me it was my last chance to come home or else he'd let Dorothy take over.'

'And are you going?'

'Of course not.' Mrs Holt opened the door an inch or so. 'I think I hear your taxi, dear.'

The old Austin came labouring up the slope from the lodge gates. Christina went out, Elwin put her case in the car.

'So next time we see you it may be for a wedding, eh?'

'May be, Elwin.'

'Good luck, then, Chrissie.'

'Good luck to you, Elwin. I hope you win prizes at the village flower show!'

Her mother embraced her. 'Oh, Chrissie, Chrissie . . . Be happy, dear – it's the important thing.'

There was a farewell party for her in London. Addie Bellhaven had invited friends and close colleagues. Their going-away present was a locket to wear on the chain given her so many years ago by Captain Dinsdorf. On the back was engraved, 'To C.H. from her friends.' With tears in her eyes, Christina threaded it on the old gold chain. She wore it when, two days later, she left for Geneva.

Someone else was travelling towards Geneva that day – from further away than London. He was on an ocean liner from New York, and his mind was full of whirling thoughts that obsessed him to the point of making him almost a hermit in his cabin.

Stephen Charlford had gone home with his father to Pennsylvania from London determined to get some idea of the kind of girl she had been, this Kristin Belu. He wanted to understand why she had parted with her baby, given him over to strangers. Dr Holt said it was forgivable – he wanted to be able to forgive.

He and John Charlford had driven from the big family house outside Pittsburgh to the Juniata Valley. The farm known as Traskanya had changed its name, they had had to apply at the records office in Duncannon to find out what it was called now. John even had to ask for directions on how to get there: it was so long ago that he'd been there, he'd forgotten where it lay.

The weather was wintry, snow lay on the ground. The summits of the Alleghenies were hidden in cloud. A sombre landscape, in keeping with the mood of the two men, father and son. John was afraid for Stephen, afraid of what fresh hurt he might be inviting by this quest. Stephen himself was grimly determined.

But his determination brought him nothing. The farm was now called by the name of its new owners, the Woodsons. The Woodsons had had the place for eight years, had bought it from the previous owners, the Larbert family.

'Serbians? You sure?' Chuck Woodson asked on hearing their inquiry. 'Never heard of no Serbians round here. We got Quakers and we got Baptists, and further to the north we got the Amish.'

'It was before the war,' John murmured. 'There was a community lived here – a man called Stefan Mesdiu and his wife, I think she was called Martita, and their cousin Kristin Belu.'

'Nope, sorry.'

In Duncannon they asked the town constable. He recalled that there had been Russians or Serbians or some such critters out on the homestead now owned by the Woodsons. Seen them about when he was a boy, he said.

'Ma Petherfold might know. She took a lot of notice of what went on and she might recall something.'

They found Ma Petherfold feeding her chickens in the early morning light of next day.

'Mesdiu, Mesdiu . . . Nope, can't say as I recall. Wait though, warn't there a girl, Sofya, used to try to make cheese? Turble stuff.'

John shook his head. He'd never heard of anyone called Sofya. 'We're trying to trace a girl – she'd be a woman now, of course – called Kristin Belu.'

'Belu! Yeah, sure, I remember her! Belu! Always used to call her Little Miss Blue.'

'You remember her?' Stephen exclaimed, with a sudden jolt to his heart that almost made him sob with pain.

'Now lemme see. Little brown-skinned girl, kind of plump. Lots of dark hair done up on top of her head in a granny loaf bun. Snapping black eyes. Spoke good English, better than that Sofya, but she never tried her hand at no cheese that I know of.'

'Dark?' John said. 'Surely not. The girl I mean was very fair: pale gold-coloured hair in two pigtails, big grey eyes, certainly not plump – in fact, rather slender.'

Mrs Petherfold shook her head with vigour. 'Your memory's mis-advisin' you. Little Miss Blue was kind of like that film star, Clara Bow – seen her?'

'Oh no,' said John. 'No, she wasn't the least like that.'

'Can't he'p you, then.'

'You don't remember a girl with fair hair in plaits that came almost down to her waist?'

'Now,' said the old lady slowly, 'there was a girl of that kind, didn't rightly belong to the farm. Seen her once or twice . . . A relation of some kind, seems to me she came two or three times on vacation, off the train at Duncannon Depot with Little Miss Blue, with an armful of books and a few clothes in an old carpet bag. I heard tell she came and stayed a while, June through September, one year: would that be nineteen-oh-nine or ten? Can't jest pin it down.'

'Nineteen-ten,' urged Stephen. 'It was nineteen-ten.'

'Was it? I didn't see her myself: she seemed to stay in and around the farm. Joe Binns used to see her a-walkin' on the far side of the valley: could always see they womenfolk, they wore sort of white wool skirts and bright jackets.'

'And that was Kristin Belu?'

'Don't know as I ever heard her name. The other one, the dark one, she sure was Belu, but it warn't Kristin, I'm sartin it warn't.'

'Do you know where they went when the farm was sold up?'

'Oh, they was goin' to make their fortunes in California,' she said with scorn. 'I'll tell you one thing for sure, they warn't going to make it selling cheese.'

Try as she might, she could remember nothing more. They thanked her, pressed some money into her unwilling hand, and drove away.

They went to New York to see Estelle. Stephen could tell it was an ordeal for his father. He didn't enjoy it much himself.

When they got back to Pittsburgh he wrote to Dr Christina about it. He wanted her to know that he could take these trials without blowing his stack.

Stephen didn't like Pittsburgh. His family – or rather the Charlford family – made its money from the coalpits that surrounded the town, but he never felt at home there.

Christmas was approaching. Stephen went to stay with relations in Philadelphia so as to see the preparations for the Mummers' Parade.

He met up with some of his school friends, did a little Christmas shopping, went to the theatre to see *Showboat* and to the cinema to see *The Jazz Singer*, donated money to the Mississippi Flood Disaster Fund, learned the slow foxtrot.

Cousin Fremont, with whom he was staying, had pretensions towards being an intellectual. He and his wife had a 'salon' every two weeks. Stephen was pressed into service to carry cocktails around and make himself agreeable to the daughters of the gentlemen and ladies of learning.

They in their turn invited the Fremonts. Willy-nilly Stephen had to go to little 'at homes' which bored him. At one such, he wandered off to the library in search of something to read, and found himself looking into several copies of the University of Pennsylvania Year Book. Nineteen-ten. That was the year of his birth. He opened it, looked through it. It appeared that their host, Greville Groose, had graduated that year. What a bunch. Clothes that year were really gruesome. Lucky for him his mother had been a Serbian peasant girl who wore loose woollen skirts and embroidered jackets.

Nineteen-eleven. Greville's younger brother, Barnard, had graduated that year. A marker in the book showed the class photograph: one of those terribly-proper young men was presumably Barnard.

He turned the page. Graduation class, Faculty of Medicine. Rows of men, a few women. Below were their names.

One leapt out at him. 'Miss Josafin Belu MD.' He counted along the row, found her. A small, dark, curvaceous girl in a dark dress. Standing next to her was a taller girl also in a dark dress, but above it her fair hair made a vivid contrast. He knew that face.

His finger ran down the page, found the caption. 'Miss Josafin Belu (Kosovo, Serbia) MD. Miss Christina Holt, (Lincolnshire, England) MD . . .'

Dr Christina!

He felt the room going round.

Later, in his room at the Fremonts' house, he got his thoughts in order.

It had to be the same Dr Holt. It had to be Dr Christina Holt, fair-haired and tallish and slender. Her hair was long in the photograph, piled on top of her head. Now it was short and worn smooth against the scalp. But it was the same woman, and after all, her home address – hadn't she said she was going home to Lincolnshire because there was some family crisis?

And her friend's name, Josafin Belu. Curvy and brunette, 'like Clara Bow, the film star.' This was Mrs Petherfold's Little Miss Blue.

Those two knew each other. That was obvious, two women among so few in the Faculty of Medicine of that year.

And now he thought about it, he was sure he had heard Dr Christina say that she studied in Philadelphia.

Next morning he rang his father in Pittsburgh. 'Dad, I've been thinking I ought to send a Christmas card to Dr Christina.'

'Why, good thinking, Stephen. What a nice idea. You go ahead and do it.'

'Dad, how come we know her?'

'Huh?'

'How did you and she get acquainted?'

'Why, I don't recall . . . Yes, wait a minute, she was at a conference in New York two years ago and the office sent me along to mingle with the guests – they were an international gathering, quite high powered.'

'She's somebody important then?'

'Oh, I think so. I believe she had a very remarkable career during the war. I did hear that when she came to Philadelphia that same year, the Medical Faculty put on a bit of a party for her. What makes you ask, Stephen?'

'Oh, I'm just interested. She was kind of nice to me.'

'That's right, she was. You send her a card, boy.'

By the time he put the phone down he had decided on his next step. If she was in any way notable and had had some social honour done to her while she was in Philadelphia, it would be in the newspaper.

He went through the files of two years ago. And there she was, her photograph occupying two columns above a piece headed 'War Heroine'.

'Dr Christina Holt, former student of Pennsylvania University and now honoured guest of this fair city. Dr Holt was awarded the Legion d'Honneur by the French Government for services with the French Medical Corps, and also the Medal of the Eagle from King Alexander for her years of work in Serbia with the Women's Service Hospital during the Great War. Dr Holt has recently been present at a medical conference in New York . . .'

Years of work in Serbia . . .

And the conversation on the telephone with the man long-distance from Geneva. Stephen had asked the nurse-receptionist, 'What language was that?' And she'd said, 'Serbian, probably.'

She had been friends with a Serbian girl in Philadelphia. That would be why she volunteered for service in Serbia during the war, because she'd learned the language from Josafin Belu.

Josafin Belu. Christina Holt. Kristina Holt. Kristin Belu.

Kristin Belu, a fair-haired Serbian girl at Traskanya, a Serbian settlement in the Alleghenies.

A Serbian name, of course.

If some girl got in a jam with a man who tricked her . . . tricked her, wasn't that what Dr Christina had said? If she wanted a place to go to have her baby without having the rest of the world come down on her, a settlement of Serbian immigrants in the Alleghenies was a hell of a good place to go.

He wasn't going to go any further with that. He was giving himself the jimjams.

There were other things to think about. Was he really going on with the idea of studying archaeology? If so, he would be going to Egypt. He had to send details of his birth and education to the Department of Antiquities.

So he went to Pittsburgh, asked his father for his birth certificate and certificate of adoption, had certified copies made. While he had them, he applied for a passport. Since he was still a minor, he had to get his father to sign the application. The passport arrived soon after Christmas.

'Well, now you're all set,' John Charlford said with approval. 'As soon as they say they want you, you can book passage for Egypt.'

'Sure thing, Dad. In fact . . .'

'What?'

'I thought of going any day now. Get on the road, you know.'

'Oh, Stephen . . .' He saw his father suppress a sigh. 'We've only just got back. And the State Department have offered me something . . .'

'That's OK, Dad. You don't need to come.'

'I couldn't let you go on your own!' Charlford said at once.

There was always someone from their circle about to leave for Europe. In the end, Stephen sailed with Mr and Mrs Baeschen, who were to bring home a daughter from trouble-torn Germany. They told each other it would be nice to have young company on the voyage.

But Stephen Charlford disappointed them. He scarcely left his cabin.

Chapter Thirty-eight

Jo-Jo met Christina off the train in Geneva. *'Mali doctoritza!'* she cried, wrapping her in a strong embrace. 'What a long time since I saw you! Are you well? What a handsome hat! Is this the London fashion?'

Jo-Jo herself was in furs against the Geneva winter. Snow clothed the mountains and lay on the lawns and flowerbeds of the city, but the Genevois have learned to live with winter – the streets were cleared, the pavements were hazard-free.

As they waited for a taxi, Jo-Jo protested yet again at her friend's plan to go back to the Hotel du Chevron. 'You must come to me – there is plenty of room in my flat as you well know.'

'Jo-Jo, it wouldn't be at all convenient.'

'Why not? You are not going to practise from home, are you? Only from the clinic.'

'It's my private life I'm thinking of, not my professional one.'

'What? Oh!' Jo-Jo gave a little gasp then produced a roguish smile. 'I see. Embarrassing for the lover, no? How could I be so tactless? Very well, you go to the hotel. But surely they don't still hold your room for you?'

'Not exactly. They put my portmanteau in store. But this time of year, there's no problem about getting a room. And before too long, I hope I'll be moving in with Laurenz and his children.'

'Indeed? You have solved the stepmother problem?'

'I don't know,' Christina confessed. A taxi came, they got in with her luggage and set off for the Chevron.

'All at once you are settled to get married, no matter what

the children say?' Jo-Jo asked with interest. 'That is a change, surely?'

'It's just that . . . recent events have made me see . . . it's silly to let a chance of happiness slip by. And I want to have a baby, Jo-Jo. *His* baby.'

'Ah.' Jo-Jo patted her hand. 'Well, I am not like you, I don't have this strong feeling towards children, but I think I understand. So you are going to take no notice of Milo and Suza?'

That was too much to say. Christina shook her head uncertainly. 'Suza . . . I think Suza was getting fond of me already. If Milo would just show a sign . . .'

'What kind of sign?'

'I don't know. All I know is, I'd recognise it if I saw it.'

At the hotel Christina was welcomed and shown up to her room, a better one than she had had before. There was a big vase of hothouse carnations on the bureau. She looked at the card. 'A loving welcome, Laurenz.'

Jo-Jo helped her unpack, had tea in the hotel room, then left urging Christina to drop in on her as soon as she felt like it. Christina had dinner in the sparsely occupied hotel dining-room. About nine in the evening, Laurenz came. He bowed over her hand, then sat down to share her after-dinner coffee in the hotel lounge.

'I'm so choked up with longing for you, I can hardly find a voice to speak to you,' he said. 'I've missed you so much, the children asked if I had the influenza.'

'How are they? I hoped Milo would write to me, but he didn't.'

'I think he began one or two letters. But he seemed to spend more time biting his pen than putting down any words.'

'I wonder if that's good or bad, Laurenz?'

'You are the child expert, my love.' And as she sat looking a little downcast he added, 'I think they have missed you. Suza has said more than once that she wished you were back. At school they were asked to write about "My Favourite Friend" and she wrote about you.'

'Yes, but Milo . . . ? Milo is the important one, the leader. If he sets himself against me, it's hopeless.'

'He will love you,' Laurenz said. 'How could he help it?'

'Oh, easily,' she told him. 'Loyalty to his dead mother would prevent it.'

They sat talking for a long time. The hotel lounge emptied. Towards midnight they went upstairs to her room, to forget their problems in each other's arms.

She went to lunch with all three Varikiavs two days later at a restaurant on the mountain slopes reached by a *téléphérique*. This was a great thrill to both children, particularly Milovan. At one point, when they lurched for a moment over a great valley, he put a protective arm around Suza's shoulders and almost, but not quite, reached for Christina's hand.

The Serbian Christmas – *Bohzich* – was approaching. It was agreed that the Varikiavs, Dr Nedjozic and his wife, Jo-Jo Belu and Christina, should go together to the midnight service in the Orthodox Church at Val d'Arve. Dr and Mrs Nedjozic would collect the others from Laurenz's apartment in the 'official' limousine after the usual celebratory supper party.

'What happens at this party, Jo-Jo?' Christina inquired. 'Is it solemn, or a family party, or what?'

'Oh, it is nothing very splendid. There ought to be a sucking pig, but I don't suppose we shall have that because it has to be roasted on a spit and I'm sure Laurenz's housekeeper would be horrified at the idea. I expect we'll get leg of pork instead. Then there will be *paklava* – you remember *paklava*?'

'That horrible sweet stuff?'

'Horrible? It's delicious! Then come the presents.'

'Ah. That was what I needed to know.'

'Only the children get presents. If grown-ups give each other something, they do it next day. But the children get presents and you say, "In the name of the Lord" as you hand them over.'

Christina went away to think seriously about presents.

Suza was no problem. She bought the little girl a very pretty dress, having noted that all her clothes – chosen for her by elderly Cousin Vela – were dull and 'serviceable'. On the other hand, Milo's present caused her a lot of thought.

Madame Pluchet, the housekeeper, had done her best for the Serbians, poor things. Celebrating Christmas after everybody else had finished, it was like running along after the procession had gone by . . . She had put up boughs of evergreen in the hall of the apartment, and tin angels which turned above the heat of two small candles.

The supper was a strange mixture of Swiss and Serbian cuisine. All the same, everyone enjoyed the meal. The children were keyed up with excitement. This was the first Christmas since Father came home. All the others had been sombre and penurious under Cousin Vela's regime.

When they rose from the dinner table, their eyes went at once to the parcels piled up on the table where the angels slowly circled above the candles. They looked expectantly at Laurenz.

'In the name of the Lord,' he said, taking up a parcel in red paper and giving it to Suza.

A pair of embroidered slippers. She hugged her father but her mind was on tugging off her shoes to try on the slippers.

'In the name of the Lord,' Laurenz repeated, and gave his son a blue-wrapped parcel.

With fumbling fingers the boy undid the wrappings. Inside he found a wrist-watch.

'Thank you, Father.' He took it out of its box, struggled to fasten it on his wrist. Laughing, Jo-Jo helped him. He held out his arm to admire the gift. A Swiss watch, and one of the best: a grown-up watch.

'In the name of the Lord,' said Christina, and gave Suza her parcel.

There were shrieks of delight. 'Pink! Pink, my favourite colour! Oh, how beautiful! May I put it on to go to church, Father?'

'Of course.' Laurenz was laughing as she darted to Christina to hug and kiss her in thanks.

Milovan stood looking at the parcels on the table. Two were small parcels, from Jo-Jo. The other remaining parcel was clearly a rectangular box, about ten inches by four by four.

Jo-Jo stepped up. After the formal greeting she presented her gifts to each child – chocolate coins in a cardboard purse. Now Christina took up the last package.

'In the name of the Lord,' she murmured, offering the package to Milovan.

He came towards her uncertainly. He took the present. The wrapping, red paper with silver stars, was slowly unwound.

There was indeed a rectangular box. He opened it. A pause, a sudden indrawn breath.

Then he took out the contents. He held up a model of one of the lake steamers, authentic in every detail.

'Oh . . . Aunt Christina . . . !' he breathed. He held it carefully, as if like fairy gold it might vanish if grasped too eagerly. 'Oh . . . thank you.'

He came across the room. Almost formally he leaned forward to kiss her on the cheek. 'Thank you,' he said again. 'I wish now I'd written to you about the timetables . . .'

As they drove towards Val d'Arve, Jo-Jo murmured in her friend's ear, 'And was that the sign, *mali doctoritza*?'

'Yes,' whispered Christina, 'I think it was.'

Next day was a holiday for those of the Orthodox faith. Laurenz, however, had to go to the Palais des Nations in the morning because urgent correspondence had to be dealt with by transatlantic cable.

Christina went round the shops with the children. It was strange to be on holiday when the rest of Geneva was at work. Suza loved the beautifully dressed German dolls in the toy departments. Milovan loved the toolshops.

'Look,' he said, dragging them to gaze in the window of an antique shop near Les Bastions. 'You see that big iron wheel? It's part of an old flour mill, I think. You see those cogs on the little wheel at right angles to the big one? That's the gear, it makes the machinery turn at the right speed.'

'Shall we go in and look at it?' suggested Christina.

'May we?' Milo asked, surprised. 'We don't want to *buy* it.'

'Oh, I think the shopkeeper would understand that,' she said, laughing, thinking that a woman and two children wouldn't strike any shopkeeper as likely customers for flour-mill equipment.

'But Cousin Vela always told us not to bother people when we went to market,' he persisted.

'I'm sure it will be all right.'

They went in. The antique-dealer came forward. Christina explained in French that they were intrigued by the cogged wheel. He bowed, pulled it a little way out of the window, and let them examine it. Milovan had a thousand questions to ask, but though his French had improved, it still hadn't reached the stage where he could ask technical questions.

But, truth to tell, neither had Christina's Serbian. She tried to translate, they all got in a muddle, Suza got the giggles, the shopman smiled, and when they left they were all in high good humour.

'After all that hard work, shall we go and have ice-creams?' Christina asked.

'Ooh, may we? Won't it spoil our lunch?' Suza said, clearly echoing the words of Madame Pluchet.

'If it does, we'll put off having lunch until suppertime.'

'Lunch at suppertime? Then we'd have to have supper at breakfast-time!'

For some reason this struck them as exquisitely funny. Laughing, they went in search of a patisserie where they could have ice-cream. It was only after they found it two streets away that Christina realised they had been walking arm in arm – Suza on one side of her, Milo the other, each holding an arm.

This is the sign, Christina thought as she watched them tucking into great mountains of ice-cream. For a boy to kiss an adult in thank-you for a special present, that was one thing. But to walk down the street, arm-in-arm, sharing an absurd joke – that was a run-of-the-mill, family relationship.

When Laurenz joined them in the afternoon for an

excursion to Montreux he found them happy with each other, teasing, joking, perfectly relaxed. He smiled at them, puzzled but pleased.

There was a Christmas reception at the 'residence' of the Serbian delegate that evening: a formal affair, attended by delegates of other countries and their wives. Christina wore a wine-coloured short dress and a string of pearls, Laurenz's Christmas gift to her. He for his part was in white tie and tails, his medals on his breast.

'We shall slip out the moment it's possible,' he murmured in her ear over the strains of the string quartet playing Smetana. 'These affairs are sheer torture.'

'But how else would I have the chance to see you in all your splendour?'

'Splendour? This stiff collar is cutting my neck in two. How will you like having a headless lover?'

'That's the kind of ghost that haunts old English castles,' she laughed.

'I shall haunt the Hotel du Chevron instead.'

Later, he glanced about her hotel room. 'I don't think I shall haunt this place,' he said. 'Haunting is done by unhappy ghosts. This has been a happy place for us.'

'I'll tell you something that I think will make you even happier, my darling.'

'At this moment nothing could make me happier.'

'S-sh!' She laid a finger against his lips. 'I think we can be married almost any day we choose.'

'Married?' He sat up to stare at her in the muted light of the bedside lamp. 'But I thought you said—'

'I believe the children would accept me, Laurenz. We must still be careful how we break it to them, but I think it'll be all right.'

'Milovan—?'

'He won't mind too much. There may be little problems, but I hope we'll be able to cope. Are you pleased, Laurenz?'

'Pleased isn't the word for it! Let's apply for the licence tomorrow! Do you know any Swiss law? Can we get a special licence?'

'Getting married is really only important from the point of view of being a mother to Milo and Suza, from the point of view of giving them a proper home. For us, in a way, it seems a mere formality. Because you see, I made up my mind before I came to Geneva that if the Fates so decide, I shall have your child, whether we're legally married or not.'

'My Christina, you are my only love, whether as my wife or my lover, for the rest of my life.' He kissed her, a long, serious kiss. 'All the same,' he added, with a little lightening of his manner, 'I should prefer to have my baby daughter born in wedlock.'

'Oh, you think we're going to have a girl?'

'I should like a little girl, just like you. And then a boy . . . Although I can't see you with a baby boy. You were meant to be the mother of pretty little daughters.'

She caught her breath. 'Don't say that, Laurenz!'

Surprised at her vehemence, he caught both her hands in his. 'What's the matter?'

She looked up at him. She said, 'I once had a baby boy.'

'What?' He spoke in puzzlement. He really didn't think he had caught what she said.

'I had a son. Years ago, when I was a student in America.'

'But, Christina . . .' He hesitated. 'I thought . . . you didn't say you had been married?'

She shook her head without speaking.

'Not married?'

'No.'

The dim light picked out little glimmers of brightness in the room, laid shadow upon shadow in the corners.

At long last she said, 'Does it make a difference?'

'No, of course not. It's just . . . why didn't you tell me before?'

'I couldn't bear to speak of him. I bitterly regretted having to give him up for adoption.'

'Oh, Christina!'

'I didn't want to. You must believe me, I didn't want to. But it seemed best. And when first I saw him again, I felt I had done the right thing—'

582

'You've seen him?'

'Oh yes. I was foolish enough to go looking for him. It was after I thought I had lost you into some mysterious world where I could never reach you. I don't know quite what I thought I was doing – trying to make a new start, saying goodbye to all that had gone before. So I went to Paris to see Stephen. He was eleven then. Such a fine boy, tall and fair . . . well-mannered . . . And I couldn't tell him who I was, I could only ask him the way to some stupid address, and walk away from him.'

'Darling!' He held her close, felt the tears against the skin of his shoulder. 'Don't cry. Please don't cry.'

'Since then I've seen him several times. Things didn't turn out for him quite as well as I'd hoped and . . . and . . . I wanted so much to put my arms round him and say, "Never mind, I'll make it better".' She looked up at him with a deep grief in her eyes. 'Laurenz, his adoptive father brought the boy to me for help after he found out he had been adopted. It hurt him very much, took away the foundations of his life. I was asked to help put him back on the right track. It was wrong even to try. Doctors and psychiatrists shouldn't take cases in which they're emotionally involved.'

'When was this?' Laurenz asked.

'Recently. It was Stephen's father who came that day – do you remember? – when you were leaving to catch your train.'

'I remember. I gathered he was in great distress.'

'With good reason. And you see, he was so sure I could put it right. I should never have agreed . . . In the end I had to put a stop to it because it was getting too dangerous, and in any case I was needed by my family. Stephen said goodbye calmly enough. But he weighs on my heart all the time, all the time!'

'Hush, hush.' He held her and rocked her, sensing an emotional wilderness within her at the remembrance of the lost child. When she was quiet once more, he caressed her, giving comfort, offering strength. He had known her in many moods: brave, passionate, despondent, joyful. Perhaps,

Laurenz thought, he had never loved her more than at this moment among the shadows of a past sorrow.

Throughout the night they talked gently together. Little by little she told him all that she had kept secret for so long. 'I've never spoken to another soul about this,' she said, almost in wonder. 'Only Jo-Jo knows, because of course she helped me at the birth of my baby.' She hesitated. 'I was afraid to tell you, I think. Because I know how strict the moral code is in Serbia . . .'

'You thought I'd be angry and disapproving?'

'Well, you might have thought I . . . I only got what I deserved by my own bad behaviour.'

'I'm only angry that you've had to bear this burden alone so long. My dearest one, you must know that I could never "disapprove" of you. Whatever you do or have done, I take it on trust that you were acting with integrity.'

'You're biased in my favour,' she sighed. 'If you only knew how near I was to telling the boy that I was his real mother. That would have been very wrong of me.'

'I don't see why?' Laurenz countered. 'You tell me that Arlette, Estelle – his adoptive mother, how is she called? Yes, Estelle – she's lost interest in him. How could it be wrong to tell the boy that his real mother still cares, still longs for him?'

'Ah no.' She shook her head. 'That's a temptation, to try to step into Estelle's shoes. But there are too many memories of Estelle as his mother. I don't think he could ever accept me as a substitute. In any case it wasn't for me to change his life by blurting out the facts. He went off to look for her, that poor little Kristin Belu. But he's found that the trail ends at a farm in the Juniata Valley in Pennsylvania and perhaps it's better to let it die there. Only a very strong personality would go on searching in the face of obstacles like that.'

'Are you saying you think he's weak?'

'Not at all. He had a very bad reaction to the news about his adoption, but he came out of it very well, and that was due to his own innate strength of character. I can guess that he still wants to find her, his real mother – there's a curiosity, a wish to know what he's inherited from her. But only a really deep need would drive him to go on with the search.'

It was towards six in the morning when he left her. Two cleaners were running a carpet sweeper up and down the main hall. The night porter was starting on his morning *café au lait* in his cubicle. He gulped a mouthful as Laurenz came into the lobby, then rose to attend to him, stifling a smile at the sight of last night's evening clothes on this early riser.

He opened the outer door for him. Snow was falling, a chill wind blew it in at the doorway.

'Oh, good lord, what awful weather! Shall I call a taxi for you, sir?'

Laurenz hesitated. He wanted to get home before his household was up and about. Was it better to wait for a taxi or to walk? Even in Geneva, taxis weren't exactly plentiful at five forty-five in the morning. On the other hand, if he walked and got himself covered in snow, he would have to leave a noticeable pile of wet clothes for Madame Pluchet to see to.

'Try for a taxi.'

The porter went to the switchboard behind the reception desk to make the call. He reported: 'They say about twenty minutes, sir.'

Laurenz took a seat on one of the cushioned benches, in a nook out of the draught. He picked up last night's paper to while away the time.

The main door opened, admitting a gust of wind. With it came a tall young man, snow on the shoulders of his gaberdine coat and the rim of his cap. He carried a small overnight bag of expensive leather, and in his hand held a piece of paper. He looked at it, then said to the porter, 'Hotel du Chevron?'

'That's right, sir.' The porter opened the hotel register, turned it ready for signature.

'No, I don't want a room, I've come to speak to someone.'

'At this hour of the morning, sir?' the porter exclaimed.

The young man frowned. 'I know it's early, but the first

train I could get was the overnight sleeper. I just came from Cornavin station. I want to speak to—'

'Wouldn't you like to take off your coat, sir? It's quite wet.'

'Is it? I suppose it is.' He set down his overnight bag so that the porter could help him out of the snow-spattered coat.

Laurenz was idly watching, simply because it was more interesting than last night's paper.

'Coffee, sir? The kitchens are just starting up.'

'No, no, nothing, thanks. I want to speak to Dr Holt.'

Laurenz sat up, suddenly alert.

'Dr Holt? I don't think I could disturb her this early in the morning.'

'Look, it's important. I wouldn't ask otherwise. I've come all the way from America to see Dr Christina.'

'America ... my word, sir ...' The porter was clearly alarmed. Claims like that were odd, to say the least – all the way from America at five forty-five on a cold winter morning. But then, he bethought himself, Dr Holt was a mind doctor. People asking for her might well be peculiar. 'You one of her patients, sir, is that it?'

'Yes!' the young man said. 'Yes, as a matter of fact, I *am*!'

'Oh, in that case . . .' He took a telephone plug from the top, began to plug the call through on the indoor line.

'Just a minute,' Laurenz said, getting to his feet and moving swiftly to the desk.

'What?' The porter, startled, gaped at him.

'Don't put the call through.'

'Here,' said the boy. 'What do you mean, butting in—'

'Are you Stephen?'

It had come to him all in a moment, when he heard the boy say in his desperate way that he had come 'all the way from America'. And that he was a patient of 'Dr Christina's' – she had told him that was his name for her. And then his age: he was just the right age. And tall and fair. And *like* Christina. Not obviously so, and perhaps only at this moment when fatigue and anxiety gave her son something of the look that Laurenz had seen on Christina's features in these last few hours: a haunted, yearning look.

The boy stood at a loss, staring at Laurenz. 'Who are you?' he said, in a hoarse whisper. A man who can conjure your name out of the air was to be feared.

Laurenz said in his heavily accented English, 'My name is Laurenz Varikiav. I work here in Geneva.'

'Ah.' Something of the fear went out of his gaze. 'The guy who rang long-distance, the guy who spoke to her in Serbian. Are you a Serbian?'

'Yes I am.' He took Stephen by the arm. 'Come along, we need to talk.' Over his shoulder to the porter he said, 'Cancel that call.'

They went to sit down on the bench. Laurenz said, 'You're just about to ask me what it's got to do with me. I explain it by saying that I'm the man Dr Holt is going to marry.'

'It figures.' Stephen nodded.

'Oddly enough, we just had a long conversation about you.'

Silence. Stephen weighed the information. It meant more than just the words. There was hope in them, because why should Dr Christina talk to this Varikiav about him, unless it was important to her? It meant she was thinking about him, just as he was thinking about her. Perhaps she often thought about him. There was that to consider – perhaps she thought about him a lot. And if she did it must mean what he thought it meant. What he wanted it to mean, what he needed it to mean. Oh God, could it really mean that?

Stephen had gone straight to New Cavendish Street when he reached London. His disappointment on finding that Dr Christina had already left for Geneva was unbearable. And he must have made Alice Lowther nervous by the intensity of his reaction because she refused to give him the Geneva address.

Frustrated, he had gone away. But next morning he thought of a way to get it, quite simply. He went to the estate agent whose board was displayed as having dealt with the sale of the lease. Might he have Dr Holt's Geneva address, his father Mr Charlford wanted to write a thank-you for Dr Holt's Christmas card? He took care not to seem too anxious this time. The receptionist gave him the address without a second thought.

The Baeschens didn't query his announcement that he was going off on his own for a few days. After all, they weren't his keeper, and their thoughts were on reaching their daughter in Germany.

The Channel crossing had been bad. The first available train to Geneva was the night sleeper. He booked himself aboard but had slept not at all. He was going to see Dr Christina, to *confront* her, to ask her . . . to ask her . . . something important.

But now here was another barrier in his path. This tall, impressive fellow, hair going a little grey at the temples, full evening dress, a row of medals . . . Full evening dress? In Dr Christina's hotel in the early hours of the morning?

He felt a furious hostility. Without knowing it, he clenched his fist and half raised it.

'Now,' Laurenz said gently. He put a strong hand over the fist and lowered it. 'We are not enemies. I love your Dr Christina. I want only what is good for her.' Stephen felt the seriousness of the words. 'Is that what you want?'

'I want . . . I want to talk to her.'

'And what will you say?'

'I'll ask her . . . ask her . . .' He faltered into silence. He wasn't going to tell this stranger anything. OK, so he said he loved her, and it was an easy guess he'd just spent the night with her, but that didn't give him the *right* . . .

Laurenz said, 'Whatever you ask, she will answer. Perhaps she is waiting to be asked your questions, perhaps it has been foreshadowed to her. She told me she was on the verge more than once . . . Well, Stephen, you have known sadness, great sadness. But so has she. So will you be kind, and let me go first to warn her?'

'Warn her? What d'you mean, warn her? I'm not going to do anything to harm her, for God's sake! I just want to hear her say . . . I've got to hear her say . . .'

'Then let me go up first, yes? Stay here, drink some coffee, and it will calm you and in a little while you will see her.'

'I'm calm, I'm quite calm!'

'But even so, it's the chilly hours of the morning and you are weary.'

Laurenz beckoned to the porter, ordered coffee for Stephen, then went up in the lift. He tapped on the door of Christina's room.

'Yes?'

'It's me, Laurenz. Let me in, Christina.'

In a moment she opened the door. She was clad in the loose silk kimono he knew so well. 'Did you forget something?'

'My love, come, sit down.' He pushed her gently into a chair. 'Your son is downstairs in the hotel lobby.'

Her eyes opened wide. She began to say, 'That's impossible!' but stopped short at the serious gaze he bent upon her. 'Stephen?' she said.

'He just walked in as I was waiting for a taxi. He says he's come "all the way from America".'

'Laurenz!'

'He says he's come to ask you something.' He knelt, taking her hands. 'I think he knows, Christina.'

To his surprise she didn't protest at that. She sat thinking a moment, then she nodded. 'There were all sorts of little psychic clues. He was edging towards it when at last I had to break off with him. Somehow he's got hold of something concrete enough to bring it to the surface of his mind.'

He chafed her hands gently, for they had gone cold. 'What do you want me to do? I told him I wanted to come up first to prepare you.'

'How is he, Laurenz?'

'Very tired. Anxious. He shies away from saying what it is that he actually wants from you.'

She moved uneasily. He let her go, rose to his feet. 'I must go back with some message, darling.'

'Yes. Give me a moment. Let me think.'

'Think? What about?'

'I'm trying to understand . . . Did he ask who you were?'

'He seems to know something about me – he remembers that I called you long-distance from Geneva.'

'Yes, of course. And soon after that, you know, he went to look for traces of Kristin Belu. He . . . he wanted to stake his claim on her.' She suddenly clasped her hands together. 'That's it. He's afraid, Laurenz! He's come here to ask me if I'm his mother and he's afraid I'll deny it! He's had so much rejection, he can hardly face any more. And you see, he thinks I've got a life of my own and a man to love, so where is there room for him in all that?'

'Ah,' Laurenz said. 'That is too deep for me. He still seems a child to me and, as you know, I don't really understand children. But I think you are right in one thing. He is afraid.' He looked towards the phone. 'And he is waiting, Christina.'

'Yes. I must talk to him.' She put her hand on the receiver.

'Shall I go?'

'I think you must, Laurenz. He couldn't bring himself to speak of anything so personal in front of anyone else.'

'And I have a taxi waiting – at least, I believe so. Very well, my Christina, I leave you to this fateful meeting. But please' – he took her hands in his— 'please let me know at once how things went.'

'I'll ring you . . .'

'Yes. And in the meantime I will be thinking of you.' He smiled. 'Of course, that will be nothing new. I always am thinking of you. But this time, with anxiety and concern.'

'I love you, Laurenz,' she said.

'I love you, Christina.'

They kissed. He smiled encouragement, then quickly took his leave.

And she was left to make the phone call to the boy who waited in the hotel vestibule.

Chapter Thirty-nine

The knock on the door was faint, uncertain. She opened it.
'Come in.'

He had his greatcoat over his arm, his tweed cap in his
hand. He unconsciously grasped and twisted the cap as he
stepped inside.

Christina had given herself fifteen minutes in which to
shower and dress. She was wearing clothes Stephen knew
well: a two-piece costume of blue wool with a white silk blouse.
Her short fair hair, still damp from the shower, was brushed
back from her brow. She knew that anyone seeing her and
Stephen at this moment would know they were blood kin.
They looked so alike: both fair-haired and fair-skinned, both
grey-eyed, both pale from nerves.

She took his coat and cap. 'Sit down, Stephen.'

He obeyed. She remained standing. He sat looking up at
her.

'Well?' she said gently.

His breath came quickly, once, twice, as if he were trying to
force the words out. 'I don't want you to think I'm here to
cause trouble,' he blurted. 'That's not it at all. I mean, I know
you've got your own life to live and everything. That guy I
met downstairs – he said you and he were getting married?'

'That's right.'

'He seems an OK kind of guy.'

'Thank you.'

'I can see you wouldn't want any trouble, I mean with
getting married and wanting a nice quiet honeymoon—' He
stopped at her little gust of laughter. 'Did I say something
funny?'

'Unconscious humour,' she assured him. 'If you only knew . . . ! Laurenz has two children. The elder, a boy, is . . . well, he and his sister had a terrible time during the war. Let's say he has problems. I don't think there's the slightest chance of a "quiet honeymoon".'

'Gee, I'm sorry.'

'Never mind about that. Tell me why you are here.'

He hesitated. 'You're always like that. You always ask questions.'

'That's the way to get answers.'

'Yeah, well, there were some answers I wanted, so I went to the Juniata Valley, but all the people at that farm where the Serbians lived, they're all long gone.' His grey eyes rested on her with speculation. 'But you knew that, of course.'

'What makes you say that I know?'

'There you go again! Questions, always questions. Well, here's a question for you. How come you went to college with a girl called Belu?'

'Where did you learn that?'

'It wasn't so hard. An old lady in Duncannon remembered a girl with long fair hair coming to spend vacations with the Serbians, and she came with a girl student called Belu. And then I looked up the Penn. U. Year Book, and there you were in the graduation photograph – Dr Christina Holt, standing next to Dr Josafin Belu. So what I want to know is, how come you never reacted when I told you my real mother was a Serbian girl called Belu?'

'Do you say I never reacted, Stephen?'

His gaze searched her face. 'Why don't you speak to me? Why do you play games with questions?'

'Are you so impatient? Your search has taken you some months. Why hurry the last few steps?'

'All right, you asked me if you never reacted. Sure, you reacted! You told me my mother had forgiven the guy who got her in trouble. I remember your voice when you said it. And when I asked you how you knew that . . . There was something then. I half knew . . . No, I didn't know . . . I don't know *now*.'

'Another question for you, Stephen. Do you shy away from knowing? Is it too much for you to know?'

He leapt up, seized one of her hands in both of his. 'No, no, I want to be sure. If you think I'll do something bad with the knowledge, be stupid about it, shove in where I'm not wanted – I won't, I promise I won't. Gee, I'm only here on a kind of a side-trip. I'm really on my way to Cairo. You won't see me around much, I'll be at work on the digs. I really want to do that, to get some groundwork in before I go to university. So you see . . .'

'Are you bargaining with me, Stephen? "Tell me and I'll go away like a good boy"?'

'No, no! Don't put it like that! I wouldn't bargain, it's too important!'

And now she had stripped away all the defences. She could see he had learned the truth and faced it. What he wanted now was the dignity of her confirmation.

He was still grasping her hand. She drew him closer to her. She had to look up to look into his face.

'I am that Kristin Belu you went to the Juniata Valley to find. I am that Kristin Belu who had a baby son she had to give for adoption, and who never ceased to regret it from that day to this.'

She had never been sure how she would tell him. When she heard her own words they sounded as if they were spoken by someone else. She had meant to say 'I am your mother', but that had seemed too great a claim. She had not been his mother – that place had been taken by Estelle Charlford.

All she could do was speak the simple truth.

And now she waited, her heart beating heavy and slow, for his response.

He stared down at her. 'Yeah . . .' he said. 'I knew, really.'

'And how do you feel about it?'

To her surprise and relief, he grinned. 'Always the questions. You know, the line of business you're in, seems to me you never say anything that doesn't end in a question mark. Is it a trick of the trade?'

'Psychiatrists are in the business of helping people to

understand themselves. The best way to help is ask questions, and help the patient face the answers.'

'Help – yes, sure, that's what you do, you help people. I understand that. You helped me, you calmed me down. I remember how furious and off-balance I was when I found out I'd been adopted.'

'How do you feel about it now?' she asked, and joined in the laughter with which he greeted the query.

'To tell the truth, at the moment I feel great,' he said when he had recovered. 'You know, Dr Christina, what hurt about the adoption was the idea that I'd just been handed over, like a parcel. But that couldn't be it, really, could it? Because you see I know you, and you're not the kind of person who'd do a thing like that without thinking it over and over. And of course, I realise what a rotten thing it was for you – the way people sneer at girls who get in trouble, and how hard it would have been trying to earn a living, and probably giving up university . . . I've had time to see all that . . . I want you to know . . . I understand . . . I do really . . . Mother.'

Tears rushed to her eyes. She brought his hand up to her breast, held it tight. 'Oh, Stephen, Stephen . . .'

'Is it OK to call you that? You don't mind?'

'Of course not! Oh, if you knew how I've longed . . .'

They put their arms about each other. He was surprised to find how slender, how fragile she was. He'd always thought of her as strong. But now she was weeping into the shoulder of his jacket, and it came to him suddenly that this had been as big an ordeal for her as for him.

He drew her to the chairs by the low table. They sat down, he still holding her hand, she with tears still streaming down her face. 'Are you all right?' he asked. 'Did I make you unhappy, coming here?'

She shook her head. 'I think I've been expecting you. But Stephen, there's a lot to consider. We're not the only people involved.' She found a handkerchief, mopped her eyes.

'You mean your friend Laurenz?'

'Oh, no, he knows all about it. I didn't mean to tell him – I never meant to tell anyone – but somehow it tumbled out. No, I was thinking of your father and mother.'

'My what? Oh! You mean John and Estelle.'

'Your father and mother,' she said firmly. 'You mustn't punish them, Stephen. They've done nothing wrong.'

'They let me think they were my real parents—'

'But that's how they were told to bring you up. And in every respect except the tie of blood, they are your real parents—'

'No—'

'Who saw you through whooping cough and measles, who saw to your education, who—'

'Who ran out on me for some cheap Broadway tenor?'

'Ah, no, you mustn't speak of her like that, son. When you fall in love, you'll discover how it can blind you to everything else.' She leaned forward to pat him gently on the cheek. 'She'll be back, Stephen. I know her rejection hurt you, but she was compelled to it – just as Kristin Belu was – by forces she couldn't understand. Before long she'll know she made a mistake.'

'We-ell . . .'

'And John, your father, he's never failed you. Do you want to hurt him, son?'

'No, of course not . . . But I don't see how it could hurt him.'

'It might make him unhappy. He might feel he'd lost some part of you, and not through any fault of his.'

'I don't know if I want to keep it a secret, Dr Christina.'

'I don't say that you must. But think about it. Don't make a careless decision. Remember, once the secret is told, it can never be recalled.'

He studied the painting on the bedroom wall. Then he said, 'Tell me who my real father was.'

She shook her head.

'Tell me!'

'No, Stephen. He's married now and with children of his own. He never even knew of your existence. It would be wrong to confront him now with the knowledge that he has an illegitimate son.'

'You never told him?' he asked, a little incredulous. 'Didn't you feel it was his duty to marry you?'

She thought back to that cruel, careless young man who had fathered him. What good could it do to tell the boy about him?

'Do you trust me, Stephen?'

'Of course.'

'Then believe me when I say he was a clever, handsome boy from an important family which would never have accepted me. I fell in love with him, but when I discovered I was pregnant I knew it was better not to tell him. You mustn't think badly of him, because though he was older than you at the time, he still had a lot of growing up to do. I won't tell you his name, I think it would only cause hurt and disappointment if you got in touch with him.' To you, she was thinking, to you – and I don't want you hurt without need.

He seemed to be listening to overtones and undertones of her words. 'You don't like him,' he suggested. 'I mean now, the way he is now, he's not a man you admire.'

She made no reply.

'I can't help wondering about him, Dr Christina. I feel I want to know.'

'Listen, John Charlford has been a better father to you than this man could ever have been. Believe me, you got a bargain, son! Don't be the kind of fool who throws away real gold to run after shiny worthless stones.'

Stephen nodded to himself. 'You really don't like him. Well, that's good enough for me. I'll go along with what you want. But gee, he must have been some fool, to let you go when he could have married you.'

She smiled. 'Don't you think perhaps you're biased in my favour?'

'Sure!' he said with emphasis. 'Why not? I think I've struck it real lucky. I mean, my mother could have turned out to be somebody I couldn't feel anything for, but you . . . you've been a friend.'

'And always will be.' She uttered the words with too

much emotion. She knew she must not make claims on him. She must return him to his parents, the man and the woman who had brought him up when she could not. She retreated into the techniques of psychiatry. 'Do you feel your father – John – has been a friend?'

'The best!' he said. 'The best!'

'But not your mother?'

He turned away from her in his chair, his face half hidden. 'When I was little . . . She seemed so beautiful, like the pictures in my story book . . . But she didn't want me to be grown-up. Having a big lanky boy about the place let other people know how old she was, I guess. She didn't like that.' He turned suddenly to say, 'When I went to see her, after I found out she wasn't my real mother, I said to her . . . I said . . .'

'What did you say, Stephen?'

'Well, I was angry . . .'

'It was something cruel?'

'I told her now she needn't try to keep me away from her friends any more – she could say, "Oh, he was adopted", and then they wouldn't bother to do sums, adding my age on to hers and guessing how old she is . . .'

'Did you tell her you were trying to find your real mother?'

'I was going to. I knew it would shake her. I wanted her to . . . to . . .'

'To suffer?'

'No, just to *notice* me!' he burst out. 'She just walked out of my life! She hadn't the right to do that!'

'You said you were going to tell her. Does that mean you didn't?'

'I never got around to it. We had this stupid argument, and then Victor walked in, and she stopped bothering about me and *he* treated me as if I were some stupid jerk, so I walked out. Maybe Dad told her. I don't know.'

She paused for thought. 'Remember we said, a moment ago, that your parents didn't deserve to be punished?'

'*You* said that, I didn't.'

'Do you disagree with it?'

'Well . . .' He coloured up. 'I just feel they . . . At least, not

Dad . . . But Mom's so . . . I just think she gets away scot-free all the time . . . And I want her to – I don't know – I want her to understand that there's a price to pay . . .'

'What price, Stephen? What price should you exact for being brought up by Estelle to the best of her ability?'

'The best of her ability! Is that what you call it?'

She touched him on the sleeve. 'How many of your friends have divorced parents, son?'

He was silent. Then, after a moment he said, 'I get it. You're saying that the other guys don't want to punish their folks—'

'Oh, they do, Stephen, they do! It's a human trait. We want to pay people out for what they've done to us. And then afterwards we feel guilt. All I'm trying to make you see is that you must think – think hard – before you say anything to John and Estelle about me. It's not that I'm ashamed – believe me, I'm happy today, happier than I ever expected.'

'But that's mostly because of that guy I met downstairs, the one you're marrying. I guess you . . . you really love him, huh?'

'Very much, Stephen. One day I'll tell you all about it. But for the moment we're talking about us, you and me. It's given me an extra happiness to have you here like this. And you're happy too, Stephen. Aren't you?'

He nodded, made a little wordless gesture with his big-boned hands.

'Do you think it would be right to spoil it all by making someone else unhappy?'

'Dr Christina, you can't be saying we should keep it a secret. You always used to say that by asking questions we brought everything out into the open.'

'But John and Estelle have asked no questions, Stephen. *You* are the one who has asked questions and *you* are the one who has found answers. Don't you think you should ask this last question: should they be told something that might hurt them?'

He got up, moved about the room, stared at the grey light beginning to creep in at the window.

'You mean, never tell them?'

'Oh, "never" is a big word. Who knows? When you've thought it all through calmly, you might want them to know. But it might be a good idea to ask yourself first why you're giving them the information. If it's to hurt your mother – to punish her, to make her "notice" you – do you think that would be a good reason?'

He laughed, a little sound that was half amusement and half bafflement. 'You never run short of questions!'

'And I have another for you.'

'What's that?'

'Are you hungry?'

His mouth fell open in surprise. Then he seized her, pulled her to her feet, swung her round, and hugged her. 'I'm starved! How did you know?'

She didn't say, because big tall young men who have travelled all night across Europe are likely to be hungry. She said, 'Let's go down to the restaurant. They'll be serving breakfast now. Did you have luggage?'

'A valise. I left it with the hall porter.'

'We'll retrieve it and book you a room. Come along.'

The ornate cage of the lift carried them down to the foyer. As they crossed it towards the desk, a figure rose from a chair in a quiet niche.

'Laurenz!'

The boy stopped short. For a moment she didn't know how the two were going to react to each other. She could feel Stephen tense at her side, ready to take offence.

Laurenz said, 'I found I couldn't just leave without knowing everything was all right.' He made a little half-bow of apology towards Stephen. 'Please don't think of it as interference. I am anxious, that is all.'

Stephen hesitated. Then he nodded. 'Yeah,' he said.

The arm holding hers relaxed, the momentary antagonism ebbed away.

Now, she told herself, now! Now is the time to bring together the two most important men in my life.

'You already met Captain Varikiav when you first

arrived, Stephen,' she said, 'but only in passing. Laurenz' –
she smiled from one to the other – 'may I present my son?'

They studied each other. Laurenz bowed.

'How do you do, sir?' Stephen said.

And held out his hand.

TESSA BARCLAY

THE FINAL PATTERN

'Tessa Barclay always spins a fine yarn . . .
gripping and entertaining'
Wendy Craig

Jenny Armstrong, mistress of the thriving Corvill and Son
weaving business, returns to her native Scotland
determined to achieve prosperity and comfort for her
reunited family. But the death of her brother Ned brings
disruption and harm . . .

Once again young Heather Armstrong is caught up in her
widowed Aunt Lucy's machinations; Jenny's rekindled love
affair with her husband Ronald is threatened and
strangers lurk in doorways to spy on the Armstrongs and
their friends. Jenny uncovers a terrible secret in Lucy's past
that still demands vengeance, and there is an unknown
enemy to be reckoned with . . .

THE FINAL PATTERN is the compelling sequel to
A WEB OF DREAMS and BROKEN THREADS –
'Just what a historical novel should be' Elizabeth Longford
'Filled with fascinating historical detail and teeming with
human passions' Marie Joseph
– also available from Headline.

FICTION/SAGA   0 7472 3542 2

A selection of bestsellers from Headline

FICTION

A WOMAN ALONE	Malcolm Ross	£4.99 ☐
BRED TO WIN	William Kinsolving	£4.99 ☐
MISTRESS OF GREEN TREE MILL	Elisabeth McNeill	£4.50 ☐
SHADES OF FORTUNE	Stephen Birmingham	£4.99 ☐
RETURN OF THE SWALLOW	Frances Anne Bond	£4.99 ☐
THE SERVANTS OF TWILIGHT	Dean R Koontz	£4.99 ☐
WHITE LIES	Christopher Hyde	£4.99 ☐
PEACEMAKER	Robert & Frank Holt	£4.99 ☐

NON-FICTION

FIRST CONTACT	Ben Bova & Byron Preiss (eds)	£5.99 ☐
NEWTON'S MADNESS	Harold L Klawans	£4.99 ☐

SCIENCE FICTION AND FANTASY

HYPERION	Dan Simmons	£4.99 ☐
SHADOW REALM Wells of Ythan 3	Marc Alexander	£4.99 ☐

All Headline books are available at your local bookshop or newsagent, or can be ordered direct from the publisher. Just tick the titles you want and fill in the form below. Prices and availability subject to change without notice.

Headline Book Publishing PLC, Cash Sales Department, PO Box 11, Falmouth, Cornwall, TR10 9EN, England.

Please enclose a cheque or postal order to the value of the cover price and allow the following for postage and packing:
UK: 80p for the first book and 20p for each additional book ordered up to a maximum charge of £2.00
BFPO: 80p for the first book and 20p for each additional book
OVERSEAS & EIRE: £1.50 for the first book, £1.00 for the second book and 30p for each subsequent book.

Name ....

Address ....

....

....